Pr

"*Bowl of Heaven* . . . the biggest sci-fi saga since—well, since ever. If only more of us could share the authors' visions, and optimism."
—*The Wall Street Journal*

"It's easy to settle in and enjoy the sci-fi smorgasbord served up by Gregory Benford and Larry Niven. . . . There's a lot to savor. Fans of so-called 'hard science fiction' will enjoy the descriptions of ionic scoop fusion drives and all the solar-powered gadgets put to practical use during deep space exploration."
—Associated Press

"It's been more than forty years since *Ringworld* and nearly that long since the Galactic Center saga knocked our socks off, and I wonder how much it takes these days to render us barefoot and gaping at the scale and scope of an imaginary world. . . . But Benford and Niven have given themselves the space (conceptual and page count) to spread out. *Bowl of Heaven* has room to accommodate both the thrill-ride and head-scratching sides of its subtradition, and I think when the second half appears, this new effort by two of the old masters will hold its own just fine."
—*Locus*

"Niven and Benford have combined their award-winning talents for storytelling to create a series opener that should find a welcome reception from fans of the authors as well as those who love hard science and mental challenges."
—*Library Journal*

"A solid work that will appeal to fans of classic hard SF."
—*Publishers Weekly*

BOWL OF HEAVEN

AND

SHIPSTAR

GREGORY BENFORD

AND

LARRY NIVEN

TOR

A TOM DOHERTY ASSOCIATES BOOK | NEW YORK

BOWL OF HEAVEN AND SHIPSTAR

Bowl of Heaven copyright © 2012 by Gregory Benford and Larry Niven

Shipstar copyright © 2014 by Gregory Benford and Larry Niven

Illustrations in *Bowl of Heaven* by Don Davis.

A Tor Book
Published by Tom Doherty Associates
120 Broadway
New York, NY 10271

www.tor-forge.com

Tor® is a registered trademark of Macmillan Publishing Group, LLC.

ISBN 978-1-250-25952-3

Our books may be purchased in bulk for promotional, educational, or business use. Please contact your local bookseller or the Macmillan Corporate and Premium Sales Department at 1-800-221-7945, extension 5442, or by email at MacmillanSpecialMarkets@macmillan.com.

First Edition: February 2020

Printed in the United States of America

0 9 8 7 6 5 4 3 2

CONTENTS

BOWL OF HEAVEN

CAST OF CHARACTERS

Cliff Kammash—biologist

Mayra Wickramsingh—pilot, with Beth team

Abduss Wickramsingh—engineer, with Beth team

Glory—the planet of destination

Captain Redwing

SunSeeker—the ramship

Beth Marble—biologist

Eros—the first drop ship

Fred Ojama—geologist, with Beth team

Aybe—engineer, with Cliff team

Howard Blaire—engineer, with Cliff team

Terrence Gould—with Cliff team

Irma Michaelson—plant biologist, with Cliff team

Tananareve Bailey—with Beth team

Lau Pin—engineer, with Beth team

CAPTAIN REDWING HAS FOUR CREW ABOARD *SUNSEEKER*

Jampudvipa, shortened to Jam—an Indian bridge officer

Ayaan Ali—Arab woman navigator/pilot

Clare Conway—copilot

Karl Lebanon—general technology officer

ASTRONOMER FOLK

Memor—Attendant Astute Astronomer

Asenath—Wisdom Chief

Ikahaja—Ecosystem Savant

Omanah—Ecosystem Packmistress

Ramanuji—Biology Savant

Kanamatha—Biology Packmistress

Thaji—Judge Savant

(The Adopted, those aliens already encountered and
    integrated into the Bowl, will have further names used
    in Volume 2.)

FOLK TERMS

TransLanguage

Long Records

Late Invaders

Undermind

Serf-Ones

the Builders

Third Variety (Astronomer variety)

Astronauts (Astronomer variety)

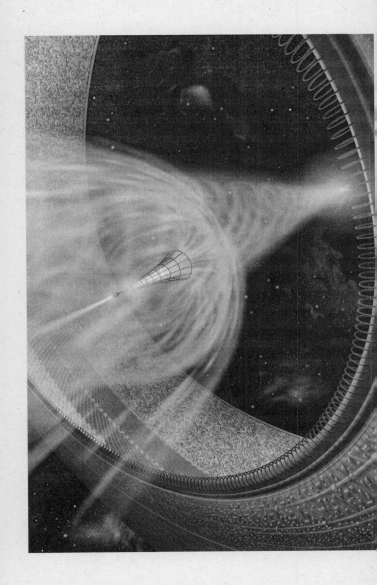

PROLOGUE

Here about the beach I wander'd,
nourishing a youth sublime
With the fairy tales of science,
and the long result of Time
—TENNYSON, "Locksley Hall"

THE LAST PARTY

Cliff turned from the people he was saying good-bye to and looked out at the world he would never see again.

The party roared on behind him. Laughter, shouts, hammering hard music. The laughter was a touch ragged, the music too loud, a forced edge to it all, and an electric zest fueled a murmur of anticipating talk. They had said good-bye already to relatives on Earth. Now, *SunSeeker*'s crew and passengers had to say farewell forever to the starship construction teams, the training echelons, the embodied political and economic forces that were about to launch them out into a vastness beyond experience.

The view was razor sharp, but it was of course a screen, adjusted to subtract the station's centrifugal gyre. So Earth held steady and he could see the tiny silver motes of flung packages headed toward the *SunSeeker* complex. They trailed back toward the flingers on Luna, and another line of specks pointed toward the fatter dots of manufacturing complexes in higher orbits. A dingy new asteroid was gliding in on its decade-long journey. Already, silvery bee swarms of robo-factories accompanied it, hollowing out its stony core for a smelter colony. Glass-skinned biofactories waited for the work crews that would pounce on the asteroid prey, their liquid riches hiding behind fogged domes for sunlight to awaken them.

It struck him how much like artworks machines seemed in space. Here they suffered no constraints of gravity, and so looked like contorted abstracts of Euclidean geometries, cubes and ellipsoids and blunt cylinders that made mobiles without wires, moving with glacial grace against the faint jewels of brimming starlight.

Within the geostationary orbit, he could not see distinct satellites, even after he hit the magnification command and the screen narrowed in. Here, the busy swarm held luxury hotels for ancients now well over two centuries old. Religious colonies were more common but rather Spartan, and ships flitted like dappled radiance everywhere in the incessant sprawl of commerce. The solid Earth swam in a countless froth of tending machines.

He leaned sideways and caught the sheen of the

Fresnel lens at the L1 point, a gauzy circle seen nearly on edge from here. It hung between Earth and the sun, deflecting sunlight from the still rather overheated planet. Adjusting patches twinkled in slow splendor.

"Y'know, it'll all be fixed up fine by the time we even wake up." Beth's soft words came from behind him.

Cliff turned and his eyes brightened. "But we'll be this same age."

She blinked and grinned and kissed him back. "Hard not to love an optimist."

"If I didn't think we'll wake up, I wouldn't go."

She wore a sheath dress that definitely wouldn't be going to Glory. It clung to her lithe body, wrapped close around her neck, and anchored at amber bracelets on her wrists. Her right showed bare skin colored like chardonnay as the dress polarized, giving him quick glances of flesh. The silky dress had variable opacity and hue she could tune with the bracelets, he guessed. He hoped this show was for him. People nearby were making a great show of not noticing. Just as most ignored the profusion of plunging necklines, built-in push-up bras, spangles, feathers, slits, and peekaboos. Plus codpieces on some of the guys, muscle shirts, the hawk hats that made a man look like a predator.

"A lot of overt signaling tonight, isn't there?" Beth said dryly.

Not his style. "Bravado, smells like." So he simply took her in his arms and kissed her. That was the usual best move, he had learned early on, especially if he could not think of something witty. Her green eyes blinked. Everyone continued not noticing. He wouldn't see most of them ever again, after all.

This thought got underlined when a banner rolled across the room's suspension ceiling. It was from the assembly teams who for years had worked with the crew, outfitting and running *SunSeeker*.

HOPE YOU ENJOYED GIVING US THE BUSINESS
AS MUCH AS WE ENJOYED TAKING YOU FOR A RIDE

Terry and Fred came by on their way to the bar, laughing at the banner. "Funny," Terry said. "We're going on to Glory, and tomorrow they'll be back at work on the next ramscoop. But they're celebrating harder than we are."

"Yeah," Fred said. "Odd. They're as glad to see us leave as we are to go."

Terry said, "We're all scarce types. All the psychers say so. Why wouldn't anyone grab a chance at a whole new, fresh world?"

"Instead of staying here to fix the one we screwed up?" Cliff asked. An old issue for them all, but it still clung to him.

Beth shrugged. "We finesse climate, or climate finesses us."

"It's good practice," Terry said. "The previous generations terraformed Earth first. Now it's our turn with a whole new planet."

A tray crawled past; you couldn't use float trays in low-spin gravity. The tray was piled with exotic dishes and surrounded by diners who would not be eating this well for centuries to come. Fred joined them, then Terry, edging into the crowd with minimal courtesy.

"My, my," Beth said warmly. "Ummm . . . maybe we should leave now?"

Cliff looked out over the crowd. Some Earth bureaucrat had on a leash a dog that closely resembled a breakfast pastry with hair. The dog was lapping up someone else's vomit. Three others were laughing at the sight. Apparently most of the party was having a better time than he was.

No matter. This was surely the last time he would see most of them—the crews who had built *Sun-Seeker,* the endless bureaucrats who at least pretended to add to the effort, the psychers and endless engineers and trial-run crews who would never see another sun. . . . He grimaced and relished the passing moment. All moments were passing, of course. Some, more so. "My heart is full but my glass is empty."

She gave him a rueful nod. "We won't get booze on *SunSeeker.*"

"In flight? Cap'n Redwing would frown."

"He seems more the 'throw 'em into leg irons' type."

Her laughing-eyed remark told them both that they needed celebration. It helped ward off the doubts, fears, and . . . an emotion he had no name for. *So be it*.

They stood with arms around each other's waist

and watched Earth's wheeling, silent majesty. Into the rim of their view swam *SunSeeker,* looking much like a lean and hungry shark.

Yes, a shark waiting to swim in the ocean of night. The large mouth was the magnetic funnel, waiting to be turned on, furl outward, and begin the slow acceleration out of the solar system. That scoop would yawn and first dive close to the sun, swallowing great gouts of the solar wind as start-up fuel. Behind the head complex curved the hoop of the control deck, its ruby glow alive with workers. Cliff watched tiny figures in their worker pods putting finishing touches on the long, rotating cylinder of the habitat and cryostorage sandwiched between the supplies storage vaults. Then came the wrinkled, cottonball-white, cybersmart radiators that sheathed the drive system. Its cylindrically spaced vents gave in to the fat fusion chambers, big ribbed barrels that fed the final thruster nozzles. Wrapped around these in a saddle truss were the big yellow fuel pods that would feed the beast as it accelerated into the deep dark, then fall away. From there on, it would glide through the centuries inside a magnetic sheath, safe from the proton sleet ahead. *SunSeeker* was a shark for eating away at light-years.

They had all ridden her out into the Oort cloud, tried the engines, found the flaws that the previous fourteen ships had tested. Ran the AI systems, found the errors in rivets and reason, made better. In the first few generations of interstellar craft, every new ship was an experiment. Each learned from the last, the engineers and scientists did their work, and a better ship emerged. Directed evolution on the fast track.

Now they were ready for the true deeps. Deep space meant deep time, all fleeting and, soon enough, all gone.

"Beautiful, isn't it?" a man's voice said from behind them.

It was Karl, the lanky head flight engineer. He had an arm around Mei Ling and seemed a bit bleary and red faced. From a snog-fog burst, Cliff guessed. Mei Ling just seemed extraordinarily joyful, eyes glistening.

Beth said, casting a sideways glance, "Yes—and we're counting on you to keep her happy."

"Oh yes, I will," Karl said, not getting the double entendre. "She's a great ship."

Mei Ling got it, arched an eyebrow, and nodded. "Saying good-bye to the world, are we? How do you think they'll think of us by the time we arrive?"

Beth said, "I'd like to be remembered as the world's oldest woman."

They all laughed. Mei Ling asked Cliff, "Hard to say farewell to it all, isn't it? You've been over here at the view most of the evening."

She had always been quick to read people, he recalled. She would understand that he needed merriment now. That they all did. "Um, yeah. I guess I'm a man of the world; my trouble is I'm trying to find which world."

They all nodded soberly. Then with a quick, darting grin, Karl showed off his newest trick. In the low centrifugal grav, he poured a dark red wine by letting it fall from the bottle, then cutting off the right amount with a dinner knife before it hit the glass. Three quick slices, Mei Ling rushed some glasses into place, and done. "Impressive!" Beth said. They drank.

"Got some news," Karl said. "Those grav waves near Glory? No signal in them. Just noise."

"How does that help us?" Beth asked. Cliff could tell from her expression that Karl was not her sort, but Karl would never know.

"It means there's not some supercivilization on Glory, for one thing."

"We already knew there are no electromagnetic signals," Mei Ling said.

"Well, sure," Karl said. "But maybe really advanced societies don't bother with primitive—"

"Hey, this is a party!" Beth said brightly. Karl took the hint. He shrugged and led Mei Ling away. She had some trouble walking.

"Cruel, you are," Cliff said.

"Hey, we won't see him for centuries."

"But it will seem like next week."

"So they say. What do you think about the grav waves?"

Just then a Section head broke in, using a microphone to get above the party noise, which was still rising. "We just got a launch congratulations from Alpha Centauri, folks! They wish you good speed."

Some hand clapping, then the party buzz came back even stronger. "Nice gesture," Beth said. "They had to send that over four years ago."

Tananareve Bailey spoke behind him. "It proba-

bly came in a year back and they've been saving it."
Cliff hadn't noticed her approach. She was more
covered up than most of the women, but gorgeous,
an explosion of browns and orange against black
face and arms. She stood with Howard Blaire, once
a zookeeper and something of a bodybuilding en-
thusiast.

Beth nodded. "Once we're in flight, the delay
times will mean we're talking to different generations. Spooky. But you were saying about the grav
waves—?"

Howard twisted his mouth, trying to recall.
"Look, *SunSeeker* was nearly built before LIGO 22
picked up those waves. It took all the time we were
out on our field trials to verify the detection. More
time to see if there was anything in it—and apparently there isn't. No signal, just some noisy spectrum. No, we're going to Glory because a biosphere
is there. One of the Astros told me these grav waves
probably come from just accidental superposition.
A good chance there's some pair of orbiting black
holes far across the galaxy, but the Glory system is
in the way—"

"That's what I think, too," a familiar voice said.
They turned to find a red-faced Fred, back again,
obviously a bit the worse for wear. "Can't get good
resolution on the source area, and Glory's over in
one corner of a degree-wide patch in the sky. The
grav waves could be from anywhere in there, even
in another galaxy."

Beth looked at Cliff and gave him her covert
rolled-eye look, saying, "I'm a bio type, myself."

Fred was a trifle intense, or "focused" as the psychers put it. Some found him hard to take, but he had solved a major technical problem in systems tech, which cut him some slack with Cliff. All crew had to have overlapping abilities, but for some like Fred, breadth was their main qualification. Of course, Fred was oblivious to all these nuances. He gestured at the screen. "Hard not to look at it— beauty and importance combined. The *Mona Lisa* of planets."

Beth murmured approval and he went on, talking faster. "Even now, I mean—hundreds of bio worlds with atmospheric signatures, but no better's been seen anywhere."

Irma Michaelson passed by without her husband in tow, her head turning quickly at Fred's remark. "You mean the new Forward probe data?"

"Uh, no—"

"Forward Number Five just checked in," Irma said. "Still pretty far out, can't get surface maps or anything. Plenty of clouds, got a smidge view of an ocean. Shows the atmospheric thermo pretty well, I hear. We got the tightbeam relay just in time! We might need to do some atmosphere work to make it comfy."

Beth asked, "What kind?"

"They say we may need more CO_2. Glory's a tad light on greenhouse gases," Fred said so fast, he could barely get the words out. "Surface temperatures are more like Canada. The tropics there are like our mid-temperate zones."

Now that we've terraformed Earth back to nearly

twencen levels, Cliff thought, *here comes another whole world. . . .*

He shook this off and listened to Fred, who was hurtling on bright-eyed with, "Once we learn how to suck carbon out of air really well, we can make a climate that will be better than what we were born into. Maybe better than humans ever had it."

By this time, he was lecturing to a smaller audience. He gave them a crooked smile, as if to acknowledge this, and walked off into the crowd, which was getting predictably more noisy.

"A lot of anxious energy humming through here," Beth said.

"An emotional bath," Cliff said dreamily, and nodded at Earth. "The big issue down there is our ever-smarter machines demanding back wages. What's retirement look like for a multicapillary DNA sequencer?"

Beth laughed, her eyes dancing. "I got a must-answer from SSC, asking what actor would best portray me in the series about us."

"At least we won't have to see it."

She thumped the screen. "I keep thinking I'll probably never see white curtains billowing into warm sunlit rooms on a lazy summer afternoon. We haven't left yet, and already I'm nostalgic."

"For me, it'll be surfing."

"Glory has oceans. A moon, pretty small. Maybe they have waves, too."

"I didn't bring my board."

He saw the Arctic Ocean ice was at least visible, a heartening symptom of a planet slowly backing down from the Hot Age. The big chunk of Antarctica that fell off a century back and caused all the flooding was slowly regrowing, too. The Pacific islands were still gone, though, and might never appear again, worn down by wave action. No surfing there, ever again.

He noticed a phalanx of officers in blue uniforms and gold braid, standing smartly in ranks. Most were from the Oort crew and would not go out on *SunSeeker,* so were here for formality. The leaner Glory-bound crew stood behind the tall, craggy figure blinking into the spotlight but still quite sure he belonged there.

"Captain Redwing is about to speak," a deck lieutenant's voice boomed out over the speakers. They stood at sharp attention beneath the other banner proclaiming,

STAR-CRAVING MAD FAREWELL

Redwing was in full dress uniform with medals blazing, beaming at everyone, face ruddy. Cliff recalled he had divorced the wife who was to go with him, but he had not heard the inside story. Redwing kept his posture at full attention except for head dips to junior officers. He maintained a kindly smile, as if he were pleased the other officers were sharing their nice little thoughts. Still, he was an imposing man in uniform.

"A great exit line," Cliff whispered, trying to edge inconspicuously toward the door. He cast a long look at Earth on the screen.

"Last night for separate quarters, too," Beth said. "Would you like to stay over?"

"Wow, yes, ma'am."

"I believe it's customary."

"Customary where?"

"Wherever it's Saturday night."

They threaded their way through the crowd, but the feeling still plucked at him. The noise and strumming music, the drinks and snog-fogs and quick darting kisses, faces lined and hopeful and sad, all passing by—but still, somehow, as if he wanted to freeze them in amber.

In an eerie way, this was like a . . . ghost story. All these support people, likable and irritating and officious and sexy and, soon enough—all dead. Left behind. When he and the other crew awoke in orbit around Glory, more than half of these would be centuries gone. Even with the standard life span of 160 years now, gone to gray dry dust.

It had never struck him this way. Not knowing it, but *feeling* it. All this greatness, the human prospect—all that would be far behind them when they next awoke.

Cliff smiled a thin pale smile and thought, *This is the last time I'll see Earth.* He looked at the swimming majesty of it, sighed with a sense of foreboding, and followed Beth.

PART I

WAKE-UP CALL

The possession of knowledge does not kill the sense of wonder and mystery. There is always more mystery.
—ANAÏS NIN

ONE

Life persists.

He recalled those words, his nervous mantra recited as the soft sleep came closing its grip with chilly fingers—

—and so he knew he was alive. Awake again. Up from the chill-sleep of many decades.

He was *cold*. His memory was blurred, but it told him he was on an odyssey no biologist had ever ventured on before, a grand epic. He was going to the stars, yes, and they had given him the stinky sulfur gas, yes, the first creeping chill . . . and that was . . . it.

But beyond that flash of memory, all he could think of was the incredible, muscle-shaking chill that spread like a sharp ache through him. He was too numb to shiver. Somewhere a loud rumble rolled up through his body, not heard but felt. *The cold . . .* He thought hard and with effort opened his sticky eyes.

Trouble. His gummy eyelids slammed closed against a crisp actinic glare. He must be in the revival clinic. Slowly he pried them open, still numb with cold. He focused with effort, looking for the joyous faces of his fellow colonists.

Not there. Nor was Beth.

Instead, the worried frowns of Mayra and Abduss Wickramsingh made him groggily anxious as they worked over him. Their faces swam away, came back, drifting above like clouds as the cold began to recede. He was *tired*. His bones ached with it. After decades of sleep . . .

Hands massaged his rubbery legs. Lungs wheezed. His heart labored, thumping in his ears. His throat rasped with a sour wind. He was finally starting to shiver. Sluggish sleep fell away like a mummy's moldy shroud.

Think. The Wickramsinghs were paired by ability, he recalled in a gray fog, self-sufficient and solely responsible for the three years of their watch. Mayra piloted, and Abduss was the engineer. They were fairly far down the queue, maybe twenty-seven watches. . . . How far along were they? It hurt to figure.

They turned him on his side to work on his stiff muscles. The massaging sent lancing pain, and he let out a muffled scream. They ignored that. At least he could see better. Against the hard ceramic glare, he could see that no others of *SunSeeker*'s 436 passengers in cold sleep were being revived. A capsule was running its program, though, so someone was coming out behind him. The bay was empty. Carbo-ceramic tiles were clean, looking like new.

As a scientist, he was not slated to come out until the infrastructure staff was up and running at Scorpii 3, the balmy world that everybody called Glory, that no eye had ever seen.

So they were maybe eighty years into the voyage. Not enough to be near Glory. Something was wrong.

Mayra's lips moved, glistening in the hard light, but he heard nothing. They worked on his neural connections and—*pop!*—he could hear. The dull rumble hammered at him. Interstellar surf.

"Okay? Okay?" Mayra said anxiously, mouth tight, her eyes intent. "What's your name?"

He coughed, hacked. Once his throat was clear of milky fluid, his first words were, "Cliff . . . Kammash. But . . . Why me? I'm bio. Is Beth still cold?"

They didn't answer at once, but each looked at the other.

"Don't talk," Mayra said softly, a smile flickering.

Definitely trouble. He had known the Wickramsinghs slightly in training, remembered them as reserved and disciplined, just what a cryo passenger would wish in a caretaker watch team.

And they were good. They got his creaky body up off the slab, kind hands helping, his muscles screaming. Then into a gown, detaching the IVs. Up, creaking onto his feet. He swayed, the room reeled, he sat down. Try again. Better . . . a step. First in eighty years, feet like bricks. They helped him shuffle to a table. He sat. Minutes crawled by as he felt air swoosh in and out of his lungs. He studied this phenomenon carefully, as though it were a miracle. As perhaps it was.

Food appeared. Coffee: caffeine, yes, lovely

caffeine. Nobody spoke. Next course, soup. It tasted like nectar, the essence of life. Then they told him, as he eagerly slurped down a big bowl of fragrant veggie mix grown aboard. Halfway through his third bowl, he became vaguely aware that they were talking about an astrophysical observation that required his interpretation.

"What? Mayra, Astro is *you*," he shot back. "Every pilot has to be."

"We need a different viewpoint," Mayra said, her dark eyes wary. "We do not want to bias your views by explaining more now."

"We are reviving the captain, too," Abduss said.

He blinked, startled. "Redwing?"

"It's that important." Abduss was unreadable. "He will awaken in another day, his capsule says."

Cliff felt a chill that was not thermal. Stores of food, water, oxygen couldn't be recycled forever. That was the point in riding semi-frozen: They would reach Glory with enough stores to survive until they could replace what was lost.

"Four of us. Waking too many people would run us short," he said. "What's up?"

Again, the Wickramsinghs looked at each other and did not answer.

• • •

As soon as he could walk steadily, they showed him the viewing screens, and for a long moment he could not speak.

The spectacle was striking, both for what was

familiar and what was not, *SunSeeker* was forty light-years from Earth, and yet he could identify many of the constellations he had known as a child in Brazil. Their familiar faces swam among a bright swarm of lesser lights, twisted here and there. On the scale of the galaxy, light-years did not count for much.

He immediately looked for their destination. A star not much different from Sol, Glory's primary should be a white point dead ahead. It was there, reassuringly bright, though still five light-years away. Perhaps its brilliance was enhanced by *SunSeeker*'s velocity? No, that was a small effect. More probably, brightened by his own longing to see, to breathe, to touch an Earthlike world, named Glory out of pure hope before any human eye had seen it. Pixels and spectra didn't do the job.

Other stars brimmed in the rosy night lit by *SunSeeker*'s bow shock. The ramscoop's plowing through the interstellar gas and ionized hydrogen was an unending rainbow light show, filmy incandescent streamers curving around them as they plunged into the infinite night. Beyond that prow wash lay the spectrally shifted universe. Some of the glimmering stars were intriguing, constellations rearranged—but nothing compared to the nearby red sun.

"That's the problem?" Cliff asked.

Abduss nodded. "It is a problem, but there is another, larger. We have been wrestling with this more difficult issue, but that can wait for the captain."

Can't these people ever say anything straight?

He made himself say deliberately, "Okay, tell me what's the big deal about this star?"

"We are overtaking it. When we came on watch, the star was not visible. There was a mild recombination source nearby, rather odd." Switching to another channel, Abduss pointed out a diffuse ivory plume behind the dark patch.

Cliff frowned. "How long is it?"

Abduss said, "About three astronomical units. This is a signature of hydrogen recombining, after it has been ionized. This linear feature seems to be a jet, cooling off and then turning back into atoms. That's the emission I made this map from, you see?"

"Um." Cliff wrinkled his nose, trying to think like an Astro type. "A jet from a star. It didn't jump out at you?"

Abduss tightened his mouth but otherwise did not move. "At first we did not even *see* the star."

Uh-oh . . . , Cliff thought. Best to shut up, yes.

"We had much to measure. The jet did not attract much attention, as it seemed unimportant. Yet now we can see it to be related to the star—which suddenly appeared."

Cliff nodded, smiled, tried to defuse the man's irritation. "Perfectly understandable. Our problems are inside the ship, not outside. So . . . the star popped into view because it came around the rim of this . . . thing."

Mayra murmured, "We became alarmed."

"Nobody noticed the star before? Earlier watches?"

Abduss blinked slowly. "We could not see it."

Cliff shrugged. In moderate close-up, the dwarf showed as a disk: it must be close. It was perched at the lip of a much larger arc of light. An ordinary star, little and reddish. He raised an eyebrow at Mayra.

"The spectral class is F9," Mayra added helpfully. "Most likely the plasma plume means that this star must have been recently active. Early stars often display this." Under magnification, the expelled matter looked to Cliff like a thin nebula, dim and old.

"But we don't know it's a young star," he said.

"No, stars of this class have very long lifetimes."

Cliff had never been much concerned with the fate of failed stars as they erupted and faltered. Spectacular, sure—but biology demands a stable abode. Still, he immediately guessed that this veil was a remnant of an earlier era in the star's life, when it was blowing off shells of hot gas. A good guess, anyway—but of course, not his field. These details of stellar evolution had never interested him very much, since they had little to do with his specialty, the evolution of higher life-forms on worlds similar to Earth. A largely abstract pursuit until the Alpha Centauri discoveries of a simple but strange ecology there. That was what drew him to Glory; Beth was an accidental benefit.

So he shrugged. "Gas from a small star. Why wake me up?"

"You are the highest-ranked Scientific," Abduss said.

Marya added, "And your specialty may be quite relevant."

That remark just perplexed him. He felt hungry and tired and disappointed. And miffed, yes, with a raspy sore throat. He sucked in a deep breath. "I'm supposed to assess Glory's biology, not be awakened to answer questions from the watch crew!"

They blinked, startled. He wondered if he was betraying more than the typical awakened-sleeper irritation they all had been warned about. Chill-sleep was reasonably safe, but coming out of it was not. Every crew member under its enforced hibernation cycle ran a 2 percent risk of subtle neurological damage from a revival, an irreducible price of seeking the stars. By waking him, they had forced him to double that risk. He'd be going back into the chill when he'd done what they wanted. He had rather blithely accepted the risk of several revivals when he became a senior science officer, he recalled, when it was entirely theoretical.

As well, no sleeper could be immediately returned to the vaults after revival. The medical risks were too great. So he was stuck for at least a month in the narrow rumbling quarters of the starship, eating the pallid food generated from ponics tanks. There was no way to avoid the perpetual growl of the fusion ramscoop. Filters could not erase the ever-shifting tones of turbulence as the ship surged through clumps of denser gas, riding waves of ionization—a moving electrical discharge, lighting up its neighborhood.

He had not been slated for revival on the passage at all, so his sensitivity to noise had not been an issue. And indeed, the shifting, grating clangor already irked him a bit. There was no way to damp it, so he would have to use noise-suppressing headphones. Certainly he would not have made the cut for active, awake crew.

The Wickramsinghs glanced at each other yet again, as if to say, *Humor him—he's a senior officer*. Both inhaled deeply. Abduss said, "Please tolerate our unveiling this anomaly so that you may experience it as we did."

"Um, yes." He still felt irked, but ordered himself to behave as an officer should.

Mayra said, "Notice that the luminous gas, as you put it, is very straight."

Cliff zoomed the image—and blinked. He had expected a ragged cloud of expelled debris, the star's outer layers blown off. The plume seemed to point at the star ahead. "Pretty, at least. Why so sharp?"

Abduss said carefully, "We wondered, too. None of the astronomical analysis systems had an explanation. But it did alert us to the infrared spectrum."

"Of this plume? Why—?"

Mayra switched to the middle infrared bands, and his mouth fell open. An orange circle stretched across the sky. The plume was an arrow stuck in the exact center of some target.

"The plasma apparently comes from the center of that massive infrared region. It is mostly of hydrogen, and its ions eventually find electrons and they unite," Abduss said, as if he were talking to a student. "That is the hydrogen line we see, the plume cooling off."

Mayra added, "But it did lead our attention to the huge region of soft infrared emission."

"Hey, I'm a biologist—"

"We awoke you because the infrared signature is clear. The circle we see is solid, not a gas."

His irritation vanished. Even a biologist knew enough to be startled by the implication. All he could manage to say was, "That's impossible."

Mayra said mildly, "When I first saw it, I, too, assumed it to be gas. The spectral lines prove otherwise."

He studied it, trying to allow for perspective. "A disk? . . . It's *huge*."

"Indeed," Mayra said.

"But it can't be a planet. It would be bigger than any star."

Abduss nodded. "We are approaching from behind it, and at present speed will come directly alongside within weeks. The . . . thing . . . is about three hundred AU away from us." He smiled quickly, as if embarrassed. "Allowing for that, look closer."

"This is why we awakened you," Mayra said.

He blinked. "It's . . . artificial?"

"Apparently," Mayra said.

"What? How—?"

"We have just come into view of this object, by coming nearly alongside. It drew our attention because its star suddenly appeared—presto! We could not see it before because the . . . the cap, whatever it is . . . blocked the starlight as we overtook it."

Abduss added helpfully, "Infrared study shows that it is not a disk. It's rounded. We witness it from behind, with the plasma plume coming through a hole at the exact rear center. The cap radiates at the temperature of lukewarm water."

"A . . . sphere?" He saw it then, the image snapping into perspective. He was looking at a ball with a hole in its bottom. Through that hole, the star glowed. His imagination scrambled after an old idea. "Maybe it's a, what was the name—?"

"A Dyson sphere," Mayra provided. "We thought so at first, too."

"So this is a shell?"

She nodded. "A hemisphere, perhaps—a sphere halfway under construction. Perhaps. Only—the old texts reveal quite clearly that Dyson did not dream of a rigid sphere at all. Rather, he imagined a spherical zone filled with orbiting habitats, enough of them to capture all of the radiant energy of a star."

Abduss thumbed up a reference to these ideas on a side screen. Good—they had done the homework before awakening him. But if not a Dyson sphere, what—?

Mayra said, "We have watched and run the Doppler programs carefully. The hemispherical cap is spinning about the same axis formed by the plume."

Abduss said helpfully, "Only by rotating such a shell could one support it against the star's gravity."

"Like this ship." He nodded, trying to guess Abduss's point. "Centrifugal gravity. But a complete, rigid sphere . . . spinning . . . that would be impossible, right? Gravity would pull it in at the poles."

They both nodded. Abduss said, "Still, the configuration is not stable."

They both looked at him, so he went on, thinking aloud. "The shell should fall into the star—it's not orbiting. There's some sort of force balance at play here. Odd construction, indeed. Just spinning isn't enough, either—the stresses would vary with curvature. You'd need internal supports."

Mayra said, "Quite right, I believe. My first degree was in astrophysics and I have some ideas about this object, but—" She bowed her head and shrugged.

As matters developed, there was a great deal behind Mayra's modesty. In the next day, eating five meals to build himself up, he learned as much about the Wickramsinghs' subtleties as he did of the strange object they had discovered. They were deferential toward him, unveiling their ideas slowly, allowing him to come to his own conclusions. This helped greatly as the magnitude of implication grew.

He didn't even ask about Scorpii 3 until hours later, when Abduss and Mayra were using the control room facilities to lecture him. The planet, their destined home, was a long way off still, and deserved the nickname Glory. Scorpii 3 was the second nearest habitable-seeming world ever found, after the Alpha Centauri base. A fast-burn probe had verified the bio-signatures found by deep space telescopes two generations before *SunSeeker*'s launch. A wonder, with strong ozone lines, a lot of water, and tantalizing hints of green chlorophyll in the spectrum. A dream world. No sign of any artificial electromagnetic emissions, after big dishes had cupped their ears toward it for decades. Plus the mysterious grav waves that made no sense, considering that there were no big masses in the system to send out such quadrupole emissions.

He looked at it in the high amplification forward scope, but it was just a flickering blur through their bow shock. Scorpii 3 was barely visible because it hung near the edge of the structure ahead, though it was many light-years away. He looked at the screens, trying to get his head around what that vast bulk could mean. But emotion overwhelmed him. Pure wonder.

Unimaginable, yes. Bigger than the orbit of Mercury, huge beyond comprehension, the hemisphere was an *artifact*, a *built* thing, the first evidence of another intelligence in the galaxy. Not a trickle of radio waves, but a giant . . . riddle.

He took a long breath, relaxed into the observer's chair and headpiece, and let the slow, long wavelength rumble of the starship run through his bones. And thought.

The Wickramsinghs felt it was a matter of biology. Wake the biologist!

Cliff wrinkled his nose. He had been irked, sure, but the Wickramsinghs were right: You see trouble, you call for help. But he wasn't prepared for this. But as well he saw that none of that now mattered.

Science had speculated about intelligence for centuries, as probes spread out through a desert of dead worlds. The Big Eye telescopes in the twenty-first century had found warm, rocky worlds resembling Earth, and some had the ozone spectral lines that promised oxygen atmospheres. There the promise had ended. Here and there flourished slime molds in deep caverns, or simple ocean life, maybe—cellular colonies still unable to shape themselves into complex forms, as Earth's life had more than a billion years ago. Sure, there was life, the consensus said . . . boring life.

To find an artifact of such immensity . . . it made his mind reel.

Then Abduss said, almost casually, "There is something more. Why we realized the protocols demanded that you be awakened. We have detected narrow-band microwave traffic from near the star."

Cliff realized that he should have seen this coming. "Coded?"

"Yes. It may be broadcasting from near the hole in the center—the angle is right—and we're getting some scattered, reflected signals."

"Are they hailing us?"

"There's nothing obvious that we can figure out, no," Mayra said. "There are many transmissions, not a long string. It looks like a conversation, perhaps."

"So they don't know we're here, maybe."

"We could hear the traffic once we were within

view of the hole, I believe. Perhaps it comes from within the hemisphere, and leaks through. It is not broadcast for others to pick up—or so we think. And unintelligible, at least to us."

Cliff eyed them both and said carefully, "I agree that the protocols call for my revival. But this is more than anybody ever visualized, when those protocols were invented. . . ." He was still dazed after a day awake. And cold; he rubbed his arms to get blood moving. "I wonder if you didn't wake me too early, though. We're not looking at plants and animals yet. If we wake too many of us . . ."

"Yes," Abduss said.

"We'd run short."

"We're short now," Mayra said. "That is the other problem. It is high time someone woke the captain, we felt."

"So you did, right after me? Me, because my secondary specialty is in rations and ship biology. Mostly, though, I'm a field biologist. But sure, call me up. Then the cap'n, to take over all the other implications. Right."

"And now we are happy to turn both problems over to you." Abduss gave him a broad smile without any trace of irony. Mayra beamed, too. They had faced all this together, and the weight of it showed in their evident relief.

• • •

It didn't take long to see why they were handing off to him and the captain.

The opportunity: an artifact bigger than planets.

The problem: *SunSeeker* was not performing to specs. The ramscoop drive was running at 0.081 of light speed, instead of the 0.095 engineering had promised.

Not a big difference, but in starflight it was crucial. At 0.081, their trip would take 550 years. They had stocks for a bit over 500 years.

Early space travel had been like this, with tiny margins of safety. Reaching the Moon six out of seven tries had been a miracle. They'd run aging X-planes for a quarter of a century, losing two shuttles before they built something better. Interplanetary travel still cut close to the bone, and interstellar was a crapshoot. And still there were always those who would take the gamble.

Of course, *SunSeeker* recycled everything—and, of course, the accounting never quite came out even. The flight plan had them arriving at Glory with time to find what they needed. Glory had a world with oceans and free oxygen, all carefully checked in the ozone spectral line seen from Earth orbit. And in the infrared, they had seen a broad disk of asteroids, too, comfortably farther out and with traces of iceteroids among them. The world or the rocks would give them the elements they needed: water, oxygen, dust to be turned to soil.

But this slower speed was eating their safety window.

He checked the log. Five watch cycles had worked on the problem in their ramscoop drive without really spotting a cause. None of them had wakened the captain. It was an engineering problem, not a command structure one. And they were on a centuries-long voyage.

The big magnetic fields at *SunSeeker*'s bow drove shock waves into the hydrogen ahead, ionizing it to prickly energies, then scooping it up and mixing it with fusion catalysis, burning as hot as suns—but somehow, the nuclear brew didn't give quite the thrust it had during field trials out in the Oort cloud. Considering how new relativistic engineering was, maybe this was not truly surprising.

Still, it had huge consequences. "We won't get to Glory in time," Cliff said.

The Wickramsinghs nodded together. Mayra said, "So . . ." She did not want to draw the conclusion.

"We have cut our rations to a minimum, all five watches, yes," Abduss rushed in, eyes large. "It was a major decision we made, you see—to revive you and the captain."

Cliff slurped down more coffee. It tasted incredibly good—another symptom of revival. "You've done the calculation. Can we make it?"

"Marginal at best," Mayra said precisely. "The last five watches have run at the minimum crew number: two. Plus we are pushing the hydroponics to the maximum. We fear it is not enough."

"Damn!" Cliff grimaced. Starve to death between the stars. "That's also why nobody woke the captain. One more gut, one more pair of lungs.

Until . . . yeah." Until they saw the strange thing up ahead.

. . .

He knew the deeper reason, too. What could the captain do, after all? If the engineers could not find a solution, mere managerial ability would not help. So the engineers had followed the protocols that had been drilled into them: Follow mandates and hope for the best. Especially since an error could kill them all with relativistic speed.

They gazed at him, calm and orderly and patient, the perfect types for a watch crew. Which he was not. Too restless and a touch excitable, the psych guys had said. That was fine with Cliff; he wanted to see Glory, not black interstellar space. All crew were calm, steady types, or they wouldn't have made the first cut in the long selection filters.

The Wickramsinghs were waiting. He was in charge until the captain woke up. That he did not understand the situation did not matter; he was a superior officer, so he had to make the decisions.

First, he had to rest. About that, the revival procedures were as hard-nosed as the mission protocols. At least that would give him a little time to think.

. . .

They found him twelve hours later, in the kitchen.

The first thing he ordered was a thorough study of the star they were approaching. The Wickramsinghs called up screens of data and vibrant images. This gave him a jumpy image of a star massing about nine-tenths of Sol's mass. There were plenty of those in the galaxy, but this one was not behaving like a serene, longer-lived orange dwarf. Fiery tendrils forked and seethed at the center of the apparent disk. "There is blurring in the image," Abduss remarked, "by the plasma plume."

Squinting, at first he did not understand the implication of the roiling spikes that leaped from a single hot spot, a blue white furnace. "Ah—that spot is directly under the center of the artificial bowl, the cap."

Abduss nodded. "Something is disturbing the star, making it throw out great flaming tongues. Very dangerous, I would think."

They were coming up on this system pretty fast. Cliff thumbed in the whole data field. The obviously artificial disk—okay, call it the cap, because he could sense from the image that it was curved away from their point of view—the cap was not at all far away, maybe a few hundred astronomical units, where an A.U. was the distance from Earth to Sol. You got used to such enormous distance measures, in the relentless training all crew had to undergo.

He tried to remember when that was . . . centuries ago. Yet it seemed like just a few weeks.

He looked at the image and let his eyes see it as a curved hemisphere cupped around this side of the star.

They zoomed the optics in on the disk's flares,

having to go through several settings that blanked out the blue white hot spot on the star's surface. The glare of the hot spot was fierce, actinic, bristling with angry storms, a tiny white sun attached to the bigger pink star like an angry leech.

Above the white spot raged the filigree spikes of streaming plasma. They whirled around one another like fighting snakes, burning as they rushed up from the hot spot. It looked like they should bathe the hemispheric bowl in licking flames. But before they reached the curve of the bowl, they dovetailed into a slender jet. Among the streamers, Cliff could see little blobs and bright flecks moving out from the star, swarming up along the jet, toward the neatly circular hole in the bowl and out into the sky.

Cliff wrestled with the images. "Let's see the earlier pictures, from the last watch."

Automatically, the ship kept records of the local sky. Its software was spectrally sophisticated and framed its own, limited hypotheses about the class and type of every luminous object it saw. They checked the records. The muted minds that murmured among themselves, struggling to understand the bowl, had spun endlessly in parameter-space confusions.

In the infrared, there was a glow where the "bottom" of the bowl would be. None of the instruments showed any image of the bowl during the years while the ship was approaching from behind. He thumbed through uninteresting pictures. The bowl blotted out a small dot on the sky, but nobody had noticed such a minor thing from light-years away.

The bowl's infrared radiation showed a temperature around 20 degrees centigrade. Room temperature.

"Ah, balmy," Abduss said. Across that vast curve, tropical conditions prevailed. The back face was cool and appeared stony. But the warmed side was at 20 degrees C. The star was less luminous than Sol—but, of course, the bowl was in continuous sunlight, so it would get pretty warm. No night.

Cliff had a mind's eye picture of the bowl as a colossal construction, even though his common sense was screaming. When something appeared impossible, it seemed best to simply study it until understanding emerged. And wait for the captain to wake up, yes.

The first shock came from simple geometry. Mayra gave him distances and angles and he quickly found that the area of the inward-facing cap was two hundred million times that of Earth. Hovering over its star, the rim of the bowl would provide a vast, livable surface. (The biologist would wait for the captain's take, but . . . *Air. Water. Stores to replenish a failing ship.* The Wickramsinghs nodded and smiled when he spoke of this. . . .)

On that area, peering through the small hole they could see, Abduss picked up reflecting optical emission . . . and found the spectral signatures of water. Then, with a bit more effort to see through the rippling plasma that shrouded *SunSeeker,* he found oxygen.

So it was an immense area designed for living . . . by what?

Cliff checked their distance from the bowl: 320 AU—about a hundredth of a light-year. *So close!* And coming up fast.

But they were still looking at the back of the cap, in the dark. He looked at the waiting faces of the Wickramsinghs and thought. They were left with some brute astronomical facts—velocities, times, food supplies. . . .

At their review meeting, the Wickramsinghs eyed him expectantly.

"It's beyond me," he said—and watched their faces, despite their best efforts, show disappointment.

"Surely we can learn more?" Mayra suggested hesitantly.

"Not at this distance," Abduss said. "And I doubt the captain will authorize a trajectory change to get closer."

Cliff looked at them and thought unkind thoughts. Five crews didn't wake the captain, because there wasn't an answer. They had been trained to keep the ship running. Schooled to stay steady. But here was something the Earthside planners had never imagined.

"I think we have two problems," Cliff said with what he hoped was a diplomatic tone. "Supplies, yes. And this strange . . . object. Too much here for us to deal with."

Abduss said carefully, "We had thought somewhat the same."

"Look," Mayra said directly, "it's nearly time to take the captain up to his conscious stage—"

"I want Beth Marble brought up, too."

Both of them blinked. "But she is—"

"Capable, right." He could see a lot of trouble coming, and he didn't want to be alone. Who did?

"But there is no protocol requiring—"

Cliff held up his hand and looked across the table steadily, letting them think about it. "Let's just do it."

"She is . . . not your wife."

"No, but she has ship skills and can pilot."

"Not until we can ask the captain," Abduss said. His face was firm.

TWO

They told the captain when he came out of cold sleep, bleary-eyed, stiff, still lying on a slab—and then his eyes began blinking with startling speed, alert.

Abduss said, "You aren't going to believe this."

Captain Redwing's skeptical grin crinkled the leathery skin around his eyes as he said, "Try me."

So they told him, while they gingerly massaged his stiff, cold muscles and applied the necessary chemistries. Cliff hung back and bided his time while the Wickramsinghs took Redwing through the whole story.

Redwing sat up and shook his black mane, his

bronzed skin blue-veined at the wrists, and said, "You're *sure*?"

So they told him some more. Showed the screens, the time log, and finally the close-ups of the back of the bowl. The captain stared at the bowl image, and Cliff could see him mentally put it aside to concentrate on the supplies issue.

"The drive not running to specs. Five crew changes! You couldn't do *any*thing?" He jabbed a finger at the Wickramsinghs.

"We did not know what to do," Mayra said reasonably. "There were—"

"We've run this way for—what?—decades!"

Abduss bristled in her defense, face stiff. "This was not in the protocols."

"Protocols be damned. I—"

"The leptonic drive is one issue, Captain," Cliff said, "and this thing ahead is quite another—"

"You're Science." Redwing cut him off with a chopping hand signal. "This is crew."

Cliff sat back and nursed his coffee and remembered all the rumors before launch. How Redwing was from one of the families that had made a bundle out of the Native American casinos. How he'd breezed through MIT with great grades and a wake of surly enemies. Made his rep in the Mars exploration and exploitation. Been a real sonofabitch, sure, but he had gotten things goddamn well *done*. Maybe not the worst recommendation, considering. Cliff was going to have to follow orders.

"We cannot go on like this," Mayra said, ever the diplomat. "Our external diagnostics are working well, so we are sure there is not some property of the interstellar gas that is the root of our drive problem. We rely on the microwave view to diagnose the ramscoop fields—"

"We'll review it all," Redwing said crisply. He bit his lip. "And the earlier crews—Jacobs, Chen, Ambertson, Abar, Kalaish—all top people . . ."

• • •

Redwing went through an extensive engineering review with them. Systems, flows, balances, malfunction indices. After hours of work, he was just as stumped as the ship diagnostic systems, which were better engineers than any of them. Nothing seemed wrong, but the ship could do no better. *Seeker* had performed perfectly in the first few decades, achieving their terminal velocity when the pressure of incoming matter on its ram fields equaled the thrust it got out of hydrogen fusion. They had been losing velocity through tens of light-years—slightly at first, then more.

Crews had tested the obvious explanations. Maybe the interstellar gas was getting too thin, so they weren't taking in enough hydrogen to drive the fusion zone at max. That idea didn't pencil out in the detailed numbers. The fusion drive was a souped-up version of magnetic cylinders, each a rotating torus that contained fusing plasma. Boron–proton reactions were the burning meat and potatoes, the protons shoveled in fresh from the ramscoop. The rotating magnetic equilibria held fusing plasma in their bottles, releasing the alpha particles into the nozzle that drove them forward. It had worked steadily now for centuries. It looked fine.

The next crew thought there was too much dust ahead, so perhaps the fusion burn was tamped down. They found an ingenious way to pluck dust samples from their bow shock and measure it carefully. Nothing wrong there, either.

There were more ideas and trials, and now it was getting serious. They had started with plenty of spare supplies, but now it wasn't going to be enough.

"Our big fat margin of error got . . . eaten," Redwing told them.

Seeker would arrive nearly a century late. They might barely squeeze through, if the expected level of leaks and losses did not happen . . . but nobody wanted to calculate the odds of that. Because they all knew the odds were bad.

• • •

They all slept on their problems, and the next ship-day Cliff was first up. Another revival symptom—insomnia sometimes lasted weeks. Along with that, and no surprise: irritability. The damn noise wasn't helping. The best solution was to say as little as possible. Meanwhile, his mind churned away at the deeper puzzle of the bowl that hung like a riddle on their optical viewing screens. The image rippled from plasma refraction, but Cliff could make out tantalizing, momentary patches of detail in it.

The world as a bowl, he thought, trying to think of a better term. Flamboyantly artificial. What would choose to live in such a place?

They held a meeting, and then another, without anything new turning up. At the end of another frustrating conversation, Cliff said quietly, "I want Beth revived. We need more minds on this problem, and we're stalled."

Redwing pursed his lips briefly and shook his head. "We'd better keep lean."

"Only if we're going to just forge on and hope things improve without our doing anything." Cliff said it in a rush, finally getting out what he and Abduss had agreed upon.

Before Redwing could respond, Abduss chimed in, "I found another slight decrease in our velocity this morning. Nearly a full kilometer per second."

A long silence, Redwing carefully letting nothing show in his face. The signs of strain in the man had been mounting. Little gestures of frustration, a broken cup, time off by himself, little social talk. The psychers back Earthside had a high opinion of Redwing's leadership style, but to Cliff the man had seemed to be best at bureaucratic infighting. *No managers to game around out here, though.*

"So whatever's wrong, it's getting worse," Redwing said.

Nobody answered.

Cliff said carefully, "Beth has piloting and engineering skills, pretty broad."

Only when the words were out did he recognize the pun. Mayra smiled but said nothing. *A pretty broad.* And of course, Cliff's longtime "associate," as the polite social term had it.

Redwing let a wry smile play on his face for a few seconds. "Okay, let's warm her up."

They started Beth's revival. The protocols were straightforward, but every case had variations. While the slow processes worked in her, they spent another two days looking at the slowdown problem, getting nowhere. The ship was flying hard, hitting molecular cloudlets and, increasingly, vagrant wisps of plasma. "That's the plume from the jet we see," Abduss said. "We're starting to hit the wake."

Then the ramscoop would need to navigate, and there would be no data to let it know how to work. The artificial intelligences that tirelessly regulated the scoop fields were smarter than mere humans, adjusting the magnetic scoops and reaction rates—but they were also obsessively narrow. The AIs worked as well as they could, making estimates based on many decades of in-flight experience, guessing at causes—but they could not think outside their conceptual box. "Savants of the engine," Mayra called them. Cliff wondered if she was being ironic.

"Look, we need to make a decision," Abduss insisted. "Yes?"

"I do, you mean," Redwing said. He made a cage of his fingers and peered into it. He was pale and drawn, and not all of that came from his recovery from the long sleep. Nobody had slept much.

Cliff said, "Maybe this is a godsend."

Redwing shot him a questioning glance. "You always had an odd sense of humor."

They had not gotten along particularly well in staff and crew meetings. Redwing had held out for making all Scientific Personnel de facto crew members, rigidly set in the chain of command. Cliff and others had blocked him. Scientific Personnel had their own, looser command structure that dealt with Redwing only near the top of the pyramid. Cliff was the highest-ranking Scientific Personnel officer awake. Of course, all that procedural detail was decades ago—no, centuries, he reminded himself—but in personal memory, it still loomed as recent.

He tried a warm, reasonable tone. "If we hadn't been slowed down, we'd be blazing right by this weird thing. No way we could even swing around that star—say, let's call it Wickramsingh's Star, eh? With joint discovery rights for all."

Thin smiles all around. They needed a little levity. Nobody aboard would ever make a buck from interstellar enterprises. . . . "But now, going slower, maybe we can make a small correction with a pretty fair delta-V, get a closer look at the thing."

Redwing looked blank. So did the Wickramsinghs.

Cliff said carefully, "It's artificial. Maybe we can—"

"Get help?" Redwing's mouth twisted skeptically. "I admit, that's a bizarre object, but it's not our goal to explore passing phenomena along the way. We're headed for Glory, and that's *it*."

Cliff had thought about this moment for two

days. He spread his hands as if making a deal, splitting the difference. "Maybe we can do both."

Redwing's face had already settled into the firm-but-confident expression that served him so well back Earthside. Then he paused, puzzled, and almost against his will asked, "How's that?"

"Say we use the plasma plume from the star. We're running up into the fringes already. It's rich in hydrogen, right?" A nod to Abduss and Mayra. "And a lot more ionized than the ordinary interstellar gas we've been riding through, scooping up with the magnetic funnels and blowing out the back, all these decades. For a ramscoop motor, this is high-quality input. Let's use it to pick up some speed."

A heartbeat went by, two. Cliff thought, *Keep it simple,* and said, "That jet's spurting straight out the back of the thing. Let's fly up it."

Redwing asked, "Abduss, isn't that plume moving at relativistic speeds? In the wrong direction? It'd slow us down."

Was Redwing right? Mayra was nodding. Recklessly, Cliff said, "That could work, too."

"You make my head hurt," Redwing said. "What are you on about now?"

"With what we've got for consumables, we're going to arrive dead at Glory. If we can't speed up, we'll have to stop for supplies. Here, now. Make orbit around Wickramsingh's Star. Deal with the natives."

They stared at him.

Cliff played his next card. "We're overtaking the star. Every hour makes a velocity change tougher."

Mayra's eyes widened, startled—but surely she had thought of this?—and then she nodded.

Redwing wasn't a man to leap at a suggestion. But he screwed his mouth around, eyes seeking the low, mottled carbon-fiber ceiling, and said, "Let's do the calculation."

• • •

That took another day.

While the others checked their screens and fretted, Cliff watched Beth come up out of the long dark cold and into his arms. He claimed the right to massage her sore self, rub her skin with the lotions and soothe away the panic that raced across her face, coming up out of decades'-long sleep. He watched her pretty face fill with color, rosy with freckles, her red hair still a vibrant halo. She had been uneasy about the whole prospect, kept it from him and failed, and now here was her fear again, in fluttering eyelids, vagrant jitters that flickered in her face—until her cloudy eyes focused, squinted, and she saw him hovering against the ceramic sky and a flush brightened in her, surprise racing, and she smiled.

"I . . . what . . . *cold* . . ."

"Don't talk. Just breathe. Everything's fine," he lied.

"If you're here, it's gotta be." She reached for him anyway, grimacing at the effort. It was like a new sun coming up.

THREE

Beth Marble felt life coming back into her like a muddy, warm flow. Seeing Cliff first made her last thoughts—those fears of decades ago, as the sedative swarmed up in her—trickle away. *He's here! Looking the same. It worked! We're at Glory, then.*

A few minutes ago in relative time, she had felt the old clammy panic. *This could be the last sight I see.* . . . And the adrenaline surge of dread still pounded through her. *And I thought I was so ready, so sure.* . . .

She smiled at this memory of her former self and carefully put that past aside. What was that mantra in high school? *Be here now.*

Cliff spoke, his words warm and steady. "Everything's fine."

She answered with a croaking, "If you're here, it's gotta be."

His hands on her felt wonderful and she followed his whispered orders. Lie back, just take it, enjoy. Smell the cool metallic air. The spreading glow of tissues swelling, blood flowing at speeds her cells had not known for years, tingling, surges of pleasure as her senses revived . . . *Hey, I could get to like this.*

Then she heard the growl of the ship.

The vast majority of the crew had gone into sleep before *SunSeeker* even started, but as pilot she had stayed up for over a year as *Seeker* gathered speed. It felt *good*, to be at the helm of a starship, she recalled—even if the yoke helm was nearly super-fluous, since electronics really steered the magnetics and lepton-catalytic fusion burn.

So she knew the thrumming long bass notes that told her the ship was running full bore. She didn't need to hear that; she could feel it.

And the subtle tenor in the background, when *Seeker* was in reversed configuration, and so decelerating—it wasn't there.

She listened hard as Cliff's hands welcomed her back into the world, and no, they weren't at Glory. Something was wrong.

• • •

Redwing's well-managed face was a study in guarded reluctance.

He did not like any of the alternatives on the table. Nobody did. But Cliff could see in the doubting downturn of his mouth that he did not want to forge ahead into long, lean years, hoping the drive would improve.

Abduss scribbled on a work slate. By this time, Cliff could read his expression pretty well. The man was steady and reliable, risk averse, with an automatic distrust of radical new ideas—just right for crewing the long years out here. Yet despite himself, Abduss was trying out the idea, and liking it. Now he had a share in a great discovery, and it was dawning that he wanted more. So did Cliff, for that matter.

But mostly, Cliff wanted to live. With Beth. They could marry, after the longest courtship in history.

Cliff knew enough to let the silence in their wardroom lengthen. Beth sensed the score now, and her careful look took in the tension: Redwing's folded hands, Abduss and Mayra keeping their eyes on their slates. The background rumble of the ramscoop fusion engines was like a persistent reminder; Newton's laws don't wait. Redwing stared into space. In the end, Abduss looked up. "We could make such a maneuver, yes. But very vigilantly."

"What do you make of it, Beth?" Redwing asked softly.

"I'm pretty sure the ship can be helmed in that accurately," she said. "It's within specs, the delta-V and aiming. I can tune the comm deck AIs to smooth it a bit. It'll be a ten-day maneuver. But I do wish I knew why the engines aren't working to design."

"Don't we all," Redwing said ruefully, unfolding his hands. "But we play the hand we're dealt."

It was as though fresh air had come into the room. Four faces awaited the captain's word.

They had awakened him to make this decision, and so far he had shied away from it. Now Cliff had a slender moment to wonder at his own ideas, if he'd followed them far enough. *Life's a gamble.* He had a gathering, foreboding sense—and a heart-pounding curiosity that would not give him rest. *Life persists.*

Redwing's mouth firmed up. "Let's do it."

• • •

Beth had the flight plan Alfvén numbers tuned just about right. She found it gratifying to see the ship respond to her helm, even though it was a bit spongy. It took eleven days to make the swerve. There were dark days when it was not clear whether *Seeker* was responding correctly to the maneuver. The magnetic scoops rippled with stresses but performed to code. With Abduss checking her every move, she brought them through, though not without some polite arguments.

Cliff and Beth spent a lot of time in their room together. The warm comforts of bed helped.

She preferred taking ginger snaps from her recovery allotment of "indulgences." These she had selected for just this, a crisp bite floating on sugar, to the richness of chocolate chip, which she also had because Cliff liked them. Though with either she always had a cup of cocoa, the warm brown mama she needed, Cliff had carried none but stern Kona coffee in his wakeup stash. No cookies at all.

"What do you remember about going into the chill-sleep?" she asked while they licked crumbs off each other.

He smiled dreamily. "They said I would feel a small prick in my left hand and I thought that was funny but couldn't laugh. Could barely crack a smile. Then—waking up."

Beth grinned and finished her cocoa. "I thought of the same dumb joke. Not that, in your case, I know what a small one feels like."

The remark got more laughter than it deserved, but that was just fine, too.

Beth said with a thin voice, "Y'know, looking at that round thing from this angle, first thing I thought was, it seems like a giant wok with a hole at its base."

"You're thinking about food again. Time to eat."

Her old fear subsided while she worked, and to keep it at bay she indulged herself with Cliff. He was the sun of her solar system, had been since the first week they met during the crew selections trials. Her parents had both died the year before in a car crash, and that cast a shadow over her application, in the eyes of the review board. They wanted crew with a long history of steady performance, no emotional unsettled issues that might boil over years later.

Losing the two central figures of her life had eclipsed her joy, made her withdraw. She had not thought of the affair with Cliff as an antidote to her grief, but its magic had played out that way. He brought out the sun again, eclipse over, and it showed up in everything she did. Especially in her psych exams and, more tellingly, in the return of her social skills. Later, in training, she had learned that about the time she met Cliff, she was slated to be cut in the next winnowing. As she put it later, "Then Cliffy happened to me." The visible changes in her had saved her slot. Then her performance at electromagnetic piloting, a still-evolving new discipline, had excelled.

She was here because of him. She let him know that, in long, passionate bouts of lovemaking. Sex was the flip side of death, she had always thought—the urge to leave something behind, ordained by evolution way back in the unconscious.

Their sweaty hours "in the sack" (not a phrase she liked, but it sure fit here, because Cliff used a hammock) certainly seemed to confirm the idea, as never before in her admittedly rather scant love life. At meals, she was afraid that it showed in her face, which now reddened at the slightest recollection of how different she was now, wanton and happy and well out of the eclipse shadow.

One evening, after she had set them in a long, curving arc toward the bowl, the captain allowed spirits to be broken out. They held a sort of impromptu group brainstorming session, with Mayra presiding as de facto referee. Ideas flew back and forth. What would they find up ahead? What the hell could the bowl *be*? Squeezebulbs were lifted, and lifted again. Beth got them all laughing. There was singing, predictably awful, which made more laughter. The captain drank more than the rest of them put together and she began to understand the pressures the man was under.

• • •

The maneuver they were planning was astonishing. The jet was far denser than any plasma *Seeker* had been designed to fly into. But *Seeker*'s specs were broad enough to include collisions with molecular clouds. You never knew what you would run into in interstellar space, Beth thought. Never the bowl, not that, but *SunSeeker* had been made robust.

Stars buried in a cloud could ionize spherical shells around them. *SunSeeker* might have to brave a cloud, and so the plasma spheres. Its prow sprouted lasers that could identify solid obstacles up to the size of houses, and vaporize them with a single gigawatt pulse. The lasers were tough, hanging out in the plasma hurricane near *SunSeeker*'s bow shock. They were going to need that.

Wickramsingh's Star was moving counter to the galaxy's rotation. That was somewhat unusual, though not rare. They were headed the same way, because Glory's system lay behind Sol, in the sense of the rotation most stars share in the immense bee-hive pinwheel that is a spiral galaxy. That was why they had not noticed the star's oddity before—the bowl cupped around the star, so they could not see it from *SunSeeker* or from Earth. As *Seeker* overtook the system, moving directly behind, the star had suddenly seemed to pop into existence from behind its shawl. And it was quite nearby.

"Mmmmmm. It's moving how quickly?" Beth asked in the next meeting. Five of them just fit five monitor chairs in the control room.

"More than ten thousand kilometers per second," Mayra said.

"Look, that's damn fast."

Mayra beamed. "Yes. I was keeping this precise fact for the right moment."

"And that's nearly our ship velocity. Sure seems high for a star."

Abduss nodded. "A bit less than ours, so we overtook it. But yes, unusual for a star."

They glanced at each other and Beth wondered why the Wickramsinghs liked unveiling mysteries one step at a time. A cultural thing? Maybe they just hadn't wanted to shock her too much, so soon after revival? She had to admit, her head was still feeling a bit woozy—and not from the cold or the drugs. Conceptual overload. If she hadn't seen the thing on the screens with her own eyes . . .

Try to think straight. Beth asked, "Could . . . could the flares we see at the center of the star be responsible?"

Mayra shook her head. "How? Surely they are caught by the cap."

Beth drew herself a sketch with an unsteady hand. "The flares point toward the cap, and the star is accelerating away from the cap? And there's a hole in it."

Abduss said, "I wondered about that. The cap keeps away, even though the star's gravity attracts it."

She thought of such colossal masses in flight, the balance of forces necessary to keep them from colliding. How? "What's moving all this?"

"The jet escapes, driving the entire configuration forward," Abduss said. The Wickramsinghs shook their heads, apparently still amazed at the immense contraption. She could see why they had awakened Cliff first, rather than Redwing. Cliff's specialty lay in dealing with the oddities of life that Glory might hold, at being flexible. A biologist, true, not an astrophysics type. Yet he had devised the idea of flying up the jet, and they hadn't.

A long still silence . . . and an idea came, lifted an eyebrow at her. She recalled suddenly that old phrase for understanding: to see the light.

"The missing element, it's—the light," she said. "The whole setup has to be using the starlight from Wickramsingh's Star."

"How?" Redwing asked skeptically.

"Let's get as many spectral views of this thing as we can on the approach," Beth said.

She had her add-ins working so sent a question and got back

SPECTRAL SYNTHESIS-BASED ABUNDANCE

MEASUREMENTS OF FE AND THE ALPHA ELEMENTS

MG, SI, CA, AND TI—

—so she realized she would just have to rely on ship's diagnostics visually presented. This was going to be the perfect collision of shipboard smart systems and the unknown—with her in the middle. At hallucinogenic speeds.

She had a big fat intuition and nothing more. Everyone had a right to their own intuitions, but no one had a right to their own facts. Best to let the facts speak.

• • •

Now came Beth's moment. Piloting is not a committee event. Even Redwing could only watch and make decisions, while the artistry of magnetic steering lay in Beth's hands.

"Wish me luck," she said with strained bravado as the ship drifted into the pearly plume of the jet.

Cliff hugged her and kissed her cheek, but she

was already riveted on the lively screens curving before her acceleration couch. He whispered, "Good luck," and retreated to his own couch, within watching distance.

Wickramsingh's Star was a smoldering beacon seen through the knothole that let the jet escape. "What'll we call it?" Beth asked from the board.

"Knothole, then," Redwing said tensely.

Near the star's hot spot, at the foot of the blossoming jet, coronal magnetic arches twisted in endless fury. Storms jostled one another all over the star, brimming with X-ray violence. It almost seemed as if the red dwarf had a skin disease.

They swept in behind, lining up. The speed of overtaking was now visible from hour to hour as the bowl swelled. Beth went with little sleep, aided by mild performance drugs that she carefully monitored. Abduss and Mayra spelled her when she started to nod off. She stayed with the board, trying to remain steady through her jittery anxiety—*but aren't pilots supposed to be rock-steady, girl?*—and couldn't help but speculate. The bowl's outside, seen in infrared, was crusted and simmering in the eternal starnight. Colossal structural beams coiled around it in a dark longitude–latitude grid. It hung there, spinning, dutifully following behind its parent star. Its cool nightside scarcely reflected any of the bright stars.

"The spectra look to be some metal–carbon composite," Mayra observed. "Not like our alloys at all."

Cliff had no important role in all this. He made

the meals and washed up while the crew worked their bridge stations with unrelenting devotion. Every plot change they checked and rechecked. Beth could tell that Cliff was impressed by their close teamwork, once the goal was clear. They could focus on technical details at last, and were obviously happier to do so.

Cliff made himself fade into the background. He had little role here, but he didn't sleep much either. Beth could read his unspoken thought: If he was going to die, at least he wanted to be awake.

In the unending din of the scoop engines, it was a struggle not to let feelings overly influence her thinking. Irritation mounted as she tried to do precise calculations and maneuvers. She projected all kinds of fantasies upon the growing mote as they screeched around, the ramscoop fields readjusting to a turning maneuver they had never been designed for. Artfully, Abduss and Beth used the star's gravity to swing *Seeker* into the exact vector that the dwarf sun was patiently following.

Beth got edgy with their eyes on her—or was that the fatigue talking? Redwing sensed this, so he and Cliff spent their time writing the report for Earthside, with full data and visuals. They were on the bridge, sending it out through the laser link at their stern, when it struck her. What were the odds that *SunSeeker* would come upon Wickramsingh's Star when their velocities were aligned?

Redwing looked startled when she pointed this out. "We're both headed toward Glory. Damn."

"They want to colonize Glory, too?" Mayra asked.

"Can't be," Abduss countered when he came onto the comm deck. "What would be the point? That bowl has tens of millions of times the area of a planet."

This seemed an obvious killer argument. Still . . . their velocities were aligned. Bound for Glory. With Sol dead aft.

"Maybe they just wander from star to star?" the captain asked. "Interstellar tourists?"

Nobody answered.

Redwing said cautiously, "You were briefed on the gravitational waves?" and looked around.

They all nodded. "Can't keep secrets from the tech types, boss," Beth said without moving her eyes from the shifting displays.

Abduss said, "You suggest perhaps this construction, this bowl, is seeking the source?"

"Makes sense, I'd think. A puzzle, isn't it?" Redwing looked around again.

Mayra said, "It is noise, or so scientists thought when we departed."

"Any chance this bowl thing could be the source of the grav waves?" Redwing gestured. "Maybe this jet?"

"There are no masses of size that could make such waves," Cliff said. "I read up on it while Beth was waking."

Abduss said, "The Glory system has no obvious enormous masses either."

Redwing thought. "Maybe they're going to Glory for its grav wave generator?"

Cliff shrugged. None of their ideas sounded right.

"Not that intuition is a reliable guide here," Beth said wryly, over her shoulder. She never took her eyes from the panels. Soon enough they got back to work, plotting and piloting. The intense work was a relief to them, a respite from the uncertainties of their lot. Beth saw Cliff come onto the bridge; he clearly envied them. At least their days were full.

They vectored in on the center of Wickramsingh's Star's bowl, keeping a respectful distance. Beth trimmed their velocity by cutting back the engines. "Maybe letting them rest a bit will make them run better later," she said, but she didn't believe it. The jet plasma running through the Knothole had plenty of fast ions in its plume, and these pushed steadily against their ramscoop fields. Shudders ran the length of the long ship. The deck hummed with long, slow tremors. For the first time in her life, Beth felt like an old sea captain, riding out a hurricane.

Now the jet was visible to the unaided eye as they neared it. They could see it as a pearly churn lit with darting flashes of blue and yellow—recombination of the plasma, Abduss said, atoms condensing out of the torrent and sputtering out their characteristic spectra. The control deck lights were ruby for visibility, stepped far down. A direct view through a window would have burned out their eyes and set the room aflame.

As it flowed away from the bowl, the long jet was

oddly tight. Beth close-upped the views. "Looks like the jet narrows down at the Knothole, then flares out. Look, some regularly spaced bright spots in the outflow."

"An instability, I would gather," Abduss said. He was fidgeting but he kept his voice calm. "The jet must have been magnetically squeezed as it passed through the Knothole."

Corkscrew filaments crawled along it, Beth saw, like one of those old barber poles. They could now see longer along the luminous lance of the jet as it speared through the opening, an exact circle far bigger than the span between Earth and its moon. Mayra trained all their scopes on the rim of the circle. The microwave spectrum crackled with bursts of noise from the spaced bright spots: pinched-in electrons singing their protests.

• • •

Abduss close-upped the bowl at a good angle and Cliff felt his heart leap as the resolution grew.

In the side-scatter of the star's somber rays, they saw what looked like enormous coils, bathed in lukewarm beauty. "Those are bigger than mountain ranges," Abduss said in a whisper.

Without thinking it through, Cliff had expected that whatever built the bowl had long since died out. Decay, collapse, extinction—these were the fates of whole species hammered on the anvil of time, not merely of civilizations. This thing had to be *old*. But it still worked. The star's solar wind got funneled stably into the jet, pushing the whole vast construct to high velocity. What could have thought of this, never mind actually build it?

Beth began getting stronger signals in the microwave spectra—a rising buzz of electromagnetic signals as *Seeker* neared the cap. Mayra began to detect a haze of watery nitrogen at the innermost edge of the circle, farther in than the coils.

"Air?" Beth asked aloud. No one answered. Cliff thought about the inner surface of the bowl, a land holding millions of times Earth's area.

And more: Close-upped through the churning refractions of *SunSeeker*'s plasma shroud, the shell clearly rotated as a single piece. "Of course," Mayra said. "Centrifugal gravity."

They merged their measurements and built up an image on the main screen. The bright plasma jet pierced the bowl's hemisphere through a ribbed hole. "Kind of like a weird teacup," Redwing said. "Cupworld."

For long moments no one spoke. Then Redwing said with elaborate casualness, "Abduss, check if there's any new tightbeam traffic from Earth."

"There has been none for—"

"Now," Redwing said firmly. Beth understood: Abduss needed something to do.

The deck took up a long, deep vibration none of them had ever heard before, an ominous bass note they felt rather than heard. "We're entering the edges of the jet," Beth said tersely. "Picking up— well, plasma surf, I guess you'd call it."

Redwing frowned. "Full brake. Cycle the magnetics."

"Roger." Beth worked the large board, eyes never still.

The bowl seemed to swell quickly. "We're locked in on the jet." The deep bass note swelled. "And— slowing. We're flying straight up the jet."

SunSeeker made its agonizing turn. To pivot the ship on its plasma plume demanded the skill of an ice skater, combined with an acrobat, spinning in three dimensions under thrust. In interstellar space, where most hydrogen is a gas and not broken into ions and electrons, *Seeker* ionized the gas ahead with a shock wave driven by its own oscillating magnetic snowplow. The pressure waves plunged ahead, grabbing the electrons available and smacking them into the hydrogen gas molecules. Properly adjusted—which took Beth only moments to tune—there was enough time for the hydrogen to break up into protons and electrons. The gas fried into a torch of fizzing ions. That left a plasma column just ahead of the ship, ready to be netted and swallowed by their magnetic dipole scoop, then fed down into the fusion reaction chambers. The trick was to torque the ship while riding atop this angry, spitting column.

Seeker curved sideways by a mere few degrees, letting the target star gain a little on them. Then they curled behind it. Lacy filaments played before them as the jet grew near. They swerved fully into the jet with a hard, wrenching turn that slammed them all against the left arms of their couches for . . . forever.

· · ·

Starships do not easily change directions. Sweat popped out on Beth's brow; a swipe of her hand on a touchpoint started a cool breeze. Throughout *SunSeeker,* joints strummed, echoing in the long corridors. Auxiliary craft shifted and strained on their mountings. Beth wondered if the ship could take it, and then if *she* could.

Finally they straightened and felt the push of the sun's jet against their magnetic collector fields. Beth surged forward from the deceleration, straps cutting into her. In the wraparound omniview screen, set to all parts of the spectrum, plumes of incandescent plasma skated and veered around their prow. Their total speed was higher than the star's, but as they came around under the great bowl and into the furious jet, another force came into play. She felt it, became alarmed, then understood. *SunSeeker* began to twist, corkscrewing steadily around in the rushing plasma torrent. They all felt the grinding force of it, a giant's slow twirl.

"Y'know, I was kinda wondering what held this jet so straight and tight," Beth said in a conversational tone, her hands moving quick and sure over the many induction controls. "Magnetic fields do the job, generated by a current in the jet itself."

"Uh, so?" Redwing said. He was not a technical type, she recalled.

"Somebody's designed this to use the star's own fields, sucking them into a jet. They form those helical filaments we saw on our approach."

"Currents?" Mayra was alarmed. "We are mostly metal, a conductor—"

"So the currents are running around us, but not into us. Conveys angular momentum. Same as airliners flying through lightning on Earth. But—what a ride! Feel the twist!"

Beth turned to grin at them all and saw startled dismay. *Okay, not everybody likes surfing.* An acquired taste.

"Hey, I've got us under control. No sweat. It's a big magnetic helix." *Put forward the best news, worry about the rest later.* "And that means we'll follow a longer path, take more time—so we'll get more deceleration out of the jet."

No change of expression. *Passengers!* No fun in them . . .

• • •

They ran hard and hot for hours and then hours more. Beth felt the strain, but somehow didn't mind. Riding the plasma knots without battering the ship was . . . well, fun. Her heart was pounding away joyfully. Excitement did that for her as nothing else could. She had been a skydiver and surfer and skier, savoring the sensation of dealing with artful speed. *Zest!*

But whenever she grinned, Redwing frowned. After a while, claiming that she needed the stretch, she got out of her harness and couch and stood while she worked the board. The AIs were laboring hard, carrying out a lot of the minor adjustments. For a while there, the ship gained a lot of charge on seams and edges, and Beth was afraid something would start shorting out. Too many electrons jockeying on the skin. But then she blew the charge off with a proton-rich plasma pulse—pure inspiration, plus freshman physics—and they got right with Mister Coulomb again.

She stayed standing. This was like surfing the longest wave in the universe, buffeted and sprayed and *rough*—but it thrilled her to her soul, every zooming kilometer of the way.

And here came the Knothole. She got back into her couch. *Fun's over . . . maybe.*

Somebody was talking behind her and she let it go. Pilots don't listen to passengers, not if they're smart.

Beth lunged painfully forward into her shoulder straps. The bowl ahead yawned like a flat plane—with a bull's-eye target. She could see intricate ribbing around its polar opening, a ridge around the Knothole. *Engineered current-carrying circuits, bigger than continents?* Something had to make the magnetic fields that shaped plasma from the sun, fields that were also pushing against their ship now with a fierce, blinding gale. Something huge.

"No trouble decelerating now," she said matter-of-factly, to calm the others. She need not turn to look at them; she could *smell* their fear. They swam upstream against the jet. Now the magnetic braking was worse than anything *Seeker* had ever been designed for. The ship popped and groaned. The bowl came rushing at them. Deep bass notes rang through the ship, vibrating Beth's couch, rattling everything. . . .

Focus. She flew through the bowl's exhaust Knothole, hugging the edge to avoid cremation. A noose of magnetic fields at the Knothole boundary tightened the jet like water in a constriction. Flow velocity rose against the ship. Running creases crossed the shock waves they rode. She saw the bowl was thicker at the Knothole than elsewhere—to carry bigger stresses? And eerie lightning played along the Knothole rim.

She dispatched an AI to map the Knothole magnetic geometry and in seconds a color-coded 3-D map unfurled on a screen. "The noose we're going through is bounded by dipolar fields," she said abstractly. "And the dipoles are kept in line with another field, perpendicular to the dipoles—so the magnetic stresses can't reconnect and die. Neat."

Murmurs from behind her egged her on. Analysis, tension-relieving talk, cheers—all just a chorus she ignored.

"Plus, ladies and gentlemen, it's radioactive as hell around here," Beth said, adding brightly, "but an interstellar surfboard—that's us—is designed for that."

They slammed ahead, losing speed. She surged forward in her harness, adjusted, and surged again. *Surfing the big one. Ride of a lifetime. If you survive . . .*

The prow tried to fight sideways but she jockeyed it back. Again. And again. Each time she got the feel of it better. Offhand she noticed she was drenched in sweat. *No wonder I can't smell their fear anymore. . . .*

She caught a glimmer refracted through the streaming plasma ahead, a small sphere wobbling toward them—Wickramsingh's Star. The bowl flattened, became the sidewise horizon. The ship howled with its labors.

For Beth, time ceased to mean anything. She countered every veer and vortex, kept them straight, swore, blinked back sweat—and they were through.

The sky opened. Abruptly they were rising above a silvery plain. The jet hammered at them still. "Wonderful!" Cliff choked out, still hanging forward in his harness. Hollow cheers, ragged. They were rising above a vast white plain, but slower, slower—and then they turned again.

"Getting out of the jet," Beth said, as if passing the butter. If they stayed in the jet, they'd be slowed further, back through the Knothole and out again.

"We're taking a lot of ohmic heating in the skin," Abduss said, voice tight with worry.

"I can barely hold the vector," Mayra said calmly. Cliff knew by now the subtle tones of tension in her voice.

The white-hot jet plume thinned, then seemed to veer aside. Rough turbulence struck, slamming them around in their couches, bringing fresh metal shrieks from the ship.

"Out!" Mayra shouted. "We're out."

"I'd say we're in," Redwing said.

They cheered and all eyes were on the screens.

Now they could see the inside of the bowl . . . and it was a vast sheeted plain brimming with light. They rose swiftly, peeling off from the jet to the side, plasma falling behind, vistas clearing. Again there curved away over the misty distance great longitude and latitude grids in sleek, silvered sections the size of worlds. The sections had boundaries, thin dark lines, demarking different curvatures of a greater mirror—and from that their eyes told them that these were all focused far away.

Silence. In a whisper Abduss said, "Mirrors . . . reflecting the sunlight back, inward, onto the star. That's what causes the hot spot."

Beth nodded, awed. Yes—otherwise the huge curved mirrors would have blinded them instantly.

They slewed to the side, turning, the screens taking in, across the immense celestial curvature, hazy tinctures of . . . green. She zoomed the scopes pointing inward along the great spherical cap. The lower latitudes of the inner bowl teemed with intensely green territories and washes of blue water. Lakes—no, oceans. The eye could not quite grasp what it saw. They were cruising along near the jet axis, and before them unfurled a landscape of arcing grandeur.

Beth calculated angles and distances. Any of the grid sections had a larger surface than the entire Earth. Each boasted intricate detail, webs strung among green brown continents and spacious seas, framing immense areas.

And her vision was all getting foggy with fatigue. Aches seeped through her.

"I've had enough," Beth said. "Climbing up that jet burned away our velocity enough. The bowl and star system were moving pretty fast, and now we're in their rest frame. We're marginally trapped in the potential well of that star."

Captain Redwing said, "You what?"

"Captain—"

"No, it's okay, I get it," he said suddenly. "The scale of this thing, it's just mind-scrambling, Beth. The bowl is the size of a little solar system, right, and you can just leave the ship circling the sun, right? Are we too close? Will we heat up too much?"

"We'll be okay." She visibly straightened, her pale lips firming. One last effort. "I'll leave the ramscoop idling, keeping the fields high, so we won't be sprayed with radiation. It runs rough that way, but we have no choice. We've matched velocities with the system, so it'll be *months* before we could be in trouble. We'll be in an eccentric orbit, right, Abduss? I'll be back at the controls before anything can happen, but somebody stay on trajectory watch, please."

Redwing looked puzzled.

Beth gave him a weak smile. "I'm going to sleep."

She staggered out. Behind her she heard Redwing's, "How can anyone leave *this*?"

And then Cliff was with her, guiding her, but lurching a little himself.

FOUR

Beth thrashed and jerked awake. The hammock shuddered. Her legs and arms were cramping from armpit to fingertips, hip to toes.

The dream faded. The controls weren't under her hands; the ship wasn't roaring through a plume of star-hot plasma. She hugged herself and tried to sleep. Cliff wasn't there. How long had she been sleeping?

Presently she gave up and went to the bridge, her boots thumping, bringing her fully awake. Her hands were trembling, though. Not what you want in a pilot . . .

"Hi," Cliff said, grinning. "Redwing left me on watch. Abduss is computing an orbit for us, unless he flaked out, too."

Beth was famished. She got out bread and fruit and ate as she watched the displays. She was just a little jealous of the others, who must have been watching for hours. And it was glorious.

Structures fanned out from the Knothole. She was now watching from the other side, gazing down at a vast sprawl. Her eyes kept tricking her, making her think this was all nearby, like looking down on Earth . . . but she was gazing over interplanetary distances. The tubing around the Knothole must be tremendous, the size of continents.

Far below the ship stretched away the wok-shaped mirrored shell, faring into a ring of green-tinged ocher. Between *SunSeeker* and those lands was a shimmering layer—atmosphere, she guessed. Held in . . . how?

She squinted and thought she could catch a sheen, the star reflecting from some transparent barrier. A membrane? She squinted at what seemed like millions of square kilometers of clear plastic sandwich wrap. The diffuse layer stretched away toward the distance, where she saw the lands of the belt—the great cylindrical section that formed the thick rim of . . . Cupworld? She didn't like Redwing's term but couldn't think of a better one. No mirrors there. Continents, yes, cloud-shrouded and green. Deserts as well, sandy and bright under the unending glare of a star that never set. Indeed, never set on all this colossal construction. *And what lives here?*

Her hands were trembling even more.

This immensity was impossible, too much; Beth looked away.

"They've made a world . . . a habitat out of the bowl," Mayra said wonderingly. "A vast green thing."

Beth took a long breath. For safety—*pilots must be focused*—she took her hands off the command boards.

Cliff thumbed up a display board. "We worked up a sketch to get the essentials of this thing in one view. Have a look."

She studied the line drawing, feeling woozy. "Yes, right. You've labeled the regions out from the axis with the equivalent gravs . . ."

"Yup, and the clumps in the edge plain are supposed to be topological features. Only my splotches are bigger than whole planets, a lot bigger." He waved his hands helplessly, grinning. But he frowned, too, worried at her fatigue.

"Right, hard to grasp the scale—this is inconceivable, but a sketch helps. You caught how the jet bulges out near the star."

More hand waving. "Looks to me like the magnetic fields in it are getting control, slimming it down into a slowly expanding straw . . ."

"A wok with a neon jet shooting out the back . . . and living room on the inside, more territory than you could get on the planets of a thousand solar systems. Pinned to it with centrifugal grav . . ."

"They don't live on the whole bowl. Just the rim. Most of it is just mirrors. Even so, it's more than a habitat," said Cliff. "It's accelerating. That jet! This whole thing is *going* somewhere. A ship that is a star. A ship star. We humans only built a star ship."

• • •

There wasn't much redundancy among *SunSeeker*'s auxiliary boats. Designs were modular: tanks or skeletal cargo carriers could substitute for passenger shells.

There were two fliers, Hawking and Dyson, twin lifting body designs. "We can't use reentry vehicles," Redwing decided. "We'd tear holes in whatever's holding the air in."

Abduss said, "Captain, these *are* the tankers."

"*Ceres* and *Eros* are tankers, too, for mining asteroids. We just add the tank," Redwing said.

Mayra said, "There aren't any asteroids or comets. The locals must have cleaned out everything that might have threatened their habitats, or even used it all to *build* the bowl."

"Really?"

"We haven't found anything at all," Mayra said.

"What, in four days? Four days to do a thousand years' worth of astronomy in a brand-new solar system?"

The Wickramsinghs were silent before Redwing's sarcasm. Indeed, the autoinventory had found no asteroids. "It's been vacuumed clean."

"Um," Redwing said. "So nothing hits the bowl."

Cliff listened with half his attention; this wasn't his business yet. The automatic search cameras were smart, quick. Probably Mayra was right: The whole solar system had been scoured long ago. But he didn't want to cross Redwing over a minor point; best to husband his credit with the irascible captain. The man had gone without much sleep, too. Cliff had found him pacing the corridors, checking and rechecking ship status, when he was supposed to be asleep.

He wished he had someone else to talk to about this, but the Wickramsinghs kept their own counsel. And Beth was sleeping. She'd done a lot of that, still recovering from cold sleep and the grueling flight through the Knothole.

Redwing chopped air with his hand. "Okay, for the moment we'll take that as given. No asteroids, no comets. We'll put a tank on *Eros*. It can carry water, mine it out of a comet, even—and it can *land*. Landing legs and a high-thrust fusion motor. We thought there'd be moons."

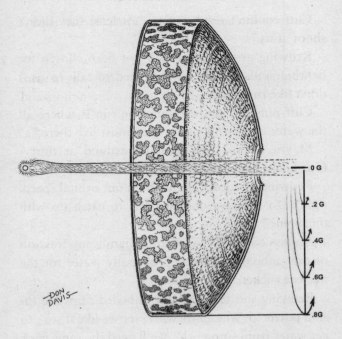

DON
DAVIS

0 G

.2 G

.4 G

.6 G

.8 G

Mayra asked blandly, "Where are you planning to land, Captain?"

"Down there." Redwing waved toward Cup-world's green-tinged rim.

"Yes, I thought so. If you land near the Knot-hole, you'll be millions of klicks from any water source, and right on top of the systems that shape the electromagnetic fields. We could be perceived as a threat."

Redwing blinked. "You think so?"

Mayra kept her face blank, apparently her way of being diplomatic. "We have no idea how the builders of this thing feel about visitors."

Cliff couldn't resist saying, "At least they didn't shoot at us."

Redwing grimaced; he had not been chosen for fighting skills. "They haven't tried to talk to us. I don't like that."

Cliff put in, "But, Captain, the rim is where all the water and farmland is. They must live there."

Mayra added, "It's spinning around at thirty-four klicks per second, too."

Redwing nodded. "Higher than our orbital speed, right? Do we have onboard fuel to catch up with that spin?"

Abduss said, "It will take a significant fraction of our onboard reserves, principally water for the nuclear rocket."

Redwing snorted. "*All* our onboard ships are fusion powered. We can fly wherever we like if we can get water from Cupworld. We'll need the same trick to use any of them. Okay, say we see a lake. We'll put *SunSeeker* in a nearer orbit and drop the lander from there. Beth will know how to do that. Cliff!"

Cliff jumped.

"Where shall we land?"

They were asking him as the biologist. "It all looks like farmland and meadows and forests," he said. "Different habitats, probably—see those ice fields? I don't know how they create those, but our telescopes can't make out individual trees. All I've got is a light spectrum, but clearly from spectral reflections, the plants are using chlorophyll, Captain. Land anywhere near water on the rim, I'd say, and refuel the tanks first thing."

Mayra asked, "Do we land on the inside of the bowl? Or the outside?"

Redwing frowned. "Inside, of course. That's where they live."

Mayra pursed her lips and said evenly, "They surely launch their own spacecraft from the outer surface. They could simply put their ships in elevators, lower them through an outer air lock, and let them go. Immediately the ships would have a thirty-four-kilometer-per-second velocity. All with no need to fly through an atmosphere, or out through the film that covers their atmosphere."

Cliff grinned. Mayra had been thinking as he did, asking how the hell this enormous contraption worked. "You think we could go in through their outer air locks? From underneath? Maybe to reenter, they have magnetic clamps or something to catch incoming craft. Maybe we could use those."

Mayra shrugged. "Suppose we do. How do we knock on the door?"

Redwing mused, "They must have safeguards. . . ."

"Even if we get in the door, they control the locks," Cliff added. "We'd be caught."

Redwing liked that. He sat back and gave them all a glassy grin. "Makes it easy to choose, doesn't it? We must retain our freedom of maneuver until we know what—whom—we're dealing with. We go down through the atmosphere, then."

"We'll have to bust through that film they have," Cliff observed.

Abduss added, "They might see that as aggressive. *I* would."

Redwing nodded. "But it's the only way not to be cornered from the start."

"Makes you wonder, doesn't it?" Cliff said casually. "They must have seen us. How come they haven't come out to pay a call?"

Abduss said, "Good, yes. I have received no electromagnetic transmissions, either."

"Funny," Redwing said. "You'd expect at least broadcast radio."

"Perhaps they use point-to-point comm, laser links," Mayra said. "Just as we do."

Redwing sat up straight, switching to his command voice. "Abduss, would we have time to hover? Pick a landing spot?"

"Not much."

"We'll take *Eros*," Captain Redwing decided. "Get it ready as quick as we can. Now, do we need to thaw anyone else?"

Maybe this was Redwing's way of "building consensus," as the leadership classes taught. Cliff said the obvious: "We'll need twenty minimum to do anything on the ground."

"Let's get started, then."

FIVE

They kept wary eyes and instruments on Cupworld while they tended to the auxiliary ships. Beth brought *SunSeeker* into a useful orbit for making the *Eros* drop. They maneuvered carefully, but though they could see landscapes far below, the distances were vast. Even orbital rendezvous took weeks. This was not a planet.

That gave them time to revive a selection they would need—engineers, maintenance people, "groundpounder" types who expected to wake up on a planetary surface. Redwing kept the numbers revived as low as plausible for the exploring party. They needed replacements for the current crew, who were all going down to the bowl, since the revived wouldn't be physically able in time.

Unsurprisingly, those woken up were quite surprised.

Just looking at the external feeds could cause these newbies to freak out. Redwing quickly learned that it was best to have the recently revived brief the next batch. Cliff got tired of explaining their incredible situation.

He spent his days surveying the lakes, rivers, and oceans of Cupworld—or as some called it, the Bowl; Cliff had tried to think of something descriptive yet high-minded, and failed. The dotted blue expanses had been well planned, apparently—no huge deserts or wastelands, good circulation of air currents and moisture.

They awoke Fred Ojama first, so Cliff could work with a geologist while making the survey. "This isn't geology," Fred pointed out immediately. "It's a, well, a building."

"A building the size of the inner solar system, yep," Cliff answered. "But somebody thought it through. Look at how the lakes, rivers, and seas follow a fractal distribution."

Fred thought that through. "Best way to distribute water. Avoids deserts, maybe . . . but that patch looks like desert. And that patch of forest might be . . . No, never mind."

"Like symbols," Cliff agreed. "Looks like writing. A super landscaper leaving messages. Like in *Hitchhiker's Guide*, the guy who designed the fjords."

Fred looked blank.

Redwing had hesitated to wake Fred Ojama. Fred's bio listed him as borderline autistic. He'd barely made the height requirement. Nobody actually knew him very well. Not all the crew were social mavens, for psycher reasons. Redwing remarked that a cocktail party with no listeners was a noise fest, and there was an analogy there about teamwork. The list claimed Fred was a near genius, too, with a history of original ideas, and Cliff had wanted that.

Cliff pointed to the boundary where the cylindrical part curved smoothly into the vast mirror dome. "I'm trying to figure out how it would be to live on the surface, when it starts to slant. The whole thing is rotating together, so as soon as the slope changes, centrifugal grav will be at an angle to the ground."

Fred zoomed on that area. "The rivers go away there. Just vanish into the sands." He snapped his fingers. "I got it. The centrifugal grav works against the inward-sloping curve of the high Bowl. So water can't flow up into the mirror area. That means the gravity alone can keep that big zone clear of life, I guess. Maybe even air."

Fred was smart. There weren't dumb people on *Seeker,* just people with other tales or people you disagreed with. An important point to remember in arguments. "Sounds right. The mirrors are important. The builders don't want them growing lichen or anything."

"So the whole structure has a clean division. The cylinder's for living, the mirror for propulsion." Fred shook his head. "What an idea."

"What kind of mind would even think of it?"

"Something with a long time horizon. This whole construct accelerates *very* slowly." Fred looked at the jet in the distance, a brilliant ivory pillar of ever-shifting tendrils. "That plasma's pushing a *star.*"

"Odd minds, gotta be. But engineering's a universal. Things work or you change them."

"You want to reverse engineer this place?" Fred grinned, nodding his bald head so it caught the gleam of the lights. "Good. Good."

Cliff had close-upped the region where sunlight reflected off the atmosphere membrane. He and Fred kept up their banter while he tried to see deeper. The shiny surface was probably some tough but thin layer to keep their air in—19 percent oxygen, 72 percent nitrogen, and traces of carbon dioxide and noble gases. Then he saw it. A patch that didn't reflect.

They used the maximum magnification of the scopes and then called Redwing. "I think we've found an area sealed off from the membrane," Cliff said, showing him the barren circle. "It's about a hundred kilometers across."

"How can they tolerate it? Won't their air leak out?"

Fred said, "Maybe they opened it for us, just recently. A thing this big can take a little loss."

Redwing looked at every view, across the spectrum, before finally saying, "Open areas, yeah. Makes sense. Apparently for landings from space?"

"That's what we figured," Fred said.

"Solves our landing problem, then," Redwing said with a thin smile of satisfaction. "Let's go in."

SIX

If your heart is large, Memor thought, and contains volume enough to envelop your adversaries, then wisdom can come into play. One can then see their transparency, and so then diffuse or avoid their attacks. And once you envelop them, you will be able to guide them along the path indicated to you by your own hard-won wisdoms.

He shook himself. This insight came from some new part of him . . . the restless part of his mind that would soon be *her* mind. For Memor was now amid the fevered straits of the Change.

Not the optimum time to confront a crisis unlike any within the last eight-squared of generations. Lifeshaping should be done in peace, but that was not to be Memor's destiny. He would be female within a few short cycles, but he had not yet lost the male's sense of reach and joy, the Dancing. He could even smell the seethe of fructifying change within him. Hormones raged; molecules fought for dominance in his bloodstream. Fevers came in like chemical reports from a raging battlefield. These changes had been designed by the Founders and their following generations, now well sanctified by endless eras. Memor knew his shifting moods and jitters paid the cost of acquiring greater wisdom. But the cost was high and hard to endure amid a crisis.

"Order descends," the Prefect called in ancient tones for the assembly of Astronomers.

"Order prevails," came the answering chorus as they took their places of rest beneath the great dome.

Memor let the details of unfurling discussion play over him. He kept his body still while his inner mind fretted at the vagrant impulses within his changing self. Even his Undermind, normally serene, showed a surface wrinkled by fretful winds. Waves of knotted concern broke across its steady currents.

The technical summary was as he had heard. A starship of boldly simple design approached from aft. Diagnostics astern had seen it turn and approach, as though their flight had not been directly for the Bowl. Perhaps they were bound for the star ahead, where the gravitational waves emerged?

The audience of Astronomers murmured. Speculation fueled their excited chatter. Monitoring the approaching ship's transmissions picked up several bursts directed back along the ship's path. Trailing satellites had picked up these, yet intensive study by the linguist minds gave little more than a simple sense of their grammar and contextual constructions. Their habits of mind as revealed in language did not seem remarkable. Linear logics, few layers of meaning. Indeed, they seemed like their ship—primitive, yes, but ambitious to undertake full starflight in such a flimsy craft. The consultant engineers—small creatures, timid in the presence of full-sized Astronomers—pointed out odd features in the magnetic configuration, and announced that they would like to inspect the long, slim craft. Much sharp discussion followed.

Memor felt distracted by the marinating changes within him. He sat out the usual time-honored dispute, Watchers—pejoratively called Sitters—versus Dancers. The Prefect called up ancient records and even voices from the far past.

Past lore supported the Dancers, Memor thought. Unsurprising—stories of change are always more interesting than stories of stasis. Change is the essence of story, built into the mind by evolution's strict dictates.

Astronomers of ancient times had fired upon many ships, usually with the Gamma Lance. They had passed by many planets, explored and then ignored. These cases did not have many stories. The Watchers kept referring back to them.

Memor stretched and tried to look alert. Watchers were boring, ponderous. But then, Memor was still male, and like Dancers favored variety, engagement. Wisdom came later. The Watchers were nearly all female.

So Memor was in the middle here. He could sense the change to come, but he hadn't lost the male's sense of reach yet.

The assembly took a long, deliberate time to glide through the vast library of the past. Memor coasted through the old records as if they were his own adventures. Zesty, colorful, shot through with ancient exploits. They enthralled him.

The Bowl of Heaven never came too near a sun. It was too ponderous for that, and with its mass could perturb the orbits of life-bearing worlds. They did send ships, of course. But the Astronomers' telescopes had always been superb; they knew the nature of a world or moon before an exploring ship ever set forth, fired into a solar system from the rim of the Bowl. Voyages to interesting planets always took hundreds of long cycles, aboard one or more great cruisers usually equipped with landers, sometimes with orbital tethers.

Memor focused on what had been mere droning history. Here, in one thrilling tale, the Bowl had come near a heavy world, too massive to support any adventurer. The mother ship hovered in the quasi-stable point beneath the largest moon. Ships angular and strange rose like sparks from the heavy world's surface, rocket propelled. There was no orbital tether. Simple technologies. This was how the finger snakes had reached them—an artful species indeed.

There followed hundreds of long cycles of negotiation, of studying one another. The little finger snakes had gained from this dialogue some trivial enhancement in their technology, nothing that could threaten the Bowl. The Bowl had learned little from them, of course.

Then 256 finger snakes had returned to the Bowl aboard the mother ship. The small colony had needed little in the way of integration. They were more dexterous than most Bird Folk, good tool-users, and crafty repair artisans. You rarely saw them now; they lived underground. Memor was impressed that such small beings had ever attained spacefaring skills, considering how they loved their buried warrens.

Lessons of ages unwound. The past scrolled on within Memor's mind. Around him, other Astronomers huffed and grunted as they, too, experienced the deep realms. An elder snored. Out of respect, all let her sleep.

Here, a bandit species had attacked approaching Astronomers' exploring ships. The Astronomers had retreated. The Bowl's defenses proved adequate, and so they had continued on, out of their range. A few scores of invaders had landed, been captured, been bred for docility. Four-limbed bipeds, they were, and they made good farmers.

These named Sil had come as plunderers; they'd seen the Bowl as a high-tech civilization and wanted its secrets. Their early days after capture proved turbulent. Training worked its slow magic. The Sil were limber, dexterous creatures, invaluable today. Space suits allowed them to work on the Bowl's understructure. Their docility was not quite dependable, even now, after twelve million long cycles.

Memor moved on through the stories. Images filled the air around him, long dead voices spoke in somber tones of musty triumphs.

Here, a gas giant planet was home to living dirigibles. Probes managed to scoop up enough infant balloons to make a stable population. They bred in air, seldom touching down. The Bowl's deep atmosphere gave them free, safe range. The bioengineers deftly tuned their genes for docility and strength. A million long cycles later, they were an indispensable part of the Bowl's civilization. To take to air without expending fuel was a great pleasure, available to all the master Folk.

Memor moved on through the annals of history, all the while fighting his trembles, fits, fevers. *Is it worth all this to become female?* Judgment is never wise while in restless agonies. He focused, lifting mind above body. His unmasked Undermind dealt with the aches and fevers, beneath his burrowing consciousness.

Here, alien visitors had failed to accommodate to their new station in life. Genetic trickery had failed them, too . . . but a life-form derived from that world had become the skreekors, a valuable and tasty prey animal that could be eaten raw for the relishing. Memor hungered for one now, stomach squeezing, just from viewing the savory pursuit-and-devour sense concerts.

Tales of successful change rolled by, all leading to today's ideal ecological and political balance. The Bowl was a living thing, not a static tool. This incoming visitor was the first in many a million long cycles. Flaming them with the flare would be easy, though not trivial: it demanded managing huge energies with a deft touch. They'd done it before.

"The Gamma Lance is primed," a senior female said. She gestured at the star bowl. The starship plainly intended to fly into their jet. *Foolish!* The senior female said.

Memor rose on unsteady legs to dispute. *But what would we all lose?* An interstellar ramjet of unusual design and audacity, at the very least. New modes of thought. Strangeness. *Adventure!* Memor sat, and others sang their vying songs. Discussion rolled on.

Memor tried to follow the discourse, while giving no sign that he wrestled with his inner self. Strange emotions flitted through his mind, mingling with the ancient records in strange symphonies of thought. The best stories were never of maintaining stasis. Change meant action meant zest. Watchers held the balance of the Bowl, but Dancers had all the best songs. Of course, there had been times when a visiting alien was simply destroyed, but where was the entertainment in that?

It might be that Memor, and Memor's peers, would give too much weight to tales of change and advancement.

Time would tell. But for now, Memor was a Dancer. He had to be.

His inner struggles and outer sweats so preoccupied him that he very nearly failed to note that the Dancers carried the argument. Only when a friend pounded him with hearty congratulation did Memor discover that he had been made Master of the Task—and would have to deal with the approaching aliens, if they should dare land.

"Why?" he asked a friend Watcher.

"Because you are inventive. Also, you have enemies."

"My enemies would—?"

"Hope you fail, yes."

Memor decided to go with the tide. He strutted a bit and bellowed hearty masculine thanks to all. *Let them come!*

PART II

THE TOUGH GET GOING

*Man is a small thing, and the night is large
and full of wonder.*
—LORD DUNSANY

SEVEN

They left a skeleton crew of five aboard *Sun-Seeker,* with Redwing plainly sorry that proper ship command protocols demanded that he stay aboard. The crew left behind were enough to handle the hundreds in hibernation and maintain ship systems.

The descent team took eleven down with them— Beth, Cliff, Fred, the Wickramsinghs, and six recently revived, who were still taking it all in. Cliff was nominally first officer, mostly because Redwing wanted to avoid the delay in reviving a ship crew officer. Cliff could barely keep the various ranks straight in his head and suspected they would soon matter very little.

Terry Gould and Tananareve started as per regulations by checking everyone's gear and organizing it for rapid use if necessary. They had field packs, rations, water, lasers, and tech gear, all compact and rugged. The lower Bowl grav made it possible to carry more, so they had packed to do so. Cliff, Beth, and Fred spent most of the long flight checking and rechecking their gear, then reviewing the many multi-spectra maps they had made. On the flat regions there stood pillars, barely resolved—not pylons, but raised land formations.

"Buttes," Beth said, sipping coffee. "Black-topped. Kinda like the American West but lots bigger. Looks like they rise all the way up to the sky roof. So the sealing barrier, that light blue stuff, ends at the rim of the butte."

"Pretty high, too," Fred added with a grin, plainly enjoying himself. "Nearly seven kilometers. Not as high as Everest, and certainly nothing compares to Olympus Mons, but worth climbing for fun. Always wanted to do Everest . . ."

Cliff kept his voice even and warm, and even managed a smile of sorts. "We'll have to arrange it for you." At times, Fred was touchy. As the ship rumbled, Cliff eyed Fred, who was lean and muscular and sported a permanent suntan. How had he gotten that in all their training time? Cliff had hardly been able to sleep. At least Fred didn't talk much now as he concentrated on work.

• • •

The last long swoop of their descending orbit was tense. The cabins filled with a sour smell and everyone was on edge. It felt odd to be coasting down toward a huge landscape that stretched away to all sides, filling the sky—and yet still be in space. The Bowl wrapped around them.

No tug of deceleration or singing of thin air. Cliff looked at the wall screens. One showed *SunSeeker* above them, a pale blue thread of flame trailing.

Another showed the top of the butte, nearly edge on and still a featureless black. Another, the "overhead" view toward the jet.

Cliff watched the ivory and orange streamers fight and roil along it. An idea struck him. "Abduss!"

The man was in the next acceleration couch, face pale, looking none too well.

"You studied the jet, right?"

"Uh, yes, Cliff . . ."

"What does it emit?"

"X-rays, microwaves, plenty of IR."

"And?"

"Not much visible light. A lot of broadband radio and microwave noise," the wiry man said, obviously glad to have something else to think about than their landing. "Very loud. Very beautiful."

"I'll bet that's why we don't pick up their transmissions—they avoid the visible region of the spectrum. Probably use direct laser feeds, instead—so no side lobes for us to pick up."

"Ah, yes, they are clever," Abduss said, and went back to looking fixedly at the land sliding below them. His mouth worked.

Lightning forked around the oval. Some kind of electrical process, like the big sheets of luminosity that came cascading down from Earth's ionosphere? Cliff watched the quick, orange streamers. They slid around the butte, with glowing fingers probing at the lip.

The atmosphere's membrane was a light blue shining sheet under them now. It was visible only at an angle. Sunlight glinted off long wave fronts that rippled in the sheet's surface, making it look like a transparent ocean. Cliff marveled at the illusion, seeing beneath it craggy mountains and long, sloping green valleys as though they lay on an ocean floor. Somehow this made the whole construction both eerie and yet like a planet.

Now they tilted and their thrusters roared, rattling Cliff's teeth. They skated along just above the membrane, and he saw that the waves were moving slowly, great undulating troughs driven by—what?

Like an ocean on Earth. Perhaps the rotation of this colossal artifact unleashed such waves, and they in turn affected the weather below. So did Earth's atmosphere, after all; hurricanes came from the planet's rotation about its poles. What oddities could they expect on this unimaginable scale?

He watched a long line of rain clouds caught in the crest of a wave. Angry blue gray clouds were corralled in the high peak, as if in rising they cooled and let go their moisture. His eye followed the cloud-racked crest to the far horizon. A marching regimental rainstorm. He felt a cold sensation of strangeness at this sight. The idea of a rainstorm that stretched long and slender over distances far greater than continents made him suck in his breath.

Now they were above the black pillar, descending. Cliff's stomach fluttered up into his throat. He clenched his teeth as *Eros* rolled and dived, wrenching around as Beth slammed them hard into their couches.

"The butte!" she shouted. "Damn!"

Abduss shouted, "What? What is it?"

Pause. "It'll be fine," she said flatly with forced calm. "I can figure this. Keep your crash webs tight. Someone should have noticed." Beth was talking through clenched teeth.

Abduss frowned. "What is—?"

"That's no butte. We're inside a hollow tube! The surface is—I don't see a surface, it's in shadow, seven kilometers down." Thrust went away. "I don't want to run out of fuel. I'm going to assume there's a floor and it's flush with the forest. Abduss, can you get me anything with radar?"

Cliff's throat was dry and his voice cracked. "Floor as opposed to . . . what?"

"As opposed to a hole that goes right through the Cupworld and out into space!"

Abduss said, "What?" His eyes showed a lot of white.

"Suppose it's a through-out tube, to save the trouble of going around the whole Bowl. That's what it looks like in a full-spectrum picture." Beth gestured at a stack set of views. In some, stars hung in the opening.

"Uh, so?"

"We could go right through. What's radar say? You can get an angle on the floor now, right?"

Abduss nodded and worked his board. He was sweating.

Cliff ventured, "We'd be picked up with *Sun-Seeker*, no problem."

"Maybe," Beth said tensely. "Unless somebody slams the door."

"There's a bottom down there," Abduss said. "Watch yourself, radar says it's not flat."

The motor thrummed again. High thrust. Pings and pops in the ship.

Cliff didn't try to speak. Beth was talking her way through it, and that was nerve racking. "It's flat, Abduss. There's a hole in it, a pit with stars at the bottom. We want to land, right? *Not* go through to the outside. Hey, there's light at the bottom! And here we go—"

Eros surged, then danced sideways under Coriolis force.

EIGHT

She set them down less than two kilometers from the butte wall, on a cluttered ledge that was perhaps four kilometers across. There was a wall along the inner rim. Beyond that, the universe peeked through a hole ten kilometers across. She made the ship linger on its jets, finding a bare spot. They thunked down and felt the tug of centrifugal gravity.

She looked toward the butte face. Pale ivory light spilled out along the bottom of the wall, from a row of windows running from tiny to huge.

They all felt the significance of the moment, but there was no time for reflection. They didn't know what waited outside, but talking wasn't going to tell them anything.

They emerged from the scout ship in full space gear. Cliff listened with half his attention to Fred reporting to Redwing. The lightspeed time gap was seventeen seconds and rising. They stood at the foot of *Eros,* looking into the light. Into a row of glass boxes of increasing size, with forest on the far side.

"Air locks," Fred said, and laughed happily. "With transparent walls." He stopped laughing when nobody joined him. "That one at the far end is fifty or sixty times as big as *Eros.* I guess they have to pass big machinery, given the scale of this, well—" He groped for a word, then laughed again. "Describing all this isn't easy. Captain Redwing, are the helmet cameras working?"

"We want one of the little locks," Cliff said.

These gigantic structures weren't funny; they were daunting. The one ahead would easily pass *Eros,* and it wasn't the largest.

Redwing, lightspeed delayed, barked on comm, "Cameras are working. Definition isn't good. Keep talking, Fred. We're lonely up here."

Beth added, "And nobody's coming out to greet us, either."

• • •

The smallest hatch that seemed to be an air lock wasn't a good choice. It was no bigger than a child. Cliff had picked one big enough to pass a couple of elephants, Beth judged. They brought the cart rovers down the ramp from *Eros* and lined up their cargo in front of the air lock. Their suits weighed lighter on them in the lesser grav.

Beth felt odd indeed, looking through two walls of faintly blue cliff to see . . . trees. Spindly black trunks, soft pink fronds, carrot-topped—but trees. They set to work opening the air lock.

Only they couldn't.

• • •

For three days, they tried to find a way into the air lock. The task took all the gear they had in the lander. Beth got tired from lugging apparatus out to the working area, setting it up, trial testing, integrating, then listening to the arguments about the results.

People under stress, she observed, need to argue. It lets off steam.

The team looked for obvious controls in the window/walls, but the surfaces were translucent, smooth, unmarked. They were synthetic diamond, at a guess. Carbon, anyway. Mounted on a blue interior wall were odd protrusions that might be controls— "For something with big fingers, or clumsy," Fred reported to *SunSeeker,* now half a lightspeed minute away. But on the outside there were no manual assists, nothing like a computer interface they could recognize, not a lever or a valve. In a way it made sense: defensive architecture.

They tested the cliff wall—a hard shell, rising straight up with a vacuum on one side and on the other an atmosphere. They could see the weather was heavy with sleeting rain the second day, and cloudy the next. Looking up the height of the transparent inner wall was like taking a cross section of the sky, with clouds sometimes stacked against it. Slowly winds blew the clouds around the enormous boundary of the butte. While the others labored, Beth and Cliff took time to watch the trees and soil and small darting things that flitted among the swaying trees. Something foxlike almost escaped a pouncing bird. . . .

An alien world. It was like standing on one side of a museum diorama, only they were in skin suits and packs. And the other side was a living world just doing its business.

Quick flitting birds like swallows, but much bigger. They were fast and sometimes flew in formations. Bright splashes of color amid snarled undergrowth looked like flowers with petals, but threw tendrils through the underbrush. Trees of curious zigzag trunks and branches. Scampering slick-skinned blue gray things—*like squirrels? same niche?*—leaping on the ground and into trees. Odd angles in the tree limbs, gnarled things like nests or goiters, a broad-winged thing flapping through . . .

Howard kept making analogies to Earth life. Sometimes they worked, but other features made no immediate sense. Strange and wondrous. Gradually Howard stopped talking to Cliff and just made notes.

Redwing got irritated that they could not find a way in. He started giving orders in a stern tone.

Eros's crew stopped answering. People got prickly, Beth noticed without surprise.

Beth figured there was some signal they were supposed to give, but the blank, smooth, slick face of the air lock wall gave no clue about what to try. Here was the abstract problem of communicating with aliens, brought down to a concrete level.

Beams of particles, laser pulses, microwave antennas brought to within a meter—none made any difference, or provoked so much as a change of color in the eggshell blue wall.

The third day they were standing around the big microwave beamer they had hauled out, Beth with her gloved hands on her hips, gazing down in frustration at the rig, which had done nothing to the barrier. Fred said very calmly, "Something moving in there."

They all turned and saw a big colorful creature walking out of the trees. Swaths of blue, yellow, and magenta seemed splashed over it in elaborate designs. A big narrow head, with a long nose between two large eyes, swiveled and watched with stately elegance. The native looked to be at least three meters tall and strode forward on legs that articulated gracefully, taking great long strides. Mouth like a stubby beak. Spindly long arms ending in complicated hands. It came forward quickly, carrying something tubular, and then three more like it appeared from the trees. They seemed to stroll, taking their time but covering ground quickly.

Beth stood absolutely still, but part of her realized that this would be the first remark at the sighting of intelligent aliens. She said quickly, "They're . . . beautiful."

"Birds," Cliff said. "Those colors—they're feathers."

"Smart *birds*?" Fred asked.

"Hey, crows are smart," Irma said. Then shrugged. "Somewhat."

Howard Blaire just gaped at the Bird Folk, his gloved hands flat against the glassy surface. He'd run a semi-private zoo in Maryland on Earth. He'd collected animals too. He'd been something of a star, bringing weird animals onto television shows. Cliff had asked Redwing to revive him because he was familiar with varied environments and animal behavior.

They stood there for long minutes and the Bird Folk did just about the same, staring through the wall. They made quick, jerky movements with their two slender arms, moving their long necks sideways and jerking their beak-mouths. It was easy to see them as birds who had replaced wings with arms, but as well, they had a lightness and grace to their gait, an elegance of motion that recalled no creature of Earthly origin. Beth found this enchanting, a sort of dance she had never seen before.

The newcomers did not make any move to open the lock. After a while, Cliff poked a finger at Fred and Irma Michaelson. Irma was one of the recently revived crew, a plant biologist. "Go forward. Make hand gestures about opening the lock."

The Bird Folk seemed excited when Fred and Irma approached, beaks flapping—but they did not answer the hand signals and gestures. They gawked. They talked to one another. They fingered the various burdens they carried on belts and vests.

Beth watched them closely—the humans were all recording visual and audio, of course—and decided the Bird Folk didn't wear clothes at all beyond appliance wear like packs and belts. They had long swaths forming colorful patterns all over their bodies, particularly at the neck. Some wore what looked like headsets, or else ornamental hats. The backs of their heads had multicolored coxcombs of astounding profusion. Every one was different, with intricate bursts of color interwoven in rubbery pink combs, some nearly a meter long. They were tall, the biggest maybe 2.5 meters high.

Redwing's voice said on comm, "Company. About time! Fred, keep me posted." Fred didn't answer.

More Bird Folk appeared, came forward, and seemed to talk to the others. Body language: strutting, bowing, fluffing of feathers. Plenty of beak flutter, speaking. Cliff reported, "We've got two species—at least two species—call them big and medium. Medium is still bigger than we are. Big defers to medium. Big carries sacks under the neck or on the ramp of its back."

First contact was turning out to be entirely a spectator event.

They stopped using their beamers on the wall for fear that the Bird Folk would take it as an attack. So everybody stood there and looked.

Beth chuckled. They had come light-years, met

an obviously intelligent species—and neither could do much but gawk.

The tension of it finally got to Cliff. "Let's all go back inside. Maybe that'll provoke them to do something."

Beth thought this was a good idea; their suits were running low on reserves of air and power, anyway.

Nothing happened the next day, either. Some Bird Folk came and went, but came no closer to the lock.

The humans made a more elaborate camp: pressure tents, stores of water, microwave stoves. Maybe that would give the aliens some idea of how they lived, Beth thought. With guard duties assigned, someone was always watching the Bird Folk, capturing every move on video.

They all invented theories about why the Bird Folk did nothing—Captain Redwing had half a dozen—but without any way to check them, it seemed futile. So they had meetings and talked to *Seeker* and tried ideas.

More Bird Folk appeared. They formed loose ranks and stretched beyond view. Over a thousand of them, by Abduss's camera-count. Irma wondered, "Maybe they don't have much technology anymore? Or are they just the local animals?"

"They're carrying things," Abduss pointed out. "Not just the neck sacks. Those three Bigs are towing . . . what? Something big, five meters long. Made of metal, looks like."

More waiting. More Bird Folk.

Cliff, mostly just to break the impasse, suggested they cut through the wall. Even diamond wouldn't stand up to what they had for tools. Go straight through the outer door of the air lock. Maybe they could find and work interior controls.

There were objections, of course. This was a crucial moment; don't make any moves that might be taken as aggressive. This view held sway for a full day, until Irma asked just how long they would wait, doing nothing. Until *SunSeeker* ran out of air? That would be centuries.

Biggest of all, there was the problem of cutting their way in. Nothing had worked before. So a team tried high-intensity gas lasers, tuned to an ultraviolet frequency that the air lock wall totally absorbed. It worked in trial runs, cutting in quickly, blowing off a carbon vapor.

They set up the laser outside the air lock. By now they had an extensive audience of Bird Folk. Beth felt uneasy working under their gaze. They just watched. Were they waiting for something? Certainly their steady stares implied a remarkable calm. Or, she reminded herself, a remarkably alien consciousness.

Redwing wondered on comm if this was some sort of test. Maybe the Bird Folk weren't interested in strangers who couldn't figure out how to get in?

They started in the middle of the outer lock door. As they worked, their acoustic detectors on the lock picked up a hissing sound. The Bird Folk were filling it with air! Celebration!

... but the lock did not open. What did this mean? The Bird Folk just looked at them, eyes glittering. Beak-mouths working. Even some odd moves, like dancing.

Pressure in the lock, with vacuum outside, made the job more difficult. Nobody wanted the atmosphere jetting out suddenly. For safety, they built a chamber around where they wanted to cut, to hold the pressure. Then the laser punched all the way through.

Through their first cut they slid a small pipe, just to sample air. Breathable, barely—high in CO_2, warm, a bit lower in oxygen, humid and with minor differences from Earth's. Had the aliens figured out human tolerances? That seemed unlikely. But the molecular ratios fit the measurements *Sun-Seeker* had made in its first studies.

"Earth's oxygen level is as high as it can be without igniting spontaneous fires in summers," Howard said. "Maybe biospheres generally run up to that limit, then stop—or else they burn themselves back to our levels."

"Never thought of it that way," Beth said, her voice hushed. "This place stays warm all the time. Maybe that draws down the optimum oxy level a little."

They were all in awe of this place, moving quietly, trying to take it all in.

Howard said, "The more I see, the less I know. Some of these plants and animals are clearly evolved from Earth. Some clearly aren't. Cliff, I think this thing—Bowl—went to Earth and picked up some life-forms. The birds are a maybe. I'd need to see a skeleton. Cliff? Anyone? What do we do next?"

This was clearly the captain's call, despite a light-speed gap of four minutes. Redwing dithered; this was far outside his leadership skill set. They all finally got him to realize that they needed an exploratory plan. Some wanted to explore the Cupworld, at least enough to restore *Seeker*'s depleted stores. But they needed crew with the lander, too. The Bird Folk wouldn't wait forever . . . would they?

Cliff won the draw to lead an exploring party through the door they would cut. As pilot, Beth stayed with the shuttle party. The two of them didn't like this, but they were short of crew, and nobody else had the right mix of skills. Beth grimaced at Cliff, and they made it up to each other that night.

Or at least that was their excuse. Nobody wanted to admit being afraid.

NINE

They started the next morning—not that there were any sunrises here.

Cliff's team were four men and Irma, all muscular and tall and athletic. Beth and Cliff did not like being more than a few meters from each other, but they overcame that.

They followed Greenwich Meridian morn, of course, because the sun never set on the British Empire and certainly not here; the reddish star always hung in the sky at midafternoon. The star's jet was a furious neon line scratched across the sky, adding diffuse shadows. The eerie landscape confused their eyes and unsettled the mind.

They could not be sure if the Bird Folk slept, though Irma had compared camera runs and found that each did take a few hours of closed-eye time, still standing up. They never seemed to sit; maybe their knees locked. Nor did they fly.

Cliff had come to think of them as like ostriches. Far prettier and more graceful, but there was a similarity. Could such birds have built the Bowl?

The gas laser took three hours to eat through the outer lock door. On broad-beam, it then cut an arc big enough for humans to squeeze through. Cliff went first. He felt very vulnerable, hurried and impeded by his pressure suit, crawling through a hole not much bigger than his torso.

By then the laser was short on charge and over-heating. The operators—two engineers, Lau Pin and Aybe—shut it down and worked over the gas chamber fittings, which were looking the worse for wear.

Irma passed him some gear, then wriggled through. Cliff watched the Bird Folk for reactions. The big ones nearby fluttered a little, stamping their big feet, then went back to their steady stares. Much rippling of feathers, glorious runs of color.

Irma was through, and Terry Gould was having some trouble. "Let's move!"

Cliff felt alien eyes on his back as he got his five through the hole. Aybe came through, and Howard Blaire. Hustle, hustle, hustle. They had planned to put a plate over the round bore hole and let one of the party partake of the lock air. Getting set up for this, Cliff happened to look behind them.

The hole had changed. It was lopsided . . . and smaller.

He blinked some sweat from his eyes, smelled the sour flavor of the helmet. He had spent too much time inside. The hole still looked lopsided. As he watched, the rim of it wrinkled, changed color, crinkled at the edges and . . . grew. Inward.

Not diamond after all.

"Block it!" he cried, lunging at the hole.

They wedged some fittings into the gap. Abduss had a hand laser on his tool belt and he cut some more metal bars to jam the hole from the butte side. These stuck . . . then bent . . . and snapped in two and flew away with lethal force, bouncing like shrapnel around the air lock as the hole tightened further.

Howard cried, *"Ow!"*

"It's self-repairing," Beth called over the comm. "Get out—now!"

"Can't—it's already too small." Cliff eyed the rate of closing. "It regrows just about as fast as we can cut it."

They stood helplessly watching the wall ooze into place, like a liquid. The laser team struggled to get it back in operation, but—

"Too late." Cliff stepped away from the narrowing hole. He scowled at the Bird Folk. "Why do I think they saw this coming? No wonder they didn't look bothered."

"They knew something else, too," Beth said. He followed her pointing finger.

He hadn't noticed the dust motes rising behind *Eros*. Cascades of white light came from everywhere.

"That dust. It's been there, ticking at the corners of my eye," Beth said. "More every minute."

Until suddenly they were all glowing, as if bright sunlight were falling into the butte. Cliff heard shocked voices in his earphone, and Beth shouting, "Into the ship! Tananareve, you at least, get into *Eros*!"

Four of Beth's team were still in the pressure box they'd built around the air lock's wall. The fifth must be Tananareve, and she was running for *Eros*. She stopped when a hexagonal thing covered with lumpy protrusions rose through the Star Pit behind *Eros*.

Jets of ice white lowered the hexagon toward the floor of the butte.

Everybody was talking over comm—panic and anger and shouted orders that made no sense. Cliff watched the thing descend in the vacuum outside, tremendous compared to *Eros*. All happening only hundreds of meters away.

It might as well have been a light-year. The hole in the air lock kept narrowing, and the ship that looked like an assembly of boxes and rhomboids and coiled tubes settled down nearby. Out of it came a lumbering machine on wheels.

Soundless, the horror unfolded. The machine had a transparent cowling that looked like the atmospheric membrane, a shimmering pale blue balloon. Inside that sat three Bird Folk, working controls, staring at consoles that flitted across the walls in splashes of vibrant color. They moved with jittery intensity. Cliff made himself study the three and saw that they had different feather markings, and looked larger than the bigger variety on his side of the air lock. They moved with a lumbering, muscular purpose.

Three more of Beth's team were free of the pressure box. Coiled tubes unwound on the wheeled tank. These reached Tananareve, caught her. They plucked her up none too gently and dropped her into a cargo hold behind the cabin. Arms reached for the other crew, yanked them up one by one, added them to the hold.

Then the tank rolled back toward its ship, up a ramp, and was gone. Just like that, Beth disappeared. Just like that.

Horror paralyzed him while his own crew still fought the hole's steady closing. Nothing worked. Cliff watched but could think of nothing to do. Their shouts came through on comm. But he heard it all through a cottony buffer, the words hollow and refracting. Meaningless. He dimly realized that he was in a state of shock, numb, unable to process the events. Part of him had shut down.

The hole sealed itself up—a neat engineering trick, Cliff admitted distantly. He did not see the flicker of motion outside. Three tall Bird Folk were standing beside the air lock. They were of the third variety. They had the same markings as the ones in the crawler outside, and with a level, steely concentration they gazed impassively in at the humans.

Something thrummed up through his feet. He turned and on one of the lock walls a set of symbols flashed, rippled, changed in a cadence. He sensed a change in the pressure. Behind the three taller Bird Folk the crowd backed away, their leathery mouths working. The three were somebody important. Maybe a funeral guard . . .

"They're going to open the inner lock door," Irma said with an odd, flat calm.

Cliff said, "Aybe!" The man's head jerked around, wide-eyed. "We're going out the instant there's room. Here, give me that hand laser."

Someone called, "We shouldn't make any fast moves. Just be—"

"We'll make a run for it," Cliff said loudly. "Everybody, get all the gear you can into your packs."

He had to try the laser himself. It worked, a brief flash. He watched the aliens. This was dangerous and he was in charge. But he was damned if he'd let his crew get scooped up like Beth.

What to do? He looked up into the bowers of the forest. Some looked dry. Last night's rain was long gone.

"Burn the trees," Cliff called. "No shots toward the birds." The lock door somehow slid aside, though Cliff could see no housing it fed into. The door just shortened along one side. A puff of ivory fog swirled around it, humidity freezing out as it expanded. Cliff shouted "Stay together!" and was first through the opening.

The big Bird Folk, third variety, were twenty meters away. The Mediums and Bigs were edging back, giving them plenty of room. Cliff aimed the laser at the trees nearby and blew hot spots in them. They burst into licking, hungry flame.

The Bird Folk backed away, all of them, arms up in defensive gestures, legs stuttering in fast, short paces. Aybe helped the fire along with dried brush he snatched up. The rest of the crew copied him, moving to their left, behind Cliff. Irma was pulling Howard along.

The trees crackled and gave off plumes of oily smoke. Cliff heard high-pitched calls that he guessed came from the Bird Folk, but there was no time to think, only to run and shoot at the trees, keeping as many burning trunks between them and the Bird Folk as he could. Bowers in the trees exploded with muffled bangs, showering the air with sparks.

The aliens did not move fast. A breeze whipped down from the muggy sky and slid down the butte wall. It gushed out at the base, pushing the flames toward the Bird Folk. Cliff and Aybe formed a team, Cliff watching to be sure they did not get flanked, Aybe shooting at more trees, the others staying close. Inside their suits, they did not have to fight the smoke. Cliff could see legions of the Bird Folk staggering away from them, into the safety of the forest.

They kept on the move long after the Bird Folk had vanished in the growing firestorm. The land began to rise and they pushed on up it, getting enough height to see. The forest ran to the fuzzy distance. Nowhere were there any signs of a town or even a tall building. The fire had gathered momentum and now surged away from the butte wall. They had created a disaster.

Cliff was elated. Panting, the others grinned . . . except Howard, who sat like a sack of potatoes as soon as the rest stopped moving. Cliff finally had a chance to look at him. A three-inch sliver of metal protruded from Howard Blaire's arm, through a slashed sleeve. Nasty and bloody—shrapnel from the attempt to block the closing hole.

Cliff gave a hand signal and they gingerly opened their suits to the outside air. Fragrant with odd odors, thick, a bit sour—but the first natural air any of them had breathed in years.

Victory, of a sort. Cliff savored the moment.

Beth and the others were back there, probably captured by now. He tried not to think about that.

They pushed on. Howard was able to run with them, but he didn't speak. He sweated a lot and seemed in shock. He'd been one of the last to be warmed up from the sleep. Cliff suspected he'd been hit with too much strangeness. Just like them all.

TEN

Beth's team took positions to cover all directions. Tensely they waited and watched. Things were moving. They crouched at the edge of the great bare plain, their backs to the closed air locks.

The space above the Star Pit had become dusty, vague. Dust motes don't behave that way in vacuum, floating, sparkling, drifting up in currents. Beth never noticed. She and the others were watching Cliff and his team in the air lock, still trapped, still trying to find controls they could work. Then— outside the pressure box, above the tremendous pit in the floor of the butte—space came alight.

All the motes were aglare, lighting *Eros* and the bottom of the butte and the line of air locks. Through the Star Pit rose a building, a skyscraper, a tremendous hexagonal prism festooned with coiled gray snakes. Metallic snakes. They began uncoiling. Some of them glared white at the head end. Others ended in grabbers, mechanical hands, clusters of nostrils that might be little rockets or sensors.

Beth and three others were inside the pressure box, up against the air lock wall. Tananareve was outside. A huge boxy thing was descending on them. "Look out!" Beth had time to call. "Into the ship! Tananareve, you at least, get into *Eros*!"

A look and a gasp, and Tananareve ran. Behind her the Big Box settled carefully. A wall in it split. A smaller wedge-shaped thing rolled out on tractor treads.

Consternation blared in her earphones. Beth turned around to see that the hole they'd burned through the aliens' air lock was closing. The Wick-ramsinghs and Lau Pin were trying to jam stuff into it, blocking Cliff from climbing through. *Shit!* Howard Blaire started to try anyway, then pulled his arm and head out and hurled himself backwards as some of the blocking struts bent, then exploded.

A snaky arm from the tractor plucked Tananareve from the shadow of *Eros* and set her inside the Big Box. Another, much larger grab reached out of the bigger vehicle and closed around the human-built pressure box. Air puffed in momentary frost, and Beth felt the pressure change. She looked for the chance to escape, to run.

The crumpled pressure box had already risen too high. If she let go, she'd be killed. Like Beth herself, Mayra and Abduss and Lau Pin were clinging hard to whatever they could reach. The pressure box descended into a much larger cargo bin in the larger vessel.

Many of the walls in the alien ship were transparent, like thick, murky glass. Beth and the rest rolled or crawled out of the wrecked pressure vessel in time to see grapplers close on *Eros* and lift it against the Big Box's hull. The thing was immensely strong.

The Big Box rose fast. In sudden hard and tilting thrust, Beth eased herself against the floor of the cargo bin, a smooth transparent surface covered with wedge protrusions so big that she had to wrap both arms around one.

Lau Pin's voice rose above the general sounds of dismay. "Tananareve? Tana—Oh, shit."

"Lau Pin? Where are you?"

"She rolled. We're over . . . up against a wall. She's out cold. Her arm's broken, I'm pretty sure."

Thrust eased. Vanished. They were falling. They clung to the tie-downs and waited.

ELEVEN

Beth shook herself, trying to keep track of time, at least.

She didn't believe her in-suit displays. Days had passed.

Beth wrenched around, feeling sluggish. Bile slid up into her throat. She clenched, swallowed, forced it back down. Not the time to get sick.

She blinked at the passing scenery. Beneath her feet lay deep space, yawning vacuum. To the sides, slabs and beams and walls stretched away.

The back of the cup was sliding past. Occasional grapplers and other machinery came into view, some of it working. No living things, just robotic arms and, in the distance, locks. A weird, stressing vision.

She moved slowly. Her body felt numb, as though senses came through a filter. It took hours to get her crew together and make them work.

Fred recovered early. He watched passing scenery, mumbling notes to himself.

They spent the time taking care of Tananareve, and tying harnesses onto the lockdowns available on the walls. Nobody else had suffered anything but bruises and banged joints. Tananareve's ulna was broken. She clenched her teeth and said little. They tried to set it and splint it, with dubious results. She had broken ribs, too, but there was little to be done about that. Mayra could inject painkillers through the suit. Tananareve fought it for a while, groaned, then went slack.

Meanwhile the Big Box rose behind the wok-shaped section of the Cupworld. Very little noise came through the walls of their chamber. Thrust came and went, with no sound of rocket motors. They must be moving by magnetic interaction, hovering so close to the cup that its curve was almost lost. They were close enough to make out hexagonal plates that made up the mirror, and tiny-looking motors on their backs, all mounted to a grid that seemed no thicker than spiderweb.

That trip was their first good chance to see anything of their tremendous prison. Stars shone in the hard black. Brute slabs of metal passed by. Clangs and grinding noises, usually with small jerks and electromagnetic noise.

A long series of plates passed by as they rose. These were a city block or larger on a side, with enormous arms to move the plate's position. Beth felt that she was seeing the rear view of a giant array, devised to tilt the laminated wedges. Yet the huge areas were not thick. What could this be?

The mirror lands. They had seen those areas on their flight along the jet. Abduss had figured they reflected sunlight back onto the star's hot spot, to boil the surface and drive the jet out. These plates, then, were able to tilt and yaw, adjusting the reflection of the mirrors on the other side from their Big Box elevator line. The whole array was like the smart telescopes Beth had seen, only these were not used to look at stars across interstellar distances. These drove their own sun through interstellar space.

The Big Box rumbled as it rose up the back of Cupworld, taking its time. Sometimes there was rattling thrust, sometimes not. The big alien Variety Three Bird Folk didn't like heavy gravity, it seemed. No wonder, given their size.

They ate the food paste in their helmets, and thereafter went hungry. Not thirsty; the suits were made to recycle. They talked about food. They talked about whether they would starve. They wondered how much those huge aliens ate, and what they ate, and if humans could eat it, too. Occasional thumps, surges, rattles, hums. Mayra collected pictures of everything on her all-purpose phone, which had no reception, of course. She watched her team bear up.

Fred—was he watching everything? Or just wrapped within his own mind?

Nothing to do but look at one another and worry. Their chronometers clocked four more days.

TWELVE

They slowed down as their adrenaline high faded. Cliff could feel the energy leak out of them. It left a sour taste in his mouth. They trotted, then walked. His own breath turned ragged, wheezing.

Cirrus clouds overhead fuzzed Wickramsingh's Star into a gauzy reddish blur. Strange, layered forest lay in all directions. There were several decks to the high trees, separated by open air. Cliff wondered if these had evolved to allow the constant sunlight to reach separate layers as the tall trunks swayed in breezes. The oddly spray-topped trees were getting bigger as they moved over a ridge and down its slope. The trees were strange, often thick at the top and with rough bark.

He glimpsed plenty of birds flitting among the branches, and some very large, broad-winged ones hanging in the sky. Odd songs and squawks resounded in the high, thick canopy. At 0.8 g, it must be easier to stay aloft. Smaller birds flitted across the sky, too, in great chirruping flocks.

He suppressed the biologist in him and concentrated on seeing if they had pursuers. No sign of it, and the first two hours went without incident. All eyes surveyed the forest. Heads jerked at the sound of small things scrambling in the bushes. They were tense at first but slowly relaxed.

"We've got to live on the land," Terry said at a break. "Conserve our supplies. Cliff, you're the biologist. What can you see that we can eat?"

"Can't tell at a glance, Terry. We need to do checks to see what here we can even digest. I've been looking for what's chasing us."

"Stay away from those aliens, right," Aybe said. "We need to figure out what's going on."

Cliff had doubts as to what was possible, but kept quiet. This was a small group, and they had to learn to work together first, and stick to essentials. "How much food do we have?"

A quick inventory showed that he was carrying more than the others. They did carry gear that worked in concert, compact food, and not much else beyond personal gear, comm, and tool sets.

"Say, let's hunt," Irma said brightly. "I used to do that. Liked it."

"Using what?" Terry's expression told them he would not have expected her to be an outdoors type, though she was tall and strong. "Lasers take a while to recharge."

Irma turned to show her hand-sized solar panel riding at her upper spine. "Mine's already done recharging. Hunting is a good way to scope out the wildlife."

"And vice versa," Aybe the engineer said crisply.

"We should find water first," Howard said, looking dry already, his clothes sweat-stained. His arm was healing fast and he showed few signs of any slowness. Vibrant health and response to treatment had been an essential in crew selection.

"We're too easy to spot up here," Cliff said, eyeing the horizon. "Water's down below. Safer, anyway."

They set off toward a denser stand of trees, using cover as they could, working down from the ridgeline. Irma insisted on taking the point position, hefting her laser intently, eyes jittery. After her came Aybe, and Cliff decided to give the man his own laser. He didn't want to be the marksman and also have to scan the terrain, figuring things out as a biologist. As soon as he let go of the laser he felt downright naked, which was the point. Not having a weapon reminded him that he was not a hunter, but rather the wary, hunted stranger. They all were, but some didn't know it yet.

Everyone seemed to accept Cliff as at least their temporary leader. It was best to appear pretty sure of yourself, he knew, so he did not share his own doubts.

So . . . What to do? Deal with the immediate. Learn, let time educate them all.

His first major decision came when he stumbled over a gnarled tree root and fell flat on his face. Getting up, tasting the sour taste of the soil here, he realized that he was tired. They all were.

His eyes felt grainy. "Let's take a nap," he said.

They groused a bit. Aybe was still pumped up with what Cliff judged to be adrenaline energy, but the others looked gray and drawn in the full daylight.

"How can we sleep in this glare?" Irma asked, fidgeting, ready to push on.

"In the shade." Cliff said it flat and sure . . . and after a long moment, they accepted it.

Aybe said, "Let's build a fire."

"We could make some hot soup, tea," Irma said, brightening.

Cliff shook his head. "The smoke will draw attention."

Irma blinked. "From who? The aliens?"

Cliff nodded. "And maybe something else that we don't know."

"What's our strategy here, then?" Aybe stood, hands on both hips. "Hide?"

"Yes. If we can."

"For how long?"

That was the nub of it. "For now, yes. Get our bearings first. Then we'll see."

Aybe sniffed. "Not much of a strategy, I'd say."

Cliff was tired, his back ached, and he didn't want to deal with this now. "Luckily, you aren't saying."

Aybe shrugged and glowered. "What's that mean?"

Cliff kept his voice mild. "We have to get oriented first."

Aybe held the glower. "You're giving plenty of orders here."

Cliff sighed. He really *was* tired. "So I am. We're in strange lands. I'm a biologist and the senior science officer in this team. Learn the life-forms first, find out what we're dealing with—yeah, seems like a good strategy."

"I don't recall us electing you."

Now Cliff shrugged. "This isn't a constitutional convention."

"I'll say." Aybe grimaced and opened his mouth to say more, and Irma broke in. "Running around here on our own, strange goddamn place, aliens, hell—where I come from, sounds like we're cruising for a bruising."

They all gave dry laughs and glanced at one another.

"Let's get some rest, guys." Irma looked at each of them in turn, beseeching.

Cliff nodded again. This issue wasn't over, but

it would keep. He might even remind them that he was first officer. Scientists didn't pay much attention to chains of command usually, but this was not a lab.

Once they sat and ate, the momentum seeped out of them. They talked little and stared off into the distance—the forest that just *felt* strange and low valleys fuzzed by blue gray water and dust haze. The view was idyllic, still. A breeze blew through, aromatic and soft. Comforting. They were each still processing the dramatic events just past, trying to get some perspective. Too much had come at them too fast.

Then in the distance, Cliff saw a round blob high in the air. Dark, small, impossible to tell how far off even with zoom lenses. No discernible movement. He watched it for a while and wondered if it was some suspended artifact. Another mystery.

Cliff drank some water and curled up under some low hanging limbs. He conspicuously pulled his hat over his face. This was an important test, he sensed, peeking at them. They looked at one another once more. Irma shrugged. They settled in.

Cliff took the hat off and said, "Aybe, you up for taking the watch?"

"Uh, sure." The lean, muscular man climbed up on a thick limb to improve his field of view.

The others laid out soon enough. Hats went on faces. Within minutes, somebody was snoring. The hard bright daylight remained.

He woke—two hours later, by his left eye watch—and sat up, disoriented. He had been dreaming of

Beth, a jangled bunch of lurching images and a vague sense of threat offstage. Aybe was lying on the branch, head turned the other way. Cliff walked around and looked up at his face. Aybe's eyelids fluttered and he jerked up. "I, I was—"

"It's okay. Sleeping rhythm's going to be a problem for a while."

They roused slowly. Howard still was gray, worn. Irma looked at his wound, and his eyelids fluttered with pain. In the enduring sunlight, they ate and drank and didn't talk much. The air was dry and dusty and a breeze had kicked up dust clouds in the distance. Cliff wondered how anybody could figure out the weather here. There might be something like the Hadley circulation in the atmosphere, since the Cupworld wasn't a perfect spherical surface— but the scales were immense. Surface gravity varied over the entire hemisphere, but not solar heating. He found it hard to think through the atmospheric dynamics. It seemed unlikely that Cupworld had seasons; no axial tilt. What carried moisture around, in what patterns? What happened to evolution, without the seasonal cycle?

He made them go downwind, slanting off the ridgeline. That way they could see whatever was interested in them, coming up ahead. Their rear guard could be pretty sure of no surprises—from animals, at least. The sapient aliens were after them with smart technology, so they could come from anywhere.

Out of the sky? Cliff gazed up into the gossamer blue bowl. Birds of many sizes flapped across the immensity. Their body designs were familiar, excellent examples of convergent evolution shaped by the laws of physics—but some were huge, oddly angular, and rode thermals until they vanished in puffy high clouds. He could not see the rest of Cupworld through the high white water haze, or the jet. No sign of industrial pollution, at least. The aliens were somewhere out there, looking for them. Their only advantage was the size of this place, its refuges.

They made their way down a valley, seeing nothing much. Yet the air of strangeness kept them uneasy, on guard. Cliff led by example—always looking around, keeping them from talking. That way they could let their ears do the advance warning.

Irma got it. "Think like we're in Africa," she said. "Lions around every corner."

The two new guys, Howard Blaire and Terry Gould, seemed capable tech types, but with little field experience. They didn't hike well, kept talking. Irma shushed them a lot. The trees got shorter, and on all sides were brown bushes and tall gray grass. Birds trilled and sang in the tree bowers and stopped whenever anybody spoke.

They crept carefully into the high grass. In the dry perpetual afternoon, the stalks rattled as they brushed by. Thirty meters in, Cliff sensed something moving up ahead.

He felt a cold adrenaline shock trickle down his spine, his chest tightening. They went to ground in tall grass and watched a bobbing, tawny spike move across their path at about twenty meters ahead. Cliff saw the spike—a tail?—turn and then stop, directly downwind of them. They all tensed.

Then it moved off again, faster, at an angle. Maybe they smelled funny to it. Or maybe, he thought, it was going to get some buddies.

Crossing the grass had been a mistake. Their lasers gave them control of a ten-meter perimeter, but that shrank to how far they could see in grass or dense forest. They all got edgy. They got out of there fast and headed partway up the side of the narrow valley, to get viewing range. They were still seeking water. Cliff had them do an inventory on the way.

He had chosen to fill out his backpack carry weight, fifteen kilos, with other gear. Luckily, he had guessed right, and brought a light sleeping bag and cooking equipment. He had left behind all the techy gadgets and gimmicks available in *Seeker*'s supplies for planetary landing. Most of those presumed a power supply and backups. One item he had found and brought was a pair of sturdy boots and, most important, spikes for climbing trees—or anything fairly soft. Light, foldable carboaluminum, they weighed little and clamped snugly around the boots. They popped out on a sharp heel-clinking command—smart tech, quite cute.

They moved carefully and kept down talk to a minimum, but they were basically city types, able to keep the expedition's technology running. Not a bad group for this place, which was, after all, an enormous machine. Their attention wandered after the first hour.

Without warning, something like a wiry, fanged slick-skinned squirrel leaped down on Irma and tried to eat through her hat. Howard snatched off her hat by its brim and hurled it like a discus. The squealing creature hung on until the hat landed in thorns, then dived into the briars and was gone.

Irma snatched at her hat as if it would fight back. She was flushed and trembling. "Why'd it do that?" she asked.

"It thought you looked like some tasty thing, I figure," Cliff said. He wondered what that thing might be, but kept the thought to himself. "Or maybe he liked your hat."

There were worried faces all around. He waved the matter away and changed the subject. "Try to listen for water. Or better, smell it."

"Smell it?" Aybe frowned. "Water doesn't smell."

"Sure it does." Aybe and Terry really were a bunch of office engineers and computer types, he thought, living out their lives indoors. And they had been inside for a long time. Good thing they didn't have to learn to build a fire or make bows and arrows. Or at least, not yet.

Except Howard Blaire, who was grinning at Aybe. Howard had run a private zoo, and collected for it, too. A field guy, he'd know the smell of water. "It smells fresh, kind of," he said.

They sniffed the air as they moved. Cliff wondered why they had seen no aircraft. It was the obvious way to search, and anyway, wasn't there routine air commerce? Anywhere on Earth, they'd have seen commercial flights by now. He recalled a glorious week rafting through the Grand Canyon, when the only sign of civilization was contrails scratched across the deep blue.

But this place was alien, and they should learn from it. What had his mother used to say? *Problems are just disguised opportunities. Sure, Mom.*

Maybe the natives were afraid of aircraft puncturing their atmospheric cap? He filed the puzzle for future study and went back to scanning the woodland they moved through.

They were halfway across a clearing when something charged them.

Irma got off a shot at something that looked like a giant red badger. The shot didn't slow it down much. Cliff and Irma both walked backwards fast. Without a word spoken, the other three ran for the trees.

Irma shot at it again, and Howard, but it didn't seem to notice. It turned away from them—for Cliff.

His fingers itched for a laser, but instead he ran for the nearest tree. He jumped, clicked his heels in midair, and had his spikes dug into the tree bark before he thought about it. Then he was up and over, just as the badger clawed up at him. He could hear teeth snap behind him. It was a pretty nasty beast, all big teeth and claws and temper. Smelled bad, too.

Cliff scrambled out onto a thick limb and looked around. His team was intact, making for higher altitude. The badger hadn't gone after Irma, not after she hit its muzzle with a laser bolt. Aybe had been light on his feet and was now far up a big tree.

They were spread out but safe. The badger jerked and snarled when Irma and Aybe gave it some encouragement to leave. Cliff could see the laser bolts spouting puffs of gray smoke from its fur. They could not get through the thick mat.

Impasse. It prowled around their base trees for hours, spitting mad. Their laser bolts made it angry, but it didn't go away. Maybe it was used to a waiting game, Cliff mused. And didn't like to climb trees.

The badger seemed mammal-like, but that was just appearances. Convergent evolution fitted life to niches. Like marsupials compared to placental mammals: similar forms but completely different physiology.

Finally, after much shouted talk, they started to quiet down. Fatigue, again. At least it was shady here. He took a deep, moist breath from the twilight air beneath the trees, and let himself relax. He could feel the tension ease from his back and legs. This was the first real rest he'd had since coming through the lock. A long time ago, yes. His stomach growled. He fetched out stiff blocks of protein/carb mix and munched them thoughtfully. Their taste burst with lemony richness in his mouth and he carefully let himself have a gulp of water. *Ah.*

Then, resting despite the badger, he heard this world. It buzzed (insects?) and barked (predator pack signaling, territory assertion?) and twanged (what the hell?). The symphony of life, singing strange in a colossal zoo . . .

He fell asleep without meaning to. And dreamed of Beth—dark images, fraught with lurid worry.

PART III

Good judgment comes from experience.
Experience comes from bad judgment.
—MULLA NASRUDIN

THIRTEEN

A Serf-One brought Memor a delicious skreekor, fragrant with the scent of its own fear. She ate it with lip-smacking pleasure while she watched the invaders.

The skreekor was an ample beast, about the size of the new invaders, but certainly far more tasty. This one was lightly spiced and big enough for a midwake meal, six or seven bites. It had been preserved by radiation; its taste was savory but slightly stale. It did not wriggle, in a final gesture of its knowledge of the right order of things. Memor paid no attention to the smaller bones that snapped as she ate. She would disgorge them later.

She'd wondered if the invaders could do magical things, tricks beyond known science. This was most unlikely. They had not presented any real problems, though the Folk had responded slowly. The aliens now seemed safely confined. One was injured or dying. Their gear was unfamiliar, but it seemed crude. They fumbled with their toys and jabbered endlessly. Primates always seemed to do that, as ancient Bowl records showed from similar adaptations of the four-limbed. In their simple forms, it made them easier to hunt, though they never seemed to learn that.

The group that escaped had shown not cleverness, but panic. Mere luck had aided them. But luck was occasional. No matter what their strange origins might be, their frenetic movements showed intelligences not able to deal with new elements. Or incapable of planning, an even worse sin. Perhaps, indeed, the only true sin.

They were dull creatures, as well. They had no coloration feathers—indeed, no feathers at all. Camouflage was therefore beyond them. How simple! From what odd world had they descended?

They seemed incapable of conveying meaning with even their elementary skin signals—and so incapable of nuanced speech. Talk from their wiggly mouths, and antic hand gestures, had to somehow suffice. The females displayed mammal signatures, bumps and curves, and lesser mass. Curious. How did sexual selection occur? Through such constricted pathways? What sour, diminished channels they used! And so tiny! Memor wondered how to teach them to speak the Tongue.

Of six Astronomers and twice that many Serf-Ones, only Memor had been trained in TransLanguage. She had long thought there would never be a chance to use her training. Vast time would pass before the world came near Target, where they expected to find their first intelligent species in many million-folds of time. Now Memor's TransLanguage and neurological sensing arts would advance her prospects. Her pulse quickened agreeably.

The Target Folk were powerful; that much was obvious to any telescope array. But they had never shown interstellar ambitions, judging by the lack of visible fusion torch signatures near their star, or large constructions.

Still less likely was this startling appearance of visitors. Such were discussed in the Long Records, but none had come for a countless time. Until now, suddenly, from behind. A crafty approach. The Astronomers were plainly disconcerted by their drawing near. A vast failing, really. Yet now that Memor was female, all seemed somehow clearer. This was an opportunity!

But at first it was not Memor's, for it had not been Memor's watch for many, many Turns. Plus, she had been *he* in those times, and thus had less judgment. Yet she, in the racked torture of the Change, had seized the moment, banding with others of the Dancers, and so now could show her newfound abilities in judgment. This would surely help her career. The prospect warmed her, beyond the pleasure of anticipation. She was on the cusp of a great era; of that, she was sure.

Memor had been trained long and diligently in TransLanguage, because one of every generation must be educated, to pass on the skills. She'd never hoped to use those elaborate methods of transcending ordinary language, designed in antiquity for speaking with these Target species, these candidate Target Folk. The Bowl's beamed transmissions at the approaching ship and at the Target had never been answered, but that did not reflect a failing of TransLanguage. There could be many reasons why the Target Folk did not reply.

Or . . . Were these aliens Target Folk at all? The thought struck her, apparently from her Undermind. She would have to trace its origin.

No doubt they might be from the Target sun, still scores of light-years ahead. Memor's great heart thumped agreeably at the very idea—but their big ramship had come from *behind* the World. Unless, of course, they thought to conceal their origins. But Memor was sure routine Astronomer observations would have picked up their fusion plume, had they approached from the Target direction.

Call these chattering things something else for the moment, then. Call them Late Invaders.

There were feeds from cameras in Sector 1126. Memor watched in hope of learning more. A second group of Late Invaders was running loose there . . . but for five wakes they never came near a camera. Perhaps they were more clever than they seemed at first?

There must be living invaders in the big ramship, too. Memor watched it on her input screen as it now arced around the sun, shedding momentum, grasping its way forward with magnetic claws. She had wondered if it would come back, if it would attempt rescue of its small invaders. But in over five wakes, it did nothing but maintain its almost-orbit, thrusting a little against the pressure of stellar gas. Perhaps they were benign. For now.

Memor bristled her feathers, air humming richly through them in a darting pride-song, to match her thumping heart. *Joy of life, that brings such opportunities.*

She opened her Undermind, a narrow window for now. This could refresh her thinking. It was like a sudden shaft of crimson light, startling to her Overmind. She could feel thoughts and emotions wrestling endlessly there, combining and mating. A rich bed of vibrant murk. She thought of these roiling notions as a sort of food for her Overmind, endlessly wriggling. *So different, so oceanic, as female . . .*

Deftly she dipped in. Notions purred. Slick sounds keened at moist harmonies. *Richness!* She might need some new combination of previous ideas, properly cast in a pale glow of fresh scrutiny, to deal with this emerging situation. Perhaps she would even have to let the Undermind churn until it produced something fresh. That had happened seldom, but the possibility was exciting. Memor would come into her own then, her talents in demand. She could ride her Undermind to become perhaps even Overlord. Thus did Astronomers rise in the pyramid of status.

Moving the invaders was going to be tricky. She needed ideas there, yes. Memor wondered how long they could go without food. They couldn't eat anything through those pressure shells, could they? Better to get them out of the vacuum.

And now the Serf-Ones were docking the Maintenance Craft. Carefully they worked, with much worried chatter, afraid of giving the slightest offense to their superiors. As was proper.

The invaders offered no resistance. There would have been no point, and this behavior showed some modicum of intelligence, plus that rarer quality, judgment. Compared to those who escaped, these might be a superior type of primate. If there were such among such a ragged, hairy species lacking any of the lushness that came from feather discourse.

Three huge Astronomers surrounded them and urged them forward with stamping feet. That signal transcended language. The invaders moved, half carrying, half towing the injured one of their kind. They huddled close together, puny things overawed by the size of the Astronomers. Their anxious primate gestures gave them away.

Seven much smaller Serf-Ones went ahead of them through the air lock, carrying gear.

The invaders stopped moving on the other side, eyes agog—an expression of wonder common among many species. Perhaps they were startled by the contrast: grass and huge trees and vast flocks of wide-winged birds, all in microgravity. Memor saw that teams of Serf-Ones had set up a force-fence. Excellent. The invaders were properly imprisoned.

Now Memor sent an Astronomer off with a flock of Serf-Ones to fetch food. She instructed the crewperson carefully: They must find something of every kind. Skreekors, hairies, bugs, fruit, bark, grasses. No telling what these things might eat, though their amino acid composition was common in Bowl experience. Memor was aware that most life-forms were restricted in their diet, their environment, cycles of sleep and mating and feeding, heat and cold . . . a thousand things, but particularly diet. These creatures might starve to death no matter what she could do.

So Memor was eager to feed them, but also to teach them. She let her Undermind purr forward on ideas of how to do so. These poor creatures must learn something of her, and she of them, before they died in microgravity.

• • •

"Mayra," Fred said, "did you get pictures of that chain of bubbles?"

Mayra looked at him. She said, "Buildings. Domes, but not just half spheres. We build that way too in lunar gravity. I snapped some pictures on my phone, but I thought you might have seen something. . . ."

Fred said, "I was too sick, and hungry. Didn't notice."

"Well, we followed a ridge after we passed the bubbles. You saw the ridge? It ran right here."

Beth said, "It's not going to matter. We're fenced in. Do you suppose they'll let us starve?"

"We're in a garden. There must be something to eat. Rabbits?"

FOURTEEN

When Cliff awoke, Irma was sitting next to him, hat tilted, standing watch with concentration. She winked and said nothing.

It still felt funny waking up in this perpetual daylight. Humans had evolved in a daily rhythm, and the strangest thing about this place was its constancy. No sway of day and night, no dance of the hours. The sun stood still, a permanent glare in the sky. He could read nothing from the slant of sunshine, since it never varied, and he missed the sunsets of the California coast. Living in perpetual day was the ultimate jet lag; it never went away. He knew from Earthside experiments, done in preparation for starship building, that people in constant illumination tended to develop longer sleep cycles.

Above, the scratch across the sky that was the jet bristled with festering luminosities. He could see tiny hairlike threads slowly flex and turn amid the tossing motes that burned with furious energy. Was this what a galactic jet looked like up close? It was brightest near the star, cooling as it coasted outward toward the Knothole. The nearer jet reddened so it sent diffuse, pink shadows rippling among the leaves. Nothing as spectacular as a sunset, but intriguing and unsettling.

The badger had wandered off, Irma told him. They gave it an hour, though, in case it was lying in wait.

They set off again, more cranky than before, from the odd sleep they had managed to get. Like a clotted rain forest, the dense copse of slender trees enveloped them in moments, fronds and puffball clumps blotting out the sky. The soil was a soft loam, with little bushy understory. This reminded him of dry eucalyptus groves in California, still and aromatic and whispery. The smells were tangy, odd, not at all like the medicinal eucalypt aroma. Game paths laced through it, hard packed dirt with some brown droppings. He sniffed some; turds appeared to have a universal pungency. The same basic chemistry, he surmised.

And more than game could use these bare throughways. Or stalk parallel to them. He waved to the others and they angled away from the easy game paths, not without some grousing.

"Carnivores lie in wait along these," he explained in a whisper. "We might look like tempting game."

"We're primates," Howard shot back.

"And nothing ate monkeys in Africa?" he retorted.

When he started his fieldwork in grad school, he could barely tell raccoon tracks from bobcat. Now he knew earthly tracks and scat and had been automatically cataloging what he saw underfoot here. Alien tracks fell into the same general categories, hooved and padded and birdlike, but some had spindly hexagonals, which he could not fathom. Scat looked pretty much the same.

They saw some game, too. These were flickers of tawny flanks among the trees, glimpses of hides with natural camouflage that faded away into the hushed silence. Howard whispered that maybe they should shoot one.

"And carry it along?" Cliff answered. "We can hunt when we set up camp."

"Near water," Irma said. Cliff nodded.

They passed under a chattering locus in the high branches and stopped to gaze upward through binocs. "Monkeys," Howard said. "Swinging around, with big tails."

"Really?" Cliff recalled the barking bands at the San Diego Zoo and used his binocs to bring one of the quick shapes into focus. A rude purple throat display, huge yellowed teeth, darting small red eyes, but—"Yeah, kinda like monkeys, anyway. But not mammals, I'd say. No obvious genitalia. Can't see teats, either."

"So primates evolved here, too?" Howard let it trail off into a question.

"Maybe they're just getting started," Cliff said softly. He wondered if, given a few millions of years, these protomonkeys could overcome the aliens they had seen. Not likely. As soon as the primates became noticeable as competition, the smart aliens would prevail. Established forms usually had the advantage, and there was nothing automatically better about primates.

"Look down there," Aybe whispered, pointing. A creek glinted green among the shade trees below.

They approached too fast, in Cliff's opinion—he called out to them to hold back. Predators liked watering sites. This wasn't Earth, where dawn and dusk were the natural hunting times, as herbivores came for a drink. Carnivores could be hunting any time at all.

But there was nothing waiting near the creek, so they all had a good long drink. It tasted cool and fine, and on impulse Cliff plunged his whole head in, glad to be free of the grit and sweat of the last few—days? There were no days here, he reminded himself. He would have to think of a new word.

He recalled a calculation Wickramsingh had

done back on *Seeker*. Take the Earth and spread it into a bowl the size of this Cupworld and it would be maybe a centimeter thick. Here in the stream-cut hills, he could see cross sections of the land. The soil was a conglomerate, like coffee grounds peppered with chunky gray rock. No strata, of course. There had been no real geology here.

To get hills hundreds of meters tall, the Builders (he thought of them as deserving the capital) must have chewed up Jovian-size masses. They had transformed a whole solar system. That explained the absence of asteroids and other debris around the star. They'd had to be removed; otherwise they could've smacked into Cupworld later, punching an unfixable hole, draining the atmosphere. He had to stop thinking of their surroundings as being just a planet. It was . . . well, a vast contrivance. With all kinds of weirdness living in it. On it.

After resting above the creek, they followed it downhill. The creek bank revealed more conglomerate rocks, round yellowish balls fixed in grainy sand. Cliff wondered how the designers of this place had laid soil and water down on a huge, spinning carousel.

Plainly they had to put down some mass, a meter or two of rock or water, to keep out cosmic rays. But the scale . . . again and again he came back to the vastness of this place. The whole idea seemed both gargantuan and surrealistic—mute testimony to the deeply alien nature of its builders. Who—what—would do such a thing? Those birds? Somehow, he couldn't see it. They didn't seem that smart.

In a while they came to a dense spread of trees and within it found a lake. Flies buzzed around a thick margin of reeds, and they found no easy way to get to the water. Cliff wondered if he could take a swim in it. His skin itched. Maybe later.

A thing buzzed by his head. It had six wings, about the size of a sparrow. Maybe it played the role of dragonflies in freshwater wetlands, he guessed. Convergent adaptation. Willowlike trees hugged the shore, but taller and with twisted, helical trunks. Convergent evolution seemed to have led to pollinator plants, too—bigger stamens and longer, twisted pistils, but the same strategy. Shrubs somewhat like laurel sumac mingled with tall trees vaguely like closed cone pines. Still, some of the plants were bizarre, with canopies permanently pitched toward the star, and bunched leaves like parabolas. There were mosses, too, bryophytes, ferns.

Howard was whispering into his phone. He was loving this.

• • •

They camped, but still Cliff thought it a bad idea to light a fire. They slept again, badly, with Howard and Irma taking watch. Voices called in the woods—chirps, snorts, ominous grunts, buzzes and bellows, oddly pleasant trilling songs. Alien melodies.

They circled around the lake, keeping to bristly brush and trees. They were getting better at keeping a clear field of fire; the badger had taught them well. Three people covered while two moved, then the reverse. This meant eyes caught any reaction among the nearby foliage. They startled game but did not fire.

Sharp odors welled up from everywhere and peculiar fowl flitted noisily. They honked and sang and sometimes sounded like fire alarms. Cliff noted that there seemed to be plenty of small birds darting in and out of the bush branches, slipping their pointed snouts into the many long-tubed, sweet flowering plants. Never was there a species he could recognize, yet the patterns were recognizable. *Sunbirds, hummingbirds, same strategy.* When threatened, some fluffed up their feathers to make themselves look larger and barked odd calls—territorial defense as in most nectar-eaters, like orioles. Others had the sharp beaks of those who preyed on insects, like wrens or the short, triangular beaks of seed eaters like finches and sparrows. Evolution here had produced skills similar to those on Earth; he found this reassuring. In the lesser gravity, birds had apparently beaten out many land animals. They were bigger, too—fat and confident. Apparently a 10 percent or so difference in local g made a big change in the balance of living types.

He'd have to talk this through with Howard when they had the chance.

He had seen flying frogs leap from stream levels to high branches, flapping short distances on webbed legs. The predators of the high sky hovered long before they dived, able to sustain their altitude with big, slow-flapping wings. The insects here were bigger, too, for some reason, though with the same many-legged gaits as on Earth. This was indeed a different place—and how different, how truly alien, they could not fully know yet.

Plus, the smart bird aliens. Was he being narrow-minded at first, thinking smart birds unlikely? But of course, these were huge birdlike ones . . . and he had not seen any fly. Maybe they resembled ostriches who gave up flying and gained technology.

Howard held up a hand, pointed, hunkered down—they were getting better at hand signals.

Along a narrow stony beach lay some long reddish brown things like bulging crocodiles, lounging in the perpetual noon. They grunted as they moved. Their bodies were long and scaly, with a short, blunt snout. A lazy yawn showed many serrated yellow teeth.

"Those are for tearing chunks out of big prey," Cliff whispered. "Our crocs dine on small fish, chickens, small pigs. These eat bigger things."

"Let's give them plenty room," Irma said.

Aybe pointed. "But what's—?"

It rose out of the deeper dark water. A long neck uncurled upward with strands of weeds dripping from its flat, rubbery mouth. The brown eyes gleamed with wet curiosity as it looked at them, mildly interested but taking its slow time.

"An herbivore," Cliff said, awed. "Like a . . ."

"Dinosaur," Howard supplied. "What the hell kind of place *is* this?"

"Convergent evolution?" But that seemed unlikely, and he stepped back as the thing rose like a slippery mountain—dark with a white belly, legs like pillars, long slick neck and tiny head. "It *is*. It's a . . . dinosaur," Cliff said, a chill running through him. "From Earth. Has to be."

Irma said, "The aliens, they stopped at Earth?"

"Must've sent ships, anyway. They must've picked up some of our—Earth's—ecology," Howard said as if entranced, eyes rapt, prophesying. "Like we were doing, bringing species alone in sleepstate— only more so."

"It's interested in us," Aybe said, taking a step backwards.

"How do we know it's not a meat eater?" Irma said.

"We don't." Terry turned to leave.

"Their native ecology here must have been over-run with alien species. So . . . Cliff? It's too good, this place, too like Earth. That's why. They imported Earth life."

"Maybe. Maybe," Cliff said, grimacing. "Reassuring, isn't it? If that's the explanation."

Irma backed away, too. "Let's go."

Cliff smiled. "Don't miss the lesson. We can eat some things here, and it can eat us."

"Y'know," Irma said, "they could've just hauled some dinosaur eggs and other life here on ships, passing by our solar system, a long time ago."

Cliff nodded, eyeing the massive, slow shape with fascination. It grunted. "So the Earth forms could've taken over parts of the Cupworld, and lasted this long."

The huge thing sluggishly waded toward them, pausing to rip reeds and lily pads from the water and gulp them down. A muddy reek came from it on the soft wind. It was slow but steady, and Cliff motioned them to back away. "It's a herbivore, I'd say, but interested in us."

"Not for eating, though," Howard said, "so why—?"

"If it steps on you, what's the difference?" Aybe was moving faster, towing a grunting Howard by his belt.

They got away from there. Irma led the way, in case some predator moved to block their exit. None did. They faded back into the forest.

Cliff now felt apprehensive. He realized that they had been taking this place as a pseudo-Earth, and indeed in many ways it was—but that also meant it held forms that summoned up in them ancient fears. None of them had seen dinosaurs except in movies, but the sight of one tapped also into a deep reservoir of primate vigilance.

Aybe said, "Now we know the trajectory of the Cupworld better. We extrapolated a naïve straight-line trajectory and folded in star motion, too. It may have been near Earth over sixty million years ago."

"What's 'near' mean?" Irma asked.

Aybe rolled his eyes as he calculated, adjusted his hat, shrugged. "Say, five light-years. How old was that dino back there, Cliff?"

"Maybe a hundred million years ago. I don't re-call the classification or the dates real well. I'm a field biologist." Abruptly he laughed. "Didn't think at the time I'd have any use for those paleontology classes."

In a clearing, Irma automatically moved to their right flank and said, "Y'know, Earth wasn't in the same place in the galaxy a hundred million years ago. So Cupworld might've been following some different trajectory, not just some straight line from Earth to here."

Howard said, "Right. Stars move a lot in that time."

Irma kept a wary eye out, whispering, "Face it, we don't have a clue what these aliens—the smart ones, I mean—are doing. Touring the galaxy on a slow boat? What kind of mind does that?"

"A slow mind," Terry said. Cliff had noted that the man didn't say much. When he did, it was well thought out. "Maybe an immortal one?"

"As a biologist," Cliff said, "I kinda doubt that anything lives forever. Once you stop reproducing, the force of natural selection stops working. Traits that gave you short-term benefits come back to haunt you."

Irma said, "But if you have biotech galore—?"

"All bets are off," Cliff admitted. "Maybe the Builders—that's what I call them, the ones who made all this—lived pretty damn near forever. But Cupworld has been on its way for at least millions of years. Maybe even sixty million—that's when the dinosaurs died."

This sobered them all as they made their way upslope, keeping their eyes on the surrounding forest. Cliff recalled a training hike into the Ecuadorian rain forests he had taken while he worked on his doctorate. The instructor had told them that the three weeks they spent upriver of the Amazon would be "meet-yourself experiences," and that seemed to capture a deep truth. Exploring made you know yourself better, like it or not. *Self-knowledge is usually bad news.* . . .

Without warning, a leathery thing the size of a greyhound came at the point man, Aybe. It ran quick and sure, as if it had preyed on something that looked like them before. Aybe shot it at a one-meter range, blowing a laser hole in its forehead. The big yellow eyes of the thing fluttered and it fell, kicking, rasping out a last breath. It looked like a reptilian dog, scaly and tough, with thick haunches and a powerful set of clamping jaws.

They stared at it. "Good shot," Terry said.

Irma said brightly, "Let's make a fire, roast up big chunks of meat."

Cliff worried about detection, but didn't stop them from gathering wood. Their amino acid scans had shown the basic same as Earth, and DNA had the same structure too. Maybe they were universal? An old folk song about moonshine cooking rang in his mind. *Don't use green or rotten wood, they'll get you by the smoke.* . . . "Don't use fresh fallen branches," he called out. "Look for dried-out ones." Terry looked scornful at this, but others nodded. They had uneven woodland skills. Cliff still had to remind them often not to talk so much, a rule every field biologist knows.

Around the campfire—carefully set under dense leafy boughs, to capture and spread the billowing gray stink, which was nearly transparent—they set into the fresh roasted haunch meat with gusto. Terry wished for a good red wine to go with it, got some laughs.

They ate but were not sleepy. So they pushed on, looking for a safe water source, a spot with clear fields of fire. Nobody wanted to spend a sleep time in trees. But what was the alternative? Cliff was still wrestling with the problem of what to do, but he had to shush them after the meal, and that made him worry more. Leadership was a bitch, he decided. More like being a schoolmarm . . .

"Look, we've got to remember one big fact: These creatures don't have any natural caution about us," Cliff said as they made their way up a steep slope under spreading canopy trees of fat emerald fronds.

Aybe said, "Doesn't that mean they'll be easy to hunt?"

Cliff gave him a wry look. "Sure. But it also means the predators have no reason to fear us. Remember that."

FIFTEEN

Memor decided to isolate her prisoners from the vast species richness of the World. Her Undermind provided the idea, and she instantly knew it was correct. She had watched the logics working in their moist, blue green connections, and understood the entire thought-chain.

The World's wealth would stun them, surely.

The blue green abundance would prove shameful to such primitives. They might even commit group suicide, humiliated beyond tolerance. Their cages she ordered made hospitable, but nothing more.

Further, her underlings saw that these small creatures found every avenue of escape blocked. Isolation was best, both for them and for scientific study. It was simple to devise transport to put them tens of millions of miles from natural air, water, vegetation, the ripe bounty of the World. Ancient records said something of the sort had worked well against the last invaders, rendering them compliant. Then again, she had to feed them.

She had found a good solution. The greenhouse was a series of verdant ledges set near the World's axis of rotation and thrust. The Jet burned a searing injunction in its sky, pointing back at the Star. Sunny and mild, this was a unique preserve, a rightful richness that fed the Astronomers and gave them restful grounds for strolling and contemplation.

Surely, as the species that tended the course and the health of the World, and so provided for their servant species, Astronomers deserved such cloistered wealth. Since time immemorial, the plants that grew there, the animals and birds that lived on the plants and each other, had all been deftly altered to match microgravity. Such was the wisdom of the Ancients.

In this lush paradise, Memor allowed the Invaders some small latitude. She had not stripped the Invaders of their equipment, because she didn't know what would kill them. No doubt some of their implements, so odd and crude, were sacred to them, or used for amusement. Very well; Memor was generous.

She and the other, lesser species watched to see if the Invaders would divest themselves of their pressure suits. They did strip the wounded one, but failed to learn from the experience. For some no doubt primitive reason, the rest remained dressed for vacuum when they went to sleep.

They slept twice as long as an Astronomer would have, and all woke more or less at once. Perhaps this was a species defense mechanism?

They stripped down then to a lower layer of cloth. So scrawny! Memor doubted they were hiding anything from her. More likely they kept themselves covered as a birth control measure, taming their primordial impulses. Or perhaps they used outer coverings to control temperature in an altogether wilder environment than the World's. Lesser species of the World had similar mechanisms, and could even use simple tools.

Memor watched carefully as they designated a toilet area, and used it in turn. No sharing. Perhaps a status ritual? They tried various bits of what Memor had set for them as food, an elaborate crescent array that would serve as a biology lecture, too. They did not eat grass or bark or water weeds, but they did eat an amazing variety of higher protein content foods. Omnivores! Memor had once wondered if they could feed themselves at all. In the World there were species that could not; they needed servants who could process and serve food. Biology had many strange flowstreams.

Some of what they had were tiny cameras. Memor watched them making records of what they saw. They spent much of their effort recording the arrays of possible food sources. When she knew they used meat, and knives, she supplied whole carcasses; they photographed these and the dressed and cooked meat, too. Plants raw and peeled. Servitors and Memor herself.

Her lessers had returned with reports on the cell cultures harvested from the Late Invaders. The Late Invaders had similar methods of genomic patterning methods. Was DNA a universal, then? Memor knew that it was not. But they could come from one of the Seed Worlds the Ancients reportedly tried to fertilize.

Memor wondered if these Late Invaders could genetically engineer tools and machines not to degrade in a biosphere. The Ancients had bequeathed enzymes to synthesize devices, so the World grew apparatus needed by the Folk.

Turning sunlight and water into machines was the Higher Way, and these Late Invaders did not seem to have mastered that pathway to greatness. They might be able to edit genes, or transplant them to another crop; such was simple. But their devices did not have the elegant cast of grown apparatuses. So they quite probably ate simple foods, too, and lived lives of primitive needs. Yet built ramscoops.

Memor pondered this and decided to try fish. She ordered admitted to their ample cage some varieties with appropriate chemistries. No need to not be generous, after all. They should be made comfortable in their final days.

SIXTEEN

Coarse, smelly, wet soil stretched away, embedded in a gray metal mesh. You couldn't call it the ground, Beth thought, not in almost zero gravity, not with a straight face. More like a sheet of stucco with plants growing in it. The stuff ran away from them in muddy sheets for what looked like thousands of kilometers.

She had climbed into one of the spindly, triangular trees and surveyed the landscape. The soaring fence was far off, tens of kilometers. "It's as if they've imprisoned us in a dull, wet, brown Australia," Mayra said. "Lots of room. Lots of space to hide."

Abduss grumbled, "We're about to starve to death, too."

"Working on it," his wife said, grinning.

Lau Pin said, "Let's at least get out of these damn suits. We can do a better splint job on Tananareve."

In the early, fractured talk the big one in charge identified itself as Astronomer—a rank, apparently. She—definitely a She, a slit wreathed by crimson feathers—used star charts and pictures to make the point, assisted by slowly pronounced words in their language of grunts, call, piping songs. The Fourth Variety of locals Beth called Porters. Like other varieties, they were feathered like flightless birds, but built more like lizards. Their limbs and toes were long and limber. In the near free fall here, they were still flightless, but they could leap long distances.

The Astronomer, whose "close-name" was Memor, had shown them this right away. Beth thought this might have been some kind of display to instill submission; certainly the long, hooting calls Memor gave sounded joyous and dominant. Most of the other Astronomers wore harnesses, and used them for carrying.

The big Third Variety who led them was a hunter. Was the alien a he—or she? Where were the genitalia? Anus under the tail, just like Earth's birds. Call it he, then—he carried a long-tubed gun and gleaming, curved knives. He looked like an efficient killer.

They never went past the fence. The Porters did the carrying. In short order they came straggling back with small corpses and bigger slabs of meat—and roots and fruit and grain and twigs, all gathered at the Astronaut's direction.

The Astronomer had big, nimble four-fingered hands, though she wasn't doing much with them. Porters did most of the work, and their long hands were dextrous too. They laid their loot in a pattern, a long arc, plants to the left, meat to the right. Swallowing saliva, stomach rumbling, Beth waited for them to finish.

The Porters backed away. The Astronomer came ambling forward, and she was huge. It amazed Beth that she could pick up such little things with her long, jerky arms: bunches of grain, a ravaged muskratlike corpse, a small globe that looked like a striped melon. The moving mountain picked up something and grunted or trilled, raised it toward her huge, thick-lipped mouth and made a warbling, keening sound—the same sound each time for that gesture.

"Eat?" Beth wondered aloud. The Astronomer made a deep bass sound. Gestured with an arm.

They were being taught.

Until Lau Pin snarled a curse, stalked forward under the Astronomer, and reached up.

People froze. Beth waited for him to die.

The Astronomer dropped the little melon.

Lau Pin caught the melon. He held it up and brandished a knife big enough for killing. "Melon. Knife." He cut the melon, "Cut," and bit into the slice. "Good," he called back. Buried his face in the orange flesh. "Eat." Lau Pin jogged back, turning his back on the Astronomer, and cut a slice for Tananareve. "Give. Eat," he said, and she did.

They all did. Eagerly.

Each time Lau Pin spoke, the huge feathered Astronomer replied with a bellow and a gesture, her long fingers tracing curves in the air. Those might be easier to repeat than the sounds, Beth thought. She noticed that Tananareve was awake and paying rigid attention. Her hands moved in response to the Astronomer's Sign language.

• • •

The Astronomers also included some called Astronauts, who seemed to be those who could patrol the vicinity of this place. They were big, lumbering sorts who barely noticed the humans. They hooted at one another in long, rolling calls.

But more important, the principal Astronomer had buckled her knees in what seemed to be
good-bye, and gestured: She had left them their
tools.

That seemed amazing to Beth. Lau Pin had used
a knife and he still had it. That was reassuring. Beth
tried something else.

She chose a slab of red meat—"Steak," she pronounced it, optimistically—and set it on a rock.
"Beamer," she said, and held up a microwave projector. They'd tried to use it to cut through the
wall of the aliens' air lock. She plugged it into
her backpack power. Turned low, it cooked the
meat in a few seconds. They set the beamer aside,
cut up the meat, and ate. Beth carefully plugged
the beamer into its solar panel charger. The meat
tasted wonderful and in her hunger she forgot
about the alien.

Mayra and Fred, of course, were photographing
everything with their cell phones, and now so was
Lau Pin. Good. The power wouldn't run out for
months.

When they were finished, they still had the beamer.
And several knives, Abduss's gun, and the pressure
suit helmets. *We must look pretty harmless,* Beth
thought wonderingly. A matter of size?

Abduss stretched, yawned, and said, "I'm wiped."

With her belly full, Beth suddenly felt the wave of
exhaustion. She thought, *Don't be silly, it's only . . .
well, duh.* The sun was at sunset, vertical to the
glassy wall and horizontal to wet soil embedded in
a coarse mesh, and it wasn't going to set. Ever.

She called to the Astronomer, "Sleep," and to her companions, "Sleep."

Memor spoke a word. She watched, and when she saw her captives turn unresponsive, she turned toward the air lock. Beth tried to watch her, but her legs dragged. She felt soooo very tired. . . .

So did the others, she could see. It was logical. They were trapped, depressed, so took refuge in sleep. It made sense. Let their unconscious selves sort out all the new, strange, and alarming. No reason to fight it.

SEVENTEEN

They had a long slog through the rumpled hills. That took days. Without more understanding, they had no plan, no destination. They needed to learn. But without a goal, Cliff knew, morale would evaporate. Even fear, which was driving them now, would ebb.

When they got tired, Cliff called a rest. Nobody argued. They soaked their hats with water and put them over their faces, falling asleep instantly. Gratefully.

• • •

They stirred themselves nine hours later, but without breakfast. Food was short.

Cliff led by example, roving through the nearby

copse of trees and bushes in search of edibles. There were plenty of berries and some fat leaves, but testing by taste was dangerous even on Earth.

But what choice did he have? He smelled them for sourness, tried a tongue touch, and if all seemed unthreatening, would bite in. Sometimes this worked with berries and the fat-leaved plants and he got a sweet burst of juice. Other candidates stung like mad and he quickly washed them away with water. He did this several times, returning with a hatful of berries or flavorful leaves. He made them memorize the plant features before eating. The others welcomed fresh food and some caught on, following him in his prowling. Irma was best at this.

The guys seemed to think that they were cut out for hunting. Howard and Terry said they had some experience. Cliff half listened to their bragging amid a discussion of guns. He had glimpsed something large in the bushes—a quick flash of brown hide, then a soft flurry that sounded like hooves, fading. If this had been Earth, he would have guessed it was a deer.

Howard and Terry went out together, making a show of it. Surprisingly, within an hour, they brought back something that looked like a large rabbity grazer, furry and with ears that pitched upward from the flat, level skull. Cliff looked at the odd ears that cupped skyward, and realized that they must be for hearing birds—diving predators, probably. He had never seen such an adaptation on Earth. It was testimony to how important flying was here.

Skinned, the critter had an interesting skeletal structure and internal organs. Cliff sectioned them out and tried to understand how they worked. Odd fans of bones, lumpy organs with no apparent function. Some made sense, most not. He needed a real lab. . . .

They cooked the pseudo-rabbit over a small fire, taking care to keep it hot and show no smoke. Under some spreading canopy trees, the little smoke that did rise got trapped and spread, so they hoped nobody could see it at a distance. Cliff thought they needed their spirits lifted a bit, and warm food again did the job. The meat was tasty, dark and gamy, and very welcome. "See anything that looked like a deer?" he asked them.

Terry nodded. "How'd you know? Four-footed, at least, and meaty—but it had teeth."

Howard added, "And antlers. Looked pretty weird. Kept sniffing the wind, like a predator. Looked like more trouble than it was worth."

Aybe said, "We should save our lasers for defense, anyway. I thought we should have tracked and cooked that badger thing we shot before."

"It looked hard to kill," Cliff said. "And we were in a hurry."

Aybe shot back, "And now we're not."

Cliff took a long breath of musky air. Might as well bring up the tough issues while they were all relaxed, bellies full. "Look, we're wandering. We need an agenda."

That brought on plenty of discussion but few ideas. He had expected that—they needed to vent.

Anxiety came out as talk, rambling and vexed. Danger and hardship made for bad reasoning, but if he could defuse their frustrations, they could all then work better together. So they talked for a while, mostly hashing over we-shouldas and we-couldas, and finally Cliff said, "The past is prologue. What do we do next?"

"Find the others," Howard shot back.

"How?" Cliff asked.

"Maybe make a link to *SunSeeker*." Howard paused, obviously not having thought very far ahead. "They can maybe link to Beth."

Cliff did not want to step all over anyone's ideas; give and take was how you worked forward. He said carefully, "We don't have anything that can reach *SunSeeker*."

"How about our lasers?" Irma said. "If we could send a simple Morse message . . ." Her voice trailed off, seeing the difficulty of even locating the ship in a sky that never darkened.

Aybe saw how this was going, his eyes moving swiftly around their little circle, and said briskly, "First, figure out how this crazy place works. That will tell us how to get on top of our situation."

Cliff agreed, but it was best to let the ideas come from others. As they tossed thoughts around, he wondered at his own developing social skills. His career had focused on technical abilities—mostly useless here—not management ones. Here he would have to get this little band through unknowable threats—much harder than just keeping employees happy, a task that had always bored him. But this was lots more interesting, and nobody else seemed to want to lead. None of the expedition's actual, official leaders were here. Though as someone had remarked in Leadership Training, the important skills can't be taught.

They kicked this around for a while and finally agreed to what Cliff thought was obvious, without his having to say a word. Good—but talk took time, and he doubted they had a lot of time to spare.

The next two Earth days, they spent moving warily across the strange yet oddly familiar landscape. Trees with limb decks, zigzag trunks, spirals—on low hills with running streams and shallow arroyos. Cliff kept track of how long they all slept and found it was steadily increasing.

Irma commented on this. "Y'know, they did Earthside experiments while preparing for starship life. People under constant illumination had sleep–wake cycles that got longer and longer. Without the sun, they lost track of time."

Terry said, "So that's why shipboard lighting follows the sun cycle."

Aybe asked Cliff, "How does anything get regulated here, then?"

"I don't know. Biology without outside timing, no day or night—we have no experience with that."

They hunted small game, using spears they made—and got nothing bigger than the pseudorabbits. Still, it was fun and they celebrated their rare victories with ragged cheers. They were urban types, and the skills of stalking came hard. Maybe it helped that the rabbity grazers were used to attacks from the sky, so were less adapted to ground predators.

But there had to be intelligent life somewhere here. They could see fields in the distance—great plains of crops stretching between the forks of two converging river valleys. Grass crops, Cliff guessed. They worked their way closer, staying in the hills and staying within the trees. Still, Cliff was startled when they came up behind a few silent, trudging figures. Not human.

"Careful," Cliff whispered. They crouched down.

The shapes were crossing a foggy slope ripe with thick aromas. Out of the mist came shambling shadows, slow and silent. Cliff switched his distance specs to infrared to isolate movements against the pale background and found the figures too cool to be visible. In the mist they were ghostly, slim shapes. Legs, but no arms.

"The farmers?" Howard whispered.

"No." Aybe peered closely at the ponderous, spindly forms. "Plants."

"What?" Now Cliff heard the *squish squish* as limbs labored.

In the murky light, they watched as crusty pods popped from the trunks of great trees. Stubby limbs peeled away from their parents and found unsteady purchase on the ground. They were about two hands high and a mottled green. The slow, deliberate birth came moist and eerie in the quiet.

Cliff watched in awe. Working their stubby legs forward with grave slowness, the roots freshly pulled from soil and then moved onto wetter ground that enjoyed better sunlight. The air brought the scent of their sharp thorns to him, a tinge of acrid poison. The young needed defenses here.

They watched the animated seeds find new spots and with great, slow care settle down to take root again. To Cliff, this method extended animal mobility to plants, perhaps made easier in lower gravity. The others looked incredulous and uneasy, though Irma nodded when he advanced his idea. Certainly these plants were not dangerous, but their strangeness unsettled. Cliff realized that they had all been thinking of this place as mildly different, just the sort of world you would see in a movie, complete with dinosaurs. Reassuringly ordinary in just the right way. He had to guard against such comfy illusions.

They moved on warily. Soon they saw spreading below their hill a vast plain of green grain. A heady aroma blew up from the crops on winds that wrote sweeping patterns across the valley.

Irma pointed. "Look—those farmer folk we saw back at the lock."

With time to observe, they could see the farmers were leathery at some joints but otherwise sported plumage that rippled with colors in intricate designs. Clad in loose-fitting coveralls, they formed teams that worked on snaking tubular watering systems, focusing the misty, arcing plumes over great distances. They worked hard in their fields, using four-footed animals to draw and plow.

"It's like farming centuries ago," Terry observed. "Hard work, very little powered machinery."

"It's not as though they can drill for oil, is it?" Aybe said.

"Plenty of solar power available," Terry said. "And this has gotta be the most high-tech place in the universe."

"Maybe they *like* manual work," Howard said. He looked at their skeptical faces and shrugged. "Just because we've been living the rugged life for a while and find the idea unappealing doesn't mean *these* things do."

Irma raised skeptical eyebrows. "Could be, I suppose. But—" She zoomed her vision and stared at the field below. "—they're coming."

Cliff looked closer. "Not the farmers. Something else."

Irma added, "Yeah. Fast."

These were even bigger, with long necks—something like elongated, feathery racehorses that strode on two legs, with long wiry arms held forward for balance as they cantered. Plenty of rich plumage but a muscular look to them, especially in the legs. Clothed only at the middle, they had thick belts with things like tools dangling from them. As Cliff watched, one of them looked around and eerily looked right at him. It was running hard but held its head fixed, the eyes large and glittering. Not farmers, no.

"Looks like they're about a klick away," Terry said. "We must've hit some trip wire or detector."

Cliff had wondered how this place could have developed different intelligent species. Specialization for labor or life niches? They probably had genetic technology, so maybe had developed new species from some early root genetics. Humanity had yet to do that.

Enough thinking; it was hard to avoid it, his head full of questions. The runners, he saw, were perceptibly closer.

"Let's get going," Cliff said, and did so.

The menacing pursuers were fast and far more than anybody wanted to fight. Terry led the way, running as if devils pursued him—and just maybe, Cliff realized, they did. Humans had invaded this biosphere unannounced. They had not surrendered meekly, but instead fled from the air lock. No negotiation. Now they were ranging around in somebody's territory, killing local wildlife to eat. The farmers seemed peaceful and simple, but that couldn't be the whole story here.

But could they outrun those things?

On the run they decided, amid hoarse, barked consultation, not to return along their earlier route. There seemed little shelter there. Instead they headed downhill from the next ridgeline. They had learned a long, loping stride that took advantage of the lower gravity. No sign of pursuit yet in the forest behind them. They stopped to listen—panting pretty loudly, then holding their breaths to hear.

A distant chippering cry. Beneath that, low growling. Coming closer. "And they know the territory," Cliff whispered.

They ran. Nobody suggested negotiations.

They hurried into a broad, low valley of gnarled trees. Some bore fruit, and Cliff felt a pang of hunger as they ran through these. It was moist here and soon they heard the snarl of water over rapids. The river was broad and Cliff wondered whether they could ford it. He glanced left and right and saw a long arched bridge. "That way!" They all veered toward the bridge, puffing heavily now.

Terry, who had started off fast, now brought up the rear. *Not a distance guy,* Cliff thought, and knew that he wasn't going to last much longer, either. He tried to think of something to do. Anything.

He studied the bridge as they slogged toward it. He could hear the high, skating cry clearly now. Closer.

The bridge was made of stone cemented together, very old style construction. On the underside, though, were thick metal beams, ribbed and with flanges at each side. Rugged.

They reached the foot of the bridge. Maybe the lighter gravity gave them some edge here, but it was all gone. He slowed, thinking frantically. Stopped. An idea flashed.

"Hey. Let—let's hide."

Aybe gave him a sharp *you're crazy* look. Irma was so winded, she just bent over and gasped.

"We'll get run down," Cliff said. "I wouldn't count on our lasers taking these things out, either—they're big and look pretty damn tough to me. And . . . they're clothed. Belts, tools. Maybe they're armed, too."

He let this sink in while he puffed, and now they could hear the cries behind them quite well. They all looked at one another, gasping, coughing, and finally Irma said, "I can't go much more. Let's try it."

The men nodded, looking relieved. Good psychology, Cliff thought—they still felt that they had to protect the woman. He trotted around to the underside of the bridge and grabbed one of the ribs. He hadn't really thought this through, but when he put his boots on the side flanges, he found they fit, barely. The others watched as he climbed up the ribs. He then turned carefully to face down toward the water that swirled and chattered over rocks. With some effort, he could strain back and support himself against the beam.

The others looked up at him doubtfully. Aybe said, "Hanging with both hands? We can't use the lasers from there."

Cliff called down, "What else can we do?"

That decided them. They inserted themselves into the nooks between the beam flanges and with some grunting got pinned into place. It was an effort and he could feel his arm muscles working hard.

"Hold on as long as we can," Cliff said. The chippering was close. "*Quiet.*"

Pounding of heavy feet. Growls from deep guts, wild shrieks, quick barks like commands. Thumps. Feet hammered at his back, or that's how it felt, and most of them passed on. But then he heard a huffing from above, heavy long breaths. Feet padded around, slapping on stone. A rumbling bass grunt that seemed to go on forever. His stinging arm muscles had locked solid, his fingers trembling. The thing above wouldn't leave. Maybe the pursuers had left one here to block their retreat?

He didn't like this conclusion, but as moments

crawled on he saw that it wouldn't matter. Irma's face was white with strain and Cliff wasn't going to last much longer, either. At least they had caught their breath.

He didn't dare whisper. Catching the eyes of the others, arrayed in the beam slots, he nodded down at the riverbank. They frowned, then got it. Cliff listened intently and caught footfalls above, a scraping that moved to the left of the bridge.

The stream splash might mask any noise they made. He nodded vigorously to them all and jumped down, landing as softly as he could. They followed as he moved to the right. Irma landed off balance, but Aybe caught her before she fell into the stream. Lasers at the ready, they ventured out from the bridge's shadow.

The shape above came back toward the high stone railing. It towered above, a long snaky head looking across the river—and Irma hit it clean and sure with a long bolt. The head jerked, looked down at them with those big, glittering eyes—and toppled backwards. They raced around, got on the bridge—and stopped to gaze at the big thing.

A deep burn at the top of its skull trickled pale blood onto the stones. The eyes blinked, but the eyeballs did not move. Cliff unbuckled the belt from the thick waist and put it around his own. The tools were odd and heavy. He was tempted to take a look at them, but—

"What'll we do with it?" Irma asked, beaming.

"Leave it," Aybe said.

"This body will float away pretty quick if we toss it in," Howard said.

They looked at one another and without a word lifted the body at several points. Getting it over the stony parapet was not as difficult as Cliff had expected. It was a bird, after all, something like a monster ostrich. They flung it over.

Irma said, "Its blood—I don't think we can mop it up easily. There's a lot."

"Let's get moving," Aybe insisted.

"Which way?" Cliff asked mildly, scanning the far riverbank for movement.

Terry said, "Across—oh, I see."

Cliff said, "They left this guy here to block our return. They're probably trying to cut us off from those hills beyond and drive us back to the bridge. Pin us against the water."

"So we stay on this side?" Irma asked. "Move downriver, say? At least it's downhill."

They looked at one another edgily and then all nodded. Collective decisions, Cliff realized, made it much easier to take if things went wrong later. Otherwise, they'd blame it all on him. They ran.

EIGHTEEN

Lau Pin hefted an eighteen-pound fish, turning it this way and that, inspecting it. A row of fins ran down each side, eleven on a side, diminishing toward the tail. Yet the fish looked odd, with ventral fins, long and wispy, narrow eyes, mottled green skin. "I'll have to be careful," he said. "Parasites."

The Astronomer had left Lau Pin a ten-inch knife. He gutted and filleted the creature and cut it in slices. The flesh was pale, like a red snapper, Beth thought. There were angry red spots Lau Pin cut out. "I think I got them all," he said. "Sushi? Or shall we start a fire?"

"Fire. Cook it," Mayra said. "I do not feel lucky. It's ugly."

They broiled the meat on twigs. It was delicious, rich in oils and savory with a strange, tangy flavor. Spirits lifted and there were jokes about finding the right white wine to go with the fish. Or maybe margaritas all round? Beth was glad to get them in a good mood. The meetings with Memor had fascinated them all, but the brute fact was that they were prisoners listening to lectures. The thrill of contact with a real alien, telling them strange new views—even that had to fade. They were not idle scientists or philosophers. They had signed on to explore a new world, make a fresh home for humanity, to sail the stars. Their patience was limited.

Lau Pin rummaged through his tool belt and then gave a startled cry. "My beamer is live. It's got signal."

They gaped. He showed them that the signal light gleamed on his handheld communicator. "It's tuned to the *Eros* systems. I'm picking up data from its onboards."

"Any internals?" Tananareve asked wanly.

"Just status reports. Everything looks normal. It's on auto-standby."

"We must be somehow in line of sight," Tananareve said.

Lau Pin scowled skeptically. "We're an astronomical unit away from it, easily. This Bowl is huge. How could we hear from it?"

Beth felt a surge of hope. "It's a smart system. If *Eros* doesn't get pinged for a while, it must amp its transmission power to get a response. Maybe Cliff's group can get it, too."

"If we can negotiate our way out of here, we can use homing to find Eros," Tananareve said.

"Yes, great." Beth made herself sound more optimistic than she felt. They had last seen *Eros* crushed into a bin in a Bird Folk spacecraft. "Lau Pin, can we use your beamer to send signals from *Eros* to *SunSeeker*?"

Lau Pin worked on it for moments, staring intently at the small solar-powered beamer that was barely larger than his thumb. "I'm trying the 14.4 gigahertz band, then the subs. . . . No, I can't do over-commands from outside. Some kind of safety precaution."

Abduss growled with frustration. They all looked crestfallen.

Beth couldn't let that continue. Best to distract them. "Let's review what we've learned, class," she said with a smile. "Mayra?"

The normally quiet woman blinked and nodded. "When Memor brought those visuals—big constructs, dazzling perspectives—I got a feeling that she did that partly to impress us. You know, show the visitors some flashy capabilities."

Lau Pin said, "I like that it—okay, *she*—uses voice and gestures. Easier to remember that way."

Mayra said, "I liked those visuals it gave us on that screen. One was some kind of macroengineering in a planetary belt. I'll bet that was their history. How they built this place."

"She's using those as attention getters," Beth said. "Then she showed us those 3-D keyboards. I think she wants us to manipulate display machines. Only—she just spoke to them."

Mayra asked, "So you think she wants us to learn their language, by picking up how to instruct those 3Ds?"

Lau Pin waved this away. "Maybe. Those images it showed us could be fauxtography, too. A phony story. Distractions, anyway. We've got to escape, not just sit and learn language."

Beth nodded. She liked the wildlife around them, wanted to learn about it—and Cliff would love it, might be loving it now—but—"Right. Our bones are getting worse as we speak. We've got to get back to gravity."

• • •

Cliff's troop were doing badly on the basics: sleep and food. After crossing broad grasslands with clumps of trees for shade, they had seen no game worth pursuing for the better part of an Earth day.

Some berries helped, and they found fresh water, a tinkling clear stream without signs of fish.

Following protocols, Irma went upstream and provided cover guard. The four men slipped into the cool waters gratefully. For several days they had all had intermittent dysentery and all needed to soak, a morale booster. In the first days, they had added a chloride pill to the drinking water but now used a solar-powered UV source in the caps of their water bottles to sterilize it.

Something broad, ribbed, and horned scuttled into a burrow at the shore. It looked to Cliff like an oval-shaped turtle with a razor-sharp crest. The burrow reeked, repulsive and rank, so they let it go.

Howard floated in a small muddy pool. He lay slack, grinning widely. "Y'know, I've been thinking. I figure our getting the runs is from chirality."

Aybe asked, "Chirality? Spin?"

Aybe was an engineer, right. "Direction of rotation of molecules. Handedness. When a molecule isn't identical to its mirror image." Howard didn't talk much and kept getting hurt, which made him even more closemouthed, so Cliff listened carefully. "Most biochemists think it was a historical accident that all our sugars are right-handed and our amino acids are left-handed. I think some of the life here has molecules opposite-handed, versus what we know."

"How?" Terry asked.

"Remember how, two sleeps back, you were all raving about how great that purple fruit tasted?"

Aybe grunted at the memory. "And got ravenously hungry again in an hour. Pretty much like Chinese food, as the cliché goes—then we all got diarrhea."

"That's why I'm always hungry?" Cliff asked. He wished they had the chirality gear in the *SunSeeker* landing supplies. They couldn't bring everything on the first lander.

"We all are," Howard said. "We're moving cross-country, burning calories, but some of our food is going straight through us—and burning our guts some, too."

"We cook the meat," Terry said.

"Sure, but all the prior biochem work we had, back Earthside, can't offset microbes no human ever met. Montezuma's revenge, y'know."

Cliff said, "That comes from microbial pathogens, different problem. I ran the DNA checks. This ecology uses the same basic double helix structure in everything I checked."

"Sure, but on other planets, the accidents of evolution could make the proteins and sugars different. If this Bowl has been cruising along, sampling ecologies, then there may be whole ecologies here based on L-glucose rather than our D-glucose, and D-amino acids rather than our L-amino acids."

Aybe shrugged. "Sick is sick."

Howard glared. "So L-glucose is interesting because it tastes just about as sweet as D-glucose, but passes through the gastrointestinal system completely unmetabolized. Throw left- and right-handed ecologies together here, and every life-form in the food chain has to choose one isomeric biochemistry or the other. Fruit sugars, fructose, will behave the same way."

Cliff recalled that Howard had been a media figure of sorts. He ran a semi-private preservation zoo in Siberia, after the climate warming ran wild there, exhaling methane. He'd never have left Earth if a disaster hadn't wiped out his patch of land, animals and all. The mission planners put him in because *SunSeeker* carried the makings of a zoo, intended as an ecology for the colony. Some critters wouldn't survive and most wouldn't be revived right away, but Howard could handle them. He and Aybe were butting heads for a bit until Cliff held up a hand.

"That explains why we get the runs? How sure is that?" Cliff said. "I thought I'd seen all the problems when I did that air sampling as we came through the air lock."

"Biology never rests." As if to illustrate, Howard slapped at gnats that swarmed around his eyes. "Better if we learned what's got our handedness and what doesn't." Howard held up his phone. "I've got notes in here, beginnings of a menu."

Cliff clapped him on the back. "Good stuff. You're the food guide now."

It made him glad to get some clarity on an issue they'd shied away from. Just talking about it and making rude jokes helped. Irma came ambling back and laughed, too.

Howard finally said, "Meat's the best for us. Kills a lot of nasty stuff. Let's find some."

"Where?" Aybe asked.

"Look to all points of the compass."

"Compass doesn't work here," Terry pointed out, and they moved on, following the stream.

At a rest stop hours later under some zigzag trees, Cliff wanted to get some game into their bellies and sleep. When Howard pointed silently into the distance, they all crouched down and peered through their binocs.

"Looks like a squashed ape," Irma said. "Meaty."

It had a gray pelt and walked with a swaying motion, hips throwing the legs forward. A narrow head kept wary watch, and it was coming toward them.

"At least two meters high," Aybe judged.

"Plenty of meat on it," Howard said. His stomach growled.

"With that thick coat, lasers won't be much good," Terry said.

Irma said, "A head shot is tough, too. Look at those eye ridges—bony and not a large skull."

"It's not carrying anything in those hands. They look nearly like claws," Howard said.

Cliff thought about killing a primate but . . . they were really hungry. He decided to say nothing.

"Let's go to Howard's points of the compass," Aybe said, "and close in on it. Maybe get some spears?"

This zigzag tree had limbs that slanted backwards as the trunk angled left, then right. They cut off four limbs that were fairly straight and trimmed them down, sharpening their points with knives, searing the points hard with their lasers. They had all gotten quick and sure, handling their field gear, and the gray "ape" was only a hundred meters away when they circled through the tree line, working around it as it moved steadily on. The quarry looked around a lot but didn't notice them.

On Cliff's signal, they all closed in. The target was bigger than they were, he judged, by fifty kilos at least. It was watching the ground as they quietly edged closer. It climbed a short knoll and crouched down among the grassy tops. This helped shield them as they moved to within twenty meters of it. The quarry's attention was focused on the ground and Terry, who edged up the slope, gave the hand signal to attack.

They ran up the slope with makeshift spears and the thing suddenly sprang up, eyes wide. Terry charged at it with a high-pitched yell and then suddenly stopped. "It's got a tool kit!"

"Hold!" Cliff shouted. They stopped, spears still at the ready.

The creature drew out a slender instrument and pointed it at them.

"That a gun?" Aybe asked.

"Doesn't look like one."

Silence. Edgy foot shuffling. Cliff now saw their potential prey was not covered in gray fur but rather a formfitting garment of close woven cloth.

From a distance it had looked like a pelt. It backed up, saw that it was surrounded, and crouched low. At its feet was a square opening, revealed by a hatch tilted back by a large handle. It had used the slender tool to unlock the thing, and the lid of turf swung wide open on a big, rugged hinge.

"It's intelligent," Terry said.

The creature stepped carefully over and took hold of the lid. It murmured something and gestured with its long, angular hands. They ended not in simple fingers but with an array of flexible, multi-jointed appendages.

Cliff dropped his spear and stepped closer. About a meter below in the hole was a complex mechanical array. As they watched each other warily, a slight rumble came from the ground, vibrating his boots. The creature bent down and tripped two flanges to a new setting, ignoring them.

It's got to be pretty confident of itself, Cliff thought.

It swung the lid back into place with a thump that broke the strained silence. It put away the tool and held out its hands, appendages up. They were twice as long as human hands and fingers.

"Is that a peace gesture?" Irma asked.

Intelligence gleamed in the quickly shifting eyes. It focused on Irma and Howard, who were standing together. Slowly it walked toward them. They glanced at each other uncertainly, and Cliff said, "Stand aside."

With what Cliff thought was supreme self-confidence, the thing walked past the humans and continued on its way. It did not even look back or seem concerned that they might follow it. They stood awhile and watched it walk into the distance with a dignified, measured pace.

When Cliff turned from watching it, Aybe had the lid up and was examining the space below. The rumble was louder with the lid off but soon faded away.

"This is interesting mechanical engineering," Aybe said. "I could squeeze down in there and—"

"I'm hungry," Terry said. "I was already figuring out how to roast that thing."

"Can't eat a smart alien," Irma said tersely.

"I suppose not," Terry allowed with a nod.

Cliff thought, *People do on Earth . . . even primates.* But said nothing.

They went back to the stream and managed to catch one of the oval turtles with the razor-sharp crest. They were all in a bad mood. They hit it with a rock and roasted it over a spit. Cracking the shell, they found leathery meat sizzling from the fire and giving off heavenly aromas. Tough, but no one hesitated.

NINETEEN

A small set of rocky ruins lay downstream. Big stones cemented in place, no obviously advanced technology. They seemed abandoned. Cliff wondered at their age.

They skirted these, and the river broadened into a lake that smelled of sulfur. A swamp dominated one side and unfortunately it was theirs. They tried moving through it but the sour muck sucked at their every footstep. A hundred meters of this made them stop.

"Leaving prints in this muck makes it easier for them to track us," Irma said.

Terry looked exhausted again. "Look, we can only run so long. We're not trained for this."

Cliff nodded. "There's gotta be a better way."

There was, but not easy. They found logs and lashed them together with vines and strips of bark from the rotting fallen trees. No high chippering cries from behind, but they worked quickly together. Their discipline was getting better; nobody spoke more than the minimum. Cliff thought to himself, *The forest always has ears.*

At 0.8 g, the raft didn't have to be as strong as on Earth. Cliff and the men took off their belts to bind together the gray logs. The mud reeked and they were glad to cast off into the shallow lake. Paddling with some broad branches was slow, but they caught a breeze and the smell got better. Cliff set them facing all four directions in case anything came after them. He could tell from their faces that they were worrying. Only partway across did he recall the dinosaur-like thing that rose from the last lake they had seen. That thing could capsize them easily here. But nothing did. Fish splashed, making them all jumpy, but nothing more came.

This lake wasn't deep enough to support something like that.

They landed in a thin forest on the other shore, a kilometer away from the swamp. Wind was increasing, sighing through the trees. At Cliff's orders—he was getting used to just making them clear and direct, when speed was crucial—they hauled the raft beyond view, into the wispy trees. Then he had them take a break. He needed a pause and they must, too.

They ate the pitifully small provisions they carried, maybe thirty grams each. Irma made a joke about losing the weight she didn't need, and they all laughed ruefully. Soon enough, it wouldn't be funny. Cliff could feel his overalls clinging to him because he was burning up his stored fat, always hungry. He wished they had time to stop and take a swim just to clean their clothes. But who knew what was in those murky waters?

So they pushed on—and found a wreck within minutes. They had seen rusting debris before, but this was different, fresher. It was a crashed light plane, made of light composites, its rear section crumpled. The passenger seats were two meters apart. A two-seater for giants, no bodies, one wing smashed to fragments. The engine had plunged out of the body and jammed into the sandy soil. Most of the fuselage was smooth, though, undamaged. Some sort of carbon composite, he judged.

Cliff again wondered why they had seen no aircraft. This wreck looked recent. Then it struck him—if a big aircraft fell, it might punch a hole through the entire structure, venting the life zone to vacuum. So only small aircraft were allowed. And not many of those.

Only a few hundred meters farther on, they stepped from the wispy forest onto a flat plain of sand. There were no hills visible in the distance through a shimmer of heat haze warping the perspectives. Warm tan sand simmering beneath the eternal sun. A steady breeze at their backs seemed to urge them into this desert.

"We sure can't go slogging across that," Terry said, his face sagging.

"But those nasties behind us . . ." Irma's voice trailed away.

"We need to get some distance between them and us," Howard said.

Cliff let them toss it around and then said, "I don't like the idea of standing out nice and clear against a desert." Not an idea, but true.

"We're trapped!" Irma said angrily. She looked wan, worn.

Aybe kicked at the sand and knelt down and used his magnifying scoper on grains in his palm. "I *thought* this stuff felt odd. Look."

They took turns peering at the grains. Cliff was surprised. "They're all round," he said.

"Manufactured," Terry said. "Maybe condensed out of a hot silicon and oxygen mix in zero grav?"

"Could be," Aybe said. "If you're building this place in high vacuum, starting from scratch, you don't have rivers and beaches to make sand."

Cliff looked at the stretching expanses, as flat as the lake had been. What moved well on—? And it came to him.

"Sand without edges has got to have less friction," he said.

Irma looked at him. "Uh, so?"

"Less resistance to a sliding surface. Let's make a . . . sail craft. Let the wind blow us across this desert."

"*What?*" Aybe was aghast.

Irma snapped her fingers. "Remember that downed plane? We could use the airfoils, cobble something together."

At first they were puzzled, then disbelieving, then—remembering their pursuers—grudgingly, they tried it.

They had to drag the cut-down body of it for hundreds of meters. Terry pried the damaged wing away, and they used the wheels to keep the thing rolling. Cliff had time to look through the tool belt he had taken off the alien body. That seemed now like many days ago. He knew this meant he was getting near his limits. That was now a bigger problem for them all—telling when an Earth day had gone by.

In his stupefied fumbling, he finally saw that most of the tools were alien wrenches, hammers, screwdrivers for pentagonal heads—and huge. Hard to use, but not impossible. One he couldn't understand turned out to be a laser. He spotted it because it had leads to attach to a solar panel that unfolded. The gear was quite well designed.

It flared on with a virulent pop. Everybody cheered. They cut through the unneeded metal with its actinic beam, slicing elegantly thin lines. It took care and contortions to shape the body into something clean and usable.

They reconfigured it into a sand-sailboat, making the usable wing of the plane into a sail. They screwed that in place with their new tools.

Luck was with them: the wind was picking up, still howling at their backs.

They set off by pushing the fat-tire wheels into the sand and then letting the wing turn into the full wind. Cliff held his breath. If it failed, they were stuck, backs against the desert.

It failed. The wheels got stuck in grit and they had to lever them out of the sand, digging with their hands. Then, with them all crowded into the long passenger compartment, they got stuck again. Sighs, drawn faces.

Terry had another idea. Cut off the wheels. Let it be a true sailboat, running on its skin. Cliff was so tired by now, he really had no faith in anything but sleep. But he let Terry shear off the wheels and struts with the alien laser.

They got out of the boat's body and pushed. Sand ground beneath it, the wind blew—and it started to gain speed. Cliff ran alongside, pushing with raw hands until it had some momentum. Only then did he call, "Pile in!"

They yelled and shouted and got inside with weary last energy. In a few minutes, Cliff looked back and could no longer see the tree line. The wind purred around their sail as it picked up. They were skating across a great sand lake with no idea of what lay ahead. Into the unknown.

So what else is new? Cliff asked himself, and fell fast asleep.

PART IV

*The real voyage of discovery consists not in seeking
new landscapes, but in having new eyes.*
—MARCEL PROUST

TWENTY

Tananareve stared at the shambling beast looming over her and made herself not cringe.

Keep your head held high, her mother's spirit reminded her. She had to, anyway, because the alien towered over her like a mobile mountain.

This thing smelled, too. Its thick musk made her eyes water and she sneezed.

Memor had brought yet again an odd thing made of plasticlike, squeezable stuff. The vast beast set the thing before her and stepped on it. It squawked, hissed, then got up and walked around on stubby legs. A life-form? Now it ran off in a panicked, lurching gait, as if afraid.

Just the way I feel, she thought. Each time, Memor brought a little thing that surprised her a bit. But what did they mean? A calling card?

Memor made a resounding speech of woofs, yips, and growls. Plus the seemingly mandatory feather-fluffs, fan displays with suites of multicolored synchronization, and ruffles that sounded like whispery drumrolls. Tananareve got the drift—was she awake?

"Of course I am," she said back, in words that

sounded more like growls. This seemed to please it. Every meeting began this way, and Tananareve still hadn't figured out why. Or the calling cards.

Haltingly, Tananareve asked Memor for help in finding food they could eat. She felt somewhat comic, mimicking the alien's huffing, bass word-structures in her high, lilting notes. But her meaning got through somehow.

Memor bowed, a gravid gesture of understanding. The huge thing lumbered around, trumpeting orders to its lessers, trying to find leafy boughs that the human could try. She caught a combination of rough consonants that seemed to mean, "fodder for eaters of meat and grasses." At least it apparently knew some organic chemistry.

She kept to the ropy vines Beth had settled her into for comfort. Tananareve felt safer here, too, lounging back among this aromatic wealth. Her dark skin blended into the shadows.

Anything was better than the awful rattling box they'd had to endure coming here. She had felt better from the moment they were shooed out of that by Godzilla-like birds.

The forest was oddly comforting. Plants here, adapted to near free fall, looked odd. The usual supporting structures were gone, so huge leaves and blooms hung in the 0.1 g from slender branches. Many had no obvious parallel to Earthly vegetation. They looked like slender spiderwebs with splashes of puffball decoration.

Serf-Ones, as the Astronomers called them, had been busy building an enclosure when the humans were harried into the Greenhouse, as they called it. The Serf-Ones inside the enclosure worked steadily but avoided people. Maybe they were scared of crushing the much smaller humans.

The atmosphere seemed to cling in her lungs, muggy and sweetly fragrant. After the ship's carefully modulated air, it was pleasant, moist and not chilly. They were still in low gravity, though. The Bowl here had just enough spin that stuff tossed up would eventually settle.

The aliens thought *big*. Their enclosure was far larger than it needed to be. Of course, the entire Bowl exceeded any imaginable idea of limits. Should that tell them anything about the psychology of those who built it?

Tananareve noticed that Lau Pin was getting restless. He paced, climbed some of the thin, layered trees, got into arguments seemingly out of boredom. After several days of this, he announced that he was going to explore. He didn't want company, either. Beth didn't like that, but she had no real authority here. She wasn't going to go herself, not with Tananareve injured and needing looking after.

She was trying to convince Abduss to go with Lau Pin when abruptly he just hiked away, not waiting. Beth shrugged and said with lifted eyebrows to the others, "Guess he just doesn't like us." Still, Tananareve knew that Beth worried. That was her nature.

Lau Pin was gone for well over a day. He returned (he admitted) when he started wondering if he could find the way back, even though he used slash marks on the large, barked trees to guide him. He reported finding nothing different, just endless vegetation. No hills taller than fifty meters, just enough to get streams to glide downhill. It was eerie, he said, watching a broad creek easing along over rocks, but not chuckling with the splashes it would have made on Earth. Low g did that, taking the zip out of life in odd little ways. He had never reached the turning back of their enclosure. Even in 0.1 g, the wall was too high to jump and its smooth lattice made climbing impossible. He guessed that the Serfs had dropped the tall, chicken-wire walls from some craft flying above. "It's enormous, this cage they've stuck us in, at least tens of klicks across," he said.

"Maybe they don't want us claustrophobic?" Abduss suggested. "Living in the Bowl, maybe they've evolved to like room."

"So we should, too?" Lau Pin rolled his eyes.

"Come on, Astronomers are *huge*. They *need* room," Mayra said. "Fred, what do you—?" Fred was glowering at one of the skyeyes hovering nearby. "Never mind."

Fred Ojama wasn't taking imprisonment well. He was withdrawn, sullen. In some ways, he was worse off than Tananareve.

Beth asked Lau Pin, "Were there more of those head-sized sensors floating around?"

Lau Pin grimaced. "Two followed me the whole way."

Nobody liked the ever-watching spheres the size of a human head. They seemed to navigate by whis-

pering jets. Lau Pin had studied them and found
there was a strong magnetic field near them. Mag
lift? Indeed, it was nearly a hundred times Earth's
surface magnetic field, running parallel to the
ground here. Abduss guessed it might have to do
with running the Bowl, perhaps helping stabilize it
with magnetic pressure.

Tananareve listened to all this behind the soft
insulation her meds gave her. She was content to
lie back and observe through cottony air. There
were plenty of vines that in small gravs didn't bow
in graceful catenary curves, but shot straight out.
These connected to plants that were crowded layers of great broad leaves. The leaves were as big
as Tananareve and firmly attached to barnacled
branches. Those long limbs were so large, she could
not see where the gradually thickening, dark brown
wood ended. Among the green and brown leaves
scampered and leaped many small creatures. They
capered among odd long, pearly white strands
as thick as her arm. These connected like spokes
across the open spaces—lanes that cut through the
thick green stands of web-trees. She could not figure out what the pale fibers were part of, unless
it was some plant of enormous size, its details lost
among the distant growths that lay along the big
tunnels that brought light and air.

She suddenly saw that her whole mind-set was
wrong here. This was not an Earthlike forest. *The
landscape is designed. Sculpted. But it looks like
Earth's nature preserves.*

Memor sent a small underling into that tangle. It

was a ferretlike thing with a big head and darting eyes. It fell from one leaf to another, slid down to a third, and landed on a catlike creature—which squashed like a pillow. With a shudder the prey died, provoking in Tananareve a pang of guilt. The cat-thing had wings and sleek orange fur. Her heart ached at the beauty of it.

Memor gruffed approval. With a few movements of its razor-claws, the ferret hunter skinned the cat and plucked off gobbets of meat and scampered to Tananareve with them. She bit her lip at the reek of the red gobbets, and pointed to the people tending their fire.

Tananareve watched as Memor's minions snatched at tubular insects and crunched them with relish into a hash. They especially enjoyed ripping big fronds to shreds, picking out packets of ripe red seeds. Tananareve videotaped them at it, watched and learned.

One of the ferret-things brought her crimson bulbs that grew profusely in grapelike bunches. Memor reassured her with feather-fans of certainty that these were humanly digestible. She reached for some, and the bulbs hissed angrily as she plucked one loose. All bluster—the plant did nothing more as she bit in. She liked the rich, grainy taste. Far better than ship food, for sure.

The taste rode atop the bland dryness of the sedative she had taken. Here she was, in the most fascinating and terrifying moment of her life—and she was injured, dulled. Tananareve stopped herself from rubbing at her cracked ribs and her upper right arm, which throbbed from a nasty break. Nothing to be done about broken ribs except not move around, as Beth said, and risk jabbing a rib through a lung. Beth had splinted her arm quite deftly. Their emergency med kit gave her some pain relief, but that didn't stop her restless mind.

She knew she wouldn't be much use for a while, even with the quick heal salve Abduss applied to her aching arm. She hung relaxed in a secured bower of vines and plants and wondered how all this profuse life had evolved in near-zero gravity. Time to sit back, watch, and learn—which turned out to be, fathom what the alien called TransLanguage.

At university she had been good at the language game, learning French and Russian. Her secondary expedition job was to be alien translation. So now she had the job of dealing with the giant who identified itself as Memor—the name itself an approximation she had worked out to a sound like a bass humming, deep in its throat. She had imagined that, if they met aliens, there would be some orderly exchange of texts and recordings and, well, a method. Something like SETI messages, maybe, across a proper desk. Not here.

The other people were distracted, finding and choosing edibles, building a shelter, classifying Bird Folk varieties—which kept appearing to do work nearby, openly gawk, and flare their brilliant feather displays, rainbows of vibrant color. Squawking, too, in a language Memor dismissed with a gravelly grunt: unimportant.

Beth came to watch with her and change the dressings on her broken arm. "That bush over there smells like cooked meat," Beth said. "Strange . . ."

They watched it uneasily. A ratlike thing as big as a dog but sporting an enlarged head came foraging by. Humans bothered it not at all. Beth pointed out that the animals here had no fear of humans because they had no experience. The rat-thing caught the meaty smell and slowed, tantalized. It lingered—and the bush popped. Spear seeds embedded in the rat. It yelped and scampered away.

"A victory for the plants," Beth said. "That rat will carry the seed, I'll bet, until it dies."

Tananareve said, "So then a fresh bush grows from the rat's body. Smart."

Memor approached, huffing and rumbling, and they both tried not to shrink from its size. It spoke and Tananareve translated to, "I, like you, have a meat tooth."

Beth said, "Uh, charmed, I'm sure."

"We try for you to find the eatables," Tananareve translated again. She thanked Memor, and the mountain of flesh and rippling feathers seemed to bow at a sideways angle, lowering its arms and head.

Memor took them for a stroll in the awkward low g, explaining, gesturing with head and hands. It felt good to walk. All this helped improve Tananareve's translating abilities. They passed by colonies of plants that clearly had a social life, communicating through pollen-sprays their needs and distresses.

Tananareve bit her lip and summoned up the

courage to ask, "How do you . . . manage all this? Your . . . world-ship?"

Memor stopped and regarded them with big, solemn eyes. She spoke in long, rolling cadences and Tananareve struggled to translate. Her voice came in bursts as she got the meaning. "Fast learns, slow remembers. The quick and small instruct the slow and big by bringing change. The big and slow urges—dammit—call it constraint and constancy. Fast gets attention; slow has power. A robust system needs twice—I mean both. There is one great commandment: Stability is all."

The sound of her voice was like stones rattling in a jug. Very large stones, boulders, in an immense jug.

Beth asked, "How old is this . . . world?"

After translations, Tananareve shrugged. "We don't have the same time measures, but it's *old*. I get the feeling Memor doesn't want to say."

"What's it—okay, she—doing now?"

Tananareve looked up as Memor tilted her head back and went into the long trancelike state she had seen before. "I don't know. She says it's like talking to another part of her mind—that is, if I'm really getting the gist of her meaning."

Memor wandered away, still in a daze.

Beth smiled and sat back into a conical bower of fleshy plants. "I'm amazed, just like all of us, at how fast you've learned."

She gave Beth a quick, flinty look. Tananareve knew that her honey-toned Mississippi vowels made most crew members discount her. *Talk that way, and people will knock twenty points off your apparent IQ,* her mother had said. But she liked the soft, supple play of her accent, the stretched vowels and rounded consonants. "I'm even more so. Who would've thought that an alien language would have sentences at all? Much less, relating in a linear configuration with structures, a system?"

"And they're not even mammals," Beth mused. "I think."

"I suppose, but we don't really know. Kinda a hard subject to just bring up." Tananareve frowned. "It was so easy to learn from Memor, just from pointing and acting out. Maybe the underlying chemistry and stuff doesn't matter so much. I guess there are essentials in language after all. Not just in vocabulary and grammatical rules, but in their semantic swamps. Gad!"

"But you did it," Beth said simply.

Tananareve shrugged. "Memor says she's using 'artful intelligences' to help her. I suppose that means she's computer linked."

"Well, we don't have that," Beth said. "Maybe that's necessary, to run a thing like this huge thing."

"Could even our most inspired programmers, just by symbol manipulation and number-crunching, have cracked ancient Egyptian with no Rosetta stone? I doubt it."

"Maybe they've met other aliens, learned something of how the whole galaxy talks."

Sobering indeed, Tananareve thought.

"Still, it means we're dealing with beings who have unseen resources," Beth said.

"Hey, just the visible resources are incredible! Yeah, that may explain why Memor can teach me so well. She's flexible. Nearly all human languages use either subject-object-verb order, or else subject-verb-object. Memor says she uses both, plus object-verb-subject, so she can adapt to us easily."

Beth sat up quickly. "Something's happening."

Animals came fast, yelping, flitting through the nearby foliage. An insectlike thing fluttered by them. It was like a dragonfly whose wing sets moved at right angles to each other. A long-limbed jumping rat streaked by, using Beth's head as a touchpoint, then gone. She flinched but managed not to cry out.

Then they both heard a long bass note sound through the bowers. Nearby, some of the long, thick white strands trembled. Something was tugging on them, sending low frequency waves ahead.

"Get down, cover up," Tananareve whispered.

The deep note was louder. Or maybe it just sounded that way since everything else got suddenly quiet.

She looked down the long strands. They laced through the foliage with a clear path around them, almost like a tunnel in the air. Every hundred meters or so, they had an anchor on one of the thick, rough trunks.

A big hairy thing came into view from the distance. Fast. Spherical and ruddy, with six long legs or arms that moved with liquid grace. It flowed as if it were swimming, flicking long, thin legs out to pluck momentum from the white cables. Soundless.

Tananareve judged it was ten meters across at least. A flying house.

She and Beth wrapped themselves away, but Tananareve left a slit open to watch the enormous creature pull and fly, pull and fly—zooming on by them with quick, nimble movements of the legs. It swept by, leaving a slight breeze with a prickly, acid aroma.

Then another. It looked the same, maybe slightly smaller, but even faster. Its legs sang with humming as they plucked, all a blur.

It followed the first around a far curve maybe a kilometer away. The sharp odor lingered.

The area around them was dead silent. Nothing moved. Slowly, slowly small rustlings started. The forest went back to business throughout the three-dimensional volume.

Beth whispered, "What was that?"

"A spider designed by an art deco mind."

"I thought Memor was the top predator of this biosphere."

"Me, too. But even we have bears and sharks."

"What'll we do?"

Tananareve thought to herself, *Send not therefore asking for whom the bells toll. And if it starts ringing, start moving.* "We'd better be getting on."

Beth nodded, eyes big, face pale, and lips drawn. Tananareve was startled to see that Beth, who had always seemed to have rock-hard confidence, was scared.

TWENTY-ONE

The moist heat here felt like it could be cut into cubes and used to build a wall. Beth was glad to feel it. It wouldn't be long before their clothes would get worn. At least there was a nearby stream running through so they could bathe and drink. Plus, the Astronomers let them make fire. She had wondered if Memor would intervene when they used the tools they wore around their waists, too, but apparently the immense aliens thought puny humans could do no real damage.

Damage, no. But maybe they could escape.

It had been several days since the huge spiderlike things came zooming through. Beth hadn't been able to sleep well after that. Others remarked that the huge beasts—Abduss called them spidows—had ignored the humans. Maybe they weren't predators at all, just large herbivores. But Beth had seen their bristly palps moving in a blur as they clutched the thick strands. It called up a fearful image of spiders that still made her shake.

Tananareve was healing quickly from the speed-heal salve Abduss had in his med store pack. But they were all getting restless, now that they had food and the basics. Mayra deftly climbed to the top of a particularly tall frond tree, lashing herself in with ply ropes when she got above a hundred meters' height. She found feathered lizards that sported gorgeous fan plumage and could fly among trees, apparently evolved toward a monkey lifestyle. One variety she called mammoth monkeys. Like many things here, they were huge but not gorilla-like. They were shy, with attenuated, long arms and long torso, just built big and limber as a snake. They liked to swing on vines, apparently for amusement.

She could see farther from there, she reported, above most of the tree canopy.

Lau Pin and Mayra spent their time with heads together, inventing one scheme after another to escape. They even got Fred involved. His notions were crazier than theirs, but nothing stood up under examination.

Find if there's some key to their enclosure, steal it. Only there didn't seem to be anything obvious the Serf breeds used to seal and unseal the boundary.

Find a way to fly away; in low gravity that should be pretty easy. But that wouldn't get them out of their warm prison. It just meant they would be on their own, without the serf breeds to help them find food.

Surrender. Somehow. Already they were talking, sort of.

Lau Pin hotly objected to this view. "Should we sit here, as prisoners? We can explore a whole huge world out there!"

Tananareve said mildly, "How about those spidows?"

That sobered them all. Beth let their discussion run; it kept them busy and they might find a good idea. She got up to get some water from the daisy-cup cistern Lau Pin had made. Far up among the bowers, orange flashes arced and snapped from treetops into the gray, clouded sky. Only moments before, those clouds had been cheery, popcorn-white puffballs. Now they slid aside to reveal angry purple towers that tapered to infinity. Her hair stood up on her neck, and a warm wind tickled her hair, sure sign of air freighted with electricity. She turned to say something—

—and got knocked off her feet by percussive force. It felt like getting hit with a baseball bat and blinded by a virulent yellow flash. The others were sitting in the giant leaves and nearly got walloped by a felled tree that crashed through nearby. The air reeked of ozone. Small creatures lay around, some twisting and the others clearly dead.

None of Beth's people were hurt, but they were certainly shaken. There had been no warning except the instant when she felt her neck hairs rising. She had always thought lightning struck golfers out on fairways swinging 4 irons to the sky, or farmers sitting on tractors in flat fields. Earthly lightning descended on anything taller than the rest of the landscape, like a sailboat on open water. But here she had been among trees and massive foliage.

Abduss said, "You were the only one of us standing."

Beth frowned. "So?"

"Lau Pin measured a strong magnetic field here. We are on a spinning conductor that carries a strong field."

Lau Pin snapped his fingers. "The same as a

generator—a rotating magnetic field drives current. Charges move around on Earth because of that, so it's the same for the Bowl."

Abduss grinned. He always seemed happiest, Beth knew, when he was solving a puzzle. "Lightning is the celestial housekeeper, balancing out the overcharged land with the ionized top layer of the atmosphere."

Beth said. "This came up through the ground, though."

"Upside-down lightning, yes," Abduss said thoughtfully. "Somehow opposite from our experience on Earth."

"Upside down can still kill you," Tananareve said. *Goes with the territory.*

They returned to the discussion. Tananareve repeated her remark about the spidows, and Beth said, "They get into this enclosure anyway. If we escape, we can just stay away from tunnels in the foliage. Back off if we see the spidow strands."

They all nodded, but she could see they were grudging nods. Abduss made the point that they had now set up "housekeeping" here, had food and water and help from Memor's servants. "Meanwhile, we know nothing whatever of Cliff's group and of *SunSeeker.* They could be negotiating with the locals right now. Let's wait. Give them a chance to make some progress."

More talk as they ate some of a spongy, spherical fruit, and Abduss's view emerged as the consensus. Beth had to admit there was some logic to it. "But we can negotiate, too."

Tananareve said, "I'm getting better at translating. I'll approach Memor about a deal. But what's on our want list?"

In the way group decisions often occur, this was the signal to abandon escape plans. More talking to Memor got everyone off the hook. Their faces said they were glad to play for time. Escaping would be scary, and they had been scared plenty already.

TWENTY-TWO

The tiny primate learned quickly. Memor had the Serfs bring in a mindscan. This was an oddly compact version of the ancient devices. At her order, the techserfs had been working on it diligently since Memor summoned forth the customary device used by scholars, but scaled down to these small bipeds.

Here in the Greenhouse Terraces—a privileged verdant garden of vast natural wealth the size of the Old Continents—dwelled many vibrant, quite different creatures. The Astronomers had studied them since ancient long-gone eras of the Voyage. Their mental processes, as viewed in mindscans, told of the slow press of evolution even under the constant condition of the World. But now such crafts could aid in dealing with the Late Invaders—an idea that had come to Memor while letting her Undermind gush up into full view.

Memor persuaded the translator primate to enter the machine. Indeed, it—yes, *she*—seemed to like the prospect of leaving the corral. Serfs had erected the scan tunnel near the corral entrance, and the primate gazed about with quick interest at the technologies assembled.

Memor spoke warmly, using soothing tones and feather-fans of quiet resolve. Serfs attended the cautious Invader, chattering in their simple tongues, and soon all was ready.

The device worked surprisingly well. The Serfs had tested it against the arboreal simians, simple forms that were the nearest approximation to these Late Invader aliens. The primate female submitted to the device after being told that it would help the translations. False, of course. But useful, as so many passing illusions are when dealing with those less adroit. Memor sighed, a long, slow, and satisfying vibration it used to let its mind process data.

The scan revealed a brain startlingly different. Strange, yes—but Memor's Undermind could see structural connections, similarities (primitive, to be sure) to the Astronomer-class minds honed by more Cycles than time could count.

The female disliked the incisive, magnetic lacing of the scan. Clearly so. She became uneasy, and with the Serfs attending to the process, Memor could see her anxieties forking like dendritic lightning fingers through a mind cloudy, veiled, mysterious. And . . . divided.

Memor experienced the exquisite tremor of an insight. An idea emerged fresh and flowering from her Undermind.

These awkward, tenuous aliens lived in a sort

of middle scale. Their senses had evolved to perceive things on their own puny scale. Of course, they could not see bacteria, but they could sense minor dimensions. The larger scales of a world were beyond them, though—no doubt because they evolved on some gravitational mass, as Memor's own ancestors had. They had a perceptual horizon limited by the curve of primitive worlds, seen at heights no more than their own stature. They must feel trapped here.

Still more shrunken was their sense of time. Typically they sensed the grind of orbital cycles, seasons, incessant day-night, the brute revolutions of planets. They lived in the mire of cyclic mechanics, sleeping and mating to the tick of some planetary clock. Slaves to time.

Memor had the Serfs interrogate the primate's innate mind-time scales. They scampered about, using their instruments. The result was desperately plain.

The creature had a summing time of a few of its own eye-blinks, a trifling interval. It used that scale to integrate information. That meant that it could not delegate to its lesser parts the usual boring business of keeping itself alive. It had to keep incessant watch.

This was difficult to believe. The Folk had abandoned the drumming rhythm of short cycles long ago. That was the informing idea behind their pursuit of constancy—of freedom from the ticktock of early origins. Instead, the Folk dwelled on the eternal Quest through the Voyage.

This small, intense being was forced to worry about its housekeeping, such as digestion, excretion, even the intake and outblow of oxygen. Could it be so pointlessly busy? Difficult to know, but depressing to contemplate.

Such a short processing time meant that it could seldom spare computational power on issues beyond its own heart rate. It lived a poor, distracted life. Yet it had built a starship!

Did it even sense the gyre of evolution? Or of the World?

Memor pondered. Her Undermind worked, fretful and persistent as always, yet came forth with nothing. She inspected her Undermind workings, peeled back layers—yes, nothing. The Undermind was justly perplexed. So many questions remained!

Could these hairy bipeds fathom why their slavery to oscillations in dark and day made them primitive? Once even the Folk had submitted to such endless toils. But they had learned otherwise, had in the Deep Times built the World to escape such bondage to primitive cycles. In its way, this small thing represented the ancient past, brought forward by circumstance for Memor's instruction.

When the alien came out of the scanning, Memor tried to get the female to speak. It was staggering a little, waving its small arms for balance. "I see you find our insightful machines a trial," Memor said.

"You trying to pick my brains?" it—no, *she*; hard to remember; how could one tell?—shot back.

"I have analyzed your capabilities," Memor said, which in a way was true.

"You goddamn smelly elephant-bird! You have no right—!"

Its noise carried little information. Hot-eyed fervor marked it, and even more its limbs whirled entertainingly, as if they were beset by breezes. The effect was comic. She had noticed this one was darker in hue than the others, which might mean it had spent more time in starglow, and so was older, and thus wiser. That was why Memor had selected her—hoping for a faint trace of wisdom in it. Futile, perhaps. But Memor did not know enough yet.

So Memor had the Serfs return it—her—to the scan. It squalled, of course.

Ah. Revelation dawned up from the Undermind. New data flowed into Memor, and she could see it working amid the low minions of her own mind. She could flick back and forth between her own mental understory and that of this Late Invader primate. A unique experience, laced with shadowy strangeness.

So . . . could she question the female while she was in the scan? She had never known this to be done, in all Astronomer history. Yet her Undermind pushed this concept up from its ripe swamps, and Memor saw the value of the idea. Onward, then.

The Serfs stood in awe as she called up the image-data, learning from it in quick bursts. She let the Undermind hold sway. Serfs could not of course understand, as they—indeed, nearly all of Creation—were all linear minds. Unified minds, yes—but with little Undermind. Serfs used a variant of linear thinking, just as did these Late Invaders, but apparently the Late Invaders had strengths Serfs did not. Certainly no Serf could have escaped from the traps laid for generic Invaders.

She scrutinized the alien brainscan with care. Hereditary neural equipment governed them. Primitive, indeed. Their minds were divided! Straight down the middle, a clear cleft. Most of Creation was so configured. Evolution had apparently used this often as an early, rudimentary precaution. The Folk shared this property as well, and it was common in this explored region of the galaxy, at least.

But there were new features here, as well. Simple forms of animals divided functions so that they could not interfere with basics, and so interrupt the fundamentals. Later, further up the evolutionary pyramid, various utilities like digestion, heartbeat, the underlying housekeeping—all became walled off in the mind, their work uninterrupted except in emergencies.

But some fundamental features of advanced minds were beyond these Late Invaders. Higher intelligence needed not mere utilitarian modes, but rather the creative ones. The source of cross-association, and thus ideas, had to be accessible. The Undermind was common to all sentient creatures—yet these primates could not see theirs! Only a mind unified at the upper levels, above the shop floor of bodily business, could have deep ideas, surely? Then a mind could manipulate them, force them on the twin forges of reason and intuition, into great leaps.

These aliens had no such ability. Their greatest

drives, intuitions, associations—all lay concealed from their foreminds, the running agents and authorities of the immediate, thinking persona. They were primitives.

Yet they had built a starship.

Memor was shocked. In her Undermind she found no lurking answers. Perhaps the Undermind needed a rest. Often, sleep brought ideas.

TWENTY-THREE

Beth listened to Tananareve's summary intently, brows furrowed. Better to hear it first and hash matters over, well before calling a group meeting.

"Incredible! They put you into some kind of device and then asked you to *think about* things?"

Tananareve shrugged. "A sort of CT device, I suppose. So I thought on command about astronomy, about *SunSeeker,* about what my left hand was doing while they put my right hand in cold water. Memor found it interesting, I guess."

"Um. We have to use this. . . ."

Beth realized that she was acting instinctively like a leader now. *Think, judge, act.* That was what irked Lau Pin, she knew. But she intuited that the others didn't want the sometimes impulsive, emotional, very young Lau Pin to take over. Too bad Lau Pin didn't know that.

"It didn't bother with the rest of your body?" Abduss asked intently. "No medical exam?"

"No, just that suffocating box with its foul scent. We had some of that in our physicals, remember?" Tananareve shuddered. "But this time—creepy, like snakes swarming over my skull."

Mayra put an arm around Tananareve. "Maybe it was trying to improve translation?"

Tananareve snorted derisively. "I doubt it."

"What did it feel like?"

Tananareve gazed off into the distance. "Like fingers in my head. I'd think something, then feel it slip away, as if something was . . . feeling it."

"Um. Creepy."

"You bet. Next time, if Memor does it again, I'll deliberately think of something lurid. Just to poke at her."

Beth started diplomatically, "I know how you feel, but that might provoke—"

"Hey!" Lau Pin shouted, and came trotting over to the bower where the women sat, using the leafy enclosure to muffle their voices. His eyes danced. "I got a beamer signal—a message!"

"From *Eros*?" Tananareve asked.

"No, that's what's amazing. It carries *SunSeeker*'s bitcode. Message is loading now."

Beth felt her pulse quicken. Lau Pin's little beamer beeped and he put it to his ear. And scowled. Lips pressed into white lines, he handed it to Beth. "Captain Redwing. For. You."

Redwing spoke rapidly in his usual growl, as if afraid the connection would drop out. She restarted the recorded message. "We saw the big electrical discharges up near the top of the Bowl. Filtered out the noise and found this beamer flag frequency. So if this works, here's our situation: We can't get much out of signaling the aliens. They acknowledged us, but they take their own sweet time about getting back to us when we transmit. We demanded your return. They say they're learning our language 'in person,' so it's more efficient to keep you. It's just you, too, Beth. They won't tell us anything about Cliff. So for now, try to transmit back. Beamers don't have any real focus, but we're now to the right of their star, as you see it, maybe thirty degrees. I'm focusing all our high-gigahertz-range antennas on that spot where the big electricals went off. We're seeing flares, lightning the size of continents. Hope that didn't fry you! Over and out."

Beth smiled. The old-fashioned *over and out* was typical Redwing. To her surprise, she felt affection for the old hardnose. He butted his head at problems until they got solved.

She glanced at Lau Pin and saw it was time to mend fences. "Here, try to send. Tell him we're okay but captive. Trying to talk to the aliens. Ask if there's any chance they can send us supplies in one of the auto-landers?"

Lau Pin nodded and his mouth lost its irritation. "I'll send some visuals, too," he said. "Mayra? Mayra! Can I have your file of photographs? I'll send mine also."

"Sure," Mayra said, and handed over her phone. "I don't see what use he'll get out of them."

"Not him." Lau Pin looked at Beth and said, "He'll get Cliff sooner or later. We've been photographing what we can and can't eat. Cliff's party needs to know that." His smile said, *Why didn't you think of that?*

Cliff might have starved by now, she thought. Beth walked out into the middle of the little clearing they used as a gathering spot and called with more joy than she felt, "Hey, everybody! We caught a break."

TWENTY-FOUR

Memor was puzzled. Only lowly beasts used divided minds. That was a known method of letting parts of the mind work separately, so that some efficiencies emerged from specialization. But it also meant that the mind could not function with all its many parts in the mix. That stunted split minds. This was conventional evolutionary theory, well verified by contact with many planets.

These Late Invaders had brains split into hemispheres that did not always interact. Yet they had built high technologies! Quite shocking. Some of them had even evaded the Folk, as well—a shock in itself. These affronts to both experience and even reason demanded explanation.

So Memor summoned the female she had tested before. Had she overlooked some essential clue? Perhaps another viewing of her divided mind in action, plus active simultaneous use of her Undermind, would reveal an insight.

To do this she had to do the necessary mental work first. Carefully, she isolated herself from the Serf breed chatter. First she withdrew, letting sight and sound drop away from her. Inner peace came, sliding slowly. The world fell away. Gingerly, to avoid startling the working elements of her mind, she opened the vistas within.

Into her higher levels swept ruminations galore. Some of these thoughts mixed senses, as the unruly Undermind often did. Liquid amber lightning shot through her Inmind with a sharp, bristly scent—and Memor knew she was amid the chemical swamp of associations. Buzzing red flaps peeled back to reveal punctured pathways.

She was ready. So prepared, she began inspecting the biped's mental landscape. Alarm rang down its corridors.

She delved into this and felt something else, a sort of . . . memory. Only it came freighted with feelings of desire, moist expectation, flaring scents. She saw the female as if in a mirror, looking at her and yet—yes, it was locked in embrace with a large male. They were lunging at each other.

She shot a glance at the female, lying flat on the preceptor bed. She was agitated, moving her legs and hands, clasping herself—

Memor realized that she was showing Memor how her kind reproduced.

Then, unmistakably, she heard her cackling rise. Laughter, it must be. The biped was making fun of Memor.

She rocked back, red anger flaring. This tiny

thing was jeering at her, using her mind to send the insult.

She let her Undermind deal with this fresh event. Soon soothing cadences passed through her, damping the prickly irritation into milder currents. As this happened, she saw that the biped was now back to a normal state. Perhaps it—she—felt that she had made her point, and was now calming down.

Very well. She would do the same. This had taught her something profound—the bipeds were quick-witted beyond their limitations. She must remember that her brain was as large as Memor's own.

The biped spoke directly to her. "I want to go back to my friends now."

Of course. These were social creatures, and she felt—she could see directly—fretful emotions down in her Undermind. The Late Invader female could not feel this clearly, though, because she could not directly see her own mind.

Instead, she sensed a vague unease. In such moments, apparently, she wanted the company of her kind. Now that Memor saw this, she understood with her Overmind the sense of it. Evolution had to converge on such social chemistries, on any world. Because more often than not, the most adaptable thing one could do to survive and reproduce was to be cooperative and altruistic. This knowledge was an Absolute, time honored and proved often in the enduring history of the Bowl. Evolution never slept, even in the great constancy of the World.

Memor answered her warmly, trying to defray her inner, vexing storms. These aliens showed much mental evolutionary selection. Whether this arose naturally or from their own genetic tailoring, she could not perceive. Their hidden Underminds were an adaptive unconscious that let them size up their world quickly, set goals, decide. Of course: these bipeds had evolved in a place where speed was vital. In contrast, the Folk prized long-term judgment, because they planned for a larger scale of time. These primates were a fresh, young species, untried.

Somehow the bipeds' methods worked, even at the chemical maintenance level. Their minds worked largely out of view of their "running-selves," the surface mind that thought it was in charge, simply because it could not see its own minions below. Indeed, she now recalled that this female had used an expression, once: "I just had an idea."

That must mean that notions simply appeared in their Overminds. They had no concept of where the ideas came from. Worse, they could not go and find where their ideas were manufactured. Much of their minds were barred to them.

Astounding! Yet it worked.

Still, the danger of this strategy was their lack of true awareness. These creatures were strangers to themselves. So they decided issues without knowing the true elements behind the decision. Perhaps they did not even know why they chose mates!

This implied a further thought.

Did they have *more* mental freedom than the Folk . . . or less? To mask the Undermind from view—could that convey some benefit? Even though it was clearly a fearsomely destabilizing element, as the ancient history of her species had shown? The Undermind could unleash vast passions that swept whole societies. Unless, of course, their deep natures could be seen and regulated.

She had never thought this of another intelligence—that there could be any advantage to concealing the Undermind. The question struck at the boundaries of the Folk, their superiority—even their freedom.

She knew that one must believe in free will, despite the ability to analyze the mind to great detail. This rule applied even to these aliens. Its logic was simple: If free will was then a reality, one had made the right choice. But if free will did not exist, one had still made no incorrect choice. One had made no choice at all, not having free will to do so.

In this, the Folk and the Invaders were equals.

These tiny creatures had a rich mental life, but it was actually deeper than they knew. They had no overlook, from which they could view the vast continents of the adaptive unconscious below. They did not see the sobering landscape of the mind in all its fervent glory.

In their curious vessel, they voyaged amid a ship environment surely unlike their natural world. Perhaps they had not considered building a Ship Star for proper exploration of the galaxy. Or more likely, they could not attempt it, and so set forth in simple machines. They were young and raw, willing to suffer.

Their situation was then tragic. They had launched

forth into the stars with brains evolved to deal with a world that bore only slight resemblance to the vast, messy crowds of information in their present, awkward mind-machinery.

Perhaps, then, their deaths would be a proper release from such unnatural tortures.

TWENTY-FIVE

The message from Redwing had given them a lift. But the mood faded before a clear, quick question: *So what?*

Lau Pin's beamer couldn't rouse *SunSeeker*. It was a long shot, of course—Redwing could focus a megawatt of 14.4-gigahertz power on them, but Lau Pin's beamer, even fully charged, delivered only a watt or two of unfocused signal.

So they were stuck. Beth watched them react to this. Then Abduss produced his own miracle, after a desultory day of chores.

"I have a bit of joy here!" he called to them all. In his hand was one of the useful flasks the Serfs had given them for their own housekeeping. Now that they had established their chore routines of getting and preparing food, the usual details of a stationary life, they had time to amuse themselves as they wanted. So they assembled, not expecting much. Abduss passed around the little cups the Serfs had made for them, ladling into them a murky fluid. "Toast!" he said loudly.

They drank. "Moonshine!" Fred called.

Abduss looked hurt. "Wine. It is a wine I made from the esters of the fruit they give us."

Lau Pin and Mayra both said, "Rotgut!" Mayra even hugged her belly in comic relief.

But they liked it anyway. Beth waved away her second cup and watched the others. They grimaced when they drank but that didn't stop them, or their increasingly high-pitched laughter, the rude stories, obvious lies, bright eyes. They needed release, after all that had happened. Alcohol was the easy road to all of that. *Let this pass,* she thought. She watched Fred Ojama, but he only grew more torpid. Presently he said, "I shouldn't," and set the cup aside.

The next morning most of them were hungover, griping and shaking their heads. They got their housekeeping jobs done and sat around and then the lumbering, smooth-feathered Serfs brought in cylindrical canisters, laying them at the feet of Mayra. She opened them carefully. Sniffed. "It's—it smells like alcohol."

Beth grimaced. The aliens had caught on that fast. To keep the prisoners quiet, give them the ancient chemical that consoles without illuminating. Smart, in a worrisome way.

Lau Pin, to his credit in Beth's view, said, "I don't like that they watch us. This proves they're trying to . . ." He didn't complete the thought.

Beth said, "What? Keep us sedated?"

Mayra objected, waving her arms. "They're just catering to us!"

Lau Pin twisted his mouth into a sardonic curve.

"Worse. They've got organic chemists, sure. But we're lab animals here, not guests. The alcohol is an experiment to see how we react."

Beth agreed. They broke up, since it was time nearly for lunch—according to their suit clocks, not of course to the unending sunlight here. Lau Pin drew the job of expanding and deepening the latrine, while the others cooked the fish and vegetables they had learned to harvest from the ample surroundings. Even simple jobs here demanded some learning, since working in 0.1 g changed everything ingrained in them. They managed, though without spirit.

Beth worried. No new word from Redwing, and they were settling into a routine now. Jobs assigned, a routine set up.

Lau Pin shouted. He came running from where they'd dug the latrine. "Come see! This topsoil is only a meter deep."

So it was—which made complete sense. The Bowl was a thin layer built to face the central star, capturing sunlight. But it couldn't be very thick without imposing huge stresses on the tension that held the Bowl together, just from mass loading. Here they saw that the entire ecology was rooted in soil only as deep as needed. Lau Pin had uncovered metal sheets and pipes, the underpinning of this odd building bigger than any world.

At lunch they mused aloud at the possibilities. "How about tunneling through?" Mayra asked. "How could we use that?"

Fred smiled derisively. "And let the vacuum suck

us away? These aliens have some way to patch really fast, I'd guess—but not before we die."

They all nodded. Beth looked around at their faces going slack and thought, *We need to have a goal. Otherwise, we'll turn into passive prisoners.* She had learned what to do from her training. Get them focused. *Do the next right thing. Now.*

She knew it was true. In a tough situation, don't avoid acting just because it's easier or comfortable. Don't lapse into a passive state. People who give up, die.

Abduss mentioned something in passing that cut off Beth's reflections. "I found these strands of spidow web, must've been tossed aside when a Spidow repaired the network. They spin this stuff out, just as Beth said they must. I saw one doing it. Creepy! Anyway, I got the strands to fuse—"

"Fuse how?" Beth pressed him.

"With a laser. Just warm the ends, stick them together." Abduss smiled, obviously happy to have something to do. He produced from a sack he carried two meter-long pieces of the filmy white stuff that made the spidow web. "See? They can be retied, with heat. I suppose these pieces got cut off in some way—"

"Then they can be made into long ropes," Lau Pin said, eyes on Beth. "So we can use them."

Beth smiled. "To get out of here."

TWENTY-SIX

Never before had Tananareve wished so fervently for a blessed night.

They had all slowly adjusted to sleeping in the incessant daylight, wrapped away in the long, moist, flexible leaves of the giant bowers. With pieces of the stuff, Mayra made them masks that helped them all get some shut-eye. Still, sleep was always troubled, her alarm senses waking her often to the occasional scamper, rattle, or caw. So when they agreed to arise and move, she was thick-eyed and muzzy.

Now they had to sneak away without the Serfs catching on. That was hard. Lau Pin led them stealthily away along routes he had explored. Tananareve had insisted she go, too, even though she had trouble getting through the root-rich terrain. Thin soil meant that trees spread their roots along the surface, making for tricky footing.

Abduss had risked his life for the long, ropy strands they carried in teams. He had walked kilometers away along the flat, forested terrace that confined them, to separate his acts from the others. A simple precaution, in case the spidows discovered him at work. Then he cut long segments of the spidow fibers and carried them away from the thread-corridor before a spidow came to repair it. This meant only minutes. Slicing through a thread sent a signal along the webs, and the huge things raced to make repairs. They looked and moved like a night-mare on a caffeine high.

"Time to light out for the territories!" Tanan-areve said gladly, when they had it all assembled. She saw Fred's grin; nobody else got the reference to *Huck Finn*. They were tense, ready.

Time to go, then. But the pace wore her down.

Tananareve struggled to keep up with Fred and Lau Pin as they hauled the coils along on their shoulders, with leaves to separate the fat threads so they did not stick together. Her arm was mostly healed, but it hurt now and sweat popped out on her brow, trickling into her eyes in big fat drops, and stinging. Sweaty work, silently done, as they crept away from their campground. Serfs did not all sleep at once, apparently, and Tananareve had monitored them to find the time when a minimum of them were awake. The Serf sleep cycle took about three Earth days, by her reckoning.

They quietly stole away, leaving behind dummies of wood wrapped in the leaves, looking somewhat like sleeping humans. No Serfs raised an alarm.

Moving silently took concentration. The air seemed to coil up into her nose, filling her lungs with thick musk. They reached the barrier just as Tananareve was starting to feel woozy. Her arm ached. Lau Pin thought the tall, slick wall was slightly lower here, due to some sagging. A huge tree had fallen into it from the other side, pulling it down somewhat. It was uncomfortably close to a spidow corridor, too.

Quickly they deployed their loops of spidow

string. Lau Pin and Abduss began linking the coils, fusing them together with quick bursts of laser light, raising a stench like burnt milk. They had practiced this craft and now could seal the ends within seconds, playing the beams along the ends until they bubbled.

Tananareve took her position along the barrier, as they had drilled. The wall was transparent and slick, probably to keep animals from climbing it. Easily a hundred meters high, too. She looked through the wall at the jungle beyond. The wall was like ancient glass, with whorls and ripples that toyed with the view. She realized that that must be exactly what it was—glass so old, it had warped through its slow slide downward, for glass was a fluid. These must be some sort of standard wall, used for keeping animals within their range. But not, apparently, smart animals.

Working quickly, Lau Pin and Abduss fused the end of the coiled filaments to a chunk of wood. Lau Pin had cut and sized these days before. He had proved handy at woodcraft and more. The ropy, rubbery vines nearby he had built into a curious kind of slingshot—taut vines, a cantilevered flinging pouch, artfully angled struts. He and the others cocked his array back, grunting. The men had practiced this and seemed confident it would work. A tanned and stretched leaf held the wood block payload, the ropes straining at it. They all took their positions as Lau Pin counted down.

Tananareve had to admire how Lau Pin had made this with Abduss. The entire taut machine was like something from the Middle Ages—and they had built it from scratch.

"Fire!" Lau Pin couldn't resist whispering.

The energy stored in the stretched vines sent Abduss's payload shooting upward, arcing high. It cleared the barrier lip and started down on the other side. In 0.1 g, a slingshot had ten times the range it would have on Earth. That simple physics had led to many comic miscalculations as they learned to walk and work here on the terrace, but now the difference paid off. The soaring block pulled the spidow thread smoothly out of the coils. The block struck the ground with a thump she could barely hear.

"Over!" Lau Pin called.

Beth scrambled up the threads, hand over hand. The pale fibrous stuff was strong and slightly sticky, just enough to get a hold. She went up fast in the low g.

But something moved behind them.

Tananareve turned and saw two spidows moving off the threads about a hundred meters away, in the channel of their threads. *How did they know?* she had enough time to think. *Vibrations? The stench?*

Then the spidows came at them.

Abduss turned and fired his laser at both the approaching shapes. The spidows kept coming. He hit one in the four eyestalks and it bucked back, showing a mouth of converging black teeth like pincers. They made not a sound, but the wounded one reared up, as if to frighten them with its size.

At that moment, Tananareve fired her laser into its belly. The thing came down with a crash. It didn't move.

But its partner did not slow. It brushed aside big trees as if they were saplings, ripping some out by their roots. Abduss held his ground and Tananareve saw the others were going up the thread, hand over hand. She fired again but the second spidow seemed invulnerable. It took the bolts without a pause. She heard from it a high, thin shrill.

"Go!" Abduss called to her. "Up!"

She fired one last time at the spidow. It was moving slower but was only twenty meters away. Tananareve tucked her laser into her belt and leaped for the thread. Her arm gave a sharp spike of pain. She favored that arm and went up, hand over hand, kicking off against the wall to try to get more momentum.

The spidows could climb the thread, of course. She had not thought of that before. They had worried about the Serfs and Memor, but the spidows were the present threat.

She was halfway up when she heard a scream. She could not help looking down.

Abduss was under the spidow, and with a gurgle the screaming stopped. But the spidow did not linger. It tilted up and with its arms it grabbed at the thread. The arms were long and sinewy and moving so fast, they were a blur.

It launched itself upward. Behind it, Abduss looked like a tissue someone had crumpled up after a nosebleed.

It was coming for her. The thin, cutting shrill was loud now.

She pulled furiously at the thread, kicked with her toes. She could hear the huge thing sucking air in and out now with long, windy breaths.

The thread jerked with the weight behind her. She looked up and there was Lau Pin, aiming down from the top of the wall. A crisp sizzle raked the air near her head. Dazzles flashed in her eyes, evaporated away. Another sizzle. Her breath rasped and she ignored the snap in her shoulder.

Lau Pin held out a hand and when she took it he lifted her bodily free of the thread. With one hand he brought her to the lip and she angled herself over, rolling to stay out of his way.

He said, "No way I—" Another sharp sizzle near her hand. The thread went limp in her hand.

She canted over the lip, gasping. Her hands grabbed it and she tumbled over, facing the wall. The brown and gray spidow mass was just below her. She thumped against the wall, mashing her nose. Blood drooled down her face.

She looked around. Lau Pin was falling away below her. He had laser-cut the thread and—the spidow was falling. It went straight down, getting smaller in slow motion. No sound now.

She hung there, holding on, watching it thud below. And flatten down, graceful and quick as a cat. Scrabbling legs, a long low mournful sound. It got larger then. It had absorbed the fall in its legs and now—it leaped for her.

Missed. Fell back. Would try again.

She let go with one hand, the weak arm, and turned her back to the wall, clunking into it.

Below were faces. The thread had fallen into coils below her and the others looked up at her. A long fall, over a hundred meters. They waved their arms and their mouths moved, but with the pulse pounding in her ears she could not make out what they said.

The spidow was coming. Maybe it had a way of clinging to the wall. She did not wait to find out.

A treetop beckoned about fifty meters below. It looked leafy and thick, with few branches showing. In this low g—no, not the time to do a calculation.

She gathered her feet and pushed off—toward the treetop.

She tumbled and tried to come down on her boots. When she hit, the leaves lashed at her. Branches snapped against her boots, arms; one caught her smack in the face. She hit a large limb, pain lancing into her ribs. It hurt badly as she tumbled headfirst through—into clear air—and managed to get her boots under her.

She hit hard. Collapsed. Rolled away, trying to get a look up at the spidow.

It came through the tree after her. Slamming through, snapping even the big branches, showering leaves and limbs down. It had punched its way through and crashed to the ground right beside her.

Beth shot it through the enormous, many-eyed head. It jerked, gave a high, thin wail—and went still.

When Tananareve looked through the wall, she could see Abduss, as still as the spidow.

PART V

Nothing in biology makes sense
except in the light of evolution.
—THEODOSIUS DOBZHANSKY

TWENTY-SEVEN

The Citadel of Remembrance loomed larger than Memor recalled from her young days, so long ago. The high ramparts loomed like mountain cliffs over the gathering assembly. Fog trailed strands of pale luminance that frayed into brilliant amber fingers, like a twisting dome over them all. She admired the new additions to the Citadel, feeling the immense powers lodged here. That august force seemed more like a state of nature than a power, but such was the point.

That the Citadel could well be her place of execution did not fully overcome her awe. Instead, it gave her a delicious blend of fear and strangeness that her Undermind relished. She could feel the strumming presence of it and knew she would have to keep it carefully controlled. Her Undermind could slip words and even phrases into her speech, in its eagerness. And eager it was; she could feel the hopeful spikes of feeling. Drama was rare in an Astronomer's life.

She shuffled her feet in the required way, said the right things, and needed scarcely any promptings from her inboards. They knew the steps but not the sway, and it was safe to ignore them here.

Memor hung back from the slowly ambling crowd of Astronomers, relishing the trumpeting salutes of greeting they gave. She always used the tone of these as a diagnostic of the collective mood, and today seemed more testy than usual. Some glowered at one another, while others passed in stiff silence, feathers turned to muted tones. Riffs and small songs danced among the bass notes of the many, a leitmotif. These came from the few young males, who walked quickly and greeted loudly, joy-fully.

Memor had been male when young, of course—the great, vibrant stage of life. Then that Memor of vivid passions and great conquests had gone through the Revealing. It had been a passage of legendary ardor and travail. Mercifully, most such memories had been blotted away by the experience itself. Yet the lessons of being masculine lingered and blended with the feminine insights she was now acquiring. This merging led to the path of wis-dom.

As with all mature Astronomers, Memor became a She of the Folk, after learning by direct experi-ence the male view of the world. While a He, there came to the higher Folk the legendary great desires, an easy willingness to risk, to change and inno-vate. This phase of zest and emotion lasted nearly twelve-squared Annuals. Memor still recalled the He sadness when those vivid feelings fled, and the bodily shifts began. Memories remained, leaving their residue of longing for a He who could never be again.

In the Revealing's changes, Memor had felt His/Her body shift with wrenching desires. The pains and startling fresh urges were also the focus of much Folk literature and dance and raucous jokes, but few were nostalgic for that jittery chaos.

From the Revealing, Memor had acquired the long views of a She, while retaining the experience and fathoming of the He era. This conferred judgment and sympathy-from-experience on the Astronomers, a vital stabilizing element evolved by the Folk over many twelve-millennia in the truly ancient past.

This essential balance—more a dance, truly—between the He and She Memor now struggled to apply to the most unsettling event of her long life: the radical alien primates. Luckily, she had the Revealing when these aliens first appeared. That dual view of them should help her now.

"Memor! We have not greeted in longtimes," came a solemn, deep voice.

Memor turned and saw the slim head of Asenath, the Chief of Wisdom. To be welcomed by such an august figure was surely a good sign—or was it? "I have longed to see you again," Memor said. "I need your counsel."

"And you shall have it," Asenath said mildly. "I like your problems—they are more intriguing than our usual fare."

Asenath turned to use her bulk as a sound screen, anticipating the arrival of someone out of Memor's field of view. Memor did not have time to turn to see. Asenath said deftly, "Boredom need not come with every task, Memor, but it may seem so as you go forward."

"I am honored," Memor said with a suitable sub-murmur of respect. She filed the words pointedly with her inboards for later review. She was about to say more, but another voice intruded to her left, "I shall have much interest as well," in tones more threatening.

Memor turned with a sense of dread to confront Kanamatha, the Council's Biology Packmistress. "I hope to please you," Memor said.

Kanamatha said, "I shall have many questions," and in her quick-tongued way turned to Asenath and said, "Following yours, my dear."

Memor knew she should say more, but the chimes sounded final call. Amid heady perfumes and sweet music, the cohort assembled beneath rippling lights. In their twelves they began entering the high chamber in all its splendor and beauty. In reverent silence they passed gleaming alabaster edifices, oversized onyx statues of the Builders lining the inward paths to the Citadel of the Council, small temples dotted with animal gods in ancient dress, grottoes for quiet negotiations—and perhaps for amorous assignations, when the time was ripe.

The following retinue included scribes, small musicians burdened with their instruments, waykeepers, lampists and mathists, stewards of the Savants, oil masseurs—and all trailing sycophants galore.

Formalities consumed some time, and then routine

reports. Each bloc applied their own torque to the proceedings, peppering the reporters with questions.

The Council had three major factions—the Farmers who ruled the vital living self of the Bowl, the Governors and Bowlcrafters who integrated the Farmers' intricate networks with the Bowl's physical structure. Overseeing all this in the larger perspectives were, of course, the Astronomers.

All three sought more power, though of course none wished to be overtly seen as desiring it. Humble achievement was the goal. But having a particular goal could not be too obvious, or one would never attain it. Memor remained silent throughout this. The occasional reports came next, and Asenath declared a mealtime to separate the two. The twelve-squared all retreated to the banquet hall, nominally to feast but actually to make deals and sniff out new alliances.

Memor ate little, wanting to keep her wits sharp. When they returned to their seats, Asenath nodded to Memor.

"Please lead me," Memor said to place the conversation in the right ranking order. She reported at length on the primates, their odd actions and even odder bodies. Full pictures of them floated in the chamber air, rotated to point out features. The genitalia were unexceptional but their carriage caused remarks. Memor skipped over the escape of some, stressing instead her studies of those captured. She showed the neural and brain interrogations and estimated their capacities—below the Folk, of course, but perhaps somewhat above others of the

Adopted, those aliens already encountered and integrated into the Bowl.

She bowed with regret to report the escape of the second party, as well, from the high latitudes. Her ending was of course humble. "Apologies to you all for my failure to retain or recapture these strange primates."

A rustle of reaction, hard for her to judge. The Council had many questions. Obviously, some had not read or even prior-memoried Memor's reports.

Why did they wear clothing here in the Bowl's mild climate? Was their world colder or more hostile? These coverings over all but head and outer extremities—were these rank symbols? Could the clothing hide subtle weapons? Or could their bodies be perhaps recently reengineered, and still fragile, needing to be wrapped?

When Memor described how the primates remained clothed except when sleeping, others asked if they were competing with one another, making declarations of self with clothing?

The primate hindfeet had thick coverings. Had they evolved on a world where their every step was threatened? How to explain that curious gait—their continual, controlled toppling must be a transitory style, surely? Bowl creatures used more certain gaits, to avoid falling injuries. Two-legged forms were few, and most had evolved tails, for balance.

A Crafter had a detailed set of questions, embedded in her description of inspecting the primates. The teeth appeared to be all-purpose, but did that mouth truly need an ugly protruding flap of muscle? A proper design would have sheltered the protruding eyes better, yes? Did the tiny knob nose mean they could not smell well through the tiny nostril bump-with-holes? How useful could those modified forefeet be, versus the obvious better choice to remain on four legs and have arms as well? This sounded odd to Memor: Astronomers were bipeds.

They seemed to use base ten, rather than the more efficient base twelve. Why?

"Their hands have ten digits."

"Surely the obvious advantages of twelve—first three fractions are integers, many other easeful facets—would outweigh that, in an intelligent species."

Memor could not contest this, and so moved on. "They display an odd adaptation—"

She showed short clips of several humans talking, their odd mouths flapping rapidly. Across their narrow faces quick muscular changes flew, a darting sequence of eyebrow lifts, shaped lips, eye moves, nostril flarings, tilts and juts of chin and jaw.

"They have this much expression, yet never evolved feather flaunting?" Biology Savant Ramanuji asked.

"Apparently they use their heads alone. Plus hands."

Sniffs and rumbles of disbelief chorused through the high vaulted room.

Omanah the Ecosystem Packmistress said slowly, "A collective good, I would predict." This came in feather tones designed to convey her well-earned wisdom, and augmented by self-deprecating, somber themes in a three-layered suite of browns and grays.

"How so?" Memor said. "Lead us."

"These facial moves are apparently signals from their Underminds. Thus the speakers do not know all that they convey."

"Surely they must!" a young Astronomer spoke suddenly. All turned to gaze, and the young one realized she—or was this one in the neutral Revealing phase?—had overstepped.

Omanah twisted her crested head and rippled her ambers and grays subtly. "Memor's points elude you. They do not know how to access their Underminds. So, in a kind of evolutionary retaliation, the Unders speak in ways the Overs cannot know."

Another stir of respectful understanding worked through the gallery—huffs, sighs, soft flares of ruby tribute to Omanah.

"I kneel to your insight," the young one said, eyes closed.

Omanah said, "Here is an example of group selection. The party speaking does not know fully what it says—*but the listeners do.* For they can see the Undermind voicing in swift flurries of expression, the signals flitting by, using little muscular movements in eyes, mouths, jaws. So the group learns the true thoughts and emotions, yet the speaker does not fully comprehend."

Memor added, "Thus the species gains a collective good."

Omanah bowed in agreement. "And so it was

with our self-modifications. The Uncovering made the Bowl possible by revealing to us our Underminds."

A large, thick-plumed Overseer Astronomer asked in slow-sliding words blended with singing, sharp chirp signatures and plume-shaking, "Do you imply, Flock Head and Packmistress, that these primates have deliberately engineered this face-flutter method?"

The Packmistress pondered this, and in the respectful silence Memor saw the assemblage's feather tones shift from bright attentive colors of magenta and olive into hues tending toward grays and subdued deep blues—signs that they, too, contemplated, trying to anticipate what the Packmistress would say. Time crawled as each of the members consulted their Underminds, trawling deep, long, and slow for insight. This was how the joint Undermind of them all, in concert, learned—accumulating in linear additions, all cross-correlated to achieve greater force—the steeped wisdom of collective thought.

Asenath as Wisdom Chief called them back to Uppermind. "Of course, these creatures have features from which we can learn. At least we recovered the body of one dead primate—not killed by Memor's efforts, I remark—and have learned much from it. Their DNA is like ours, as it is with several of the Adopted. This fits the accepted view that earlier life dispersed through our galaxy on wings of sunlight."

Then she turned with dramatic effect and called,

"Attendant Astute Astronomer Memor! How to deal with these escaped aliens—*that* is our issue. And you let them escape."

So here it was. Memor dodged with, "Knowledge speaks, wisdom listens, Ecosystem Packmistress Asenath."

"I expected more of you."

"I can explain some features, Packmistress, and then describe—"

"On with it."

"These primates have to live with a spectrum of desires driven by natural selection, as do we all. Their starship is a simple design, as if from a society that has developed quickly. That surely means they now operate in a world much different from their primitive lives. Yet still driving them are their deep desires. These, as our own species long ago learned, are hard to govern with learned experience or even medication. Their morality, as did ours, often fights with their desires. So to understand themselves is impossible for them, unless they can *see* their inner, unconscious minds."

"They are retarded, then," put in an Ecosystem Savant. This provoked feather-ripples of amusement, but no one made noises of glee; the occasion did not invite such.

"Indeed," Memor said. "We could help them with this—"

"Help them?" Asenath showed vibrant oranges and reds in a dancing pattern, half in jesting colors, half in rebuke. "They got away from you!"

Memor stepped back, bowed, hooted in the notes

of sorrow and beseeching. "They proved more clever than their ship implied."

"Certainly more clever than their approach suggested," Judge Savant Thaji injected. "They simply landed and came through our air lock. No caution! So young!"

"I can see that as misleading," Asenath remarked without a single feather display. "Or subtle. They gained entrance, we thought we had them—then they got away."

"And now they roam at will!" the Judge Savant said. "Doing damage! We have reports of several dead in 12-34-77 district—their doing, no doubt. They captured a car, as well."

"Very grave," a Biology Savant said. "Grounds for removal."

"Or a more exacting measure," the Judge Savant said with display of scorn and censure, gray and violet fans dancing in rebuke.

Memor stood and let the discussion run, for it would harm her cause to speak now. Instead she let her Undermind rule the moment. It conjured up for her a memory of a visit to the funeral pit, in all its elegant yet somber majesty. At its center was the Citadel of the Honored Dead, who would be churned into a matrix they shared with plants, animals, insects, and the depleted topsoil the honored would enhance. Subtly hidden machinery adjusted the slowly roiling mud-fluid for bacterial content, acidity, temperature, trace elements. First the Pit, then the Garden: the fate of all.

When the Undermind let go of the memory and

was satisfied, Memor turned attention to the argument rustling all about her. Harsh things had passed her by in a flurry of hot words. She deliberately let these go, as was best in such heated moments. Insults are best not remembered. She let it all go, following the long-ranging talk but not engaging with it. Here, the Undermind helped.

The Judge Savant pressed her case for execution, calling it "a just recycling." Others differed, calling for Memor's replacement. Much talk. If Memor had followed it, laid it deep and solid in memory, she would then go through doubt and regret—which would in future impede her work. Better to let the moments glide by.

Yet questions about the primates called her out of her needful reverie. Refreshed, Memor pointed out that she had used classical methods of psychological control, since these primates were strongly social animals. She began by keeping them in comparatively small areas, and gave them just enough food to be sure they did not starve. "Still, hunger began to play a role in their behavior. Within ten of their sleep intervals—they seem to come from a planet with a fairly long day—they showed classic symptoms. Some began to communicate with us more often. This was obvious food-seeking. Slowly, I believe, they began to identify less with their fellows, and more with us—specifically, me."

"Yes, very good," a helpful underling allowed himself to say. All else ignored him, of course.

"Within five more sleep intervals, their mood shifted. Disputes began, often in their talk during meals. This, too, fits classical theory—eating brings food to the front of their minds, their hunger drives competition, then disagreement."

"You broke down their social code? Their solidarity?"

"In part," Memor said, hoping this would come over as modesty. In fact, though, she was unsure that she had. Hurrying on, she said, "They were obviously crew on a distant voyage, so we cannot expect to break them down quickly. Time is our friend here."

"Any signs of the early stages of Adoption?"

"I believe so. They often brightened when one of my team gave them a bit of food, or allowed a small favor."

"Your analysis of their minds suggests they can be Adopted?"

"In time, yes."

This gained her shuffling fan-gestures of approval, and the air eased.

In the end it came down to a vote. Memor suffered through the moments as each voter consulted her Undermind and finally cast an electronic signal. Asenath displayed the results, and—a shocked hush.

"You have survived in your office," Asenath said, letting a pitch of reluctance skate among her words. "But I shall monitor you, and report you to this assembly when needed."

Memor allowed herself a relieved bow. There came hoots of derision, and a background soft melody of approval, expressed in sighs and foot-claps of applause.

In the great vault the gathered began a rhythmic chanting. The Protocols called for some group expression, and the momentum of the moment gave it forth. The chant called out an ancient rhythm. It spoke of what the Essence is not, instead of what it is. This set the Citadel into a great rolling call, amid hooting songs and vibrant bass notes. *Joyful joined we are, eternal. . . .*

This was clearly a rebuke of Memor, a reminder of what the Universe of Essences demanded of all the Folk.

She felt grateful to escape with a mere reproach. She even roared and stomped and joined in with the chorus. The humming calls grew and she began to enjoy it all. Release.

But the memory of the Pit, then the Garden—these remained long after.

TWENTY-EIGHT

Cliff awoke to feel the ground trembling. Blinking, eyes gritty, he looked around at the small copse of ellipsoidal ferns they had sheltered under. Nothing visible in the shadows. No odd scuttlings.

But he could make out a faint, ominous rumble from below. There was no actual geology here, so it had to be machinery moving on the outer face of the Bowl. He got up and walked barefoot, feeling the vibration. It seemed louder in one direction and as he moved, the ground trembled a bit more. Birds rustled and chirruped in response to it.

Then it began to fade, though he kept walking, and by the time he reached a slab of fused rock, he could feel nothing. The source must have passed, so maybe it was a moving platform on the other side, an elevator or similar.

Then he noticed he was out of the trees. Feeling vulnerable alone, he glanced at the mercifully empty sky and quickly sought the canopy cover. *Like a terrified rodent,* he thought ruefully.

But he couldn't get back to sleep. He had been deep in a softly erotic dream of Beth. Their biggest problem was the unending day. They all had trouble sleeping because there was always something up and active, rustling through foliage, setting off their apprehensions. Now, though, the others were snuffling and snoring and he envied them. At least he could use the time to think, to plan.

He lay back and looked through the canopy at the dim presence of the star. The jet was a scratch across the sky, flexing with whorls and tendrils. Near the star little flashes of brilliance lit the base. He was getting used to this sky, to this place—and that was dangerous.

So much here had a familiar feel—the sudden sizzle of lightning splintering a sky, a patter of rain, moaning breezes—but the tremor just now gave him an important warning. Here they all lived with a strangeness made all the more discomforting by its deceptive likeness to a world they all knew.

So they had to use everything, especially deception. They were torn between the need to stay out of sight and the drive to explore. They had disguised their craft, making it sand colored. From a distance, the sand ship made no impression, but close up it did move and attract the eye. The fixed wing aerial surveys they occasionally saw in the distance had missed them. Cliff hoped their pursuers were losing interest, because the fliers were getting spotty. Luckily, no intelligent aliens seemed to live in this vast desert.

But his gang of five was getting surly and hungry. They had learned to spot and shoot the large, savage lizards that lived in the rock outcroppings. The meat was nearly as leathery as the brown hide, but over a roaring fire of hardwood that did not give off smoke, it supplied protein they badly needed. No talk; they ate eagerly. Carbohydrates were harder to find, and water always an issue.

He had tried to forage for edibles, but the problem was tough. Not only was this an alien ecology, but it was also one that worked without night. What did that do to plant evolution? What kind of defenses did plants have here? On Earth, poisons were defenses against predators—tobacco was a particularly effective one in the tropics, where there was no winter to kill off the insects.

But in this Bowl, no winter saved plants or animals from constant predation. So Cliff expected to find plenty of poisons, deceptions, disguises. He had already seen plants that looked like rocks or even skeletons. The leathery lizards could bound sideways, because they had two forelegs and one hindleg designed to give them startling leaps. What hunted the lizards? He expected that the evolutionary arms race meant that a big predator was around, but he saw none. Maybe the lizards ruled this region, the top predators.

Humans were new here, so creatures mostly took no notice of them. But big birds smacked them in the head, or dived for their eyes, apparently mistaking them for some easier game—but what creature was that?

They had all lost weight. Howard, who was always recovering from some accident or injury, was now downright pallid and scrawny. They all leaned on Cliff to find more edible foods, and he had some successes—but was running out of ideas.

He heard some movement nearby and turned, automatically reaching for his laser. "You woke me up," Irma said, sitting down beside him.

"Spotty sleep is better than none," Cliff said, holding out a piece of the odd fruit they'd found. It looked like a puffer fish with spokes of purple hair, but tasted sweet and dark.

"Good call on this one. Better than mangoes, even."

"Sliced it, smelled it, tip of the tongue—that's all we've got to go by. I wish I had some testing gear to use on candidate food."

Irma nodded. "Those woodlands we first went into, the soil was more acidic and moist. The soil here, though, seems alkaline and dry."

"Like most Earthside deserts."

"Right, so we can use our intuition from what works there. Look there—"

Within a few meters were fernlike plants, thorny bushes, prickly globes dangling temptingly from enormous trees. "Okay."

They climbed partway up the crusty bark of the tree and brought down two of the large oval fruit. "Funny," Irma said. "They trail these coarse leafy strands, look more like tendrils."

He cut into one. "There's this fuzzy red tinge to the skin, like blister rust on Earth. But what's that mean here?"

He sniffed the rosy skin and found no stink of decay, but again, what would rot smell like here? So he sliced off a chunk, bit in—and found a gusher of warm soft sweet succulence burst in his mouth. "Maybe poison, sure, but soooo good . . ."

She grinned. "I'll wait, see if you topple over."

He waited to see if his stomach rejected it, but nothing happened. Irma said, "I think we should sleep in shifts. Keep two guards up, spell each other every four hours."

"Let's try it. But it's hard to sleep on the sand ship."

"We have to keep moving if we're going to learn much."

"Yeah, sure—but I'm wondering what we're doing, running around. We sure as hell aren't getting closer to understanding this place."

She patted him on his shoulder. "Don't get down about it. The guys take their cues from you."

"Huh? I'm not in charge."

She grinned. "Like it or not, you are."

"Who said?"

"Primate politics. Ever notice? They say their piece, argue, then look at you."

He sniffed. "No, I hadn't noticed. Aybe and Terry give me plenty of grief."

"They're scared. We're all scared. Sometimes that comes out as anger."

"Uh, glad you brought that up." The scent of her, after yesterday's swim in a pond, was messing with his concentration. He felt uncomfortable somehow, so resorted to safer generalities. "I see some old patterns emerging under the stress. The guys are summoning up their inner macho, like putting on armor. Not that I'm immune, either."

"You don't flex it like they do."

He chuckled ruefully. "Look, as a teenager I practiced cool smoking in the mirror—" She laughed and he blushed. "No, I really did. Cancer sticks! I also impressed dates by revving the engine at stoplights."

She laughed. "No! You had a combustion car?"

"An heirloom, the license cost a fortune. Once I tried on thirty sunglasses to get the right ominous look. With guys like Aybe and Terry, I talked tech and .45 automatics, usually while holding a beer bulb. And—" He glanced at her. "—I wore jeans so tight, I got sore balls and a red rash."

She cackled, slapped her knee. "That's so bad, it must be true."

"Sure, it was ridiculous then, it's ridiculous

now—but Aybe and Terry are faking a calm they don't have."

She nodded. "Sometimes it's so thick, you could cut it with a knife. I see them eyeing us, hiding their fears. Good deduction, Cliff-o."

He turned to her. "We've gotten used to being scared, maybe. But I don't—"

Without warning, she reached over, hands on his shoulders, and kissed him. Held it, long and hard. Let go, sat back, looked at him levelly. "Had to say that."

Say what? he thought. "I, look, I'm—"

"Married, I know. So am I."

"I hope I didn't—"

"Give some sign? No, damn it." She took a deep breath and rapped out words in a rush. "We're on the run across a goddamn artifact we don't understand and could get caught any minute, or killed, maybe worse than killed—so, way I see it, the usual rules, they don't matter."

"I—"

"No real argument, Cliff. But you and I have got to keep this little bridge party going and, and, I'm feeling *so* lonely, so like I'm on the edge, have got to—hell, I don't know what I'm saying."

He smiled. "I don't either, but I . . . liked it."

They just sat and stared at each other for a while, letting the moment brew.

She raised an eyebrow, gave him a twisted grin. "Y'know, what anybody thinks of us means, to me, less than zero."

"You make a good case." Cliff wondered what

he was doing, mind boiling. But something strong in him knew he needed this.

"I never liked sex in daylight, though."

"I never was so picky."

• • •

Terry said, "We're getting nowhere."

Irma sniffed and poked at their small, popping fire. It burned old wood, which did not give off smoke. "We're alive, right? And I wouldn't have given us good odds on that last week."

Aybe sniffed, his wide mouth twisted skeptically. "Week? This damn place makes time meaningless."

Irma lifted her phone. "Standard time."

Techtypes all, they then ruminated on keeping a time standard here with their digital devices, which got updated aboard because *SunSeeker* had significant relativistic time effects versus Earth-normal time. Aybe cut this off as he leaned forward over the fire, where stick skewers turned and dark lizard meat sizzled. "This place was made to *erase* time, that's my point. What kind of thing makes a big thing that hasn't got seasons, change, variety?"

Cliff said mildly, "Something that likes life predictable."

Terry pounced on that. "Yes! Something really strange. Those big, feathered things we saw—they run this place. We ran away from them!"

"They were taking us prisoners," Howard said. His injuries made him wince as he adjusted his seating around the popping fire.

Terry said, "Maybe they just wanted to talk."

Irma said, "It didn't seem like an invitation."

"Hey," Terry said, "the thing about aliens is, they're *alien*. We may have misunderstood them."

Aybe shook his head. "That doesn't matter. We can't live out here forever. What's our agenda?"

Cliff sighed, but put his hand over his mouth so they didn't hear it. They all looked at him; Irma was right. He wished he were more certain, but said anyway, "Lie low. Work the sand sailer toward the mirror region. We're making good time. We could get there in maybe a month."

"Month means nothing here," Aybe said.

Irma said, "Hey, we need to keep time straight. Call it a million seconds, okay?"

They managed a low chuckle, the most they could muster as a group identity. Cliff watched their faces and seized the moment. "I'm hoping to find some access at the mirror zone. We saw that there were big constructions up there, close to the Knothole. Whoever runs this place probably hangs out there."

Terry furiously shook his head. "We need to talk to these aliens. Look at what they've built!"

Irma said, "So?"

Terry sat back, blinking. "Let's get close to one of their living zones. Stop hanging out here in the desert."

Howard said, "I agree."

Irma said, "I don't like going in under their terms. Maybe they think aliens like us should be eliminated—who knows?"

Aybe scowled and jutted out his chin. "We escaped, remember? They may not take that kindly."

Terry shook his head once more. "All I know is, we'll learn more observing them near here, instead of trying to move millions of kilometers up to the Knothole."

Irma pressed, "How?"

Aybe pointed. "I climbed that big skeleton tree yesterday, got a look at a dark patch off that way. Green, must be a forest."

Terry said, "Better game, better concealment. Let's go there, see if we can find some natives. Watch them, learn."

Cliff watched them as this got tossed around. He had realized that Terry was the sort of guy he had known in university. He liked to sit around and drink and philosophize, and if he got drunk, he would tell you what you could expect in life for the sort of person you were. That met the legal standard for an asshole, Cliff figured. When the crew was getting shaped up—centuries ago in real time, yes—he had barely met Terry. But now he knew what type Terry was and was thankful that there was no alcohol here. With a few drinks in him, the man could do real damage in a small group like this. Maybe without the drinks, too.

So now Terry was far from what his skill set could deal with. Fleeing across a huge contraption nobody had ever imagined, Terry kept himself oriented, Cliff could see, by staying sharp of chin, assured, with eyebrows clenched behind aviator glasses. Sure of himself. Dangerous.

Assurance in the face of uncertainty was a good pose for a leader, sure. But not without plenty of thought to back it up.

"I say let's vote," Aybe said.

"Sure," Howard said, his only remark in a while. He kept picking at a nasty scratch he had scabbing over on his calf.

Cliff said, "All in favor of following Terry's idea."

Three hands: Aybe, Howard, and Terry. Cliff shrugged. "Okay, after breakfast we set sail."

Irma said wistfully, "I wish I was back on *Sun-Seeker,* not hiding and running."

They all nodded.

Irma had a point, Cliff realized a bit later, but there were compensations. Here they got to deal with the crux of the problem, understanding this place, not just watching it from the orbiting ship. Plus, no boredom. *An adventure is someone else risking their life far away. . . .*

And he had just dried off from a great swim in a warm desert pond. He felt great. He drank a cup of water, and snapped open one of the pods that held tangy little silky strands, like eating sweet cobwebs. The water was far better than *SunSeeker*'s recycled, bland water, and the air here had a fresh zest. Also, their chem tests showed it had no gut-buster microbes they could not nullify. Redwing certainly wasn't breathing anything so good.

It took two days to sail to the distant forest, over crusted sand that sang beneath them. The surface was glazed, and when they stopped he took small samples to study under his field microscope. The stuff was hard yet living—bacteria, lichens, and mosses mixed into sand. Maybe all these were waiting for the next rain to flourish. They learned the hard way that their sail ship had to skirt the darker patches, which were rough and once poked a hole in the bow. Sticking to the tan-colored zones gave them better speed. Somehow the place seemed ancient, even the occasional sand dune firm and polished. There were parabolic dunes, star dunes, straight dunes with radial crests. The emptier the land, Cliff realized, the more luminous and precise the names for its features.

They passed by a raised bluff, tan and barren, and suddenly saw a canyon open in the steep stone walls. "There's green in there," Irma pointed out.

Their sails flapped in the lee of the cliff when they lost the wind. Howard said, "Let's have a look, take a break."

All heads nodded; they were getting stiff, sitting in the craft and managing the ropes to steer.

They left Howard with the sailer, since he still had a gimpy leg from a fall. Marching two kilometers up the dry canyon was hard, working against the drifts of dun-colored sand in a broad streambed. A soft breeze swept their sweat away.

The side channels looked ancient, and Cliff kept a wary eye on their shadows. Ruins of stone and twisted metal stuck out of the erosion plain. Terry tried to make sense of them, prying fragments from the soil, but most of it was rusted away. Breezes sighed around them as they came upon a larger wreck, a tumbled-down building of curiously long rock slivers, pale along their lengths and burnt at their edges. "Fire?" Aybe asked.

"Looks abandoned," Irma said, pulling a slab free of the rest. The whole stack of stone gave way, sliding down and tumbling so they had to lurch out of the way.

"What's that?" Aybe asked about a buried structure, and they spent fifteen minutes uncovering a hard metal carapace. The building's collapse had dented but not breached the boxy thing.

Aybe used up a lot of his laser charge cutting in. He used razor mode and the highest frequency, but the stuff was much tougher than any steel alloy. They levered the metal open to the music of wrenching screeches. Inside, wrapped in polycarbon, were fine metal grids and some mysterious black boxes with ports and plies in their sides.

"Hard to figure this out," Terry said, fingering the stuff, "but must be electrical."

"To do what?" Cliff asked. Not his area of techspeak.

Aybe spread the metal grids across a slab of the pale, hard stone. "Doesn't matter what it was for. Point is, what can it do for us?"

"Like what?"

Aybe grinned. He had been moody the last few days, but now a tech challenge animated him. "Amp up our antenna function. For our beamers."

"That'll be tough, getting an impedance match to a beamer."

"I like problems."

They found little else but buildings that had collapsed a long time ago. No obvious resources, no primitives among the ruins as in a bad movie; nothing.

The electrical stuff was too heavy to carry, except Aybe wanted the grids. Terry said, "Fine, so long as you carry them from here on out." On the move, everything was about mass.

As Cliff marched back to the sailer, he wondered how this huge desert zone had formed and whether the climate here needed vast, largely inert areas to function. There must be large-scale atmospheric movement of water, like the Hadley cells of Earth, but even with the occasional patterns of passing clouds, he could not figure out how things worked here. Earthly air moved in several circulating patterns, and the poles were the final place where matters got resolved. But on this Bowl, the only pole was the Knothole region. What did that do?

The Bowl and Earth both rotated, so both felt the Coriolis force—which brought all its complications, like hurricanes. But the sheer scale of the Bowl made him wonder if the same rules of thumb about weather could possibly apply. Matters of heating and atmosphere, not just the planet's rotation, set the scale lengths of Earth's circulations. Here, those scales were immensely larger, about a thousand times!

Then there were the oddities and intuitions that were wrong even on Earth, but might not be here. People thought whirlpools in baths circled differently in Earth's north and south hemispheres, but that was an illusion. It might be fun to see if that was true here, though.

All that seemed a long way off, slogging beneath the constant sun. They traded occasional comments, but it was a good idea to shut up and watch their surroundings. Except for the birds, who were conspicuously larger than Earthside ones, Cliff noticed that few animals advertised themselves. Caution seemed the universal policy.

So he mused as he helped with the steering, pulling ropes to adjust their sail, listening to the buzz as their bow rasped over the stiff sand. He watched his sweaty team and wondered how long they would hold up. Nobody in *SunSeeker*'s crew was given to big shows of emotion, shouting, brags, insults, tears and drama, big proclamations of love or hate, stomping out of meetings. No bipolars, no geniuses. Rather, they were members of the sober, hardheaded, but soft-spoken race. Educated to a fault, practical as a paper clip. Considered, deliberate, oatmeal steady, skeptical and sharp-eyed when they met new ideas, unflappable, but—and this was what cut down through the applicant list like a hot knife through ripe butter—with an appetite for adventure. An odd assortment of those realists nonetheless willing to dive down the funnel of time and come out centuries later in a strange new place, ready for the dangerous and eager for the grand. This made them short on hugs and compliments, quick with the narrowed eye, short on the soft warm armloads of comfort.

Their spirits rose as the forest grew from a distant line on the horizon to a dense stand of trees, even though their food and water were running out. They hid the sailship, ventured in with lasers drawn, and soon found a stream. Yellow big-finned fish lurked in the darker pools and Howard managed to catch five with a simple line and hook, no bait needed. A feast! And the water was as sweet as champagne.

A kilometer farther on, there were dense stands of fragrant bushes that, when they crawled into it, gave them something like a day/night ecology. They fell asleep immediately.

Over breakfast of more fish, Terry said, "Time to set up a base, drop some of our body gear. I'm tired of backpacking everything we've got."

Aybe nodded. "And reconn."

Cliff didn't like leaving anything behind, but they had a point. Even in the lower gravity, the straps cut into their shoulders by the end of a day's march.

They hid their heavier gear in a stand of angular, skeletal trees, marked it with subtle signs, and moved out, using their practiced methods. Aybe and Terry took point to left and right. Cliff and Howard brought up the rear to the sides, with Irma in the middle. No talking, hand signals only, stay out of clearings.

The foliage here was strange. Vines made convoluted turns, as if trying to find a way out of their thick mats. Small, unseen animals clattered and called in the canopy. Birds gave fluttery songs, not like Earthly chirps. Then they heard ahead a low, ominous hum and circled it. A dense clump of webbed brown plants teemed with brightly turning leaves that sounded like bees. Cliff could see no role for this in plant dynamics, unless—"Maybe they're windmills generating power," he whispered to Irma.

"For what?"

"Dunno."

They skirted the humming network, which was a hundred meters wide. He wondered if this artificial ecology used directly generated electrical power somehow, reactors and plants, and not just solar energy. The whole structure could be a giant electrical grid. Only a few meters away lay the high vacuum of space, and the understructure of metal could conduct electricity to distant points. For the usual question—*why?*—he had no answer.

"There's some odd noise that way," Terry said, pointing left. A clatter, some yips and snorts. They followed his lead.

After a few minutes Irma said, "Over there, a hill. Let's get up in those trees to survey."

They found a slight rise of a few meters and shimmied up the zigzag trees at the top. Howard stopped halfway up and whispered, "The birds."

Cliff worked his way out on a limb that kept jabbing him with tiny spikes, the big tree's defense against some sort of predator. He got a view of a distant meadow where odd things hovered. Four aircars, holding a meter or two above the emerald green. Inside their open tops were two or three of the Bird Folk. The aircars moved in a circling path, and Cliff saw their prey—a large thing that dodged across the meadow, hemmed in by the aircars. It had three legs and danced away from the encircling hunters, its big hairy head jerking around, seeking an escape.

A lance arced out from one of the aircars and hit the big animal in the haunch. It yipped, a high insulted cry, and dashed away. A big Bird stood up in its aircar and threw another lance at it, missed. The aircars rushed around in some kind of pattern, weaving in and out as if this was a game, or some ritual. The animal yipped again and screamed when a lance caught it in the middle.

It collapsed, gasping so loud, Cliff could hear the plaintive cries. Another lance ended that. The thing slumped.

The Bird Folk landed and Cliff wondered at the vehicles' soundless grace. Were they magnetically suspended? That made sense if they carried powerful electromagnets in their thick undercarriage. The Bowl's conducting frame a few meters below the meadow would provide the surface that opposed the magnetic fields, allowing the aircars to ride on the magnetic pressure.

"That thing's a carnivore," Irma whispered. "Mostly bone and muscle. The birdies are hunting for *sport.*"

She was right, Cliff saw. Nine of the Birds had formed a circle around the dead creature and did an odd dance, strutting in, whirling, dancing out with spindly arms raised, making quick leg movements. Then came a honking shout. They circled the beast, raised the lances they had pulled out of the carcass, and hooted again.

It looked primitive and yet understandable. Terry said, "They're like primordial hunters!"

Howard said, "They're not using impact weapons, like guns. I saw some with long spears, arrows, a flung garrote."

Irma said, "Maybe low impact because they don't want to damage the underpinning of the Bowl? It's only a few meters down in spots."

They nodded and climbed down, moving away from the Bird Folk. Cliff realized that this immense world was a park, in a way. For the Bird Folk.

They spent hours working through the dense vegetation, returning to pick up their gear, then moving on to explore further. It was too risky to leave anything behind—except for the sailcraft, their escape route into the desert lands.

Cliff and Irma took note of the many life-forms they saw, including a long thing like an armadillo. It crawled without legs, using its sliding plates of armor to inch forward. "An armored snake," Irma said. Terry wanted to kill it for meat, but Cliff was unsure it would be edible. And he hated to kill creatures on spec, even when they were hungry.

They found enough of the nasty lizards lurking near streams and shot them. They were aggressive but stupid; it was simple to kill them. Aybe gathered dry wood to keep their smoke down. As they ate the greasy lizard meat over a low fire, they tossed around ideas about the Bird Folk, and what they had seen. Not reassuring, no.

They napped, got up with the usual aches from sleeping in the open, and after a breakfast of more lizard, moved on into denser woods. This was a search-and-understand mission, and Cliff moved carefully, not letting the uncertainties get to him.

A distant high noise came rolling through the tall trees as they moved forward. A *skreee* came from their left and they cautiously moved that way, faces puzzled. Some bass rumblings, then more *skreee*. They saw a broad clear area and circled it, Terry gesturing to keep low.

A chattering alarm burst out in the branches high above them. Cliff felt his pulse rate rise as he duck-walked forward through low brush. The whole forest was alive with excitement and arcing above the din came the shattering calls he recognized as those of primates they had seen before. Monkeys, though larger and stranger. But the *skreee* sounds had structure, chopped notes floating on the underlying base line, like sung words. These were different primates, riffing up in the high canopy.

He peered through the ropy strands of a vine plant. Much movement. He brought up his binoculars and studied the moving figures.

The Bird Folk. On foot this time.

About two hundred meters away, moving right to left across a broad, rocky plain. They ran in long loping strides, eight of them, carrying instruments in their long arms. Their feathers rippled with flowing patterns of yellow and magenta. Their heads were tilted back, which pointed their long, broad noses forward, their two large eyes glittering.

Knobbed legs articulated gracefully, eating up the ground between them and their prey.

Bunches of running figures were nearer to Cliff. Primates, running with their own loping grace. The primates were tall with long arms and even longer legs, running it seemed from a stand of zigzag trees several hundred meters to his right. Their angular heads jerked around, looking back at the birds, who were angling toward them from farther away. Cries spilled from the primates—harsh, barked shrieks. They ran faster and broke into groups of threes.

At first Cliff had thought the ragged, fleeing band were, somehow, humans. But these were primates nearly as tall as the Bird Folk, and had four arms. They ran in clumps of three, the one behind turning to fire something that looked like a crossbow at the Bird Folk. The shots were inaccurate and the Bird Folk dodged them anyway. The primate that fired then ran ahead while a companion in the group of three stopped, aimed, fired. The one in the middle was reloading.

Arrows flew everywhere. Primates and Birds shrieked and howled and chattered—a din.

An arrow hit one of the birds, but it simply lodged in the thick feathers. The Bird plucked it out and tossed it away. Then the primate ran on and the next one stopped to fire, a classic delaying tactic. This shot hit home. A Bird went down in a tangle of legs.

A long, hooting cry came from the Bird Folk. Angry rumbles came from the surging Birds. They sped up, long legs taking great bounds. They closed in on the primates and swept to both sides, a flanking pincer movement.

Something bright flashed from the huge running Birds, and a loud boom rolled across the open plain. Several fired at the same time, and primates burst into flame. Shrieks, bodies falling, limbs jerking.

Cliff smelled an acrid tinge and watched the remaining primates panic. They scattered, bunches breaking up. Some fired arrows but most fled.

The Birds ran them down. Some they did not shoot with the quick, darting beams, but instead ran up behind them and leaped high in the air, coming down on a primate in a crushing fall. Cliff could hear bones snap.

The last primate turned and howled at the Birds and they simply ran it down, trampling the body again and again.

The Birds danced on the bodies. Their mouths opened wide and they emitted sharp, harsh calls, like trilling fire alarms. With their stubby beaks they stabbed the primate bodies. Spindly long arms shot toward the sky, jerking with joyous energy, and they circled, making a quick-footed dance, shrieking in a melodious chant.

Cliff backed away from the spectacle, shaken. He straightened up a bit and retreated, duck-walking backwards. Terry came alongside him and whispered, "My God."

"Yeah. Yeah." Cliff could barely absorb what they had seen.

The party came together, united in a single purpose—move fast, get away.

Cliff remembered thinking that this place was a park, in a way.

Certainly not for mere primates.

TWENTY-NINE

Redwing dipped into Meal 47, a pomegranate-rich sauce and artificial meat mix with long grain brown rice, green vegetables on the side. It tasted the same as always, of course—pungent, hearty. And since he'd had it more times than he could count, boring. Still, its savory tang was somewhat enjoyable because it appealed to the dimmed senses he had developed in the austere, rumbling caves of *SunSeeker*. And every meal reminded him of their dwindling supplies.

Any semblance of a sensory life was heartening in the ceramic claustrophobia here. At least when the ship was driving through interstellar plasma, noise-canceling headphones could subtract most of the sound. Not here, now, when *SunSeeker* was laboring hard, its Reynolds bosonic drive coughing in electromagnetic stutters. Some crew said they just forgot about the engines' steady din, but Redwing could not—though he hid this, of course. He had to seem calm, steady, oblivious of their desperate uncertainties.

Getting contact with the Beth group had been

their sole breakthrough. Before that, Redwing found himself commanding a ship that had constant navigation problems and no contact with the ground. He had nearly written off the whole landing party.

Redwing raised an eyebrow at Ayaan Ali, who came and sat at the mess table, waiting respectfully. Ayaan was an Arab woman who dressed in deck uniform like everyone else, but occasionally at dinner wore a stylish veil and glinting emerald earrings. "Ah, good," Redwing said formally. "Report?"

"We've got the high-gain antennas ganged together."

"How's Beth's signal?"

"Strong and—"

"Can you get me visual?"

"Hell, Cap'n, we're working with a damn field phone signal here!"

"Answering my question comes first, then the complaining."

Ayaan's face stiffened and there was a three-beat silence. Then Ayaan said slowly, "No, sir, don't really know yet about visuals. Doubt we have the bandwidth."

"It's a bandwidth problem, or a signal to noise and coherence mapping?"

"At this stage, that's rather a moot point."

"Ah." He looked at the slabs of illos she showed him in a long silence. "Good, then. No complaint?"

Ayaan blinked and her mouth firmed up. "No, sir, and no excuses."

"Excellent." Redwing permitted himself a slight smile.

Ayaan laid out a diagram on his slate, pointing to the array she had mounted outside, jury-rigged from interior structural beams. "As soon as we work the kinks out of ganging the dishes, and optimize Beth's incoming, we'll have a coherent, linked system."

"Which means you can go after Cliff?"

"Yes, but remember, we don't even know what gear they have."

"Field phones, too, as I recall."

"But have they hung on to them? I'm getting no pings back at all."

Redwing understood the tech enough to know that grouping all their microwave range antennas together outside was a hell of a tough problem. Software and hardware together had to gang the antennas so they were coherent in phase, like making them into one big eardrum. Doing that on a constantly moving platform swooping above the Bowl, and focusing them on spots in the moving landscape—he couldn't even begin to imagine the problems. "You're doing a great job, Ayaan. I know the problems. Just keep trying for a ping."

Ayaan blinked rapidly at the notoriously rare Redwing praise. "Yes, sir."

Redwing nodded and strode with visible energy—more performance for the crew—the five meters to the bridge viewscreen. The whole hemisphere had been converted into a complex display that could flit from real images to overlay dynamics charts.

Look too long at them, flip back and forth, and you had to sit down and let it seep in. He had ordered that their interior centrifugal grav be Bowl normal, 0.8 g. They would all be ready to go down and help, if that was necessary. But he wasn't going to put another boot on the ground until he knew more.

He felt a sudden surge, twist, and correction strum through the deck and walked over to the operations chair.

"How's the induction coil?" Redwing asked the pilot, a short man named Jampudvipa, always shortened to Jam.

"Sputtering. I got it back right, using the three-zone thrusters. We're getting barely enough plasma to keep the system from going into parasitic oscillations."

"Damn. Can we make the delta?"

Jam wrenched his face around and shrugged. "Perhaps."

The Bowl image spread across most of the glowing hemisphere. It always made him stop and stare.

The landscape unfolded at speeds hallucinatingly fast, because they were moving at about ten kilometers a second over it, orbital speed. So much wealth: forests brimming with green promise, clouds towering a hundred kilometers high over shallow seas, spare bare deserts of golden sand, crawling muddy rivers snaking through valleys rimmed by low hills. Hurricanes roaring and churning across continents larger than Earth itself. An immense, impossible geography. A contraption devoutly to be wished, yes. But, by whom? By . . . what?

He watched the comm bands. Beth's signal was down to zero, but her party had gotten through earlier for a few minutes. To keep Beth within range, Redwing and Jam had to maneuver the ship constantly, spelling the watch with Clare Conway, the willowy blond copilot. But the solar wind here was a puny wisp, barely enough to keep the induction chambers from shutting down. Space was everywhere a very good vacuum, but the red star's wind was even thinner than Sol's. Plasma blew off stars, but this smaller sun's somehow got swept up into the jet. Magnetic focusing, apparently, though how it was done seemed a mystery to the engineers. Indeed, Redwing thought, this whole weird place was an implied slap in the face to human endeavors. Even *SunSeeker* was a mere bauble compared with it. A huge bowl whirling around so fast, it covered a perimeter bigger than Mercury's orbit, every nine days.

Jam's job in all this was to keep them close enough to the Bowl's atmosphere to let Beth's weak phone signal get through to them. He steered them so close, the land seemed like a flat plane below them, an infinite wall of blue green dotted with clouds hundreds of kilometers high, of seas bigger than any planet. All of it hung under the constant glare of star and jet, which cast different glows across the deep atmosphere, in long blades of shadow and radiance.

Redwing could see the strain in Jam's face, but the man would never mention it, of course. "How long can we keep doing this waltz?"

"A day, perhaps two."

"Then what?"

"We must use the reaction motors."

"We can't afford to burn real fuel."

"I know." Jam's watery eyes studied Redwing's face. "But I cannot alter the laws of mechanics."

"To me, Jam, that means something between diddly and squat. Time to do some hard thinking, or we're going to lose touch with our people."

Redwing had almost said *my people,* but thought better of it. Too possessive, even for a captain. He had to seem sober, focused, yet somehow above the fray, thinking about the larger prospects.

To give Jam some time, he walked the length of the full deck, eyeing the display boards for signs of trouble. They had few crew up, to conserve on supplies, but heads looked up as he passed, his face observing yet detached.

He passed by the Bio Preserve and on impulse cycled through the lock. A strong stink of dank animal sweat wrinkled his nose. One of the pigs had gotten out of its enclosure. It ran up to him, squealing, sniffing, and farted. This turned out to be an overture. It crapped on the deck, turned, and dashed away.

Damned if he would clean it up. He called out to Condit, the field biologist, and pointed to the mess when the woman appeared. She shrugged. "Sorry, Cap'n. It got around me while I was recharging their food."

"What do they eat?"

"Anything. Table scraps, human dander from the air filters. Even their own dung if you let them."

"Maybe you should. Serve 'em right."

She nodded, taking him seriously. "It might help in the nutrient recycling, yes. We trap eighty percent of nitrogen value in our urine, but getting much out of solid waste is hard. Maybe we should feed our wastes to the pigs."

Something in Redwing liked that idea. *Let them eat shit! Marie Antoinette had it right.* But he kept his face blank and said, "Look into it."

Back in the central corridor, he sucked in the dry, stale ship air with relief. He had to carefully avoid letting his sense of humor off its leash.

He hoped nobody here had access to records of his older self. Decades before *SunSeeker* was building, he had scorned the whole idea of interstellar arc-ships, and written a tongue-in-cheek send-up of the program. He proposed that they simply send out robot ships with a single message that read, *Make ten exact copies of this plaque with your name at the bottom of the list and send them to ten intelligent races of your acquaintance. At the end of four billion years, your name will reach the top of the list and you will rule the galaxy.*

A joke, quickly forgotten. The Review Board that passed on starship command hadn't seemed to turn it up, anyway. Or they overlooked it. But now he couldn't be that jokester.

As Redwing returned, Jam looked up. "Cap'n, I think we could—" He paused, as if this might be too much of a leap. "We could, ah, perhaps gather some reserve plasma by, by approaching the jet again."

"Too dangerous. We nearly lost it all, flying up that thing."

"We can come close to it, without entering the turbulent heart."

Redwing smiled. *Turbulent heart* wasn't a bad description of how he felt. "Scoop up plasma, store it?"

"I believe we can, using the capture cross section of the magscoop, when we extend it again."

"That'll take us away from the Bowl, though. A big delta-V."

"We can make it up, I calculate, with the reserve plasma gathered by an approach."

Jam's steady eyes said, *Your call.*

"We'll lose touch with Beth, right? No hope of reaching Cliff's party with Ayaan's jury-rigged antenna, either."

Jam nodded. "Surely true, yes. But we can make a strong boost when we arc down along the Bowl, and return within perhaps ten days."

"Plan it out," Redwing said slowly. "I want to give Ayaan a crack at reaching Cliff, then we'll see."

"Yes, sir."

Redwing paced again, wishing he had more options. Regret that he had not gone down in the landing party surfaced again—a gnawing black dog, but he submerged it. His judgment had been right, even if it did mean he spent his time bottled up here.

In some of the preflight training, to help them deal with the media, he had attended a showing of older ideas about interstellar travel. It was both funny and appalling. One of the earliest, from the Age of Appetite, had featured a dashing starship captain who always went down to planetary surfaces to investigate. Nobody questioned the practice! Of course, they had lots of other wish fulfillment trash ideas—faster-than-light travel (and this was after Einstein!), aliens who spoke English of course, teleportation for quick jaunts wherever they wanted. Nobody explained why that didn't yield an economy with infinite resources. After all, the transporter could just as easily make extra food or devices or money; anything at all, even people.

Yet those Age of Appetite people had the dream, too. They just didn't think much about how it would take hardship and death in the teeth of the unknown.

He made himself smile and say encouraging things as he paced the deck, and kept his musings to himself, as always.

THIRTY

They were rattled. Cliff could see it in their faces.

"I wonder," Irma said as they ate cold meat beside their sailcraft, "if the Birds planned to hunt us, back when we came through the lock?"

Aybe snorted. "Of course not! They were treating us as equals—"

"—and they tried to capture us," Terry finished for him.

"We didn't give them much chance to negotiate," Aybe insisted.

"They grabbed Beth's party," Irma said. "And look at what they did to those odd primates. They were tool users, too!"

Howard said mildly, "We can't gamble that they'll treat us differently."

"I agree," Cliff said. "Focus on what we do next."

Terry said, "I still think we should see what their society looks like, but at a distance maybe, see—"

"Too dangerous," Cliff said.

Howard nodded. "But sailing along in the desert zone, that's dangerous, too—and doesn't teach us much."

They all agreed. Terry said, "I'm getting tired of sitting in that rig, boosting it over outcroppings when we hit a snag, searching for water. And the dust storms! We've got to get some better transport, or we'll be hunted down."

More agreement. Cliff began to see an upside to the horrifying kills they had witnessed. Fear concentrated attention. "Let's hunt up meat, grab some sleep, move away in the morning."

Howard and Terry brightened. They actually enjoyed hunting the nasty lizards, so they set out toward the nearest dry area. The black and brown things usually lived under cairns of rock they had shouldered into place. The trick was to catch them outside, and Terry had shown a talent for luring the quick-footed, hissing beasts with the old game meat left over from previous kills. They didn't seem to mind eating their own kind. "Maybe they're alien lawyers," Irma had said, and got a laugh.

Aybe fished out the mesh he had found before, unfolded it, and began tinkering with it, using his tool kit. Irma went looking for likely edible plants, but as their discipline demanded, always stayed within earshot. Cliff tried to relax. He had not been sleeping well. This ever-warm, sunlit prospect was as good as he was going to get, the new norm in his life—so he dozed.

Only to be awakened by a shout from Aybe.

"Uh, whazzit?" Cliff said, coming out of his sleep. He had been dreaming of Beth and didn't want to leave the warm comfort of the illusion.

"I got it!" Aybe had arrayed the mesh in a tree for support. His beamer was patched into it and he excitedly waved the phone at Cliff. "I got *Sun-Seeker*'s carrier indices."

Cliff snapped awake. "What? You can talk to them?"

"Damn low power, audio might not work—but I'll send them a text message."

Cliff watched and Aybe's face danced. "They answer! It's Redwing."

Aybe stared at the phone and called, "Sending a file!"

Long minutes dragged by while Cliff and Aybe stared at the phone display screen. Finally it chimed and a picture appeared—a big purple globe. A green upright finger symbol stood at the bottom right of the screen. "I've seen that thing," Aybe said. "The finger, green—maybe that means it's okay to eat?"

"Hit the next page," Cliff said.

A dozen pages confirmed several plants they had eaten. Cliff said, "How'd Redwing get this?"

"Must be from Beth's group," Aybe said, "relayed through *SunSeeker*."

"Just what we need," Cliff said. "I saw one of those. That other one, too. Wait—I got it. This is a menu!" The next pages gave plant and animal pictures with two red fingers crossed, clearly warnings. "And an anti-menu. The red ones are dangerous to eat. The blue, okay." He looked up, grinning madly. "Boy, that Lau Pin is sharp."

Looking through the menu, Cliff thought about the colors of edible food here. Evolution geared animals and people alike to like the colors of things that were good or benign—blue for skies and clear water, white for snow. People disliked browns and dark colors linked to feces and rotten food, and reds that might mean spices or poisons. Plants had evolved those as warding-off signals. He hoped Beth hadn't taken risks to discover all the menu's contents. Then—

"Wait," he said to Aybe. "I'll bet they got that data straight from the aliens."

"So they're still in captivity. Um."

"Maybe. The important thing is, we're back in contact."

"Sort of." He sighed. "I lost *SunSeeker*'s signal again."

"They're moving, in orbit. Not easy to stay within range, even with these narrowband phones."

"Good thing they were designed to work at long range." Aybe chuckled ruefully. "Nobody thought they'd have to work over interplanetary distance, though."

Hearing from Beth brought up a subject he hadn't wanted to confront: that one quick moment of passion with Irma.

Sadly he remembered an old joke: *A conscience is what hurts when all your other parts feel so good.*

• • •

By the time Irma returned, Aybe could tell her which of the plants she had gathered she could toss and which to keep. Howard and Terry brought in an odd-looking two-legged thing like a badger, which was edible. They skinned and roasted it and felt joyous.

Then they sailed away into the desert, to get space between them and the magcar Birds. Half an hour of skimming slowly over the fine-grained sand got them into a region of rocky ridges. None they couldn't avoid, but it slowed them considerably. Howard was scanning the horizon for a better route when he called, "Something big coming."

It was a dot in the distance that steadily swelled. "We're more exposed out here," Aybe said. "If that's—"

"A magcar," Irma said. She had binocs and counted out, "Two, no, three Birds in it."

"No point in trying to run," Terry said. "Those are fast."

"But do we fight?" Howard asked.

Irma said slowly, "We don't know for sure they're hostile."

Aybe said slowly, "Angling for a mangling, we are."

Cliff silently cursed himself for not thinking how exposed they would be. "We can't run or hide, so let's do a reverse. Wave, hail them if they get close."

They all looked at him as if he were crazy. "Keep your weapons concealed. If things turn sour, we shoot. But first I'd like to get up into that magcar."

Howard said, "It'll all be in the timing. If we have to shoot, I'll take the one on the right. Terry, you get the left one. Irma, the third, wherever it'll be."

Irma followed the growing dot with her binocs and called, "Still coming, going left—ah!—they just turned toward us. We're spotted."

"Okay, now we look as though we want to be found," Cliff said.

"And keep our lasers out of sight," Howard added.

They spread out around the sailer as the dot grew rapidly. They started whooping and waving arms, dancing around. The magcar slowed, lowered until it was two meters off the ground. Three heads bobbed in the passenger area, and they still reminded Cliff of ostriches. As the magcar neared with a thin whining sound, he could see they wore harnesses that held odd-shaped tools. One was piloting, and all wore helmets.

The car stopped above the sailcraft, and he could hear a steady thrumming from it. He wondered how magnetic pressure could support such a mass so far from the conducting surface, which had to be meters below the soil. The Birds spoke to one another in high, chittering voices. Their heads jerked around, feathers danced in complex patterns. *Is that part of their speech?* The magcar rose to three meters.

This seemed ominous to Cliff. He backed away from the car and said to Irma, "If they produce weapons, we'd better shoot first."

"Yes," she said, "you call it."

He called to the others, "If I say 'start,' then shoot them."

Terry said, "I don't think that's necessary—"

"Let's *show* them we're peaceful," Howard said, spreading his arms with hands held open.

Seconds crawled by. Cliff's hand poised, tense, ready to go for his laser.

Two of the Birds stood up, and the magcar shifted a bit. It tracked a bit to the left, so the humans were bunched on one side now.

"Let's try harder," Aybe said, and called up to them, "We *are* peaceful." He spread his hands.

Terry echoed him, showing bare hands. "Speak mildly," he said. "Let them know—"

A net flew out of the magcar so fast, Cliff could not tell how it was flung. Quickly it wrapped across both Terry and Aybe—*sssssssp*. Somehow the net's perimeter slithered around them and jerked hard—*ssssip-klick*—closing them in.

There was a snaky, thick ropy line at its peak, leading back into the magcar. It snapped taut. The net swept them off their feet. The line began hoisting them up.

Cliff was so shocked, it took him several seconds to realize that he was supposed to be in charge. "I— *Start!*"

He looked up. Three laser shots hit the Birds. One was hit in the head. It toppled back. The other two shrieked and reached for something in their harnesses. Four shots threw them back and down, out of sight.

Cliff had fired one shot—and missed. He stuffed his laser away and sprang at the net. He snagged hands in the webbing and went up it fast. His boots hit Terry, who cried "Ow!" Cliff surged using Terry's back. He grabbed the line and hauled himself up. The Birds were milling around on the magcar floor, shrieking.

Over the lip of the magcar, tumbling, he fell on a Bird body. Feathers made it soft; then he struck the hard body beneath. He struggled up, breathing in the thick, sultry smell of the aliens.

The bodies were bleeding red. Two didn't move. One was twitching, but its eyes were closed. As he stood, he slipped on the blood, recovered, shook his head in the adrenaline haze—and looked down at a surprisingly simple control board.

Terry and Aybe were shouting, but he ignored them as he studied the board. To the right was what seemed to be a simple lever and release. Everything else looked like press plates and displays. The lever, then.

He tried it, and the line started to draw up into

a receiver with a rasping noise. Cliff reversed the lever, and the line played out. He tried the release, thumbed it hard looking over the side, and the net dumped the men.

"Ow!" Terry hit the ground with Aybe on top of him.

"Wow," Aybe said, standing up. They all gaped at one another, amazed at what they had done.

Irma said, "That was so fast. . . ."

"Good shooting!" Terry said.

Cliff called down, "Let's grab this. Shinny up here, bring all our gear."

Terry said, "Think it's safe?"

Cliff considered for several seconds. "I can't tell if they sent any alarm. Seems unlikely, though."

Aybe said, "I never thought we could—it was so fast!"

Irma said, "That magcar is better than this damn sailer. Let's go."

Terry started, "I wonder—"

"Think later," Cliff said. "Act now."

They all looked up at him from below, faces scared and joyous at the same time. Seconds passed. Then, as if some unspoken agreement had been reached, they scattered to their tasks.

Howard came climbing up, and the two of them inspected the bodies. Their lasers had punched holes in vital organs, bringing shock, and then the aliens had bled out. Together they tried to detect signs of life. No pulse, and certainly there would have to be a heart. No reactions, no breathing, eyes blank and staring.

"Turd-ugly, aren't they?" Terry said, and kicked a body. "Solid, too."

There were many facets of these aliens Cliff wanted to explore, but there wasn't time. They got the harnesses off the bulky bodies before he and Howard pitched two Birds overboard. Cliff kept the one less damaged. Aybe started to argue with him and then shrugged.

By this time the rest were passing up gear. Howard said, "If they did set off some alarm, we'd better get away."

Everybody agreed, and voted Aybe into the pilot's chair, since he had flying experience. The chair was too big for humans, but the seat wrapped anyone who sat in it with a gauzy strap restrainer, and Aybe managed to settle into it. He set to work systematically learning the control panel.

Cliff climbed down to check the bodies he had tossed out. Autopsies are best done fresh, and he learned a good deal in half an hour of cutting. Aybe shouted, "Hey, look!" and made the magcar perform some maneuvers. To their applause he announced in a stentorian voice, "Flight is leaving, folks."

They all laughed hard, letting the tensions out.

He helped Irma carry some gear from the sailer. She whispered, "Great attack! I knew you could do it."

"Well, that makes one of us."

THIRTY-ONE

The hell of it was, Redwing thought, that *Sun-Seeker*'s magscoop seemed to act better as a brake than as an accelerator.

The deck veered and flexed under his feet, seams groaned, a low rumble echoed. The magscoop expanded, breathing like a lung, and *SunSeeker* slowed. Contract, and the ship accelerated.

Redwing hated the rumbles and surges, maybe because they echoed his own anxieties. To maintain flight control and keep their magnetic fields up and running, *SunSeeker* had to feed its engines with plasma. But the plasma density here was low and the ship had to keep flexing its magnetic screens to stay in burn equilibrium. So the whole ship followed a troubled orbit, skimming along above the Bowl and trying to pick up weak signals from their teams.

"Jam, can't we smooth this out?" he asked.

The slender man stared intently at the control boards and just shook his head. "I am trying, sir. Ayaan's array is slewing as we change velocity."

Ayaan herself called from a nearby control pod, "I can't get coherence! My antennas cannot focus."

Redwing felt frustrated, out of his depth technically. A ramscoop of *SunSeeker* class was an intricate self-regulating system, and no one could master even a fraction of its labyrinthian technology. It was not so much a ship as a self-tech entity, with artificial intelligences embedded in every subsystem. It behaved less as a ship than as an electromagnetically structured metallic can run by a dispersed mind, itself electromagnetic.

Beside it, an ancient automobile was an idiot savant, working because analog feedbacks and what the techs called "self-regulating networks" operated well enough, arrived at by incessant trials and some considerable deaths. Autos arose through a form of driven evolution. *SunSeeker* came from a two-century-long evolution of directed intelligences, none individually of great capability. Indeed, the subminds embedded in *SunSeeker* were no better than ordinary human intelligence, and some much lesser. But the sum of these subminds, as with whole human cultures, was greater than linear. Modern human civilization was surely of lesser station than its greatest intelligences, such as Gödel and Heinschlicht. So was *SunSeeker* an anthology of self-critical and disciplined minds. Each mind lived its life with a reward system and constraints, dwelling in a community of diverse talents. All that properly propelled *SunSeeker* into a social intelligence, one that ran beyond what the ship could entirely comprehend. In this it was much like human societies. While it nominally served Earthly society, the ship also had evolved over the centuries of its flight into its own, original society. Smart networks had to.

It could innovate, too.

"Cap'n! Our subsystems found a way to amp the coherence," Ayaan called out. "I've never seen it do that before."

Redwing walked behind her acceleration couch and watched the screens display a dazzling graphic. It showed linked armories of smart systems, adjusting in milliseconds to the fits and snarls of *SunSeeker*'s trajectory. The hundreds of elements in Ayaan's array glided to compensate, like a retina that caressed the light falling on it.

The signal grid shifted, its colors cohering. Suddenly, a strong pulse came through. "It's from Aybe's phone," Ayaan said, excited.

"Send Beth's bio data as soon as you can."

"Got it inserted already, right behind the carrier signature," Ayaan said crisply.

"What's their situation?"

"Here's their text."

GOT FREE OF ALIENS.

MAKING OUR WAY ACROSS THICKLY WOODED

TERRAIN. HEADED OUT OF DESERT ZONE.

"That's it?"

"I had to synthesize their signal three times to get even that."

"Can't they send up some detail?"

"I'll ask them to use store and transmit. That lets them set the phone so when it acquires us, it sends a squirt at optimal rates."

"No audio?"

"Too noisy for that. I squeezed this out of repeated text messages. Lucky it got through, considering."

"Considering what?"

"How weak their signal is, how fast we're moving, the whole problem of using a dispersed antenna—"

"I get it," Redwing said. "Outstanding work, Lieutenant."

She smiled and added, "I'll send what text I get to your address."

"I wish we had more people to analyze this," Redwing said suddenly, feeling his isolation.

Again, Ayaan smiled kindly. "Our experts are on the ground, gathering information."

He nodded, then lifted his head a bit. He shouldn't let the crew see his uncertainty. An old rule: If people can see up your nostrils, you're keeping your chin at the appropriate alpha angle.

"Has Aybe got the food stuff?"

"Just did. Sent back an acknowledgment—whoops, there goes the connection. Damn."

Redwing paced and turned back to her. "Y'know, just before they went down, Cliff was afraid they wouldn't be able to digest any of the food down there. Kind of funny. Now we're sending him menus."

Ayaan chuckled. "It's a major discovery, I should think."

"Really? Still seems like common sense to me. Food is food."

"Most biochemists think it was a historical accident that all our sugars are right-handed, while our amino acids are left-handed. It could easily have been the other way round."

Redwing blinked. He kept forgetting that crew

were multiskilled, so the loss of one specialist couldn't crimp them a lot.

"Well, turns out otherwise," he said. "Beth's team said they had some dysentery at first, but some of their med supplies put them right. Prob'ly Cliff's did, too."

"Beth's text messages said she got most of her lore from the aliens."

Redwing nodded once more. "They knew the poisons, and maybe those are pretty near universal? Interesting idea."

Ayaan was observing him closely, he noted. "Sir, I understood Cliff's point, and indeed, I agreed with it. Particularly his suggestion that they do thorough sampling of the alien air, to see if it would be dangerous to us."

"Which they did. And it wasn't."

"Beth reported some flulike symptoms, dysentery, too—but, yes, nothing fatal."

"They caught a break, maybe."

She shook her head. "What interests me is that these ideas of Cliff's, and mine, they were quite plausible. Yet you ignored them."

"Not exactly. I said be careful but keep going. We had to go down there, had to take our chances."

"Yes, and that is what I find admirable. You made the decision, despite our worries."

He wondered briefly if she was just sucking up to him. But no—she wasn't that kind of woman, a brownnose climber. "That's my job."

She beamed. "And I am glad it is not mine."

"You're going to have to make decisions, too, as

this whole thing plays out. Here's a tip: The biggest mistake is being too afraid of making one."

They both laughed together and it felt good.

• • •

That evening he lay in his bunk thinking about the day and what Ayaan had said.

All the media back Earthside had played the whole ocean/space analogy to the hilt, making Redwing's job sound like that of Captain Cook or Magellan. But those sailors had plenty of experience, had worked their way up the naval ladder by sailing to nearby ports, learning command, getting navigation right, and gradually making longer voyages. The first generation starship commanders had to make a huge leap, from piloting craft around the solar system, then the Kuiper belt and fringes of the Oort cloud, then to interstellar distances. That was a giant jump of 100,000—like sailing around the world after a trial jaunt of about three football fields.

He had piloted a ramscoop on one of the first runs into the Oort cloud, and done well. But in all the trials, *SunSeeker* hadn't topped a tenth of light speed more than once, and they had run at that for only a week. Five ships had gone out before *SunSeeker*. In the first decade, none reported ramscoop troubles like theirs.

They were sailing uncharted waters here, Redwing thought, to use a nautical phrase. Magellan, he now recalled, had gone ashore and gotten tangled up in conflicts in the Philippine Islands, and died in a battle he chose to start. He had been convinced that the angel of the Virgin Mary was on his side, so he couldn't lose, even though he was outnumbered by a thousand to thirty. Later generations named a small galaxy after him, but he had made plenty of dumb decisions, especially that fatal one, out of emotion.

So maybe analogies could be useful, after all.

PART VI

*Action speaks louder than words
but not nearly as often.*
—MARK TWAIN

THIRTY-TWO

Even Tananareve was keeping up, moving steadily with grim, sweaty determination, but Mayra wasn't. She hadn't been making good time since their last sleep. Her forehead wrinkled with grave, deep lines and her lips moved in an interior dialogue. Beth could feel what it was doing to her, the loss of her husband eating into her morale.

That was how she had to think of it, Beth realized. Morale. Keep the unit together and deal with what happened. Leadership, they had called it in crew training. Every crew member had to be able to assume leadership if the circumstances demanded it. Which meant if the actual leader got killed or disabled or broke down in the face of things nobody had imagined before. Leadership.

She slowed her own pace, then watched as Lau Pin burrowed into the thick, leafy undergrowth and was gone in seconds.

Beth bit her lip. She would not yell after him. They were fugitives, best to stay quiet. She followed the torn foliage, thinking how easily a Serf-One tracker could do the same, or just follow his nose. The smell of smashed vegetation was rank.

But Mayra wailed and threw herself down among the springy leaves.

Beth glanced after Lau Pin, then touched her shoulder. "Mayra—"

"He's *dead,* and what's it for? We're just *running*. We're all dying of bone loss anyway in this low g!" She spat the words out, pressure released.

"Oh, Mayra, I'm so sorry." Best to just let this run for the moment, get the words out and be done with it. The emotion was the point here, not the health issue. There was plenty of experience in low gravs, and this region seemed to be about 0.3 g. Maybe not too bad—if they didn't spend months in it.

"And, and—where are we *going* that it was worth so much?"

Beth said softly, "We had to get out. We all agreed. He was a fine man, and he dealt with that spidow brilliantly. Bravely." Beth patted her arm, feeling useless in the face of such sorrow.

Mayra nodded, tears running down her face unnoticed. "He was just so, so—"

"I know." That was all there was to say, really. Sympathy seemed useless, but it was essential all the same. If the bereaved felt isolated, they got even worse. "I'm so sorry."

In a flash, she recalled her own feelings, looking at Abduss. A thick smell rose up from the body like fumes, stinging the nose. The spidow had flattened Abduss, and the bladder and bowels had let go. Already blood had crusted into reddish brown rivers and the face was squashed beyond even parody of the man who had once enjoyed sharp, symmetric features.

She had worked up spit and swallowed, taking deep breaths, and managed not to vomit. Then she walked away, expelling her lungs and getting rid of the dregs of the smell. Every encounter with death stayed with her, but this one would go to the head of the line.

Even the memory made Beth wonder if Cliff had survived in this strange place. She made herself stop thinking about it and sat beside Mayra, putting an arm around the woman who was sobbing softly.

Fred spoke, slow and even. "So am I, Mayra." A pause. His head jerked toward the horizon. "Either way we decide to go, we should stick to the ridge."

This startled Beth; Fred could go for a day without talking. The other women blinked, glanced at one another, and decided to let the moment move on. They tended to look around when Fred spoke. He did it so seldom, so gravely.

Lau Pin was back in time to catch it. "Fred? We can't. It'll make us conspicuous."

"Not *on* the ridge," Fred said witheringly. "Keep it in reach. It orients us. Look—" His hands sketched a tented line. "When they brought us here, do you remember passing that line of bubble buildings? Then the ridge just went on, dead straight for thirty or forty klicks, under the wall and into the Garden. Under the dirt and rock, it's a, a structural member, don't you see it? How shallow the dirt is? If you're building here, you anchor the important stuff to the load-bearing . . ." He trailed off, hands waving.

Beth was nodding, hoping this would move them away from Mayra's grief. There was no solution for that but time. "Along the ridge, right. Stay off to one side and don't go near the spidows. Keep close watch, and we can see the spidow corridors."

Fred nodded, too, so she went on. "We already know some of what we can eat. Cook it with the guns so they can't follow the smoke. There's no dry wood here, so it'll smoke for sure. Folks, we need to think about not getting caught. No more ripping through undergrowth. We move along the tops of the trees. Tricky, but we can do it."

Lau Pin frowned. "Dangerous, and that'll slow us down."

"Safer, though," Mayra said, coming out of her mood. "How much spidow rope have we got? Lau Pin—?"

"I took Abduss's share of the rope," Lau Pin said, pointing to the loops of it around his waist. Beth realized that the way to keep Mayra involved was to present decisions to be made. Draw her into the group.

Tananareve said adamantly, "I think Beth's right. And it's only for a short distance. So, which way, Fred?"

Lau Pin said, "That was a spaceport, that line of bubbles. I never saw them clearly, I was too dizzy. But, but it has to be a spaceport, doesn't it? And warehouses and so forth."

"Could be," Mayra said, blinking some more and

visibly bracing herself, getting back into emotional stability. "But that's just where they'll look for us."

"Yeah. Yeah," said Fred. "But if we follow the ridge the other way, we'll find something important."

Tananareve asked, "Like what?"

"Say, something that wants a solid anchor."

"Okay. Which way is the ridge?"

They looked at one another. Beth took a big breath, thinking, and said, "We need to climb."

• • •

From the top of a braid tree the ridge was obvious, a couple of kilometers away. They were on its long, gentle flank. Moving along in the treetops was more like swimming than climbing. The low grav helped a lot, giving their movements a slow-motion grace as they swung among the long, rubbery limbs of the tall trees.

Beth could see immense distances: the landscape was concave, unlike Earth's. Distant things rose up and got noticed. The ridge was conspicuous, a bony scrabble of boulders at the crest, four or five kilometers away. Beyond was a frenetic sky, the bright pink sun, and the glaring, restless white flare. The Jet cooled into rolling reds and strands of amber as it neared the Bowl. She watched a filament weave around another, each making a helical dance, like snakes dancing to slow music.

They stopped short of the ridge to talk it through. "Spaceport," Beth said. "We need to find a way back to gravity. How's our dead reckoning working today? Fred, which way is that row of bubbles?"

Fred's eyes danced anxiously and he nodded toward his left.

"Should be that way. Left," Lau Pin gestured.

Tananareve used her binocs and said, "Folks, can't you see it? Like a black froth, that way. Left, like you said, Lau Pin."

"You've got good eyes. Anything to the right?"

They looked. The ridge dwindled, dwindled . . . nothing, nothing . . .

"Spaceport," Beth commanded, keeping her voice firm. "I wish I knew how to be less conspicuous. We're not hidden." She ducked suddenly. A big black bird with bright yellow canard fins just back of its head cruised above them, inspecting, unafraid. It swooped and dived away, honking.

"Ah, lunch," Fred said.

Lau Pin laughed. "Those will help. The Astronomers won't find us by our heat signature, not while the sky is full of big birds. If we can catch a few for dinner, we might use their feathers for camouflage."

• • •

Marching away from the spaceport, they would have left behind them vehicles that could take them back to gravity. Lau Pin was right: the spaceport was their obvious target.

Too obvious.

Canard bird flesh tasted like meat-eater, dark and rangy, a little like lion, Beth thought. She'd eaten lion at a theme restaurant, centuries ago now. She pushed away the thought that of all those she had ever known—parents, friends, lovers—only the *SunSeeker* crew were still alive.

She smacked her lips and focused on the meat. They conscientiously ate all of any game they got—fat, gristle, crack the bones and suck out the marrow. You never knew where your next meal was coming from here. They'd caught only four of the turkey-sized black canard birds before the rest caught on. Now they had to dip down into the forest to get anything to eat. Water they found pooled in leaves. Shooting from the trees was easy, though; the midsized animals didn't seem to regard the sky as a threat, and just ambled along.

They'd used the black feathers to decorate themselves, smiling as if at a masquerade. Now they crossed the forest tops in low leaps, like flying squirrels. They'd tied spidow line in loops, to catch themselves in case of a fall. All their Earthside training in fieldwork paid off.

Snaps, pops. Branches thrashed without a wind, off to the left. Lau Pin halted, motioned them back. Fred reached, not for a weapon but for his camera phone. They watched for long seconds. Then Tananareve aimed a low-level laser into the rustling branches.

Branches fell, thrashing loudly on the long way down. Branches? "Tree octopus," Lau Pin said. "I swear, that's what it looks like."

"Couple of snakes, mating," said Mayra.

Beth said, "Seems more like a bunch."

Fred was replaying video in slow motion. "Snakes with two or three tails," he said. "Very strange." He showed them the phone. "See? Tails with . . . might be fingernails, or rattlesnake rattles. Look, they caught some lower branches."

They all paused to listen and heard rustlings below. Lau Pin suggested, "Go down for a better look?"

Fred began working his way down, without waiting. Beth called, "Fred! We need to keep moving."

"I see something."

"They could be venomous!"

Fred didn't answer. Mayra videotaped him until he was out of sight.

And here he came back moments later, waving something the size of a pillow, the shape of a sausage. "They dropped it," he said as he reached them. "Look, it's about as wide as they were, thirty centimeters around, snake-shaped. It's got straps. And—"

"Don't tear it!" Lau Pin said.

Rip. "Velcro."

Beth reached in, stirred the contents. A haunch of red meat wrapped in cloth. A knife with a peculiar handle. Tool with a button: Flashlight? Communicator? Both? Dared they try it?

"Folks, we have to keep moving," Tananareve said presently. Beth agreed. They resumed their flight, with the sausage pack tied at Fred's hip.

"What if we have to leave the forest?" Lau Pin wondered. They rested on the broad leaves that were the size of the main deck on *SunSeeker.*

Beth didn't have an answer. Outside the forest, they would find a vertical landscape. There might be nothing to grab on to. But the greenery seemed to run as far as that row of dots, which was beginning to look like hemispheres of varied size and color. They had decided to move toward large buildings in the distance.

Braid trees became scarce. Vegetation hugged low to the ground. The big canard birds were avoiding them now. *That last meal might have cost us,* Beth thought. Her stomach rumbled.

They prowled through the low scrub bushes and used their binocs. At any movement they froze. Astronomer-sized Bird Folk were wandering among the buildings. And canard birds wheeled over the trees near the bubbles, cawing and diving.

Their approach was slow, methodical. No shadows for cover, and the sky seemed hotter here. The first dome was a sphere as big as a ten-story building, standing up from the jungle on a single leg. Reeds and ferns surrounded it, of types the Bird Folk had used for food.

Beth carefully watched the distant figures as they moved at their bobbing pace, their long necks weaving back and forth to keep their heads stationary as their long legs stroked forward with lazy grace.

Walking out from the spaceport, Astronomers would reach this structure last, she saw. It would be the culmination of their path, a final lesson, with a vast garden of delights beyond.

They crept forward warily. The air was fragrant and lush, and Beth listened for suspicious sounds, but there were none.

So what was this bubble? She studied the designs on its outside. Brown abstracts, some with white traces, and each shape surrounded by a dark blue. Almost like—

"It's a globe," Tananareve said in her ear. "A globe map."

"Damn, you're right! This garden, it's some sort of . . . gallery of planets?" She peered at the more distant globes—and, yes, they had the same color patterns, continents swimming in seas. But the spheres were comparatively tiny, not all the same size but no bigger than train cars or even the largest Bird Folk.

Tananareve asked, "So this one—their home planet maybe?"

"Or one they passed by, explored."

"They're headed the same way we are, so maybe it's Glory? At this range, their telescopes could pick out continent-sized features. And look, there's another big one at the far end of the chain."

Beth saw it: barely more than a dot. "One is their home world, and the other's maybe their ultimate target—yes, it could be. You'd think the home world would be treated specially." The Astronomers might actually know the shapes of Glory's continents, or this could be some planet they just mapped with big lenses as they passed by its system. If a world wasn't interesting, they might not land on it at all.

Lau Pin whispered, "What's up?" so they shared the idea. Beth stared at the nearer sphere, then began circling anticlockwise. The rest came with her, moving in irregular jumps, staying hidden.

It mapped a planet, all right. There were no ice caps; where were the poles? The thing wasn't rotating fast enough to tell. It might not be rotating at all, though it stood on a single axial pole. Oceans were a mottled blue; land was red and brown. The land masses were all clumped, and white streaks showed chains of snowcapped mountains. It was somewhat stylized, the continent and islands colored more like gems than landscapes, and the blue oceans—three-fourths of the globe's surface—were translucent, the deep sea floors showing through, subduction zones and midocean ridges clearly defined. Look hard enough, and you saw shadows moving in there. Life-forms the size of mountains? By now they knew that it was indeed rotating, but very slowly.

Tananareve whispered, "Somebody coming."

Fred sprang up on a strut and surveyed. "Yep." A handful of bird shapes were moving toward them. Lau Pin said, "We need to hide."

Fred jerked his head again—"Inside."

"The only way in is that post holding up the sphere," Lau Pin said. He loped away.

Beth said uneasily, "I saw motion in there. We don't want to have to fight anyone."

"I looked," Mayra said. "Holograms. Something's making pictures."

"Audience?"

"Nothing I could see."

Lau Pin waved an arm, and they followed silently, swiftly.

The spindly metal pillar that held the ten-story globe would have collapsed in normal gravity. The interior was a spiral stair, steps narrow near the axis, several feet wide near the walls. Lots of room. Accommodation for various species, maybe not just Bird Folk.

They were hidden as soon as they entered the giant stairwell. Tananareve suggested staying in the stairwell, but even she wasn't pushing it. Wonders waited above.

They entered armed, as best they could.

The inside was even roomier, with a ceiling ten meters high above a single gigantic space. It looked like a museum: items standing free or floating on thin wires Beth couldn't quite see, all squashed into whatever space would fit. A vast ceramic green ramp ran round the spherical wall.

"Watch for anything moving," Lau Pin said. "Fred, Mayra, Tananareve, you in the middle. I'll take point. Beth?"

"Rear guard."

Here on the floor was a shifting mound, almost flat but with ridges and pools. Patches of ocher and pale green writhed and then spread out. After a minute, it repeated. It made no sense at all until Tananareve said, "Continental drift."

Beth said, "We still don't know—"

"Which planet. True."

They walked among what must be model space-ships, and with a flicker were suddenly in a three-dimensional movie. As they crossed some unseen threshold, it rose abruptly all around them, a starscape riddled with swarming dark dots.

Beth stepped back quickly. The dots vanished. That much furious motion, anything could be hidden . . . but there wasn't anything alive here except her own people, visible as long as she wasn't in the hologram. They had spread out a little, looking for enemies—barring Fred, who stood stock-still, caught by the dancing dots.

She stepped back in. Chaos danced in flickering light around her. Anything could sneak up on them under these conditions, but she couldn't look away. Fred sighed beside her, mesmerized.

THIRTY-FOUR

The sensaround opened in deep space.

A tiny knot of yellow white sat at the exact center of the display. The field of view was a hemisphere so big, she could not grasp it without turning her head. Stars sprinkled the sky, but she could recognize no constellations.

Slowly the point of view rotated. Maybe that was the nearest star? But, no—a ruddy yellow disk swam into view at her far left. The disk fumed with small storms, and she could see magnetic arches soaring above the brimming bright churn. Clearly this star was smaller and redder than Sol and pocked with dense black spots. The vision slid farther, the star moved right, and tiny ships came in view. They had blue bubbles midship, probably fuel blisters. They tugged huge hexagonal containers, hundreds of ships all heading toward . . .

A vast pale crescent swam into view. She watched the framework of long, spiky girders that curved around complex guts. Between these were long loops like wedding bands, glowing. The thing was so large, it cast deep shadows over a bee swarm of ships, all tending to the large structure like worker insects.

Farther away orbited tumbling rocks, mostly tinged with white. Flames shot along their faces, and fumes billowed out in spheres. Those must be immense smelting systems laboring in the high vacuum. Big clouds of white and amber gas rose from them, expanding until they dimmed to transparency and faded. The view crossed a smaller star, glare white, brighter than the rest of the sky.

Still smaller ships flitted among the mining operations. Some hauled massive girders through cylindrical arrays. Out the far end emerged long struts with a glaze on them, shimmering in the orange red starlight. Some kind of hardening process?

Dirty gray blobs hovered in the distance. Beth realized these were iceteroids, like those humanity exploited in the Oort cloud of Earth—condensed out when the sun was born, rich in volatiles. Beside them flitting ships shepherded enormous orange balloons. These filled with gas that was born in the tiny orange fires at their base. Mass and elements for the construction, she guessed.

Then the milling swarm of mote-sized ships became a blur. Time speeded up. The huge thing they were building took shape. Girders aligned and layered. Scaffolds unfolded and crossbars buttressed those. Joists and brackets the size of planets formed in the haze of buzzing motion. An enormous geometry emerged. It was the Bowl.

Flitting shapes, too small to see clearly, wove a tapestry of black lace around the budding hemisphere. This array glowed suddenly, a flash of white light. Gas blew away from the structure like a fading fog.

This is a history lesson, Beth thought. *The natives here must want to keep aware of how they came to be . . . and so leave places like this so the message is not lost, a tradition sent down through deep time.*

The camera eye view closed in. Beth could see intricate maneuvers of silvery ships as they worked their way across the surface of the Bowl in the making. They laid down layers and pillars that lapped around the hemisphere, and the camera eye followed them, sliding over the lip of the Bowl into . . . a thick flock of ships, all ferrying volatile bags, the orange balloons she had seen before. Flashes like lightning arced through the bags of gas. Above the bottom of the Bowl, these came free. They slipped through holes in a nearly invisible upper layer, gliding downward toward the floor of the Bowl.

The field of view closed in on the shimmering layer.

It was the atmosphere's boundary shield. This billowed out as it held in the pressure of gases emptying forth. On the Bowl floor, gushing geysers spouted thick ivory clouds. Other ships skimmed along the ribbed understory of the floor, spewing masses of brown and black—the topsoil, falling into place.

This was an Origin Story. Somewhere, the small red sun had spawned the creatures who built the Bowl. Why didn't it open on a planet where the builders began? There were none in the black sky. If the red star had planets, they were small. So maybe the creatures' world was far away, orbiting the first bright spot she had seen. Maybe the builders came from near a distant companion of this small sun.

Now the measureless basin turned. The bee swarm of working ships was an earnestly working fog as they spun up this world in the making. The soil settled and blue haze spread throughout the skin of atmosphere. Darting flashes lit the troubled high clouds. Monsoons swept the ragged continents, and seas sloshed.

The system evolved. Storms lashed immense, windswept lands. A joist on the backside popped free and the bee swarm surrounded it as gouts of dirt and gas became a volcano into a vacuum. Patched, the system ground on, spinning up. The shimmering sheet holding in the atmosphere flexed and rippled as angular momentum warped it.

Time ran faster. She was not sure how she knew this, but surely it would have taken a very long time to form a working biosphere. Yet now she saw the air clear and gray clouds form in high stacks like pancakes. Green lands spread like a bacterium overwhelming a curved petri dish.

Beth could see the Knothole now through the clearing atmosphere. In an arc around it, mirrors blossomed in lines, like yarn wrapping around the floor of the Bowl. The dark patch of the Knothole bristled with large gray shapes that she supposed must be large magnet cores being built. Slowly the center resolved and she could see stars winking in it.

The winding up of the mirror fields slowed as the last strands of it popped into being. Now the mirror fields jittered and flashed as they came alive. Her view tilted and swam toward the edge of the Bowl, where knuckles of burnished metal grew. Quickly the mirror field gained a slick metallic sheen. Fitful sprays of blazing colors worked in it.

The mirror fields showed sparkling oranges and reds. They threw images of the small star into view, flickering and finding their patterns, settling in. Abruptly a thin line of boiling plasma arced in and played in the spaces above the Bowl. The plume steadied, stuttered—and lanced through the Knothole.

Thin at first, the luminous Jet thickened. Snarls worked along it. Dark spots. A filament broke free and lashed across the envelope that held in the atmosphere. The Jet snapped off. But the damage was done: the atmosphere's skin darkened and massive plumes of air shot out. A blur of worker ships stopped that.

The view turned toward the reddish star. Its corona boiled with hoops of magnetic force, making giant high bridges around a white-hot point. That was the mirror focus spot, and more ships tended to it with anxious energy.

With a jerk the Jet lanced out again. It speared exactly through the Knothole. The repaired skin of the atmosphere reflected a pale image of the Jet.

Now this Bowl of the past resembled the vibrantly alive presence of today. The point of view backed away from it, and the constantly flickering swarm of worker ships faded.

Imperceptibly, the system of star, Jet, and Bowl began to move. It swam across the blackness, the Jet's raging brilliance drowning out the icy stars. The vast contrivance glided with aching slowness away from the distant yellow white star.

Leaving the system, she guessed. It could not make a pass near that star without risking disruption of whatever planets might orbit there. The Bowl became a vessel bound for the distant pale lights, the firmament of beckoning stars.

Only the starscape remained.

Lau Pin, Fred, Tananareve, and Mayra looked around themselves. It was, Beth thought, a little like being on LSD. A trip into a distant, wondrous time.

In the dark she could see through the globe's smoky glass. Gigantic Bird Folk were walking underneath.

Fred said, "I think I see."

Mayra said, "We all saw, Fred."

Tananareve said, "I think I see why primitives died out when they ran across advanced civilizations."

Lau Pin said, "It strikes me that if there's only one way into here, there's only one way out."

Beth: "We can't leave now. We're surrounded."

Lau Pin: "If any of them come in—"

Mayra: "We're dead. Let's keep looking. All the secrets are here. By the way, Beth, this has to be the map of the origin world."

"Oh . . . almost."

• • •

Over the next hour, two dozen Bird Folk passed them by. The human folk spent their time examining hundreds of spacegoing tools. Most were too cryptic even to be described. Mayra took pictures.

They gathered at one point to share dried canard bird meat. It was all they had left, save for a bar of chocolate Tananareve shared out.

"I think the Bird Folk are gone," Beth said. "Do we feel lucky?"

"We feel hungry," Tananareve said. "Somewhere around us, there must be something to eat."

THIRTY-FIVE

Six little world-globes ran in a row, three or four meters in diameter, half a kilometer apart. Worlds— big enough to show as spheres—but not all Earth-like. One was featureless blue, bigger than the rest. One was stark ice white, cracked around the equator. None of them had windows or openings.

The final bubble, an hour away, was another

glassy sphere marked with land masses in a great blue sea. They moved carefully now, slipping from clumps of immense ferns to the shelter of occasional tree stands. Bird Folk of a variety Beth didn't recognize were streaming into a great arch. Beth's troupe moved carefully, but the Bird Folk were paying no attention at all. They murmured and whooped with odd, high singsongs.

Tananareve crept close against the glass, around the curve from the entrance. "Dancing," she said. "It's a dance hall."

Lau Pin was beside her now. He stared awhile, then said, "Mating ritual."

Beth said, "There's a difference?"

The chuckles that followed this weak joke told her how tense they were.

Beth was up against the glass now. Slow, thumping music with skittering undertones. A simple song, cascading chords ornamented by lots of percussion. Lurching bodies, heads turned upward to the ceiling.

With sun and flare behind her, she and Tananareve might look like ferns, if they held still. There were platforms throughout the interior, on narrow pedestals, some topped with . . . sofas . . . nests? Thousands of Bird Folk, including a few gigantic Astronomers, were paying no attention to anything but one another. Some were dancing, some fighting, some . . . head to tail . . . that must be mating. But the Astronomers weren't doing any of that. Were they there to supervise? Or as voyeurs?

"Nothing for us here," Mayra said primly.

"But, Mayra, it must be a map of Glory! It's the last globe in this park."

"Get some photos, then."

They did that, then went on.

The ridge continued toward the Bowl's inner well. Vegetation was sparse here, offering less cover. There was nothing to eat.

And the next dome was silver, as big as several football fields, with a tremendous square opening and tracks running into it. Floating railroad cars ran in and out. They were open cages, and inside—

"Live animals," Tananareve said.

"Plants, too. Warehouse," Lau Pin said. "Anyone hungry?"

They crept in, hidden by the shadows beneath a slow-moving car, and rolled away before the cars reached the unloading dock.

There were Bird Folk around, one of the big varieties. Some might be guards, but most were working, moving stuff on and off the cars. What went on the cars was recognizable: crates of melons and plants and creatures from the humans' garden-prison. What came off were ferns and reeds and grass, tons and tons of it. It must all be food for Bird Folk of various types, Beth thought.

She got the rest to hang back until they could see the patterns of movement. Once offloaded, the workers ignored the food. The humans waited, stomachs rumbling, and then approached a cage car. They kept to the shadows of squashes and melons as big as automobiles. They carved into the underside of one of these, juice gushing out, and began to feast.

Fred pointed to a grid on the wall, with a wind blowing into it. "We should be there," he said.

"Why?" Beth asked.

"We stink," Fred said.

They looked at one another . . . yeah. Nods. Bird Folk mostly had big nostrils. They would have a powerful sense of smell. Beth's team moved under the air conditioner, taking melons and fruit and a dead mammal with them. The wind there was refreshing.

• • •

They feasted, and slept, and feasted some more. "The easiest way to carry food is in us," Fred said, and was jeered for it, but they ate anyway.

"I think I see . . . ," Fred said.

Conversation had already stopped. Beth said, "What?"

"It's going to sound crazy."

Beth looked around her. "We're living like mice in a gigantic alien supermarket," she said, "inside a wok the size of the solar system. We're all lunatics here, Fred."

He said, "A lot of stars come in pairs. Maybe most of them."

Heads nodded.

"I think that sphere was a map of Earth. Earth before the continents split up."

Lau Pin asked, "Why would they build a globe of Earth?"

"They're dinosaurs."

Lau Pin laughed. "Yeah, right." The others were grinning.

"Some dinosaurs got smart. They developed space travel. They did some exploring. They visited Sol's companion star. Anyone ever wonder how the dinosaurs stayed warm enough? Sol used to be cooler, remember."

Lau Pin was still grinning. "Come *on*."

"Companion star," Tananareve said. "They stole it?"

"It was theirs. Earth was theirs, too. Left the solar system as it was, but maybe they took the planets around Wickramsingh's Star. Grist for the mill."

Beth noticed that Mayra had lost her smile, which meant she was thinking again of her lost husband. She put an arm around Mayra and listened as they talked Fred's crazy idea around.

She tried to think about it without a snicker. They'd watched the building of the Bowl. If you weren't here, on and in it, the Bowl itself would be . . . a laugh riot. Cupworld. The advanced version would have night and day, provided by orbiting tea bags. A spaceport in the handle. But Fred was so earnest.

Intelligent dinosaurs. Evolving into Bird Folk. Must have had feathers already. "It could fit," she said not quite seriously. "Dinosaurs think big."

Talk continued. It was good to distract them from their situation for at least a few moments. Beth began to think about how to get them moving. They weren't hungry and they weren't prisoners, but low gravity would still make them sick if they stayed here. Their bones would get brittle; neurological functions would steadily erode.

Lau Pin and Fred were watching the distant workers while they nibbled at a great wedge of green melon. Now Fred said, "Those are the same variety that were guarding us."

"Feeding us, too," Lau Pin said.

"No. A little different. That star pattern on their flanks, see? They're not moving stuff, they're just . . . meandering?"

"Hunting us."

"Yeah." Fred swept his arm across an arc. "They're moving in a wave. We stay here, they'll have us."

"They're not very good at searching or we'd be caught by now."

"Probably out of practice," Beth said, and peered at Fred. "Have you got some idea? Because I don't see any way past them."

"Hide in a melon," Mayra suggested. "Or two or three. Wait while they go around us."

"I want a better look at that air outlet," Fred said.

They brought ferns with them, for cover. They lay beneath the grille in a howling wind, examining the grille and watching the searchers. The Bird Cops weren't all that big . . . bigger than humans, though. Earthy smells brushed past them: manure, crushed grass, big animals.

"There's plenty of room for big birdy engineers to work in there. We can get around the fans," Lau

Pin said. "Carefully. We don't want to turn them off. The cops would notice."

They took as much food with them as they could carry. They didn't have any way to preserve it. Outside, maybe they could make a fire and smoke the animal they'd butchered. Then on to the spaceport ledge and try to find a ride. Or die trying.

PART VII

*You can't depend on your eyes when
your imagination is out of focus.*
—MARK TWAIN

THIRTY-SIX

"Slow down!" Cliff called out.

His stomach wobbled and lurched as the magnetics torqued them. The motors surged, growled,
hummed. He held on as Aybe wrenched the magcar
around, spinning it hard, testing its abilities. Up,
down, around—surges faster than some damned
amusement park twister, and not amusing.

Terry stood up to restrain Aybe, and a swerve
sent him halfway over the side. Irma grabbed his
arm and hauled him back in. "Damn it, stop!" she
shouted.

Aybe brought the craft out of its spinning mode
and the motors beneath their feet eased. "We gotta
know what this baby can do!" Aybe laughed with
glee. He took the magcar up and it slowed, stopped.

"Careful," Howard said. Terry and Irma did not
look pleased.

Aybe's engineer eyes widened as he took the craft
up. He pushed a simple control yoke forward to the
max, and the magcar slowed against gravity, then
stopped. "Looks like we can't go above six meters."
He moved it forward, and the speed crept up.

"Let's get the hell out of here," Terry said. Cliff nodded.

Aybe took them down to near the ground and then away in a fast horizontal path. Cliff looked back at the bloody sprawl of bodies. Leaving these aliens was a dividing point, he felt. Once this incident became known, from here on the natives would probably give no quarter.

Aybe experimented with altitude and speed, getting the feel of the magcar. They got ten kilometers away before they found a narrow gulch that concealed them among billowy trees, swaying in a steady, strangely musky wind.

The others went through the dead aliens' gear while Cliff stood watch. He scanned the sky for pursuit. Nearby, undisturbed by the magcar passage, birds in flight broke from their immense, triple-decked formation. They curled in banks, forming a sphere, cawing and yawing in squawking concert. The sound was a rolling *skkkaaaaa!* and distracted him so he did not see coming from above the cause of it all. A huge slender shape shot down from a cloud and dived into the bird ball. Its jaws opened and scooped up several birds at once. He lost it in the thickness of the swarming birds. It poked out the far side an instant later, jaws closed now and turning away. Like a shark, he thought. A sky shark.

Irma sat beside Cliff and asked Aybe, "This wind is too much. Can't we shield it?"

"Yeah," Aybe said brightly, always happy to greet a new problem. "There must be . . ."

After a few minutes of his trying the oddly shaped controls, a narrow pole abruptly poked up from the magcar center, where the engine housing bulged, humming as Aybe drove them forward. It rose to three meters' height, and suddenly the wind pressure and sound eased away. They were all impressed. Aybe figured it was some field effect, and when Howard poked a finger over the car lip he got a shock. "Defensive, too," Howard said, nursing the finger.

Irma said, "We should decide where we're going."

"Shelter, I guess," Terry said.

"We have to think long term," Irma said. "What's our goal?"

Howard said, "Learn and stay free."

Aybe shrugged. "Learn what? How to find Beth's group? Or get back to *SunSeeker*? Or—what?"

Irma looked around at them. "Once I was supposed to meet a friend in Old New York. The whole comm grid was down, so I couldn't reach her—and she was a Primitivist anyway, so usually didn't carry tech or have any embedded. So how was I to find her?"

"Go to obvious places," Howard said.

Irma brightened. "Exactly!"

Howard nodded. "So you went to the Empire State Building museum, and there she was."

"No, Times Square, but—yes. Let's do the same."

"So what's obvious here?" Aybe barked as he steered, never taking his narrowed eyes from the landscape.

Everyone thought, looking at the alien landscape whipping by. They were going up a slight slope, and low hills framed the steel blue horizon. Green and brown vegetation clumped at the bases of hills and in the erosion gullies where Cliff knew predators would be waiting.

Terry said, "The Jet. It's the engine moving this system, and it passes closest to the Bowl at that opening, the Knothole."

"Ah!" Irma nodded. "So maybe whoever runs this place lives near there?"

Shrugs answered. "Seems dangerous," Howard said. "If that Jet breaks free—and why *is* it so straight?—I wouldn't want to be near it."

"Okay, but look." Irma called up on her phone a picture taken from *SunSeeker*. The big band of mirror territory gave way near the Knothole to a green zone. In a close-up view they could see complicated constructions nearer still to the Knothole. "Somewhere in there."

Aybe shook his head. "That's maybe a million klicks from us!"

"I'm not saying we fly there in this little car," Irma said. "But look, we're living in a *building*. There must be some big, long-distance transport around this place."

"Where would it be?" Cliff said, face blank. He had no idea, but ideas came out in talk like this and Irma was right to kick it off.

"Something obvious," Howard said. "This place is so big, there's got to be some structure that contains transport. To be large range, it's got to be large. Irma's right, it's a *building*."

"Okay, let's look for structures." Irma held up more views from *SunSeeker*.

Looking at them, the angled views of the Bowl, Cliff recalled what was now a distant life. He had lived for only weeks after revival on *SunSeeker* and now—he checked his inboard timer—months here, on the run. Somewhere up there, *SunSeeker* soared serene and secure. *If we could get more than spotty contact . . .*

All this experience was new, while decades of growing up and getting educated in California were the true frame of his life. Yet that world was gone forever from him. In a moment, the entire prospect of his life—finding Beth, setting sail to Glory on *SunSeeker* to explore a world and make a whole new life for humanity—all collapsed around him. *Beth. God, I miss her.*

All his past life was a dream, one that had to be tossed aside now for a frank reality on an enormous construct. He sat, speechless.

"What's that grid?" Terry pointed at Irma's small flat display.

Cliff looked, trying to yank himself out of his reverie. Redwing had talked of "morale problems," but this was more like a moral problem. What did any of their grand plans matter, against this brute reality?

Irma was responding to Terry by refitting her map with keystrokes and voice commands, using elevations gotten from *SunSeeker*. As *SunSeeker* approached the Bowl, they had made a clear mapping of the near-hemispherical crisscross weave on the Bowl's outer skin. Those features stood out, a knitted basket that supported the enormous centrifugal forces caused by the Bowl's spin. A miracle of mechanical engineering carried out on the scale of a solar system.

She flipped the display over to view the living zone of the Bowl's interior. These maps were much more complicated, since huge continents, seas, and deserts overlaid everything. But clearly, as Irma worked the analysis, a cross-mapping of the outer grids had their parallels on the inward face.

"Ridgelines, that's it," she said. "There's a consistent matching of the support structures. The Bowl's ribs are big curved tubes. We find them on both sides—the mechanical basis of ridges here in the life zone."

Howard said, "Where's the nearest?"

"Ummm, hard to tell." This went back to the whole problem of conformal mapping of the Bowl's curves and slants that had bored Cliff on *SunSeeker* and did now, too. When he came back to the Irma–Aybe–Howard conversation, they seemed to have resolved the issue and Irma said adamantly, "I'm sure it's at least a thousand klicks, that way—" and pointed.

Aybe had another objection and Cliff went back to watching the terrain. Aybe could fly the magcar around obstacles with the surprisingly simple controls, and still keep up a steady stream of disputation with Irma. Cliff got bored and rode shotgun in the sense of watching for trouble to their flanks. They were gently rising over terrain that got more bare and stony.

While the three argued, they came upon some hills of actual rock—cross sections of layers, some showing rippled marks that bespoke the eddies of an ancient sea. There were hollowed-out openings, some big enough to walk into. Parts of the walls had the curved sheets that meant sand dunes, each seam of differently colored red and tan grains sloping smoothly, an echo of where ancient winds blew them. These rocks had to come from some planet's surface.

"Hey, I'd like to look at those," Cliff said. "Let's take a break."

The tech types broke off and Irma surged up. "Yes! Need to pee anyway."

They came behind as he scrambled up the slopes. Puffing, he scaled a climb into one of the caves. So the Bowl builders had kept some of their home world? Intriguing—

He blinked. Pink paintings marked the cave roof and walls. Simple line drawings showed lumpy animals. One was clearly a running stick figure like the Bird Folk, a slender long neck and arms carried forward. Before it ran smaller animals. The Bird carried a . . . spear? Hard to tell.

Something told him these were truly ancient. They reminded him of the aboriginal paintings he had seen in Australia. Those showed kangaroos and fish and human figures. Not as sophisticated as the French cave paintings, but very much older, dating back to fifty thousand years.

But these—these were alien artworks of . . . how long ago? Impossible to tell. The Bowl builders had brought this here, perhaps—these hills stuck out above the bland rolling terrain below. Probably this was an honored remnant of whatever world the Bird Folk came from. Their planetary origin, lost in time.

The others came up and all stood, silent before the strange artwork. There was a dry smell here, like a desiccated museum.

They left it silently, as if afraid to disturb the ghosts from far away in the abyss of time.

THIRTY-SEVEN

Memor made her clattering ritual steps and buzzing feather-rush display, bowing as she took her seat. Warm waters played down the walls of the huge chamber, tinkling and splattering on rocks, which calmed her for the duel to come. Though this was to be a small meeting—the better to get things done—the Minister had chosen to use this largely ceremonial hall, perhaps to stress the gravity of Memor's errors.

Her only friend here, Sarko, hurried forward, hips swaying. "Welcome, one-under-scrutiny. Let me help you."

Sarko was tall and elegant compared to the

more pyramidally shaped Folk. Theirs was an unlikely friendship, since Memor was more the grave, solemn type. Yet both realized that the other had needed social skills. Sarko's willowy manner made her an excellent social guide. She made a point of knowing everyone and let Memor know just what intrigues were afoot. In return, Memor shielded Sarko from complaints that she seldom really contributed ideas to the general purpose. Social gadflies were useful, after all, to lubricate the grinding machinery of Folk hierarchy. Sarko's friendship with Memor went back to the ancient times when they had both been male. Such scandals they had narrowly averted! Gossip they had barely survived! The rich old days.

"Thanks, fond one," Memor said. "What can you tell me?"

"There'll be the usual minor business you'll sit through, of course. The Adopted—not that your primates are, ey?—fall under the Code, nominally. Especially if—" Here Sarko gave a flare-flutter of mirth. "—they are rampaging over the landscape."

"They are clever," Memor allowed herself.

"And hard to catch! We had abundant testimony to that last meeting. Pity you weren't here—exciting. I gather these primates are not like ours, not simpletons hanging around in trees. Anyway, no wonder they escaped, they seem quite clever. Tricky! I gather they got away from several large search parties, and now have—" Sarko paused in her usual headlong talking. "—have killed several Folk? . . . And captured a car? . . ."

Memor gave an assenting wave of feather-fan. "True enough. Word leaks out, I see. They have made the case against their kind quite well."

Sarko peered into Memor's face. "You do fathom that the best way to save your career is to agree that they must be exterminated."

"Oh, quite."

"So you will? Please."

"I think we play with fires we do not know here, and should be careful." Memor had planned that sentence; might as well try it out on a friend.

"That will not go well with the Profounds, old friend."

A slow side glance. "Friend, I can count on your support?"

A humble bow. "I have little power, alas."

"Use what you have. I have survived the Citadel of Remembrance, though not without scorn."

"May you do so well here!" Sarko said, her expression returning to her usual happy state, with blue eye-feathers furling.

Memor followed Sarko's guidance through the formal labyrinth, enjoying her quick, birdlike movements. Sarko was a quick but not deep intelligence, open to larger mental vistas but preferring the light joys of the social give-and-take.

As an Ecosystem Savant approached, Sarko fell back. "Would you have sustenance?" came the customary offer.

"Not before any other," Memor made the usual counter. The Ecosystem Savant ruffled colors of routine admiration and the introductions were complete.

At this formal moment, a Packmistress entered, seated herself, and nodded to all with a fluttering plumage neck-arc of authority. "We will commence." A flutter of acceptance ran round the moist chamber.

The first item was an anticlimax. An ecosystem engineer presented the latest problem. In Zone 28-94-4578, water temples controlled flow to terraces, preventing Folk tribes upstream from using it all, and so avoided impoverishing those below. Yet rainfall had slackened, despite the best Eco management. To prevent the highlands from withholding water without conflict demanded social cement. These Moist Temples used customary *subak* rituals to link the communities with full mingling ceremony and mandatory cross-breeding. Otherwise, they would be snatching at one another's feathers. Absent such community, crops would fail. Ancient forests would be overrun with loggers, potters, shepherds, and thieves, seeking what they could wrench forth. This evolving crisis challenged lands larger than whole planets.

The biology of all lands shifted in time, of course—nature's restless seekings making species that, in the evolutionary sense, pass by each other on their way to somewhere else. Adapt, evolve, or die—the eternal rule. But drought hastened nature here.

Memor watched as several Profounds tossed the problem among themselves. Much verbal artistry could not conceal the hard choices. There seemed no merciful solution. Accordingly, the Packmistress let each side play out, stating cases, pleading for more aid.

Then the Packmistress showed a crescent display of resolute judgment—a bad sign. She said, "No extensions for longevity throughout the threatened domain. No appeals, no exceptions."

There it was. A hush fell upon the chamber. Memor could hear the gentle splashing of the calming waters on the walls. The Packmistress had condemned millions to their natural extinction. They could not claim special aging preventives.

The Packmistress ordered a recess for contemplation. Sarko immediately appeared at Memor's flank. "Perhaps such stern justice will be of help."

"Or set the tone," Memor said dryly.

"I have been circulating. . . ." Sarko always opened with a teasing promise, fluttering side feathers near her eyes. "Some say you know the most of these aliens, so should lead the hunt."

"Are you sure?"

"Yes, those who spoke at all seemed quite friendly to your cause."

"I do not seek to lead a hunt."

Feathers ringing Sarko's neck fluttered. "But you fathom these strange—"

"Has it occurred to you that I could *fail*?"

"Ah, no. You have such a sterling record—"

"This is the first alien invasion in countless twelve-cubed Cycles. We are inexperienced. As well, no one has ever dealt with such evil little creatures."

Sarko's elegant head jerked, weaved. Feathers fanned the astonished violet-rimmed eyes. "But you! Everyone says—"

"Everyone hasn't walked in my path. I do not wish to exchange one route to death for another. This hunt could fail, the aliens could do much damage—and there will be victims among us, then."

Sarko's joyful face collapsed. "Surely you can't—"

The summoning chimes sounded, reverberating in the high chamber. Memor drew in the soft air, but tasted a bitter hint—her own bile?

Back in chambers, more Eco deliberations droned by. Movements of the Folk were not following the Design. Memor let her Undermind rove as she half listened.

All life was properly in movement, on the grand plains of the Bowl World. But the bigger, lower-grade-intelligence Folk, who lived as primitives and augmented their diet browsing shrubs and trees, were to move on—to give grazers a chance to live on the grasses that followed the loss of shrubs. These primitives were not crop-raising Folk, and should remain in their wild condition.

So populations had to be forced to move, and not set up camps and villages. The Packmistress made quick work of this matter, directing Suborns to destroy the primitive camps and force the sub-Folk to move on. They had their role in the Design, and should be reminded of it.

She reminded them all that the Originals had learned the Great Truth that governed all: that given vast new lands, the Folk then quickly invade these spaces, wreak destruction, and when resources grow short, fight with neighbors for more. Under the first rush of exploding populations in the Original Times, wildland had to pay or perish, to persist. Poachers and loggers turned lands into battlefields.

Only after much strife that threatened the Bowl itself did the Codes come, managed by the Savants. There was no alternative to a constant, assuring order. Another revelation was that death did not permit one to stay out of the Cycle. In some Bowl societies, the Folk tried to deny their own role, and so put their dead into coffins and mausoleums, burned themselves in pyres, even suspend themselves in cold for future resurrection. All were a wrongness, for the Bowl needed these bodies.

"Mites and worms *should* have us," the Packmistress said. "This is the Cycle and it must be obeyed. Such is the Design. The Code does not protect lands and seas from the Folk, but rather *for* the Folk—by taking the long view. The Code teaches humility, because it engages us with Nature in the eternal dance with all other species."

Memor bowed her head at this obvious platitude and wondered how it would affect her—well, *trial* was not quite right, but the stern faces of those around her did not bode well.

At this moment Sarko piped forth, "I suppose the message here is, just remember that you can never predict the behavior of a system more complex than you. And if you want a project to stay on track after you're gone, you don't give control to anything that's guaranteed to develop its own agenda."

Ah, Memor thought. Sarko was drawing fire to defuse the tension in the room. And it worked. Those clustered around made derisive noises, though some just fluttered their feather-fans. "Surely that is too simple," an elderly Savant hooted. Others just laughed.

The Packmistress allowed a flicker of irritation to ripple through her feathered corona. "For we—Savants, Profounds, all those in the tier below Astronomers—corruption of purpose means simple bribery, graft, or nepotism. But for lower Folk who enjoy their lives in the unchanging state our Bowl ensures, corruption has an entirely different meaning. It is the failure to share any largesse you have received with those with whom you have formed ties of dependence."

Sarko said, "Surely that is predictable, my—"

"Our view of corruption makes sense in a culture of laws and impersonal institutions," the Packmistress rolled right over Sarko. "But theirs is a small world whose defining feature is the web of indebtedness, of obligations that ensure the social order. So to them, not to give a job to a cousin is corrupt, even if others are better qualified. Not to do deals with tribesFolk because better terms may be found elsewhere is also corrupt. Reducing corruption of this sort demands—" The Packmistress let her voice fall to a grave tone. "—resolve."

A sobered silence from those who saw what was going on.

"It is useful to recall the full brunt of our measures," she began, displaying a somber arc-pattern of grays and pale blues. "I remind us all that while such social dissension occurs on occasion, there is a rogue element afoot, and not far from these territories where the water temples are failing to make a benign equilibrium."

With this she cast a significant long look at Memor. "Witness, I bid you, the current state of those we have condemned for committing offenses of this type." With a great sway of her body, she signaled the attendants. The dome over their heads surged with popping energy, and a wide image played upon it. Memor shivered with fear when she recognized the context.

The greatest preventive the Astronomers had, used against only those whose actions threatened the Bowl's environment and fate, was the Perpetual Hell. Mention of its very existence could silence a crowd.

Those who violated the Code could face having their very minds mapped, and their bodies then executed. They would then awake suspended in a virtual, mental Hell from which none escaped. Ever.

Memor had gone through the mandatory sampling of a mere single Hell, and would never forget it. And now here it came again, splashed across the ceiling.

A glowering sky, shot with red and amber. Beneath lay a vast swamp flooded with fuming lava, the stench—the Packmistress had ordered the full sensorium to come into play across the chamber—so strong, it now crawled into her nostrils and stung throughout her head.

"Attend!" the Packmistress commanded. Heads had already averted the images, eyes snatched away.

Memor looked up against her will. Rooted in this acrid slime were . . . the doomed Folk. They writhed and screamed in tiny shrill voices. Fires danced upon them as they twisted. A din of shrieking pain played across the bodies. They could not wrench free of the fires and so endured it like trees whipped by winds of agony. Eyes pleaded with them all—for those in this place knew they were watched; it was part of the torture—begging for release from agonies she could see but do nothing about. Rocks fell from the smoldering sky and smashed the fevered mud.

The first time she had to watch this, the intent was to educate her, and the lesson never left her mind for long. Now the Packmistress meant to instill discipline. Memor trembled, for the message was clearly focused on her.

At a nod, the image and scents fled. Sighs and worried murmurs laced the air as the Packmistress settled herself, looking satisfied.

All waited and the Packmistress let tension build. *She's toying with me,* Memor thought. At last the Packmistress said slowly, "The Bureau of the Adopted had as its Research Minister a Profound of the most high stratum. He will present their views now, and our guest, Memor, will answer. Attend—these are the firm results of our global staff, an analysis of the nature of these . . . aliens."

Memor watched as the Profound—a male, of course, since males push at the boundaries, as a rightful, youthful function—gave a rather hurried talk. He swept his great head about to stress his points, feathers ruffling constantly at his neck for emphasis. Masculine energy surged through his sentences.

"These are clever creatures, a form we never saw evolve in the Bowl." The Profound tipped his head at his audience, mirth playing in his eyes. "This may come from their tempting role as game—" This brought a storm of laughter, obviously a release from the tension of watching the Hell. "—but we can deduce aspects of their evolution from their surprising intelligence."

Memor knew where this was going. She was not so far from the male phase; she could still anticipate the channels of their thoughts; after all, that was a core female talent. Evolutionary theory would predict a clear pattern in the aliens, and males loved the mechanisms of theory. Selection pressure on some world had favored the climbers of trees, and then had somehow shifted, so the climbers came down to the ground. There they learned to hunt. As strategies go, hunting in groups compelled social communication, to find prey and coordinate attacks. That drove speech and language. In turn, intelligence acted on social cues so that group survival became enhanced, in conflict with other hunting groups of the same species. That drove cooperation. Particularly, selection would favor both the charismatic minds that could lead, and the analytical ones, which would see deeper. The social pyramid would have a bulge in the middle, of the variously competent.

"But this is a commonplace," Memor injected, a calculated move whose risk made her heart pound. She tasted in her breath the tang of her own sour apprehension. "We can all see where the argument goes. We ourselves evolved in something like this manner, in the Home."

Invoking the Home was a bold move, but she had to make it. Memor made a fan display of rattling colors. "But these creatures are tiny! They would lack the advantage of size, and so should not be very successful."

The Profound gave a jut of his head and a jaunty spray of derisive colors. "Size can become an instability, as surely even nonspecialists must know." This dig provoked a titter among some. "It is simple to grow large and dumb, yet remain secure. We—the Folk—found a balance. We became smart and yet our size let us develop the civilized arts. Our societies matured. We learned to sustain, the greatest of virtues. We learned to Adopt other species through modification of their genes, our great skill—though, of course, even the Adopted at times need recalibration."

Memor rose to her full height to challenge this. Rising was a risk, for it could offend. But her life was at stake here. Plainly, the Packmistress had chosen to subject them to the Perpetual Hell to make this point without speaking of it. "You speak of strategies we do not in fact know at all. Adopting is our method here, yes. But, I might remind the Profound, we do not know how *we* evolved!"

Memor had not expected this sally to deflect the Profound's argument, and it did not. He said, "Standard theory declares that this skill, plus our extraordinary social coherence, was decisive. I am not surprised you do not know this, for you are untutored in the evolutionary arts."

"Do *you* know what sort of world we came from?"

"Of course. The best parts of it were much like our Bowl."

"You mean the Great Plain, the Knothole, the Zone of Reflectance, or—what?"

He shot back, "That is a specialist question, beyond the concerns of—"

"You do not know, do you?"

"I did not say that. I think it beside my point."

"Let us note the Profound did not answer the question."

"Halt!" the Packmistress ordered. "We are getting away from the reason for your appearance here, Memor, *and* I note you are using this diversion to delay our proper considerations."

Memor saw she had gone too far and so made the ritual bow with coronations of dutiful apology—three fan-trills and a rainbow display of self-dismay. The attendees nodded in approval and a few even sent quick fan-toasts at Memor's performance of a difficult salute. That seemed to calm everyone, but Memor knew it was mere polite manners.

The Profound said slowly, voice filled with deep sour notes, "Memor here has allowed to *escape* the *only* of these aliens our Security had captured!

They are far away from the other primates, who escaped immediately when they entered."

"How did that occur?" a senior figure asked.

"Inexcusable oversight. I might add that the commanders responsible have been recycled."

"That seems brutal," a voice at the back called. "We are unaccustomed to invasion, and do not have anyone living who has experience."

The Profound said slowly, "As well it might, but word of recyclings spreads, and aids in discipline."

Silence. A senior member said, "We still cannot find those, the ones who got away at the air lock?"

"No, and that is the salient threat. These primates are vicious—they have killed some of us!—and at a demonstrably lower stage of evolution. But they are infernally hard to find, catch, and kill."

"We have *none* in captivity?" The senior figure rustled head feathers in surprise.

"Exactly so—" The Packmistress's head swiveled. "—due to Memor. The only dead primate we have found, left behind by his companions as they fled, apparently died from a large predator—which the other primates then killed. All this occurred during their escape from Memor." She ended with a long stare at Memor, aided by fan stirring of rebuke at her shoulders.

Memor disliked such smug orations but kept still.

The entire body turned and looked at Memor. She decided the best tactic was to stare right back.

The Profound did not hesitate. "There is a further issue. These are not truly rational minds. They cannot view the Underminds and so do not know themselves."

Gasps, frowns. Memor started to object to this intrusion into her own area. "Ah, I—"

The Profound waved her off. "For these primates, there is always a silent partner riding along in the same mind. It can get in touch with their Fore-selves. Yes—we do owe this discovery to Memor, I'll grant. But! Their Underminds can speak to them only through dreams during sleep. Memor showed that they have ideas that come to them out of 'no-where.' Not words or exact thoughts, just images and sensations."

"Surely these cannot be significant ideas?" a se-nior asked. "They are unmotivated."

The Profound shook his head sadly, a theatrical move that made Memor grind her teeth. "Alas, I must report to you—again, due to Memor's work— that this primate 'silent partner' is the wellspring of their primitive creativity."

"But that is inefficient!" the senior Savant in-sisted.

"Apparently not, on whatever strange world these tree-swingers came from in their crude ship. Evolution must have preferred to keep their minds divided between the conscious self and the silent."

The Savant looked incredulous—eyes upcast, neck-fan puckered red, snout cocked at an angle. "Surely such disabled creatures, even if they have technologies, are no threat to us."

The Profound flicked a command, and the dome above them popped with an image—the alien primates gathered around a campfire. The audience rustled. "These look quite helpless," the Savant said.

"They are not," the Profound said, and cut to an image of three Folk sprawled, their bodies stripped of gear. Burns at their necks and heads had singed away many feathers. Brown blood stained the sand around them, and surprise lingered in their staring eyes.

"And now we turn to the cause of these events," the Profound said quietly.

Memor recognized the images she had sent in reports. Of course, the Profound had put his own interpretation on her brainscan data, slanting it to his pointed ends. Memor stood. "I am not the cause, my Profound. I am the discoverer."

"Of what?"

"The sobering implication that these primates undermine our understanding of our own minds."

"That is nonsense."

"You are a male, my dear Profound, and so should be more open to ideas, since you are young as well. These events imply a painfully fresh insight. These creatures somehow avoid the risks of an unfettered intelligence. The implications—"

"Are many, but the threat is clear," the Profound snapped. "*You* let them escape. The only concrete knowledge we have comes from the single corpse they left behind—being primitives, I would have expected them to at least try to bury it. Studying that body explains their archaic origins. They have organs that barely function, some clearly vestigial, particularly in their digestive tracts. Natural selection has not had time to edit out these simple flaws. And, tellingly, there is *no* sign of artificial selection."

Clucks of doubt greeted this news. An elder asked, "How could they become starfarers without tailoring their bodies?"

"They were in a hurry," Memor said dryly.

The Profound's eyes narrowed. "They must come from quite nearby, to reach us in such simple craft. Yet I checked with the Astronomers, and there are no habitable planets within several light-years."

Memor saw this digression was to mollify the crowd, by seeming reasonable. She said, "They caught up to us and slowed to board. They obviously do not come with an attitude of awe, as with prior aliens. Customarily we pass by a star, and any intelligent, technological life-form comes to us with great respect for the Bowl, its majesty. I doubt these, who apparently found us by accident, will join the Adopted without great trouble."

The Profound's eyes glistened as he saw an opportunity. "Then you agree they should be killed?"

"Of course. But the implications they bring—"

"Will not matter when they are dead, yes?"

"You speak of that as an easy thing. My point is that it will not be simple. They have resources I cannot fathom."

"But that is subject to demonstration, yes?" The Profound yawned elaborately, amused.

"If we muster—"

"I assure you we are receiving reports from varying Folk communities. I have not gotten reports from the party you let escape, alas." With this, he gave a derisive feather-flicker. "But other Folk do glimpse the primates who stole an aircar. They've been sighted as they pass in the distance."

"Then you— Wait, why do the Folk not attack them?"

"They proceed through a zone of low habitation. None who sighted them had weapons of such range, for obvious reasons."

The Folk communities had only low-power armaments. Large explosives could breach the shell and open the Bowl to vacuum. If such were used by the infrequent Adopted rebellions, disaster would follow.

Memor could sense the shift in the audience. A senior Savant said, "If you are correct, our Profound, we must use those who know these strange primates."

The Profound turned, puzzled. "I have made a case for extermination—"

"But only Memor knows how they think, yes?"

Memor said, "I cannot pretend to know, but I can at least sense how they respond."

The senior was puzzled and asked for explanation with a classic ruffle and coo.

"I can predict many actions of these primates, yet without understanding their motives."

The Profound sent his crown feathers into a circling pattern of blue and gold. "I think Memor has proved she does *not* know how—"

"She is what we have," the Packmistress said suddenly. "She studied these aliens."

"But the risk!" the Profound said, turning to make the strut-challenge to the entire room. "We know from prior eras that aliens drawn to us from planets arrive with a planetary view of life. This cripples them. Of course, once having seen and lived upon the Bowl of Heaven, they saw their errors and found a quiet equilibrium. The Adopted have been quite useful to us and, once rendered docile, improve the lives of us all. Yet inevitably such aliens suffer for reasons built deeply into their genes—a nostalgia for planets that necessarily suffer the pains of days and nights, of axial seasons, of uncontrolled, hammering weather. So the Adopted are susceptible to incitement. These Late Invaders could excite such nostalgia into rage, vast violence, and then—"

The Packmistress held up her arms, and the room fell silent. She did not react visibly, but turned to Memor and gazed steadily. "You will find a way to draw them out."

Memor hesitated. "But . . . how can I . . ."

"You know them. You have seen their ways of bonding, of talking with those curious faces of theirs. The idea of an intelligence that does not fully control expression, showing all to any who see—and so lets others know what emotions pass within! Use that! You have two bands of aliens moving across the majesty of the Bowl. They are communal animals, yes?"

"True, they daily meet and speak and—"

"Good. Use that."

"Lure them?"

"If you can devise a way, surely."

"May I have use of the Sky Command? I can cover territory quickly with the fliers. And especially the airfish."

"I suppose." A sniff.

Memor hesitated, then bowed. Her caution warned her not to go further, but—"What of their ship?"

"Eh?" A Packmistress is not used to being questioned.

"Their starship orbits about our star. Suppose it has some powers we do not know?"

"That is for the Astronomers, surely." The Packmistress stirred, as if she had not considered the issue. "I heard at Council that our mirror complexes probably cannot adjust quickly enough to focus on their ship. It has capacity to maneuver, and could evade a beam."

A senior Savant added, "No small ship could damage the Bowl, in any case."

"Ah, that is consoling," Memor said with a bow and a humble submission-flurry of crest feathers. Then, as she rose, she had an idea.

THIRTY-EIGHT

When they stopped for a rest after a long journey in the magcar, Cliff searched for food. It felt good to get out of the car and into the "sorta-natural," as Irma called it.

There was little of animal prints or scat here,

he noticed automatically. He found ripe berries, spotting them from experience. Some large trees had fruit growing off their trunks, an oddity that he used. With Howard he shot several of them off the bark by laser. He had developed a small poison detector, using the gear he had brought. That time of their landing—going through the air lock and then on the run—seemed far in the past. He had expected a few days on the Bowl, mostly doing bio tests, then back to *SunSeeker*.

The fruit was a succulent purple and tested okay.

But the purple sap drew tiny flies that went for the fruit and then tried to suck the moisture off his eyeballs. They darted into his ears and dwelled there, prying deep inside. Dozens of them danced in the air, looking for suitable targets. Only running left them behind, and not for long.

This just led the flies to the others, who batted at the buzzing irritants. It got bad and they decided to fire up the magcar and flee. Aybe was irritable; they had stung him on the neck repeatedly. He took out his ire by "trying out the dynamics." This meant more acrobatics. Howard had measured the magnetic fields around the magcar and found it was an asymmetric dipole, with field squeezed tight under the car. With all aboard, the car sped faster by hugging the ground, so they skimmed along at only a meter in altitude. The more weight, the faster they could go. "Counterintuitive," Howard said. "Must be the fields grip the metal belowground better."

Aybe nodded. "I figure the Bowl underpinning is metal with magnetic fields already embedded."

Irma said, "Maybe those big grid lines we saw on the outer skin? Could be enormous superconductor lines. Howard, what's the magnetic field intensity at ground level?"

"Strong—so much, I can't measure it with my simple gear. At least a hundred times Earth's, maybe a lot more."

Soon a ridge of mountain loomed before them. Aybe took them straight at it and Irma said, "That's not far from the gridding I found. Maybe it's a city?"

"Then let's not go there," Howard said.

But under binocs, the rising ridge looked like bare rock and there were no signs of locals. Aybe worked them around the narrow canyons that led to the base.

"No signs of life," Aybe said. "Maybe it has some structural role?"

"We can get some perspective from up there," Cliff said mildly. He had wanted to see further around this immense place but until now could not think of a way to do it, short of capturing an aircraft. Yet they had seen few of those in the skies.

They started up the slope of the spire. It was mostly bare rock, but here and there they could see in the gullies some metal, as if the frame were showing through. The magcar handled well.

Howard said, "I think the magnetics are getting stronger."

Aybe nodded. "I'm feeling more grip now. We can go uphill pretty fast." He brought the magcar down even lower to the rock face and they lifted steadily.

Cliff watched the terrain fall away. Forest, grasslands, rumpled hills. The spire steepened steadily but somehow the magcar held on, groaning, and propelled them up its flanks. He wondered what drove it—a compact fusion scheme? The oscillating rumble under his feet suggested that, but alien tech could—no, would—be alien.

As they rose he saw immense decks of clouds rising like mountains in the distance. The atmosphere was so deep, such stacks could form and drift like skyscrapers of cotton. The Bowl rotated around in about ten days, and this drove waves and eddies in the huge atmosphere. The clouds followed this rhythm in stately cadence. He had seen the effects on the thin film that capped the atmosphere, and in the deep air below—ripples that shaped the winds, tornados here and there spinning like vast purple storms, resembling a top on a distant table. How could anyone predict temperature and rainfall in something this big?

Aybe had taken them far up the spire now. It felt like climbing a building with no safety net. They were above the layer of air where small clouds hung, and now the view reached farther. Opposite the clouds was a clear zone. He was looking away from the rim of the Bowl, toward the Knothole. The Jet slowly wrapped and writhed, a slender red and orange snake. He followed its dim glow toward the Knothole but could not see past the foggy blur there. But nearer, beyond the vast mottled lands, lay a strange, huge curved zone—the mirrors.

He was about to turn away when he saw something new.

Glinting pixels struck his eye. The whole zone seemed to teem with activity—winks and stutters of light. Were the mirrors adjusting to tune the Jet, to stop the snarling waves that rode out on it?

"Let's go there." Cliff pointed. "That's got to be where whoever runs this place lives."

"Up to high latitudes?" Howard said. "We haven't any idea what's there!"

"We haven't got *any* ideas!" Irma burst out.

"Then we need some," Aybe said.

• • •

They kept moving up the rocky flanks of the immense tower, then had another sleep stop. At their rest site were some of the helically coiled, willowy paper bark trees they had found before. These they used for toilet paper, but they also cooked fish wrapped in it. Terry discovered a local herb that, roasted inside the fish, gave a pleasant taste to the big slabs of white meat. Cliff gutted the fish they caught in the surprisingly rich streams and ponds, and kept notes on his slate about their guts. There were oddities to the usual tubular design, such as one that excreted to the sides, not at the tail, and another with a circular comb around its flanks. Disguise? Defense? Hard to know.

They all enjoyed the view. To one side, a gunmetal blue sheen of sea yawned in the distance. The seemingly flat horizon to either side disappeared into a haze; the water gave no impression of being concave, only vast. Here, Cliff mused, masts would not be the first sign of an approaching ship.

There were a few Earthly analogues to this place, he reflected. Earthside, deep sea creatures lived in constant darkness, the opposite of this steady daylight. Here the sun stayed put in the sky, so animals could navigate by it. They all hid away to sleep, except for some lizard carnivores he saw dozing in the eternal sun. Beyond those bare facts, Cliff could not see how to generalize.

Terry came and sat beside him to admire the views. They walked around a bluff to see the other side, silent. They had exhausted their small talk long ago. The unending days were wearing on them all. Their clothes, though of Enduro cloth, showed popped linings and ragged cuffs. They bathed whenever they found a stream or lake but often smelled rank. The men had ragged beards, and Irma's hair kept getting in her way. They didn't cut hair, though, because it kept their UV exposure down. Though everyone with a *SunSeeker* berth was exceptionally strong and tough, living in the open wore them down. Worst of all was the strong expectation that none of this was going to change soon.

"That way," Terry said, pointing, "that's up-Bowl, right?"

"You mean to higher latitudes?" Cliff tossed a rock onto the steep slate gray rock below them and

watched it bounce and scatter until he lost track of
it in mist below.

"Yeah, past the mirrors. Must be a hundred million klicks away from here."

"Pretty far, right," Cliff said, distracted by something he had glimpsed. He brought up his binocs
and close-upped the mirror zone. It was flashing
rainbow colors, tiny pixels of blue and white and
pink rippling. He had seen that before, but this
time whole regions of mirrors were forming the
same color, making—*an image.*

He stared at it, mouth open.

"Look up close," he whispered to Terry. "What
do you see?"

"Okay, I—good grief. It's . . . a face."

"Not just a face. A person—human."

"What?" Terry grew silent. "You're right! A
woman."

"Moving, too—it's . . . it's Beth."

"My God . . . yes. It's her."

"And her lips are moving."

"Yeah. I used to lip-read, let me . . . She's saying
'come,' I think."

Cliff found he had been holding his breath.
"Right."

"Come . . . to . . . me. Repeats. That's it."

The face on the mirrors repeated the words over
and over. Her face rippled and snarled in spots
where wave coherence failed.

Terry said, "Does that mean they have her?"

"These are aliens. Maybe their contexts are

different. It could mean they want her to go to them. Or it's directed to us, and me, and says, go to Beth."

"Damn," Terry said.

Cliff stared at the repeating pattern and frowned. He seemed to float on the shock of it, suspended, seeing a face he had longed for. He had dreamed of her so much through these desperate days, imagining her dead or in some alien hellhole. . . .

"Unless . . . it could be Beth sending the message."

THIRTY-NINE

For Cliff, dreams made it all worse. The next "day," he awoke with the scent of roast turkey in his mind. When he was a boy, his idea of heaven was Thanksgiving leftovers. He had loved chopping onions beside his mother, stuffing the bird with green cork tamales instead of regular stuffing, as Grandmother Martínez did. The other side of the family did ground lamb, rice, and pinyon nuts. Drifting up from sleep, he tasted the Arabic stuffing flavored with prickly spices and a little cinnamon. He blinked into the constant dappled sunlight, not wanting to leave the dream. His stomach growled in sympathy.

Food dreams . . . He had them every sleep now. They ate simply here, but his unconscious didn't have to like it.

He got up, yawning and reaching for some fragrant fruit they had found the day before. They managed to get enough small game, shooting from the magcar, and they all gathered berries and herbs to avoid hunger here—but his sleep turned to fragrant feasts nearly every "night." He suspected food stood in his dreams for some deeper yearning, but could not figure out what it might be.

He mentioned this to Irma as the "day" was drawing to a close, and she said immediately, looking him in the eye, "Beth. Obviously."

This made him blink because it was obvious and he had not seen it. "I . . . suppose so."

"Just as I miss and want Herb." Still the direct stare.

"Of course." That was his filler phrase while he tried to think, but Irma wasn't having any.

She shot back, "You don't remember Herb, do you?"

"Uh, engineer, right?"

"No, he's a systems man."

"Well, that sort of engin—"

"Redwing was going to revive him to work on the drive problem, but we got too busy."

"And you miss him. . . ." Cliff resorted to a leading phrase to get away from the Beth issue, but it didn't work.

She said, "We're helping each other through the hard stuff, Cliff. I want you to know that's all it is."

"Of course." Pause. "Not that I don't have, well, real feelings toward you."

She smiled. "I do, too, but they're—how to say?—not deep."

"Sex does have what the psychers call a 'utility function,' yes."

"As long as we both know that. And speaking of it, I'm not really tired . . . yet."

This was clearly a lead-in, so he smiled and said, "I've got to take a stroll before settling down."

The team followed a set procedure when they slept. Find a secure place, often one that surveyed the land around them but was in shadow. Be sure nothing could approach silently by rigging lines that would rattle some gear if tripped. Post a guard if the situation looked risky. Have a spot where people could retreat for a toilet, perhaps even fresh water.

Today—the term meant nothing more than their awake interval—they camped under a broad canopy of tall trees. Wildlife chattered and jeered above as they walked through dense vegetation. Cliff always kept aware of his flanks and regularly turned to look back, to recall the path. They kept silent, wary. What he called a smokebush bristled with its tiny branches, easing slowly toward them as it sensed their motion. It could snare only insects and small birds, but a moving plant still gave him the creeps.

Irma checked above, head swiveling regularly, and they were a few hundred meters from camp when she abruptly turned and kissed him. He responded to her quick kisses and short, panting breath, and only when her clothes were mostly off did he notice that there was no comfortable place to lie down. "Maybe we should walk some more that—"

"There's a slanted tree, see?"

"Yeah, those zigzag trees. I think they exploit the sun's constant position. See, they stage tiers of upward-facing limbs and leaves, to cup the sunlight. Each layer is staggered to the side, so a single tree, seen from above, makes a broad emerald area, captures more sun."

"Faaaa-scinating."

Her dry tone made him turn and she kissed him hard and deep. *Oh yeah, we came here to—*

She backed him onto the broad, slick-barked wood. He shucked his trousers down to his ankles, and she smiled when she saw he was ready.

"There." She settled on him. "That's better, isn't it?"

"Lots better."

"Stay still."

He wheezed with her weight as she moved. "Oh . . . kay."

"Hold me . . . here."

In the long moments he felt the breeze caress them with soft aromas and listened for any sound that might be a threat. Fidget birds that were always chattering and scattering chose this moment to go jumping through a nearby bush. He glanced to check, then focused on her eyes, which were drilling into him with concentration.

You're never off duty, he thought, and she whispered, "Slow. Don't rush it. Slow. Keep doing that. Oh yes. God, Herb, yes, that's it. Just like that."

He said nothing about the name, just concentrated. A small tremor came from branches above, then stopped. Wind whistled, wood creaked. "Lift up a little."

"That?" he gasped out.

Then it got fast and intense and he lost all sense of place. When he came, it was hard and the scents of the woodland swarmed up into his nostrils.

"Ah . . . Okay." She exhaled a long, fluttery sigh and something fell on them.

"Snake!" she cried, and rolled away. So did the snake. It was long and fat and slithered away.

Cliff stood and snatched up his pants, which were caught in his boots. *Not smart,* he thought just before the second snake appeared. It paused, rearing up to a meter height on a fidgeting stand of short tails. The beady eyes jerked around, studying them. *It's smart,* he thought, and saw two more snakes come weaving out of the leafy background. They smelled like grease and ginger. Their eyes yawned wide in surprise.

Then they all paused. Cliff could now see all four snakes, taking their time as they studied Irma. He plucked his laser from his belt and said, "Just stay still. Don't look threatening."

"*Me* don't look threatening?"

This provoked some signals between the snakes, their slim heads jutting as they rasped out soft sounds. *Do they recognize that we're using a language?* Their sibilants also seemed like words, modulated with clicks and head-juts. He noticed suddenly that two snakes had a belt tightened near their heads, and small slim things like tools tucked into loops.

The moment hung in the soft air. The snakes eyed one another, heads jerked back to regard the humans, they rapped out a few more short bursts—and then darted away.

Cliff started after them and Irma called, "Let them go!"

He didn't fear them somehow. They hadn't bitten. Maybe this was just an accident.

They were just strange enough to make him follow the wiggling shapes through the understory of thrashing green limbs, long stems with leaves, and flowering plants. After thirty meters he was going to give up, but the snakes, moving in parallel now and weaving in sequence like a wave, turned toward an out-jut of dirt. They went into a hole about twenty centimeters across, each taking a turn while the others turned to confront Cliff. The last one hissed something loudly, turned, and slipped quickly inside.

Irma came up beside him. "What the—?"

"I want to know more about those."

"Hell, they made me wet myself."

"They're tool users. I—"

"Snakes? Come on."

"And they're smart."

"Snakes!"

"They got away from us, didn't they?"

FORTY

They came down the spire easily, cushioned on magnetic fluxes that Aybe treated like a rubbery ski slope.

They got him to slow down, but he always took a slide when there was a catch basin below. Then he would fetch them up against the opposing slope, braking with the magnetic fields that were surprisingly strong within one meter of the rock.

Most of the catch basins held deep blue water. The look of mountain lakes rimmed by trees reminded Cliff of hiking in the Sierras, which were much the same as centuries ago, judging from the Ansel Adams photos he had studied.

After all, humans had restored the ancient world they destroyed in the twenty-first and twenty-second centuries, the Great Rewilding. In Siberia, people had even carried out a Pleistocene rewilding, bringing back wolves, lynx, cougars, wolverines, grizzlies, and sea otters—top carnivores driven nearly to extinction. Once the human population fell back to two billion, there was room.

Cliff had helped in that when a boy. Nothing biotech or major, just clearance of invasive species. He left near dawn in summers, wearing oiled pants to fend off chaparral scratches, carrying a big knife, a pick mattock, and binocs. *Who meets the dawn owns the day,* his father always said—and remembering this, he felt a pang that the father who had said good-bye to him with a firm handshake at their parting was now dead over a century.

In those bright summer days, he had killed invasive pampas grass, flamboyant blond plumes that sucked nutrients from the California soil and fed nothing. He cut and gouged down stands as big as his house. He was a bio-bigot supreme, angry at tough, foreign plants that took all and gave nothing. Far better than going after trout or deer, and better, rougher exercise. It felt good to yank pampas grass up. Then the chem death—spray the roots and dug-out ground with an herbicide sting.

The memory made him think of how any mind could build this Bowl and make it work. It was millions of times larger in area than the whole Earth. How did they deal with species and change?

Even California was hard to manage, demanding lots of gut labor. The golden hills where he grew up were in fact an outcome of invasive Spanish grasses. Those outcompeted the native bunchgrasses, whose deeper roots kept them green through the year. But the climate warming of the twenty-first and twenty-second centuries favored the feisty, talented travelers people called weeds—which just meant a plant someone didn't like—that were more robust compared to the local Spanish grasses. So change came again, and the Bowl would face such sweeping alterations, too.

Moodily mulling this over, he hardly noticed when Terry nudged him. "Something big."

Aybe saw it, too, and angled them over into shelter

below a ledge. A long blue green tube was drifting high up across the sky. It was partway through a turn, coming around so the nose pointed their way.

"It's seen us," Terry said. "And coming down. Speeding up."

Aybe said, "Same old deal—you trade altitude for velocity."

"So they've got blimps," Terry said. "Makes sense, with this deep an atmosphere."

"Yeah," Aybe said. "Got no fossil fuels, hard to run a plane without 'em. Might as well float."

Irma pointed. "Not a blimp. Fins moving. Rowing in the sky? Look—" She close-upped with her binocs. "—it's got eyes."

"A living blimp," Cliff said. "That's one adaptation I didn't think of."

Through his binocs he close-upped the warty hide of the thing. Bumps and gouges expanded into turrets and sealed locks. Yet the thing had big eyes and ample fins like the sails of a fat ship. They canted to catch the wind and he saw other eyes toward the stern of it.

How could such a thing evolve? He had seen floating birdlike things with big, orange throats they could expand. But he'd guessed that was just a sexual display, not a navigational trick. There were odd slits in its side. At extreme magnification he saw things moving along there and abruptly knew he was seeing through a transparent window. The tiny shapes visible there looked like the Bird Folk. "Living, sure. With passengers."

Irma said, "I can see the tail as it comes around.

Big! It's sure hard to judge distance here. From the detail, I can see it's a long way off, ten klicks at least."

Terry said, "So it's *really* large. . . ."

"We'd better run," Aybe said, and took the mag-car whooshing down the slope. He popped up the field screen to deflect the wind.

Terry said, "Circle round, block their view so they can't see us as they approach."

"Right," Cliff said, thinking. "Run into those canyons and stay low. We'll be hidden then."

They continued down, Aybe deftly buffeting them against the magnetic fields. This took them frighteningly close to the sheets of rock that made up the spire. "Stay near the trees, at least!" shouted Terry. "If we smack those rocks at these speeds—"

"Don't bother me!" Aybe shouted, and narrowed his eyes, gripping the yoke tightly. Sweat ran down his brow and dripped off his chin.

They got into a narrow canyon just as something came arcing through the sky. It was a slim airplane with visible pilots. "Should've known they'd send something faster. Think they saw us?"

"We were visible only a few seconds—"

The canyon wall exploded. Shards and chunks of rock rained down. The windshield proved to be better than that. Cliff jerked his head up at the *wham* of impact and saw a rock larger than his head fall, tumbling, then sag into the field shield and bounce off.

Aybe threw the yoke forward and they accelerated, a meter above the rough ground. The car jittered as the magnetics dealt with the onrushing shelves of rock in the canyon floor.

Cliff heard somebody's breath rasping in and out. He had heard it before. It was his. The others were hanging on as Aybe made a hard left into a narrow side cut. *What if this is a box canyon?* Cliff thought but decided not to say. It was too late. They rounded the sharp curve and another *wham* behind them threw rocks and gravel against the magcar. Cliff looked up but could not see the plane. Aybe took a hard right into a passage that angled steeply up so only a sliver of sky showed.

Irma said, "If we get trapped in here—"

"We're not running, we're hiding," Aybe said flatly. "I don't think they can see us this far down in a crevice."

Terry said, "You decided that without a word?"

"There wasn't time. They threw missiles at us so fast, I could barely stay out of their view. They'd catch us eventually."

Irma said, "You're right. Or anyway, we have to stick with this now."

Terry hunched down and twisted his mouth skeptically. "What if they just use bigger warheads?"

"I doubt they can. Punching away at the under-structure of this Bowl is risky," Cliff said. "I'd bet they don't use heavy ordnance."

"Let's hope," Terry said.

So they sat. They kept the screen up, which in turn muffled outside sounds. They sat so they could watch in all four directions, including up at the crooked line of blue sky. That soon went white from clouds scudding in. They could hear no sounds of the plane or the colossal balloon creature, and neither crossed the crack of sky.

Purple clouds slid across the narrow slit above. For a moment they drew down the windscreen and listened. A breeze stirred the sand nearby but they could hear no odd sounds. "We'd better just stay here, lie still, draw no fire," Aybe said.

So they waited a long hour. Then another.

Terry got impatient. They dropped the screen again, and everyone got out to pee. Cliff squatted in a side passage and had just finished up using the paper tree bark to clean himself when suddenly big raindrops smacked his head. More spattered down as he ran back, getting soaked. By the time he got there, torrents were hammering on the magcar and bringing a prickly tinge of ozone as lightning forked and crackled. He was last and they all got more wet when Aybe dropped the screen to let Cliff in.

They sat and watched noisy water splash down the rock walls. Streams rushed by, gathering force and lapping at the car.

"We'd better get the hell out of here," Terry said.

Aybe scowled skeptically at the rushing water. "Okay. I'd rather get caught than drown."

"If water gets drawn up into our undercarriage—" Cliff stopped. "Never mind, we don't really know how this thing works anyway."

This had been bothering him, but it did no good to say so now. *You learn more with your mouth shut,* he thought. *Amazing, how often that's the right way to go.* No one said anything as streams slid down the screen, blurring the view.

"Somebody could come up on us here and we'd never know," Terry mused. "But movement draws attention," Terry added.

Cliff recalled his father saying, *The early bird may get the worm, sure, but the second mouse gets the cheese.*

"We can't just sit here," Aybe said adamantly. "That living balloon will come looking, use a search grid."

Irma nodded, her hair bedraggled. Aybe tried the controls and got a comforting hum from the floor. He lifted them above the muddy, frothing waters. Gingerly he found a side channel and went up it. After cautiously following that for minutes, Aybe paused to see if any danger lurked. A broad canyon yawned ahead, ghostlike in the sleeting rain that blew by in gusts. "This is a real break," he said, looking back at the others, who were still wringing water out of their clothes. "Looks like a long valley. I think I'll make time up that canyon so that air whale can't find us."

"Unless they can look through rain in nonvisible wavelengths," Terry said. "Then we'll be a nice fat moving target."

Irma said, "And we *are* a target. Aybe, don't worry—you won't get caught. They're shooting to kill."

Silence as this sank in.

"Um," Aybe said. "I'll hug the walls, then."

"Might help," Terry said, "but—" He glanced up at an angle, saw nothing through the hammering downpour. "—we don't know where that sky whale is."

"And we won't know," Cliff said. "That's our problem."

Aybe grinned. "Indecision may or may not be my problem. . . ." They all laughed, breaking the tension.

Out they went. The canyon snaked a lot and through the screen looked like dim blobs. Without saying anything, Aybe turned up the speed, elevating another meter for safety. At a speed Cliff judged to be at least sixty klicks an hour, the driving rain seemed to miraculously go away. Water swept around the sides and Cliff realized this was from the speed, clearing the view far better than wipers could.

They sat and pretended not to worry, which only lengthened the silences between them. Cliff realized that while they had been running from aliens for long weeks now, the odds had changed. The birdlike aliens were trying to kill them now. If cornered, what should he do?

He knew he wouldn't beg. That would be an insult to all humanity. He felt this immediately, without thinking.

The others were probably thinking about this, too. He could see the strain in their averted eyes, the sagging lines of fatigue in Irma, who was still futilely trying to wring out her hair. How much longer could they take of this?

Aybe concentrated, flying them past rock walls, which zoomed by like ghosts that slid out of the storm, flashed by, and then fell away into mist. Cliff realized that rain was the only cover they or any living thing had here. No creature could take advantage of darkness, ever. He saw some animals running nearby and wondered if they, too, were repositioning themselves. Or using the rain as cover to mate?

"Y'know, maybe it's no accident that most people have sex at night," he said suddenly. "Or at least indoors." He had to get them out of this funk, if only because *he* had to get out of it.

"What?" Irma shot him a sharp warning look.

So he told them in roundabout fashion. Start with fear of attack while coupled, so do it in the dark and under shelter. Then frame it as really important to everyone. Give social signals, so nakedness implied you were willing to have sex—why else were people so embarrassed to be seen nude, as though they had revealed some deep secret? Set up tribal rules so couples don't get disturbed then. Make it important, not just a quick jump-on in the dark. It was a contrived theory, made up on the spot, but it did its job.

As he had guessed, Aybe made the first joke. It wasn't a very good one, but Terry followed that with a real groaner. They got to laugh and sport, and the lines in their faces faded. Talk came fast, short, punchy, delicious. Their group training came out unself-consciously—how to lift the mood, knit up the small abrasions of working together.

Cliff knew he had droned on during the long times they were sand sailing, and now in the mag car for days, so he made use of that history.

After the laughing, he went on just to distract them from the danger they were in and could take only so much of, and still stay steady and focused. So he told them what he thought about this strange huge place. He noticed that there were flowers, pretty unsurprising as a convergent evolution—but here they always bloomed. Trees didn't drop leaves unless they were dying, since no chill was coming, ever. Animals had no downtime—so burrows where they rested were large, and guarded. Small animals defended their nests ferociously since they had to have a sheltered spot in near darkness to rest, recuperate, and, of course, mate.

Irma gave him a skeptical look and he knew his little seminar was boring them again. When he paused, she said, "Why's this so big? And why's nobody here?"

Terry said, "You mean, why so much open land?"

Aybe said, "They don't like cities, maybe? We haven't seen anything more than towns."

Cliff nodded. "Even from *SunSeeker* we didn't see big metro areas."

"Maybe the Bird Folk like countryside, not cities," Irma said. "I know I do."

They came around a long curve and suddenly the rain died. Without prompting, they all stood and surveyed as far as they could. Terry called, "It's there!"

The balloon creature was a distant tube hanging

above a rocky headland. Cliff hadn't thought till now that the balloon was subject to the winds that brought the storm. It was plain bad luck that the wind moved the creature to block their path.

Looking through his binocs, Terry called, "They just dispatched one of those silent planes. It's turning back toward us."

Only then did Cliff glance in the opposite direction and see that the spire lay behind them. "Damn!" he said. "We have to go back where we were." *So much for running away.*

Aybe expertly turned the magcar and took them away, using the canyon walls to keep them screened from the airplane's view. They ran hard for the spire canyons, which were deeper and afforded more shelter. They all sat in silence. Being hunted was now a gray fear they all carried at the back of their minds, with no letup.

Aybe slowed a bit and let out a yelp. "I got it! I've been wondering about that spire. Cliff, check me. We saw a pattern of them from *SunSeeker,* right?"

"Uh, yeah."

"I know why. They're in a grid because they're part of the construction. They're stress juncture points!"

They looked at him blankly. "They're like counterweights, see?" Aybe took his hands off the yoke and gestured, palms perpendicular to each other. "They draw support cables and pair them off against each other in bridges, see?"

Irma said vaguely, "This spinning bowl, it's like a bridge?"

"Yes," Aybe said eagerly, "one with both ends tied to each other."

"Why's it a spire?" Terry asked.

"I'll bet there's a counter-spire on the outside of the bowl, too. It's all about matching stress." To their hesitant looks, he added, "Think of it as like an arch, each side supporting the other."

"An arch works against gravity—," Terry began.

"And this place works against the centrifugal force—which we feel as gravity," Aybe said triumphantly.

Cliff liked Aybe's getting them out of their funk, but had to ask, "So what? I mean, that's cute but—"

"Don't you see?" Aybe asked, wide eyed. "The natural place to lay out a transit system is along the stress lines. That's where the heavy mechanics gets resolved. Plenty of support for rail lines, things like that."

Cliff thought he got it, but—"So some transport stops here? Like a train station?"

"Or elevator," Aybe said. "Same thing, really, in a damn weird contraption like this."

Cliff called up some pictures he had from the *SunSeeker* surveys. Under high resolution, he could make out the tiny needle points jutting off the back side, pointing at the stars. They formed a grid around the hemisphere and had seemed unimportant at the time. He had been overwhelmed with the whole idea then, just getting his head around it.

"So?" Terry asked. "We've got airplanes looking for us—"

"And we can hide, but who knows what kinds of

detectors they have?" Aybe rushed on. "So we have to go to ground, get out of their view—"

"Into that subway system you think correlates with the spire, right?" Irma said brightly.

Aybe jerked a thumb up. "Yep! You're right, it's more like a subway, buried below us."

"And where is it?" Cliff said soberly.

"At the spire, of course. Makes engineering sense. I was stupid not to see it before."

They were all standing and Cliff slapped him on the shoulder. "Great! Sniff it out, then."

Irma hugged Aybe, and Terry shook his hand, but as he did so, they heard a distant whispering burr. Terry jerked his head. "The plane. It's coming."

"We'd better find this subway pretty damn soon," Cliff said.

They set off, moving fast.

PART VIII

ONE MAN'S MAGIC

One man's "magic" is another man's engineering.
—ROBERT A. HEINLEIN

FORTY-ONE

This alien technology had a strange effect on him. Cliff looked at it with foreboding as they approached.

The towering sides of great obsidian-dark slabs let intricate designs play out in the elongated perspectives. Bladelike sheaths of a gleaming yellow metal soared up the flat faces, ornamenting it with geometric shapes that tricked the eye into confusions of perspective. Or Cliff's eyes, anyway. Triple vertical vents like shark gills suggested a cooling channel.

It loomed above them as they dismounted from the magcar. In the last few hours, they had chased down innumerable narrow canyons, looking for Aybe's "train station" somewhere near the base of the stony spire. After several false leads into literal blind alleys, their nerves got frayed. Coming back out of a canyon they knew would serve as a perfect trap for their pursuers above, they wondered what waited in the sky. Airplanes swam like sharks in the pale blue and seemed to frighten big flocks of birds into flapping anxiously away. Aybe hugged the magcar to the stone walls, moving into the open only when they were low on the horizon.

Then the magcar nearly ground to a halt, strumming and grinding in its bowels. Aybe had a hard time getting it to inch forward. After a tense while, it surged again. Following a winding gorge that slowly widened, they came upon what Cliff now realized should have been obvious—a broad, steep canyon of what seemed to be a conglomerate blending into green sandstone, water cut and layered. This canyon spread out after a few kilometers into an enormous plaza of rough stone, baking beneath the constant sun. They circled this, still keeping to the walls, until across the expanse they saw a lofty construction sunk into the mass of the rising spire. Cliff judged it to be at least a kilometer high. It took them nearly an hour to circle around to near its base. Then they paused.

Irma said, "Look, tracks."

Wheeled transport had passed this way many times, leaving a spaghetti snarl of trails. Most were so faint, Cliff had to avert his eyes to see them.

Terry gestured. "Some gouged their way."

Deep ruts were spaced about ten meters apart. Whatever had come this way stressed the very rock it moved on. The rut rims were rounded, so it must have been long ago. "They go straight into that," Irma said, pointing to the open entrance at the center of the black façade.

They all hesitated. Aybe moved the magcar forward but again it slowed, muttered and snarled, and slowed even more.

"I hope it's not failing," Irma said.

"I can't figure what's up." Aybe shrugged. "Tried

the registers in these funny displays, popped open what I could. Most of it's sealed tight, or has key slots I don't have tools for. Not like I have the operating manual."

"We've been driving it pretty hard now—" Terry glanced at his right, which meant he consulted his interior software. "—thirteen days. Maybe it needs an oil and lube."

Irma sniffed. "Smells like a lubricant coming to a boil."

Cliff let them talk it out, knowing there wasn't any real choice. He turned his e-gear toward the sun. Once inside, he suspected there would be no chance to get a recharge.

"It makes sense," Irma was saying. "And we're at the entrance of this place, so—"

"So we hide the car and see what's inside," Cliff said quietly. "Beat it if we find trouble."

• • •

It was big. Also empty.

More deep ruts in the flooring showed where the big weight had come from. They followed, eyes constantly moving.

In the middle of a huge, high-ceiling foyer stood stonework on a pedestal. It was the size of a big man and rotated slowly on a magnetic suspension. All surrounding light seemed to radiate out from it, sparkling as rich facets shifted up and down the color spectrum.

Cliff moved his head, and fresh detonations of

blue and yellow lanced out. The stone did not seem to have a fixed shape. As facets shifted across its surface, the very boundaries of the thing seemed to alter. "It's hypnotic," Aybe said.

Its light came from within yet played on what light fell on it—brilliant, soothing, stunning in its sense of eternal hard beauty.

Irma took out her laser and down-tuned it to flashlight level. She played it over the stonework, fetching forth bright, coruscating waterfalls of spectral glows. "What an artwork," she said admiringly.

So it was, Cliff thought, but—"Turn your laser off. Maybe it's an alarm."

Irma blinked and backed away. The stonework subsided, its splintered light dimming. Plainly it fed on incoming light. "Let's move," she said.

They backed away from the stonework and followed the ruts toward a high arched entrance. Inside the next large cavern, they saw a huge door divided in two. "Looks like an elevator, all right," Terry said.

"No button on the side to summon it," Irma noted.

"Over millions of kilometers?" Aybe shook his head. "It'll have to work like a train to—"

Faint sounds from behind them. A rustling, then a clang. Cliff looked around. "There, lower left on the far wall. Could be a door."

They scrambled for it. On close approach at a full run, Cliff saw it was much bigger than a human door and had a lumpy embedded ornament—maybe a lock?—in the middle.

As Cliff skidded to a halt, Aybe said, "Why run? Let's take them on."

"For what?" Irma spat out.

Cliff ignored them. The door didn't respond to a simple shove and it didn't look as though their lasers could quickly cut through the heavy metal around it—brass? Iron? He couldn't think. The thumping noises from behind them were louder now. The ornament had a complicated opening at its center. And now he heard clumping footsteps and rumblings of something heavier.

He fumbled with the collar around the center and then Irma said, "Let me." She took a tool kit out and tried several long slender instruments. It seemed incredible to Cliff that this could be an analog lock. He started to brush her aside but then thought, *What would last here?* Not digital nets, whose elements decay. No—simple hard metal.

Irma struggled and tried another tool. A third. A fourth. The sounds behind got stronger and now Cliff could hear some muffled jabber making sounds like words, but he was too frazzed out to think about them. Irma twisted hard—she had two levers in the complicated slot—and it gave.

The door was heavy and it squeaked as Irma and Terry shoved it open. Beyond lay darkness. They all stepped through and carefully tugged the door back. Irma turned her laser to illumination mode and they saw the rugged lock apparatus on the door's center. Terry shoved one of Irma's tools through the stay to stop it from locking them in, and they all pushed the door into its frame. No click.

"Is that smart?" Cliff whispered. "They can just push and know someone's come in through it."

Irma frowned. "Maybe so. They came so fast, as if they're answering that alarm—must be from nearby."

Aybe said, "If they're caretakers, they'll conduct a search. Maybe they can extract images from that stonework and know what we look like."

"Let's lock it behind us," Cliff said. "Now."

They did, releasing the rod and watching a big clamp take hold. "Now what?" Terry said.

They turned to peer through the gloom. Big machinery ran along one wall, secured with chains. Dust tickled his nostrils and coated his lips. It felt fine and acidic, the grime of millennia. Somehow this felt luxurious, as if he could fall into its soft domain. He had not realized how the silky texture of the restful dark felt like home.

"Cliff, come on," Terry called, and he went to explore.

They were in a framing room that apparently wrapped around the "railroad" and held repair equipment. Large transparent walls showed them the railroad itself. There were indeed two sets of rails in the middle of the large corridor, running flat on the ground and tapering away into blurred distance. A blue radiance showed collars lining the rail tunnel, pale frames with luminescent inner rims of white.

"Big rail cars, must be," Aybe said.

Cliff said, "Boxcars the size of a house."

"That white light is getting stronger," Irma pointed out.

"I feel a breeze," Terry said. Howard was coughing in the dust that swarmed up from the floor.

Cliff could see four of the collars brighten, and the breeze got stronger and suddenly the white collars flared. In the hard flash, a crackling came sharp as something shot by and a muffled *whump!*—with a quick flicker—told them the thing had passed at high velocity. The window rattled—

Then the true surge wrapped through the side rooms, and the heft of it knocked them down. It was quick and delayed just enough so that Cliff knew what had happened only when he found himself flat on his back, blinking up into the dimly lit dark. He got up, rubbing his head where it had hit the dusty floor. He sneezed.

The others were up and wandering. Irma stood, legs spread and head down, gasping in the low oxygen. Howard rubbed his head, cursing. Terry got to his feet and leaned on the wall beside the big window and breathed in and out in a systematic way, eyes ahead.

Aybe got unsteadily to his feet, slipped, caught himself. His eyes wandered and he shook his head, gasped. "See those?" he asked, pointing at slim, shiny fibers, electrical ribbons attached at all four sides. "They're dischargers. That flash—even through this thick window, my hair stood on end. This must be an electrodynamic system."

Cliff remembered e-lifts Earthside that worked by charging elevators and then handing the weight off to a steady wave of electrodynamic fields. This might be similar.

"Did you feel that tremor as it passed?" Aybe said. "It didn't just shake—the floor, it sank a bit. That 'train' is heavy."

Terry said, "How do we get on one?"

"Find out how to stop one, first," Cliff said.

Terry smiled. "Then—where do we go?"

The big question. "Away from here," Cliff said. "That's what we've been doing all this time—move, dodge, try to learn."

"What about finding Beth's team?" Irma asked.

Cliff paused and felt their eyes on him. "I'd like to, sure. As far as we know, they're in the hands of the Bird Folk. But where?"

"Maybe near the mirror zone?" Aybe asked.

"Because they sent that image from there?" Irma shook her head. "Could be just suckering us in."

Cliff held his tongue. He hadn't known when it happened how to discuss with the others the Beth image. He still didn't.

"Y'know," Terry said, "we're going way out on a limb here."

"Out on a limb," Irma said, "is where the fruit is."

Aybe said impatiently, "We need to get away! Why not take the first one we can get?"

They all looked at one another, as if realizing how little they knew and how few options they had—and nodded.

Cliff sensed a slight breeze. "Another one coming."

They braced themselves. But this time there was no gale, just an amiable breeze carrying a *whooooosh* that ebbed away. A long series of blocky cars passed, slowing, slowing—

That distracted them from seeing the black carapace of a machine that stood on three legs beside a side wall. Its slender arms manipulated controls on a panel. It made a final move and the train stopped.

Down a side alley of the vast alien platform came bulky gray robots. Soundless, swift, they ran on tracks and held their big arms up, as if saluting. A team of six opened the side of one car and started unloading capsules stacked within. They moved with surprising speed, all coordinated and specialized— lifting, loading, moving the capsules down the alley and into the distant reaches. None of the robot heads turned to look at the humans watching through the viewport nearby; they worked like monomaniacs, which of course they were.

"See that control box against the side wall?" Howard pointed. "That machine used it and the train stopped."

They studied the machines working, and Cliff felt a tremor beneath his feet. Again he had the sensation of something massive moving nearby. It seemed to pass perpendicular to the tracks he could see. "There's another level," he guessed. "The other axis of a grid, must be."

"Sure, longitude and latitude on the Bowl," Terry said.

"These tracks run to higher latitude," Aybe said.

Irma asked, "How can you tell?"

Aybe grinned, nodded to her. "I have an innate sense of direction. In basic, remember when they set us down in a forest and told us to find our way home?"

Cliff did. He had flunked. It had made him fear being dropped, though he did well in the other field tests. "So?"

Aybe's grin got wider. "I beat your asses, remember? I watched you straggle in."

It had been embarrassing. Cliff felt his face burn at the memory. The Georgia pine forest was utterly flat, the trees packed in tight to get the best yield for pulp paper, so the going was tough—and the sky cloudy, so he couldn't use the sun to navigate. He had finally paired up with a guy, then another, and they had found their way by using a search pattern, each staying within calling distance of the others. Not really a way to track in wilderness, when there might be predators or enemies, but it had worked. Sort of. Later he learned that he had nearly lost the cut for *SunSeeker* because of that. Even though he had been an Eagle Scout.

Irma's mouth twisted sardonically. "So?"

Aybe glared. "Just that these are the tracks we should take to higher latitude. This train is headed the right way. It's freight, no passengers we can see . . ."

"And?" Terry asked.

Aybe was making them wait for his wisdom. "Let's have it," Cliff said sharply.

"If we jump on this one, stay in the vacant cars, nobody will see us."

Hop a freight, Cliff remembered reading in a novel somewhere. A classical expression, apparently.

Irma looked dubious, eyebrows raised. Terry snorted. "We'd be stuck in a box!"

"Aren't we stuck right now?" Aybe shot back.

"These are freight cars—"

Aybe held up his phone, thumbed it to a slow replay. "I got this while the first cars whizzed by." The lead car had windows, and through them they could see oddly shaped seats or couches. There were rectangular machines on the far walls. "Looks like passenger seats. Nobody in that one, as far as I can see."

Terry said, "Seems risky."

Cliff held up his hands. "How do we do it, anyway? I don't see a way—"

"There—" Aybe pointed down a side corridor. "I saw a doorway to the left, and I'll bet we can get to it that way."

Terry shook his head. "I doubt we—"

A clanking came at the big door they had come through. It was locked and secured with a metal bar Irma had found. They stared at the heavy door as the noise—rattles, bumps, jarring hits—got louder.

"They found us . . . ," Terry said. "Damn—"

The rattles stopped and so did Terry. Pause. A buzzing sound from the large door.

Cliff said, "They're cutting in."

Aybe said, "Let's get out of here."

Irma raised an eyebrow. "To . . . where?"

Cliff looked at the robots. They were nearly done unloading. He leaned against the hard, transparent window and saw in a long perspective other dock-ing platforms, with milling robots. It was a long train.

He didn't like being forced into a move. *If you're on the run, though . . .*

"Let's do it," Cliff said. "Now."

Nods, some resigned sighs. They had brought most of their gear in backpacks and stuffed cargo pants. They ate some of their food as they watched the robots finishing up; less to carry. Cliff worried about getting on this train, but there seemed no other plausible option. How would they eat? When should they try to get off?

The robots were nearly done when they angled down the left side corridor. There were periodic windows. Cliff could see similar robot teams un-loading or loading other cars. They trotted along, looking for the passenger cars. "Let's pick it up," he called out. If the train left and they were trapped . . .

They ran for five minutes until they saw the sole passenger car, the leader of a long line that stretched far into the rear. This one was longer than the freight cars and had big windows. And it looked vacant.

No robots seemed to be around it. They went through a kind of lock with a pressure seal flexible frame, and onto the dock. Robots labored in the distance but took no notice of the humans. The car door slid easily aside, and they spread out to see if anyone was aboard. Nothing, though the place had a damp smell like a zoo. A forward-viewing win-dow showed the tunnel ahead, lit every hundred meters or so by phosphor walls giving an ivory glow.

They tried the rectangular machines bolted to one wall and found that they yielded food—or what passed for it here. Punch and grab, an analog system. Some wrapped things fell into the hopper. They looked like dried cat litter but smelled not bad.

They stayed out of view of the windows. Cliff felt tired. Howard looked worse. There was blood in his scalp.

They watched carefully, but the machines that passed by outside seemed unaware of anything wrong. Just as he sat down, the train accelerated away without any warning. Irma had found a big door with pressure seals on it and was about to open it when the train started. She sat down hastily and they found the seats adjusted to their shape automatically, and warmed to a comfortable temperature as well. After so long in the magcar, Cliff let himself relax.

But the train kept accelerating. He sniffed the air and tasted the tang of ozone. The ride was smooth and he went forward to see. They were hurtling forward at a speed he estimated, from the rapid fluttering of the passing wall phosphors, at over a hundred kilometers an hour. Yet the acceleration increased still.

He sat next to Aybe and said, "We're still accelerating."

"This is a big place. This system is already better than any e-train I ever rode on. To move around it in, say, a week, means this thing has to get into the neighborhood of a hundred kilometers a *second*."

"Um. Maybe they take longer."

"I hope not. Those food machines can't—wait, maybe they *can* make food from scratch." Aybe blinked at the thought.

Cliff worried that he had led them not into a trap, but into a death voyage.

FORTY-TWO

Redwing watched the Bowl's enormous landscape slide by in the distance and reflected on how, decades ago, he had been something of a scientist, too. He had become a spacer because of that.

And from that he'd won the habits of mind that led him to lead a band of scientists and engineers to a new world. This thing, the Bowl, was not a world, but a huge contrivance. It gave the appearance of being nearby, because he could see patterns resembling those he had watched for wonderful hours, in low Earth orbit. Yet it was tens of millions of kilometers away, its sealed-in atmosphere deep and strange.

The comparison deceived his eye. Here the atmospheric circulations he had studied as a young man were utterly different and vast beyond comprehension. The star's light fell uniformly, or nearly so, across the Bowl. But it never set, and so drove none of the night-day winds that shaped the movements he had studied, the stately currents of atmospheres on Mars, Earth, Titan, Venus. The Bowl always kept the same attitude toward its star, too. That meant no seasonal variations, no hard winters or hammering summers. He had savored long ago—centuries in real time!—crisp autumn skies, with their bright, blazing fall colors, and then after the cold months, the promise of spring. None of that happened here. Aliens had designed in the steady shine of a small star and its jet. No night. What would want to live in endless day?

So air currents did not flow up from the spot where the star was directly above, since there were none. Or rather, it was the Knothole, where the Jet passed through. No Hadley cells, polar swirls, trade winds, or barren desert belts wrapping around the globe. Instead, here the effect of spin held sway.

He could see long streaming rivers of cloud begin above the ample dark blue seas, then arc over distances larger than the separation between the Earth and its moon, driven to higher latitudes of the immense Bowl. Purple anvils of sullen cumulonimbus towered up to seven kilometers above landscapes of mottled brown and red. The scale of all this violated his sense of what patterns could be possible. Clearly the whole vast contraption had been designed to hold everything constant—steady sunlight, no big differences of temperature to drive storms or trade winds. It left him with no intuitions at all of how weather got shaped.

Climate came from the spin, then. To pin its

inhabitants to the ground, they spun it—and then got curious Coriolis effects.

Abruptly the name alone brought back his grad student days. That had been more than half a century ago, and there leaped to mind a drunken song of the climate modelers.

ON A MERRY-GO-ROUND IN THE NIGHT
CORIOLIS WAS SHAKEN WITH FRIGHT
DESPITE HOW HE WALKED
'TWAS LIKE HE WAS STALKED
BY SOME FIEND ALWAYS PUSHING HIM RIGHT!

Apparently Coriolis had been a mild man, but his force made hurricanes, tornadoes, jet streams, and assorted violences. Those should occur here—and as he thought it, he saw a brilliant white hurricane coming into view of the screen on his office wall. That slow churn of darkening clouds was the size of Earth itself, spinning its gravid whirl toward the shore of a huge sea. *Trouble for somebody,* he thought. *Or something.*

The knock on his door drew him back into the humdrum reality of *SunSeeker.*

Karl's lean face was all smiles, which could be good news. *There's a first time for everything,* Redwing thought. But the lean man folded himself into the guest chair and unloaded the bad news first.

"There's a progressive crazing of those transparent ceramic windows we use for the astronomy," he began. "Caused by mechanical stress or maybe some ions that get through the magnetic screen. Limits their working life."

"You can fix it?"

He waved a hand lazily, somehow sure of himself. "Sure, got the printer making new ones right now. The external robos can slap them on when done, and I'll feed the old ones in for materials stock. Not why I came to see you, Cap'n." The slow smile again, above dancing eyes. "I've got an idea."

"Good to hear," Redwing said automatically. This was maybe the twentieth notion Karl had delivered this way. The man did deserve some credit, for he had spruced up the ship and made it run better. But the man was so focused on his machines that he was not much further use as a deck officer. Redwing could see Karl was settling in to bask in the tech details, and it was more efficient to just let him work through it.

"I've been tuning our scoop fields for the plasma we're getting from that small star," Karl said. "It's not like protons incoming at a tenth of light speed, so I had to retune all the capture capacitors."

Redwing knew the big breakthrough that made starflight possible, though it relied on tech you never saw from the bridge. The method of catching the sleet of protons, slowing them down between charged grids for electrical power, then funneling them into the fusion chambers where a catalyst worked the nuclear magic—it all happened in the halo around the ship, and then the burn occurred in its guts, where no one could ever go. *We ride on miracles.*

He nodded, waiting for the idea.

"So we're flying with a scoop a thousand kilometers across now, all supported by nanotube mesh. Bigger funnel than we had before, 'cause the plasma's weaker. I tuned it all up—had to use the full complement of our external in-flight robos, too."

"I like the ride now," Redwing allowed. "It doesn't wake me up nights."

Karl beamed. "Glad to hear it. Lowers the structural stresses, too. Then I thought—this scoop arrangement we've got isn't optimal for where we are, so what would be better?"

Redwing wanted to ask him to just spit it out, but that didn't work well with tech crew. "I'll guess—the Jet?"

Karl's face fell. "How did you know? If—"

"What else do we have in this system?" Redwing asked with a grin. "Had to be the Jet. Plus, you know we flew in here through that Jet. What a ride!"

Karl looked surprised at Redwing's enthusiasm. The man was elaborately casual, but conservative to the bone. Useful in a deck officer, where a captain had to balance personality types against one another. A captain had to know when to take risks, not tech lieutenants.

Redwing had always thought that life's journey wasn't to get to your grave safely in a well-preserved body, but rather to tumble in, wrecked, shouting, *What a ride!* But he could see from Karl's puzzled expression that the man thought captains should be sober-minded authority figures, steady and sure, without a wild side.

"Well, sir, yes—I looked into that. The scoop settings we had then weren't as good at sailing up the Jet as the ones we have now, so . . ." Karl hesitated, as if his idea was too risky. "Why not use *SunSeeker* as a weapon?"

Now *this* was an idea. Not that he understood what it was, but the flavor of it quickened his pulse. "To . . ."

"Let me walk through it. Remember when we saw the mirror zone changing, painting a woman's face on it? I was outside with robot teams to repair the funnel struts. I could see it direct, right out my faceplate. Incredible! It was Elisabeth Marble, the one they captured with her team, mouthing words."

Redwing gestured slightly to speed him up and Karl took the hint. "Even that—which lasted maybe an hour, then repeated every day or so—had an effect on the Jet. Gave it less sunlight, I guess, or just rippled the light over the Jet base. Big changes! A day or two later, I saw little snarls propagating out from the base of the Jet, at the star. They grew, too, moving out."

"We all did." It hadn't seemed much different from the variations Redwing had seen, over time—knots in the string. He was still amazed the bright scratch across the sky was so stable.

Karl leaned forward, eyes excited. "The mirrors focus on that spot, delivering the heat to blow plasma off the star's surface. Plus, there are stations circling the base of the Jet that must somehow generate magnetic fields. I'm guessing those big stations then shape and confine the Jet. So—" Karl cocked a jaunty grin. "—why not show them what we can do to the Jet?"

Redwing exhaled a skeptical breath. "To do what?"

"Screw it up!"

"So it—"

"Develops a kink instability. The disturbance grows as it advances out from the Jet base. It's like a fire hose—you have to hold it straight or it snarls up and fights you like an angry snake."

"Then when it gets to the Bowl . . ."

"I'm thinking we could force the kink amplitude to grow enough, it'll snake out sideways. If it hits the atmosphere containment layer—that sheet that sits on top of the ring section—then it can burn clean through it."

Redwing studied Karl's eager face. This was world destruction on a scale Redwing had never imagined. Should he have?

"Then there's the sausage instability—we get those sometimes in the funnel plasma, before it hits the capacitor sheets and slows down. A bulge starts in the flow, say, starting from turbulence. That bulge forces the magnetic fields out, and that can grow, too, just like the kink. You get a cylinder of fast plasma that looks like a snake that's eaten eggs, spaced out along it."

"So it gets fat and can—"

"Scorch the territories near the Knothole, where the Jet passes closest to the Bowl. Knock out their control installations there, I bet." The words came flooding out of the man. "I've studied them through our scopes, and they're huge coils all around the Knothole mouth. I bet they're magnets that keep the Jet away. Magnetic repulsion, gotta be."

Redwing was aghast, but he couldn't let Karl see that. "We do this by flying into the Jet?"

"More like tickling it. I can work out how we can zig across it, then zag back at the right time and place to drive an instability."

"Near the Jet base, by the star?"

"Okay, so it'll get a little hot in here, I grant you that."

Good to know he would grant something, at least. For a man proposing to kill the largest imaginable construct, he seemed unfazed.

"At no danger to *SunSeeker*?"

"I can tune the funnel parameters, do some robo work on the capacitor sheets. Fix 'em up." Karl smiled proudly. "I ran a simulation of running *SunSeeker* across the Jet already. There's a problem slicing through the hoops of magnetic stresses at the Jet boundary, sure. We cut through that and it's smooth sailing, looks like. Statistically, a Monte Carlo code shows we don't get bumped hard—"

"I recall a statistician who drowned in a lake that was on average fifty centimeters deep." Redwing smiled dryly.

Karl hastily retreated. "Well, we can just skim the Jet first, try it out."

"I'd like to see the detailed analysis, of course." He narrowed his eyes deliberately. "Written up in full."

If this crazy idea ever got anywhere, he wanted it documented to the hilt. Not that there would be any kind of superior review in his lifetime, Redwing mused, but it was good to leave a record, no matter what happened. Karl nodded and they went on to discuss some lesser tech issues.

After he left, Redwing stood and watched his wall screen show the unending slide of topography he still thought of as below, though of course *Sun-Seeker* was orbiting the star, not the Bowl. The hurricane was biting into the shoreline now, sowing havoc. Somebody was suffering.

He had seen that this Bowl, like a real planet, still had tropical wetlands, bleak deserts, thick green forests, and mellow, beautiful valleys. No mountain ranges worthy of the name, apparently because the mass loading would have thrown something out of kilter. But terrain and oceans galore, yes, of sizes no human had ever seen. But some minds had imagined, far back in ageless time.

The truly shocking aspect of Karl was not his idea, but the eager way he described ripping open the atmosphere cap. That would kill uncountable beings and might even destroy the Bowl itself. Redwing watched the Coriolis forces do their work. He tried to see how the global hydrologic cycle here could work—and then realized that this wasn't a globe, but a big dish, and all his education told him nearly nothing he could use.

Still, there were beings down there of unimaginable abilities. How could they survive a storm that lasted for weeks or months? That was the crucial difference here—scale. Everything was bigger and lasted longer. How long had the Bowl itself lasted?

And the creatures who made and ran it—they had both great experience and long history to guide them. Surely they would know what had occurred to Karl.

Just as surely, they would have defenses against visitors such as Karl.

FORTY-THREE

The e-train zoomed on, at speeds Cliff estimated to be at least ten kilometers per second. Astronomical velocities, indeed. Maybe Aybe was right, arguing that to get around the Bowl in reasonable times demanded speeds of 100 km/s. The blur beyond their windows showed only the fast flickering of phosphor rings as they shot through them, until even those blended together to become a dim flickering glow.

They broke up to explore the long passenger car. There were roomy compartments with simple platforms for sitting and sleeping, and rough bedding supplied in slide shelving. Howard discovered the switches after the first hour aboard, while searching for more food. Cliff heard his shouts and came running.

"Look!" Howard said proudly when all five were there. He slid to the side a hinge switch near a compartment door. He slid a switch on the wall, and the compartment ceiling phosphors dimmed to utter dark.

They hooted, clapped, and Irma did a dance with Aybe. It was as though they had gained their freedom—freedom from sunlight.

Irma favored exploring the rest of the car, and they did. Compartments varied in size and style, mostly in the arrangement of platforms. Irma remarked, "These can accommodate passengers of varying sizes and needs. Fit to species, I guess."

Cliff nodded. "The Bird Folk are big, sure, but some of the forms we saw from a distance were smaller. Interesting, to have intelligence in a range of body types."

"But why is nobody here?" Terry insisted.

Aybe added, "And nobody at the station, 'cept robots."

"Maybe they don't travel much?" Irma wondered.

No answers, plenty of questions. The passenger car was over a hundred meters long and ended with a pressure door, where the car narrowed down. "Let's not go further," Irma said. "Great find, Howard, that light switch. Let's use them, huh?"

Aybe found something that sounded like a grinder in the tiled floor of an otherwise bare room. "That's gotta be the head," Terry said. Starships used nautical terms, and soon they were calling the train's nose the bow.

They ate before sleeping. All along, mealtimes had been important, just as they had been in their interplanetary training missions. On the Mars Cycler,

Cliff had learned ship protocols and how to deal with short-arm centrifugal gravity (which made his head lurch the first week when he walked), but the most important lesson was the social congruence. Eating together promoted solidarity, teamwork, the crucial judgments of strengths and flaws they all needed to know. In a crisis, that knowledge let them respond intuitively. Here, where danger was never far away, those unspoken skills had quickly become crucial.

"What do we do when we pull into the next station?" Terry asked, munching one of the odd foods that he had squeezed out of a tube—which then evaporated into the air with a hiss, once emptied. How it knew to do this was a topic of puzzled discussion. Cliff watched them as they all—judging from expressions as they ate, each reflecting inwardly after the excitement of pursuit—wondered what they had gotten themselves into.

Too late, Cliff thought but did not say. He recalled another favorite phrase of his father's: *Life is just one damn thing after another.*

The train ran on in its silky way, electromagnetics handing off without a whisper of trouble. Cliff lay back and relaxed into the moody afterglow of eating more than one needed. The low hum of the train lulled him but he summoned up resolve to say, "We need to stand watches, same as before. Terry, you're up first."

Groans, rolled eyes, then the slow acceptance he had come to expect. Cliff made the most of it, standing up and trying to look severe. "We don't know anything here. We're not camping out anymore. This is a *train*, and it stops somewhere. When it does, we've got to be able to hide or run."

They nodded, logy with the meal, as he had planned.

Howard said, "We should break up, too. Don't clump up, so they can bag us all at once."

Cliff didn't like the pessimism behind that, but he said, "Good idea. But not alone."

Long silence. Terry glanced at Aybe, and Cliff suddenly remembered that one of them was gay. Which one? For the life of him, he could not remember. *Damn! All this time—*

Too late. Didn't matter anyway: Howard, Terry, and Aybe would be sharing. Nobody alone. Cliff and Irma—

Terry and Aybe looked at him, long steady gazes, and he realized that they knew. He would be with Irma and the compartments sealed off very nicely, thank you. Never mind who was gay, the big issue here was about him and Irma. He had been ignoring it. So consumed with his own emotions, he had not thought through what happened to a small band with cross-currents working below the surface. Now that they were inside again, back in a moving machine, somehow everything suppressed in the pseudo-wilderness of the Bowl melted away. It was about the old elementals—survival, sex, the splendor of the deep sensual accents. Life.

Realizing that left him speechless, which he also saw was a good idea. *Life is just one damn thing after another.*

"So what happens," Terry said evenly, "when we stop at a station?"

Irma said quickly, anxiously, "We need an exit."

All agreed. They trooped to the back end, *aft on the starboard side,* to consider the pressure door. "We've got to try it," Terry said.

The door opened with a shove. It led to a short lock chamber, and in the wall was a simple pressure gauge—long-lasting analog, of course—with release valves. Simple stuff, artifacts so clear they could serve generations without an instruction manual.

They factored through into a dark room that lit up slowly when they entered, phosphors brimming with sleepy glows.

"Freight," Terry said.

Dark lumps of webbed coverings secured units the size of Earthside freight cars at multiple points. It all looked mechanically secure and professional, robot work of a high order by Earthside standards.

Aybe said, "We fall back to here?"

"We don't have much choice," Terry said.

"If we start to slow down, send an all-alert," Irma said.

"Who's up on watch?" Terry asked innocently.

"You," Cliff said. He hadn't much hope the thin, angular man would stay awake more than five minutes beyond the rest. But it was good to set some standard, even if it was obviously not going to work. In their tired eyes he saw that they knew this, too.

So they went back, chose compartments, and

cut the phosphors. For the first time in their new, strange lives here, blessed night descended.

• • •

Cliff sat up. A subtle long slow bass rumbling came through the floor. He blinked, thinking fuzzily that maybe he was under a tree, maybe some animal was nearby—and suddenly knew that this was real, solid darkness. Not shade. It wasn't going away.

He found the wall switch and powered up the phosphors. Irma jerked, shook her head, shot a palm up to block the light. "Uhh! Noooo . . ."

"Got to. We're slowing down."

Cliff clicked on his phone, sent an all-alert. Until this moment he hadn't wondered if the walls of this train would block the signal. Well, too late—

"I'm up," Irma said unconvincingly. She got unsteadily to her feet, pulling on her gray underpants.

Cliff couldn't help himself. He started laughing, quick bursts of it. He bent over, tried to stop, couldn't. The laughs slowed, developed a hacking sound.

"What?" Irma said, struggling into her cargo pants.

He made himself stop. "I—I was thinking about . . . sex."

Skeptical frown. "Uh, yeah?"

"No, not now. I mean—just that—I worried about us and them, Terry and Howard and Aybe.

Last night. Never realized that sleep was the big thing we all wanted."

She grimaced, yawned, stretched. "Well, yeah. This is a sleep high—feels *so good*."

"Wow, yes. I musta slept—" He glanced at his phone. "—oog . . . fourteen hours."

"And you thought about sex?" She tried to smile, failed, rubbed her eyes.

"Not really. Just thinking about the team, y'know—oh, hell. I'm not up to speed."

"Speaking of—"

Yes. *The train was slowing.* They had been so joyful, they'd ignored it. He hastened into his own pants, boots, backpack, field gear. All he had, now. Into battle, maybe.

He went out into the corridor, pulling up his backpack harness. He had run away from enough threats to know that you never can count on going back for your gear. Terry and Aybe were already there, standing warily as they looked out the windows at the dark sliding by.

"Y'know," Irma said, "we should've looked for underground places to sleep."

"We did. We ran into nothing like this train station, but yeah, we shoulda looked harder."

The phosphors were pulsing as the train passed by, their gray hoops fluttering so slow now, he could see the flicker. "I see a platform up ahead," Aybe said.

Cliff went forward. Harder glows showed the prospect ahead. He close-upped it with his binocs.

There were teams of robots, standing in gray files. Beyond them . . . figures on the platform.

"Back into our rooms," Cliff said. Irma came up, still a little bleary eyed. "Seal the doors, too."

"What if some Bird Folk are assigned to our room?" Terry asked.

"Then we deal with it as it comes," Irma said, rolling her eyes.

The small surges of deceleration came slower now. Each segment of the rail line handed off to the next smoothly. Cliff went into the same compartment as Irma and they fell silent. This one had a window and they crouched down to be invisible from outside. The train slowed without any braking sound. Cliff felt hungry and fished out some of the salty food stock he had gotten from the machines. With plenty of water, it was bearable. They were long past the point of testing everything before eating now.

The train stopped. They waited. Distant clanks and rumbles. Irma and Cliff finally cast darting glances out the window. This went on and on. Robots trundled by, some as large as a car, their forward opticals never wavering. Irma put her hands on the floor, to feel any vibration from doors in their car.

"How do you feel?" she asked.

"Like a snowball in hell."

Footsteps outside, faint and hesitant. Stop, pause, then going on. Again. And again, closer.

The footsteps stopped outside. Cliff took out his laser and held his breath. The door had a mechanical lock that, despite their supposedly having secured it, now rotated. Cliff stepped forward and jerked it open.

A sleek, tawny creature held up its large, flat hands and said in slurred Anglish, "I share no harm."

Cliff glanced along the corridor, saw no one, gestured inward, and stepped back. The alien moved with grace, shifting its body to wedge into a corner, leaving the most space for the humans.

Irma said, "You speak . . . our language."

"Astronomers shared language with lessers, to make hunt easier. I loaded into my inwards. Please forgive my talk error. We were to seduce you into friendship giving out."

Cliff said, "Is anyone else coming on this train?"

The slim alien paused and consulted some internal link, Cliff judged, by the way it cast its gaze to the side. Cliff realized by standing they were visible to the platform and quickly squatted down. The alien mimicked this, bending as though it had no joints, only supple muscle.

"No. Distribute was to be, but I erased the possibility."

Its skull was highly domed, with high arches and a crest running along the top. Those and its short muzzle would give it strong jaw muscles, a classic predator feature. Yet it had no retractable claws, or maybe they were just relaxed. As he watched, the thick fingers extended sharp fingernails. *Ah!* Cliff thought. Binocular vision, too, with eyes that flicked restlessly from Irma to him.

"Erased?" Irma said cautiously.

It spoke with a low, silky growl that carefully enunciated vowels, as though they were strange. "Intersected controls so alone could greet you. And in keeping-with, deflected the pursuit team to the train orthogonal to this line."

"So we are safe here?" Irma persisted, focused intently on the alien.

"For short times."

"Why are you here?"

"To achieve consensus with you. We must bond to our joint cause."

"Which is?" Cliff said, bouncing quickly up from his squat to see the platform. Robots moving, no life-forms.

The alien made a short, soft, snorting sound. "Return to full sharing life."

To Irma's puzzled look—had it learned how to read human faces?—it said, "For all the Adopted."

"Which are—?" she asked.

"Many species, low and high. We are bonded here. We seek-wish to return-voyage our home worlds."

"You are from—?"

It made a sound like a soft shriek. In its large round eyes Cliff saw a kinship, an instant rapport that he did not need to think about. For one who dwelled in his head so much, this was a welcome rub of reality. The sensation of connection unsettled him. Why did he feel this way?

Then he had it—this was a smart cat.

"We will help you, if we can," Irma said. He saw at a glance that she felt the same as he.

"But we are only a few," Cliff hedged.

"You share-voyage with many in a ship that can damage-share the Astronomers." This came out as a fast, hissing statement, eyes widened.

A forward lurch came then, rocking them all on their haunches. Cliff stood up with some relief. Nobody on the platform. The train surged into its heavy acceleration again, pressing at them.

"Oops! Let's get into some chairs," Irma said. "And tell Howard and Aybe and Terry. Breakfast!" She broke into a broad grin that cheered him up, out of his confusion.

FORTY-FOUR

Memor was glad she had not brought her friend, Sarko, for this was a rude and joyless place.

From their vantage here, she could see the long flanks of composite rock, carved by ancient rivers. This was bare country, left behind when topsoil had fled downhill in the far past. Now its canyons had a certain majestic uselessness for habitation, which made it perfect for an assembly of search parties. They could survey the low gravity forests that began at the canyon mouths below—a blue green ocean. Long, undulant waves marched across that plain of treetops, stretching into the distant dim oblivion.

Those lofty reaches ranked among her favorite natural wonders, the gift of low gravity. There, one could "swim" in the trees, buoyed up by their fragrant multitude. The vast trees stood impossibly tall, swaying in the warm breezes that prevailed here at high latitudes. And the aliens lurked among them, surely.

"Do you have any amenities?" Memor asked the attendant, one of the lesser forms known as the Qualk, who sported an absurd headdress. Perhaps it was meant to impress her? That seemed unlikely, but one never knew.

The Qualk fluttered in tribute for the attention paid to him and gestured with an obliging neck-twirl toward the refreshments. Memor moved forward with grave energy, aware that all those in this field station watched her.

A Savant approached. "Astronomer, we have heard stories, ones we cannot believe—"

"Inability to believe is no insurance," Memor said, but laconic irony was lost on this small, squirming one with anxious eyes.

They were assembled for her. More fretful eyes, from a variety of the Bird Folk and some minor members of the Adopted. Memor allowed suspense to build as she quaffed a tangy drink and munched a crunchy thing.

"You are all here, leading your teams, to find the escaped aliens. How is that proceeding?"

Some restless shuffling, sidewise glances. The governing Savant moved to the fore. "The Packmistress sent us—"

"Never mind your prior instructions. What did you encounter?"

The Savant flicked looks around but could not avoid Memor's gaze. "Of course, we have not found the aliens. By the time we hear of them, they are gone. We could follow—after all, we have mobile troops, total air cover, local sensors—but they elude us."

"Why?"

"They seem able to move across terrain without regard for borders or the ancient constraints we all feel. They came over our regional boundaries, moving in natural terrain with concealment. We backtracked them and saw that they skirted our settlements and found ways around our checkpoints."

"You are not alone. There are two of their parties, far across our lands, and they both seem better at this than we."

The Savant nodded, said nothing.

They would come to her, this murderous band of Late Invaders, Memor thought. She had set upon the mirrors a portrait of the leader of the primary group, a face many worlds wide. "Come to me." The leader would certainly know that she had not sent that message, but the others would not. They had every motive to link somehow, and then they could all be caught.

But there was no certainty in this, and a worse danger loomed. So Memor persisted, "Is it the Adopted?"

"What—what do you imply?"

"Do they speedily report?"

"Well—" More furtive glances. No escape.

"I take it your reply is no?"

"Ah. Yes."

"You mean no?"

"Yes."

"And why is that?"

"The Adopted somehow—I have no idea why!—do not obey. They have heard of these aliens."

"And so?"

"They somehow . . ." The local Savant cast more anxious eyes. "These primates are unAdopted. Many ages have passed since the last invasive intelligences gained a foothold on the Bowl. This I truly do not understand—but many of the Adopted see them as . . . admirable."

A voice nearby said, "Improper genetic engineering, then. Or else there has been a slide in the Adopted's conditioning, occasioned by genetic drift."

An image from their Underminds, more likely, Memor thought. *An ancient archetype running free, from the times when the Adopted were on their own.* She huffed, worried, but gave no other sign of her true reaction. She had read and seen images of alien invasions, far back—many twelve-cubed Eras ago. No Astronomers now living were alive then. Though Astronomers were the longest-lived of all the Folk, even they faced a hard fact: The Bowl swam by life-rich worlds seldom. Still rarer were those planets inhabited by sentients—those who could perceive and know—which were of use to the Folk. Still more rare were aliens of sapience—entities who could act with appropriate judgment. The universe gave forth life reluctantly, and wisdom, far more so.

These alien primates, alas, had both—in quantities they surely did not deserve, given their primitive levels of development. Plainly some harsh world had shaped them, and cast them out into the vacuum, untutored.

But she was forgetting her role here. She snorted out anger, spat rebuke, and gave a reproaching feather display of brown and amber. "Admirable!"

"I regret to deliver such news."

"I had no such reports before."

"This was a regional problem, noble Astronomer."

"It is now a global one. These are dangerous aliens, afoot in our lands."

Murmurs of agreement erupted. But Memor did not want agreement; she wanted action. "We do not know what they want. We cannot allow them to remain loose."

The Savant caught her tone and lifted her head. "We shall redouble our efforts."

Memor supposed that was the best she could expect of these rural provinces. They slumbered, while mastering the Bowl fell to their betters. She sniffed, gave a flutter display, and was turning away when the Savant asked quietly, "We hear tales of the alien's excursions. . . ."

Obviously a leading question. How much did this minor Savant know? "You refer to—?"

"One of the alien bands, these tales say, discovered a Field of History."

"I believe the primary group stumbled upon one, yes. So?"

"Then they know our past. And can use it against us."

"I scarcely think they are so intelligent."

"They have eluded us." Short, to the point. This Savant was brighter than she looked.

"You worry that they will know we once passed by their world? These primates were not even *evolved* when we were nearby."

"We gather from the History that these invaders came from a world whose ancestors we once extracted."

Memor trembled but did not show it. These unsuspecting types were lurching toward a truth they should never glimpse. She stretched elaborately, looking a bit bored, and said carefully, "Yes. I researched that. They were without speech, had minimal culture, few tool-using skills. Scavengers, mostly, though they could hunt smaller animals in groups, and defend against other scavengers. Those primates, once Adopted, further evolved into game animals. Not particularly good ones, either."

This at least provoked a rippling laughter. Beneath it ran skittering anxiety in high notes. The Savant persisted, "They do not seem easy to Adopt. They may be angered to see what has become of their ancestors."

Memor did not let her feathers betray her true reaction. The Savant was right, but for reasons Savants were not privileged to know. Rely on cliché, then. No one remembered them even a moment later. "The essence of Adoption is self-knowledge."

The Savant nodded slightly, letting the matter pass when an Astronomer so indicated. Clichés, Memor reflected, were the most useful lubricant in conversation. Thus she missed the Savant's next statement, which was a question—and so soon had to give a summary of what she knew of the aliens. How this could help, she had no idea, but it deflected attention from the real, alarming issue.

She began, "These spacefaring primates have a linear view of life that extends forward and backwards in time. I discovered this while examining their minds while they functioned, and realize that some of what I say may seem implausible. It is not."

This provoked some tittering in the crowd, but Memor plowed on.

"They are very interested in the beginning of the universe, despite the general uselessness of this information now. Even more oddly, they fix upon the long-term fate of the universe, and have strong views on these matters. Some are even religious! To Astronomers, these are matters subject to many unknowns, too many to lend a sense of urgency to the issue. Yet the Late Invaders feel urgently concerned."

A Savant asked, "How can that matter?"

"It has sent them out in their tiny, dangerous ship, yes?"

"To answer such vague questions?"

"Not entirely. Their deep drive, which they

seldom know consciously, is to *expand their horizons*."

"Why? What use can that be?"

"An anxiety fills them, drives them out. I could see it simmering in their Underminds."

"I doubt such creatures could be Adopted," the Savant persisted.

"It is our task to enlighten them." Memor retreated into cliché again. "To erase this hunger for horizons, which evolution dealt them."

"Do we know their origins?"

Memor disguised her lie with a ruffle-display of purple guilt. "I fear we cannot say yet." It was truthful, in a way; she could not say.

"I meant, not what planet they are from, but why they have this anxiety?"

Memor had not considered that, and in a moment of guilty truth-telling, said so. Discussion wafted through the audience. She could see the teams who searched for the primates wondering why the discussion was so theoretical, but that was not crucial. The tone of this meeting was, though.

She took command again with, "We suspect they had to flee a hostile territory, and that crisis forced their evolution. Perhaps their numbers became too great for their environment, and the ambitious moved on to fruitful lands. This forced evolution of better tool-making and general, social intelligence."

Now that she said it, the idea had some appeal. How *did* the primates get the urge to voyage forth in such frail ships? Because they were born on the move.

A Savant said, "They would flood our lands!"

Memor quieted their murmuring. "We can certainly contain that. We outnumber them by twenty orders of twelve-magnitude."

Until this moment she had not fully appreciated how strange the aliens were, even though she had seen into their minds. This was the nub of it: They loved novelty, excitement, and motion—even though it might mean death.

Whereas the Folk wisely lived in the perfect conditions for them, precisely to give life a constancy, a gliding sense of time that belied the issues of beginnings and endings. The reward was a place beyond the natural places, a machine for living that spun, as did worlds, and yet did so to maintain the constancy that was the point of the Folk. They froze time for the span of their species and perhaps beyond. Evolution of the Folk of course occurred. But the aim of artifice was to constrain this, maintaining a close watch, so that the Folk could be in their exalted state. Thus they had thrived now through immense long tides of time, a fact well understood by each succeeding generation. The highest function of a species was surely to suspend the rude, blunt blow of happenstance, and control their own destiny. The Astronomers governed not just the relations between the Bowl and the heavens, but the Bowl Lifeshaping as well.

She thought on this, all the while letting the comments and open disputes work themselves through the assembly. When it had played out, she said with due gravity, "The primates may know some of our history—but it is so vast! They cannot comprehend it."

This brought applause. The Adopted held as a matter of faith and history that the Bowl's serene constancy was the goal of all wise life. So did all the intellectual classes—Savants, Profounds, and Keepers. So what if primates knew a tiny fraction of the Saga?

Of course, her true mission here was to damp their fears. She reminded the audience of their resources, and let members of the search teams tell of their glancing contacts with the primates. None from the party who had lost their magcar, because the primates had killed them all. She mentioned this, to set the stage.

Now they would rehearse the enveloping movement planned to ensnare the roving primate band, the one that had found what they called the Field of History, which Astronomers termed the Past Worlds. A distant team would carry forward that hunt.

Memor asked, "So much for abstractions. I am here to direct your hunt for those who have already killed some of the Folk. I gather you recorded their entry at a Conveyance Station?"

Some of the Adopted nodded eagerly. "Yes, Astronomer! We have the sky creatures ready to depart."

"Most excellent. A long while has lapsed since I experienced the thrill of running down dangerous prey. Let us take to the air, then."

Nothing would get in their way now, since

they had the primates located to a region. When captured, she forbade any questioning of them. A few chance remarks could wreck entire established structures of Bowl society. She could take no chance that anyone should come to know of the Great Shame.

FORTY-FIVE

The alien regarded them with its large eyes and made a curious squatting motion, its sinewy arms held out to the sides. With the large pancake hands and thick fingers, it formed a twisting architecture in the air. Its name was Quert, its Folk the Sil. Its graceful form moved restlessly, pacing among the odd chairs where the humans sat and ate. The train was moving fast now, and the staccato *snick-snick-snick* of the electromagnetic handoffs propelling it forward rang constantly in the background.

Quite deliberately it said, *"Bon voyage. Buon viaggio. Gute Reise. Buen viaje. Viagem boa. Goede reis. Ha en bra resa. God tur. Bonum iter. Καλό ταξίδι!"*

Silence. They all looked at one another.

Irma said brightly, "Those are words for parting. We are joining."

"Misalignment?" the alien said. "Then—" And silky words came from it, *good-bye* in several human languages.

Irma said slowly, carefully, "We are happy you

have learned our languages. Very good. We all speak Anglish."

"I have compressor knowledge. Now can adjust."

Cliff said, "Where did you get such data on our languages?"

"Astronomers. They sent all to hunters."

"You are a hunter?"

"We Sils, true. Also others."

"What kind of others?"

"Others of Adopted."

"Who are—?"

"Those brought here. Not species made in Bowl."

"From other planets?"

"True." The big yellow eyes studied them all in turn. "Like you."

"We haven't been—"

"Now to be Adopted. That is goal Astronomers."

Irma asked, "Adopted . . . how?"

"Genes. Social rules. Status adjustment." This came out as hard, firm statements from the narrow mouth. Cliff wondered about inferring emotions from facial signatures in aliens, but this case at least seemed clear. The constricted face oozed resentment.

"What next?" Terry asked, puzzled.

"Large sharing comes soon," the catlike alien said. "Onto here I—we came to speak and share help. Have time now little."

"Why?" Aybe asked. They were having trouble understanding the slippery slide of Quert's words and the odd context.

"Stop soon, will. Others come."

"So we—?"

"Leave next stop. Must."

Quert flexed its hands. They had six fingers ending in sharp nails. The palm was broad and covered by fine hairs. Now that Cliff studied the creature, he saw it was clothed in a subtle woven fabric that mimicked the tan-colored fine hairs. Perhaps that helped camouflage it?

"How long do we have until the next stop?" Aybe asked, looking edgy.

"Short." Then Quert stopped prowling and looked at each of them in turn. "The Sky Rule will come."

"Those who are after us?" Aybe asked.

"I have fellows there. We may share violence."

"We all?" Irma asked.

"Must quick," Quert said with slippery vowels, and fished from its clothes an oddly sloped cylinder with a transparent lens at one end. "You carry force?"

"You mean weapons?" Terry asked.

"Wea—yes. My vocabulary adjusting. Do I need of your tongues other?"

"Those languages?" Irma thought. "No. But— the Astronomers gave you all those?"

"They had from other primates, or so said."

"You can un-learn a language?"

Quert's eyes then did something startling. They elongated up and down, an expression with no human parallel. Cliff realized it must mean surprise or puzzlement. Quert said, "Must do. Am crowded and slow now."

Then the graceful creature sat at last and closed its eyes. Its eyelids vibrated as if shaken from behind and it did not move. Cliff noted the slowing of the *snick-snick-snicks*.

The electromagnetic handoffs now turned to braking. "Should we hide?" Howard asked. "If we're to get out—"

Quert abruptly sat up, shook its head. "Gone. Better." It looked around at them quizzically, as if coming out of a deep sleep. "Yes. Get down so they not see. Then leave we."

They went back into rooms and crouched below windows. A pale light rose in the walls outside, and they all brought out their lasers. These were nearly fully charged, since they had followed strict recharging rules in the magcar.

Quert crouched as the train slowed. Cliff sprang up as it stopped with a solid jolt and there were robots everywhere outside.

"Go time," Quert said, and they went.

Out onto the platform, identical to the one at which they'd boarded. Robots of gray and green worked steadily on the freight cars and ignored them as they passed. They ran.

After some dim corridors they came out into a broad high-arched plaza under the relentless sunlight. Cliff slowed, stunned.

Hundreds of howling creatures like Quert sent up a warbling, sonorous call. They carried tubes and packs and looked well organized, formed up into ranks. They greeted Quert with high-pitched shouts and words that came over more as shrieks to Cliff. In the eyes of these aliens he saw jittery vigor, anxious turns of heads, a fearful energy. They seemed oddly human, but made small dances that broke out among them, knots of spinning joy within rectangular ranks. This stirred and confused him. The smell was like a crisp, fragrant corral. The humans ran through a corridor of celebration.

They nearly made it. Outside in the raw sunlight, the surging bodies made an impressive display, but halfway across a big canyon floor some zipping pulses came down abruptly from the ramparts above.

Screams, loud hollow thumps, panic. Cliff stuck close to Quert and ran for the canyon walls.

They got into a cleft in an orange conglomerate rock and were working back through it, led by Quert, when a heavy rolling blast caught them and slammed them to the ground.

Quert got up unsteadily. "Come . . . they."

Strange whistling sounds came from the plain outside. Cliff glanced back as they jogged down the cleft. He could see a lancing green light surge down, a hard fizzing spark like a lightning flash you could see in full daylight. Answering deep explosions rocked the air. Pebbles and sand streaked by them with a *whoosh*. They ran harder.

They came out into a side canyon where more of Quert's kind clustered. They grouped around black angular snouts that thrust up into the air. *Guns,* Cliff thought. No matter how alien this place was, form followed function. They stopped and Quert said, "We show now."

The guns erupted in short, spatting flashes. Cliff ducked at the noise and tried to see what they were firing at. The narrow barrels recoiled like howitzers, but no spent shells ejected from their base. The barrels tracked slowly and the alien teams cheered.

"Get we over!" Quert yelled in a high, rasping voice.

"Where?" Irma shouted over the banging salvos.

Quert gestured to a rock bluff hundreds of meters away. There were at least a dozen of the long-barreled guns firing and aliens ran everywhere, shouting orders. *We're in a war,* Cliff thought. *And I thought we were getting away from trouble on the nice train. . . .*

"Better do what they say!" Aybe yelled. "We dunno what's up."

Understatement, Cliff thought, and nodded. They started running, weaving away from the gun crews.

They got about halfway across, led by the swift Quert, when suddenly horrible screeches rose from all sides. Quert barked out a congested howl and fell to the ground. But Cliff felt nothing.

The guns stopped. Screams of agony came from all around.

"It's some kind of pain gun!" Aybe yelled. "Gets them, not us."

They hesitated. He had once been the kid who stood at the top of the waterslide, overthinking it. Finally he had learned to do, not think, and navigate the chute as it came at you. A big moment, back when he was six years old. Now here it was again. Same answer: *down the chute.*

"Go!" He picked up Quert—surprisingly light, as if it had no bones—and sprinted forward. Where? With no guide, he just ran across the canyon. There was a tunnel in the canyon wall and the humans fled to it. Shrieks of terrifying pain came all around them. It was a long run through chaos, three hundred meters as fast as they could go. They made it, to the tunnel, leaping over writhing alien bodies, driven to hammer forward by barely controlled panic. He put the alien down.

Panting in the shadows, Irma gasped, "I couldn't see who was shooting."

"Up in the sky," Aybe said in a hoarse voice, winded. "A smaller version. Of that living blimp. We saw before."

Cliff looked down at Quert, who was sprawling, dazed. He edged out and looked up. A scaly brown football with fins was waltzing lazily across the sky. Big flat antennas hung down from it, probably the source of the pain ray. It moved like a fat, preying insect. The green beams cast down their burning lances.

He remembered feeling a pain flash once. His flesh had cried out, *I'm on fire!* He had looked down at his arm where the invisible beam was landing, and tried to say, *This is just my nerves getting jangled, I can take this,* but that didn't work. The body ignored his mind, which knew the 95-gigahertz radiation was stimulating the nerves in his skin. His skin just kept screaming, *I'm on fire!*

Same effect here, different frequency. The aliens had different wiring. If you wanted to hurt them, you tuned for the wavelengths that forked into the nervous system and didn't let go. Electromagnetics were the same everywhere; you just had to know the right frequency. Pain flowed into you on invisible wings.

The other aliens were running away. No, *herded* away.

The brown football was churning across the sky, angling its antennas toward the crowd it swept before it. He watched the hundreds of fleeing figures rush down the canyon. A rabble.

"Maybe they're rounding these up," Irma said at his side.

"Nope," Aybe said beside her. "Getting them out of the way, yes. They're after *us*. That was our reception committee, Quert's people. The ones up there are running them off. I think—"

Then there was no more thinking as the brown football forked down more of the green rays. This time the enormous hollow *whoosh* thundered on for endless moments. They ducked. Debris blew by them. Pebbles rattled against rock, and big orange, broad-winged birds fell from the sky, squawking as they died.

They stood and watched as the dust cleared. Cliff didn't want to acknowledge what had happened, resisting what his eyes told him, until at his elbow Quert said in its slow, sliding sibilants, "Know we share with you. They kill us."

"Where can we go?" Terry asked in a dry croak, eyes jittery.

Cliff felt the same—dozens of Quert's folk had

died a few hundred meters away. Thin screams came from there. And the football was moving this way.

Quert, too, seemed shaken, its face a frozen stare. Slowly the alien drew its eyes away from infinity and said softly, slowly, "We share under ways. Must cross open spaces now."

"Why is that—" Terry groped for a word, failed. "—that thing in the sky shooting at you?"

"You they seek," Quert said simply, eyes still dazed.

"So they're after *us*?" Aybe asked, eyes wide.

"We heard you come. They know also."

Aybe eyed the living dirigible. "So they'll come after us."

"And we. Oppose Astronomers now."

"Then we have to nail them," Aybe said firmly.

Cliff saw the logic. Their pursuers knew the terrain; they didn't. "But we have no—"

"Use *their* guns. Can't be that hard."

The cries outside diminished. They looked out carefully and saw the big balloon was dealing with their victims, slamming down shots at them. "Distracted," Terry said. "Let's blow a hole in them. They're in range."

If the enemy's in range, so are you, Cliff thought but did not say.

• • •

Of course, the brown football turned and started beaming their pain gun again. The burst caught

Quert while it was showing them how to aim and fire the auto-fed gun. Quert doubled up with the pain and went into thrashing jerks, head lolling back, eyes popping out as though pressure built inside its head. An awful sight.

With Terry, Cliff carried Quert into shelter. The pain gun cleared the area swiftly. Howard got a gun going and showed Terry how to manage another. They fired them intermittently as the brown football slowly made its way toward them. "Must be done killing the others," Terry said laconically. "We got maybe ten minutes before they can do that to us."

Cliff looked at the big lumbering thing in the sky, working its fins and—were those fans running under it? Yes, pushing the strange hybrid of life-form and engineering across the distance, maybe ten kilometers. Worse, the wind was with the thing.

They poured on the fire. The smart rounds burst into fragments as they neared the target, tearing into the wrinkled hide. Primitive weaponry, Cliff thought, and suddenly saw why. Quert's kind were unused to warfare, he gathered. No steady gun crew discipline, a lot of strange shouting. They had not done it before, and these guns were their first real try. Battlefields, Cliff reflected, are not the best place to learn your lessons.

Abruptly came the counterfire. He saw green stabs for an instant and then the cliff wall nearby shattered. He knew this only as he shook his head, on the ground. It had slammed him down and now he saw everything through a spatter of fractured light and clapping, hollow explosions. *Shock,* he thought. He drew in a big lungful of air, flavored with the tang of dirt. He got to his feet and helped Irma up. Dust clouds blew away in the wind and he saw that their artillery piece was shattered where a large rock had hit it. A few meters to the side, and it would have killed them all.

"Other . . . other guns still work," he croaked.

They limped to one nearby and Aybe jerked open the breech. "It's loaded. Let's give 'em hell."

They got it to firing, following shouted instructions from Quert. Cliff knew he was still dazed and stood aside as Aybe and Terry aimed it. There were systems that did sighting mounted on the gun deck, pictures that homed in and locked. Quert told them again how to work it, speaking patiently and slowly from shelter. The pain gun was still going, he could tell—the Sil who darted out to help others jerked and cried with the sheeting pain.

The gun slammed out shots at the approaching target. "Aim for the underside." Irma pointed. "There are portals there."

Aim changed. Shots exploded into shrapnel just short of the yellow ports lining the bottom seam of the big balloon creature. They could see the impact, kilometers away.

"That's a living thing," Aybe said. "It's gotta hurt."

The creature was unused to this. It flinched when the rounds struck—long waves broke across its skin, like slow-motion impacts of a huge fist on flesh. It began to turn.

At its side, a smaller craft burst from a green pod. It was a slim airplane and fell away in graceful arcs. All the action was smooth, slow. Then their guns ran dry and a silence fell on the canyon.

"Astronomer goes," Quert called weakly.

The huge creature hung in the air and small things began emerging from it. They crawled like spiders across the skin and covered the gaping red wounds with white layers.

"Fire some more?" Aybe asked. He had used up the ammo store.

"Don't think we have to," Irma said. She was getting her composure back, patting the dust from her pants and blouse, and even brushing her hair into place.

Everyone quieted down. Faces human and alien alike were drawn, tired.

Apparently that meant the battle was over. Soon the pain gun antennas were out of view and the effect ended. The Sil who had stayed came out of shelter, and a great mournful dirge sounded. Their voices merged in a long, rolling chant. They moved among the fractured bodies, turning them to the perpetual sun. The song rose up and reverberated from canyon walls. Quert splayed arms to the sky and joined in the deep long notes. It was eerie and moving and Cliff let himself be drawn into it for a long while, despite his pounding heart.

But at last the feeling ebbed. The flapping balloon creature was moving languidly away across an empty sky as teams crawled over it, mending. Quietly the humans left their post and Quert seemed to revive, shaking itself in quick vibrations of arms and legs, as if shaking off a mood. Quert led them away and into a long, narrow passageway through the far side of the ruddy canyon.

They walked in silence, absorbing what had happened.

"May return," Quert warned. "Go."

They hurried through an underground passage. They spent five minutes of running, pounding down channels as the chants behind faded away. Quert showed them what looked like an air lock and they went through it fast. Beyond was a dimly lit tunnel. In this they ran for at least half an hour, just Quert and five other of the aliens—who ran with unhurried grace, their paces light, long, and quick—and following them came the humans, slogging on with thumping feet.

Like gazelles, Cliff thought, and then went back to pondering what might lie ahead. He had led them into this and for quite a while now he had not known where it was going. Wandering and staying out of the hands of the Bird Folk had seemed obvious. Plus trying to learn—and those were the last things he had been certain of for a long time.

They reached a dock suddenly. But this was a vertical one with no-door elevators, chugging along at a speed that made it easy to step onto a descending plate. Quert showed them how and Howard jumped too heavily onto it, lost his balance, and fell to the floor. That made Terry laugh in a high-pitched way, while the others piled on.

Howard got his breath and they all looked at one

another, aliens and humans alike. There was some odd commonality here he was too distracted to think about right now. Just assume it and see if it worked. Not a theory, but a plan.

Cliff staggered. His right leg went from a dull ache to a steadily building throb. *Adrenaline high is fading*. He felt the warmth from it flowing down into his boot. He sat down sloppily and breathed deep, sucking in air to calm his racing heart. Gingerly he felt the wound.

Irma said, "You're bleeding."

Cliff nodded, panting. "Flesh wound."

Howard said, "We're short of bandages."

"I'm not as badly hurt as we've seen," Cliff said. He tried a shrug. "I'll get by."

Irma had thought to take some of the clothing off the dead aliens. She handed him something shirtlike, cottony. With Irma's help, he tore it into lengths and folded one to make a pad. He tied that over the wound, pulling to get it tight, and the compress seemed to stop the bleeding. He did this automatically, recalling practice they had all gone through. *Centuries ago*.

They went on, Cliff limping.

They came down steadily in darkness and stepped off onto a metal frame in the rock. Beyond the elevator was no rock at all, just ceramics and fiber beams and even burnished metal. There were struts and the usual squared-off construction in a gravity well, but also curved arches and round hatches. Quert led them through support structures, and suddenly one wall was transparent and Cliff was looking into blackness pocked by tiny colored lights. *Stars*.

"It's . . . the backside of the Bowl," Aybe whispered.

Somehow the view was at an angle to vertical, not straight down through the floor. Local gravity was different here. Cliff watched a distant craft swim across this night sky, lit only by starlight. Then a nearer sphere came into view, with three small ships nosed against it. A fueling station? It slid by fast and Cliff realized they were the ones moving, spinning to maintain centrifugal grav at half a thousand kilometers per second. All you had to do to launch a ship was let go of it.

He pressed his face against the cold transparent window, just as the others did, and looked at long lanes of structures stretching away in all directions. Endless detail into the distance, with gray robot forms working over some towers nearby.

Quert's long vowels intruded on his thoughts. "Can see later. Now go."

It was hard to leave the view. The perspectives reminded him that they were never far from the vacuum of space, no matter how familiar some of the Bowl could seem.

"Come!" Quert took them onto another dock and then very fast into a narrow capsule. They fitted into horizontal slots with support straps, and as Cliff got his into place they took off to a swift sucking sound.

Cliff unwrapped the bulky bandage he had made,

and the sight was not good. A dark stain had pasted his pants leg to the wound. It smelled bad and was suddenly popular with nasty little flies that came swirling out of nowhere. With Howard's help, Cliff shed the lower half of his peel-out trousers, unzipping to reveal the damage. There was an entrance wound on the right side of his calf and a matching, larger wound on the left. Water brought by the Sil washed off the crusted dark blood. The puckered openings were red and swollen.

Irma brought her first aid kit and pooled its resources with the kits of the others, each kit somewhat specialized. "Looks like some shrapnel went right through your calf muscle," she said calmly. "The leg's going to purple up."

"It's hard to walk on."

"Then don't."

She and Howard worked for a while, injecting him and putting clean compresses on the leg. Cliff watched the sky where puffy gray clouds raced one another.

Irma patted him. "You're not going to die."

"That's a relief. Don't have to call my insurance guy."

"You won't lose the leg."

"Even better. Hurts though. Got some fun drugs?"

That brought chuckles. "Ran out," Howard said. "My fault."

Irma said, "And your next question would be, 'Where are we?'"

"And the answer . . ."

"Going to a Sil refuge. Their casualties are in the cars ahead. They lost a lot of dead."

He didn't know what to say to that. And his head was feeling like a balloon that wanted to soar into the sky.

The trip lasted a long time amid bare dim lighting. He thought of talking to the others, but now he knew it was smarter to just rest when you could do nothing. He fell asleep, dreamed of discordant sights and sounds and colors, and just as on the train, came awake only to the tug of deceleration.

PART IX

I intend to live forever. So far, so good.
—STEVEN WRIGHT

FORTY-SIX

Beth stood in the entrance of the cave and listened as thunder forked down through immense, sullen cloud banks. They were stacked like a pyramid of anvils with purple bases. Down through them, leaping from anvil to anvil, came bright, sudden shafts of orange lightning. Fat raindrops smacked down, lit up by the flashes. Some of the glaring lances raced from one shadowy cloud to another and came down near them, exploding like bombs as they splintered trees.

"Majestic," Fred said at her side.

"Terrifying," she countered, but then admitted, "Beautiful, too."

"Look at those." Mayra pointed. In the milky daylight that filtered through the pyramid clouds, they watched moist plants move with a languid, articulating grace. Slowly they converged on the lightning damage. They came forth to extinguish the fires from those strikes.

"Protection, genetically ordained," Tananareve said.

"Sure they're not animals?" Fred asked.

"Do they look like animals?" Tananareve countered. "I checked, went out and lifted one. Roots on the end of those stalks. Roots that slip out easily from the soil when it rains."

"But the rain will put out the fires."

"Maybe they're healing something else. We really don't know how this ecology works, y'know," Tananareve said.

"And the ecology's only skin deep," Fred said. "Ten meters or so down, there's raw open space. Maybe the lightning can screw up subsurface tech."

Beth listened to the full range of sounds rain makes in a high, dense forest. Pattering smacks at the top, gurgling rivulets lower, as the drops danced down the long columns of the immense canopy. The orchestrated sounds somehow encased her, lifted her up into a world utterly unnatural but somehow completely secure, while seeming still so strange.

Somewhere in this immense mechanism Cliff was . . . what? Still free? Captured and interrogated? Her skimpy communication with *SunSeeker* confirmed that he got through to them intermittently and was moving cross-country. That was all she knew, yet it would have to be enough.

The rain, wind, and lightning daggers swept her along in a sudden tide of emotions she had kept submerged. She longed for him, his touch, the low bass notes as he whispered in her ear of matters loving, delightful, often naughty. Lord, how she missed that. They liked making love while rain spattered on the windows, back there centuries ago. It gave them a warm, secure place to be themselves, while the world toiled on with its unending business. They had ignored the world for a while, and it ignored them.

Fair enough. But this whirling contrivance could not be ignored. It could kill you if you did not pay attention, and very probably would, she imagined. They would probably die here, and no one—Cliff, Redwing, Earth—would ever know, much less know why. Beth's small band certainly did not remotely understand this thing. Why was it cruising between the stars at all—driven forward by engineering that eclipsed into nothingness all that humanity had achieved? Why? . . .

"Fred, that idea of yours, where'd you get it?"

He shook himself from his reverie. "Just came to me."

"Straight out of your imagination?" Tananareve scowled at him. "Some imagination you got, to think dinosaurs—"

"I didn't *imagine* it, if you mean I concocted the idea. It just . . . came to me. Pieces all fit together. In a flash." As if in agreement, a big yellow bolt knifed down through the shimmering sky and slammed into the rock of the hill above them. Stones clattered down.

"There's no evidence for it," Lau Pin said.

"That globe we saw," Fred said. "It's like Earth, but the continents are wrong. All mushed together."

"Maybe the geologists got the continent details wrong," Beth said. "It's a long chain of reasoning, back seventy or so million years."

"Never mind that!" Mayra suddenly said. "What

fossil evidence is there for any early civilization? Where are the ruins?"

"That much time?" Tananareve scoffed. "Nothing left. Subducted, rusted away, destroyed in a dinosaur war, maybe. Look, guys, the Cretaceous–Tertiary Boundary shows where the asteroid hit. It shows through in only a dozen places around the Earth. Why would you expect anything to be left at all?"

Lau Pin swept an arm out at the churning trees, the walking plants, lightning slicing down from towers of dark clouds. "What's the leap from some smart dinosaurs to *this*?"

"I don't know." Fred shrugged. "Depends on what the smart ones thought, how they saw their world."

"There's no fossil evidence for smart dinosaurs," Lau Pin said. He went back in the cave to turn their fire. It was cooking the last of the big carcass they had brought from the warehouse, and the yamlike roots. It had started smoking again, probably from rain blowing in, and they all had a coughing fit.

"You can't judge intelligence from the size of skulls," Beth said, "and anyway, dino skulls are plenty large. Look, they had grappler claws, a start toward hands. Later on, some dinosaurs had feathers—that's where birds came from. There's plenty we don't know about that era."

Fred nodded and then said quietly, "There was one clue. When I saw that great holo of how they built this Bowl, I looked at the star in the distance. It looked a lot like the sun."

"That's it?" Lau Pin snorted dismissively.

Another shrug. "Started me thinking."

"They were really smart, built this—and got wiped out by a rock even we could deflect away centuries ago?" Mayra said. "Come *on*."

Fred shrugged yet again. "No answer. Maybe they got caught in a cultural phase where they stopped watching the skies. Look, it's an idea, not a complete theory."

As Mayra argued with Fred, Beth watched her. The deep furrows on Mayra's brow had gone away and the worry lines at the eyes, too. She seemed better about the death of her husband, and had even laughed a bit. But Beth was sure that Abduss was never far from her mind. Nor was Cliff from hers, of course. She would never forget the squashed Abduss she had seen, still breathing for a short while in milky spurts, frothy saliva dripping like cream down to his ears while his cracked skull leaked brown blood into his eyes.

Beth shook her head to sweep away the image. She left them to their discussion and sat down near the cave entrance to savor the scent of the rain. As a little girl, she had loved that smell—freshness enveloping her, fragrances boiling into the air. They weren't on Earth, but it *felt* the same. "This Bowl has a lot of similarities to Earth, yes? Maybe the really strange stuff, like those walking plants, are from other worlds."

Fred nodded eagerly. "Or tens of millions of years of directed evolution."

"Point is," Beth said, "even if Fred's right, *how do we use the theory*? How can it help us?"

Lau Pin stretched, drew in a clean lungful of moist air. "Sleep on it, I say. Fred, you get your ideas how? Dreaming?"

"No, but I have them when I wake up. I go to sleep thinking about things, problems—and when I wake up, there's an idea there. Maybe wrong, but . . . it's like getting a note from another part of myself."

Beth got up and patted Fred on the shoulder. "I suspect that's why you made *SunSeeker* crew, too. Didn't you figure out the high-voltage capacitors in the ramscoop?"

He smiled. "Yeah. That was fun. That was a neat puzzle."

"Sleep again, after you take the first watch. Maybe the part of you that never sleeps will come up with more ideas."

Beth unfolded her cushion from her backpack and inflated it with long, deep breaths. A part of her eyed Fred's lean stance framed by the cave's mouth. *Wait a bit, get it on with him? You're horny, alone—do something.* But she brushed the impulse away. *Don't complicate a team that's barely getting by.*

By the time she was ready to sleep, the rest were distributed back through the small cave, grateful for some shade and the storm's muting of the constant sunlight. She squinted through the clouds and could barely see the star's disk.

As she dropped off to sleep, she thought of Cliff again. He had always been better at fieldwork than she was, and she hoped maybe he understood this weird place better. Would she ever find him in this huge world-machine? "G'night, Cliffy. Wherever you are."

She hugged her blow-up pillow and smelled the rain and thought of places secure and warm and far away.

FORTY-SEVEN

Memor had always enjoyed the serene voyaging these living craft afforded. She looked down on the slow passage of rugged terrain and breathed in a luxurious sweet aroma. The mucus of this great beast had been engineered to carry a delicate fragrance unlike anything else. Its scent was a luxury and settled the mind, though chaos raged all about them. She allowed herself another lingering taste, then turned with an appropriately severe expression.

"This is truly absurd," Memor said. "We have dozens of airfish aloft and much airplane coverage. Yet the prey keeps ducking belowground, eluding us."

The Captain of this armed airfish gestured with indifference. "We will turn them up. They exited the Longline transport at the station below. They can surely not go far— Wait, see those Sils?"

The reed-thin male peered at a large wall display. Small life-forms filled narrow canyons of tan rock. More of the Adopted species, one Memor had not seen before, were coming into the crowds, arriving apparently by foot. Good—an agricultural culture, with low technologies and simple ways.

The Captain drawled thoughtfully, "They cluster in several canyons. No dancing, no parades or ceremony. This is not their usual communal gathering."

"You know well these . . . ?"

"Sils, we term them. Always an unruly lot. Not the first time, my dear Astronomer, that I have taken to air to discipline these."

"The problem persists?"

"Yes, has worsened steadily. The Sils are among the worst of the Adopted. They are not much evolved beyond carnivores, so I suppose we should not be surprised. Herbivores—why did we not bring more of *those* aboard?" The Captain blinked, taken aback by his own outburst.

"Because herbivores are seldom intelligent," Memor said dryly. "Good eating, though—we do have some of those."

"Of course, of course." The Captain turned and barked out quick orders to his staff officers. They were taking more rattling fire. The great beast that carried them protested in long grumbling notes that rolled through the walls that ran with juice.

Memor watched the living opalescent walls run with anxiety dewdrops, shimmering moist jewels hanging and spattering with an acid odor. Skyfish expressed their deep selves through chemistry, an unreliable, or at least largely unreadable, medium. They were perhaps the most successful of the Adopted. Taken from the upper atmosphere of a gas giant world long ago, they found the deep atmosphere of the Bowl a similar paradise to cruise and mate and turn water into their life fluid, hydrogen. Somehow the great ones of the early Bowl had managed to make these living skyships merge into the blossoming Bowl ecosphere. To cruise the skies in them was a voyage into history.

She turned when the Captain, now quite distressed, was done. "Can we disperse this crowd? They hamper our finding these primates."

The Captain gave an efficient flutter of feather-arcs: agreement. "I can use standard suffering methods."

"Do so."

The Captain gave orders and the great belly of the skyfish began its laborious turn. Memor circled the observation deck, scattering small crew before her, to see how the Sils were moving. Streams of them came from all directions. Such crowds! Many walked, some ran with a dogged pace, others rode animals. They looked up at the skyfish. Some stopped and shook themselves, their rage evident. At what? Their target was the Longline station.

"Captain! When might the primates arrive here?"

"They could get here soon, Astronomer. It is possible. But we do not expect them to follow a simple route, staying on the same line. That would be too obvious." This last sentence provoked an involuntary submission-flutter of amber and brown as the Captain saw the implications.

"They may realize we expect evasion."

"Our strategy command thinks that unlikely—"

"Humor me."

"These Sil have no way of knowing—"

"There are always betrayers, Captain. Information crosses patchwork boundaries, though we try to stop it."

"I wonder, Astronomer, why your esteemed presence came here. Surely the primate invaders would not take a simple route—"

"Do not presume to estimate the rationality of aliens. Nor their clever nature."

"Surely you do not expect them—"

"These Sils gather for a reason."

"But how could—? Of course, these Sils have given us trouble since my grandmother's time. They see this as another device to—"

"You are wasting time."

The Captain hurried off to alter his commands. The skyfish eased lower as it wallowed across the air, toward the stony ridges that marked the Longline here.

Memor took some moments to review on her private mind-feed the background of these Adopted, the Sil. The Bowl had passed near their star as the Sil were still in hunter-gatherer stages. The Bird Folk found Sil promising, and brought many aboard. Those early Sil were long since left behind genetically—crafty they had been, yes, but not that smart. Something close to the far older Bowl primates, but with ambition, tool-making and better social skills, developed through group hunting. As usual, their first tools had been weapons. This always led to a spirited species, which could be positive—but not, alas, for the Sils. They made their periodic rebellions, and were periodically re-instructed, often genetically.

These Sils evolved first in trees—often a source of later troubles, for it gave them dexterous use of several limbs. Thus the Bird Folk bred quite deliberately for higher intelligence and tool use, by increasing artificial selection, testing the results, and directing their mating to enhance the effects. The Sil were domesticated and made smarter, suiting them better for the technological jobs needed to tend the Bowl. Troubles came when these wily ones rebelled, or worse, tried to expand their territory. The tragic solution was to be avoided, of course, but even that didn't always work.

"Crews! Begin firing!" the Captain called.

Memor braced herself. This was the inevitable problem with using living beings to fly in the Bowl's deep atmosphere. Of course, they could not use chemical fuels for every aircraft, as that would tax the farming regions beyond their endurance. Electrodynamic flight was preferred for long stays aloft, but was too delicate for the long skirmishes that regional patrol officers had to carry out. Skyfish, though, could bear up under the typically archaic weaponry Adopted species could bring to bear. Further, its immense vault of hydrogen made it ferocious in close air support.

As Memor watched, the crew used their flame guns on scattered Sil groups on the ridgeline. These were apparently spotters, for they were armed with simple chemical explosive weapons. As the skyfish slewed slowly to the left, it brought its flame spouts to bear. Gouts of rich golden flame raked the ridge. They were so close, Memor could hear angry shouts from the burning ridge, often followed by shrieks and screams as their last agony came to them. Not a delicious sound, but reassuring, yes.

Then the pain projectors came into play. Memor watched as the Captain adroitly directed the assaults, driving the Sil. The running, struggling Sil looked like herd animals in a panic. Then the green laser pulses destroyed them in densely packed groups. It slashed down, annihilating in fire and ferment. The Sil broke into fleeing remnants.

But the skyfish was taking hits as well. The simple Sil had fixed artillery set up with surprisingly mischievous warheads that blew shredding blasts into the underbody. Memor felt the floor vibrate as the great beast reacted, flinching from the wounds. A deep bass note rang and the wall membranes fluttered. In answer the gun crews poured on more pain projector power. Soundless, this was the standard weapon to terrify opponents.

Yet the artillery fire did not abate, even under maximum power. "The Sil surely cannot withstand—" Memor broke off as she saw on the viewer the gun crews.

The Late Invaders had come. "Captain, use your lasers."

The male displayed a corona of dismay. "Their fire has disabled our forward batteries, Astronomer. I apologize for—"

The skyfish writhed as shrapnel struck it. Long rolling waves warped the moist walls. Equipment smashed down from their perches. Crew ran by, babbling of emergencies. Memor ignored this and said, "Your sting does not take with these primates. They have different neurons. You must use the gas-fed lasers."

"We will get them up and running. A few moments—"

A volley from below slammed into the great beast. Memor carefully descended, feet seeking a balance as the floor shifted—down a great curving stair and through a polished plate glass dilating door into the skyfish bridge. Chaos.

The Captain turned and bowed. "We have taken many hits, Astronomer. Perhaps we relied on the agony projectors too much—"

"Perhaps?" Memor scarcely thought it necessary to point out that the skyfish was floundering, spewing fluids from multiple wounds, losing altitude, veering erratically. "Perhaps?"

"I propose we withdraw—"

"If you can."

"We can mend and rearm at higher altitude—"

"If you can reach it."

Skyfish had all the advantages of living technologies, but they had their own life cycles as well. The marriage of life with material was a great ancient success that made the Bowl biosphere work, but of course with drawbacks. Life-forms needed rest and could self-repair, and even with help could reproduce—and all that took time. In battle, at times knowing the organism's limits meant having the wisdom to withdraw.

"This beast is badly damaged. It's frightened—feel it?" The floor and walls were vast lapidary membranes that now shook with a neurological spasm. Smoldering fumes rose amid the clanging discord.

"We relied too much perhaps on the agony projectors. In future—"

"You have no future. We are so close to these primates, yet they prevail."

"I can—"

"Get me to my pod."

"I believe we have the situation in hand, or soon will," the Captain persisted. "My crews can quickly bring the laser—"

"If the hydrogen vaults are breached, we shall have no further disputes. I will have my pod *now.*"

Memor loved the moist, fragrant membranes of skyfish, but prudence demanded that she not risk herself while this great being floundered and perhaps even failed. She swiftly followed the running escorts, down a long ramp and to the side farthest away from the rattling battle. Here her pod waited, with crew looking anxious. "Depart," she said, "with speed."

As they dropped away from the great belly of the beast, Memor wondered what this reversal might mean. There had been regional revolts before, of course. These Sil fit the age-old pattern—an Adopted species suffers some cultural or even genetic shift, and becomes difficult to manage. Standard strategy was to contain the conflict, using reliable nearby territories. Such struggles set up larger scale rivalries, of course, and with adroit handling, these could lead to calm. Once the regional Profounds played factions off against each other, stability emerged.

That would have to be done here—unless the aliens upset the usual forces. These Sil were canny creatures, a fairly recent addition to the Adopted. A mere twelve-triple-cubed Annuals had passed since their genetic alteration had pacified them. Perhaps it was time for a more fundamental solution—pruning.

But the primates had now shown that they were too destabilizing. Their ship, which might hold technologies of some use, might as well be destroyed. Those at large would have to be exterminated. It was a pity, for their minds were a fount of oddities, and study might reveal some of the features of the Folk in far antiquity—even before the opening of the Undermind.

Well, perhaps Memor could conduct some research with them, before the executions. That would be a just reward for her, after all the annoying troubles they had brought.

FORTY-EIGHT

Sitting on a riverbank beside lounging aliens, Cliff recalled his father showing him how to cast for fish.

The rhythm, first—how to cast the line with his elbow doing the real work and his wrist firm while the left hand payed out the line. A quick rainbow trout had leaped for it in a silver flash. He had felt it tug back and forth as it fought. When he reeled it in, the gasping body was a sacred, beautiful thing. He had thrown it back, on impulse, and his dad had laughed, comprehending the wonder of it.

No such goal here. He landed a big, floppy thing that watched him with huge round yellow eyes when he dragged its bulk up onto the shoreline. Oddly, once out of the water it did not fight. Maybe it expected to be tossed back in? If aliens did catch-and-release, maybe so.

He fidgeted the hook out—the fish mouths were bony and complex here—and turned with the heavy body in his arms. The Sil danced their heads around and made a high, murmuring noise. Slowly it dawned on him that this was their way of applauding.

One Sil came forward, took the fish, and did an astonishing thing. It cast the fish up and with a flashing knife blade caught the skin, tossed the fish up using the leverage, and spooled the skin off. It was a miraculous trick, skinning the fish—and then the Sil sectioned the fish, too, in slashing cuts as it turned in air. One of the Sil offered Cliff a hand-sized slice of sashimi.

Cliff took a bite out of courtesy. It was near taste-less, something like tai.

These creatures were quicker than the eye could see.

Their lands were different, too: lush greenery, few rocky landscapes, odd trees and big-leafed plants rich in fruit. Plenty of scampering small game, too, which the Sil must relish hunting.

He sat and thought about the Sil for a while and then of Beth. He wondered where she was, what she had learned. He recalled the soft brush of her hair on his chest when she hovered over him, sighing in low, sliding notes. He longed to see her, share the eerie wonder of this place with her. There might be trouble over Irma, but . . . *but what?*

He had deliberately not thought about the problem. Irma had been a refuge from the increasing tensions that came from roving in hostile territory, yes. . . . But was there more to it? He didn't know.

Face problems as they come, he realized, had become his working rule. Irma sat down lazily beside him. "If you leave out these meaningful silences, I won't fall asleep."

Cliff shrugged. "No meaning at all. I'm just feeling good."

She yawned. "My dad always said—" She did a deep, boisterous male voice. "—it's never too late to have a happy childhood."

"I already had mine."

"Did you follow all that talk from Quert?"

"About being an 'Adopted' species?"

"Yeah, that whoever runs this place takes on board species from worlds they cruise by."

"They have the room for it."

"Not really a new idea, just bigger scale. I mean, we humans invented our own little niche evolution when we domesticated wolves."

"Sure, and when we turned bottle gourds into

containers. But equally, that let dogs and gourds colonize the human niches—catch a ride on an opportunity."

"The Bowl is an opportunity passing by, with land to spare."

"This is a clue to why they built this thing. It's impossibly big, sure, using materials so strong, they rival the subnuclear struts we have in *SunSeeker*. But they haven't let the smart species here overrun the natural environment."

She sat up and watched a Sil try Cliff's makeshift fishing rod. The Sil had their own, but were curious. It spun a line out a long distance with one liquid move. "You mean, they haven't done what we did to Earth."

"Right. And got to go star-hopping while they do it."

"We evolved to take short-term predictions and make snap decisions using them. Long term isn't our strong suit. Just look at the Age of Appetite—it ran more than two centuries!"

"Must have been fun."

He applauded as the Sil caught a fish, uglier and even bigger than his. His noise made Sils nearby turn, startled, and give them long looks. Cliff recalled that if humans stared at each other for long, it meant they would either fight or make love. With the Sil, staring was clearly more complex. Their graceful faces used the eyes as much as humans used their mouths for signaling. Apparently right eye squinting and left wide open meant puzzlement.

He contented himself with just waving. Their eyes widened in appreciation.

"The 2100s were about digging out from the damage, getting the climate stable. Only way to do it was with a big presence in space, metals and rare earths from asteroids, a solar system economy. Then we got hungry for the stars."

"They must've, too."

"Then why not just send out ramscoops, like us?"

"Maybe they did. Maybe came to Earth and left no trace."

"Haven't we seen Earth species here?"

He nodded. "I've seen plenty of things I recognized. It could be parallel evolution—function calls out form, the same shapes. Like that fish. It's god-awful ugly, but so are some fish I saw in the Caribbean."

"Bet it tastes good, though."

His stomach growled. "I'll start a fire. That's a good point—the twist of molecules, the chemical hookups here. They're close enough to ours so we don't starve."

Quert appeared from the rich foliage, carrying a pack. "Swimmer! Good." In one swift sweep, he took it from Cliff and said, "Cook we will."

Cliff sniffed the air. "Woodsmoke. They already knew I'd catch something."

"They're smart. I wonder why they took such losses just to pluck us off that train."

"They want out from under the boss who runs this."

"Well, we sure can't help them."

"Probably not. We're damned lucky to be alive."

"Did you think we'd last this long?"

"Not really." Cliff took a deep breath and plunged on, feeling awkward. "I . . . didn't think we'd become lovers, either."

She blinked and looked hard at the river flowing past, clear and cool. Avoiding his eyes. "We're not, really. At least, I don't love you."

"Me either. 'Utility sex,' wasn't that what you called it?"

She giggled nervously. "I did say that."

"You and your guy were going to have a standard contract marriage?" he said to be saying something.

"Yup, when we got settled at Glory. Then I'd bring out my stored eggs and have a family. We figured a twenty-five-year contract would do that nicely."

"Beth and me, we hadn't gotten that specific. In all the training, there wasn't time to . . ."

"To really think it through? Actually, it's feeling it through that does the trick."

"Um. 'Love is not love which alters when it alteration finds.' I suppose."

"What? Oh, Shakespeare. Well, this is alteration"— she waved a hand at the Bowl, which hung like a shimmering haze across the sky—"beyond anything I imagined."

"So . . ." He savored finally getting some use from his high school English, then sobered. He wanted to get something settled but didn't know how. "We keep up with the . . . utility?"

She shrugged. "It helps." Then she gave him a wicked grin. "That's my story for now."

"Might be trouble when we meet our mates."

"Face that when it comes."

He stood, stretching. He watched distant dust devils climb toward the roof of the sky, in an atmosphere so deep, he could see huge dark clouds that hung like mountains in the high, fuzzy distance. How were they ever going to figure out this place?

Aybe, Howard, and Terry arrived, carrying some plants they had harvested with the Sil. "Shoulda had you along, Cliff, so's you'd know what these things are, if we can eat 'em. Howard spotted a lot of this."

"My God, Terry, you're drunk!" Cliff took the plants and checked them; they looked reasonable. But he couldn't take his eyes from Terry and—yes, Aybe also had a bleary look.

"They gave us a drink, said it was refreshin'," Terry said.

Howard said, "Tastes a little like pineapple wine. Bland. I was not tricked, boss." He thumped his chest. "Alcohol."

"I'll say. The chemistry here really is similar." Cliff waved them to the riverside. *Might as well relieve the pressure when they can....*

Was ethanol a universal? It appeared in low densities in star and planetary system forming regions: simple organic chemistry. It was just sugars turning bad, so they formed a hydroxyl with carbon. Chimpanzees used it, too. Maybe all higher intelligences sometimes needed to escape from the prison of reason?

"So," Aybe plopped down and said with the

owlish manner of a drunk trying to pretend he's sober, "where do we go from here?"

"There's a price on our heads, boys," Irma said. "I say stay here, rest up, learn from these Sil."

"We can eat," Howard said. "Nev-ever a given."

"We need a plan," Aybe said.

"A goal without a plan is just a wish," Irma said. "But what's our goal?"

"There's enough room here," Terry said with leaden profundity, "for everybody cold sleepin' on *SunSeeker* to live."

"But this isn't a planet, it's a park!" Irma shot back.

"Seems big enough for a million planets. Strange aliens. Room to make somethin' new." Terry nodded to himself.

Irma's eyes and nostrils flared. "We didn't cast off everybody we knew to come to this place!"

"Well, we're here anyway," Aybe said solemnly. "We don't even know if we can get *SunSeeker* started up right again."

"There's damn plenty we don't know, right," Terry agreed.

Cliff eyed them and saw this was an idea brewing for some time among them. Carefully he said, "Look, we're in a crazy place. But don't let your preoccupation with reality stifle your imagination. We're bound for Glory."

In their pealing laughter he heard joy.

FORTY-NINE

The inhabited section of the Bowl, its vast ring-shaped rim, was what Redwing had come to call the Great Plain. Now *SunSeeker* crossed softly over the rim of the Bowl, and the Great Plain fell behind. Far below, the cellophane sky dropped to touch a rise in the Bowl's understructure, bulging outward by a few kilometers, as they crossed the Bowl rim. "Stay well clear," Redwing told Jam again. "We don't want to burn holes in their sky with our magnetics."

Jam grinned as if at a joke. "Yes, sir. Do your enemy no small injury." He added, "Machiavelli."

So the great ship floated past the rim with 100,000 kilometers to spare. Redwing watched, mesmerized, until Ayaan whacked his back with her fist. "Captain! I've got Fred Oyama!"

"Hot damn! Patch me through. Fred, need update on your condition."

Ayaan said, "Talk past him. You're eighteen minutes apart at lightspeed, and all they can send us is text. Talk and I'll text-connect it."

"Yeah. Fred, we're cruising around back of the Bowl to see what we can see. Our last contact with Beth's team had you in a cluster of caves. She was worried about what low gravity is doing to your bones and such. Otherwise you're safe, right? You should have at least a couple of months' grav therapy, once we get you into *SunSeeker*'s hospital section."

"We've solved the problem with *SunSeeker*'s

motors," he said, and decided not to give details. The ship had been delayed by the Bowl's head wind, just enough to matter. Maybe *SunSeeker* could have veered around the Bowl's wake and kept on to Glory, stretching their supplies to the max. But the Bowl was a bigger game, really. An unimaginable jackpot—if they survived it. Glory could wait.

Redwing watched Ayaan working their antenna system to keep him on target. Their technology was at its very limits, communicating over such vast, constantly moving ranges.

"We've fiddled some with the menu, including some biochem information, so I'll beam you an update, *now.*" Ayaan nodded and pressed a key to send the prepared squirt.

"I'd like to pick you all up. We should at least plan to meet. It would be great if we could find a meet place. The trouble as I see it is that any site big enough to see from here would be like arranging to meet in Australia." Redwing laughed, then remembered that he wouldn't hear a response. "Too big. But if we could find something like a radio station, we could find each other there. We'll look for antennas of any kind while we're here."

He paced the deck, trying to wedge in every thought before they lost the connection. "Of course, there's no docking or refueling arrangements for us that we understand on the outer skin. Of course, we've lost one of our landers. Never mind, we still have the *Hawking* and *Carson* and *Leno.* Your team has been without medical treatment for four months now. We need to debrief you."

Not the best time, a link just when they were coasting out over the rim. "I'm looking at the back of the Bowl, seeing quite a lot of structure. Blems, bubbles, angular structures, crisscrossed lines . . . I'm zooming on an intersection . . . those are tubes networking . . . maybe a transport system. Looks like spiderwebbing.

"Bigger, shorter tubes right at the rim. Knobby gray structures big as . . . well, little moons. Like Ceres. Several of 'em. I can see the nearest one in motion. Really big. Too big to be a weapon. Helical lines running round the inside—"

Redwing's internal alarm bells went off. "Karl, what do you think?"

Karl was standing alert, almost crouching. He said crisply, "Looks like they're encased in magnetic field coils. Maybe some sort of offensive weapon."

"Or telescope," Clare said.

Karl shook his head. "Astronomy? Nah. No need for that long cylinder. Could be a laser of a kind we don't know? Huge, in any case."

"Looks like old-style cannon," Redwing said. "Except bigger than makes any sense."

Clare Conway said, "Maybe they fight planets. *Big* cannon. Captain, we'll be looking right into that tube in maybe twenty minutes."

Karl said, "The nearest of them is swiveling to engage us, sir."

Redwing frowned. "Okay. Jam, start us turning. Stay away from the focus of that thing. Ayaan, do you still have Fred? Fred, give me some good news, will you?"

Jam said quickly, "With your permission, Captain, I'll bring us back above the Great Plain."

"Do that. Fred, we'll be out of touch in a few minutes. We have a message from Earth. I'll squirt it *now*."

. . .

They lost the Fred link. What Clare had called a cannon continued to follow them. Jam and Clare rolled the ship to escape. The magscoop flexed and fought as it reconfigured, seizing on whatever ionized solar wind it could grasp. They dropped down below the Bowl rim.

"No telescope could be that big," Clare said. "Right? Captain?"

"Jam, is she right?"

"I'm going lower," Jam said, concentrating on their trajectory. Long rolling waves hummed through the ship. "Scopes don't need to be long, just wide to capture light. But to emit light . . ."

They were over the Great Plain now, decelerating a little to bring them past the rim. Clare said, "That does it. That long tube isn't following us anymore."

"Doesn't want to fire on the Great Plain." Redwing made it a straight assertion based on his intuition. That hid some of his relief.

Jam said, "Maybe they can't. If it's a cannon, and if it could swivel down to fire on inhabited turf . . . a civil war could get really nasty, couldn't it?"

Redwing didn't know, so he didn't answer.

Ayaan said, "My lucky day. I've got fresh text from Cliff's team. Spotty and noisy, but the software cleaned it pretty well. Want to see it?"

She put the long message on all their screens. Cliff's team had discovered a tram system and learned to use it; had met aliens and fought a war with them as allies; those aliens had led them into the Bowl's structural undergrowth. There were low-res pictures. They were eating well enough, and grateful for Beth's menu instructions.

"Mostly they're staying alive and moving," Redwing said. There were smiles all around. "Great news."

"But even if they're not captured, they're getting nowhere," Ayaan added.

Redwing was getting near the end of his watch so handed off to Karl and went to his cramped quarters. They had snagged a cluster of messages from Sol system while beyond the Bowl's lip, and the AI had them crisply decoded on his private computer. He told it to speak the messages as he ate dinner alone—Sri Lankan rice and chicken in a deep tangy sauce. One of the biggest threats to stability in a spacecraft was sensory deprivation of a subtle sort, and tasty food helped a lot. So would sex, but that was a dead end for a captain. There was a certain lady he'd like to revive, but the circumstances had to call for it—probably, when he needed large ground teams. There was nothing official between them, no contract, no conditional agreement. And big ground teams didn't seem to be a good bet here anyway. He sighed, watched the great construct roll on below, and turned to the tightbeam communications.

There were some tech updates on the grav waves from Glory. He set them aside for Karl after a glance and read the executive summary. After centuries of study, Earthside didn't know a whole lot more. The wavelengths and wave packets still implied huge masses waltzing around each other in complex patterns. Yet large aperture studies of the Glory system showed no such masses at all. Maybe grav theory was wrong, one message said. Or they were watching a source accidentally in the same spot in the sky and much farther away.

He read that ". . . final merger of two black holes in a binary system releases more power than the combined light from all the stars in the visible Universe. This vast energy comes in the form of gravitational waves, bearing the waveform signature of the merger." Far too much power to be the Glory signature, but the waveforms were like those from the merger theory.

Or else, the summary said, ". . . the effect is fictional, made up somehow to deceive us." Fictional? Maybe the language had changed. Facts never had to be plausible; fiction did. He snorted.

The last century or so of messages had taken on an odd flavor of exhortations to the same refrain— the glories of their mission and urging them on. Sometimes these carried overt religious tones, but this one was an eco-sermon. He told his software to mine it for real information.

Most of the real news was on biosphere management: Earthside, the carbon sequestration that had worked well was having side effects. The warmed, expanded oceans were building up their carbonates, a product from the deployed farm waste carbon dropped into them. Now some was coming back out. Seeding the ocean to capture CO_2 by sweetening the ocean dead zones had also capped out, and the climate engineers couldn't stuff more in. Alarm bells . . .

All the things put off for a few centuries were now biting back. The only thing Earthside had truly planned for on a centuries-long timescale was the starships. . . .

He turned on his wall screen and looked at the distant landscapes drifting past—low mountains crested in snow, vast forests, river valleys the size of Earthly continents. How *did* these creatures run their Bowl? It had to be far more complex than managing a mere planet.

Could the Bowl teach Earth something crucial about terraforming? That alone would be worth stopping for.

He made himself run through the rest of the tightbeam signals. There were some updates on performance modes of their onboard AIs, some hardware issues, suggested upgrades here and there. Most likely these came as feedback from other starships. *SunSeeker,* too, had tightbeamed back such reports. He was pretty sure the summaries he had sent about the Bowl were the most bizarre ever transmitted.

He captained a starship, but this enormous thing was a star that drove a ship, was the propulsion, a star that was the essence of the ship itself. It ran on fusion, too, like *SunSeeker*. It was a . . . shipstar.

So . . . who captained it?

ACKNOWLEDGMENTS

We conferred on scientific and literary matters with many helpful people. Erik Max Francis, Joe Miller, and Joan Slonczewski gave detailed comments on the manuscript. Don Davis, Mark Martin, and Joe Miller and James Benford were of great help in technical issues. And of course, Olaf Stapledon and Freeman Dyson were first.

SHIPSTAR

This book is for John Varley, Arthur C. Clarke,
Bob Shaw, Paul McAuley, Alastair Reynolds,
Iain M. Banks, Robert Reed,
and others of the Big Object Society.

On to larger things!

ACKNOWLEDGMENTS

We conferred on scientific and literary matters with many helpful people. Erik Max Francis, Joe Miller, and David Hartwell gave detailed comments on the manuscript. And of course Olaf Stapledon and Freeman Dyson were first.

Cast of Characters, Common Terms

SunSeeker Crew and Terms

Captain Redwing

Cliff Kammash—biologist

Mayra Wickramsingh—pilot, with Beth team

Abduss Wickramsingh—engineer, with Beth team

Glory—the planet of destination

SunSeeker—the ramship

Beth Marble—biologist

Eros—the first drop ship

Fred Ojama—geologist, with Beth team

Aybe—general engineer officer, with Cliff team

Howard Blaire—systems engineer, with Cliff team

Terrence Gould—with Cliff team

Irma Michaelson—plant biologist, with Cliff team

Tananareve Bailey—with Beth team

Lau Pin—engineer, with Beth team

Jampudvipa (shortened to Jam)—an Indian
   petty officer

Ayaan Ali—Arab woman navigator/pilot

Clare Conway—copilot

Karl Lebanon—general technology officer

ASTRONOMER FOLK

Memor—Attendant Astute Astronomer

Bemor—Contriver and Intimate Emissary to the Ice
Minds

Asenath—Chief of Wisdom

Ikahaja—Ecosystem Savant

Omanah—Ecosystem Packmistress

Ramanuji—Biology Savant

Kanamatha—Biology Packmistress

Thaji—Judge Savant

Unajiuhanah—Senior Mistress, Keeper of the Vault
Library

OTHER PHYLA

finger snakes—Thisther, male; Phoshtha, female;
Shtirk, female

Ice Minds—cold life of great antiquity

the Adopted—those aliens already encountered and
integrated into the Bowl

the Diaphanous

FOLK TERMS

Analyticals—artificial minds that monitor Bowl data
on local scales

TransLanguage

Long Records

Late Invaders

Undermind

Serf-Ones

the Builders—the mix of species that built
the Bowl

Third Variety—Astronomer variety
Astronauts—Astronomer variety
Quicklands
Kahalla

PART I

ESSENTIAL ERROR

It is better to be wrong than to be vague.
In trial and error, the error is the true essential.
—FREEMAN DYSON

ONE

Memor glimpsed the fleeing primates, a narrow view seen through the camera on one of the little mobile probes. Simian shapes cavorted and capered among the understory of the Mirror Zone, making their way to—what? Apparently, to the local express station of mag-rail. Very well. She had them now, then. Memor clashed her teeth in celebration, and tossed a squirming small creature into her mouth, crunching it with relish.

These somewhat comic Late Invaders were scrambling about, anxious. They seemed dreadfully confused, too. One would have expected more of ones who had arrived via a starship, with an interstellar ram of intriguing design. But as well, they had escaped in their scampering swift way. And, alas, the other gang of them had somehow evaded Memor's attempt to kill them, when they made contact with a servant species, the Sil. So they had a certain small cleverness, true.

Enough of these irritants! She would have to concentrate and act quickly to bring them to heel. "Vector to intercept," Memor ordered her pilot. Their ship surged with a thrumming roar. Memor sat back and gave a brief clacking flurry of fan-signals expressing relief.

Memor called up a situation graphic to see if anything had changed elsewhere. Apparently not. The Late Invader ramship was still maneuvering near the Bowl, keeping beneath the defensive weapons along the rim. From their electromagnetic emissions, clearly they monitored their two small groups of Late Invaders that were running about the Bowl. But their ship made no move to directly assist them. Good. They were wisely cautious. It would be interesting to take their ship apart, in good time, and see how the primates had engineered its adroit aspects.

Memor counted herself fortunate that the seeking probe had now found this one group, running through the interstices behind the mirror section. She watched vague orange blobs that seemed to be several simians and something more, as well: tentacular shapes, just barely glimpsed. These shapes must be some variety of underspecies, wiry and quick. Snakes?

The ship vibrated under her as Memor felt a summoning signal—Asenath called, her irritating chime sounding in Memor's mind. She had to take the call, since the Wisdom Chief was Memor's superior. Never a friend, regrettably. Something about Asenath kept it that way.

Asenath was life-sized on the viewing wall, giving a brilliant display of multicolored feathers set in purple urgency and florid, rainbow rage. "Memor! Have you caught the Late Invaders?"

"Almost." Memor kept her own feather-display submissive, though with a fringe of fluttering orange jubilance. "Very nearly. I can see them now. The primate named 'Beth' has a group, including the one I've trained to talk. I'm closing on them. They have somehow mustered some allies, but I am well armed."

Asenath made a rebuke display, slow and sardonic. "This group *you* let escape, yes?"

"Well, yes, they made off while I was attending to—"

"So they *are* the escaped, I take it. I cannot attend to every detail, but this was a plain failure, Attendant Astute Astronomer. They eluded you."

Memor suppressed her irritation. Asenath always used full titles to intimidate and assert superiority— usually, as now, with a fan-rattle. "Only for a short while, Wisdom Chief. I had also to contend with the other escaped primates, you may recall, Your Justness."

"Give up everything else and get us that primate who can talk! We need it. Don't fire on them. If they die, you die."

Memor had to control her visible reaction. No feather-display, head motionless. "Wisdom Chief? What has changed?"

No answer. Asenath's feather-display flickered with a reflexive blush of fear, just before she faded.

She was hiding something . . . but what? Memor would have to learn, but not now. She glanced at the detection screen, ignoring her pilot. Beth's group had disappeared into a maze of machinery.

There were heat traces in several spots, leading . . . toward the docks. Yes! Toward another escape.

There had been six of these Late Invaders when they escaped. Now the heat traces found only five, plus some slithering profiles of another species. Had one died or gone astray? These were a social species, on the diffuse hierarchy model, so it was unlikely they had simply abandoned one of their kind.

"Veest Blad," she said to the pilot, "make for the docks. We'll intercept them there. *Fast.*"

TWO

Tananareve Bailey looked back, face lined, sweat dripping from her nose. Nobody behind her now. She was the last, almost keeping up. Her injuries had healed moderately well and she no longer limped, but gnawing fatigue had set in. She was slowing. Her breath rasped and her throat burned and she was nearly out of water.

It had been a wearing, sweaty trip through the maze she thought of as "backstage." The labyrinth that formed the back of the Bowl's mirror shell was intricate and plainly never intended for anybody but workers to move through. No comforts such as passageways. Poor lighting. Twisty lanes a human could barely crawl through. This layer underpinning the Bowl was the bigger part of the whole vast structure, nearly an astronomical unit across—but only a few meters thick. It was all machinery, stanchions, and cables. Control of the mirrors on the surface above demanded layers of intricate wiring and mechanical buffers. Plus, the route twisted in three dimensions.

Tananareve was sweating and her arms ached. She couldn't match the jumping style of her companions in 18 percent gravity without a painful clicking in her hip and ribs. Her pace was a gliding run, sometimes bounding off an obstructing wall, sometimes taking it on her butt—all assisted by her hands. It demanded a kind of slithering grace she lacked.

Beth, Lau Pin, Mayra, and Fred were ahead of her. She paused, clinging to a buttress shaft. She needed rest, time, but there was none of that here. For a moment she let the whole world slide away and just relaxed, as well as she could. These moments came seldom but she longed for them. She sighed and . . . let go. . . .

Earth came to her then . . . the quiet leafy air of her childhood, in evergreen forests where she hiked with her mother and father, her careless laughter sinking into the vastness of the lofty trees. Her heart was still back there in the rich loam of deep forests, fragrant and solemn in the cathedral redwoods and spruce. Even in recalling it all, she knew it had vanished on the tides of time. Her parents were dead for centuries now, surely, despite the longevity treatments. But the memories swarmed up into her as she relaxed for just a long, lingering moment.

Her moment of peace drained away. She had to get back to running.

In the dim light, she could barely make out the finger snakes flickering ahead of the long-striding humans. They had an amazingly quick wriggle. Probably they'd been adapted through evolution to do repairs in the Bowl's understory. Beth had gotten fragments of their history out of the snakes, but the translation was shaky. They'd been here on the Bowl so long, their own origins were legends about a strange, mythical place where a round white sun could set to reveal black night.

"Beth," Tananareve sent over short-range comm, "I'm kinda . . . I . . . need a rest."

"We all do," came the crisp reply. Beth turned up ahead and looked back at her, too far away to read an expression. "Next break is five minutes."

"Here I come." She clamped down her jaw and took a ragged breath.

Their target was an automated cargo drone. The snakes had told of these, and now the bulkheads and struts they passed were pitched forward, suggested they were getting close. Up ahead, as she labored on, she could see it emerge, one in a line of identical flat-bellied cylinders. Tananareve could see the outline of a great oyster-colored curved hatch in its side, and—*was that? Yes!*—stars beyond a window wall. She felt elation slice through her fatigue. But now the hip injury had slowed her to a limping walk.

Without the finger snakes, this plan would have been impossible.

She limped up to the rest of them, her mouth already puckering at the imagined taste of water. The three snakes were decorated in camouflage colors, browns and mottled blacks, the patterns almost the same, but Tananareve had learned to tell them apart. They massed a bit more than any of the humans, and looked like snakes whose tails had split into four arms, each tipped with a claw. Meaty things, muscular, slick-skinned. They wore long cloth tubes as backpacks, anchored on their ridged hides.

Beth's team had first seen finger snakes while escaping from the garden of their imprisonment. Tananareve surprised a nest of them and they fled down into deep jungle, carrying some cargo in a sling. The snakes were a passing oddity, apparently intelligent to a degree. Her photos of them were intriguing.

Now it was clear the finger snakes must have tracked and observed their party ever since. When Fred led the humans to an alien computer facility, they were not in evidence. Fred had found a way to make the computer teach them the Bird Folk language. Among his many talents, Fred was a language speed-learner. He got the quasilinear logic and syntax down in less than a day. Once he had built a vocabulary, his learning rate increased. A few more days and he was fluent. The whole team carried sleep-learning, so they used a slip-transfer from Fred's. By then he had been somehow practicing by himself, so it was best that he got to talk to the snakes first.

They just showed up, no diplomacy or signpost-
ing. Typical snake character—do, don't retreat into
symbols or talk. When the finger snakes crawled
through the door, somehow defeating Lau Pin's
lock, Fred said hello and no more. He wasn't exactly talkative either—except, as he often rejoined,
when he actually had something important to say.

So after his hello, and a spurt of Snake in reply,
Tananareve was able to yell at them. "Give you
honor! We are lost!"

Five snakes formed a hoop, which turned out to
be a sign of "fruitful endeavor commencing." Tananareve made a hand-gesture she had somehow
gotten from the slip-transfer. This provoked another
symbol, plus talk. Formal snake protocol moved
from gestures and signs into the denser thicket of
language. Luckily, the highest form of Snakespeech
was a modified Bird Folk structure that stressed *lean*
and *of sinew* as virtues, so their knotted phrases did
convey meaning in transparent, staccato rhythms.

The finger snakes were rebels or something like it,
as nearly as Tananareve could untangle from the cross-
associations that slithered through Snakespeech.
Curious, also. Humans were obviously new to their
world, and therefore they began tracking the human band in an orderly, quiet way shaped by tradition. The snakes worked for others, but retained
a fierce independence. Knowledge was their strong
suit—plus the ability to use tools of adroit shape and
use. They went everywhere in the Bowl, they said,
on engineering jobs. Especially they maintained the
meters-thick layers between the lifezone and the

hard hull. In a sense, they maintained the boundary that separated the uncountable living billions from the killing vacuum that waited a short distance away.

The snakes wanted to know everything they could not discover by their intricate tracking and watching. They knew the basic primate architecture, for their tapering "arms" used a cantilevered frame that bore a warped resemblance to the human shoulder. This, plus a million more matters, flew through their darting conversations. Snakes thought oddly. Culture, biology, singing, and food all seemed bound up in a big ball of context hard to unravel. But when something important struck them, they acted while humans were still talking.

When it was clear that humans would die if they stayed at low gravity for too long, the finger snakes led them here: to a garage for magnetically driven space vehicles. Snake teams did the repairs here.

• • •

One of the finger snakes—Thisther, she thought—clicked open a recessed panel in the drone, so the ceramic cowling eased down. Thisther set to work, curling head to tail so his eyes could watch his nail-tipped fingers work. The wiry body flexed like cable. Phoshtha turned away from him, on guard.

Tananareve was still guessing at genders, but there were behavior cues. The male always seemed to have a tool in hand, and the females were wary in new surroundings. Thisther was male; Phoshtha and Shtirk were female.

Phoshtha's head dipped and curled as she turned around, seeking danger. Shtirk wasn't visible; she must be on guard. Tananareve sensed no obvious threats, barring, perhaps, a whistling just at the edge of her hearing.

Phoshtha wriggled to meet her. "Thisther knows computers-speak," she said. "King of computers=persons. Will write thrust program for us quick, person-comp-adept, she is. Are you sick?"

"Was injured," Tananareve said. "Not sick. Am healing." Both spoke in Bird talk, its trills and rolled vowels chiming like a song.

"Is well we know."

The curved side of the cargo drone slid up with a high metallic whine. Green verdant wealth. The drone was filled, jammed with vegetation—live plants standing forth in trays, rich hanging streamers. Lights in the curved ceiling glared like suns. Thisther continued to work, and suddenly trays were sliding out and falling. Half the trays had piled up on the deck when it stopped.

"Keep some plants. Air for us while we travel," Phoshtha said. She wriggled away.

Lau Pin jog-hopped in the light grav, springing over to help Tananareve. "You okay? Shall I carry you?"

"I'm fine. What's that whistling?" It was loud and now had a low rumble to it.

"We need to get aboard," Lau Pin said, glancing around at the snake teams at work. "Quick." He tried pulling her along by her belt, desisted when he saw her pain.

Tananareve walked over to a copper-hued wall, leaning against its warmth. The finger snakes chattered in their jittering bursts and oozed across the platforms with wriggling grace. She studied them amid the noise, and . . . let herself go.

She was back in the leafy wealth she had grown up in and, yes, knew she would never see again. She allowed her head to tilt back and felt her spine kink and lapse as it straightened and eased. Amid metal and ceramics, she thought of green. This odd construction they were moving through, a weird place bigger than planets, had its own version of green paradise . . . and was the only reason she had survived in it. The vast, strange canopies with their chittering airborne creatures; the stretching grasslands and zigzag trees; animals so odd, they threw her back into her basic biology—they were all natural in some way, yet . . . not. Someone had designed their setting, if not their species.

Those sprawling lands of the Bowl had been tolerable. These mechanical labyrinths below the Bowl's lifesphere were . . . not. She had seen quite enough, thank you, of the motorized majesty that made such a vast, rotating artifact. *Rest,* that was her need now. She had to descend into blissful sleep, consign to her unconscious the labors of processing so much strangeness.

She let go slowly, head lapsing back. Easing was not easy, but she let herself descend into it, for just a moment before she would get up again and stride off, full of purpose and letting no soft moments play through her . . . Just for a while . . .

"Looks like the male is finished playing with the controls," Lau Pin called.

Dimly she sensed the snakes moving by her. This-ther wriggled into the hold . . . then Phoshtha and Shtirk.

Tananareve came out of her blissful retreat slowly. Voices echoed odd and hollow around her. Lead infected her legs; they would not move without great strain. She made herself get unsteadily up onto two uncertain feet. Clouds in her mind dispelled slowly—something about green wealth, forests of quiet majesty, her parents . . .

She made her chin snap up, eyes fluttering, back on duty . . . and slowly turned to survey the area. *Where's Beth?*

Clouds still grasped at her. *Breathe deeply, keep it up.*

Tananareve strode off to check around some angular buttress supports. No human about.

The snakes had crawled into the ship, fitting somehow into open spaces. Lau Pin jogged to join them. He glanced back at her, waved a hand, turned, went away. . . .

Still there were clouds. She listened intently as she tried to put one small foot in front of the other. Remarkably difficult, it was.

Rumbling, sharp whistling, chatter. Tananareve walked a bit unsteadily back toward the ship. Her vision was blurred, sweat trickling into her eyes and stinging.

The great curved door closed in Tananareve's face.

"Hey," Tananareve said. She stopped, blinked. Clouds swept away on a sudden adrenaline shock—

"Wait!"

The drone slid out of line and away, slow at first, then faster and faster.

"Dammit!" she shouted. "Damn—" She couldn't hear herself over a whistling roar. Hot air blasted her back.

• • •

"Wait!" Beth Marble shouted. She could feel the acceleration building. The finger snakes were wrapped around support pillars, and her crew were grabbing for tie-downs. She found handholds and footholds while thrust pulled massively at her.

She wailed, "Tananareve!"

"She was sick," Phoshtha said, recessed eyes glittering. "Thrust would have killed her. She would have slowed us."

"What? You let—" Beth stopped. It was done; handle the debriefing later, in calmer moments. The snakes were useful but strange.

They were accelerating quickly and she found a wedge-shaped seat. Not ideal for humans, but manageable. There was little noise from the magnetics, but the entire length of the drone popped and ponged as stresses adjusted.

Lau Pin said, "I have *SunSeeker* online."

"Send Redwing our course. Talk to him." Beth couldn't move; she was barely hanging on to a tie-down bar. "Use our best previous coordinates."

"Okay. I'm having it compute from the present force vectors." Lau Pin turned up the volume so others could hear. "Lau Pin here."

"Jampudvipa here, bridge petty officer. Captain Redwing's got some kind of cold, and Ayaan Ali is bridge pilot. What's your situation?"

"We're on our way. It went pretty much as we'd planned. Hardly anything around on the way but finger snakes. We've got three with us. Uh . . . We lost Tananareve Bailey."

"Drown it," the officer said. "All right. But you're en route? Hello, I see your course . . . yeah. Wow. You're right up against the back of the mirror shell."

"Jampudvipa, this drone is driven by magnets in the back of the Bowl. Most of their ships and trains operate that way, we think. It must save reaction fuel. We don't have much choice."

Some microwave noise blurred the signal, then, "Call me Jam. And you don't have pressure suits?"

"No, and there's no air lock. No way to mate the ships."

A pause. "Well, Ayaan says she can get *SunSeeker* to the rendezvous in ten hours. After that . . . what? Stet. Stet. Lau Pin, we can maybe fit you into the bay that held *Eros* before we lost it. If not . . . mmm."

Lau Pin said, "The finger snakes don't keep time our way. I think it's longer for us. I'll make regular checks and send them."

"We'll be there. And you all need medical assistance? Four months in low gravity, out in the field—yeah. We'll have Captain Redwing out of the infirmary by then, but it only holds two. Pick your sickest."

"Would have been Tananareve."

• • •

The drone was gone. The system's magnetic safety grapplers released with a hiss. Tananareve stood in the sudden silence, stunned.

A high hiss sounded from a nearby track. She turned to find a snake to stop the drone, call it somehow—and saw no snakes at all. All three had boarded the drone. Now the shrill hiss was worse. She stepped back from the rising noise, and an alien ship came rushing toward the platform from a descending tube. It was not magnetic; it moved on jets.

Tananareve looked around, wondering where to run. The ship had a narrow transparent face and through it she could see the pilot, a spindly brown-skinned creature in a uniform. It looked not much bigger than she was and the tubular ship it guided was enormous, flaring out behind the pilot's cabin. The ship eased in alongside the main platform, jetting cottony steam. Tananareve wondered what she should do: hide, flee, try to talk to—?

Then, behind huge windows in the ship's flank, she saw a tremendous feathered shape peering out at her, and recognized it. Quick flashing eyes, the great head swiveling to take in all around it, with a twisted cant to its heavy neck. She gasped. *Memor.*

THREE

Redwing looked out across the yawning distances, frowning.

Far down, there were all the artful graces of land and sea, suspended before a warming sun like a rich, steaming dish offered on a steel-hard plate. Everything was larger, grander, and strange.

The Bowl seas were light blue expanses larger than Jupiter, bounded by shallow brown edges. Across those ran arcs of grand wave trains, immense ripples that must roll on for years before finding a shore. At finer resolution, sediment plumes of tan and chocolate spread across shallow seabeds, feeding kelp straits of festering ripe green. Rumpled hill ranges were larger than Asia. Never driven by continental drift, these crosshatched the vast lands, carved by rivers that could cut no farther than the Bowl's hull. Indeed, he could see places where wind or water had worn away the living zone, leaving patches of rusting metal. Under close-up, he and Karl watched teams repairing such erosions.

The deserts were huge, too. Tan lands of grass went on over distances greater than the Moon was from Earth, with only dots of green beckoning where an oasis sprouted. Sprawling dry lands ended where water found its way to make moist forests. Storms spiraling in immense white-bright pinwheels churned with ponderous energies, raking across deserts larger than planets, and over forests so deep, no one could ever walk out of them.

How did anyone design a thing like this? A vast trapped atmosphere, oceans the size of planets, lakes like continents, yet no real mountains—maybe that was a clue. Of course, putting an Everest on the Bowl would make it lopsided and complicate dynamics. There could be no plate tectonics and so no volcanoes, but how did this biosphere circulate carbon and water? On Earth, a complex cycle a hundred million years long did the job. As well, Earth's tectonic ranges forced air over and around them, generating the moving chaos humans called weather. The Bowl's dwellers did not suffer from mountain wind shadow, or the combing winds that raced through narrow passages. Mountains made for stormy trouble on Earth. The Bowl was a milder place than planets could be.

But why build a whole contraption like this, when you could just move to Florida?

The question wasn't just rhetorical. If he could fathom what built such a thing, and why, he might have a clue about how to deal with them.

Ping. His autosec reminded him of lunch.

He thought of it as the mess, very old school, but Fleet said it was a Starship Wardroom. He sat as usual for Meal 47, his current choice: classic turkey dinner, rich cream sauce and cranberries. He made himself not think about the simple fact that it was all made of ingredients centuries old; after all; so was he.

He had kept mistaking what Mayra Wickramsingh said at every meal: *Nosh for me,* it sounded like. After she and her husband, Abduss, went down in the disastrous descent to the Bowl, he had looked it up. The Linguist AI had a transform function, so it learned even through his mushy pronunciation; the AI found it was an Indian phrase, *naush fara-maiye,* meaning "please accept the pleasure of savoring this meal," which seemed like *bon appétit* to Redwing. Suitable. "*Naush faramaiye* to you all," Redwing said, bowing his head. The crew bowed back. Clare looked puzzled.

"Cap'n, I'm having trouble with the Artilect coherence," Jampudvipa said.

Redwing still used *AI* as a shorthand for the shipboard systems that patiently oversaw operations, since that's what everybody called them when he was growing up. But Artilect was the actual Fleet term, since integrated artificial minds constituted a collective intellect. It was useful to think of the systems as different people, engaged in a constant congress, discussing the ship's current state. "What's their problem?"

"They want to go back into full scoop mode."

"In a solar system? We can't get the necessary plasma densities."

"I know." Jampudvipa shrugged. "I think they're showing mission fatigue."

"Have you tried to give them some shut-eye time, one by one?"

"They resist it."

"Enforce it. Tell them they need a psych reboot, only make the language prettier."

This got rueful laughs around the wardroom table. "Diplomacy—not our strong suit," Clare Conway said. She was more personable than most pilots, one of the reasons she had made the crew. Redwing had gone through her file while making his selection of whom to revive.

Ayaan Ali frowned. "It is serious problem, Artilect coherence. They start to disagree, to have their own ideas—trouble."

"They want what's impossible," Karl Lebanon said. He folded his hands and leaned back against a bulkhead. As general technology officer, he shepherded Artilects through daily problems, plus a dozen other jobs. "We can't go back to interstellar mode."

Clare sipped her coffee. "They have to adjust our ramscoop intake in ten-second intervals, to optimize. That burns their attention reservoir, makes their duty cycles long. Stresses them pretty hard."

"We're getting system clash in our magnetic scoop system," Karl said. "It'll tire the Artilects and we'll start getting torques, surges, inductive effects that wear down our gear."

"Same small-scale coil problem?"

"Yeah. The system's pretty stressed. Never made for this kind of low-velocity maneuvering. We can't get into the magneto components to adjust them."

Clare said, "A mechanical problem, fixable—but only if we could get a bot in the inductive chamber. Those we could maybe make, but present bot complement can't do it. That choice set is not even in the partition menu."

"We can't downtime them?" Redwing knew the answer but if he let people talk, they felt better. All three chimed in with their versions of the same hard fact: A ship designed to work at interstellar speeds was a bitch to control in planetary orbit, and have any actual maneuvering capability. The Artilects were taking the brunt of it.

Redwing nodded as each spoke but ran his own inventory as well.

By this time his knees were sending angry messages that they wanted a trial separation. His weight workout this morning had pushed the limit too far, again. A warning sign: When he overexerted, he was working out unconscious worries. So he concentrated on Clare's detailed tech talk and focused outward, nodding and keeping his gaze on her while thinking about all the crew. They worked well together, as the Psych Artilect Adept predicted, before Redwing had wakened the new members. How well would they do when Beth's team came aboard? Only four left out of six, but— the ship would get more crowded and irritations would begin to build. He had a time window before he would have to decide whether to get out of this entire situation and cast off into interstellar flight again or—what? Go down onto the Bowl in enough numbers to accomplish a resupply and . . . what? *Too many unknowns.*

He let the crew run on for a while, noting that their uniforms were getting a tad messy, hair uncombed, beards a few days old. He would have to sharpen them up a bit, and now might be the time.

At least this crew would look better then, when and if they got Beth's team aboard. They'd have to double on berths. Working spirit and order would be more difficult. A clock would start ticking.

He said mildly, "Officer Jampudvipa, with the Artilects going moody, should we be letting them run the bridge alone while we have lunch?"

Blinks, nods. Jampudvipa looked rueful, mouth turning down, and got up hurriedly. "Yes, sir. They're in collective agreement mode but—yes."

That let him focus on the others. "Beth's team will be aboard in a few hours. That's if we're lucky and solve the problem we have to focus on now. Still, I want everybody spruced up—clean, shaven, bright eyed." Nods all around, some repentant. He turned to Karl. "But the major problem is, how do we get them aboard?"

"I've got her photos of the vehicle they're in— basically, a magnetic train car with locks facing outward, to vacuum," Karl said. "But they don't have their suits. The aliens, these 'Folk,' took those at capture."

"So . . ." Redwing let them think a moment. "Can we match velocities and run a pressured conduit?"

"Not easily." Karl's mouth fretted as he thought. "We've got EVA gear, sure, but it's one-man, for repairs."

"How about the *Bernal*?" Clare asked. "It's for freight transfer, but we could maybe refit it for a fix-up flexi passage."

"I don't trust anything flexi to stand up to torques and stretches," Karl said. "If we try it, yes, *Bernal* is the best craft."

Redwing had used the repair bots to inspect *Sun-Seeker*'s hull soon after entering the Bowl system, and he privately agreed with Karl. In interstellar mode, their strong magnetic fields had kept the ship from the blizzard of neutral atoms and dust. *Sun-Seeker* was less effective dealing with erosions while it maneuvered at low thrust around the Bowl. The externals looked pitted and scarred now, and he wondered about whether the repair bots could spot flaws that could prove fatal in a personnel transfer. Or if the flexi would sustain pitting from random debris. A thousand questions nagged at him.

Redwing said, "We could try a fit with our dorsal hatch. We'd have to rig some kind of docking collar."

This they liked. Redwing let them toss ideas around for a while as he tried to envision exactly how that configuration might work. Ayaan Ali had little to say, but he saw a quick widening of her eyes and nodded at her, holding up a hand to draw attention.

"I . . . have an idea," she said quietly. "But we must work quickly."

FOUR

Beth watched the Bowl's outer hull, a fast-forward world flittering by below the hard black of space. Even protrusions the size of skyscrapers were just passing gray blurs. In contrast, though the Bowl itself had a surface rotation speed in the range of many kilometers a second, the array of gas clouds and nearby suns hung still. Even high speeds on the interplanetary scale meant nothing to the solemn stars.

Their tubular craft traveled down the outside of

the Bowl, hovering close on magnetically secured trap-rails. She watched enormous plains of gray steel and off-white ceramic flash by. Images jittered so fast, she could not tell what was important. A wall with crawling maggot robots, doing unknown labors. A sliding cascade of liquid metal fuming in high vacuum as it slid into jet-black chunks, then ivory cylinders, then shapely gray teardrops—all to descend into intricate new works, objects meant for mysterious use. All that went by in a stretched display she processed in a few seconds—an entire industrial process carried out in cold vacuum, far from the Bowl star's intrusions. It seethed with robot motion. Fumes danced, billowed, and evaporated away in lacy blue streamers.

Now enormous tangled structures the size of mountains flowed by them. She could see lattice works and cup-shaped constructs but not what they did. It was difficult to keep perspective and their speed seemed to increase still, pressing her at an angle. She was sitting in a chair designed for some other being, one wider and taller. Windows on all sides showed landscapes flitting by, lit by starlight and occasional bright flares amid the odd buildings. From above her head came occasional clanking noises and whispery whistles—sounds of the mag-rail.

"All this industrial infrastructure," Fred said quietly beside her. "Kept out of their living zone."

"Ah, yes," Beth said, not taking her eyes from the images flashing by in the big board window. "We hardly saw any cities before, either."

"Sure, the Bowl's land area is enormous, but then

you realize that their whole mechanistic civilization is clinging to the outer skin. So they have twice the area we thought."

Beth glanced upward into the "sky," where the hull's burnished metal gleamed beneath fitful lights. "And anyone who lives here, does so wrong way up. Centrifugal gravity pushes them away from the hull, so the Bowl is always over their heads. The stars are at their feet." Beth laughed softly. "An upside-down world of its own."

"Smart, really." Fred was watching, too, his eyes darting at the spacious spectacle zooming past. "You can do your manufacturing and then throw your waste away in high vacuum."

Beth shook herself; enough gawking. "Look, we're in a cargo drone. We have to be ready in case we stop and get new passengers."

"Relax. We'll feel the deceleration, get ready."

"At least we should search for food dispensers. This passenger compartment is for whoever's accompanying the cargo—"

"Plants, yeah," Fred said distantly, still distracted by the view. "Those finger snakes arranged to escort the plants, fit us in. Neat."

Beth smiled. Fred had summed up days of negotiations. Their halting efforts had been beset by translation errors and mistakes. Even sharing a sort-of common language, a mix of Bird and English, there were ambiguities that came from how different minds saw the universe. The snakes used wriggles and tiny movements of their outsized faces to convey meaning, and it took a while to even notice that. Words meant different things if a right-wriggle came with it, versus a left-wriggle. The snakes had similar troubles reading "primate face gestures" as they termed it.

Fred turned to her. "You're worried about Tananareve."

"I . . . yes."

"You're surprised I noticed."

"Not really, I—"

"Look, I know what's in my personnel file. I'm classic Asperger's, yep. But I hope I make up for it by, well, my quirky ability to see how things work. Or that's what the file says."

To stall for time she asked, "How did you see your file?"

Fred was honestly surprised. She realized he did not actually know how to be dishonest, or at least without detection. "An easy hack."

"Well . . . yes. I read everybody's file before we left *SunSeeker*. Standard field-prep method."

"So I should overlook how you fret about us, especially Tananareve."

"She's not really recovered, and I should've noticed she didn't get in here with us."

Fred gave her an awkward smile. "Look, the place was confusing and we didn't have any time. She wandered off. There were the finger snakes making a racket and shooting questions at us." A sigh. "Anyway, put it aside. We've got the boarding problem coming up."

She sighed. "Right, of course." *So much for Asperger's patients not picking up on social signals.*

What had that training program said? "Cognitive behavioral therapy can improve stress management relating to anxiety." Yet Fred seems calmer than the rest of us. . . .

Fred pressed on. "The snakes say we're due for a stop about where *SunSeeker* could rendezvous with us. But we have to come out at high speed, so they have to match us. But—"

"Nothing like pressure suits aboard," Lau Pin said. "The snakes say they can't make anything like that, not in time."

He and Mayra had come up, carrying a bowl of what looked like gruel. Mayra scooped some out with a spoon, tasted it. "Bland, but no harm on my bioregister. This comes out of a dispenser in the next car."

So they all fell to eating. Beth was hungry, so the lack of taste in the muddy mixture of carbs and sugars didn't stop her. She was thinking, anyway. Silence, except when two snakes came by and chattered in their high, fluting voices. Beth ignored them while Mayra carried on a halting conversation with the aliens. *Intelligent aliens, the goal of centuries of searching, and I don't have time for them. . . .*

Her hand stopped with her spoon in midair as she stared into the distance. Slowly she turned to Mayra. "Ask them if we can disconnect this car from the track," she said.

• • •

The big problem was hard to sense when you were blithely standing in fractional gravity and not paying attention to the sky. Here on the mag-train, that sky was filled with stars, and it took an hour or two to notice that they were moving. As she thought, Beth watched a bright star move off the window where she sat. The Bowl rotated in thirty-two hours, so the night sky seemed to move a bit slower than it did on Earth. She recalled how, in elementary school, she had been amazed that while sitting at her desk she was really whizzing around at well over a thousand kilometers an hour. The Earth's rotation did that, and its orbit moved her at thirty kilometers a second, too. Now she was sitting in a fast train car and also moving with the Bowl's rotation, hundreds of kilometers a *second*. Leaving the Bowl meant launching into space at that huge velocity.

Mayra said, "They're scared. Why would you want to—?"

"Can they do it?"

"Yes, at the next stop. There's a launch facility they use for traveling off the Bowl, but—"

"How do we shed the velocity?" Fred said.

Beth said, "Carefully, I bet. If they can launch, they must fire us off against the Bowl's rotation, to bring the exit speed down to a manageable level."

"*SunSeeker* must be moving at a few tens of klicks a second," Fred said. "To lose half a thousand klicks a second . . ." His voice trailed off into a croak, apparently at the magnitude of it. ". . . that's not the way to do it, though."

Beth watched the landscape zoom by outside. Were they slowing?

Mayra said, "They call it the Jumper."

"A launch facility?" Beth asked. "Fred, what did you mean?"

"The obvious way to get off the Bowl is to go near the axis, where there's nearly no centrifugal grav, so not a high speed. Then leap off into vacuum."

"We're headed that way, but—" Beth stopped. "Where is this Jumper?"

Mayra chattered to the snakes, and then said, "The next stop, if we take the right shunt. They say." She looked doubtful, as if this was all moving too fast. *Which it is,* Beth thought, *in more ways than one.*

The finger snakes rattled their "shells," which seemed to work like fingernails. She had seen them use those with lightning-quick skill, to manipulate the intricate tools carried in their side pouches. Now they made a noise like castanets—or, she noticed, like a rattlesnake about to strike. Each snake had four of them on their four fingers. Beth saw Mayra drawing back, her face a mask of alarm. "What's—?"

"They sense great risk," Mayra said slowly, "in taking a Jump in this hauler."

"Not space rated?"

"No, a lack of 'life caring'—habitat gear, I think. That noise, though . . . Ewww."

"Yeah, kinda hard to take," Beth said. The snakes were weaving now, standing on leathery, strong "arms" and straining up into the air. Their bodies seemed all ribbed muscle, eyes glittering as they glanced at each other.

Fred said, "Maybe they're deciding whether the risk is worth it."

"Worth what?" Mayra asked, her face still tight with alarm.

"Worth going with us," Fred said. "That's what you meant, right, Beth?"

"I figured there had to be a way to launch into raw space without going to the pole, the Knothole, to get the speed down. I guess there is."

Mayra said, "That's what the finger snakes imply. They're working out whether to help us do that . . . I think." A wry shrug. "Not really sure."

Beth leaned forward, eyes still on the scenery flashing by above the perpetual night sky below. Yes, they were moving slower. Definitely. And was the grav here lighter? So they were moving toward the Knothole? "They can handle the tech for a Jump?"

"Yes, they say. But . . . they say it will be hard on us. A lot of acceleration, and—"

The snakes chattered and rattled and Mayra bowed her head, listening. "The seats will self-contour, so we will . . . survive."

"It's that hard?" Fred asked.

"High. We don't have suits that baffle us against sudden surges." Mayra shrugged. "It is not as though we could have carried them with us, all these months." A slow sad smile.

Beth saw she was recalling her husband, who had

died when they broke out of confinement, crushed by a hideous spiderlike thing. "What else?"

"They say there is little time to do it. As soon as we reach the next station stop, they must gain control of the shunting system. They say they can, the attendants there—mostly finger snakes—are old friends. Then they must move us into a cache that will ratchet us into a 'departure slot' as they call it. Then we move into line and get dispatched by an electromagnetic system. It seizes us, in a manner independent of the precise shape of this hauler . . . and flings us into space, along a vector counter to the Bowl's spin."

Mayra had not spoken so much in a long while. Beth chose to take that as a positive sign. She was right about gear; they had little and would be forced to use whatever came to hand. The seats here were oddly shaped and not designed for humans. The finger snakes had couches to strap into. Not so the bare benches she was sitting on. Still less so for the latrine, which turned out to be a narrow cabin with holes in the floor, some of them small, others disturbingly large.

She signed. "I know it may be uncomfortable. But it's the only way."

Silence. Even the snakes had gone quiet.

Lau Pin said, "We're dead if we stay down here. They'll catch us again. We escaped once; that trick won't work again."

Mayra and Fred nodded. *Collective decision, great.*

Beth noted the snakes watching her. They had

somehow deduced that she was the nominal leader of these odd primates who strode into their lives. Maybe all smart species had some hierarchy?

"Okay, we do it. Notice we're slowing down?"

Fred nodded. "Yeah, felt it."

Lau Pin said, "We don't have much time. Got to hit the ground and move fast. The snakes will tell us what to do."

"Right, good," Beth said. She glanced at Mayra. "And . . . what else?"

"Well . . ." Mayra hesitated. "It's the finger snakes. They want to come with us."

FIVE

Redwing plucked a banana that grew in a weird toroid, peeled and ate it, its aroma bringing back memories of tropical nights and the lapping of waves. Cap'n's privilege.

His comm buzzed and Clare Conway said, "We'll need you on the bridge presently."

"On the way."

Yet he hesitated. Something fretted at the back of his mind.

Redwing had read somewhere that one of his favorite writers, Ernest Hemingway, had been asked what was the best training for a novelist. He had said "an unhappy childhood." Redwing had enjoyed a fine time growing up, but he wondered if this whole expedition was unfolding more like a

novel, and would be blamed on one person, one
character, the guy in charge: him. Maybe you got a
happy childhood and then an unhappy adulthood,
and that's how novels worked.

His mother had made it happy. His father was
away at one war or another while he grew up, and
when he was home seemed absorbed by sports
and alcohol. But that didn't include playing catch
with Redwing or coming to his football games. His
mother had given him a birthday gift of a telescope
and microscope, and a big chemistry set. He bought
chemical supplies by selling gunpowder and other
pyrotechnics to the local kids. So science had been
in his bones from the time he could read. But there
were other currents in the mix. He bought a bicy-
cle and a better telescope with gambling cash. His
mother, who was a bridge Grand Master, always
played penny-ante poker with Redwing while they
waited in the car for his music lessons to start. He
then applied what she had taught him to the neighborhood kids. They didn't know how to count cards
or compute probabilities from that. They also paid
to see him blow something up or dissect some poor
animal as a bio experiment. He was without prin-
ciple but soon had enough principal to advance. A
university career and PhD led to space, where he
really wanted to go. But *this far?* . . .

Maybe, considering a "fault tree" analysis of his
life, having a father who never gave him much time,
Redwing figured he was socially unhappy enough
to satisfy Hemingway. But finding fault wasn't like
solving a problem, was it?

He had been gaining belly weight in these long months skimming along the Bowl structure. Onboard physio analysis said cortisol was the culprit, a steroid hormone prompted by the body's "fight or flight" response to stress. It had bloated him, listening to the plight of his teams fleeing aliens, and damn near nothing he could do to help.

He paused outside the bridge, straightened his uniform, and went in with his shoulders straight.

"Cap'n on bridge," Ayaan Ali said crisply. Unnecessary, but it set the tone. Going into battle, if that's what this was, had a way of quickening the heart.

"We're skimming as close as we can to the Bowl rim," Ayaan Ali said. "Having thruster problems."

Redwing made a show of staying on his feet, taking in the screens, not pacing. "Seems like cutting it pretty near."

Karl Lebanon, neatly turned out with his general technology officer uniform cleaned and creases stiff, said, "That magneto grip problem is back, bigtime. Sir."

Redwing gave him a nod. "Hand-manage it. Stay with the scoop Artilect all the time, ride it."

"Yes, sir. It knows what's up, is running full complement."

"Stations," Redwing said quietly. Old trick: speak softly, make them stay sharp to hear.

He didn't want to call out of the cold sleep enough people to crew this any better, much less to populate some kind of a big landing expedition. Defrosting and training them would burn time and labor. Even after the reawakened came up to speed, at Glory system in some far future, the whole crew would all have to triple up on a hot hammock schedule, skimpy rations, and shower once a week. Under such stress, how could they perform? He didn't want to find out. Not yet, anyway.

SunSeeker had five crew defrosted, including Captain Redwing. Beth's remaining four would make nine. If he had the chance to rescue Cliff's team, they'd be fourteen aboard. A bit crowded, but they could do it.

"Coming up, sir." Ayaan Ali stared intently at the screens. "Rim looks the same, but that big cannon thing is swiveling to track us."

"We're in that slot?"

"See those walls?" Below he saw where the atmosphere screen was tied down. There was a rim zone with big constructions dotted across it, out in the vacuum. Ayaan had found a slot between two of them that kept below the cannon declination and now they were gliding through it, a few kilometers above the edge zone. Complex webs of buildings and immense, articulating machinery slid by below.

The Bowl's outer edge loomed before them, bristling with knobs and bumps the size of nations back on Earth. Looking at the rear screens, he saw the thin, smart film that held in the Bowl atmosphere shimmering in slanting sunlight, blue white. This was the closest they had coasted in to that atmosphere blanket. He hoped they wouldn't take ground fire, though the Bowl's Great Plain was a thousand kilometers away, and any projectile fire would puncture their filmy cover. But yes, Karl was probably right, just from elementary geometry.

Still . . . "We're low enough?"

"Yes, sir. They can't depress that snout to aim into the Bowl structure."

"Smart sociology. If there are wars here, at least nobody can blow a hole in their life support."

We keep below their firing horizon, so we're safe. Or so went the theory. So many theories had gotten blown away, ever since they sighted this huge, spinning contrivance. But if this one failed, they'd be in easy range of what looked like, Karl said, a gamma ray laser.

"Karl, what's the emission gain?"

"They're running something that gives off a lot of microwaves. Chargers, probably. Running up capacitor banks, I'd guess."

"To discharge against us, through some plasma implosion, giving them the gammas?"

"That's my estimate, sir."

"What do you make of our situation?"

"I had the usual basic training in remote warfare. The find-fix-track-target-engage-assess decision tree, with Artilects providing the live data. That's all I know."

"No course in alien strategy and tactics?" This got him a round of chuckles around the bridge, as he had planned. Let them get a little steam out.

"Uh—no, sir. Not on the curriculum, couple centuries back."

A quiet jab, well delivered. Redwing nodded and smiled in tribute. "Then full speed ahead." In a tribute to ancient naval traditions, he added, "Give us some steam."

"I don't like to flex our magnetic scoop system any more, uh, sir," Karl said.

"Same small-scale problem?"

"Yeah. The system's pretty compressed. We can't get into the magneto components to adjust them. It's a mechanical problem, not just some digital e-management thing."

"Do your best." Not the time for more techno-speak. Though that was all that kept them alive, of course. "Belay any repairs until we get Beth aboard. How's the flexi gear straightening?"

"Programmed on the printer," Jampudvipa said. "Fold points and tension web seem sturdy enough to compile at pickup."

"Excellent. Clare?"

"Look at the screen. The laser pods are above us now."

What's the old saying? "Come in under their radar" *means something else. This is running in under the guns of a fortress that cannot fire down into the Bowl lifezone.* "Um. Can we skim that close to the atmosphere?"

Karl pointed to the blue sheen cast off by the boundary film of the atmosphere. This close in, it spread like an ocean landscape, yet the eye saw through it to lands and seas below. These stretched away in infinite perspective, intricate layers basking in unending solar radiance, free of night. The eggshell sheen of the boundary tricked the eye into seeing it as an ocean, with lands on the floor below.

There were even long rolling waves to the boundary, flexing in slow, marching rows.

Redwing had to admit the design features here were clever beyond easy measure. Rather than fading off in the familiar exponential, like planets, the Bowl's air ran up and into a hard boundary. The air was thin there, hundreds of kilometers high—but the multilayer smart film kept the errant wind streams and vortices at bay, spreading the energies across vast distances, smoothing them out. No molecules leaked away forever, as they had for poor Mars. The Bowl's own magnetic field gave a spiderweb defense against cosmic rays and angry storms flailing out from the persecuted star that powered all this. Its fields were like spaghetti strands wrapped around the atmosphere, layers of argument against intruding particles wanting to plow into innocent gases.

Redwing said, "What other weapons does this place have?"

"More than we do," Clare said mildly.

"Look," Jampudvipa said with an irked twist to her mouth, "this thing's unknowably old. Ancient! Beyond ancient. On Earth a century was a huge time for weapons to evolve. I read up on this in preoutbreak history, back when we were on one world. Amazing stuff. In the same century as the first nuke got used, we also killed each other with bayonets and one-shot rifles. So how can we think about—*this*?"

This outbreak of consternation made them all sit back, think.

Karl said solemnly, "The laws of physics constrain everybody—even the Bowl Folk, whoever they are. Or whatever."

"Tech has its own evolution," Clare said. "What's in those big domes at the Bowl rim?"

"No way to know. Fly low, is all we can do," Redwing said. *Taking my ship into uncharted waters . . .* It was liberating to be simply honest.

They slid on a blithe arc over the quickly spinning lip of the Bowl. Sensors set on the big domes and their enormous snouts registered no change.

Cruising over the Bowl's lip and down the swiftly rushing hull brought quick instructive views. *Sun-Seeker* had come at the Bowl from the side and below, along the axis of revolution and through the Knothole. Now Redwing could see the detailed and intricate lattice that framed the hull's support structures, threaded by long ribbed structures that looked like enormous subways and elevators, some with spiky turrets protruding at the junctions. But here and there were sections clearly retrofitted, yellow and green splotches of newer joints and fix-up ornamentations of mysterious use.

Additions and afterthoughts, he judged. Some reminded him of accumulated grime, touch-up attempts and insertions. *Like the yellowing varnish on a Renaissance masterpiece,* he thought. *Strip away the accretions, and beneath is the original brilliance. Interstellar archaeology.*

SIX

Karl deployed the smart flexi with an electric shock. Under a kilovolt surge the velvet blue shroud billowed out—so thin, he could see the gyrating hull grinding past in the distance. Starlight lit its eternal churn. A certain serenity enveloped the view, for the background was the eternal spread of stars. The approaching dot was for the moment nothing.

He had static-fixed the flexi to the *Bernal*'s hull. Its sensors would follow inbuilt commands he could activate. *Well, here goes . . .*

The flexi popped open at the electro-command. Yet the micro sensors at the far end remained live and ready, he saw from his wrist monitor. The flexi bubble furled out as liquidly as a cape cast off a shoulder, though all this was in high vacuum, no gravity or atmosphere to command its dynamics. Such a thin fabric of layered smart carbon could be made and trained in the ship printers, but he had never tried anything this complex before. Now they had to use it to rescue Beth's team from the big train car that came swarming up at them, the dot assuming a velocity a bit too high. Problems, yes. Perhaps not fatal, entirely. Yet.

Karl had not been thawed when *SunSeeker* shot through the Knothole, so all this gigantic architecture was new to him. He stared, momentarily lost in detail.

"Coming up on rendezvous prompt," Jam sent on comm. "Bogie on vector grid."

"Got it." He eased the flexi controls, using both hands. For ease of manual operations, there were no left-handed crew on *SunSeeker*. Karl had made the crew cut because he was genuinely ambidextrous. In college he had made extra cash as a juggler.

"It's coming up too fast," Jam said urgently.

"I've got mag fields on, maybe I can push it off." Karl ran the mag amplitude to the max. That was a stressor in a thick-hulled freighter like the *Bernal;* he could hear tinny *ping*s.

He was looking out a true port, not a screen. Living inside a starship with only screen views felt disconnected. There was something about capturing the actual starlight photons bouncing off the Bowl that made it more real. This huge thing had to have incredible strength to hold it together, he realized. *SunSeeker* had a support structure made of nuclear tensile strength materials, able to take the stresses of the ramjet scoop at the ship core. Maybe the Bowl material was similar. So he scanned the Bowl's wraparound struts, the foundational matter, on the long-range telescopes on his bridge board. It was only a few tens of meters thick, pretty heavily encrusted with evident add-on machinery and cowlings. Which meant the Bowl stress-support material had to be better than *SunSeeker*'s. *What engineers they were. . . .*

Jam said, "It's braking. Must have some maneuvering ability."

"I can see them," Kurt said quietly. He ran his scopes to the max. There were windows in part of the hauler and human heads peering out at him. He had to admire them. They had made it through captivity, struck out across unknown alien territory, stolen transport, liberated themselves—and were coming back to the ship to report.

Jam said, "Ease them in. Careful."

"I read their roll at near zero, yaw zero point three five, but correcting—and pitch seven point five degrees." Kurt rattled off the numbers just to be saying something while he used hand controls to turn *Bernal* into a plausible alignment.

"Bearing in," Jam said. "Just got confirming signal. Ha! As if anybody else were meeting us out here."

"Aligned. Now's the hard part."

Center ball was smack on, horizontal bar of the crosshatch dead center with vertical bar, and the bulky burnished train car that looked like a shoe box came to rest in the *Bernal* rest frame. With both hands he triggered the flexi with an electro-static burst.

The flexi skirted across the gap like an unfolding velvet blue scarf. It unfolded and clamped on to the boxcar metal around the simple air lock. It anchored and popped him a message: PRESSURE SEAL SECURED.

"Got it." Kurt palmed the pressure valves, and air rushed into the flexi corridor between the ships. Of course, the craft weren't perfectly matched. But the flexi compensated, extruding further lengths of itself to accommodate the vagrant torques and thrusts as the two spacecraft wobbled and rocked in the magnetic grasp. *Pressured. Secure.*

"The flexi's working!" Jam's words came compressed, excited. "Ayaan was right. Programming them to double-seal solved the pressure problem, straightened them out."

The boxcar's lock popped and he saw the first head appear, looking around. Beth he recognized from her photo.

"Tag 'em through." It happened fast and he had to keep them aligned with the mag grapple. Kurt watched the people come out through the boxcar air lock. The flexi was so transparent, he could see them kick against the sides for momentum and glide through the channel into the *Bernal*. He counted them. But—

"What's that with you?"

"Snakes," Jam sent the audio through a direct link.

It was Beth. "Smart snakes. They helped us."

"Trouble," Kurt said to himself.

SEVEN

It was a rough ride, irritating for Memor. She was cramped in the rattling hot cabin, subjected to rude accelerations. Her pilot seemed to take relish in throwing them into wrenching swoops and pivots. Magnetic ships moved more smoothly, of course, but Memor had chosen a rocket vehicle: it would not have to hover so close to the outer hull of the World. Memor braced against the surge and wondered if her pilot could be among the disaffected. This might be a small way of expressing smoldering anger. Best make a note for future use?

Surely not. Veest Blad was of an Adapted species, but he had been with her for years, back before Memor became female. Veest was too smart not to be loyal.

"Ah!" And *there*, her prey were in sight. That limping one was Tananareve. And those ropy things the probes had seen, now wriggling into one of the cargo cars in a magnetic train, were finger snakes.

Treason! They must be assisting the escaping bipeds. Finger snakes were a useful species, but their adaptation to civilization had always been chancy.

The car's side closed. The whole train lifted, eased away from the docks, and moved into star-spattered space.

Memor considered. She had the acceleration to catch the train. Could she shoot out the magnetic locking plates without harming those inside? But Asenath had forbidden that—and the primate Tananareve, Memor saw abruptly, was still standing on the dock.

Tananareve had been the language adept of this band, with many sleeps spent acquiring the Folk language. Thus, the most important, for Asenath wanted a speaking primate, for reasons unknown. But . . . the creature seemed ready to fall over. How far could she get before Memor claimed the rest of them and came back for her? Perhaps she would not even be needed . . . but wait—

"Veest Blad, land near the biped. Not too near. We don't want her fried."

"Yes, lady."

So what was that about? Memor had countermanded her own decision. A moment's brief look into her Undermind told her why. The abandoned female looked to be dying, and she was the one whom Memor had inspected, had trained, had grown to know. The others—perhaps they could be caught, perhaps they might all be killed by Memor's overbuilt weapons, true—but they weren't needed while Tananareve was here.

• • •

Tananareve wiped sweat away and watched the bulbous vehicle settle a good distance away, engines throbbing. Still teetering a bit, feeling woozy, she stood in the hot moist wash of rocket exhaust, waiting. Running wouldn't help her. She'd seen the tremendous creature's speed.

Memor opened the great target-shaped window and rolled out. It looked painful: the rocket vehicle was cramped for her. Memor walked to Tananareve, huffed, and bent low, her eye to the woman's eyes. In her own tongue she asked, "Where have they gone?"

Tananareve groped for a lie, and it was there. Beth's team had discussed destinations, and rejected—"They've gone to join Cliff."

"The other fugitives? The killers?"

"Cliff's team, yes."

"Where?"

She said, "I don't know. The aliens knew."

"The limbless ones? They are Adopted, but often rebellious. We must take action against them. Tananareve, how goes your adventure?"

"We were dying for lack of weight," she said. "Lost bone and muscle. What choice did we have?"

Memor seemed to restrain herself. "No choice now. Come. Or shall I carry you?"

Tananareve took two steps, wobbled, and fell over.

She woke to a vague sensation, a hard surface with big ribs under it: Memor's hands. She flexed her fists and shook her head, trying to get her mind to work. Now they were in the ship, her face close against a wall dotted with icons for controls. Something rumbled, vibrated. Language? And now the wall took on the appearance of a distant forest of plants grown in low gravity, like the place she'd escaped from. A creature like Memor stepped into view and flexed a million multicolored feathers.

No way could Tananareve follow a conversation that was largely the flexing of feathers and silent subsonic tremors that shook her bones. Memor was holding Tananareve like a prize, and the other was snarling. . . .

• • •

Asenath the Wisdom Chief was not of a mind to be placated. "One! You have one, and it is dying!"

"I will save it," Memor said. "I will take it . . .

her . . . down to the Quicklands, where spin gravity can restore her muscle and strengthen her bones. I know what she eats and I will procure it. This female is the one who understands me best. Gifted, though in many ways simple. She knows Rank One of the TransLanguage. Wisdom Chief, will you question her now?"

"What would I ask?" Asenath's feathers showed rage, but that was a plumage lie. Memor's under-mind had caught the truth: She was in despair.

Memor found that revealing. Earlier the Wisdom Chief had been trying to bring about Memor's disgrace and death. What had changed? Memor decided to wait her out.

Asenath broke first. "There comes a message from the Target Star, from our destination."

All Memor's feathers flared like a puffball. The human, engulfed, tried to wriggle free. Memor said, "That is wonderful! And dangerous, yes? Can you interpret—?"

"There are visuals. Complex ones. The message seems aimed at these creatures. At your Late Invaders!"

Memor's feathers went to chaos: a riot of laughter. "That is . . . endlessly interesting."

"You must care for your talking simian. We will try to make sense of this message. It is still flowing in. If I call, answer at once, and have the human at hand."

• • •

Tananareve had caught little of that. She was nibbling at a melon slice now, slipped to her by Memor.

She was enraged—tight-lipped, squinting in the strange glow—that she'd been caught again, but grudgingly grateful that Memor had brought provisions. The huge thing did not seem to mind carrying on conversation in front of a human, either.

What was that about? Hard to follow. Was Glory inhabited? And had someone there sent a message? Surely not to Earth; that would be foolish, when the Bowl was straight between Earth and Glory, and so much more powerful.

The captain should be told. He and his crew would figure it out.

Rockets fired, accelerations gripped her—and Memor's ship was in flight. Tananareve sagged into the pull. The hard clamp was too strong to allow movement. She relaxed against the floor and tried to get into savasana pose, letting her muscles ease, hoping that her dinosaur-sized captor wouldn't step on her.

EIGHT

They couldn't all get into *SunSeeker*'s infirmary. Beth and Fred and Captain Redwing hovered around the door, watching as Mayra and Lau Pin were led to elaborate tables. Tubes and sensors snaked out to mate with them. Jam, acting as medic now, watched, tested, then asked, "Are you comfortable?"

Mayra and Lau Pin mumbled something.

"I'm sedating you. Also, you're being recorded.

Mayra Wickramsingh, I understand you lost your husband during the expedition?"

"Expedition, my arse. We were expi . . . expiment . . . animals for testing. Big birds had us—"

Redwing said, "Come with me. You'll both be on those tables soon enough, but for now we'll give you gravity and normal food."

Beth resisted. "You're testing her while she talks about Abduss? He was slaughtered by one of those monstrous spider-things."

"We'll need to know how badly that traumatized her. The rest of you, too. How are you feeling now?"

Fred said, "Hungry." He lurched up the corridor toward the ship's mess, then sagged against the bulkhead. "Feeble."

Beth asked, "How is Cliff? Where is he?"

Redwing allowed a vexed expression to flit across his face, then went back to the usual stern, calm mask. "Holed up with some intelligent natives, Cliff's last message said. The Folk tried to kill them all. They were shooting down from some living blimp—sounds bizarre, but what doesn't here? The locals helped Cliff's people get away. Aybe sends us stuff when he can. We have pictures of a thing that looks a lot like a dinosaur, plus some evolved apes. I sent those to you; did you get them?"

Fred spoke over his shoulder. "We got them, Cap'n. The Bowl must've stopped in Sol system at least twice. Once for the dinosaurs, once for the apes, I figure. And we found a map in that museum globe."

"You sent us the map," Redwing said, ushering them along the corridor. A pleasant aroma of warm food drew them. "How did that strike you?"

"Strange. Might be history, might be propaganda for the masses."

"There's a difference?"

She smiled. "It was in a big park, elaborate buildings, the works."

Fred wobbled into the mess. Beth was feeling frail, too; there were handholds everywhere, and she used them. Surely she'd been longing for foods of Earth? There had been almost no red meat in the parts of the Bowl she'd seen. Beef curry? Its tang enticed. The mess was neat, clean, like a strict diner. Already Fred had picked a five-bean salad and a cheese sandwich.

Redwing dialed up a chef's salad. "We're recording everything we can get in electromagnetics from the Bowl surface, but there's not much," he said.

Beth asked, "What are you doing with our allies? I mean the—"

"Snakes? They kind of give me the willies, but they seem benign. We're helping the finger snakes unload that ship you hijacked. Those plants will do more for them than for us, don't you think? Shall we house them in the garden? We'll have to work out what to give them in the way of sunlight and dirt and water. Want to watch?" Redwing finger-danced before a sensor.

The wall wavered, and yes, on the visual wall there were finger snakes and humans moving trays out of the magnetic car. Beth saw these were new crew. Ayaan Ali, pilot; Clare Conway, copilot; and Karl Lebanon, the general technology officer. The ship's population was growing. They moved dexterously among the three snakes, struggling with the language problem.

Beth muted the sound and watched while she ate. Silence as she forked in flavors she had dreamed of down on the Bowl. No talk, only the clinking of silverware. Then Fred said, "The map in the big globe? It looked alien, but it's blue and white like an Earthlike planet."

"Could that have been Earth in the deep past?"

"Yeah. A hundred million years ago?"

Redwing said, "Ayaan says no. She pegs that clump of migrating continents to the middle Jurassic. Your picture was upside down, south pole up. Argue with her if you don't agree."

Fred shook his head. "I can recall it, but look—I sent Ayaan my photo file, so—"

Redwing called up a wall display. "There is a lot of spiky emission from that jet. Seems like message-style stuff, but we can't decipher it. Anyway, it fuzzed up your pictures and Ayaan had a tedious job getting it compiled. She compiled, processed, and flattened the image store. Piled it into a global map, stitching together your flat-on views—here."

Fred read the notes. "Of course . . . All those transforms have blurred out the details, sure. So now, look at South America. Just shows what looking at things upside down and only one side, will do. Now, right-side up and complete, I can see it. How could I have missed it?"

Beth said kindly, "You didn't, not really. We were on the run, remember? And this doesn't look a lot like Earth, all the continents squeezed together. But you were right about the Bowl having some link to Earth. Tell the cap'n your ideas."

Fred glanced at Redwing, eyes wary. "I was tired then, just thinking out loud—"

"And you were right." Beth opened her hands across the table. "Spot on. Sorry I didn't pay enough attention. So, tell the cap'n."

Fred gazed off into space, speaking to nobody. "Okay, I thought ... wow, Jurassic. A hundred seventy-five million years back? That's when the dinosaurs got big. *Damn.* Could they have got intelligent, too? Captain, I've been thinking that intelligent dinosaurs built the Bowl and then evolved into all the varieties of Bird Folk we found here. Gene tampering, too, we saw that in some species—you don't evolve extra legs by accident. They keep coming back to Sol system because it's their home." Fred remembered his hunger and bit into his cheese sandwich.

A smile played around Redwing's lips. "If they picked up the apes a few hundred thousand years ago, then they could have been en route to Glory for that long. They're definitely aimed at Glory, just like we were. Beth?" Beth's mouth was full, so Redwing went on. "All that brain sweat we spent wondering why our motors weren't putting out enough thrust? The motors are fine. We were plowing through the backwash from the Bowl's jet, picking up backflowing gases all across a thousand kilometers of our ramjet scoop, for all the last hundred years of our flight."

Beth nodded. "We could have gone around it. Too late now, right? We'll still be short."

"Short of everything. Fuel. Water. Air. Food. It gets worse the more people we thaw, but what the hell, we still can't make it unless we can get supplies from the Bowl. And we're at war."

"Cliff killed Bird Folk?"

"Yeah. And they tried to repay the favor."

• • •

Beth had expected some shipboard protocols, since Redwing liked to keep discipline. But the first thing Redwing said when they got to his cramped office was, "What was it like down there?"

Across Beth's face emotions flickered. "Imagine you can see land *in the sky*. You can tell it's far away because even the highest clouds are brighter, and you can't see stars at all. The sun blots them out. It gives you a queasy feeling at first, land hanging in the distance, no night, hard to sleep . . ." She took a deep breath, wheezing a bit, her respiratory system adjusting to the ship after so long in alien air. "The . . . the rest of the Bowl looks like brown land and white stretches of cloud—imagine, being able to see a hurricane no bigger than your thumbnail. It's dim, because the sun's always there. The jet casts separate shadows, too. It's always slow-twisting in the sky. The clouds go far, far up—their atmosphere's much higher than ours."

"You can't see the molecular skin they have keeping their air in?"

"Not a chance. Clouds, stacking up as far as you can see. The trees are different, too—some zigzag and send long feelers down to the ground. I never did figure out why. Maybe a low-grav effect. Anyway, there's this faint land up in the sky. You can see whole patches of land like continents just hanging there. Plus seas, but mostly you see the mirror zone. The reflectors aren't casting sunlight into your eyes—"

"They're pointed back at the star, sure."

"—so they're gray, with brighter streaks here and there. The Knothole is up there, too, not easy to see, because it's got the jet shooting through it all the time. It narrows down and gets brighter right at the Knothole. You can watch big twisting strands moving in the jet, if you look long enough. It's always changing."

"And the ground, the animals—"

"Impossible to count how many differences there are. Strange things that fly—the air's full of birds and flapping reptile things, too, because in low grav everything takes to the sky if there's an advantage. We got dive-bombed by birds thinking maybe our hair was something they could make off with—food, I guess."

Redwing laughed with a sad smile and she saw he was sorry he had to be stuck up here, flying a marginal ramscoop to make velocity changes against the vagrant forces around the Bowl. He didn't want to sail; he wanted to land.

She sipped some coffee and saw it was best that she not say how she had gotten a certain dreadful, electric zest while fleeing across the Bowl. Redwing asked questions and she did not want to say it was like an unending marathon. A big slice of the strange, a zap to the synaptic net, the shock of unending Otherness moistened with meaning, special stinks, grace notes, blaring daylight that illuminated without instructing. A marathon that addicted.

To wake up from cold sleep and go into *that*, fresh from the gewgaws and flashy bubble gum of techno-Earth, was—well, a consummation requiring digestion.

She could see that Redwing worried at this, could not let it go. Neither could she. Vexing thoughts came, flying strange and fragrant through her mind, but they were not problems, no. They were the shrapnel you carried, buried deep, wounds from meeting the strange.

PART II

SUNNY SLAUGHTERHOUSE

*After the game, the King and the pawn
go into the same box.*
—ITALIAN PROVERB

NINE

Cliff stood at the edge of the ruined city and tried to get his eyes to work right.

This world looked . . . strange. Shimmering green and blue halos hovered around the edges of every burned tree and smashed building. The jet scratched across the sky had its usual twisting helical strands around its hard, ivory-bright core . . . but there, too, an orange halo framed it, winking with vagrant lights.

Okay . . . shake the head, blink. Repeat. The colored halos dimmed. He made himself breathe long and slow and deep. Acrid smoke tainted the dry air.

In the second Folk attack, he had gotten hit again. Irma had stitched the wound in his right shoulder and then . . . he slept. It was strange to sleep for days and nights—though those words meant nothing here, where the ruddy star hung forever in the same spot in the sky. Yet he had slept long, his irked back and aching bones told him.

He had come out of it, stiff and dry and jerky. A bit foggy, he watched the Sil deal with their wounded and put out the widespread fires. He had just woken up and now, after a breakfast of odd foods and stale water, felt pretty well. The halos ebbed, faded. With Irma he stood watching the Sil work. Their lithe bodies slumped and sagged. They were naturally limber, dexterous creatures, but not now.

Irma said, "The skyfish came over this part while you and I were trying to help carry that heavy ammo the Sil use. Blasted everything."

He nodded, dimly recalling the fevered hours of carrying heavy cargo on rolling flatcars. Their wooden frame carriers held long cylinders of shaped shells with elementary fuses on the underside. It paid to be careful with them. Hard, dumb, sweaty work it was, while they heard hollow hammer blows rain down like a distant drumming wrath of sky gods. The concussions rolled over them and he had learned pretty quickly not to look up or back too much, because the occasional orange-hot fragment or buzzing shrapnel came that way. Once he had seen a zigzag tree burst into flame after a sizzling meteor slammed into it. He had helped throw water on it, then dirt when they had to. The burning city took all the reservoir water, and then that ran out, too.

After they got it put out, the humans went back to hauling ammo. The Sil guns hammered hard, trying to take down the skyfish. The brown and green football blimps churned across the sky and aimed lasers, antennas, and some kind of fire weapon down on the city.

He distracted himself by thinking how the skyfish could work at all. Its elaborate fins could flare out, capturing wind like a sail, and driving the gas-bag forward. He guessed the huge creature could trim on this by shifting mass inside itself, getting a torque about its center of mass to navigate. This can be somewhat like a ship sailing at angles to the wind, tacking with its big side fan-fins spread out. It had big eyes and blister pods, maybe evolved from some balloonlike species. A bioengineered creature used to slowly patrol the air above the Bowl.

He had watched the battle and recalled how this place had been only a short while before. The Sil had their pride, of course. Their first full awake time in this large Sil city, the five visiting humans had to be led around, shown the town. They saw ancient majestic buildings of stacked stone, gleaming shiny statues to great dead savants, beautiful swooping curves and ramps and towers, then spindly ceramic bridges over moist green gardens and sprawled homes. They exhausted their reserves of *ooh*s and *ahh*s. It was indeed a fine city of untold ancient origin.

Not now.

During the battle, at least five of the living skyfish had circled, covering each other against any Sil artillery. When the guns barked up at them, a shower of beams and missiles cascaded down, silencing the crews. The pain beam was terrifying. When it struck, Cliff could see the shocked fear come into the Sil faces. They turned and ran, some snatching at their skins as though they were on fire. At the sensory level, they were.

The pain gun was a microwave beam that excited

Sil nerves with agonies that made them fall, writhe, scream. It deranged some, who howled and jerked and ran in chaotic bursts. Others had the sense to run steadily out of the beam, if they could. The effect was intense, immediate, and ended Sil resistance where the beams struck. The pain projectors were soundless, which made them even more horrifying. These were the standard Folk weapon to panic opponents, and they worked their silent terror well.

But humans did not feel it at all. Some difference in the neural wiring made them immune. So Cliff, Aybe, Terry, Howard, and Irma hauled ammo and tried to stay alive. The skyfish wallowed across the air above the Sil city and brought flame spouts to bear. Some forked down green rays that seared buildings and people alike. The enormous living sky creatures systematically burned along geometric paths, and whole blocks of homes and factories burst into yellow flame.

The Sil brought their archaic weaponry to bear and blew shredding blasts into the skyfish underbodies. Once Cliff heard an enormous hollow *whoosh* that thundered down like a bass note. He and Irma looked up and saw a skyfish belly explode. A huge yellow ball licked around the green skin and trailed up the sides.

"Hydrogen," Irma said brightly. "*That's* their buoyancy gas."

Howard said, "Helium must not give them enough lift. Tricky."

"Oh, come on, where would they get helium?"

Another skyfish was floundering now, spewing fluids from multiple wounds, losing altitude, veering erratically. The city below it boiled with flame. The great beast slid down the sky through realms of smoke. Its crash was like a green egg crumbling in slow motion as it burned.

The destruction lumbered on amid roars and bangs and the sour stench of flame. Not long after, a nearby explosion Cliff never saw caught him. He took hot fragments in his left side and arm and went down. Then it all got fuzzy, the licking flames filmed over by a gray screen of pain.

He recalled seeing the skyfish turn and begin their ascent. They rose quickly, buoyed by the spreading fires below. Someone said the huge blimps would mend and rearm at higher altitude and might come back . . . and then it all went vague and he fell away into troubled sleep.

So now, getting his eyes to see this place right again, it seemed odd to have the big world go rolling along without him. Sils labored nearby and gave the humans no notice whatever. There was a gray silence to their movements, but they kept on stolidly.

Just like it will keep on after you're dead, Cliff thought. *The wide busy world of muscle work, weather changing, window washing, future judging, fast joyous dancing, racing heart in great passion, nose picking, fun talking, and bug swatting—all that will go merrily yea merrily along. If these aliens were never aware of your presence, they won't be overwhelmed by your absence. But*

*the same is true of the people you know, too. The
world picks up the pace and moves on. Eternally.*

They were standing apart from the men—Terry,
Aybe, Howard—at the city's edge. The humans
had all slept in a makeshift cave in the surrounding hills, to avoid the constant light. Here there
were scraps of the lush greenery on the slopes amid
the rocky landscape, with some odd trees and big-
leafed plants rich in fruit. They were eating some of
these, rather bland with lots of pale blue juice. Irma
said, "Quert looks worn down."

Cliff turned to see the slim alien approach, its
usually light-footed stride slow and lame. Quert's
voice was grainy, flat. "Onto here I-we came to
speak"—a jerky hand gesture—"and wish share
help."

Quert's Anglish was still improving, and quite a
few of the other Sil had managed to share the language upload and integrator AI. Cliff still found it
striking that the Astronomer Folk had widely distributed—"among the hunters," Quert had said—a
software that taught Anglish with a few immersion
sleeps. He had seen the squat little machine that
"learn us" as Quert said, but had no idea how it
really worked.

Irma said, "We can labor beside you."

Quert's large yellow eyes studied them all in turn.
"Medical we are now at. The dead rot."

"They be many," Irma said. The Sil had the most
trouble with the irregular forms of *to be,* so they
tried to use simple forms.

"I sad be for our acts."

"You could not know the Folk would exact such a price," Terry said, coming up to the group.

"Many dead. Have not known before, fire on our city."

"You have lost the city, too," Terry said.

"No. Do not hurt for the city. We build again fast." Quert paused for a moment, eyes distant, then said, "The city speaks what has happened to us. Everywhere on the Bowl, the wounds, they show."

"Sure," Irma said.

"When we have more to say, we rebuild, the city speaks again," Quert said. Irma didn't understand, then.

The Astronomer Folk had apparently hoped the varying species of this area would rally to the Folk cause, and use the Anglish to somehow ensnare Cliff and the others. For the Sil it had worked in reverse. The Sil had been festering under Folk rule for a long time, and had seized the opportunity of uniting with their small human band. Now they suffered for it repeatedly, as the Folk tried to find the humans.

How long will they bear up? Cliff wondered. *We've caused them huge losses . . .*

"How we help?" Aybe asked.

Quert stood silent as its large eyes elongated up and down, rhythmically. The yellow eyes closed and the eyelids vibrated, as if shaken from behind. These expressions had no human parallel. Cliff had thought before that this must mean surprise or puzzlement, but now the alien made a curious squatting motion, its sinewy arms knotted in front of it.

With the large Sil pancake hands and thick fingers it shaped a twisting architecture in the air.

Then its eyes jerked open and it stood. Cliff was cautious in inferring emotions from facial signatures in the Sil, but this case at least seemed clear. The constricted face oozed sad resolve.

"Dead are many. Have time now little."

Irma said softly, "You wish help with the dead?"

"We may share violence. Share our ends also."

• • •

The finely tended Sil city was now a chaos of jagged building shells, of splintered statues to great Sils now shattered into lumpy gray shards, of cratered streets, of angular trees sheared off at their roots or burned to cinders, of vehicles sitting gnarled and toasted, and the only sounds those of stones falling from half-crumpled walls. No groans, anymore. A city of dead.

A grim procession clogged the few cleared routes. Sil shuffled along with blackened faces and torn skins, mournful angular faces with eyes that saw little before them. Some of them bore wounded; others bore their dead. None spoke. None needed to.

The stench came to Cliff as they strode down from the surrounding hills. It rose as they entered the ruined precincts. Terry made masks for them all that proved essential as they labored through the endless day.

There was a code for burying the dead, something to do with recycling their substance into the Bowl's sealed ecology. Especially here, water seemed scarce and the bodies went into a kind of pit that had a flexible blue cover and drains at the bottom.

Cliff hated going into the buildings and avoided them. He came upon a big Sil body that had a family gathered around it. They were rolling it in a pale green sheet. They stepped back and looked at Cliff. They were short, thin, and probably could not easily carry the body. He nodded and squatted to pick up the stiff fragrant mass. He got it standing on the rigid legs, then tipped the body onto his shoulder. As he stood up, the pressure forced gas through the voice box and a ragged croak rattled out. It sent shivers down his back. For a long second he wondered if the alien was protesting. He made himself look into the contorted Sil face, gone rigid. A purple tongue stuck out between the small knobby Sil teeth. The eyes had burst and goo ran down the angular cheeks.

Cliff looked away, stopped breathing. He took short jolting steps and the family followed him silently, all the way to the pit. He was sweating when he edged the body gently into the opening flap. The family just stared at the green sheet as it slid in, murmured to each other, then turned and walked slowly away. No sayings over the body, no ceremony. There was something dignified in the utter lack of ritual.

None of the Sil had looked him in the eye. He wondered what that meant.

The first day was hardest. After that, a numb resignation set in. The bodies got loaded on wagons and taken to parks—the only large, open areas in the city not filled with rubble. Some places the Sil got funeral pyres going, burning the bodies to keep them from stinking and from spreading disease. "Dirt takes not all," Quert said. Cliff supposed that meant the soil processors were overloaded by such massive numbers.

Many corpses were underground. The job became an elaborate Easter egg hunt, Irma remarked sourly. They would bust into a shelter where often Sil had taken refuge, sitting in orderly rows. The humans were just helpers beside the Sil who would gather up valuables from the Sil laps, where often the dead had held what they felt was most dear. The Sil did not attempt identification anymore. They just turned the valuables over to an escort team. Then Sil would come in with a tubular flamethrower and stand in the door and cremate those sitting rigid inside. Get the precious metals and jewelry out, Cliff supposed, and then burn everybody inside. *An alien Belsen,* he thought, *and in the end, our fault.*

The first bodies the human team had carried out, they treated with care and respect, loading them onto stretchers provided to give some semblance of funeral dignity. But after the first day of working on the piles and acres of wrecked bodies, humans and Sil alike became more casual. Bodies got stacked and carried for convenience. After that, a rank callousness descended and they used racks to group the bodies, then drag them with electrical haulers like sleds of dead.

The Sil called this entire bleak spectacle, the elegant stonework buildings smashed and seared brown and hard black, something that sounded like *scleelachrhoft*. But they all spoke little. In answer to questions, Quert mostly had an eye-move that meant "yes" or a side-nod that meant "no."

Then came the patient patrols through the gray stone rubble. Here a leg, there an arm. Just pickings at first, parts to bag, but then they hit a treasure vault of tragedy. A reeking hash of a hundred had assembled in a basement. Cliff stepped in and found the tiled floor was awash in a still-warm broth of rank water and viscera. When the burst water mains had erupted, Cliff deduced, some of them had tried to escape through a narrow exit in the back. Their bodies were packed in a tight passageway. The dead did not bear burns. From their stiff, bloated condition, he gathered they had died of the smoke or oxygen loss as the firestorm sucked it all away.

Their leader had made it halfway up a ramp, only to be buried halfway up to her neck in a plaster goo and stone chips. She looked delicately young, smooth of skin still, though it was swollen and had begun to pucker with brown and blue welts. He carried her out himself.

Humans were bigger and stronger and came from a higher-grav world, so they got assigned the harder jobs. When they went into a typical shelter, usually an ordinary basement, it looked to Cliff like a streetcar full of Sil who'd simultaneously had heart failure. Just sitting there in their chairs, all dead. A firestorm may occur naturally in forests, but in cities becomes a conflagration attaining such intensity that it creates and sustains its own wind system. Cliff had watched the first stages of it from a distance, as wind whirls darted among buildings like dust devils of pure yellow and burnt orange flame. Those danced among tall apartment buildings like eerie flame children having fun.

Cliff became used to the hovering ruddy heat that seeped through the clouds still overhead. Smells came rising from the dead and made all the work gangs speed up their work. The bodies were not alike but strangely specific. Some clutched purses, others wore jewelry, and a few who had prepared for what they thought the worst wore rucksacks full of food. Some of the Sil work teams took these, and Cliff just looked away, not knowing what to say or do or whether to care at all. A young boy Sil had a pet, a four-legged furry thing Cliff had never seen the likes of—still leashed to the boy, eyes still gleaming.

They were at their work, doggedly going from apartment to apartment, when a Sil woman suddenly appeared and hurled herself at Cliff. She shouted incoherent abuse and battered at him with tight fists. Another Sil rushed over and pulled her off him. She broke down sobbing, chanting, and was led away. He stood stolidly for a long while, emotions churning.

Once some Sil work partners found a small cellar of what seemed to be a winelike drink. When Cliff passed by them a while later, carrying a Sil body, they seemed to be roaring drunk. He saw them later, too, and unlike those teams nearby were working energetically and maybe even enjoying it. So whatever they drank, it seemed a blessing.

It went on and Cliff stopped even estimating the dead. The number was beyond thousands and probably in the tens of thousands and he did not want to think about it anymore. The fiery death penalty applied to all who happened to be in the undefended city—babies, old people, the zoo animals. . . .

The teams talked less and less and the work days seemed to go on infinitely, down a dwindling pipe. A day toward the end, when they could see there were few streets left to cover, they were combing the shattered shells of the last buildings. With scarcely a whisper, a flittering craft came over and dropped filmy oval leaflets that drifted down from the sky. The curious script meant nothing to the humans, of course, but a Sil read it in broken Anglish:

> *We destroyed you because you harbored the Late Invaders. They will damage our fragile eternal paradise and bring disease, unease, and horror to your lot, and to all who dwell beneath the Perpetual Sun in warm mutual company. We struck at the known location of Late Invaders and those helping them to elude our capture. Destruction of other than targets of high security value was unintended and an unavoidable consequence of the fortunes of safekeeping of our eternal Bowl.*

The Sil became angry when reading these notes. They hurled them to the ground, stomped on them. Then others gathered them up and marched off with piles of the filmy sheets. Cliff wondered at this and so followed. The Sil went to their collective lavatory. Since he was in need, he went in and found the propaganda stacked for use in wiping asses.

He understood all this emotionally. Gathering up body parts in bushel baskets, helping a sorrowed male Sil dig with hands and shovels where he thought his wife might be . . . the events blended, endlessly.

TEN

Irma said, "You have a flat affect."

"Um, what's that?" Cliff had just awakened from another long sleep. He looked out the narrow opening of the cave they called home. Beyond lay the same stark sunlit landscape of despair he had become accustomed to. He yawned. At least the halo effect in his vision had gone away. Not much else had.

"It's a failure to express feelings either verbally or nonverbally—that would be, just using your usual grunts and shrugs."

He kept watching the view out the cave opening and shifted uneasily on the inflatable bedding the Sil had given them. It was a bit small. "Can't say much after what we've been through."

"I learned this in crew training. They gave it to us because we could go through traumas if we get to Glory—"

"*When* we get there. This Bowl, this is an . . . interlude."

"Okay, *when*. There might be pretty heavy events to get through on Glory, our trainers said. So we trained to deal with shock, combat fatigue, stress disorders. Recognize the symptoms, apply a range of therapies. You've had low affect for days now."

He could not claim he didn't feel differently, so he said nothing. That was always easier.

"Look me in the eye."

Reluctantly, he did. Somehow it was easier to peer out at the blasted and sunny landscape . . . though now that he thought of that, it made no real sense. Still—

Irma leaned forward, took his head in both hands, and looked fiercely into his eyes, shaking his head to get him to focus on her. "Good! Trust me, this is a problem and we both need to work on it. They told us to expect it especially when a subject—"

"Now I'm a subject?"

"Okay, a fellow crew member. It's when people talk about issues without engaging their emotions."

"I'm . . . sorting things out."

"Another symptom is lack of expressive gestures, little animation in the face, not much vocal inflection."

"Um. Ah. So?"

"Do you split your feelings away from events?"

"Not . . . by design. I'm just trying to hold it together here."

"Taking pleasure in real things can help that."

"Um."

Pleasure. Good idea, quite distant from here . . .

He looked out at the ever-bright sunshine that was beginning to weigh on him. The stellar jet cut across the sky, adding its neon glow to the hammering sunlight. They had experienced some darkness here and there on this long "expedition" through the strange, incomprehensibly large Bowl . . . and in his dreams now, he longed for more darkness. He dreamed of diving into deep waters, where a murky cool leafy world wrapped itself around him. He was always sorry to wake up.

He was thinking of this when he realized she was deftly pushing his buttons. Her voice turned furry, intimate. Hands stroked, caressed. Pretty clearly she wasn't being made wanton and reckless by his fabulous magnetism.

This was therapy. Not that the fact mattered.

It became a matter of silky moments and building readiness. Then a gliding delight, sweetly enclasped, and a long exultant shudder for both of them. The artful ease lasted him into a sliding sleep. . . .

When he woke she took him through some softly worded moments he only later saw were exercises. Irma asked him in her soft, insistent voice to report the lurid dark nightmares he had. She walked him through those, tracing out moments like the rattling wheeze of corpses, the leaden weight of stiff bodies, the sharp acrid stench of rot . . . and then she asked him to watch her hand weave, left to right to left . . . a sway of motion that somehow called up calming spirits in him, let him lapse into a silent, quiet place where he could rest and feel and not swirl back down into those tormented whirlpools. She sighed and stayed with him while he sobbed silently, yet at least not alone. And slept again.

He woke while Irma slept and reflected on good ol' plain human sex among all this strangeness. Making love worked just fine here. He knew that aliens would have other such modes and they would be odd indeed. Earthside, male honeybee genitals exploded after sex; wasps turned cockroaches into zombie incubators; male scorpion flies produced wads of saliva to feed their mates—a nuptial gift that distracted her front end while her hind end mated. He had learned a basic lesson here: *Expect the unexpected.*

More dozing. A lot later, it seemed, he asked vaguely, "We should go . . . somewhere. . . ."

"The mass funeral festival of the Sil. We must go."

"When?"

"Get dressed."

• • •

She had gotten him into a halfway presentable mood with the most direct possible method. Smart, with talents he could not anticipate. He had always tried to work with people who were smarter, quicker, and more naturally adept than he was, plus those who had talents he could not even anticipate. Irma was all of that. In this incredible mess of an interstellar expedition, she kept her wits.

He realized that he, on the other hand, had exceeded his limits. He had no combat experience and yet had somehow gotten through the first Folk assault with just a wound. That had nearly healed when the Folk came back with not one skyfish but six—to kill so many Sil that nobody could count them. No doubt the Folk hoped to catch the humans and burn them, too, but that could not have been the reason for the hours of unrelenting flame war.

The Folk wanted discipline, and knew how to get it. Discipline meant punishment meant order meant stability meant this giant spinning contraption could go on its ancient trajectory, bound for Glory and stars beyond.

Learn to think the way the Folk do, he thought. That was the only way to survive this bizarre, strange, and wonderful-but place.

He slowly got from Quert a way to deal with all the violence. After all, loss was everywhere. Everyone on *SunSeeker* knew when they departed Earthside that they would never see family or friends again. Cliff tried to phrase what seemed to work. *You will lose someone you can't live without, and your heart will be badly broken, and the bad news is that you never completely get over the loss of your beloved. But this is also the good news. They live forever in your broken heart, a wound that doesn't seal back up. And you come through. It's like having a broken leg that never heals perfectly—that still hurts when the weather gets cold, but you learn to dance with the limp.*

ELEVEN

Cliff listened to the deep rolling music of the Sil dirge. This was an honor, he realized—to witness the public mourning of these lithe aliens, their voices soaring in a long, rolling symphony he could understand, at least emotionally. It was truly so—music had fundamentals common here. Their flowing melodic line had tricky interior cadences, subthemes, and as it gathered force, these merged to become a high, howling remorse laced through with beautiful, somber notes. In the carved rock amphitheater, the Sil stood as they sang, sat when they did not, their angular heads lifted up to show faces twisted with grief.

They had lost many in the assault by the remorseless, hydrogen-fueled sky beasts. Those vast creatures had killed so many Sil almost as an afterthought, punishment for hiding humans. Apparently firing into crowds was permissible, and the Sil seemed unsurprised by these events.

Cliff sat and thought of that as the music wrapped around him. It immersed them all—he could see this strong music had its effects on those beside him. The Sil had many subtle eye-gestures and the odd elongation of the flesh around the eyes apparently meant mourning. All because of the humans . . .

His small band had been on the run for a long time, and now had met the sobering fact that those Folk who ran this huge, spinning machine would kill others just to stop a few humans. But . . . why were they important? It puzzled him and gave the slow, solemn proceedings of public mourning a gravitas he respected.

Their song rose and fell; their long bass notes reverberating from elaborately carved walls. The Sil leader Quert stood tall and splayed arms to the sky as the large wind instruments among them—not separated, as in a human orchestra—joined in the deep notes, pealing forth as the longer wavelengths resonated with those reflecting from the walled basin. It was eerie and moving and Cliff let himself be drawn into it. Grief made its same choices for the Sil as among humans—gliding, graceful themes, deepening as the growing amplitude plowed into more somber courses. Then, suddenly, that ended in a stunning trill the voices held for a long while, as their instruments boomed forth.

The silence. No applause. Just grief.

They all—Howard, Irma, Terry, and Aybe—sat respectfully until told to move, as they had learned was considered polite here. Howard was nursing a bad cut and a bum knee, Terry and Aybe had burns and bound-up wounds, but altogether the humans had minimal damage. They kept their heads down, perhaps from politeness, but Cliff lowered his eyes because he did not want to look into the eyes of the Sil more than he had to. The Sil filed out, their slanted faces seeming even longer now, no one speaking. Their instruments caught Cliff's eye. The laws of physics set design constraints for woodwinds and stringed players—long tubes, resonant cavities, holes for tuning—but the music that bloomed from these oddly shaped chambers and strings was both eerie and yet familiar. It had an artful use of counterpoint, moments of harmonic convergence, repeating details of melodic lines. There were side commentaries in other keys, too. Was music somehow universal?

As they emerged from the stone bowl, he looked back at the now-empty crescents where the seats each had a slight rounded depression for sitting. Once in Sicily he had seen an ancient open theater that looked much like this. But here the stones were pale conglomerate, not limestone, and far older. Yet the same design emerged.

Still obeying the code of silence, they walked into the sprawling community. This part of the Sil cityscape had escaped the fire bombing. It was a vast relief to be away from the charred precincts where he and the others had worked for . . . he could not even recall the count. At least a week, though now it seemed a boundary between a past where he had felt in control of his world, and now . . . this. . . .

He pulled his mind away from the memories. *Focus*. His crew training made this possible, but not easy.

The Sil chose habitats, he noticed, the way a seasoned soldier instinctively chooses cover. Here a wall gave an angled exposure to the star. Another wall stood oblique to that, to allow the jet's glow to have its say with redder luminosities, so each shadow had different colors at play. One wall gave protection from the prevailing wind, with an apartment perched to take advantage of the cooler prospect, big open windows facing away from the field of bright, fine sands that bounded the Sil town. There was a lake nearby, not deep but enough to fetch a tranquil blue from the hovering sky. Sils lounged in shadows for delicious rest, on a spongy plane, their bodies prone on the soft jade green. Sil crowds gathered there, their trilling speech low and reflective. A moist breeze blew through the crowd, and streamers of fog danced among the zigzag trees.

All eyes followed the humans. They had all agreed to affect a casual disregard of this. "Think of it as like being a movie star," Irma had said.

And it was. The Sil at least hid their sliding gaze by turning heads a bit away, but Cliff felt the pressure of their regard.

"They wonder what to make of us," Howard whispered.

Aybe said, "We're enough like them—two arms, two legs, one head. Maybe that's an optimal smart alien design? Makes us sorta simpatico. Better than the Bird Folk, anyway."

"And the Sil know to keep a distance, give us some room to take them in, too," Terry added. "It's kinda fun. Here are real, smart aliens who aren't chasing us."

"Or killing us," Irma said sardonically. "Beth's team wasn't so lucky."

This memory sobered them as they passed by a truly ancient-looking stone edifice, erect on its bare site, the huge blocks sweating with every gush of mists from the lowlands. Cliff savored the moist breath. The winds here stirred with minds of their own, sinewy and musical as they hummed through the Sil streets. The homes somehow generated music from the wind, hollow woodwind notes in lilting harmonies that seemed to spill from the shifting air.

The sky was clear, a flight of huge lenticular clouds sliding past like a parade of ivory spaceships. The sky creature had been of that size, moving with ponderous poise. Beautiful in its way, and lethal. These clouds poured rain onto distant hills, and the fragrant breeze brought the flavor to them.

As they often did, the humans watched the strange landscapes around them and tried to figure out how it all worked. Aybe and Terry maintained that there had to be tubes moving water around the Bowl, since otherwise all fluids would end up in the low-grav regions near the poles. Irma pointed out that some photos of the Bowl, taken when *Sun-Seeker* was approaching, showed just what Aybe and Terry thought—huge pipes running along the outside of the Bowl. Cliff listened to all this and sorted through his photographs. He had nearly filled his comm-camera's digital storage with photos of plants and animals and had to edit out some to free up space. Already he had decided to ignore algae, bacteria, Protoctista, fungi, and much else. He kept snaps of purple-skinned animals loping on stick legs across a sandy plain. He had captured flapping, flying carpets with big yellow eyes, massive ruddy blobs moving like boulders on tracks of slime, spindly trees that walked, birds like big-eyed blue fish. A library of alien life.

Cliff knew he had missed a lot of creatures

because they had quick and good camouflage to conceal themselves. They discovered this by stepping on what looked like limbs or lichen or dirt and turned out to be small animals that knew the arts of disguise. He sucked in the moist air and recalled that on Earth, desert plants defended against losing moisture by keeping their stomata closed in the day. They opened at night to take in carbon dioxide without evaporating too much water away. On the Bowl, though, without night, the air had to hold enough moisture to let plants respire, venting oxygen. That meant a lot of water. It explained the heavy rainstorms and thick, flavored air, the sprawling rivers they had to work around, the mists that shrouded even small depressions in the land.

Yet some aspects here were like an Earth that had vanished long ago. Standing nearby was an enormous version of something he had seen Earthside, embedded in coal beds: horsetails. These resembled a first draft of bamboo—thick walled, segmented grass, tan and tall. The trunks popped as they swayed in the wind, eternally fighting for space and sun and soil just as did all the others. He had seen creatures that excreted through pores in their feet—surely not from Earth. Their speech sounded like whistling and farting at the same time. Both used flowing gases through a pinched exit, but . . .

Quert broke off from a murmuring crowd. Moving with efficient grace, it came up to them, its big yellow eyes heavily lidded, and said, "Thank delivered in kind. We now speak, want."

Its language ability came in simple stutters of words. Cliff could usually guess the content. Quert moved with rippling muscles. *Like brilliant gazelles,* Cliff thought. The Sil were limber, dexterous creatures that worked on the Bowl's understructure. They lived in small towns, mostly, so this now-ruined city was unusual. Quert said Sil were peppered through the immense lands of the Bowl. They seldom met other Sil groups larger than the few thousand here, since distance isolated them. They received instructions from the Folk and carried out their labors. Otherwise, they governed themselves. Populations were stable, by social conventions handed down for countless generations. This was a standard Folk method, apparently. *Divide and rule,* Cliff thought.

Throngs of Sil followed their mourning with festival. The humans stood aside as the lithe forms began to move, sway, sing. All around them spontaneous movement broke out. The warm sun and lancing jet stung their skins and they danced until a kind of glow spread on their skins. "Maybe the exercise changes their surface circulation?" Irma wondered as the pumping music swelled, bodies glided and kicked, and the golden richness of Sil skins seemed to give off its own moist radiance.

Quert led them to a low building, its walls slanted sheets of ivory rock. Beneath their feet was blond gravel that as they entered a small room turned green, each pebble wrapped in a translucent skin of slime. Quert bent and carefully unhinged from some sculpted seats small blobs that seemed to be slugs that had adhered. They sat and the seats adjusted to their bodies with a slithery grace.

There was a long wait, but as protocol required, the alien spoke first. "We need know goal Astronomers."

"They want to catch us," Terry said. "Or kill us."

"Whichever is easier," Aybe added.

"Capture best for them. Folk want know what you know." Quert said this flatly.

"About what?" Irma asked.

"Ship you ride, plants you carry, bodies you have, songs. Possible is." The swift slippery slide of Quert's words belied a calm the feline alien wore like a mantle. Plainly Quert was a leader.

The talk went on, speculating on why the Folk had fired into a Sil crowd. Yes, humans were among them, but why did that matter? Cliff watched the alien and reflected on what could come next. In his experience people centered their lives around money or status or community or service to some cause, but the Sil seemed to live learning-centered lives. Here little bits of practical knowledge were the daily currency—Howard had given them a Möbius strip to amuse the children—and their main vocation was to be preoccupied with some exciting little project or maybe a dozen. As one Sil had told him, it was quicker to list the jobs he didn't hold than the ones he did.

There were teams completing a pit to turn manure into electricity, plans to build a micro-hydroelectric generator in a local stream. They devised and built their own lathes and saws, tough enough to carve into the hard wood of the big trees that ringed their sprawling village. The Sil seemed shaped by what Cliff saw as a frontierlike culture. Here they drilled into trees to make body lotion or designed cement hives for swarming insects, as if to foil a creature that sounded to Cliff like honey badgers. *They're isolated,* Cliff thought, *no other Sil for great distances, or other intelligent species . . . out here in the bush, lost in their experiments.*

His attention had wandered. Aybe had been peppering Quert with questions, and nobody understood its answers. Then the alien leaned back, yawned to show big teeth, and held up its hands. "Not right thing, you speak for. Folk want all Adopted to obey. I-we, you—" A liquid pointing gesture. "—not made in Bowl. Danger badness comes from us, say Folk."

This came out as hard, clipped words, not the sliding sibilants Quert usually used. It was tricky inferring emotions from alien facial signatures, Cliff's judgment warned him, but the narrowing eyes and tensed lips made a constricted face that oozed resentment. Cliff said, "You came before us."

A quick blinking, which seemed to convey agreement among the Sil. "Not Adopted over long time. We move, live, work. Folk give us things. We do their commands."

Irma said, "You said earlier that you move often?"

Quert looked puzzled, as it always did by the human habit of conveying a question by a rising note at the end of a sentence. "Our kind rove."

"But you have buildings."

"Young must learn by doing. This I-we know.

Costs to know. Must pay. No such thing as free education. And buildings, cities used to talk."

"Talk?"

"Adopted can see our work from everywhere in the Bowl. We shape our cities to make messages. Small messages. Big shapes for streets, parks, buildings. When we know, they know, too. What Folk want from you."

The Sil had a way of leading you toward what they meant, then letting you go the rest of the way. Maddening, at times. Asking them again, or in a different way, got nowhere, banging on a door that wouldn't open.

The Sil preferred to show them. Quert took them to a site where the ground seethed with a tan, stretching substance. It came out of the Bowl when the Sil triggered it, Quert said. Then they tuned it somehow. Cliff inspected one of their handheld devices but could make nothing of the ribbed and fissured face of it. The Sil apparently took in information and gave instructions by feel, not visually. This seemed odd for ones who had so many eye-moves to express themselves. Cliff was still wondering at this when the slick tan surface began to ease upward. It became grainy as it rose, wedges emerging from the big bubble that blossomed above them. It firmed up into walls and crossbeams as windows opened like sleepy eyes along the edge. A thick cloying scent like drying cement filled the air and Cliff stepped back with the others, not able to follow the complex moves the "constructors," as Quert termed them, made to shape the thing, through signals he could not fathom.

After an hour or two, a fresh building stood two stories tall. The floors were rough and there was no clue how the inhabitants could get water or electricity, but the oval curves of its walls and sloping floors of the interior were elegantly simple. The roof sported an odd array of sculptures that imitated Sil body shapes and cups pointed at the horizon.

In the entire growth of the home, Cliff felt a tension between order, as seen in the room gridiron pattern, and a spontaneous, discontinuous rhythm to the wrinkled walls and oblong windows. It had just enough strangeness to be expressive, though he did not know what the Sil made of it. They seemed to think it played a role in reconciling them to their lost friends and shattered city.

Nomadic, Cliff guessed. Each generation set up shop in a new area, hunted and gathered, devised their own kind of town. A species with a wandering curiosity, alighting on interesting parts of their environment. The Bowl was big enough to accommodate that style. But buildings as messages? "Do the Bird Folk read your building messages?"

"Think not." Quert made a rustling sound in its big chest and said quietly, "I-we lost many. Sil like you, many parts, all lost."

There was a sadness in the long, sliding words. The self-forming building seemed to play a role in their reconciling what had happened. Yet none cast glares or stares at the humans. He could imagine no reason why the Sil should forgive the humans for bringing all this upon them. But then he was yet again seeing them as thinking like humans, and they did not.

The talk continued for a while as Cliff listened intently, trying to judge how Quert saw the world. Having an alien who had already learned Anglish was an immense advantage, but Quert's short, punchy sentences gave only a surface view of the mind beneath.

"If I were a lizard, I'd be a belt by now," Irma said at one point, and for the first time they saw Quert laugh. Or something like it—barks that could just as well have been a summons, but accompanied by eye-blinks and sideways jerks of the head. As Quert did this, the eyes watched the humans, and there came a moment of—Cliff grasped for the right word—yes, *communion*. A meeting of minds. This cheered him up a great deal.

Then Quert said there were meetings to go to, clearly meaning to end on a high, light note. They broke up and returned to the cavelike place the Sil had given over to the humans. It was a rude warren built of rocks rolled together to form corridors and rooms. A thick tentlike sheet drawn over the top of the whole sprawl of rock made a roof. At certain places detachable patches let in sun for the rooms, and were easily pegged back in place for sleep. Utilitarian and, Cliff realized, quite portable—just roll up the sheet and find another field of boulders. The Sil apparently used whole gangs to move the rocks, a communal effort.

The whole team was tired and somehow the Sil dirge had quieted them. They went to their rooms. Cliff took a side corridor to his own small cubbyhole; Irma gave him a smile he could feel in his hip pocket.

Cliff had never fancied himself much of a lover, but since they had been taken under the protection of the Sil, they were at it every sleep period. This was no exception. They slept awhile then, and when he woke up she was looking at him. With a lazy smile she said, "When the chemistry is right, all the experiments work."

"I'm more of a biology type."

"That, too. Y'know, you've learned how to keep this pack of people together, too. I watch you do it. You've learned how to pull their strings."

"Um—yours, too?"

"Not so much. Learning to pull men's strings is one of a woman's major skills, of course. I can see you do it in your own guy way." She softened this, though, with a grin.

He felt uneasy thinking about being manipulative, but—"I learned on the job."

"You let everybody have their say, then let them do the calculation. Who's with them, who's not. Most of the time that solves the problem."

"Well, they think I have your vote already."

She laughed. "Touché! But not because of fun in the sack."

They were indeed in a sack, of sorts. The open, braced hammock fiber somehow stayed flat though it hung from straps, a smart carbon sheet. He didn't like discussing how to manage their little team, though. He now trusted his intuition and was relieved not to think about it. He leaned over, kissed her. "What do you think we should do next?"

"If you keep caressing my leg, I'll tell you."

Cliff laughed and kept up a smooth, steady stroking of her tawny leg. He hadn't noticed he was doing it. "I don't see how we can find Beth or stay away from the Folk, much less figure out this place."

Irma shrugged. "I don't either. Yet."

"What makes you think we can?"

"Well, for one thing, it's us. And we have smarts."

"Smarter than what built this contraption?"

"Well, there's street smarts on Earth—remember that phrase? Means you can get around on your own. Maybe here we have planet smarts."

"Which means?" A pretty obvious way not to give away what he thought, but people didn't seem to notice it.

"This place seems to be deeply conservative. You have to be, to keep a contrivance like this running. Hell, even at first glance, I knew it wasn't stable. If the Bowl gets closer to the star, the biosphere heats up *and* starts to fall toward the star. To correct that, I'd guess the locals have to fire up the jet stronger, propel the star away, and get back to the right distance for heating. Then there's the problem of what to do if I stamp my foot and the Bowl starts to wobble. It must be they have correction mechanisms in place. On a planet, inertia alone, and Newton's laws, keep you going if you do nothing. Not here."

"Ah, the spirit of an engineer. You didn't answer my question."

She chuckled. "You noticed! I'd say stay here, try to get back in touch with *SunSeeker*. Let Redwing figure a way to help us."

"He doesn't seem to have a clue. Unless you're down here, it's hard to get a grip on the quiet, odd ways this place is so different from a planet."

"Such as?"

"It's impossibly big, but it's mostly vacant. Why?"

"It suits the Folk mentality, must be. Lots of natural landscape—okay, not natural, but it's shaped to feel natural. It's a park, really. The Sil fit in here, too."

"Nomad habits of mind, right. And the Bowl is a nomad, too. Wanderers living on a wandering artifact. A big, smart object."

She pursed her lips. "Smart? Because it has to be managed all the time, kept from falling into its star?"

"It moves forward in a dangerous way, just like us. Any two-legged creature has to fall forward and catch itself. Aside from birds, there aren't many Earthside animals that do that. The most common two-legged one is us."

She considered this. "The Bird Folk are two-legged, in a way. Though I saw them move on all fours, too, since the forearms can help them for stability. Maybe they're concerned about not falling, because they're massive."

"So they have the same gut instinct—move forward, even if it's tricky. I—"

Shouting in the distance. Irma got up and pulled on her rather tattered uniform, stuck a head out through the curtain of her chamber. "Quert? What's—?"

The alien came into the room in the quick, sliding way the Sil made look so liquidly graceful.

"Come . . . they."

Cliff hauled out of the hammock, feeling his joints ache and eyes sticky. His fingers fumbled as he got dressed. Irma went with Quert. By the time he got to the entrance, they were all staring up at something humming in the sky. Not the balloon creature that had fired on them all, something smaller, faster. It skimmed low, wings purring. A slim, winged thing of feathers and a big crusty head that scanned the land below systematically. Its big glittering eyes saw the Sil settlement and turned toward them.

"Like a huge dragonfly," Irma whispered.

Quert said, "Scout. Smart one. High value, so Folk must—"

The thing surged as it turned toward them. Cliff said, "Inside!"

The nearest building was ceramic coated with crusty, bronzed metal. He ran toward it as he looked back. Howard was watching with binoculars the slim body as it canted in the air, wings furious. "Howard!"

Quert was faster than the humans and got into the building entrance. It caught the big hinged door and swung it nearly closed as people ran under its arch. "Howard!" Cliff called, and then went in.

"We must be inside," Quert said. "Scout smart with—"

A humming in the air washed over them. Cliff saw Howard jerk and grab with frenzied fingers at his head. A startled yelp from him turned to a high, shrill scream. Howard fell and was snatching at his legs, head, chest. His jaw yawned wide with a colossal cry. His eyes bulged white.

Quert slammed the heavy metal door closed and drove a latch into place, cutting off Howard's shriek like a knife.

Cliff stood blinking at the big door, unable to push away the sharp image of Howard frantically slapping at invisible demons.

The humans looked around at the crowds, dazed. There were many Sil already inside, providing a chorus of their sliding speech, feet shuffling, eyes shifting uneasily at this latest attack. Others, though, slumped against walls and let their heads rest back, eyes closed, as if resigned to absorbing yet one more disaster.

"They get to shelter fast," Irma noted. "Seem to be riding it out, pacing themselves."

There were no windows in this place. Phosphors lit the narrow rooms. Cliff went through the Sil crowds, their eyes tracking him, and down a corridor, searching for a way to see out. The air hung thick and carried an odd, sour flavor.

He turned back and found Quert following him, who said, "Hurt come through glass."

"You come here to get away from the Folk microwave weapon?"

Quert made the odd, waggling sign of assent. "They Folk change to do your kind."

Irma had followed Quert through the claustro-corridors. "This time it hit Howard. The Folk must've found the right frequency or power levels."

"Folk know technologies well. Adjust fast. Always have."

"And sent it on that scout?" Cliff wanted to see how Howard was doing. "If I could get a look—"

"No window this place." Quert made a hand gesture that they had learned, during the long days of burying the Sil dead, meant "rest peacefully, no cares."

The Sil would not let Cliff find a way to look out. One of them came down a chute and, speaking quickly in the sibilant squirts the Sil used, through Quert reported that the fast-flying scout with the big gleaming eyes had circled until it tired, fired down randomly at some Sil, then flew away.

Irma said, "It's come before?"

"Only metal stops hurt." Quert looked weary, long lines running down its pale face and leathery neck. "Keep tight."

Cliff knew that microwaves in the spectral region that plucked at the human nervous system were about three millimeters in wavelength. The Sil must be vulnerable to a different wavelength, since humans had not felt the pain gun used in earlier assaults. So the Folk must have developed something that hurt Howard a great deal, and done it within a short while. Something around a hundred gigahertz. Impressive.

Irma said, "So they must know you Sil very well—"

"The *aquladatorpa* knows us. It look for you."

"You've been living a long time with the Folk. Under them, I should say. How do you bear it?"

Quert thought awhile and Cliff let him, not interrupting. Humans had a nervous, intrusive way of interrupting each other, a social gaffe of some consequence among the Sil. Then Quert sighed and said slowly, "You have word, 'enchant,' means our *ochig*. Or like it. Enchant comes from light, from sun and jet. Living essence, is enchant. *Ochig* comes down streaming. Plants, animals, Sil, and now human grow and learn and think from *ochig*. Bowl turns to keep us here so *ochig* can bring enchant passing through us. Sil in world, human in world, Folk more in the *ochig,* thick in *ochig*. Moving through world, *ochig* makes pattern. Folk see pattern. Get pattern wrong and Folk do wrong."

"They don't seem any better than you Sil."

"Not better. But in right place."

"They're in the right place when they slaughter you?"

"Right will come. *Ochig* endures."

This was the longest Quert had ever talked about anything, indeed the longest speech he had ever overheard among any of the Sil. They had an air of paying attention to the passing moment. He envied that.

Cliff wandered aimlessly, still seeing in his mind's eye Howard slapping at himself and shrieking. He came upon Irma, who had found a little cranny and was sitting on the bare cold stone floor, sobbing. He sat beside her and took her shoulders in his hands and drew her close. Soon enough he was murmuring and clutching her, letting out emotions he did not wish to name. Just holding her helped. He kneaded the tight muscles in her neck and shoulders. She did the same for him and in the long dim time between them some comfort stole over their bodies and then deeper. He could not cry but she could, letting the soft sobs out one at a time. Time eased around them.

They spent more hours inside before the Sil unwrapped the shelter. They coiled up shiny sheets that they had triggered to cover all the door hinges. Intense electromagnetic waves with millimeter wavelengths can leak around slim edges, even those less than a millimeter wide.

Cliff looked out a small window and saw Howard curled up on the ground with no Sil within view. They came out a side door and surveyed the empty sky. Aybe rushed forward, unhooking the first-aid kit . . . and they all stopped where Howard sprawled.

Howard did not resemble a man now nearly so much as a twisted, red, roasted chicken. Lips blue and bloodless, arms a blotchy purple. His eyes peered up at them as though asking what had happened.

Cliff stared at the face a long time. This man had been under his leadership since they left the ship, since they went through the lock at their landing, and then across long weary paths and through sudden panics. Howard had a habit of getting hurt, missing jumps and landing wrong, some scrapes and sprains, despite his physical stats. The ground truth, as their training had told them, was the final fact, and no tests or training could tell you what happened when plans met reality in a usually brutal collision. Swift came reality, and it took no prisoners. Cliff had not seen this coming and Howard had lagged a step or two behind and so was now forever gone. On his watch.

Quert said quietly, "Is quick. Hurt is where beam hits."

They buried Howard with the other Sil in the collective grave site. Cliff said little and they were walking back from the site when a faint hum filled the air. Heads turned. Sil nearby rustled with alarm.

The slim shape skimmed low, wings whirring in the sky. Sil began running. Their yellow eyes raced with jittery panic.

"Go time," Quert said. They went.

PART III

Status Opera

*Scientists study the world as it is; engineers create
the world that has never been.*
—Theodore von Kármán

TWELVE

Memor watched the primate scream. She tried to lunge out of the beam and tripped. Sprawled. Gasped. The armaments team dutifully tracked her as the poor dim creature scrambled to crawl away. She kept up the sobbing little shrieks as the weapons crew tuned their large antennas further. It went on until Memor waved an impatient fan-display and the team cut off the pain beam.

The team was pleased, their feathers fluttering with joy, though they kept discipline and said nothing. They had correctly adjusted their weaponry and hit the right resonance for nerve stimulation in the alien.

"Tananareve," Memor in her best learned accent, trying to address the primate by name in its own awkward tongue, "you can survive this level of agony for, you would say, how long?"

Free of agony, the primate leaped to her feet. Eyes narrow, mouth tight, voice high. "You torture me like a lab animal!"

"A legitimate use," Memor said mildly, "in warfare."

"War? We landed on your world-thing, tried to open negotiations—"

"No use to revisit the past, little one. We are on to other matters, and this experiment was useful to us."

"How?" The primate sagged to her knees, then sat, wiping sweat from her forehead. "How can slamming me with that damn fire-beam help?"

"We need to know how to . . . negotiate . . . with those of your kind."

"You mean *fight* them."

"The opening struggle comes first, of course."

Tananareve's face took on an expression Memor had learned to interpret: cautious calculation. These primates managed to convey emotion through small moves of mouth, eyes, chin. They had evolved on some flat plain, apparently, without benefit of the wide range of expression that feathers conferred. Tananareve said slowly, "I'm very glad they're still free. It means you don't know how to deal with them."

Memor disliked the sliding logic of this creature, but knew she had to get around it. "We need the means to bring them to order. Inflicting pain is much more . . . virtuous . . . than simply killing them, I think you will agree?"

Tananareve shot back, "Do you have anything you would die for? Your freedom to make your own way, for example?"

"No, dying seems pointless. If you die, you cannot make use of the outcome of the act."

"Die to save others? Or for a belief?"

"I certainly would not die for my beliefs. I could be wrong."

Tananareve shook her head, which seemed to be how these creatures implied rejection. "So you experiment on me, to see what power level of your beam works best?"

"That, and tunable frequency. How else are we to know?"

Thin lips, narrowed eyes. Anger, yes; Memor was getting used to their ways. "Don't do it again."

"I see no need to. You obviously felt a great terrible agony. That will suffice."

"I need . . . sleep."

"That I can grant." In truth, Memor was tired of this exercise. She did not like to inflict stinging hurt. Yet her superior, Asenath, had commanded that a fresh weapon be developed, capable of delivering sudden sharp pain. The customary such radiator, which worked well on the Sil, had failed in the first, clumsy battle. Memor did not like to think of that engagement, which had killed the skyfish she rode in. Her escape pod had lingered long enough to witness the giant, buoyant beast writhe in air, its hydrogen chambers breached by rattling shots from the ground cannon below. Then the hydrogen ignited in angry orange fireballs and the skyfish gave a long, rolling bass note of agony. The mournful cry did not end until its huge cylindrical body crumpled, crackling with flames, against a hillside. What a fiasco!

Now Memor had to redeem herself. She could do so by developing and delivering quickly a pain projector, one that could damage the primates without overloading their nervous systems, and thus killing them. And now she had. Further, at the insistence of the weapons shops, Memor's stroke of insight had been to carry out earlier testing on small tree-dweller primates, gathered from the Citadel Gardens for the purpose. They seemed to have similar neurological systems and vulnerabilities, and so were the optimal path to this success.

Memor swelled with pride. The trials on the Sil city had been preliminary, and it was difficult from the skyfish to discern if humans had been affected at all. But these tunings made that probable. The Sil had needed discipline, and the possibility of death-stinging the humans hiding among them was a bonus, of course.

"We will speak later," she told the primate. "I have more interesting experiments in mind for us to work upon together."

The primate made a noise of deep tones—nothing more than grunts, really—perhaps some symptom of a residual pain. Memor thought it best not to notice this as she departed, her small attendants and the weapons team following dutifully.

THIRTEEN

Memor hated when her insides wanted to be her outsides.

She did not like the testing of new weapons upon her charge, the primate. To do so made her nauseated, her acids run sour. Yet Asenath had ordered quick results quite clearly, and to preserve her position Memor had to comply. She accepted the logic, however distasteful the experience.

Looked at another way, the slap of pain did not merely withhold: the slap imparted. It conveyed precisely the knowledge of greater power withheld. In that knowledge lay the genius of *using*, the deep humiliation it imposed. It invited the victim to accept a punishment in pursuit of a larger purpose, one that might have been worse—that would in fact be worse if the use wasn't accepted. The pain-slap required that the higher goal be understood.

Of course, the primates could not understand this, but in time with their Adoption that would come. If they could not be so opened, then they would have to be extinguished, well before their vagrant abilities could be a threat.

Memor relaxed a bit by regarding the aged wonders nearby as she passed down corridors and through yawning archways. The teeth of time wore long on the Bowl. By its nature it must run steadily. Engineer species must fix problems without the luxury of trial and error experimenting. That meant engineer teams relied on memory, not ingenuity. Intelligence was less vital than ready response to situations that had occurred before, and so were lodged in cultural recollection. Species had their mental abilities shaped to do this. It was the Way.

Memor thought on this as she watched some mutants being culled. They were small variants on the repair snakes, long ago acquired from a world with rapid tectonics. They had evolved swift, acute responses to those treacherous lands, a driver of their crafty intelligence. Memor had witnessed the underground cities this kind built, when allowed, in the underskin of the Bowl—labyrinths of elegance and deft taste she had been much impressed by. Memor remained surprised that these snakes had subsections of their genome that made them resist the nirvana of the Bowl. Surely here they should be endlessly joyful, for they were free of the frightening ground-quakes, foul volcanoes, and hammering ocean waves that often dashed their hopes and their subsurface homes to oblivion?

These, however, had a touch too much of their crafty independence. They were in a nearby chamber with transparent walls, where another research team had tried to correct the mental errors in the snakes. Apparently, this corrective experiment had failed. The researchers were exterminating them by gas, and Memor paused to watch the agonies of these smart serpents, who under duress flung themselves into twisting knots. It was revolting, writhing bodies and pain-stretched mouths. At least she could not hear them, as she had Tananareve's shrieks. Gazing through the wall at this, she could not help but reflect upon the fate of the primates, should they continue to provoke.

They would face the fate of the Sil, whose rebellion had united with the renegade primates and brought down Memor's skyfish. That had made the reprisal destruction of the Sil city inevitable—though it came first as an idea sprung from the slim though weighty head of Asenath, the reigning Chief of Wisdom.

Memor sighed and trudged on, putting the image of the snake agonies behind her. Now she must go to Asenath and confer, though she sorely disliked and feared the Chief of Wisdom, who was known to be capricious.

An oddity of long history had placed the confinement and punishment chambers together with ancient honoring sites. They were all now encased in a great Citadel that loomed above the lush green landscapes here. She lumbered past large, luxuriant stone structures of vast age, moss clinging to the doorways of crypts polished by time. Some bore blemishes of tomb raiders, but even those harsh, jagged edges had smoothed. These chambers held ancient dead who had been allowed burial, in a far-distant time when that was possible, and before the realization that all mass and vital elements must be reprocessed. Surely that was the highest honor, to be part of life eternally, not a mere oxidized relic. The bodies inside had long returned to the air, of course, with only shriveled bones remaining as a small, unharvested calcium deposit. No doubt the grave goods—ornaments and valuable family remembrance-coffers that some added to the sepulchers of that age—had disappeared long ago, at the hands of vagrant intruders. The past was the easiest venue to rob, after all.

Though not to fathom, came a vagrant sliver of thought. Memor stopped, shocked. Her attendants rustled, unsure what to do. With a feather rattle

Memor bade them stand away. The sudden thrust of *not to fathom* carried guilt and fear wrapped around it. Memor *felt* the thought-voice and knew it had come lancing up from her Undermind. Something had festered there, and now propelled out, calling to her. She would have to deal with the unruly, understand what this shaft of emotion meant. But not now. She forced herself to resume her stroll, not letting her aides see her vexed condition. Best to rattle her feathers, sigh, casually move on.

She noted there were pointless messages for the unknowable future, here: TO BE READ UPON YOUR WAKING, from some lost age when minds stored in silica or cryo could, they hoped, work forth from their decay into some future with vaster, smarter resources. None awoke, for there was no shortage of minds in the Bowl. Nor of bodies, for the number of walking, talking minds was a matter of stability, not wealth. Minds were not the point of the Bowl, but the long-run destiny of the Folk was . . . and of course, of those lucky species who came onboard through countless Annuals of time, to help make the Bowl sail on, *sail on,* to witness and grasp the great prospect offered by the whole galaxy's own vast, strange, ponderous assets. Whoever or, indeed, whatever wrote TO BE READ UPON YOUR WAKING lived in some illusion of past times. They now drifted as fragrant dust beneath Memor's great slapping feet.

She looked around, savoring. Some mausoleums carried chiseled epitaphs noted for their charm, which may have preserved the blocky tombs' hard

carbo-concentrated walls in their revered sanctity.
Here one referred to

> I, THE FAMOUS WIT, PLONEJURE,
> SOOTHED PAIN WITH COMEDY AND LAUGHTER.
> A PERFORMER OF PARTS, SURE I OFTEN
>   DIED . . .
> BUT NEVER QUITE LIKE THIS.

Another was more dry:

> DIUREAUS SAW THE OTHER FOLK BESIDE HIM,
> GUILTY, TRUE, AND SQUARE, AND WORSE,
> HUNG UP ON A HIGHER CROSS THAN SHE,
> DIUREAUS DIED HERE OF FURIOUS ENVY.

Pleasant, to think that wit was ancient. She
wished that the Chief of Wisdom Asenath had a
touch of wit in her genes. One more tomb inscrip-
tion caught well Asenath's melancholy spirit:

> THEY TOLD ME, HERADOLIS; THEY TOLD ME
>   YOU WERE DEAD.
> THEY BROUGHT ME BITTER NEWS TO HEAR, AND
>   BITTER TEARS TO SHED.
> I WEPT WHEN I REMEMBERED HOW OFTEN YOU
>   AND I
> HAD TIRED THE SUN WITH TALKING, AND SAW A
>   JET-CURL CARVE THE SKY.

Since this passage was carved, Memor noted, whole
worlds had evolved to harbor life, and others had

been scorched of life by ancient brutalities. Yet the image *saw a jet-curl carve the sky* endured.

Ah! Here was the entrance; no more time for rumination. *Step proud and high—*

Memor marched in grandly, head held high with casual grace, her attendants trailing beneath the grand arches of this Citadel of Remembrance. Herald music rumbled and sang to greet her. Pungent mists fell in tribute and out of duty she sniffed, bowed, fluttered a quick ruby tail display. Skin-caressing life fell in curling display around her, caressing her head leathers, whispering faint blessings and salacious compliments. Invitations whispered in her ears, promising succulent delights, then fluttered away. Aromas of heady prospect swarmed up her nostrils and tainted the air with ruddy promise.

Impatient, she shook these off and looked around for the right portal to find Asenath. From the court rabble here dawdling came much sensory babble, greetings, aromas, electric skin-jolts, high hails, a murmur of veiled gossip—all usefully ignored, for now, to show that she was above the insolent fray.

High ramparts trimmed in grace notes of colorful mega-flowers loomed like cliffs over the noisy gathering crowd, most of them come for the extermination ceremonies. They knew the ancient rules against recording in any medium, sight or sound or scene—a ritual death—and so came for the immediate experience. They did carry magnifier scopes and had an anxious, eager air. Skittering voices surged with a hunger that had no proper name. All these she avoided.

Administrative high offices were disguised from those unwelcome, which meant of course the crowd schooled in mere sensation—and the even greater number of the unknowing, unschooled, blunt of mind—all got shielded away by pale luminances that misled the unwary, sending them down dank corridors to their elemental raw pleasures. In such holes the halt and lame of mind would find some passing delights, and forget why they came, forget for their short vexed time the whole point of the Folk. Good enough.

Yet the dancing sheaves of prickly glow were smart sensors, and the walls knew well whom to admit. Those embedded intelligences, ever circumspect in their ways, sent fraying brilliant amber fingers to direct Memor down somber, ancient corridors. Crusty, glistening rock winked her forward past a sensor net of embedded eyes. She drew in the soft moist airs. There were always fresh changes in the Citadel, yet the Ancient Zone captured best the colossal powers lodged here. The rough stones held much elegant and courtly wisdom of ages past, canny knowledge set in stone. Memor heaved a sigh. She *belonged* here.

A quiet, delicious blend of dread and strangeness flowed in her Undermind; she sensed it with a tingle of relish. She forgave it the sudden lance that had jarred her, and concentrated on the immediate. That strumming presence knew that this primordial, welcoming Citadel could well be her place of execution. Should she not perform well, and fail with the primates that were fully her charge now, she would receive little mercy.

Yet this did not fully overcome her awe at the majesty here. Of course, her Undermind often used its trickster mode, slipping words and even phrases into her speech, in its keen, eager way. Jokes about Underminds escaping control were a staple of classic literature and current japes. She could feel its hopeful spikes of muted zeal and would have to keep it carefully controlled now. *Though not to fathom,* indeed.

Drama entered seldom in an Astronomer's life, and for that she was grateful.

Ah! The correct portal. She entered into a small knot of Astronomers, to be greeted by feather-riffs in orange and emerald, then small trill songs that echoed complimentary status-signals. Heads turned. Eyes widened. Bass calls of friendship resounded. A shield, of course, for what all knew: Memor had been summoned and they were looking forward to the show. Anticipation danced in their eyes and neck-feather-flutters.

She had to wait while a Revealing ceremony concluded. It had been a passage of legendary ardor and travail. The recent male, unsteady and weak-eyed, now advanced toward the welcoming cadre, where she knelt with gravid solemnity. The new She looked around in a many-wrinkled face full of bewildered puzzlement. She blinked with surprise, her feather-fan awash in ripples of wonder and flourishes of muted purple hope. Memor recalled this stage, when the male dwindled away into memory and a new *She* emerged, dewy-eyed.

From this fresh female's Revealing she would, through the difficult next Annuals, acquire the long views of a She, yet retain the robust memories of prancing, exploring thrill that had marked her vivid He era. Memor could not help joining in with her deep soprano the rising fulsome joy-song, full of deep welcoming tones, and from above, the high, tenor resonances—all celebrating the conferred judgment and sympathy-from-experience that the Revealing summoned forth. This new She would in time, and with much further study of the essential astrophysics and the Vast History, join the Order of Astronomers. From this essential balance—more a sure dance, truly—between the He and She, wisdom could and thus would come.

Striding forward, clumping with big solemn feet, Memor took note of this new Her-name: Zetasa. In time this new She could, and so might, bring a new, vital stabilizing element to their colloquy—a wise method evolved by the Folk over many, many twelve-millennia in the truly ancient past. This was the essential, time-honored, and stabilizing truth. She relished it.

"Memor!" came Asenath's solemn, deep bass voice. "We have not greeted in longtimes, I do say."

Untrue, but perhaps useful. "I greet in tribute, and wish to confer on present problems," Memor said in long sliding tones, with a penumbral, light-yellow feather display. This drew an attendant twitter of speculation. As tradition demanded, Memor ignored the light trilling soprano chorus of conjecture.

"Which have multiplied, I gather."

"I captured one of the primates and am learning much from her," Memor said. "As we speak, skyfish descend upon the Sil lands, to either capture the primates remaining on the Bowl, or else kill them."

"Ah! As Governors, we must attend to the dismay of the Bowlcrafters, who do not relish such punishments." Asenath made a flutter-rush of red and gold to signal concern, but Memor thought it was only a pretense. Something else was in play.

"Please lead me," Memor said to place the conversation in the right ranking order. Asenath had to take the lead.

"You showed us results of your neural net and brain interrogations of these primates, I recall. Eukaryotic multicellular bilaterians, they are, with unexposed Underminds—fascinating, I am sure. You then estimated their capacities as well below we Folk, and perhaps somewhat above others of the Adopted. Yet they continue to elude us, and now half of them have *fled the Bowl*."

The attendant minor figures drew in their collective breath at this. *To escape!* was their clear, unspoken message. Memor made a half turn to block most of them from Asenath's piercing gaze. She was saying, "Now they have returned to their plasma scoop starship. Do you *still* feel they can be integrated into our Way?"

Making a ritual humble-flush, Memor said, "Apologies most firm indeed, for my failure to retain or recapture these strange primates. I believe their curious gait—a continual, controlled toppling upon those hind feet that have thick, artificial coverings—must be a key clue to their ability to improvise. They can hop to new ideas far more readily than we anticipated. Their ability to form a quick bond-alliance with the Sil is an example—another two-footed species, I remark, which perhaps helps explains their rebellion. The primates arrived on train transport, and immediately engaged with the Sil in a battle against our skyfish. How this came about with such speed is a puzzle. Perhaps there is a species-signal here that may explain it in part."

"I would think their two-legged forms were adaptive on a more aggressive and quick-fighting world."

"So . . . you would urge extermination."

Asenath saw she had been maneuvered into a hasty conclusion, always a mistake. "Perhaps not immediately. Their ship has interesting features of magnetic control I and others feel would be useful to examine."

"Ah, wise. Perhaps a consultation, then?" Memor motioned Asenath into a speaking cloister. She took the feather-flush hint. They made it seem they were merely strolling as they spoke. Memor dropped the shimmering, electric-blue sonic cloak behind them once in the narrow confines, where luminous walls gave a warm green glow.

"I did not want to refer to our continuing trouble with the jet flare guidance," Memor said.

"You venture that primates could help somehow?" Asenath's neck fringe fluttered with skepticism.

"They are inventive—"

"Surely you do not imagine that we could allow them to touch what is most sacred and vital to the Bowl!"

"I was trying to—"

"The very idea would be transparent heresy to some of the Folk." A slow, studied gaze, no feather signals at all. "Perhaps . . . including me."

There was surely danger here. Asenath's feather tones shifted from bright attentive colors of rose-purple and olive into hues tending toward pewters and subdued solemn blues. They rustled, too, with an air of menace. Betrayal by Asenath could take several avenues, all hard for Memor to counter. So—admit failure, and do so quickly and first.

"I mention that possibility only because my own narrow escape—when they and the Sil attacked my starfish—was essential. I had learned that the primates could quickly use the chemically driven Sil weaponry. Our assault teams needed to hear that. The primates are swift, original, unpredictable. I wished to report this firsthand—"

"Your death at their hands would have carried the same message," Asenath said dryly.

Without hesitation at this sally, Memor said, "I brought recordings, Wisdom Chief, to analyze—"

"Which show that these Late Invaders are erratic, impulsive, volatile, capricious—yes, all qualities we Folk have suppressed, in order to preserve the Bowl of Heaven. Yet these very same Late Invaders you now propose to *use,* to harvest, to—"

"No, no! I think they could show us new technologies, aid us—and perhaps bring word of a world we do not know, have never visited."

"And then?"

"Of course, if they cannot be Adopted into

our society, then they and their odd ship must be erased."

Asenath gave a subtle fan-salute, undercut with a skeptical throat-wash of dubious red. "I must say, Attendant Astute Astronomer, that you maneuver well here in chambers, though alas, not on the battlefield."

"I was not commanding the skyfish!"

"I hear otherwise. . . ."

Too late, Memor recalled giving orders to the skyfish Captain. She had been unnerved while the simple Sil artillery hammered loud and strong at the great beast's walls. There was some panic then, before the hydrogen vaults were breached. Only her own quick commands had gotten her into her pod. Her parting sally to the doomed Captain had been, *Soon we shall have no further disputes. I will have my pod now.* The Captain had of course not appreciated the ironic tone. Memor had not looked back as she quickly departed. The Captain had gone to his proper reward.

Memor had been a bare short distance from the lumbering gray-skinned beast when a Sil shot struck a girder-bone and ricocheted into a hydrogen vault, then through the outer wall. Surely that had been a lucky shot, which Memor witnessed at a distressingly close distance. The hard slam of the exploding hydrogen had very nearly thrown her fleeing pod into a fatal yaw and tumble. She had shuddered as the skyfish bellowed a long, hoarse cry, realizing its imminent death.

Memor sensed she had been silent too long, reflecting on the sudden memory welling up. Her

Undermind had not processed those harrowing moments then. But now was not the time to dally over the past. "I made a few suggestions to the Captain, all in the heat of the moment."

"It became even more heated as you escaped," Asenath said with brittle brevity, eyes narrowed.

"Had I not, you would know little of the engagement."

"You are aware that you are already in disfavor?"

"I know that my efforts have not been widely recognized. These primates are difficult to reason with, for their mental structures suffer primitive modes we have not dealt with for a great while."

"At least you recaptured one of those who escaped in the original party. Yet the others now divide into two groups: those ones we have never captured, somewhere among the Sil, and as well a party of four, who escaped the Bowl entirely, and now return to their ship. This last is most infuriating. Their ship somehow glides just below the firing field of view of our gamma ray lasers on the Rim."

"Yes, most regrettable." Memor made an apologetic display of amber and blue gray, rippling her feathers to convey remorse. "I did note that our defenses are deliberately unable to be aimed downward at our Bowl, and this decision was made by Elders long ago, after the Maxer Rebellion."

"Your history is correct. Alas, the Maxer Movement is not completely extinguished, and I fear this flaw in our defenses can be laid at their door."

"I did not know!" Memor did not have to pretend; this was indeed bad news, a defense flaw coming at the worst time, with Late Invaders at large.

"It is not your matter, Memor. Concentrate upon the Late Invaders."

"You mean, capture and kill?" That would be easiest, and would get Memor out of the spotlight. Though she would regret their loss, for they were intriguing in their odd mysteries.

"No! I felt that way before, but there are now new issues. To understand, and keep these discussions secure, we must visit the Vaults."

Memor felt a tremor of unease ripple up from her Undermind. Grave matters came to those who had to consult the Vaults. "But why?"

"That you must ask Unajiuhanah, Keeper of the Vault Library."

The idea itself was puzzling, and filled Memor with dread.

FOURTEEN

About Unajiuhanah there was a timeworn joke, that she loved to sing the ancient songs at public events, even at funerals. Asked if she had performed at a recent high burial, Unajiuhanah answered no, and the riposte was, "Then it was a merciful death indeed."

"Compliments to you, Asenath," Unajiuhanah began with a ritual rippling feather salute in gray and violet. This achieved the feat of representing the Great Seal of the Vaults in an actual fluttering picture, a striking image on Unajiuhanah's high fan display. Memor could even see a jittering vague white patch that stood for the formal writing of ancient times, indecipherable now but signifying the weight of vast history. It shimmered like a mute reminder of the long purpose of the Bowl and thus of the Vault.

Asenath introduced Memor, which proved unnecessary as Unajiuhanah brushed aside a summary of Memor's life details and turned to address her directly.

"Memor, I will entertain your notions because I knew your great ancestors and feel I owe them some indulgence. Indeed, I live because a certain fine SheFolk many generations ago stood and fought against an insurrection that very nearly toppled all order in this Vault. That ForeFolk stands before me now, represented by a minute genetic fraction—in you, Memor."

"I am most grateful," Memor said with a simple mild flourish of ruby, embarrassed neck-fringe.

"Now I have a surprise of sorts for you, to bring you into our deliberations. Here is your other self."

Unajiuhanah paused, her voice rising to call, "Bemor, come forth."

"Be More" Memor heard, the very name plunging her backwards into her young days—while her eyes fixed on the big, somewhat ungainly senior male that was . . . she saw, breathing hard . . . herself. At least, genetically. *Bemor! Lost brother!*

They had been separated long before Memor went through the Revealing. Now with "Bemor" she heard again the joke between the two of them. It had been funny then while young but had turned sour many twelve-cubed Annuals ago . . . *Be More*. More than Memor. Be smarter, swifter, know more, exert power, fathom more deeply, stand taller, command power. *Be More*.

"Brother!" Memor called, for Bemor had not suffered the Revealing's agonies and transformations—all done in their youth, by high design. Be more . . . be male.

"I thought this meeting should best come as a surprise, or else one or the other or even both of you would surely dodge it." Unajiuhanah gave a mirthful display, fluttering ruby breast-feathers discreetly. Clearly she was enjoying this.

"Your great turbine of a mind reports you well," Bemor said as overture. "I've sensed your reports. Quite complex and deep."

"Sensed?" Memor realized her own whole-mind scans, carried out routinely to monitor performance, were not private. Usually they were, but of course not in matters of high security.

"They are also quite entertaining," Bemor said. "You remember well, and your Undermind is a source of insight. The facts you confronted alone are high drama. I could scarcely imagine such odd aliens as these Late Invaders. What zest!"

"You mean, how did I let them escape?"

"No, I mean they have a crafty nature we could use."

Memor was sure *Your great turbine of a mind* was an ironic salute, but best not to draw Unaji-uhanah's attention to it. "If we can Adopt them, perhaps—"

"I think not. Too unstable, as species go. They can be better used to carry out our larger cruising agenda."

This was new, beyond the time-honored precepts of the Astronomers, and indeed, of all other castes. *Larger cruising agenda?* Memor should be shocked, she knew, but had no time for that now. "I acted to constrain their actions, under Asenath's direction."

Bemor waved this aside with a cluster-flourish in green and sea blue. "Those orders now vanish. There is new wisdom, falling upon us from the stars."

Memor contented herself with a fan-feather gesture and let Asenath carry the conversation. She was still staggering mentally from the sudden meeting of her near-self: the path not taken, if somehow she could have stayed a male. Bemor had a quick, brusque way of saying things that swept away the niceties of diplomacy and polite evasion. Quite male. Best to change direction.

"I was discussing how I was forced to carry forward the reconnaissance of the Sil, who had sheltered the primates. They proved better at bringing down our skyfish with their simple chemical cannon, admittedly. I—"

"Fled, as you should." Bemore spoke kindly, shuffling his large feet in a faint echo-dance of welcome—*to soften what was to come?* "The primate ingenuity combined nonlinearly with that of the Sil, who were always an irksome and crafty kind."

"Destabilizing," Asenath added, "still." But then she backed away, as if to let the twins negotiate their own newfound equilibrium. So did Unajiu-hanah, with a muted bow. Memor saw this meeting was arranged to divulge information, in a way slanted to make best use of the perpetual jockeying for position in the Astronomer hierarchy—and of course, in the status of the Vaulted, who tended the most ancient records, integrating them with the emerging new.

So, take the momentum away from them. "What new wisdom intrudes?" Memor chose to use an ancient saying, said to come from the Builders, though across the sum of Bowl eras, no one truly knew.

"We fathom more of the gravitational waves, and their true origin," Bemor said.

"As I recall, they come from Glory, or from some source well beyond," Memor said, for this had been the received wisdom from before she was born.

"Not so," Bemor said. "Not beyond. The source is in the immediate Glorian system."

"There is no plausibility, as some argued, that the gravitational waves came from a chance coincidence in the sky? From some cosmological source far away?"

"Not even close. I see your early education has been a waste of time."

Memor knew this gibe, a lancing shot at her earlier ranking in the rigorous status queue of the elect, pre-Astronomer examinations. Quadlineal calculus had always eluded her somehow, and Bemor had never let her forget it. . . . She now *had* to get back some position in this conversation playing out before their elders.

"But surely there cannot be heavy masses moving near a planetary system. That would render unstable the orbits of any planet nearby—"

"No, that must now be considered untrue. Facts say otherwise. We have heard from our Web trading partners."

"What can they—?"

Bemor beamed, yet kept to his clear, factual mask. "You may recall some long Annuals ago we asked them to erect gravitational wave antennas to concentrate upon Glory. They have so done, and with felicitous trading strategies, we have secured their data."

Very well, play for time. And *think*. "I did not know that. Expensive, I suppose?"

Bemor was enough similar that Memor could easily read the quick, darting expressions in feather-flutter—quill rattle, spines flexing so hues slid from steel blue to indigo sheen—that bespoke anticipation of an opportunity to make a veiled boast.

Asenath raised some pink neck-rustle as a deft, ironic signal. Memor realized this was what some intimates of the court termed *Status Opera*, the only true game when the social structure must remain static, for the sake of Bowl stability. Maneuver for position, yes, but carefully, deftly, for the system must always endure, above all.

Bemor was in his element, and so took his fulsome time. "I engaged three other Galactic Web partners, one of whom knew nothing of gravitational waves whatever, and how to detect them. As expected, those who did know had technologies smaller and less sensitive than ours."

Bemor delivered this in a flat, factual way, almost offhand, and with a subtle wing-shrug—a good precursor to a revelation. Memor appreciated the method, as it was hers as well. They were twins, after all. . . . Though Bemor seemed to do it with more verve, as if knowing their audience would approve verve.

"I had to trade valuable arts and science to induce their cooperation," Bemor said. "We barter and gain, delayed for many Annuals, of course. I employed a rich trading language to describe our wants, and used the artificial, intelligent agents we had installed in those societies long in the past."

Memor was at a disadvantage here, since she had learned little of such distant diplomacies. She did know that the Ancients had seen value in establishing agents, transferred as sealed minds in code, to distant worlds. Interstellar commerce over huge distances made sense only if exchange of knowledge—arts, science, engineering, the equivalent of patents—could be traded for some return value. Such a market occurred, mediated among artificial intelligences run solely inside mutually agreed upon containment: the Mind Province established among alien societies. Elaborate protocols ensured that no artificial intelligences could run outside the Mind Province. They were safe there, too, to run their code without corruption.

This protected Bowl secrets from the alien locals, and in turn, the local infosphere from the agent.

"I chose truly distant worlds for two reasons," Bemor said. "They had to be displaced from our trajectory, so that we could gain triangulation on Glory. I then—"

"You transmitted double-encrypted?" Asenath demanded. "You are sure the gravitational wave signatures were unwrapped in secrecy by our sequestered agent?"

"I received the coded instant return notice, yes. I got it back many Annuals before the official trading partner even acknowledged receipt."

"Meaning? That they pondered it long before even notifying us?"

Bemor was not disturbed by these thrusts; he seemed bemused. "Caution is admirable, do you not think so? The first reply came from an insectoid civilization, apparently hungry for further astronomical knowledge. They trade such wares eagerly and built the needed detectors with speed."

"How distant are they?"

"Over a twelve-squared light-Annuals, at a high angle with respect to our trajectory. The second reply came from a similar distance and a different, large angle. We paid them with techno-lore, methods our prior history implied would interest them. These were duly lodged in the host species' banking system. Credits not spent locally may be transmitted, securely encrypted, between solar systems, of course. Then came a third reply, also willing."

Bemor made to condense around them a shimmering shell display of the realm around the Bowl. The three agreeable trader stars shone bright yellow, all at considerable angles away. One lay very nearly parallel to the Bowl, along the trajectory axis they followed, ending in Glory. The simulation showed message flags denoting ongoing info-commerce transporting among all three, as well as their links to the Bowl.

"So they set to work, these trade partners—"

"Ran their gravitational wave detectors. Learned our skills. And nailed firm the site of the waves. It is in our destination system—Glory."

Memor said slowly, "Agents do amass more and more knowledge about their host species. They report back. Do these worlds have any opinion about the cause of the waves?"

Bemor looked pleased, with a body-flutter of magenta flush. To Memor this was a giveaway: a salute, really, as if to say, *I recognize!—you can leap ahead, see what's coming.* "They could not resist diagnosing the long wavelengths and their resonances. And . . . there are *messages* within."

Asenath gasped and could not resist: "Saying what?"

Bemor's elation collapsed, his neck wattles compressing to thin red layers. "We do not know. These, too, are apparently deeply encrypted."

Memor felt a tremor of awe, that emotion mingling fear and wonder, so seldom sensed in a calm, regular life. It swept her like a tidal slap. "Sending coded messages, by oscillating huge masses to make waves of gravity itself?—in organized ways? That is . . ." She was about to say, *impossible*—but caution ruled. ". . . improbable, in the extreme."

Asenath added wryly, "We are approaching something strange and perhaps quite dangerous. Glory seems innocuous, but they send gravitational messages—somehow. The escaped primates are headed that way, too—or were, until they decided to land upon the Bowl of Heaven. They seem—" She preened with an oddly insulting fan-gesture, ominous and foreboding. "—ambitious."

Memor decided not to rise to the bait. "They are able and may be of use."

Unajiuhanah came in then with a gentle, sad wing-shrug. "I enjoy your sparring, but there are larger issues, you twins." A nod to Asenath, to proceed. "Our larger cruising agenda, recall?"

Asenath said, "The Glorians, as we term them, have sent an electromagnetic signal."

"Directed at us?" Unajiuhanah prompted.

"I . . . suppose." Asenath looked puzzled.

"There is no distinction in spatial coordinates between the Bowl and the primate star rammer," Bemor said. "That may explain the content."

"Which is?" Memor asked, impatient with this parrying.

"Cartoons," Unajiuhanah said. "Such as primitive cultures employ. They might as well be painted on cave walls, but for the fact that they move. Showing violence, often physically improbable."

Silence. "I would truly like to know some way to discover if these abject signals are insulting, from a culture that has devolved so deeply that it thinks these are useful, or even amusing."

Bemor said, "Beings who can hurl huge masses to make messages would not be so. All our knowledge of cultural evolution, gathered in your archives, Unajiuhanah, says so."

"I would so believe," Unajiuhanah said simply.

"Or else . . ." Memor hesitated. "We are mistaken in our assumptions."

"Whatever can you mean?" Asenath said with a nasty rebuke-rustle.

"Suppose they are not sent to intersect us, or the star rammer." Memor envisioned the line of sight—Glory, the Bowl, and upon it the alien ship, orbiting above . . . and beyond, at an unknown distance, farther from Glory . . . "The Glorians may be transmitting to hail and instruct, and so to warn . . . the primate home world."

"But then—" Bemor hesitated. Fevered rattles came from his wing, a note of harried distress at what he glimpsed.

Imagination helps, Memor realized. The insight had come from her Undermind, direct and unsaid until now. . . . She felt a rumble of discontent from deep within her—of knowledge pent up, unexpressed, and so vagrant and wild. Fear surged in her, but she suppressed it, focused on the moment. She had been in a duel with Bemor here, and now there was a sally she could use, at last, an advantage coming from within, uninspected, yet sure, she felt, *sure*.

Memor said, not without some pleasure, "They are afraid not of us, but of the humans."

PART IV

SENDING SUPERMAN

Nothing fails like success, because we do not learn anything from it. The only thing we ever learn from is failure. Success only confirms our superstitions.
—KENNETH BOULDING

FIFTEEN

It was possible to exercise at Earth gravity on *SunSeeker,* just by jogging six-minute kilometers in the direction the deck was rotating. Beth sweated but didn't make that speed, running on the spongy turf and sucking down the chilly ship air that always seemed to taste faintly of oil. An hour into her slogging, choppy run she felt better in the odd way that returning to good gravs did—a sensation of solidity, of the body's chugging machinery settling back into its groove. If she ran fast in the same direction the deck rotated, she increased her speed of rotation, and so increased her weight. She reversed for her hard-pounding finish. Going fast against the rotation, she nearly floated like some sticky angel on air, her bare feet barely skimming the soft fabric. She sped around the outer habitat circumference in her shorts and sopping T-shirt and lurched into the showers, gasping and happy.

The shower next to her went on. She leaned around the corner and saw a finger snake wriggling in the spray.

"Phoshtha?"

"Hello, Beth. This device is delight." The thin, sliding voice somehow fit the dancing eyes.

"Yes, but do not use it too often. We can't recycle the water very fast." Beth stepped back in and turned the shower on, a giggle tickling her lips. The finger snakes had no sense of privacy.

She got herself in order, feeling much better. Exercise calmed, made her world brighter. Ready for Redwing. Maybe.

Ten minutes later she rapped on his door. He was wedged behind his desk, leaving her more room in the narrow captain's cabin. His wall display showed the slowly passing infinities of Bowl landscapes—at the moment, low mountain ranges in a low-grav region, with cottony cloud masses stacked above them. She had seen such clouds from below while swinging through the spindly trees on vines of thin, flexing strength. The clouds were nearly as tall as Earth's entire atmosphere, and from the ground looked like an ivory cliff that tapered away to a speck.

"Hope you're feeling better," Redwing, rising— unusual for him, indeed—to shake her hand. "Admirable performance down there. I'd like to get some background from you, away from the others."

"I think if we met as a group and—"

"A unit commander always reports first." Redwing's crusty face wrinkled into a grin, but she knew beneath the wry, leathery look he was absolutely serious.

"Oh." *Back in the navy we are, yessiree.*

"Before we get to specifics, bring you up to speed, I want to know what it was *like* down there."

She was prepared for this, because the shipboard crew all asked the same thing. They had spent months eating canned food and breathing desiccated air, gazing down at a whole vast *thing* gliding by, like having a terrific top view and no way out of your cramped apartment.

Still, she struggled to put the experience into words. Wonder, terror, hunger, spurts of fear, aching weariness fringed with a lacing anxiety that every time you closed your sticky eyes and fell into sweaty sleep, you could wake to find yourself about to die . . . "A tailored wilderness. For days you forget you're not on an alien planet but on the skin of a furiously rotating machine. The star is always there and after a while, even after you've learned to sleep in shade and heat, you hate it. Darkness—I can't tell you what a luxury it is to *turn out the light.* There's weather, for sure, lightning that seems to be sheeting yellow all around you, and the jet—like a golden snake twisting across the sky. Always on the run, looking to see if something's coming up on your tail to eat you, going for days without a bath, running without water even, feeling your steps get lighter because you've lost weight without even noticing it, hunger being sometimes the only thing you can think about—"

She made herself stop. With the crew she had been able to hold back but here, with Redwing, she couldn't . . . and realized that something in the smile, his head nodding as she spoke on and on, the eyes dancing with interest, had made it happen. *How did he do that?* Maybe it was something you had to learn, from commanding ships all over the solar system.

"I know some of that," he said, face now open and eyes far away. "You don't get to pick the nightmare that wakes you up at four A.M.—it comes looking for you, again and again."

This was a startling moment, taking her unaware. He was a man in a hard place to be, and she read in his gentle downturned smile a rueful regret that he could not possibly, as captain, go down there.

She made herself sit up straight, regain some composure. *Keep your smile in the upright and locked position.* "My mom used to say, a truly happy person is one who can enjoy the scenery on a detour."

He laughed, a hearty, full-throated roar in the metal echo chamber of his cabin. "Good one! Damn true, this whole thing is a detour."

This last sentence came out of nowhere, with baritone notes of regret. He sat back and took a moment to see the mountain range far below slide away on the wall, a huge glimmering eggshell blue sea lapping against the mountains' slate gray slopes along a narrow beach.

He knows how to pace this conversation, let it breathe.

He swiveled back to gaze at her with deep blue, penetrating eyes. "Tell me about . . . the food."

She held her breath for a long moment, comparing the bland, warm forgettable dishes she had wolfed down in ship's mess, realizing that while she ate eagerly it left no trace of memory. "I . . . there was something we could shoot out of the trees, when we were desperate. A fat primate thing, in the low-grav region. Stringy meat, yellow fat, looked like a big roasted monkey, but when you'd gone two days without anything but a kind of thick-leaved grass, it was . . . heavenly."

"Taste human?"

"How the hell would I know?" Then she saw he was grinning, and laughed. "Not that I would've cared."

"You could digest it?"

"Surprisingly, yes. Of course, we had all the biotech compatibility injections and a handful of pills. I had all of us start taking them as soon as the aliens—they call themselves the Folk, just like primitives on Earth—gave us food. We held out on our own rations for a while, then I had us cook the live game they gave us—"

"Live?"

"Yes. They were smart enough to let us prepare it our way, which they watched closely. We dispatched them with our lasers. Simmered some, with some herbs tossed in, it stayed down pretty well. But once, when we were hiding near somebody—some*thing*—searching for us in the tall tree region, we ate fish, raw. In fact, I had to be still and not give us away, afraid to get out my knife or laser, so I ate it while it was . . . alive."

"Not for long, I bet. Sashimi still moving."

"Unpleasant . . . for me and for the fish."

"You all lost weight."

"Even after eating yummy dried worms, very ripe, like sticky Jell-O. Live antlike things, as big as dogs in the low-grav zone. Crunchy embryos in the shell, tasted good but I felt horrid after it, dunno why. A fried scorpion-like thing, two tails. The head was bitter but I ate it anyway." She paused; it came back so easily. . . . "Trying to forget that one. Bizarre, memorable."

Redwing smiled fondly. "Hey, I ate haggis once in Edinburgh. So . . . uh, thanks."

She blinked. *Thanks for what?* Then she saw; the yucky food made him yearn to go down there a little less. And he had gotten her to unload some, too, get some of it behind her. A ship's captain is always about moving on.

"So I wondered—what kind of weaponry can they have down there? Gray goo bombs? Nerve flatteners? Old-style shaped charge with spinning flechettes?"

"I didn't really see weapons."

"Um. Cliff did—I'll get to that in a moment."

Cliff! The crew had been evasive about him and his team, but they did say the "Cliff team" seemed healthy and still free—quite a tribute, they said, considering. She had thought to shoot back, *Considering how we got snapped up right away?*—but didn't.

"Point is, what can we expect from them?"

"I think they want to control this, keep us around—preferably, in a nice, spacious prison like the low-grav one we were stuck in—while they figure out who we are, and if they can use us."

"Use us? For what?

"Maybe make their big whirling machine work better? New tech?—though it's hard to believe we could tell them anything. They built this—"

"You're sure?"

"Well, they run it, anyway. It must be really old. Maybe somebody else built it? The big one who interrogated us, Memor, was evasive on that."

He frowned. "Hiding something they don't want outsiders to know?"

"Yes, it's a puzzle. Or maybe a really ancient mystery. I wonder if even the Folk don't know where the Bowl really comes from. They do know the terrain, though. There are life-forms that dazzle any biologist, some I couldn't figure out at all. Cliff must be in heaven—he likes taxonomy. I filled up my digital photo files keeping track of the plants and weird animals. Some are bizarre, and others are kind of like Earthside, but changed. Larger, for one thing."

"Because the grav is less, point eight?"

She nodded. "That, yes. Could also be the island effect."

"Which is? . . ."

"We see it Earthside. Small islands have smaller animals. The last mammoths lived on Siberian islands, the smallest of their kind because the resource base is less."

"So . . . continents here are sure bigger. Some are larger than Earth. So are oceans—seas, I guess we should call them, they're shallow. I've studied them in close-up scan while you were down there."

Redwing brightened. Here was something he knew and Beth didn't. He flashed pictures on the wall and she realized he had cooked up a slide show. He went through it eagerly, describing how and where he had found the images. He and Karl had worked up a Bowl version of longitude and latitude. Numbers marked each slide.

"So much open territory! Forests as big as North America, not a town anywhere. But cities the size of countries back home—hell, bigger than our continents. I'd sure as hell like to know who made it, and how."

Beth nodded. It had been an impressive show. "The Folk may have built it, or know who did. They're unlike anything I've ever seen—think of elephant-sized, two feet and a heavy tail, big eyes and mouths—and feathers they flutter around all the time, like it's some kind of coded fan dance."

He grunted and frowned, which she took as encouragement. She knew she had to write a report, but telling it helped shape the story. Enthusiasm began to steal into her voice. "They examined Tananareve for long times in a big machine that seemed, she said, to read everything in her body. Plus her mind, somehow. She could feel tingling all over her, sensations like quiet little sparks, she said. There were plenty of other smart aliens around, most with handlike things that Earth never evolved—a sort of wriggly tentacle that split out into feelers, like you might see on an octopus that could make tools. They worked for the honcho—the big Folk creature in charge, named Memor.

Terrifying thing, when it loomed over you, huffing hot smelly air in your face. Memor was in charge, all right. Once I saw it—her, whatever—eat something that was still alive, a kind of crunchy armadillo the size of a pony. It bellowed as she chewed it up. Disgusting! But sights like that were just getting started—"

Redwing gave her a concerned look. "Um, if you could . . ."

"Sorry, once I get started—okay. It'll be in my report."

"Everything you recall. Anything could be vital; we just don't know enough."

Beth nodded. It had all come rushing out, the pent-up emotions and thoughts of months on the ground, every day tense and wearing. . . . She took a deep breath. "Anyway. This Memor seemed to *read* Tananareve and ask questions about how her mind worked, what she thought of, how it felt to think—odd stuff."

Redwing pursed his lips and looked down at the vast clouds coasting by far below. His wall screen amped the image to the max, so they both watched huge purple cloud-anvils towering over a seemingly endless sea. There were sand bars the size of the Rockies lounging in the sea's green shallows, like tan punctuation marks. Vegetation dotted them, and one dot she judged to be the size of Texas.

She had learned to let him have his silences, as he let her experience settle in with all the rest of what he knew. Beth sucked in the dry ship air and tried to recall the cloying thick, aromatic atmosphere they had wondered about, *alien air* they called it because of the syrupy way it filled your lungs with a heavy, cloying sweetness unlike any flower she had ever known. The smell was still on some of her carry-gear. Up here, in dry antiseptic rooms, she sniffed it and liked the aroma and body. Breathing it in, she felt something like nostalgia.

Redwing nodded as if making a decision. "You can review Cliff's messages—some text, some voice. Short, to the point. Don't be alarmed by them. He had not much time to report in. Reception is bad, we should have sent you down with more robust comm."

"Our good comm gear was in the landers."

"Of course. That's how the Folk found out our operating frequencies, broadband patterns, encryption. For the landers and for the hand comms, too, damn it. So he and you could get through only a short while, then the Folk autoscreens went up and it was all fuzz."

"Look, Cap'n, we had no way of knowing—"

"I should've been more cautious." He shook his head abruptly, face pinched. "I used the landing protocols we rehearsed Earthside—simple stuff for an uninhabited planet. No defensive measures. I went by rote, when I should have been wary of anything like this—an impossible machine churning through space, managing its own star to—"

He broke off, she saw, knowing he shouldn't vent his inner doubts to officers or crew. Yet it helped him, she was sure, and he needed it. A man like Redwing had spent his life wanting authority, getting some, then some more, all the time finding out how to make it work, how to move up a ladder everybody wanted to climb. Nobody had a captaincy forced on them. Nobody told them it meant keeping yourself to yourself for long years and decades and, for starships, the rest of your life.

He swiveled his chair away from the constant landscape sliding by and looked at her with an expression made rigid by force of will. "Cliff described a mass slaughter. He was hurt—not too bad, but he took days to even be able to call in. Wounds, fever, the cruds."

"We had the cruds a lot of the time," she said to be saying something, keep him from lapsing into a monologue again. *This captain needs help. But then we all do.*

"I got reports just this watch. From Cliff, pretty noisy. The Folk killed a whole damn city. Some kind of living blimp—he sent two pictures, hard to believe even then. And Howard . . . died."

"Oh no. He was—"

"Always thought he was a little too inquisitive, couldn't move fast—I down-wrote him in an operations report during crew training, but Command ignored me. He didn't come into a shelter fast enough, Cliff said. Got burned with a weapon tuned to our nervous system. Heats up the skin some, overloads the neurological system—fries it, really. Pain like he'd never felt before, Cliff said."

It was Beth's turn to look away. "We had it easy."

"But these 'ally aliens' as Cliff calls them, the Sil—they had scavenged around in the blimp thing.

Got some Folk comm gear they'd never seen before. Those Sil are smart. They got it running, broke the encryption barriers on the Folk message center, pried out all sorts of stuff they can use—and something bigger than that. Lots bigger, that we can use. The Folk had a message, just came in recently, the tags said—" Redwing leaned across the desk, laced his hands together on it, spoke directly at her. "—from Glory."

Beth had been in sympathetic mode, trying not to think about Cliff's wounds, Howard being fried, and all the rest—but this made her snap out of it. "Earthside never picked up a peep from Glory. No leakage, no ordinary surface EM traffic—"

"I know. This is plainly different, directed at Earth."

"How do you know?"

"Here." He thumped his desk, and the wall turned from sliding perspectives of a tan grassland swept by waves the size of continents—and became . . . a cartoon.

Line drawings, vibrant color. Purple background. Traceries of yellow on the edges, twisting like snakes. A strange red-skinned asymmetric being with what looked like three arms stood alone, facing the viewer. It began a rhythmic move, arms rotating in their sockets in big, broad sweeps—except the third, which somehow lashed up and down, then made a wide circular arc with a sharp snap at the end. *Athletics?* Beth thought. *Or some diplomatic pose? Ritual? Kabuki theater among the stars?*

The thing wore tight blue-green sheath-clothes that showed muscles everywhere, bulging and pulsing. The covering seemed sprayed on, showing a big cluster of tubular—genitalia? If so, male—not between the legs but above them, where a human's belly button would be. They, too, bulged as she watched.

The skintight covering ran all over the body, including the wide gripping feet. But the arms and its head were exposed; the head was triangular and oddly ribbed. Two large black eyes. No discernible nose, but three big holes in the middle of the face, echoing the face's triangle, with big hairy black coronas around each hole like a weird round mustache. A large mouth with two rows of evenly spaced gray teeth.

For a moment the viewpoint closed in on the head, which looked like an Egyptian pyramid upside down—ferocious, with mouth twisting, thin lips rippling with intricate fine muscles around the gray teeth, which kept clashing together. The front three teeth in both rows were pointed—evil-looking things—and the mouth had puffed-out lips to accommodate them.

"So far, just an introductory picture, looks like," Redwing said. "No sound. But then we get action."

Beth was still blinking in pure astonishment. Her father had centuries ago called this a *whatthehell moment*. . . . She had met uncountable aliens, fled from some, killed some, eaten many—but *this* . . .

The viewing angle expanded, and walking in from the right was a . . . human. Beth gasped.

The man wore a blue skintight suit with a red cape, big head, black hair—clearly a man, yes. Muscled, striding forward proudly—and the alien third arm struck out, caught the human in the face. A nasty slap. The man staggered back. The alien made a half turn and thrashed the man, slamming him away and then grabbing him by his right shoulder, twisting him into full view. There was a large red S on the man's deep blue chest.

"Superman!" Beth did not know whether to laugh or just gape. She did both.

The alien leaped, twisting in air, kicking Superman in the gut. He went down hard on the rocky ground. The graphics were good—Beth could see Superman's shock, surprise, pain. Dust puffed up where he fell. Vigorously the alien leaped high, paused while it made more mouth-gestures directly toward the viewer—and came down hard on top of Superman with obvious relish, slamming down with both big feet. Superman's mouth opened in shock and surprise, eyes bulging, showing white. The alien fanned its two arms, whipped the third one that seemed slim and sharp—and brought it down on Superman's head. The lash brought blood streaming from Superman's left ear and—incredibly, splashed big red gobbets on an imaginary window between the scene and the viewer. The blood ran down in rivulets while the alien raised all three arms into the air, head back.

The effect made Beth rock back, as if the blood had flown in her face. She gasped.

Prancing, whip arm twirling, the alien proceeded

to dance on Superman. It sent more kicks to the head and gut as the opportunity arose. The alien looked full at the viewer as it pranced, eyes even bigger. Its image swelled to fill the screen, and the eyes glowered at the viewer.

Stop.

A long silence.

"Pretty clear message, I'd say," Redwing clasped hands across his belt and leaned back in his flex chair.

Beth could not take her eyes from the alien head, its threatening expression frozen. "They eavesdropped on something, TV I guess, or . . ."

"And chose to send a message a child could understand: *Stay away.*"

SIXTEEN

Cliff had handed him a problem from hell. How to stop the Folk from killing a lot more of an alien species, to intervene with big things Redwing had never seen, minds unknown . . . or else do nothing. "Nothing" looked like the right answer, but he didn't have to like it.

He had the shipmind call up readings on this from the ancients available on the ship's database of all human cultures. These long-dead voices had never confronted any remotely similar problem, but came as close as humans could: Saint Augustine, Spinoza, Churchill, Lao Tzu, Kant, Aristotle, Niebuhr, Gandhi,

King, Singh. Interesting, thick reading—but it made him think about his life in perspective. Maybe he could use that if he survived this whole huge thing. But for now, alas . . . No help there.

The best solution was to get Cliff's team out of that place. Then the Folk would stop trying to capture or kill them. Bargaining could begin.

The brief comm burst Cliff had managed to get through to *SunSeeker,* fighting through the electromagnetic haze-screen the Folk had put up, gave the cartoon files and some optical spectral data that fit Glory exactly. No question where it came from.

It couldn't be a coincidence. The Glorians were sending the Bowl a threat. But it used imagery of Superman, of all things—an antique "superhero" (he had to look the term up) from the expansionist phase of the Anglo-Saxon era. Technically, of course, that era was not over. It had merged with the larger economic unification of Earthside. English was the obvious unifying language—larger, richer, with simple introductory grammar. Irregular verbs galore, of course, but by the time the interplanetary phase of economic expansion was well under way, there was no competition. Mandarin, Cantonese—they came from a productive society, as did Hindi—but nobody could write them well, and they didn't work simply with digital culture anyway. Plus the Chinese culture didn't have the flexibility of the Anglo structure. The other Asian cultures did a bit better, but English was as set into the world culture as the qwerty keyboard. History ruled.

So a comic book figure like Superman, his Pedia base said, fit with the modern social structure, too. Other archetypes like Dracula, Sherlock Holmes, Frankenstein had clear roles, but fit uncomfortably with the world culture. The other superheroes of the twencen were modeled on men like animals—bats, spiders, apes. Superman, tellingly, was an alien. Yet he fit into human society seamlessly.

Superman's key assumption was that his disguise was just to put on glasses and business clothes and be an everyman. Then nobody, even Lois Lane—a character that reminded Redwing of his ex-wife—could spot him. *Every man a Superman.* What could be more obvious? Do your job, toe the line, the daily grind—but all the time you are free to imagine yourself leaping over buildings, flying through the air, flattening the baddies. Maybe even getting a date with Lois.

Redwing shook his head. Cultures could best be understood in the rearview mirror. Superman might work among the multitudes of Earthside, but such guiding archetypes were not what you needed in deep space. The interplanetary culture spawned Smoke, Ellipso, Whitethighs, and others. Such larger-than-life figures helped cultures understand themselves, turn their lives into stories.

So . . . Here among the worlds and stars, *this* was a frontier. Earthside hadn't had one in centuries.

But the aliens spoke in that antique visual language. They must have used big antennas to pick up all sorts of popular media, broadcast over hundreds of years. Then, apparently, they finally saw the

Bowl headed toward them. So they sent a brush-off message, using the cartoons that swerved around language and slammed home the point. Aliens stomping on Superman, beating him up, kicks to his head and gut, the finishing glower straight into the viewer's face—classic, in its way. Any chimpanzee would get that right away. Even a smart one with a starship.

There were intelligent, technological Glorians who knew something about images with power—and they didn't want the Bowl to appear in their skies.

Well, who would? It had immense mass and its own star in tow. It couldn't approach a planetary system without scrambling up planetary orbits. Coming to call meant the bull comes into your china shop and is in no hurry to leave.

A warning was understandable. Threats, comic book or not, might work.

But . . . no curiosity? No desire to embrace the strange, the alien, the obviously huge technology the Bowl implied? What kind of aliens were these Glorians, anyway?

Beth had said shakily, "I need to think about this," and departed.

A sharp rap startled Redwing. He glanced at his desk, which pulsed with a reminder color.

Karl had knocked smartly on the door, right on time. Redwing got up and met him, shaking hands as he did sometimes with crew to show this conversation was more than ordinary. After all, the close quarters and endless waiting led, in classic fashion, to rumors, imaginary problems, and endless speculation.

"I carried forward those points you brought up," Karl began.

"You're done integrating the new crew?"

"Nearly. They're slow, dazed. Some sleep pods didn't work just right, it seems."

"Anything serious medically?"

"No, just slow recovery rates." Karl looked tired. Redwing knew that rumor-mongering went double for the newbies. Some of the freshly revived had the checked-my-actual-personality-at-the-door look of people absorbing and not able to react. It *was* a surprise, yes. Not Glory on the viewscreens, but an immense, whirling landscape. Redwing had decided to let them get into the work cycle, then get to know them, see what teams he could shape from them. Dealing with the Bowl to get what Redwing wanted was going to be a complex game.

They needed supplies of volatiles and fusion fuel catalysts, just to depart and head for Glory. That was only the beginning, though.

Best to get things back on firm ground. He leaned forward, hands clasped on the desk. "You and I need to have a clear understanding of how the dynamics of this Bowl and star system work. It may be the only leverage we have over the Folk."

"They've been running this place for a very long time," Karl said. "I doubt it has any vulnerabilities."

"Start with that jet. You'd think they'd have reached cruising speed and been able to shut off the plasma jet by now, but never mind that—"

"They can't!"

Redwing looked skeptical. He liked playing this role, letting crew "educate him" and tumble out their ideas. While a lower-rank officer dealing with the myriad specialists a ship needed, he had learned that you could get to the point much faster this way. These were tech types first and crew members a distant second. "Ummm . . . Maybe they can't."

Karl rose to the bait. "Look, a grad student can show that the Bowl isn't statically stable. I know, I checked with a shipmind nonlinear analysis, and I'm just an engineer."

"Why not?"

"The Bowl's not in orbit around the star. Turn off the jet, the star draws it in by gravity. It hits the star."

"So the jet has to stay on."

"This whole thing is dynamically stable, not static—same as we are when we walk. We take a step, fall forward, catch ourselves—only way to get anywhere."

"So what makes the whole star-and-Bowl scheme work?" Redwing had a hunch, but he liked to check it against somebody who really knew. It helped the intuition. Karl was just the type he needed.

"The jet comes off that glaring hot spot. The Bowl reflects a lot of the star's own sunlight on that spot, making the corona far hotter than you ever see on the surface of a star. Somehow—here's the real magic trick—the star's own magnetic field gets wound up in that spot. Notice the star's *spin-*

ning—so it generates magnetic fields deep in its core, a dynamo. That leaks out, forms the whole region dominated by the fields—the magnetosphere—and that hot spot draws field lines in, wraps them around the jet as it forms. Then the field takes off with the incredibly hot plasma, trapping that pressure in a wraparound like rubber bands—and it all escapes the star. The magnetic field lines wrap around the plasma like tight invisible fingers, squeeze it, make it spurt out. The jet carries forward, slim as you like, straight for the Knothole—and passes through. The jet thrust makes the whole damned thing move forward, star and Bowl and all."

"So?" Redwing knew he could appear incisive by just asking the obvious next question, interrupting the headlong spinning out of a whole complex story.

It worked. Karl blinked, seemed to come out of his techno-daze. "So . . . the magnetic fields hit the Bowl's fields—"

"What fields?"

"The Bowl's a huge conductor, spinning fast, with electrical currents running in it. It makes its own magnetic fields. I checked the lander data from when the teams went down. Strong fields, even at the top of that deep atmosphere. Keeps cosmic rays away, sure, but its real reason is—"

Karl blinked again and sensed he was going into lecture mode. Redwing just nodded. *Keep 'em anxious but focused,* his old cycle-ship commander had said. *They never really notice you're leading them.*

Karl slowed. "The Bowl mag fields, they catch

the fields from the jet. I've got plenty of mag-depth photos of this. The Bowl shapes the jet and binds to it, both. That links the Bowl to the star. Of course, gravity's making the Bowl want to fall toward the star—after all, it's not in orbit or anything, just spinning around. But it can't fall into the star—there's a sort of dance between them. The star's running away, thanks to the steady push it gets from the jet. So the Bowl is chasing it. To make the ride less bumpy, the system has those nice magnetic fields, acting like rubber bands you can't break. See, magnetic fields always form closed loops."

"Why?" Even Redwing knew this, but it was best to throw the occasional bone.

"Old Doc Maxwell. It's the law."

"So—"

Karl jumped right in, as Redwing had known he would. "The fields massage the Bowl, cushion minor excursions, smooth out the ride."

"So the Folk can't turn it off. Ever."

"Do that, the Bowl crashes. I estimate it'll take about a year to fall into the star. I'd love to see it—gotta be spectacular."

"But it can't happen. Because of the jet. So—how do we screw around with it?"

Karl blinked yet again, twice. "But . . . why . . ."

"We have people down there. Must be billions of smart aliens on the Bowl, too. We have to make a deal to get our people back. To get on to Glory."

Karl looked at the Bowl view sliding by on the wall—forestland now, dotted with twinkling small seas, whitecaps outlining some where a strong wind blew down from somber gray mountains. "They've been safe for millions of years. Longer."

"How long?"

"I don't know. But to make something like this— you have to have some large-scale ambition in mind."

Redwing looked skeptical. "Touring the galaxy?"

"While you get a permanent suntan, yes." Karl grinned. "And never get cold."

Redwing nodded. "Never get cold—maybe a motive? Not just a small thing like going interstellar, but never leaving your home?"

Karl thought awhile and Redwing let him. When Karl spoke, it was a whisper. "Taking a whole culture, a world, so many species . . . on a ride that could last forever. Not just colonizing some planet. An eternal voyage. That's got to be it."

Redwing shrugged. "Over millions of years, your own species has got to change—maybe go extinct."

"The whole thing will go unstable if you don't have somebody to do the tweaks, keep watch, fix accidents."

"For sure. Then there's cultural change. But you can't let the society decide the whole Bowl experiment is a bad idea. Then you die!"

Karl hadn't thought this way. *Engineers don't,* he mused, and then recalled that his three degrees were in electrical, mechanical, and astroengineering. *Okay, usually.* "Look, Karl. A few hundred years ago, we called people savages because they pierced their ears, ballooned their lips, wore trinkets in their nose, cut their hair so it looked wild or had no hair at all. They did weird stuff, had strange noisy dances and rites, and tattooed their bodies. Then, when I was growing up, everybody called that stuff hip and fashionable."

"Uh, so?"

The lands below were back to mountains and seas—beautiful expanses, larger than the whole Earth–Moon system. Redwing never tired of it all. . . . "We can take cultural change, even stuff that comes back from our ancestors and looks odd. But we're expanding, moving out into the stars."

"Well, sure."

"And so are the Folk. I guess they can take tattoos. It's fashion, which means it's over by the time people like us even hear about it. But I doubt they can take big new religions or political mobs that want to, say, take over piloting this contraption. They can't allow that."

Karl got it. He nodded eagerly. "And we thought we knew what conservative meant."

"They can't risk the wrong kind of change. And that's exactly what we new-kid-on-the-block humans represent."

PART V

MIRROR FLOWERS

A man who carries a cat by the tail learns something
he can learn in no other way.
—MARK TWAIN

SEVENTEEN

Cliff and his party followed Quert at an easy, loping pace. The lower gravity made long strides easy, but the humans could not match the ease of the Sil's fluid grace. There was no ground transport except the Sil city subway, but that had been damaged, too. Quert said it was intermittent and unreliable, "Smoke go in there. And . . . some say . . . be worse things."

They made their way beyond the ruined Sil city and broke into open woodlands. It was a relief to suck in soft, moist air and just *move, escape*. No one looked back.

They paused on a short hill and Cliff could not resist a last perspective on the blasted landscape. Its once-proud ramparts and arches, its residential precincts, its lofty spires of what might have been elegant churches—all burned or hammered down to rubble. The Folk had no mercy. Yet he could see rising from rubble the tan buildings they had watched self-forming with a quiet, eternal energy. Seen at a distance, the fresh shoots of new life moved like stop-motion videos, eager plants rising to begin anew a city that surely, in the immense history of the Bowl, had been rebuilt myriad times. Cliff sighed and clasped Irma to his side. "It's coming back. Slow but steady."

"This place was made to replace itself. A technology that *counts* on having to regenerate. I wonder what it runs on."

"Solar energy, reprocessed waste—did you see that molecular printer Quert used to make us your new carry-pack?"

She nodded and shrugged the new pack, easing the straps. "Great, some kind of light composite stuff. Made a molecule at a time, Quert said. It's built exactly like the old busted one. Minus the broken frame, from when I fell down."

Cliff shrugged. "If you hadn't been down, that flame beam would've burned you."

"Yeah, lucky break." She puffed her overhanging hair back from her eyes, a classic gesture of bemused frustration. "Dumb luck. Poor old Howard ran out of luck."

"Damn shame. He was always getting hurt, breaking something, even getting lost to go pee."

"Some people are like that. Crew selection was by Fleet merits, y'know—not backpack experience. Résumés don't account for plain old bad luck that keeps coming back."

"Sure 'nuff—a big mistake. Next starship I'm on, I'll remember that."

She laughed and punched him in the arm, which drew sidelong glances from Terry and Aybe. Even Quert noticed. *Well, let 'em,* Cliff thought. *Not like it's been a lot of fun lately.*

Then they pressed on, turning their backs on the burgeoning city that would live again.

Quert led the way, with other Sil flanking them. They all carried weapons, long slim tube launchers. Their faces were grim, focused, and they did not seem to tire.

Relentless sunlight streamed down through the symphonic play of ivory clouds. Tall and cottony, they were so vast that parts of them were laced through with blue tinges of moist anvils. Clouds as anthologies: the anvils hanging in the soft mist of larger puffballs, lightning sheeting across denser, purple knots, all of it like separate cities of the sky, tapering away into the far heights. Here and there clots condensed out, their understories fading into rainfalls—sheets of pale blue falling great distances, then absorbed back into the air before ever striking the Bowl.

Cliff said to Irma and Aybe, "Relax into tourist mode," and they all chuckled, not because it was funny but because everyone needed an excuse to smile. They came into a flash of green, almost pornographically abundant in the smoky, almost rotting aroma of turned black earth, rains sweating down from passing squalls, air thickened with rich purpose. A vehicle purred past and from its big tail-pipe a lush pale blue cloud gushed. Irma drew in a breath of it and said, "You can almost smell dinosaurs in that. It smells like a fossil fuel."

Aybe sniffed. "Probably ethanol, but it sure smells rich."

None of them had actually ever smelled the

exhaust of a true oil burner, on an Earthside that was scrupulous about emissions. Only jet airplanes using turbines rated fossil fuel use, back when *Sun-Seeker* left the solar system. Cliff wondered if by now Earthside biotech had engineered anything like the skyfish here, living beasts that could float and fight.

He doubted it. What biological substrate could they start with to develop such bizarre forms? That made him consider how the Folk had ever engineered their skyfish. From some airborne floaters, found on some planet where thick air and light gravity made that an optimal path? Big, slow, made invulnerable by its size, like elephants or whales or a brontosaurus? *This place is like a museum of other life-forms,* he thought, *but one that keeps evolving. Maybe that was part of the point of building the Bowl itself? An ongoing, moving experiment with more room than a million planets?*

They entered a broad plain of short grass, and there was a trampled, much-traveled track stretching into the hazy distance. Straight up in the air, though, momentary openings between the towering clouds gave a dim vision of the Bowl hanging in a pale eggshell blue sky. Cliff watched the watery vision of huge lands shimmer, a vision from all the way across this solar system. *Only it's not any solar system we ever envisioned,* he thought. *More like a huge contraption made of a system's parts.* Back on *SunSeeker* before they came down, Fred the engineer type had estimated the Bowl's mass, and got more than Jupiter, more probably than there was in the Kuiper belt or the Oort cloud. Somebody had scavenged an entire expanse of space, maybe all the worlds that circled Wickramsingh's Star, to make this thing.

Along the trampled path, occasional Sil held out strings of fish, stringy rootlike vegetables, a gauzy plant like a haze of wire. He realized these were for sale, but of course, the humans had nothing like Sil cash. Passing these hawkers, making poor imitations of the Sil *no no no* eye-gestures, they went by. Here and there a Sil stepped forward, lowered its head, and held goods up, waving them toward the humans—an offering. This struck Irma as an eye-widening surprise. Cliff knew enough to take some food, with eye-moves of thanks, and then wondered how to cook the food that began accumulating. All this occurred silently, for the Sil seemed to relish a gentle, still presence. It was usually hard to get them to talk at all, and when they did, they were terse.

Across the plain came small, darting vehicles sheathed in shiny silver metal. Some moved toward the humans, though most went their own way. A knot of about a dozen Sil cars eased up in the purring machines and shut them down. With proper greetings they got out to address Quert. They had a conversation taking at least twenty minutes.

That was long enough for the humans to sit near the cars and find out which of the gift foods they could eat raw. "Hand meal" the Sil called this. Sil talked while they ate. When Irma asked about that, Quert had consulted an electronic aid he sometimes used to translate, and said, "Sportive verse." This apparently meant creating poetry, a ritual perhaps parallel to humans drinking alcohol and singing together.

They were hungry. There was a pleasant nutty spiral fruit that left a peppery taste. They ate it all and had moved on to a nearly rhomboid-shaped bittersweet fruit. Quert and three other Sil came over to the humans, doing the head-moves and eye-signals that always came before an important discussion. Cliff reflected on how much they had learned about Sil culture by simply watching their social cadences. Humans talked all the time, Quert had noted with genuine wonder, as though that were uncommon on the Bowl.

Quert said, "They gift movers to us."

"We are gift happy," Irma said, smiling and nodding. She was better at ferreting out the meanings of the clipped Sil sentences and echoing their manner. She kept track of the myriad eye- and head-gestures and tried to imitate them, though not always with much success. There had been some amusing errors, such as when she had inadvertently asked Quert if sex was part of their diet, or where the beds were to be, and then walked into the rather primitive male toilets. She could not then tell male from female Sil and had to be told, with furious elbow signals.

The small, squat vehicles were actually simple to drive. They used hands and feet, just as Earthside cars did, and ran on an auto-gear system with adjustable constraints, mostly apparently magnetic. Indeed, its propulsion seemed magnetic, but it never rose more than a meter above the broad plain. Everything here, even the homes, seemed powered by electromagnetic induction, through the Bowl's substructure. There were solar collectors everywhere, befitting a land where the sun always shone, and the self-shaping buildings were driven that way, too. Cliff could tell by the occasional tingling of electrical discharge that ran over his skin when he stood near the walls, as they surged up and formed elegant cusps and arches.

Quert showed Cliff how to drive the magcar, seeming to insist it was a guest's privilege. That let him take the little thing out onto the broad plain, Quert in the copilot seat, and Irma and Aybe in the rather cramped rear seats. Their backpacks and gear went in racks on the roof, secured by a curious self-wrapping lattice that figured out its own way to secure the arrangement, tripped by a tiny tapping from Quert.

They headed on toward distant mountains, cloud-shrouded and mysterious. Quert then went into comm mode, using the inbuilt dash system to get in touch with other Sil, using a system Quert said the Folk could not intercept. Quert apparently had embedded acoustic receivers, for it peered ahead intently and subvocalized, face giving nothing away. Irma sat in the back, and the others were in another car, following close on the right side. Cliff took the odd magcar up to its highest speed as other car traffic thinned out. They were moving away from the Sil concentrations, but Cliff had no idea of their destination.

He did not notice nearby cars or anyone following until abruptly one drew up alongside them. It
deftly came in and blocked them from the other human car. The two Sil inside did not look at him, but
they matched exactly his velocity. Then the magcar
started coming in closer. He thought nothing of it
until they were only a car-length away. He slowed.
They slowed. He sped up. So did they. Another
magcar came in from his left, moving fast. Its driver
also didn't even seem to notice the three cars moving now together. They all peered straight ahead.
Maybe they're a guard party? he wondered.

Closer, closer . . . Cliff had time to say, "Quert—
Quert?" interrupting the alien's concentration, its
eyes slowly coming fully open, as if it had been in a
trance. "I think something's—"

A third car came over fast from the left, slightly
ahead. It slewed hard and set itself up exactly in
front of their car.

Irma said, "Are these—?"

The lead car slowed, its big tail signal sliding in
ruby red pulses across the back. Cliff had to step on
the mag brakes, and the car hummed loudly. He tried
to maneuver to the left, then right, but there was no
room now, and then the car ahead braked harder.

Cliff slammed on the brakes. The three that had
boxed him in hit theirs a few seconds later. The
brake howl was a high *skkkrrreeeee,* all of them
losing speed as fast as they could. The cars were
identical, so they hardly separated at all as the
howling deceleration threw Cliff forward. They all
wore odd net belts that stopped Cliff from being

heaved onto the windshield. His few seconds' lead
in decelerating meant he was now about ten meters behind them all as they slid to a stop, throwing
gray dust and the humming loud and shrill.

Irma was saying something and Quert, too, but
Cliff focused on the six Sil who jumped out of the
magcars. They called short crisp orders to each
other and reached into their workbelts. *Going for
weapons,* Cliff thought. *Not guards.*

The Sil ran around their cars and formed an orderly bunch, intent on Cliff's car, shouting now.
Quert gave its gravel growl and took off its web-
belt. Irma gave an alarmed cry.

The only weapon we have, we're inside.

Cliff saw what he must do. He slammed on the
acceleration and shot forward. The car shook as he
hit the Sil. Impact scattered them across the blunt
shiny hood. Bodies struck their windshield and
rolled up it, tumbling over the roof—dull thumps—
and Cliff kept his foot on the accelerator until just
before they hit the forward car.

They slammed in hard and the magnetic bumper
pushed them back, lessening the impact. Their magcar's hood crumpled. Alarms blared an odd hooting
call in Cliff's ears. Quert cried out in surprise and
Irma went silent.

"Okay?" Cliff said, surprised at how mildly he
said it. "Irma? Quert?"

"O-okay," Irma said. Coughed, gasped. Aybe
said, "What the—?"

Quert caught Cliff's eye and gave the assent signal. Its mouth sagged open.

He had scooped up all the Sil. Some had rolled off to the side and others over the cabin. They had all absorbed the full hard impact of the car, giving off sharp, surprised cries. He watched where they had hit the plain. None bounced back up.

They wanted to grab us, maybe kill us. No negotiation. Went for their weapons.

Some of them had gotten their odd little guns free and lay stretched out, guns in hand but arms not moving.

Cliff backed out, turning to his left so the car glided over the bodies on that side. They crunched beneath the magcar. He got ten meters behind the bodies and shifted. He moved forward very deliberately and ran over the ones sprawled on the right. Moving fast, he slewed to ride over the two in front. Each body nudged the car up, no more, but that brought the full pressure of the magcar down on them.

He knew the bumps meant smashed bones, organs, spurting gouts of fluids lost into the soil. Agony, screams, the light fading behind terrified eyes.

None of them moved as Cliff then backed all the way out and drove around the whole mess. No point in checking to see if anyone survived.

Irma said, "The other car's gotten free, too. Looks like they have a Sil driving."

"My mate," Quert said quietly. "She fine. Drive hard." Cliff glanced at the alien, who seemed as quiet and calm as ever.

Terry was in the other car and waved at them, holding thumbs-up. "They must've done something similar," Aybe said quietly. "Wasn't watching . . ."

Cliff amped the acceleration and had them up to max speed by the time the cars and bodies were just a dot in his side rearview screen. He was surprised that he did not need to think much at all about what had happened. The three-car team had tried to grab those he cared about and were willing to use force to do it. That meant they had crossed a line.

Cliff had spent endless days stacking and processing bodies, and now knew he was not the same man. He had done what he had to and had not taken any time to think it through. Before he came down to the Bowl, he had been another sort of man entirely. This place had taught him a lot, and most of it he could not say but perhaps comprehended it better that way. It was in his nervous system now, experience digested and made part of himself.

Maybe that was what Quert had. Indeed, maybe the Sil had it without having to learn. In the silence of the magcar he felt himself relax. The mountains ahead loomed large now beneath their mantle of anvil clouds, bellies ripe with purple richness, ready to rain as they climbed the slopes. Already he looked forward to that. He would get out of the car and let the falling big drops hammer him with their wealth and feel each moment for what it was, for the joy of it entire.

"Those wanted capture," Quert said.

"I figured that," Irma said. "Killing us is easier."

"Our chances would be not good in their tender care," Cliff said.

"Give us to the Folk, show loyalty." Quert made a head-shrug.

"So . . . you killed them," Irma said.

Cliff nodded. "Probably so."

Irma let that ride and then said, "They would have gotten in their cars and come after us."

Cliff thought that was obvious and kept his attention on their rearviews and the mountains ahead. No visible pursuit. He reminded himself that attack could easily come from above. A skyfish could be hovering a kilometer up and—he glanced out the window—not obvious until it was too late. *Worrying isn't thinking,* he thought, using a saying he had honed in the long, unending days of pursuit when they were first on the run across the Bowl. Perpetual alert could degenerate into a floating anxiety that robbed the mind of concentration, sent it skittering into pointless knots. Not returning to the same damn subject was a learned skill, he saw.

"Where do we go now?" he said directly to Quert.

"Into cold."

EIGHTEEN

They went under the mountains, not up them.

Before entering the underground maze, Cliff looked down through a short pass at the lands beyond the lofty mountains. Beyond lay the first mirror zone he had ever seen. Big hexagonal patterns gave some sparkling side-scatter of sunlight. They filled a valley and dotted the hills above. Lush vegetation filled the spaces between, but clearly most of the sunlight reflected back at the star. This was how the Bowl fueled the jet that boiled up from the hot arc light inferno at the center of the stellar disk. Expanses of mirrors, incomprehensible in scale, focused on the central fury. Somehow, the *SunSeeker* engineers said, magnetic fields got drawn into the perpetual hellhole. These fed outward with the jet as it escaped the focal point. The brilliant plasma billowed out at its base, and then the magnetic fields gripping it in rubbery embrace disciplined the flow, narrowing it. By the time the luminous jet reached the Bowl's Knothole, it passed through easily without brushing the heavily armored walls.

As he watched the enormous sheets of reflecting metal in the distance, Cliff mused that this was how the star provided its own thrust, from sunlight that first bounced off the hexagonal mirrors, returned to its parent source, and propelled the jet. *Riding on light,* he thought, and held his phone up to the star itself, letting the device consider it. In a moment, the back panel said

K2 STAR. SIMILAR TO EPSILON ERIDANI (K2 V). INTERMEDIATE IN SIZE BETWEEN RED M-TYPE MAIN-SEQUENCE STARS AND YELLOW G-TYPE MAIN-SEQUENCE STARS.

Yet he recalled the watch officer who revived him had said it was an F star. It had turned out later that the spectrograph was saturated by the hot spot glare, and got its signatures wrong. Classic field error.

And indeed the star seen through the phone's polarizer was a troubled disk, speckled by dark blots that circled the base where the jet blossomed. The whole star rotated around the jet base, which meant the builders had started their mammoth final touch there, perching the Bowl as a cup high above the original star's pole. Fascinating to consider—

"Come!" Cliff noticed Quert glance back at him with irritation, eyes jouncing in the Sil way. He rushed to catch up with the others.

Their party neared the underground labyrinth and found they were not alone. There were zigzag trees in dense blue green forests near the entrance. Sil moved under the canopy, bands trotting with deft speed. They kept to well-defined bunches, entering the weaving corridors under the stony flanks. The corridor's external locks yawned. Even in the rock hallways, yellow orange plants hung, emitting light to guide the constant line of Sils and humans. The Sil barely glanced at the humans. Quert and mate moved together in the swift shuffle Sil used, like loping in light gravity, as easy as swimming in air. All in silence.

Cliff saw as they fled that many Sils had small, betraying injuries. Parts missing—splayed knobby fingers with one gone, just a blank space of gnarled red skin. A conical Sil ear half sheared away. Marvelous purple-irised eyes clouded by some past collision with life. Mottled skin; scars adorning slim legs, feet, inflamed two-step joints that served as elbows in their arms; faces sporting red scars that wrapped around as though some enemy had used a curved blade. Cliff felt oddly embarrassed at the humans' smooth clear skins, unmarked by a life of labor and hardship, or battle and disaster. Without even thinking about it, the humans paraded around with skins and sturdy limbs that spoke of city comforts, the easy life away from fear and pain, a softness not earned.

The unseen Sil damage was perhaps more lasting.

He watched Irma as they sped down internal corridors of the Bowl, following Quert and its team along the gradual downward slope. She was changed, subdued and reflective. Her eyes peered ahead but were focused on some internal scene. He recognized the symptoms because he had known them, back there amid the wholesale slaughter of the Sil. She had announced his own blunted responses to him, using her jargon—diminished affect, emotional isolation, a thousand-meter stare, a general emotional numbness, stress disorder.

Now it visited her. Maybe Howard's death had done it, tipped her over the edge. Or the fast way Cliff had crushed the Sil who wanted to grab them.

He thought of this as they kept their steady pace, moving away from the big thick doors of what seemed to be the occasional air lock. Since he and Irma started having sex—neither of them called it love-making, and in a fundamental way, it wasn't—they had drawn closer. The other team members had seen that, and aside from a few wry references, nobody said much about it, or seemed to let it irk them. They were a field team, not a social circle. Howard's death had made that clear enough.

He watched Irma's concentrated expression, ever alert to what lay ahead, but clearly introspective. He cared about her now and had to understand what she was going through. They had lost Howard in a way nobody saw coming, and for Cliff there were no afterthoughts, because he knew he could have done nothing different. In the sudden deadly moments, everyone was truly on their own.

Maybe Irma didn't see that yet. *Something would have broken her sooner or later. She would have come up against some hammering event that changed how she saw the world. If she had stayed Earthside, she might have gone into late old age before it happened. The ones with no give, the ones with the carefully guarded, clear-skinned little porcelain selves, shatter in the end. Some chips and splinters get lost, so that when mended, little fracture lines show. Nobody gets through life immune to the hard collisions. The blackness always follows a step or two behind you, hand raised to touch you on the shoulder. That tap, when it comes, shakes you and hastens your step. When the indifferent world breaks your illusions, that shattering takes something out of your own inner cosmos. Something dies within. Irma will never fit together quite so well again. Neither will I, of course.*

They came through another of the bulky air locks, and when the intermediate chamber closed, Cliff saw that their escort Sil were the only ones left with the four humans. The fleeing Sil had gone elsewhere.

At the other side, the cool, clammy corridor

sloped steeper still, and now they passed into a different kind of passageway. The flooring became transparent and then the walls. The orange glow of luminous plants dimmed because there were few of them on the ceiling. Through the floor he could see nothing but black and then abruptly, as they passed a ribbed steel seam—stars. Wheeling slowly across their view through walls and floor, red and blue and yellow.

"Ah!" Aybe said. Irma sighed. Quert made the gesture of approval and eye-bulge.

"We're on the outside of the Bowl," Cliff said needlessly, hearing the joy in his voice at the same moment he noticed the air before him fog with his breath.

The wheeling sky lit a twilight world.

They all stood and took it in. The whispering drone of the airflow masked any sounds that might come from the outside world. They stood on a pathway looking up at the Bowl skin, visible in starlight through cylindrical walls transparent in all directions. Their passage stretched into the distance, below a flat plane above them that even looked cold, a land showing silver ice and black ribbed lines that marched away like longitudes and latitudes.

"Ice and iron," Irma said.

Between the black support struts was a rumpled terrain of dirty ice. The stars moved in lazy arcs above. A few craters pocked the ice, broken by strands of black rock and—

Glimmers on the plain. Cliff turned and looked behind them, where the long shadows of a quick dawn stretched. And sharp diamonds sparkled white and hard.

"Reading 152 K in starlight from that surface," Aybe said, peering at his all-purpose detector/phone/computer.

"Nearly as cold as the Oort cloud," Terry said. "But why is there a tube to take people—well, Sil—up above the Bowl skin?"

Quert said nothing.

Irma pointed to bright points of light winking on and, after a few seconds, off. "It's always dark here, just starlight. Maybe that's mica reflecting from rock?"

"Too bright," Terry said.

A flash came from nearby. They turned and looked at a pinnacle that forked up from the silvery plain below. "A . . . flower," Terry whispered.

Fronds spread up from a gnarled base, which itself sat firmly on the icy crust. Light green leaves speared up, tilted toward them. "A paraboloid plant," Aybe said.

The thing was at least five meters long and curved upward to shape a graceful cup made of glossy, polished segments. The plant turned steadily as they watched, and as the direct focus of it swept over them, the reflected beam was like a blue-tinged spotlight.

Irma looked over her shoulder and said, "It's tracking that big blue star."

The plant turned steadily away and Aybe said, "Look down at the focus point." Where the glassy frond skins narrowed down, they became translucent, tight, and stretched. The starlight collected all along the parabolic curve, about a meter on a side.

Cliff close-upped it in his binocs and made out an intricate tan-colored pattern of lacy veins. "Chloroplasts working in this cold? Impossible."

"It's not so cold at the focus, I bet. That's the point of concentrating starlight," Irma said. She gestured at the horizon, which seemed sharp even though it must have been thousands of kilometers away. "A whole damn biosphere in vacuum."

"Running on just starshine?" Terry asked. "Not much energy there."

"So this plant evolved to work like an antenna," Aybe said. "They live here, hanging upside down on the outer edge of the Bowl."

"Where did a star flower evolve?" Irma asked wistfully. They saw now the thick dark stalk that supported and held the flower, swiveling it as the Bowl's fast rotation swept stars across the sky. "To track starlight and digest it."

Aybe snorted. "Life evolving in vacuum?"

Cliff noticed that Quert was letting them work through this.

"Doing its chemistry by . . . starlight?" Disbelief made Aybe grimace. "How's that happen?"

"Folk bring," Quert said.

"From were?" Terry asked. "Why?"

Quert paused and struggled with the language problem, eyes jittery and trying to convey nuances, Cliff thought, that were simply beyond human capacities. "Light life we term them. Here when we came. Learned to get out . . . live from ice . . . find star."

Irma said, "Maybe they started in a warm core of an asteroid? Or iceteriod? Got to the surface and used sunlight? Far out from its star, maybe no star at all nearby. Survived. Made leaves to be sunlight concentrators. So then parabola flowers just evolved, out in the dark."

"Long time," Quert said.

Irma shrugged. "Maybe a long way from a star, too. So the Bowl comes by, grabs some? But . . . why?"

Cliff watched across the flat plain and, yes, glimmers came from everywhere as—he glanced back—stars rose and the light-seeking flowers tracked them. Or one of them. The slow steady sway of the focusing plants swept the sky, selected the brightest, fixed on it. The big flowers locked on a bright blue-white star. *Light vampires,* Cliff thought.

He judged the humans and Sil stood perhaps a kilometer or two above the Bowl's outer shell, looking down at a wonderland of deep cold night. Yet it lived. He watched a forest of strange, attentive life-forms that tracked across the moving sky, clinging to the outer skin of this whirling top. All this cold empire—stretching far away, perhaps around the entire Bowl—worked on, as it moved through starfields and brought heat to kindle their own chemistry. An entire vast ecology lurked here. *Sun-Seeker* had flown by it and seen none of this, Cliff recalled. The whole Bowl was so striking, nobody registered details. They had taken the huge ribbed outer structures to be the mechanical substructure it seemed. Nobody noticed icefields or plants; they were on too small a scale.

He close-upped some of the points of light and saw shiny emerald sheets moving all together, following the brightest star visible. They never saw the star that drove the Bowl, of course, only the eternal spinning night. There were translucent football cores at their central focus. In a nearby parabolic flower, he could make out how the filmy football frothed with activity at the focus—bubbles streaming, glinting flashes tracing out veins of flowing fluids. Momentary Earthly levels of warmth and chemistry, from hard bright dots that crept across a cold black sky. Flowers rooted in ice, hanging under the centrifugal grav. Driven by evolution that didn't mind operating without an atmosphere, in deep cold and somber dark. Always, everywhere, evolution never slept.

Irma said as they moved along the transparent tube corridor, "Y'know, we've found piezophiles that thrive under extreme ocean pressure, and halophiles grow in high salt concentrations. This isn't all that much stranger."

Aybe said, "I wonder if they cover the whole outer surface. They could be the most common form of life in the Bowl."

Terry pointed. "Maybe even more than we thought."

They gaped. Terry said, "Like a . . . cobweb. Stretching up." The thing hung on several stringy tendons that sprouted from an icefield in the distance. Their eyes had adjusted so even in starlight they could make out five sturdy arms of interlaced strands. It climbed away from the Bowl and into the inky sky, and all across it were more of the flowers, their heads slowly turning to track the brightest blue-white point of light above. It narrowed as it extended and cross struts met branches to frame the huge array of emerald flowers. These were larger than the ones on the ground. The colossal tree tapered as it reached out.

"A cold ecology," Terry said. "The flip side of the Bowl's constant sunlight. A steady night."

Irma asked Quert, "Why do the Folk need this?"

"Soft fur, sharp claws. Same animal."

This seemed enigmatic to Cliff, so he said, "They get something from it—what?"

"Their past." Quert's slim face struggled for the right translation. In the dim starlight, the alien face showed its seams, its lines drawn by tragedy. He reached for his mate, a willowy Sil who seldom uttered a word, but whose eyes slid and danced expressively. She clasped Quert to her, they embraced, and there was much eye movement between them. Apparently such signals were more intimate and effective among Sil—and certainly so, compared to the talky humans.

Cliff had learned to look away at such moments; Sil had a different code for privacy and display, and apparently did not mind expressing emotional intimacy in view of others. Cliff was not used to it, and wondered if he ever would be. Quert turned from its mate and nodded toward the cold fields of paraboloid flowers. "Soft fur of Folk."

Quert turned back to the humans and visibly made itself stand firmly, looking at them all. Speaking slowly, to let its inboard translation training give it the human words, Quert said, "The plants are always here. Stars power them. They store. Always Bowl skin is cold. This be—" Quert gave a sweeping gesture, eye-moves, and said in a whispery tone, "sacred memory."

Irma said, "You mean their . . . data store?"

"History," Quert said. "Big history. Sil want to read it. You can help?"

PART VI

THE DEEP

The Mind, that Ocean where each kind
Does streight its own resemblance find;
Yet it creates, transcending these,
Far other Worlds, and other Seas.
—ANDREW MARVELL

NINETEEN

As soon as Memor sat down, she noted that the Late Invader Tananareve was carefully watching the bulk of Contriver Bemor settle into place. Bulging eyes, lips tight-pressed and white, body tensed as if ready to flee—Tananareve showed the classic primate fear signals.

Fair enough; being the smallest creature in the ample cavern, more slight even than Serf-Ones, must draw up primordial dreads of being trampled. Memor tossed Tananareve some glossy sweatfruit to ease her trembling. She took it, bit, considered the taste. Gave a small smile. No sign of gratitude, however.

Intelligence generally emerged on worlds only after earlier forms exploited the advantages of being large, slow, and stupid. Size was a ready defense inspiring no selection pressure toward more complex neuro systems and forward-seeing capability. Indeed, Memor had learned about such creatures as Tananareve in her study immersions. They were among the class that built models of their external world, all the better to predict where food might lie, or what predators would do, and still later, what others of their kind would think of them. Somewhere along that axis of change their internal models learned that other creatures also had models running behind their anxious eyes. Thus emerged advanced societies.

"We merely wish to question you about aspects of your species," Memor said as a preliminary.

"That last session—where you 'slapped' me with that pain gun? Was that asking questions?"

"You understand, we were developing—quite successfully, I must remark—a tool to use in making contact with the others of your kind."

"They're still alive?" The primate seemed to honestly doubt.

"Of course. They are taking their pleasure with travel about our vast lands."

"You haven't caught them, have you?"

One of Tananareve's least attractive qualities, as a medium-level intelligence, was her way of leaping ahead in a discussion.

"We have not exerted sufficient effort to capture them, if that is what you mean. They did elude us at the very moment we took custody of you Late Visitors. We decided to let them remain at large, as experience of our wonders is the best lesson we can give."

"Do you understand our word 'smug'?"

"I do. Our reading of your entire dictionary— both active that you use, and passive that you merely recognize—shows you have levels of nuance."

Memor had meant this as a compliment, but Tananareve gave a dry little cackle that meant derision.

"I think you should consider our relative status before invoking your 'smug' word."

"Ummm. Smug is as smug does."

This elliptical remark brought a dismissive rumble from Bemor. Memor's twin, though still held at the male First Life, let his words sprawl forward, languid, as if he wished the small audience to savor them. "We desire your counsel, little smart monkey. Your fellows have done harm to several castes, from Serf Prime to even a few at the lower rungs of the Folk. All this—" Abruptly Bemor belched out a bass snarl. "—because they would not submit to diplomatic engagements."

Tananareve laughed again. "Loud bluster is still just bluster."

Memor admired how Bemor did not allow emotion to flare further in his speech. This was evidence of an Undermind fully and well integrated, unlike the turmoil Memor felt bubbling up from her own. His voice and feather display suddenly smoothed, becoming a cool refrain. "I wish you all now to focus upon our slow, steady response to the Glorian crisis. This goal we have long sought, for it is the plentiful world long observed but never understood—and so we pursue it."

"Because we seek the origin of the gravitational messages," Asenath interjected. "And now, the electromagnetic sendings from Glory are so simple, we can at least decipher those. Yet they do not speak to us."

Bemor allowed this interruption, though only marginally within conversation protocols, and gave a feather-rush of agreement. "Indeed. As we approach, suddenly these Late Invaders appear in our skies. So arrive the primates in their adroitly engineered magnetic funnel fusion rammer—and we receive a message from our destination. The simple drawings carried in electromagnetic codings are of the primates, not of the Bowl. These two events *are not coincidences*. They come so very close together in the great abyss of galactic time." Bemor reclined in his chute, easing his bulk. "The Glorians convey a strange warning message. As Memor noted, they warn away these smart monkeys, *but not we of the Bowl*. So we must act. The vectors of our circumstance demand so."

Memor turned to Tananareve. "Your expedition knew none of this?"

"Right," Tananareve said, eyeing them both warily. "Your—what do you call it?—Bowl, that was enough."

Memor began, "Their story is that they did not suspect our presence or trajectory. As well, their ship lacked supplies—"

"I know all that." Bemor gave a feather-fan shrug. "And their star ramship rode a prow of ionization that absorbed the microwave emissions we saw, so they could not have received them in flight. Their own communications are simple digital amplitude-modulated laser beams—and those are directed back toward their star, not ahead."

He waved an arm-fan at Tananareve. "You have

said your ship did not receive messages from your home world for a long time, then did. Why?"

"Political instability, we think. We did send reports, but apparently our people went through a phase of no interest in the interstellar expeditions." She sat stiffly, Memor noted, as though reluctant to admit this.

Bemor looked skeptical, his eyes turned upward derisively—though Memor knew Tananareve could not interpret this. "Why this lack of concern?"

Bemor saw this primate was unable to follow their discourse, and so waxed prolific in his remarks. Memor cocked a scarlet at him in ironic interest, for this was unusual for him. Bemor said, "We have only a few long-flight expeditions, such as this one. Most are from stars we pass nearby, who see us in their night sky. Those mount an expedition, those who have interplanetary abilities. In that sense, we inspire progress among slumbering civilizations, simply by appearing to them in passing. Those that have arrived had great trouble living in the biospheres they found. Microbial mismatches, food-production difficulties, and some unknown health problems."

"But we did receive a message about the time we discovered your . . . Bowl."

Tananareve was still edgy, and yielded this information only, Memor saw, because she feared Bemor. Something about an inherent caution with males? Bemor's rank musk was a bit overpowering. Or had the earlier pain gun incident made this primate more willing to cooperate? If so, it had been a good move.

"Ah. The primates did not expect to receive signals from Glory, suggesting that this is their first attempt to reach that star. So—" Bemor turned to Tananareve and whispered in her tongue. "—I hope you are telling true?"

She returned his gaze. "Right, we're the first expedition. Your Bowl . . . We knew none of this."

"You had no plan when you invaded our paradise?"

Tananareve snorted. "The team I was in, Beth Marble's team—until we escaped, we had as much control over what happened as a kitten does in a clothes dryer. Cliff's team is showing you what we can do, I hear."

Bemor gave a bemused eye-flutter with his delicate purple fringe. "I saw in your vessel a high level of ingenuity, more than expected of First Stage intelligences."

"Which is . . . ?

"Curiosity, as you display in that admirably simple phrase. Artifice in magnetic engineering, particularly the ingenious flux conservation mechanism in your scoop. We have studied it, following the fluorescence of decaying ions, and so mapped your magnetic artifice. Your configuration can navigate on the skimpy ion density gathered from our star. Admirable!"

Tananareve blinked, unsure how to respond. Memor began, "I, too, am surprised that you manage to—"

"Moving on," Bemor said, turning away from Tananareve and Memor alike, "I believe you, Asenath, have questions for the primate?"

Asenath fluttered forward—glad of some attention, finally, Memor guessed. She questioned Tananareve, with Memor supervising occasionally, and learned nothing new. Bemor became bored. They were still close enough in manner—since, after all, they shared the same genetics—for Memor to know that Bemor was remaining politely present, but in fact was importing signals from elsewhere in the Citadel. Perhaps from superiors?

"This Late Invader is most useful for studies of the structure of her mind," Memor said, trying to introduce what was for her the most original Late Invader trait, their submerged and unreachable unconscious.

But Asenath went on, her agenda becoming apparent. "The message from Glory is aimed at primates. The Glorians think primates are running the Bowl!"

Cackles, hoots, coughs, and murmurs. General hilarity, even among the assistants, who normally suppressed any show. "Good!" Asenath said. "Let them keep that misapprehension. Make the true rulers, ourselves, unpredictable."

"We surely are that," Bemor said sardonically. Yet something in his tone conveyed ironic skepticism.

Asenath made a submission-display flutter, but it was unconvincing. "Ideal setting for an entire suite of deception-maneuvers, yes. We will need cooperation of the primates to bring this off."

Bemor turned to the primate and said in its tongue, "You follow this?"

Memor was surprised that Bemor articulated the alien fricative consonants quite well, directing breath with his tongue over the sharp edge of the teeth and into the capture hollows of his cheeks. It gave Bemor a solemn, echoing way of pronouncing the rather simple constructions the primates could manage. Memor had taken several sleep-times to master that, and her words still came out reedy and thin. Worse, the primate understood Bemor immediately, saying, "I don't know your language."

So Bemor gave a guarded version of their conversation, keeping it minimal, giving away nothing, omitting of course anything the primate could use. Artfully done, Memor had to admit.

Tananareve's first comment was a question. "What about the light-speed problem?"

Bemor said, "We think long. Perhaps few of us will live to arrive near Glory."

"So you want to reply to their signal? Deceive them?"

Memor felt the primate showed insufficient respect for their company, but Asenath chose that moment to recover some role in the conversation. "My team is putting together a response for Glory. No great hurry, but there may be a time limit."

Tananareve shot back, "What if the Glorians send out an exploring expedition of their own?"

"We can surely see it well in advance and defend properly," Asenath said with a fan-flutter in ivory that said, *Such is obvious.*

"You know about the gravity waves, right?"

Bemor said, "You imply, we should be wary of what weapons might they have?"

Tananareve stood, stretched, plucked some sweatfruit from an ample bowl. A show of indifference? Perhaps this was all the primate could do, since it could not give feather displays or more subtle signals. With a mouth partly full of the fruit—a grave social error for the Folk—she said, "Well, I sure would be."

"I believe," Asenath said, "and Contriver Bemor may amend this, that the Lambda Spear can be revived?"

Bemor made a ring-show of blue and green, meaning "yes," for he knew the primate could not grasp this.

"What's that?" Tananareve said.

"It is a truly terrible device, able to alter the fundamental constants of a small region of space-time, upon command," Memor put in.

Her eyes widened. "You use this . . . how?"

"With great care, obviously," Bemor said. "We can project such an effect only over long distances, so to avoid being in the realm affected. It is appropriate for defense on a system-wide scale."

"It comes to us," Memor added, "from the Time of Terror."

"I'd love to hear the story," Tananareve said.

"I can show you a worked example of how we avoid such dark times, soon enough," Asenath said with a mild feather-rustle. "I have an appointment at a Justice Rendering. Duty summons."

TWENTY

Cliff and the others were glad to get back into the warmer precincts of the Bowl underground. They rested in a large view space that gave them warmth, yet through a broad portal gave a closer view of the "vacuum flowers," as Irma termed them. They ate the food they carried, and the Sil leading them brought water from a small delivery system lodged in the hard rock walls. The Bowl's outer hull was intricately woven through with passages, rooms, narrow little living quarters, and shops for what looked like repairs. As well, they passed by warrens that seemed to be where the finger snakes lived and worked. In some of the shops, snakes wearing harnesses labored at rack arrays, doing metal and electronics work. They were intense little creatures of glistening, gunmetal blue skin, beady eyes focused at close range on implements usually smaller than a finger—a human finger, not the bigger boneless ones the snakes used.

"Y'know," Aybe said, "it's kind of reassuring that in this incredible place, they're making flanges and hex joints, pressure sleeves and shafts with ball joints."

"Engineering," Terry said, "is a universal."

Some of the snake teams were working now on a large, intricate wall. They worked with a fevered energy, clacking and hissing to each other and slithering adroitly over copper arrays. This wall lay behind where the humans watched the dim landscape of the hull. Hull ice was thick here, and vacuum flowers lapped against the transparent portal. Cliff touched the window and had to snatch his hand away at a sudden sharp pain. He feared it was so cold, his fingers would freeze to it. Quert had said there were multiple vacuum layers in these transparent walls, but the cutting cold came through.

"That's it," Aybe said, "these corridors are below the mirror zone. We're at the edge of a big mirror area, too. This whole section of the Bowl must be chilly."

It seemed so. So the land beyond was extremely cold, dotted with rock that formed roofs over areas of gray ice steeped in dark. Following Quert's advice, Irma played her laser beam, set on dispersed mode, into those dark spaces. In this flashlight mode, they were surprised to see odd, ivory-colored things moving with agonizing slowness.

Aybe asked what these were. "On our way here we saw bizarre life-forms feeding on ice, but those—"

Irma said, "Those slow creatures with mandibles and eyestalks, yes—like lobsters, but living in high vacuum and low temperatures."

Terry eyed the moving gray things. "These shapes are amorphous. More like moving fluids."

"Ice life," Quert said. "Kin to ice minds."

Irma said, "So, ah . . . You brought us here to . . ."

Quert let the silence lengthen, then said, "Sil want speak."

"To . . . ?"

"Ice minds."

"What can we do?" Irma asked.

"Ice minds speak to you." Quert made eye-moves that might imply hope or expectation; it was still hard to tell.

"Won't they speak to you?" Terry asked.

"Not speak Adopted."

Irma said, "You mean, species brought onboard the Bowl? Why not?"

"Ice minds old. Want only new."

"Y'know, those blobs in the shadows are moving, together. Toward us," Aybe said.

"Watchers," Quert said. "Allied with ice minds."

Cliff said, "So you were ignored before—," and saw that now the vacuum flowers were opening and turning. "Why . . . why are those doing—?"

Quert gestured at the vacuum flowers that abandoned their slow sweep of the sky, dutifully tracking nearby stars for their starlight. They rotated on their pivot roots toward this transparent wall.

The company fell silent as the flowers began to open fully, from their tight paraboloid shapes that focused sunlight on their inner chemistry. Slowly they nosed toward the wall where humans and Sil watched. As they did so, they blossomed into broad white expanses, each several meters across.

"They're really large," Irma said. "Still hard to imagine, plants that can live in vacuum, and bring in starlight from over a large area. To feed . . . Quert, did you mean these flowers provide energy for the whole biosphere living out there, on the hull?

Quert simply gave eye-signals, apparently a

"yes." Then the Sil said, "Commanded by cold minds," and would say no more.

The thin glow of the jet brimmed above the horizon here, and some flowers seemed focused permanently on that. It seemed an unlikely source of much energy, for the plasma was recombining and emitting soft tones in blue and red. On the other hand, that was steady though weak and some flowers had perhaps evolved to harvest even such dim energies.

They were all transfixed as the radiators spread open and completed their pivot toward the humans. There was silence broken only by the faint sound of air circulating, as the field of flowers—Cliff swung his head around to count over a hundred within view—then began to pulse with a gray glow. Behind the flower field the stars still wheeled, cutting arcs in the black. The humans stood mutely watching, their heads tilted up to see the spreading flowers, who in turn clung to the rotating hull. The gray glow built slowly, the whole flower display assuming a shape like a giant circle flecked with light, staring at them. Cliff felt a chill wash over his skin that was not from the temperature. *This is truly alien. . . .*

A pattern began to emerge. In the dim light their eyes had adjusted, and so the brighter flower circles made blotchy spots while the darker flowers accented a contrast . . . and the entire array began to form a speckled image. . . .

A picture came into view. Irma gasped. "It's Beth's face—again!"

The picture was crude because there were fewer pixels to be had from the flowers, but still Cliff found it unsettling. He gazed at the cartoon of Beth Marble while others talked on. Finally he said, "Reasonably close, too. Whoever commands these vacuum flowers knows the method they used with the mirror zones. They're using this to get our attention."

Quert gave a rustle of agreement. "Ice minds."

"At least her lips aren't moving," Terry said. "That gave me the creeps."

"So . . . no message," Aybe said. "Just a calling card."

Quert looked around and pointed to the wall behind them. The snake team was still working, this time with some armatures like waldoes. They had somehow extruded a flat tank from the wall, and snakelike machine arms were completing it. This was not repair but construction. They worked by coaxing features from a substrate that simmered with flashes of orange light. The whole working team was laboring with new members. A big lizard-like thing of crusted hide had four tentacles, each of which alone was larger than a finger snake, fissioning into more small ones that snakes did not have. Cliff watched one use fingernails, too, that deformed into helical screwdrivers, snub pliers, a small hammer. It was trimming away and adjusting features freshly drawn from the wall. Cliff glanced back at the Beth portrait, still frozen in a smile. When he turned, the work team was slithering away across the wall, as the central oval they left brimmed with orange glows.

Letters and then words seemed to drift to the surface of the wall, as if bubbling up from deep ocean water.

"It's Anglish," Terry said. "How do they know?"

"Ice minds," Quert said. Across the Sil's face— and across those of the other Sil with them, who had been quiet all along—the skin stretched and warped, framing the eyes. Did this mean joy? Fear? Impossible to tell. But there were no other signs of concern in the body, which remained still.

The script ran slowly.

We have ranged the Deep and kept history near.

We are not of you carbon-children of thermo-nuclear heat and light.

We ride here to preserve the greatness you have found now.

Long ago we shaped this traveling structure, when the warm folk came to us from deep within the whirlpools that girdled our suns. The warm folk gave us tools to build large. Some of us stayed among the comets, but we here have clung to the Bowl. We live through eons of time, and so have seen the many thousands of faces intelligence can assume. We dealt with them in turn. We are the Bowl memory.

Irma said, "This looks like a prepared lecture."

Aybe nodded. "Must be. They've used it before. I

guess if there are thousands of years between passes nearby other stars, you work up an all-purpose greeting."

Terry smiled. "Boilerplate, huh? This doesn't look like a greeting, though. More of an announcement, I'd say."

"Intended to awe, yep," Cliff said.

"As if this place didn't impress us enough? Their Anglish is good," Irma said. "They must have access to the Folk's experience. But are we missing a point? These—Ice Minds—claim they built the Bowl."

"Shaped it. Designed it, maybe," Terry corrected her. "After intelligent warm life found them. After they ranged through the solar system and then the planets of this other little companion sun, after they worked their way into . . . would you say a mutual Oort cloud? And found these forests of supercold life. And the Ice Minds used them for engineering."

"Or they could be bragging," Cliff said. Nobody laughed.

They watched as the words faded and a long series of still pictures followed. Each came in at an easy pace, as though there were all the time in the world to show images of planets—crisp and dry, cloudy and cool, cratered yet with shimmering blue atmospheres—and stars, sometimes in crowded clusters, at times seen close-up and going nova in bright, virulent streamers, or in tight orbits around unseen companions that might be neutron stars or black holes. Wonders the Bowl had seen while driven forward by its jet. Portraits of the early Bowl years, Cliff gathered—the jet flaring and trembling in tangled knots of ruby and sharp yellow as the vast cup got under way.

For these ones that Quert termed Ice Minds there was indeed all the time in the world. The screen visions streamed on and the humans sat with backs against the rough walls to watch them. Strange landscapes loomed.

"They call us warmlife," Quert added as the screen showed an iceworld. Against a black sky odd lumps moved, in a lake lit by a smoldering red light. There were dune fields, ponds, channels. The lake sat in a convoluted region of hills cut by valleys and chasms.

Aybe said, "I'd say that looks kind of like Titan, Saturn's moon."

"There was small life there," Irma said. "Microbial, some pond scum, nothing more."

"There're moving forms on that screen," Terry said. For this view the screen showed sequential shots. The lumps seemed like knots of fluid, assisted by sticks that crossed through the globular bodies. Blobs that somehow used tools like rods? These coherent colloids moved across bleak fluid that might be hydrocarbons like ethane. On the beach the lumps moved ashore with viscous grace, pulling themselves forward with extruded feelers that managed the sticks. "They're clustering around that domed thing that looks like a termite mound," Irma said. "Even blobs can build."

"Those forms we saw in the shadows out there—" Terry gestured to the ice plains beyond.

"—might have some connection to these. Except these are on a planet."

"Life adapts," Irma said. "A big leap, from a Titan-like cold around a hundred degrees Kelvin, with high atmospheric pressure, to those vacuum flowers and the rest of it, all holding on to the outside hull."

"A big jump," Terry said. "But there must have been incremental steps, and they had billions of years to do it."

By this time the image had faded, replaced by a view of a dense jungle. This one, though, had spiral trees, whipped by high winds against a purple sky of shredded clouds. The stilled storm had a big beast in the foreground, something like a dirty brown groundhog, its head tucked in against the wind.

The show went on and then on some more. After a while even exotic alien landscapes became repetitious: blue green mountain ranges scoured by deep gray rivers, placid oceans brimming with green scum, arid tan desert worlds ground down under heavy brooding brown atmospheres—

"All planets," Terry said. "They're not showing us comets. Not showing us themselves."

—iceworlds aplenty beneath starry skies, grasslands with four-footed herds roaming as volcanoes belched red streamers in the distance, oceans with huge beasts wallowing in enormous crashing waves, places hard to identify in the swirling pink mists. *Life adapts, indeed.*

After a while, the slide show was over and more Anglish words appeared.

You warmlife now learn to journey from star to star.

We have seen your kind before.

You expand outward at great cost to you, for fleeting quicklife reasons.

Most warmlife comes in small ships, as do you.

The dream of this Bowl enticed us with its capacity. Its slow progress fits our minds, our style. Over eons we have seen little need to change its design.

Through voyages we gain passengers warm and cold. This is only part of us. Other ice minds live elsewhere in the Bowl's shadow.

We deeplife are one in fluidity.

We address you now because this is an unusual time. This Bowl approaches a fresh world. As do you.

We have no reason to intervene in warmlife affairs. We act when the Bowl faces threats to its stability and endurance.

You will help us.

"We will?" Aybe said.

"They're probably listening in some way, y'know," Cliff said sternly.

Aybe blinked and said loudly, "Ah, yes, we will. If we know how."

Irma stood and gazed out at the dim icelands where the vacuum flowers still held Beth's image. She fanned her laser and said, "Those blobs, they're moving, all right."

"Maybe these Cold Minds keep those forms around because they're related by mutual evolution?" Terry asked. "Hard to know. If these Cold Minds are as old as they say, there's not much that can be new to them."

Cliff said, "And even less that's interesting."

Liquid life-forms? he thought. Trying to think on huge time scales was hard. *Maybe warmlife is just a buzzing, frantic irritant to them. And there is something in their manner, dealing with us warmlife, that suggests immense distance. These things had probably evolved in the outer fringes of solar systems. They could travel on comets, maybe, bouncing from star to star. So maybe they freely roamed the galaxy while the most advanced warmlife consisted of single-celled pond scum.*

None of this was reassuring.

"What did you have in mind?" Irma addressed the screen.

TWENTY-ONE

Memor watched Tananareve carefully as their party entered the chamber for the Justice Rendering. The primate studied the walls and ornamental traces with a quick and ready eye, as though cataloging all she saw. Quite natural for an explorer, who expected to report back to her superiors. That might well not happen, but no need to give the primate a hint of that.

They sat in high rows above the steeply inclined vault. Above them hovered ancient tapestries of gold and ivory, while the funnel at the vault's floor was an ominous jet black. Bemor sat higher than Asenath, Memor, and the primate, as fitted his rank. He spoke with the Highers, even the Ice Minds. Memor knew—and envied, of course. Though Bemor was her twin genetically, but for those genes that expressed sex, he had been reared to deal with long-term thinking and abstractions at a level Memor had not. Perhaps that explained, Memor thought, the tenor of irritation that crept into his sentences when discussions flagged or failed to reach a sharp point of usefulness. Male traits indeed, she recalled.

A clarion call sounded deep and long in the vault. It comprised some high trills, playing against long strumming bass notes that Memor knew were resonant with the body size of Folk, and so would be felt rather than heard. Such musics instilled an uneasy impression of immensity and whole-body involvement, a tool persuasive yet hard to recognize. It instilled an apprehensive awe.

Tananareve watched and listened, saying nothing. Her eyes darted with quick intelligence. Only her tight pale lips told of some inner tension.

Resonant chords came from the music walls. At a signal, a team of brawny Folk strode from the witnesses gathered on the lower level. With prods, these forced each of the Maxer Cult members forward ... closer to the edge ... their legs slipping in the slime ... then at the teetering brink ... as a deep voice extolled their violations of the Great Pact. At a second hooting call, the Folk thrust the Maxers into the pit. Some flailed in resistance. Others turned with resigned shrugs and jumped. Cries, shouts, shrieks.

"This is a most useful spectacle," Asenath said mildly. "Well done, too."

The music rose to a triumphant chorus, high notes rejoicing. Barely audible beneath the sound was a chanting—

"Live in this moment. Give in this moment."

"Ritual reprocessing is too good for those who undermine stability," Asenath said, spitting out the words. "They endanger us all."

"So may we," Memor said, and at once regretted it.

Asenath shot back, "Not if we exterminate the humans as we have these!"

They had apparently forgotten that the primate sat among them, Memor saw. Tananareve's head jerked up for a moment; then she bowed it ... which meant, Memor knew, that the primate had learned some of their speech. Had understood Asenath's remark. These creatures were smarter than she knew.

There was a long silence after the ceremony, hanging in the heavy air.

Bemor said softly, "We Folk must conquer our own festering anxieties, as well. These reprocessings are necessary for stability and for life it-self. We Folk in our own wide variety, along with the multitudes of Adopted, should accept the hard, simple fact that we ourselves and all we encounter are transitory, ephemeral, beings of the moment. We matter little. We should embrace the beauty and pleasure of the world, knowing it will cease for us, inevitably. We are not the Ice Minds. Such is the Order of Life."

Memor added her agreeing fan-display to that of Asenath and other Folk within range of Bemor's deep bass voice. For her it was a satisfying moment. Bemor could make these matters far more resonant and inspiring than she; just another sign of his abil-ity range. When they were both young, cared for by their long dead Principal Mother, he had early on shown his ability to handle higher-level abstrac-tions and find the nugget of wisdom in passing mo-ments. She admired him.

But Asenath would not let it be. She said, "These primates do not see such wisdom. They are an ex-pansionist species, such as has been seldom seen in the Bowl for great ages. Their ship has maneuvered below range of our defense gamma ray lasers. Their parties afoot elude us. It is time to marshal efforts to eliminate them." A pause and vigorous fan-rattle. "Obviously."

Bemor gave an agreeable rainbow flourish with mingled eye-frets, but then said soberly, "There have been, down through the vast generations, un-counted acts to restore stability. All these carried a penumbra of drownings, starvation, sad sickness, massacre, looting, ethnic scourges, laser conflagrations, air-cutting slaughters, assisted group suicides, expulsions into vacuum—the list trudges on."

"You seem saddened by this," Memor said—a bit presumptively, but after all, she was his identical.

Bemor yielded on this with an embarrassed flutter. "I recall when young—you were spared this, my twin—assisting the more militant among us. We walked on corpses, sat on wrecked bodies to rest, stacked them as they stiffened to provide us a momentary table to eat upon. The delay in recycling them into the Great Soil meant they had to be assembled and even defended, against predators both feral and intelligent. But it had to be done."

Memor said kindly, in mellow tones, "Brother, I do not follow—"

"The Bowl grows errant beliefs like mutant species. There were obscure faiths and ethical theories that held the body was some kind of holy vessel, whose owners had not yet departed. Or else such spirits would require the body, even though rendered into dust, to be made animate again. So they resisted return to the Great Soil, a true sin."

He looked around at nearby Folk, who regarded him with varying displays of doubt. "You flutter your fan-feathers with disbelief, yes—but I have seen this in historical records, and even in person. Sad sights I regret witnessing now." Bemor sagged a bit as if borne down by history, his feathery jaws swaying. "Alas, my memory is long and I cannot erase those laid down with such feeling."

Crowds come to witness now shuffled out of the

Vault. Other Folk dispersed until it was Asenath, Bemor, and Memor, plus of course the primate.

Asenath said, "Your report is due, Memor. Your hunt for the bandit crew still loose among the Sil continues?"

Memor duly reported finding the Late Invaders among the Sil. With a quick air display of images, she told of the attack upon the Sil city, the vast destruction.

"Approved by upper echelons?" Asenath asked severely.

"I ushered it through," Bemor said mildly, eyeing Asenath but making no feather-display at all. Lack of fan-signal was a subtle sign of coolness, but Asenath missed this and rushed ahead, eager with a point to make.

"And they are dead?"

Memor suppressed her usual feather-rainbow to convey irked response and said, "No. I had surveillance auto-eyes study the Sil buildings. While they are rebuilding themselves, they involuntarily shape new messages in their forms. This is not a language but a gesture-speak. The influence of building style plainly shows a vagrant presence among the Sil, and I deduce that the humans survived the assault."

Asenath pressed forward with full fan-clatter. "So. You failed."

"I did not command the skyfish. Those who did not achieve their goals were demoted. But recently one fast-fly craft caught this." Memor flicked an image into the air surrounding them. A down view showed a primate running between recently shaped buildings. A pain beam rippled over it, and the figure crumpled. The beam stayed on and the writhing thing kicked and thrashed and then lay still.

"A single kill?" Asenath said with downcast tones.

"We now know we can hurt them at will over distance. My primate here"—a gesture at Tananareve—"was our test subject. But I found also that the Sil have secured access to my own surveillance."

Bemor said, "So the Sil are watching you, too?"

"I withdrew immediately, of course. In that interval the primates made their way toward a nearby mirror zone."

Asenath brushed this aside, pressing on. "Memor, we have not heard your report on this primate of yours. I take it she has been well fed and often exercised?"

Memor puzzled at Asenath's apparently friendly tone, suspecting something. "Of course. I brought her here to higher gravities, for her health. Her species was clearly not made for lightness—indeed, their bone and joint structures suggest a world of heavier gravitation than even the Great Plain."

Bemor asked, "You have read her mind structures enough? Your reports mentioned this odd character, inability to see her own Undermind."

"Yes, obviously an early evolutionary step. Imagine building a large, coherent society of individuals who could not know their own impulses, their inner thoughts! Touring her mind was instructive. I got most of what I need."

Asenath fluttered with appreciation. "I shall depend upon your ability to monitor this primate. We will need her cooperation to convey our response to their ship's attempts at contact."

Memor hid her surprise. "Now?"

Asenath said sternly, "We must deceive the Glorians about who commands the Bowl. Your primates can do this for us, if properly handled."

PART VII

CRUNCHY INSECTS

*It is a common experience that a problem difficult
at night is resolved in the morning after the committee
of sleep has worked on it.*
—JOHN STEINBECK

TWENTY-TWO

"These snakes are incredible," Beth said to Karl. It was pleasant to have time to relax and just watch without feeling endlessly responsible. She had gotten used to that on the Bowl.

"If you'd asked me before I saw them, I'd have said more like improbable." Karl could not take his eyes from the screen. "Hard to see how evolution worked out skills like this."

They were watching some aft zone electronic repairs carried out in the narrow spaces near the magnetic drive modules. The snakes wriggled into spaces that would have taken her and Kurt hours to unsheath, disconnect, monitor, diagnose, and fix.

Karl called to them, "Go left at the condenser bank. They're cylindrical drums with oil valves on the upper side, colored yellow. Then spin open the double diode—they're the blue plates."

The Maintenance Artilect took this from Karl's mike and translated it into the sliding vowels and clipped sharp notes that made up the finger snake language. On the screen they both watched the snakes make the right moves. They each had a tool harness that they plucked small instruments from.

With these they deftly inserted, turned, levered, and adjusted their way through one task after another, with speeds almost impossible to follow. The interior cameras were tiny light pipes and gave barely enough definition to make this work. All the while, the ship hummed on and occasional thumps and surges hampered the work. *SunSeeker*'s magscoop was operating close to its shutdown threshold already, and repairs while operating were the bane of all ships—but it had to be done.

Beth was out of her depth here—*hell, I'm a field biologist!*—but regs said nobody worked alone on ship maintenance, ever. Flight deck officers were full up, conning *SunSeeker* as close in to the Bowl's atmosphere levels as they could, while still grabbing enough plasma from the star as they could. Just maintaining flight trajectories while watching for bogies was burning up all their attention.

Beyond tending to the hydroponics, certifying the air content, and helping turn algae into edible insects and porridge, Beth had nothing more to do. She helped a little with the preliminary "fault tree" analysis of this maintenance run, but that meant mostly giving instructions to the Artilect, which plainly knew far more than she did about what she was supposed to be doing. So she used a wise saying she'd learned from Cliff: *Never pass up a chance to shut up.*

Which was harder to do than she had thought. "Uh, can I help?" she asked for maybe the eighteenth time.

"No, I got it." Kurt never took his eyes from the

screens, and his headphones whispered constantly with updates from the Artilect. "Going well."

Man of few words, bless him. At least Karl didn't ask her over and over about living on the Bowl, like the rest of the watch crew.

The snakes wriggled some more, did scrub procedures on some parts, and with surprising speed got a discharge capacitor line back up to specs—part of the booster system that allowed them to amp their magscoop when needed. "Okay," Kurt said, "come on back out. You guys need a break."

The snakes dutifully turned and started on their tortured way back out of the engine labyrinths. "Amazing what they can do," Kurt said, nodding his head. "Makes me wonder how we got by without them."

"Barely," Beth said.

"You're bio, how did smart snakes ever evolve? They sure didn't Earthside."

"Something about their home world, one of them said. It had plate tectonics gone wild, crazy surface weather, storms that would take the paint off metal. So smart life stayed underground."

"How about earthquakes? Volcanoes?"

"Their world had 'bands of furious turmoil,' they said—their language has considerable poetic power. Their landmasses butt against each other, kind of like Earth, with its baseball seam wrapping around the globe. Stay away from those, and life underground is somewhat easier, they learned. Where are you from?"

"Gross Deutschland. You?"

"Everyplace, mostly away from California—after the Collapse, we had plenty of migrants from there."

"Okay, snakes got smart, but *mein Gott* they are wonders at handling mechanics."

Beth grinned. "Look, we don't even know why we're relatively hairless, compared with the other apes. Why we walk on two legs and can outrun anything over distance. Why we're so damn good at mathematics, at music—you name it. So understanding where an alien species came from is hopeless."

The finger snakes came wriggling out of the narrow cap passage into the drive's innards. Ordinarily she and Kurt would've used smart cables to get in there, running them with a control panel. To her astonishment, the snakes broke into a high, wailing song—*chip chip, duooo, rang rang, chip, duoo duoo*. Not entirely unpleasant, either. At least it did not last long. Then they formed a "wriggle dance" as Redwing called it, arcing over each other and forming intricate curves that included bobbing in and out of the circle, rolling over and doubling up to make O's, then back into the throng—still singing, though less shrill. They finally ended up standing halfway erect on their muscular tails, their fingers wriggling at the dumbstruck humans in comradeship—or so whispered the Artilect in Karl's ear.

Then, with good-bye hails, they went off to eat in the algae pits, where a repast cooked up by Beth earlier awaited.

Karl said, "They're so coordinated. As if it was completely natural for them."

"You mean instead of how humans do it—drill, train, discipline, drill some more?"

"Pretty much. The snakes—look at them, off to their home in the biospace. All together, chattering . . . Some species are better at collaboration than we are. How come?"

"We're pretty new at it. About two hundred fifty thousand years ago Earthside, group hunting became more successful than individual hunting. That started the logic of shared profits and risks. Penalties kept alpha males from dominating. There emerged a kind of inverted eugenics: elimination of the strong, if they abuse power. And the cooperators won out."

"Wow, you know this stuff. It'll be fun seeing you work out all the aliens on the Bowl."

Beth opened her mouth to say something modest but . . . he'd brought up what she'd already missed. Back onboard, but dreaming at nights of the Bowl. "Uh, yes. Look, it's time for that self-cook in the mess," she said.

• • •

Fred was talking while he pounded a wad of bread dough. Physical work opened him as well as anyone could, so Beth tried to pay attention. "I kept wondering, y'know. The Bowl map shows Earth as of the Jurassic period, when all of the biggest dinosaurs emerged. Y'know, apatosaurs and so forth. I think I finally have the sequence right."

Beth nodded while she did her own kitchen work. He slammed the dough down and punched it for punctuation. "A variety of intelligent dinosaurs emerged first. *Oof!* They must have been carnivores. They invented herding. *Uh!* For millions of years they must have been breeding meat animals for size. *Ahh!*"

He looked around and realized that nobody was listening except Beth. "You mean all those theories about dino evolution are wrong?" This was interesting to her but apparently not to the others. The crowded kitchen buzzed with low conversation as they worked on aspects of dinner. Fred's jaw closed with a snap. She knew the pattern—if people didn't listen, he didn't talk.

Karl handed Beth a handful of roasted crickets that reeked of garlic. "Try these. Crunchy." He had pitched in with the cooking before she even got to the ship's mess.

"Yum," she said. Next came a basket of aromatic wax worms ready to cook. She tossed aside black ones: that meant necrosis. "They go bad fast; hell, I harvested them two hours ago," she apologized. "The rest are pupating—just right." Deftly she peeled back their cocoons and tossed them into the electric wok.

Captain Redwing came in and watched, standing straight and tall, smacking his lips slightly. "Wax moth larvae, a gourmet favorite." The crew laughed, because he always pretended to like the food in the mess, no matter how implausible that was. Or else he ate alone in his cabin. After their last culinary disaster, a motley mashed-up dish everyone disliked and called Stew in Hell, he went on dry rations alone.

Karl turned and swept brown roasted crickets up, salted them—salt was easy to extract from the recycler—and with head tilted back, trickled them into his mouth. "How come when you have less to eat, it tastes better?"

"Less is more," Redwing said. Everyone around him raised eyebrows. "Look, we're in a tough spot, carrying forward maneuvers nobody trained for—" He nodded at Karl, Beth, Ayaan Ali. "—and exploring a big thing nobody even imagined. We've got to do with less until we see our way out of this."

Everyone nodded. Redwing finished with, "So on to Glory—and let's eat."

The moth larvae weren't all done. The crew watched the chubby white larvae sway and wriggle in delirious fits as the heat took them. Insect protein was simple to raise on algae and, if well cooked, had a zest that the rest of the menu lacked. Fresh from a skillet, they had a kind of fried fritter some called "pond scum patties" to go with them. The ship couldn't afford the room or resources to raise muscle and sinew. Some crew came from the North American Republic and weren't used to insect food, or else from experience regarded it as beneath their standards. A few weeks' exposure to the stored rations usually fixed that. Some things, like the trays of gray longworms, few could bear to look at. Those

Beth thought it best to grind into a paste for a fake pancake.

Beth spread the larvae into a frying pan, where they fell into a fragrant, fatty goo Ayaan Ali had made. They squirmed as they sizzled and then went still. She stirred them, thinking *Amazing what you'll eat when you have to* . . . and then recalled things she had gratefully ingested when she had to on the Bowl. Sometimes, admittedly, while deliberately not looking at them . . .

A zesty aroma rose from the crusty larvae and as soon as she set them out, crew descended on them.

Redwing had saved a morsel for this moment, and now trotted out from his personal stock a bowl of—"Honey!"

That made the dish work. Everyone dug in. "As insect vomit goes," Karl said, "not at all bad."

Ayaan Ali asked Karl, "Done with that flight analysis?"

Karl barely slowed his eating to say, "Realigned the simulation, yes. Fitted it to isotope data from the scoop over the last century."

Beth asked, "Meaning?"

Ayaan Ali said, "We're still trying to understand why the scoop underperformed. It might help us fly it now in this low-plasma-density regime."

Redwing said casually, "How's the detector mote net working?"

Beth knew this was one way Redwing liked to turn social occasions into a loose staff report meeting. Certainly his approach made hearing tech stuff flung about a tad more appetizing.

Ayaan Ali gave herself an extra helping of sauce—much needed, since to Beth the woman seemed rail thin and low energy—and crunched up some more insect delicacies before saying softly to the others, "Karl and I deployed, on the captain's direction, the diagnostic fliers we'd planned to use when we came into the Glory system. They would give us a good three-D map of the mag fields and solar wind when we came in."

Redwing said, "So I decided we could send them out on a short leash. They can tell us details about the plasma turbulence, density ridges, things that we can't get a good reading on inside *SunSeeker*'s mag cocoon."

This, too, was a Redwing method—let the crew know there was logic behind his orders, but do so ex post facto. Playing along, Beth asked, "Short leash?"

Karl said, "I'm pretty sure we can reel them back in. They're marvels, really, size of a coin but able to propel themselves by using tiny electric fields that let them sail on magnetic energy, to sense plasma and measure waves, and report back in gigahertz band. We've got them spread over a big fraction of an astronomical unit, sniffing out ion masses and densities, picking up plasma waves, the whole lot."

Beth was impressed with *SunSeeker*'s abilities and kept quiet while the others kicked around their lingo. They loved their gadgets the way ordinary people cherish their pets. The thousands of "smart coins" sending back data were working well. That they could be fetched back, told to return home for reuse—amazing stuff. Plus they had useful results right now.

Ayaan Ali waved one of her augmented fingers, and a 3-D vision snapped into view, sharp and clear above their table. Hanging in air, it showed schematics of the Bowl in green, with *SunSeeker* a tiny orange dot swimming above it. The ship had to stay below the rim of the Bowl to avoid the defensive weapons there. But it also had to skate above the upper membrane that held in the Bowl's atmosphere. That left a narrow disk of vacuum for *SunSeeker* to navigate, riding the plasma winds that came direct from the star. But more important, they got plasma spurts from the traceries and streamers that purled off the yellow-colored jet. The churning jet was big in the 3-D view, a slowly twisting nest of luminous threads that drove forward. As the crew watched the display, it shifted smoothly, since the Bridge Artilect tracked human eye movements to display what interested people. They witnessed the jet narrowing further as it flowed out, then piercing the Bowl cleanly at the back, through the Knothole and out into interstellar space.

Deftly Ayaan Ali pointed to the safety zone disk where *SunSeeker* flew and the 3-D dutifully expanded until they could see bright blue dots swimming in a grid formation all across the huge expanse. They were sprinkled over a distance of about an astronomical unit and when Ayaan Ali waved her hand, they answered with momentary violet flares, a ripple slowly expanding away from the ship's position.

"They report in steadily, each staying a good distance from the others. We get plasma signatures in ample arrays. The coins feed on the plasma itself and change momentum by electrodynamic steering." She could not restrain herself, beaming. "Beautiful!"

Karl nodded. "And they got good news, in a way. Remember, before we sighted the Bowl, our scoop underperforming? Turned out it was eating a lot more helium and molecular hydrogen than ordinary interstellar space has. Some of it got ionized by our bow shock and then sucked into the main feeder."

"Ah, but it doesn't fuse—got it," Fred said. This was the first time he had spoken during the entire meal, and everyone looked at him. "Hard to tell from inside the ship that it wasn't getting the right food."

Beth didn't see, but wasn't afraid to ask, "So?"

"Those useless ions slowed us down, just pointless extra mass—and not fuel." Fred dipped his head, as if apologizing. "Sorry if I get too technical. My obsessions don't translate well."

Everyone around the table laughed, including Redwing's rolling bark. "Don't put down your assets, Fred," Redwing said. "Even that dinosaur idea."

Beth appreciated Redwing's methods but wanted to move this along, so she asked, "So our drive's okay? We're managing to keep it flying in interplanetary conditions, after all—which it was never designed to do."

"That's what the smart coins tell us. We're actually getting more plasma than we would if we were in near-Earth space," Karl said. "The jet snarls up some, so we get a bit more blowoff plasma from it."

"That star isn't behaving like a main-sequence one, either," Redwing said. "I had the Astro Artilect look into it. It says we got the spectral class wrong at first because of the hot spot—it swamped some spectral lines. But as well, the whole jet formation active zone makes the star act funny."

Ayaan Ali asked, "You mean those big solar arches we keep seeing? Big billowing loops. They dance around the hot spot, and every week or two they blow up in huge, nasty flares."

"Right," Karl said. "Those help build the jet, somehow—I really don't see how to build so stable a pillar of plasma from the storm at its feet. Those storms give the jet its power and blow off other plasma, too. The jet's base storms also spatter out a big, highly ionized solar wind—which helps us scoop up more fusion fuel, too."

Beth nodded, feeling more than a bit out of it. "Pleasant to have some good news for once."

Redwing said quietly, "So the smart coins tell us we have some room to maneuver. Good indeed."

Smiles all round. Fred nodded enthusiastically.

A new flight deck officer Beth didn't know well, one of the recent revivals, came into the mess. "Captain, we're getting a tightbeam laser signal from the Bowl. Did a translation in digital format. It's in Anglish. Visual's cutting in and out. But we can tell who it is—it's Tananareve."

TWENTY-THREE

As he sat waiting for the signal to stabilize, Redwing recalled the hammering noise that worked through the ship's plates in the trial run, as acoustics bled from the ramscoop magnetic fields into the marrow of their bones. At the departure reception, a president of one of the major ship builders said lightly of the din, "To me, it's the sound of the cash register." It had been a major achievement not to deck him right there.

And even better later, when the medical teams were putting him under, to reflect that when he next opened his eyes, the ship builder would be dust.

Now the background rattles and pops and long rolling strums were second nature. He listened all the same, as a captain should. Now he heard a crackling and a carrier hum. Then "—hope this gets through."

To Redwing, Tananareve's smoke-and-whiskey voice said she had been through a lot, but the timbre of it spoke of her resolution. The screen was blank, but audio came with little pips and murmurs in the background, perhaps static, perhaps the background noise of some alien place.

"How goes it?" he said.

After a delay of only five or six seconds, her shaky voice answered carefully, "It goes."

Then she coughed. "They . . . they here want me to talk to you about cooperating on a message. You've seen the feed from Glory, right?"

He saw a bottom-screen crawl line from the bridge comm system say they had picked up the full feed. The screen flickered, and then suddenly an image of Tananareve snapped into full color view. Against a black rock background, she looked haggard and pale but her eyes flashed with flinty energy. Nothing more in view. Her clothes were the field-issue pants, shirt, and jacket she had gone down in, looking beat up and patched. She also wore an odd gray shawl around neck and shoulders. There was dirt on the left side of her jaw and scratches along the neck. Overall she looked worn down.

"Yes, we have. Very odd," Redwing said. Best to be guarded. He knew her captors were listening and wished one would step into view. He hungered for a feel of what these aliens were like.

"The Folk, these aliens call themselves, they want to work, to, uh, collaborate with us—with you, Captain—on making a message. Something to send to Glory." Her eyebrows rose on *you,* and Redwing wondered what that meant.

Something in her voice had roughened, maybe from being in the field so long. It was Anglish with the corners knocked off. She laughed suddenly. "The civilization at Glory, they seem to think we're running the Bowl. My, um, mentors, they want to leave it that way. Keep themselves in the shadows, at least until they know something about Glory. But they need our help for that."

"Outstanding. What do they want to say to the Glory Hounds?"

"Captain, they're still fighting about that. They'll have to talk to us first."

"That's it? What about Cliff's team?"

He could see conflict flicker in her face. So could Beth and Karl, sitting behind him, judging from the way they stirred in their seats. They were in Redwing's cabin because he wanted to keep this first transmission from the aliens, after months of silence, from the rest of the crew. It was always a bad idea to let crew see policy being made, especially if it was on the fly, as this might have to be. "I . . . don't know anything . . . about that."

Her hesitations told more than the words. She was probably trying not to let the Folk know how much she knew. Then, to confirm his hunch, she very carefully gave him a wink with her left eye. Left: something wrong. A common code in visual reporting, all across the Fleet. Right meant things were right but more was to be said.

"So why don't they let Cliff's team go? And you?"

Hesitation, a side glance at whatever was directing her. "They need me as translator. . . ."

"And Cliff's team?"

"And as for Cliff, they don't know where he is." A right-eye wink this time. What could that mean? That the Folk knew something but not enough to use?

"So if we work with them on a Glory message, what do we get?" It was time, he judged, to put something on the table. Let them go first.

"You are all welcome down here. There is plenty

for us." She said this straight, no inflection, staring straight at the camera as if this were a rehearsed line.

"Thanks, but mostly we want supplies for the ship. And information."

"I believe they want to help with ship repairs." Again the straight stare, no eye movement.

"We don't need repair. We figured out that we'd been fighting their jet backwash for a century. Once we're full up on ship stores, we'll be on our way."

For the first time, she showed a darting, skeptical squint of the eyes. "That isn't what they have in mind."

"Tell them we will exchange delegates, perhaps. We can't house more than one or two—"

"They want you, Captain, for negotiations in person."

"Not until they release you and Cliff's people. They've been in the field a long time, need medical and some R and R. You, too, Tananareve."

"I believe they have something more . . . lasting . . . in mind."

"Such as?"

"They mentioned a generation or two. Enough time. They say, for species to get to know each other."

"I'm a ship officer with orders to carry out. I'm conveying colonists to Glory and cannot change mission."

Hesitation, side look, pursed lips. "I . . . gather they like to sort of collect species, to live here, to work with them."

"I can't spare people. Colonizing a whole planet takes teams, and they're barely big enough as it is. Cut our numbers and then downstream both halves— those we left with you, and those we took—would get inbred."

A pause, her eyes dancing, looking off to the side. "They . . . they say they find us very interesting." The flat way she said it told him that she was also not saying a lot, and he would have to guess it. But what?

There came a sudden voice, swift chippering sounds underlaid by deep notes, as if someone was speaking in two tones at once. Redwing thought it was the first truly alien thing in this transmission— speech built like a symphony, with several elements rendering part of the message in different sliding tones, sometimes highs and lows scampering over each other. Some notes rang hollow, others full. Yet all this was also oddly resonant, as if the play of words—if the screeches, grunts, trills, and mutters were that at all—made a larger work of greater scale.

He really wanted to see who made that voice. The six-second delay was driving him nuts.

She considered for a moment, looking off camera, and then said slowly, "They welcome us with . . . total hospitality. We can live here. They will assign a huge territory to us and help us set up a civiliza- tion comparable to—" She paused. "—well, what we had Earthside."

"Um," Redwing said, keeping his face blank.

"And . . . from what I've seen, there are rules

to keep this whole big habitat working. They impose . . . order. They're very, uh, firm about that. Make a mistake here, and you could endanger the whole place."

"Like any spaceship," Redwing said. "Open a hatch the wrong way, and you die. Maybe everybody in crew dies."

She nodded and her eyes slid briefly to her left, then back. "I think so. They do say we should know for the long run that there are generous upper limits on population. We could have territory bigger than Earth itself. Really, we could choose what part of this whole huge thing we wanted. I'd guess we'd probably want to be on the Great Plain, where it's point eight gravs and pretty calm, I gather."

"You make it sound pretty fine," Redwing said in a flat voice, no inflection at all.

Her tongue darted out, and she looked uncertain. "It is, in its way."

"We all have to come down? Leave the ship in some orbit?"

She paused. Redwing now sensed a presence near her, the target of her glances. Somehow from the small sounds of muffled movement, shuffles, and long slow breaths, he felt something nearby. The source of that strange voice, yes. Maybe more of them, several aliens watching, listening, no doubt knowing through their technology what he meant as soon as he said it. And what else would they get from this conversation?

"I . . . suppose so. They do want to study *Sun-Seeker*, they say. There are some aspects of the magnetic throat and drive they might be able to use. One of the Folk—a big one who seems in command, though it's hard to tell, really—says the techniques we use may have been known a long time ago, and lost. So they're interested."

"Lost? How old is this Bowl?"

"They won't say." She frowned. "Maybe they don't know."

Beth and the others kept quiet as Redwing's face furrowed with thought.

"And if we don't like to stay long? And give over a lot of our people?"

"They say this aspect of our interactions is not negotiable. They must acquire some of us."

"No deal," Redwing said sharply.

"Then . . . there will be . . . suffering, they say."

"We've come to threats pretty quick, haven't we?" Redwing said with lifted eyebrows.

She gave him a quick nod. Then the screen went blank.

They sat in Redwing's cabin a long time, watching to see if the signal came back on. It didn't.

PART VIII

COUNTERTHREAT

The possession of knowledge does not kill the sense of wonder and mystery. There is always more mystery.
—ANAÏS NIN

TWENTY-FOUR

"They seem as recalcitrant as you implied," Asenath said, leaning toward Memor and fluttering irked yellows about her neck. Her harsh warm breath rippled Memor's ruff feathers, an unpleasant sensation.

Bemor added, "More so."

They were ensconced in a shadowy side chamber after the transmission to the alien ship. The dark rock walls were of truly ancient times, furrowed with past attempts at adornment—panoramas that once depicted vast sagas of civilizations, long vanished. These had nearly worn away, leaving the striations and sparkles of the original grit-soil substance from which the Bowl was first built. The air of great, chilly expanses of time clung to them.

Tananareve, the last remaining Late Invader prisoner, was bending, flexing, pulling her foot to her forehead, sitting up and lying down over and over with a weight on her straightened hind limbs. The motion was distracting. They were flexible creatures, indeed. Memor told herself that the primate was doing it for her health and tried to ignore it.

Asenath restlessly gave an agree-flutter. "I do not

enjoy negotiating with those who can see so little of their true position."

Memor gave a fan-salute of agreement but said, "They are new to all this. No doubt they wish to take their best possible outcome as a beginning position."

Bemor gave no feather-signals at all, but let his voice range down into low registers. "They are not negotiating from strength."

"I think they imagine they are," Memor said.

"I could not diagnose that from their speech," Bemor said with a casual, superior sniff.

Memor still felt uncomfortable around Bemor, and tried to tell herself that his dismissive murmurs and small feather-displays were not meant to offend her. Perhaps they were mannerisms he had evolved to deal with staff and lower workers? Stiffening her resolve with this thought, she allowed herself some of what the Folk termed "lubrications" on what she had learned, using images of the primate cast on a shimmering wall projection. "I have studied their 'tells,' their limited visible methods of adding meaning beyond their words. They communicate, process, and fully feel emotions by mimicking the facial expressions of others nearby. So I studied the subtle shifts in their Captain's eyes, mouth, even the slight expansions and contractions of his nostrils. Apparently they have no ability to signal with their ears."

"Ah, their Captain is male? Unusual." Bemor looked skeptical.

"Bemor, there have been other Invaders who had

male hierarchy leadership, yes?" Memor felt this appeal to his greater range of knowledge would mollify her brother. And give a nod to the very idea of male leadership, too—though he knew well that his prominence at high levels was a planned aberration in Folk social structures.

"Of course, though we managed them throughout their Adoption to cleanse them of that destabilizing structure. They are now all proper matriarchies."

"But not the Sil," Asenath said.

"They are young, not fully formed," Bemor countered.

Asenath gestured outside the Citadel, toward where the primate was hanging from a tree limb, her legs raised to form a V. She remained in that position as the moments passed, but her eyes were on her captors. Distracting. "And that one—you watched her during the talk with Captain Redwing? She gave some facials."

"Of course. Tananareve is under therapy: well fed, often exercised. This local gravity is closer to her home world, too. A fairly simple creature, she is. And she used no unusual signals, as I could see." The Late Invader was still watching her, but surely Tananareve could not follow the swift, layered Folk speech. Simple commands, yes, but nothing sophisticated. She might overhear a word or two, but never the feather-nuances.

"The eyes," Bemor said. "What does a slow wink mean to them?"

"Puzzlement, I believe," Memor said.

"Nothing more?"

"Uh, I believe not."

"She used a long slow wink when questioned by that male Captain about the whereabouts of their other party."

"I noticed, but how much can a single small gesture convey?"

"Could it be a sexual signal?"

They all found this amusing, since sex among the Folk involved ritual feather-displays lasting through several mealtimes, classic dancing and cadences, song-trills of expectation and mutual agreed definition, then the ultimate mounting, all with urging songs and the completing union—not a matter to be taken lightly or often.

Memor was pleased that this remark drew amusement; she was known for her humor. "They are storytelling creatures, transferring useful knowledge from short-term into long-term memory, with assigned significance, all by telling a narrative to themselves."

Asenath said, "They constantly update this?"

"Without complete fidelity to the original, yes. Remembering a narrative alters it."

Bemor said mildly, "So they know their inner selves as fictional characters, written by themselves? Then rewritten?"

After more agreeable and incredulous laughter, and then a timely arrival of small tasty animals served on sticks by the attendants, Asenath said, "I fear that adds to their lack of realism. We should remind them of it."

Bemor looked skeptical, with purple rushes at his neck. "That would be . . . ?"

"Memor, fetch forth your primate."

When Tananareve came hesitantly through the arch, the contrast of her spindly, pale skin and dull-toned clothes with the three large full-feathered Folk was striking. Her feet slapped the bare cold stones in her frayed boots and her breath wheezed as she got used to the moist, salty scents of life within a Citadel. She was only a bit larger than the attendants who sat dutifully near Asenath, Bemor, and Memor, their faces always tilted upward hopefully in the ivory light, watching to see what their superiors might need.

"How do you think, little one?" Bemor addressed the primate with his rumbling voice.

Memor was shocked. Somehow in a mere few sleep-times, Bemor had mastered the Late Invader tongue, solely from Memor's reports and recordings. His pronunciation was accurate, too, strong on the clunky primate vowels. She felt a wash of cold anxiety and not a little fear. *My brother truly is quicker, sharper. Can it be because he links so much with the Ice Minds?*

"Clearly," Tananareve said. "Quietly."

Bemor gave an amused rustle that no doubt the primate did not fathom. "Quite well put," he said in Anglish. "Do you think your Captain will cooperate with us?"

"If you let go of our people, he will."

"We will compromise on that. We might very well let many of you go on to Glory."

"Nope, we all go."

"That is unreasonable."

Bemor turned to Memor and in Folk said, "This is normal?"

"They sail before the thousand breezes that blow through their opaque unconscious Underminds," Memor said. She noted the primate was looking at them, but did not worry that this creature could fathom their speech. After all, Folk had layered grammars and conditional tenses the primates totally lacked.

Bemor huffed skeptically. In formal Folkspeak he said, "Very pretty. What do we do?"

"They do learn by experience," Asenath said. "Memor herself says so. They are in a wholly strange place and may relapse into patterns from their past, fearing to face their future here."

"To face their fate," Bemor said.

Asenath said, "In them there is an undercurrent of strong neurological response to social life. In their neural patterns I read connecting elements, plainly honed by long natural selection. They evolved as hunter-gatherers within a socioeconomy where sharing and justice were critical to long-term survival. Yet these fail when extended to larger groups—a major problem of theirs, even now. Judging from the encased memories I read, even their stable societies oscillated between banquets and barbarism."

Bemor said formally, "Our long voyages have revealed much poignant wisdom. I have often viewed from the hull observatories, the vibrant stars glaring in their perpetual dark. That star swarm marks not so much a mystery but a morgue, brimming with once glorious and now dead civilizations. This I learned from the Ice Minds."

Memor rustled at this. Here at last Bemor played his strong card, the slow intelligences of great antiquity. They dozed through the Bowl's long voyages, else they might try too many experiments. In this way they were a reserve of long-term wisdom, not of mere passing expertise. They had been present at the Bowl's construction, even participating in its design, or so legend had it. How such cold creatures could know mechanics was an ancient puzzle.

Bemor used the rolling cadences of formal speech to stress his different status. Infuriating, but she could do nothing overt about it. And she was his sister twin, too. Asenath would falsely assume they worked together. Perhaps, Memor saw, she could use that in her own favor.

"You believe they wish to play a role in this Glory matter already?" Asenath asked intently.

Bemor fan-marked yellow agreement tones. "They must. The Glorians have technologies we need to ascend to a higher level of communications, with minds that have ignored us until now. The Ice Minds also surely wonder if these primates could ever fit in on the Bowl. They have implied such."

Asenath said, "The primates will have to."

Bemor said with casual superiority, "If they are able. We live among the long history of spaces and species. We encourage local groupings and discourage long travels across the Bowl. These adventurers may not fit in well. They seem obsessed with pushing beyond their horizons."

Asenath said, "Most of our Adopted give their names as 'the people'—whom they of course assume to be blessed. Others are, well, not so blessed. Each likes to see itself as central and important even among the vast tracts of the Bowl. Many live within a history of faces—bosses and chiefs, matrons and managers on high. As they adapt, these Adopted, to the majesty that is the Bowl, their history becomes simple. It is about who wore their own species' crown and then who wore it next."

Bemor fluttered agreeably. "Of course, as planned long ago. The Adopted do not any longer reflect upon great matters, beneath our eternal sun, untroubled by the universe around them. They dwell in comfort, without the horrors of unsteady sunlight, of seasons and slantwise sun. The Ice Minds see nothing but the entire universe, all around them. They are of the constant dark."

Memor thought this a bit much, attaching Ice Mind majesty to his own agenda. But she said nothing. She thought, though, upon her own past roles in this. Species grew in number until the Folk had to shepherd them to their equilibrium value. Belligerence and slaughter ran their bloody course. Borders brought a fretwork of scars, a long scrawl of history made legible on ground. With borders of sand or forest or water, Astronomer Folk shaped place to match species. Boundaries defined. When warring muddles arose, they examined yet again why territory caused them. Often this came from inept borders drawn by yawning bureaucrats far in the past.

So Memor and others thrust themselves into the ground truth of locales, letting time brew wisdom from raw rubs and strife. Such lands were often the equivalent of cluttered attics, stuffed by history with soiled rags, dented cans, and old, oily wood: a single spark could ignite them. Such running sores where species war raged unchecked, the Folk could only cleanse with great diebacks. Quite commonly, the packing fraction of religious passions in too little space was the deep cause, and had to be corrected. Folk molded the Adopted so none sprawled in an unending tide. Conversations and genetics shaped better and longer than mountains and monsoons could. Tribal beliefs in a tyrannical God figure running an imaginary, celestial dictatorship were often easier to manage. They understood hierarchy.

Such was the aged truth the Folk learned either from the Cold Minds or from hard experience. Memor had climbed up with a chilly indifference to necessity, and so now had merited the honor of dealing with the Late Invaders. *I hope I can capture the renegades and win approval,* Memor thought, suppressing her Undermind's qualms. *Or else there will come . . . execution.* She felt a shudder from her Undermind—something she could not see, a secret of great implication . . . it slipped away.

Her reverie done, Memor snapped back to attention. Asenath ventured, "So . . . we should not consider these primates good Adoption candidates?"

Bemor gestured at the primate, who narrowed

her eyes and looked intently at him. "No, I believe they can be broken to the rule of reason, in time. But their Adoption should not be assumed to be an important value to us. We need them to help negotiate with the Glory system, true. But we can then cast them aside like a sucked carcass, if we wish, at little loss."

"What habitat would suit these creatures, then?" Asenath asked.

Memor said, "I have plumbed the mind of this primate, Tananareve. I gather they want to be on a height looking down, they prefer open savanna-like terrain with scattered trees and copses, and they want to be close to a body of water, such as a river, lake, or ocean. They prefer to live in those environments in which their species evolved over millions of years. Instinctively, they gravitate toward parklands and transitional forest, looking out safely over a distance toward reliable sources of food and water. They can flee predators from land to water, or back, or to forest, where their kind once lived in trees."

"What a primitive mode!" Asenath seemed repulsed.

"Is this opinion, that the primates are mostly useful for dealing with Glory, the sole wisdom the Ice Minds wish to convey to us at this point?" Memor asked, turning to Bemor.

"I think that is quite enough indeed," Bemor said—rather haughtily, Memor thought. "But . . ." Bemor moved uneasily, feathers rustling. "The Ice Minds do not always reveal their thinking. They seem unusually interested in these primates. Still, they wish us to secure the help of these Late Invaders."

Asenath rushed to send an assent-flutter toward Bemor and turned a subtle angle toward him, and so away from Memor. "So, Contriver, I propose that we give the primate ship a reminder of their true position."

"Um," Bemor said with a skeptical eye-cant. "How?"

"They are inspecting the magnetic configurations around their ship, probably to better guide their own craft. But it could be they will use it to disturb our magnetic mechanics, as well. Their technique is to spread a wide array of sensors."

"Adeptly so?" Bemor said.

"These are craftily done, hundreds of disks the size of my toenail. I suggest we wipe our skies free of them."

"Destroy them?" Memor asked.

"It will serve as a calling card," Aseneth said with a smirk-flutter.

"I'm sure it will," Bemor said, sending an assent corona of yellow and blue. He leaned forward eagerly. "We will at least learn something from their response."

"I shall see it is done," Asenath said happily. "I believe these Late Invaders will be put in their proper place, and soon realize it."

Memor wondered if she had been outmaneuvered here. Caution would have been her policy, but Bemor seemed bemused by the idea of overt action.

"I hope you enjoy it as well, Asenath," Memor said with what she hoped was just the right tone of sardonic agreement. It was always difficult to get these things right.

TWENTY-FIVE

Blessed night, Cliff thought. The soothing qualities of pure deep darkness washed over them all. After months of relentless sun, they had all they wished of sweet shadow. It fell like a club upon their minds, sucking them into sleep.

He swam up to blurred consciousness after another long sleep, wrapped in a fuzzy warm blanket the Sil had found for them all. His team lay around like sacks of sand, feasting on the festival of dark that released their need, after so long in the field, for rest.

He was still groggy. Something had sent a twinge, awakened him. He got up, pulled on pants and boots, and left their little room carved from brown rock. His boots were getting worn down and he wondered how he could get something serviceable. As usual, the right answer was, ask the Sil.

Small soft sounds were coming from where they viewed the Ice Minds messages. He came in carefully, watching the two Sil speaking in their curious way. There was more eye and head movement than there was talk. And as usual, the most active one was Quert—who noticed Cliff and beckoned him over with an eye-shrug.

"Ask for wisdom of past," Quert said. "This got now."

On the screen were phrases that might have been answers to Sil questions.

Over long times there is no lack of energy or materials, only of imagination.

Not having resources makes species resourceful.

Anger dwells long only in the bosom of fools.

"Thanks for having them do this in Anglish."

"Did not ask. They spoke first to us. Now to you."

"What is this all about?"

"Want to deal with Folk. You can help. Ice Minds care not for us. Care for you."

"Why?"

"New Invaders know new things."

"So they brush you off with 'Anger dwells long only in the bosom of fools.' And you are supposed to forget how the Folk killed so many of you?"

Quert gave only a tightening around the eyes, and his words were in a cool whisper. "Ice Minds say we are unquiet in soul."

"You're handling those deaths better than I have done with my friend Howard."

"There is more worry to come."

Quert beckoned him toward the large portal that

gave a view of the sprawling icefields. To the side the stars wheeled and on the dim icy outer crust of the Bowl the vacuum flowers slowly tracked the brightest stars in the moving sky. This was for Cliff still a magical vision. He watched it with Quert, who after a moment made a simple hand gesture and the portal flickered. The view jerked and though the stars still swept across the jet-black sky, now there was a bright object moving counter to the Bowl's rotation, skating across the blackness. When it was nearly overhead, a sudden beam flashed into view and Cliff realized the craft was using a spotlight. A powerful green laser beam fanned out to a ten-meter circle, sweeping. The beam flared briefly as it shone directly into the portal and then moved on. The bright point of the surveying ship tracked on, away and over the horizon. The stars wheeled on.

"That was a recording?"

An assent-rachet of Quert's eyes. "They not see your kind. Saw us."

"Some Sil? If they were looking for us, then we're safe—"

"Folk say Sil not come here."

"I thought—" He stopped, realizing that he had not thought at all whether the Sil were trespassing here. Apparently they were. Once the thought occurred, it seemed reasonable. You don't want riffraff intruding into the provinces of beings who dwell in deep cold. Their mere body heat could cause damage.

"No one is to come talk to the Ice Minds?"

"Not allowed by Folk."

"So they'll come after you?"

"Soon. We move."

Cliff realized he had thought of this cool dark refuge in rock as a resting place. They were all tired of moving across strange landscapes. But now they would lose that, too.

"Where to?"

"Warm and hot."

TWENTY-SIX

Redwing woke from a blurred dream of swimming in a warm ocean, lazily drifting . . . to a melodious call from the bridge. He hated buzzers in his cabin, and so the strains of Beethoven's Fifth drew him up with their four hammering notes. If he didn't answer within ten seconds, it would double in volume. He got to it in nine. "Um, yeah."

"Captain, the smart coins aren't reporting in," Ayaan Ali said in a tight, clipped voice. In task rotation, this was her week on the skeleton watch. It was 4:07 ship time.

"How many?" He was still groggy.

"All of them. Their hail marks just winked out. I had them up on the big board along with full stereo visuals in optical. Their hails started disappearing at angle two eighty-seven, and a wave of them swept across the real space coordinate representation. It took, let's see, one hundred forty-nine seconds to sweep over all of them. I can't get a response hail from a single one."

"Sounds like an in-system malf."

"I checked that. The Insys Artilect says nothing wrong."

"You called on the other two?"

"I brought them up into partial mode to save time. With just their diagnostic subset running, I got them to review whole-system stats for the last hour. They say there's nothing wrong."

"The full Artilect is right, then." His mind scrambled over the problem, got nothing. "Run it again. And direct for an all-spectrum search. Plus look at all the particle count indexes. Everything we've got."

"Yes, sir. Shall I call—?"

"Right, Karl. And Fred."

"Yes, sir."

"I'll be there pronto."

He made it in under two minutes. His onboard coverall slipped on easily—he had been losing weight lately, working the weights and doing pace running—and he used Velcro shoes. Ayaan Ali's brow was creased with lines he had never seen before. Worry, not fatigue.

"Nothing unusual in the all-spectrum," she said, voice high and tight. "Particle fluxes normal. The magnetosonic and ion cyclotron spectrum is as usual, pretty much. But the Alfvén wave spectrum power is up nearly an order of magnitude."

The Insys Artilect visualized this spectrum, cast

over the schematic of their near-space environment. It presented as a green front of waves rolling over the zone of the smart coins, silencing each as it swamped them. With an on-screen slider bar, Ayaan Ali moved this map backwards and forward in time. "I wonder how these magnetic waves could turn off our coins."

"Tumbling them, I would think," Karl said. He had come in quietly with Fred just behind. "Alfvén waves can nonlinearly decay into waves short enough to be of the same size as the coins. That tumbles them and can kill their navigation."

"And maybe turn them off, too," Fred added.

Karl pointed to the wave sequences. "They spread out from the jet, notice. An example of what my language has a single word for—*Vernichtungswille:* the desire to annihilate."

"So this is the Folk reply to our first negotiation?" Ayaan Ali asked.

"Looks like," Fred said. "Say, what's that?" The back-time display ran into earlier hours, and Fred reached over to freeze it, march it forward. As he did, a blue wave rushed across the entire display space. He backtracked it, shifting out to larger frames. "Look, it traces back to the jet. What's blue mean?"

"High-energy ions." Ayaan Ali thumbed the resolution until they could make out a snarl in the jet itself. It was a knot of magnetic stresses that tightened, fed by smaller curls of magnetic flux that rushed outward along the jet.

"Look," Fred said. "Kinks came purling along

the jet, moving fast. They converged in that knot, and—here comes the blue."

Karl nodded. "From that we get the Alfvén waves. Very neat, really. They can control the magnetic fields in their jet, focus them."

"To kill our coins." Redwing looked around at them. "To show us what they can do."

A silence as they looked at him, as if to say, *What do we do?*

"Officers of the bridge, I want you to fly a small satellite over the rim of the Bowl. We haven't got any recon of the outside of this thing, and Ayaan Ali reports that we got a stray signal from Cliff's team just hours ago. It was text only, said they were under the mirror zone. If we can put a relay sat within range of them, on the outside, maybe we can make a stable link."

Fred looked at Redwing for a long moment. "You want to risk a satellite?"

"I think we need to know how far these Folk will go," Redwing said. He kept his tone mild and his face blank.

"As for further measures, I have a brief from Karl"—giving him a nod—"and we will meet in the mess at eight hundred hours to discuss it." A pause to let this sink in. Time to go public, he figured. "Dismissed."

• • •

He started the meeting with news. Ayaan Ali delivered it, standing beside an image that flickered onto their wall screen. All exec crew were arrayed around the biggest table on the starship, coffees smartly set in front of them, uniforms fresh pressed from the steamer presser, everybody aware that this was not just another damn crew meet.

Grimly she said, "We launched our satellite toward the nearest Bowl rim. It is a microsat with ion drive, so it accelerated fast. I took it over a mountain range that neighbors the rim edge. See the picture sequence."

A set of stills ran, in time jumps that made the craggy mountains below zoom past. Their peaks were in permanent snow despite the constant sunlight. Redwing supposed this meant that the atmosphere was thin there and the outer skin, which they now knew was quite cold, was only a short distance away. The chill of space kept water frozen out.

Now the scene stuttered forward to show the Bowl rim approaching. The sat probe scanned forward, aft, both sides. At the far left edge, the atmospheric film shimmered, keeping air confined. On the left a small bright light appeared.

"I stop it here," Ayaan Ali said. "Note the near-UV burst on this view. It appeared within a microsecond frame, apparently a precursor."

"To . . . ?" Karl wondered.

"This. Next frame." Ayaan Ali pointed to a bigger white blotch at the same location to the sat probe's left. Her smile had a sardonic curve. "And that is it."

Karl asked, "What happened? Where's the next frame?"

Ayaan Ali gave them a cold smile. "There are no more. It stopped transmitting. Here is an X-ray image of that region. I had it running all during the fly-out, just in case."

They could make out the dim X-ray images of mountains and Bowl rim. Apparently this came from minor particle impacts of the solar wind. At the very edge of the rim was a hard bright dot. "That's our probe dying. From spectra and side-scatter analysis, I believe the killing pulse, which we saw the UV precursor of, was a gamma ray beam."

"From where?" Redwing knew the answer, but he liked to let Ayaan Ali keep the stage.

"That big cannonlike thing farther along the Bowl rim, sir."

"It's an X-ray laser?"

Ayaan Ali shook her head. "This image comes from secondary emissions. I can tell by looking at the spectrum. Also, I had a gamma ray detector taking a broader picture. It gave this."

Another bright dot. This time there was no background at all, just a point in a black field. "The power in this image is five orders of magnitude higher than the X-ray fluence."

He said flatly. "So we were right. It's a gamma ray laser."

Redwing looked at Beth. Ever since she returned, he had asked her to attend tech meetings, reasoning that she might have insights called forth by new events. "As far as I know, we never found a way to go that high in photon energy. Did you see any signs the Folk had tech like that?"

Now Beth shook her head. "Weapons weren't really around us. Or maybe we didn't even recognize them as weapons. They didn't need them, I guess. We were trapped."

Ayaan Ali said, "Weapons of this class would be very dangerous on a rotating shell world. Blow a hole in the ground and you're dead."

Karl said, "There was an Earthside program to develop high-frequency lasers long ago—I mean even before we left—and it never got lasing to gamma energies. At those tiny wavelengths, a laser could focus to very small areas, so you wouldn't need very much power to blow something to pieces."

Fred said, "This is bad news. Now we can't fly a probe over the rim. They can kill any sensors we send out. We're bottled up."

"No doubt they expect us to come back to them and ask for a negotiation," Ayaan Ali said.

"Which we won't do," Redwing said. Nobody said anything. Time to change direction. Sometimes that jarred loose a fresh insight. He leaned forward, fingers knitted together. "Beth, do you think that the Folk would ever let us go forward to Glory?"

Beth sighed and looked at the screen, where the explosion of their probe was frozen in time. "They have a very hierarchical society. The big one who interrogated us, Memor, acted as if she owned the world. It's hard to think they'll let us go and reach Glory first."

Ayaan Ali said, "Which we certainly could do, since we won't be facing their jet backwash."

Redwing remembered a lecture on alien biospheres during flight training in which someone said, "Humans and animals regard each other across a gulf of mutual incomprehension. With aliens, that has to go double." Yet here he was trying to figure out the negotiating strategy of an alien mind, immersed in a civilization uncountably old. He let them toss ideas around for a while to get them used to their situation. Sending the probe out to get destroyed had given the right edge to this, he decided. And it had laid to rest any notion that the Folk were bluffing.

"So . . ." He let the pause grow; they were so quiet, he could hear the whisper of the air circulation. "Let's send a reply."

Karl got up to speak and flicked on the wall display. It showed the jet in an extreme view—magnetic field lines in ruby, the tubes of bright plasma they contained glowing orange, the Bowl itself sketched in nearby as abstract lines. "We can fire a shot across their bow. The jet is pretty narrow as it approaches the Knothole. Notice the helical mag fields that funnel and contain the plasma. Very neat."

Beth said, "So the idea is . . . ?"

"Fly into it. Disturb the jet. Let it flicker around in the Knothole."

They just gaped at Karl. He had a chance to check their teeth and noted that Beth had an incisor with some ragged damage and stains. Beth let out a breath. "I flew us up the jet, remember? *Remember?* It was like taking a sailing ship through a hurricane. Do that *again*?"

For a long moment Redwing watched the naked fear play across her face. He recalled the long hours of strain and sweat as the ship popped and creaked, the racking uncertainty Beth had showed as she stayed with it through surges and awful wrenching turns. All the crew had worked to the limits of their endurance. That had been their only real choice. Through it all he showed no uncertainty. That was his job. And in the end he did not regret it.

But this was not a necessity. They could coast here and play for time. But they could not leave. And they were eating their provisions while Cliff's team was in constant danger.

He said slowly, "I think we need to show them that we are not going along with their agenda. That we will not be docile members of their big club."

A long silence. Their faces tightened and mouths compressed to thin white lines: startled fright, worry, puzzlement. Karl then said, "I wasn't thawed when you danced through the Knothole, Beth, but I checked this out with Fred. The physics is fairly straightforward. It won't last long, maybe ten hours."

Redwing could see they were too stunned to take it in.

"We'll leave the technical aspects for later. There will be three crew rated to pilot on the bridge at all times. In fact, all crew present. Warn the finger snakes to anchor themselves."

Karl said formally, "I want you all to know I have done calculations and simulations. There is a broad parameter range of what we might face.

The Navigation Artilects have been working full bore to study trajectories, the back-reaction of the jet plasma flow on our mag throat. It compresses our prow fields and alters our uptake—but that's mostly good news, because we get more thrust from the plasma. There'll be plenty of ions to fuel our fusion burn. I think—"

"Yes, technical aspects come later." Redwing smiled and tried to look confident. "Thanks, Karl."

Beth looked him straight in the eye. "We don't understand the Folk worth a damn, sir."

"Indeed."

"I have no idea how they'll respond." Beth looked worried, and her eyes jerked around the table, looking for support.

"They understand negotiation, that's clear from our conversation through Tananareve. They've killed our coins and now our probe. Let's show them we know tit for tat, too."

They looked hard at him. Ayaan Ali still had her slightly wide-eyed, shocked gaze. Fred wore his usual expectant fixed stare. Karl was trying to look confident. Beth's face was pale and strained, eyes fixed on him.

He stood. "I want you all to know we'll reply to the Folk. But while doing so, we'll navigate toward the jet and make preparations."

They left quietly. None of them looked back at him except Beth. She waited until the others were gone and closed the door. "I have to admit it feels good to be doing something. I didn't like being in their prison. Even when we got out, it was into a bigger prison."

Redwing blinked. "One the size of a whole damn solar system?"

She laughed, gave him the high sign, and left.

PART IX

ON THE RUN

Some folks are wise and some are otherwise.
—TOBIAS SMOLLETT

TWENTY-SEVEN

Cliff was tired of traveling. The immense distances of the Bowl took a steady toll that could not be erased by dozing in uncomfortable seats designed for another species, or indifferent food gotten from dispensers along the way, or headphones that tuned out the drones and rattles of endless long transport. The Bowl was built on the scale of solar systems, but humans were built to smaller perspectives.

Quert and the other Sils had brought Cliff's team through a twisting labyrinth of tunnels, moving away from the hull where the Ice Minds dwelled. Then a mag-train. More tunnels. Occasional glimpses of odd landscapes seen through huge quartz sheets that glided by as they took barely curved speed ramps at planetary velocities.

He had felt the surges and high speeds, but after a while they did not register as distinct events, just a long symphony of lurches. At times he felt he knew where they were in an astronomical sense— alignments of star and jet and horizon, glimpsed through flickering windows. But those got confused as soon as he looked again, hours later, after being pummeled and spun.

Now they ventured out, on foot, into a terrain that reminded him of California deserts—low scrub brush, gullied tan terrain, hazy sky, occasional zigzag trees. Those seemed to grow everywhere on the Bowl. Gravity was different here, a lot less. He felt a slight tilt to his weight, too. They were closer to the Knothole, had to be.

Curious blocky buildings visible through some dust haze in the distance, maybe ten kilometers away, a tapered tower at its center. Cliff drew in hot dry air with a crisp, nose-tingling flavor and basked in the raw sunlight. It was good to be still and on your feet in sunlight. Always sunlight.

Quert beckoned the others out of the well-disguised hatch that led into the hull system. For many hours they had crawled through some conduits and once had to wade through a sewer to get onto a fast-moving slideway. Then a train. The Bowl's constant daylight threw off their sleep cycles. He'd measured this, and found that the team had shifted to a thirty-hour waking cycle. The welcome dark of the night-side hull had helped fix that. But they were worn down.

"Think we're okay here?" Irma asked Quert.

"Need go farther," Quert said, looking around. "Not safe here." The other Sil shifted uneasily and looked at the zigzag trees.

"What's the danger? At least it's warm." Irma had not liked the cold and had hugged one or the other of the men in the night, seeking warmth. Nobody thought anything of it; they were all in a pile most of the time, dead to the world.

"The Kahalla. In shape they are more like you than we. An old kind of Adopted. Loyal to Folk."

Irma frowned. "So what do we do?"

"Find . . ." Quert paused, as if translating from his language. "Tadfish. You would say. Maybe."

"There's shelter over there." Terry pointed at the low hills to their left. He seemed more alert and energetic now, Cliff noted.

"We go past that," Quert said, but the other Sil around him rustled with unease. This was the first sign Cliff had seen that they all could understand Anglish. Plainly they were worried, their legs shifting and heads jerking around as if looking for threats.

"So let's do this fast," Aybe said. He, too, looked refreshed. They all had skins worn from constant sun but not deeply tanned. There wasn't a lot of UV in this star's spectrum.

They set off at a long lope made graceful by the lower gravity. Cliff got into his stride easily, enjoying the sensation of hanging a second or two longer at the apex while his legs stretched out. As much as he had liked the dark of the hull labyrinth, the sunlit open was more his style.

"Kahalla!" one of the Sil cried. Quert stopped and turned and so did they all. Some fast shapes flitted through a distant stand of zigzags and heavy brush.

At first Cliff thought these were four-legged creatures, but as one of them sped across a gap in the rust-colored brush, he saw they had two legs. Their gait leaned forward and hinged oddly. Big angular heads.

"Here Kahalla live," Quert said.

"What should we do? Deal with them?"

"Do not know." Quert and the other Sil looked carefully at the Kahalla. There were many of them.

They all began to run again. Quert waved them away from the zigzag trees where the moving figures were and toward the buildings several kilometers away across a dusty plain. It seemed to Cliff they were needlessly exposed there but then Quert, who was in the lead, took them behind a rise and into a slight gully that was enough to shield them from direct fire. Dust from their running stung his nose. They were all running flat out. His team had their lasers and Quert their own weaponry, but they were vastly outnumbered. Until now he had not thought much about how lightly armed Bowl natives were. That seemed to imply little overt conflict despite the vast and horrible damage the Folk had dealt out to the Sil. There was an odd Zen-like grace to them in the face of horror.

As if sensing that something was up, big birds flapped suddenly from the surrounding brush and zigzags. They swarmed and turned together and made off with loud keening squawks. In the lower grav, the big wings could use the slight wind to escape. Obviously to these odd four-winged birds, the running figures meant trouble.

The dust swarmed up into his nostrils and stung. The acrid nip also snapped him into focus. He looked up at the big birds stroking themselves up into the air and he recalled his sense of relish when he saw his first Baltimore oriole. They were nearly extinct then. The Great Crash had passed but many birds were teetering on the edge, and the sight of the deep flaming orange against the rest of its black plumage thrilled him. He knew the Baltimore oriole's name came from some royalty's ancient coat of arms, but that mattered nothing compared with the small fragile beauty of it. These alien birds sweeping and cawing above had none of that, yet they still stirred him. So why had this structure, vast in size and time, kept so much rich wildlife when Earth had not? Humanity had overrun itself in vast sullen cities long ago. Its soiled vapors ruled the sky, still, despite earnest geoengineering.

That question swarmed up, awakened by this wealth of life flapping around him. Stinging sweat trickled into his eyes and he was glad of it.

He remembered the bleak gray landscapes he had seen across the American West following the Great Dry. The denuded skeleton forests of the High Sierras, where fires consumed the last needles of the demolished pine forests and layered the Owens Valley with black shrouds for weeks. The dead dry prospects of deserted suburban streets lined by abandoned cars already stripped of their paint by the hissing sands borne on constant hot winds.

His legs burned with fatigue. Cliff shook his head to throw the sweat aside. He checked that his team was staying together, and panted, and felt the ache slicing in his lungs, and ran on.

Sometimes he could abstract himself out of the moment with thoughts, memories, dreams, anything. Anything but the terrible fear that once again they were the prey. His team. Being run down again. His responsibility.

So . . . how did this enormous artifact preserve such diversity of life? It was like some goddamned Central Park in Old Manhattan, before the rising seas washed all that away. A natural place that life sought refuge in, yet it was an artifact, a managed simulacrum of the natural world. A jewel in a concrete setting.

But this place was not a dead park. It lived and maintained itself and went on. He had to concede that to the Folk who ran this place. They had evaded the excess that had nearly ruined Earth.

He ran on. The others panted and strained around him. The Sil took their long strides with easy grace and were always ahead. The humans labored in sweat and stink and gathering sour fatigue as the building complex loomed.

In the zigzag trees around them, Cliff felt the presence of the running humanoids though he could not see them. It seemed stupid to be pursued on foot like *Homo sapiens sapiens* of a hundred thousand years before. Here amid a fantastic construction they were reduced to—

Then he saw it. The Bowl, a huge facsimile of a real planet, kept itself running and stable by being larger than worlds could be. Giving life enough room to find its own way.

But how did they stop the myriad intelligent species here from expanding beyond their province? A puzzle.

And now there was no more time for idle

thought. The distant buildings were close. And his legs were made of lead.

Quick is the word and sharp's the action. Where had he heard that?

They came upon the towering great gray slabs through an outer maze of silvery metal sculptures. These depicted heavyset humanoids in various poses, mostly in combat with assorted knives, shields, lances, and the like. The nude bodies were squat and sturdy, big muscled chunks above short legs and fat feet. Their ribs seemed to wrap around the whole body and their arms turned both ways, double-jointed and elbowed. Some statues were of standing figures and in the air around these gleamed some unintelligible script that flashed brighter as Cliff looked at them. A smart system that registered his gaze and amped the label? They reached a large bladelike tower that seemed solid, standing at the center of a hexagonal open spot. Flagstones of intricate angular designs led toward this tower and up its flanks in elongated perspectives. There was a solemn air to the place as its design soared up the flat tower face, ornamented with bumps and knobs that tapered away into the sky.

They paused to drink water and Cliff stood looking at the big stonework. Slowly, about fifty meters up, an eye opened.

He knew it was an eye though it was of the same burnished tan as the rest of the tower. It had a green center like an iris. Slowly the entire oval, several meters across, turned downward to look at them. One eye.

"What . . ." Cliff could not take his eyes off the single enormous pupil at the thing's center. It seemed to be looking straight at him. A pupil in rock? An eye with lens and retinas?

"Stone mind," Quert said simply. Then he turned quickly and peered into the distance.

Cliff looked to his left and saw several of the stumpy humanoids flitting among the sculptures. There were a lot of them, moving with surprising speed. They huffed and squatted and made ready. Their brown clothes seemed to have endless pockets and they fished among those to bring out things, affixing them to the long tubes.

"Chem guns," Aybe said. "In all this high tech, the old stuff still makes sense."

"Or maybe they haven't been allowed any more advanced tech?" Terry wondered.

"We saw a humanoid like this, remember?" Irma said. "It opened a door leading down into some entrance, back there on an open plain. When it saw us, it just walked away."

Aybe said, "Yeah, maybe we should've looked into that entrance. We were getting pretty ragged, maybe it would've been good shelter."

Cliff knew this was a way of calling up an unspoken grudge. He had argued to push on and they had. "That means these humanoids are maybe maintenance workers," he said mildly. "They're working for the Folk, keeping the Bowl fit."

They broke off talk as the creatures moved. Without a word the entire party of Sil and humans turned and watched the humanoids go to each flank, surrounding them. Nobody spoke.

"Kahalla," Quert said. "They hold us for Folk. Send message."

Terry whispered, "How can we get away?"

Before Quert could speak, a long droning note washed over the area. It seemed to come from everywhere and was more like a sensation in Cliff's body than a sound. The tone shifted and a long rolling vowel played out, *aaahhhhmmmm*.

Quert said, "Sit. Listen. The stone mind wakes."

Cliff sized up their situation. There were at least a few hundred of the humanoids around them. They didn't look friendly. Many wore jackets and carried long tubes that looked like some sort of launch weapon. They were swarthy and their heads never turned away from watching the humans near the tower. They bristled with suppressed energy. Cliff wondered how he knew this and saw it was something about reading body postures. Maybe that was a universal, across species? Or else the whole primate suite of abilities converged—driven by the urgent need to communicate, no matter what world your abilities came from—on myriad subtle signs that told stories from a mere glance.

Irma said quietly, "They're dangerous. We can't fight them. Are we waiting for this song to end or what?"

"They hear the long voice," Quert said.

Aybe said, "So? How long does this last?"

"The rock being speaks of its many deaths,"

Quert said, its head dipping low and eye darting up and down, a gesture Cliff did not know.

Tones now shifted higher, into *shree*s, *kinnne*s, *awiiih*s, and *oooeeeiiinnee*es. The pressing power in it seemed to hammer the air around them. Cliff felt these as warring long-wavelength notes that made his muscles dance, his body arch and flex and stretch in resonance with the powerful sounds rolling through the dry air around them.

"It's . . . it's playing us," he managed to get out. "This sound . . ."

"It tells of its great death," Quert said. "Takes far time."

The Sil had formed a crescent facing outward against the solemn threatening silence of the humanoids. Together with Quert, the Sil flexed their arms, turning their inner elbows up to the sun. Cliff saw slender black fibers extend in the pits of their elbows. Their tips gleamed in the hard sunlight. He had never been able to tell males from females in the Sil, but it did not matter. They all had done some physiological magic and made these black lances poke out of their inner elbows. One of them abruptly jerked an arm down and the lance arced fast and sure out in a long parabola. The elegance of it struck Cliff as it watched it skewer a small wood emblem atop a hunkering stone sculpture of a big-chested humanoid. It hit the dry dark wood exactly in its center, and the black arrow flapped with energy not yet dissipated. As sure a challenge as he could imagine.

The humanoids did not respond. Their feet shuffled, their heads waggled a bit, but no sounds came. The big notes had fallen silent, and Cliff thought the song or whatever it was had come to an end. Dead silence. The Sil glowered at the humanoids and flexed their black arrows. He wondered how that had evolved. Gene tampering? An onboard defense, obviously. You didn't have to carry anything, and the black rods with their gleaming pointed tips waited for the downward yank of the arm. Their hands could be free, so they could have other weapons there, too. But . . . the Sil held no other weapons in their hands. No pistols or guns of any sort. Unlike the humanoids, who now sent forth barking calls, high and shrill.

A taunt? A rebuke? It was impossible to tell. The calls stopped and Cliff felt himself tensing, pulse fast and hard. The two bands of aliens glared at each other in what seemed another universal signal—narrowed eyes. Grunts and hisses and heavy panting. Feet stirred in the dust. Arms and chests bunched and flexed. A fevered bristly aroma came drifting on the still air, the heat of bodies exuding aromas that, he supposed, carried signals evolved long ago on planets far from this stark scene. Time stood crisp and still. Eyes darted and judged.

But then came long drawing notes from the stone tower. Echoing tones of *kinnnes awrrrragh yoouui-unggg arrrafff* . . .

He panted and watched the aliens move into position around them. Shuffling in the dust. Huffing with energy.

"We haven't got a chance, do we?" he said in a casual way.

Irma said wryly, "Looks like."

Boonnnug wrappppennnu faaaaliiiooong . . .

The humanoids lifted their heads. Their shuffling ceased. As the long solemn notes washed over them, they slowly buckled. Sat. Folded their armaments and their arms, down and low.

The long, loud notes rolled on. Cliff did not know this speech. Neither did the Sil, he gathered. But the humanoids did and they wilted before the slow steady sway of the music that poured over them. The words became a soothing song that washed over the entire stonework, itself laid out some vast time long ago, an era beyond knowing.

The warmth lulled Cliff as well. "Take a break," he said to the others. "Sit. Wait them out."

He felt the flowing wall of sound as it called, *yoouuiunggg kinnnes awrrrragh yoouuiunggg. . . .* He felt his knees go weak.

Quert was having none of this. It said, "Let them sit. You do not."

"Huh? Why?" Cliff straightened up.

"The slow song will reach them. Resist it."

"Resist? I don't—"

Quert gave him an eye-goggle he could not read.

"Let it go," Irma said. "There's more going on here than we know."

Terry and Aybe agreed, heads nodding, eyes drifting, going drowsy and vague. *Greee habbbiiitaaa loohgeree . . .*

Strange fat pauses drifted by in the warm air.

Hums and echoes. *Like corpses on an ocean,* Cliff thought, and jerked awake. *What an odd repellent metaphor of the vaguely meaningful.* His unconscious was seeping through as he got drowsy. Or was it something the words called forth? The low booming voice called . . . *biiitha ablorgh quartehor biiilannaa* . . .

To keep himself awake and not weaken and sit down, Cliff asked Quert, "This is a sculpture? With a recording? Why is it so important?"

Quert looked at him with an expression Cliff had learned to read as puzzlement. "It is alive. It awakes to speak."

Cliff glanced up at the huge eye, which was still staring down at them. Gradually Quert's indirect way of saying things unfurled the story of this place. What Cliff saw as a sculpture was actually a living thing. Alien to the Bowl, rugged and slow, it had come long ago from a world that died. "It lives to tell. It awakes when audience approaches."

Irma said, "This is a *smart rock*?"

Quert said, "Sunlight powered. From world very hot."

"It can't move, right?" Aybe asked. "How'd it get here?"

Quert found all this unremarkable. "Bowl passing by. Explored that hot world. These Kahalla asked the Bowl to take one of them to keep themselves. To speak for them."

Terry asked, "To carry their culture?"

Quert turned to them and made a gesture they now knew meant "stay steady" among the Sil. "It sings. The Kahalla decide to send one of them. Their sun swelled. They would soon melt."

Terry said, "I thought those humanoids—" He gestured at the ring surrounding them. "—were the Kahalla."

"They take name of living stone." Quert seemed to find this completely natural.

"We triggered the monument? The Kahalla stone?" Aybe asked, his eyes wandering over the landscape.

Cliff understood; it was so ordinary in a dry fashion, but there were plenty of ways to get everything wrong here. Stones and primitives, all beneath a luminous sky, elements of ancient human history and still so easy to see as simple, a tailoring of Earth history. It was nothing like that. The strange kept trying not to be strange.

Quert's eyes meant "yes." "I-us took here. Knew song was only way." The alien's eyes told more than its words, but then words were tight little symbol lines. They could easily deceive the mind.

Only way? To not get caught? Cliff studied the stern stonework that soared over a hundred meters above them. A single creature, something he would have bet plenty could never evolve: smart rock. On a hot dry world, there must have been some sort of competition. *Among rocks?* He could not grasp how they contended. Against weathering? To gain mass and so defend themselves against abrasive winds and tides? How could information flow in a stone? How could it gain intelligence, to control its fate?

This went beyond biology into geology—and yet evolution had to explain such a thing. He recalled how dumbfounded he had been when he first saw the Bowl from *SunSeeker*. This made him feel the same way.

It was harder to remain standing, but Quert insisted. The resonant voice boomed on and the Sil listened intently. Long droning notes rode the hot dry air.

"Each time, different information," Quert said.

Long song pealing on. In the next hour, Quert gave Cliff, in halting detail, some of the Kahalla's slow evolution. Planets that condensed out early near their stars necessarily must seethe and surge. Liquid metals and decaying radioactives spit energy into crystalline lattices. Order came from oblique condensations. The essentials geological were much like essentials biological: Life began from metabolism wedded with reproduction.

The first sentient Kahallans used their world's temperature and metallic difference between the core and the upper mantle as their thermodynamic driver. Along slithering seams of flowing lava, moving with aching slowness, they learned to track the shifting heat patterns. Predicting these was even better. Among the metal ions in their crystalline rhomboids, variations made their own order. Slow, slow and strange, reproduction of patterns followed. Some worked and so persisted. When shifting crystalline lattices held the basic data of early sentience, evolution's hammer could find its anvil— much like bits encoded in silicon by humans' computing chips, fresh intelligences arose without benefit of the bio world.

Size conferred advantages in energy harvesting, so the Kahalla grew ever larger, over working agonies of billions of years. They learned to communicate through acoustic waves amid the strata. Social evolution drove the geological, just as they had driven the biological.

Time stretched on. There was plenty of it.

As their world's core cooled, the Kahalla migrated from near the core and toward the surface, for their planet was slowly spiraling toward its sun, its barren rocky surface cracking with the warming—a new source of nourishment. Geological energy was like the biological—diffuse, persistent. Driven by gradients, not logic. Yet it sifted through patterns and choices.

Ages passed. Finally the early Kahalla extruded themselves onto the plains festering with swarming heat, simmering beneath a glowering orange sky that was mostly now the skin of their star. Bio life had never arisen here, but now persistently the Kahalla colonized the stark black fields graced by rivers of smoldering lava. Great strange sagas of conquest and failure played out across smoldering landscapes. Songs worthy of immortality sang across blistered lands and blighted great monuments.

Civilizations faded as tidal forces forced the planet nearer its star, ever nearer beneath a flowering culture—and soon the Kahalla saw their fatal trap.

With their gravid slow slides of silicate, they could not migrate away from the surface fast enough to evade the heat. It lanced down from a star that swept the Kahalla with furious particle storms and bristling plasma. They retreated. Not fast enough. And ahead, their silicate minds knew, lay a great brutal force. They would soon enough reach the limit where tidal stretching could wrench and wrest apart their entire world.

Their society, ponderous and unimaginative, began to disintegrate. Their muted culture was largely a society of songs—purling out through the stacked geological layers, soaring operas of driven love and inevitable death. Like all life in its long run, it strove to understand itself and so perhaps its universe.

Yet some had fashioned instruments to survey their lands, their swarming sultry skies—and caught a glimmer of the Bowl in a momentarily clear sky. The Bowl had ventured in without fear of disrupting life-bearing worlds, for there were none—it thought. It coasted clear and sure in a long hyperbolic orbit. The Bowl was a sudden beckoning promise to those slow and solid and doomed.

Somehow the Kahalla sent a signal to the Bowl. It was of long wavelength and thus carried low meaning, a slow song. Yet over time their signal persisted, and was heard.

An expedition of robots answered—the spawn of a crafter species that stubbornly managed the near-Bowl transport and mass harvesting. Much conversation came and went and came again. It became with gravid grace a slow sliding talk across barriers of time and mind and much else.

Yet still. These robots retrieved the essence of the Kahalla intelligence—slabs of silicate, laced with evolved strands of impurities, all serving as a computational matrix.

So the robots brought the Kahalla mind to the Bowl in crystalline crucibles. It was a great act of graceful tribute, ordered by the least likely magistrates of all—the Ice Minds. So did the very cold save the very hot from utter extinction.

"And this is the only one?" Cliff asked Quert. The droning long chant was still pealing on. And on. Bass thuds and hollow tones spoke *wruuunggg laddduuutt eeeilllooonnnggghh*.

"It alone stands for all the Kahalla now."

Cliff could sense the majesty of it as he watched the great vibrating rock, framed against cottony clouds that rushed across the sky. "How does it live?"

"The sun lights those"—an eye-shrug toward the hills—"and tech condenses the heat, feeds the Kahalla crystals."

"So it's like an enormous, living museum exhibit," Irma said.

"Bowl preserves. Without, life-forms die."

"All life-forms?" she asked.

"Must be."

Cliff turned to watch the humanoids who had taken the name of this mournful singing stone and saw that the Kahalla's long hours of chant had done its work. The humanoids lay sprawled in deep slumber.

"Song goes to their souls," Quert said.

"You knew it would?" Aybe whispered.

"Heard it did. Only chance." Quert turned and gave them a comical eye-shrug. Then Quert bowed and gestured to them all. "Silent go."

The long *aaahhhhmmmm loohgeree oojahhaaa habbbiiitaaa* pealed on. It was great and strange and still impossible to fathom.

They left quietly. They were tired, but the long notes drove them forward. Somehow the place now smelled ancient and timeworn without question. The very scented air told them this without instruction.

Cliff and Irma and Aybe and Terry—they were all that was left now, and they had to move. The constant sun slanted pale yellow through high sheets as they trundled on with the Sil forming a crescent escort around them. He saw rainbow clouds hovering in the vapor over their laboring heads. Their crescents spoke bold colors shimmering through the sky's firm radiance.

His team was shambling on now, sweaty and confused, truly tired in the way he had learned to recognize. Heads sagged, feet dragged, words slurred. The alien song droning on from far behind them would never end, he saw, down through however many corridors of ruin and turbulence that song needed. They were beautiful stretched songs telling of sad histories that no one would ever quite know.

There would be scholars of it somehow in the long run, but they would carve off only a sheet of it and not know it entire. Cliff looked back once as they neared a stand of zigzag trees, a whole sweeping forest waving in the moment's breeze, and saw that the round eye was still watching them.

It never blinked. They went on.

TWENTY-EIGHT

Captain Redwing started crisp and sharp, fresh from coffee, with the same questions he always used when taking staff through the planning stages of a new, untried operation. Standard questions, but always able to surprise.

They had walked through Karl's simulations and Ayaan Ali's trajectory analysis. The Specialty Artilects had put their own stamp upon the general plan, though as always they did not make judgments beyond a probability analysis. Their deep problem, Redwing thought, was that they were so much like human reason with far better data—and yet so forever uncertain.

The worst way of reviewing options was to let people make speeches. Questions shook them up, made them come forth.

He looked at the entire assembled crew around the main deck table. "First question: What could we be missing?"

Karl Lebanon answered. "Their defenses."

Fred Ojama said, "Ayaan Ali and I did a depth scan for those. Nothing obvious, like the gamma ray laser."

Beth Marble set her mouth at a skeptical slant. "They could launch craft against you from anywhere."

Petty Officer Jam scowled. "I've seen curiously few flights above their atmosphere envelope. They don't seem to launch into space often."

Clare Conway said, "Speaking as copilot, the obvious way to launch is to just pop a craft out on the hull side. It's moving at hundreds of klicks a second right away, so you zoom around the rim. Come at us from that angle."

Ayaan Ali nodded. She was wearing a metallic blue scarf over her hair and resisting the urge to toy with it, Redwing noticed. This crew was good at suppressing tension and not allowing it to change the group mood. That had been a high selection criterion. She spoke slowly. "We would have time to deal with that. I am able to turn the ship quickly now. We've learned how to use the magnetic torque technique to gain angular momentum from the fields above their atmosphere. And we may be difficult to spot, since we will be in the jet."

Karl nodded. Redwing saw they had now mentally stacked up the unknowns, which was a good moment to hit them with more. "Second big question: How will this *not* work?"

Silence. Beth said quietly, "If they have something to prevent tipping the jet awry. Something we can't guess at now."

"They've surprised us plenty before," Ayaan Ali added.

Karl added, "Right. They've had lots of time to think about this."

Clare said, "What maybe won't work? Me. I may overestimate my ability to pilot through the jet. Beth, how bad was it?"

"An endurance test, mostly. I was driving straight up the bore, staying near the middle. Had to stay on the helm every second of the way. The big problem was keeping *SunSeeker* stable in the plasma turbulence. The jet is far denser than anything this ship and its magscoop were designed for. I had to max everything we had."

Redwing wanted to add, *And we nearly overheated, too,* but he said instead, "Sounds hard. But we're thinking of a fast flight through, yes?"

"I think so," Beth said, looking at Redwing, who nodded. "Put it this way—staying alive on the Bowl was hard, too, but lots more fun."

Their faces had grown more somber already. Most of them hadn't been revived when *SunSeeker* flew up the jet and through the Knothole, but they had heard about the long hours of a creaking, groaning ship, and the dizzy swirls when they yawed and nearly tumbled. Their eyes turned introspective. He decided to loosen them up.

"Y'know, way back when I was in nav school, I asked an instructor, 'Why do people take such an instant dislike to me?' At first the woman didn't want to answer. But I nagged her and finally she said, 'It saves them time.'"

When their laughter died down—he could read their tensions by that measure, too—he said, "Point is, I'm a bug about details. Made me pretty damn obnoxious in nav school and ever since." He gave them a smile. "I learned that in nav and tactics and all the rest. Space doesn't forgive anybody. So we have to simulate all the troubles we can see coming."

Karl said, "And then?"

"I'll throw some unknowns you hadn't thought of into the simulation, the training pod, all the rest. I want you to expect the unexpected."

They nodded and for half an hour they tossed around possible unknowns. Then he said, "Question three: Will you please shoot as many holes as possible into my thinking on this?"

This led to more scattershot thinking, more debate. The jet was the big problem, and there were many ways to look at it. Redwing waved his hand in a programmed way, and the bridge wall lit up with a photo of the Bowl made when they were on the approach from the side. This was when Redwing and the small watch crew, plus Cliff and Beth, were just trying to grasp the concept of the Bowl. That now seemed so long ago, but it was less than a year.

Some of them must not have seen it before, because it brought gasps.

"I'd forgotten how beautiful it is," Beth said.

Clare said wistfully, "Some of us have only seen it up close. We missed a lot."

Fred pointed. "Notice how it flares out from its

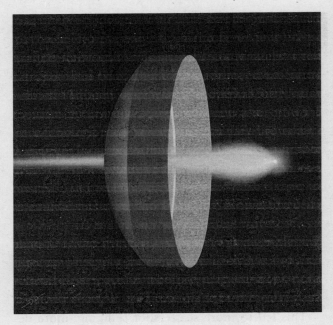

star, then narrows down a lot. That's the magnetic stresses working. Wish I knew how they do it."

Karl said, "I've fished around in the thousands of images *SunSeeker*'s Omni-survey Artilect made on our approach. That's when we got far enough ahead, while we were making our long turn to rendezvous. By the way"—a nod to Beth—"that was brilliant navigation. Hitting a moving target on an interstellar scale."

"This was all-spectra?" Fred asked.

"Exactly. Here is a view of the *other* side of their star. Away from the jet. It's in spectral lines specified to bring out the magnetic structures visible in their solar corona."

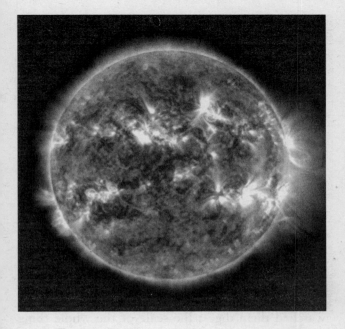

Ayaan Ali said, "Star acne," one of her rare jokes. She even blushed when everyone laughed.

Beth said hesitantly, "Those are all . . . magnetic storms?"

"Not storms, though on our sun, they would eventually blow open and make storms. Those loop structures are anchored in the star's plasma. Think of the magnetic fields as rubber bands. The plasma holds them down, and when they get free they stretch away from their feet. They're stable, at least for a while. Lots of magnetic field energy in those things. They move, just like the ones on our sun. But in the long run they move toward the edge we see and migrate. Over to the other side."

Before Karl could go on, Fred said, "To the jet."

Karl chuckled. "I should know somebody'd steal my thunder. Fred's good at that."

"So the other side of their star, which we can't see—"

"Is a magnetic farm, sort of?" Clare said skeptically.

Karl chuckled again. "You guys are too fast. Yep, Clare, that's where the star builds big magnetic loops and swirls. Then they drift over to our side of the star. They gang up around the foot of the jet. Then they merge—don't ask me how. That feeds magnetic energy into the jet—builds it, I guess." He shrugged. "I don't have a clue about how this gets done."

All but Karl had blank, big-eyed stares. Redwing watched them digest the scale of the whole thing for a long moment. *Star engineering,* he thought. *Somehow we missed that in school. . . .*

"There's a real problem here," Ayaan Ali said. "These Folk aliens you talked to, Captain—did they seem like beings who could command a star?"

Redwing pursed his lips. He liked to let things speak for themselves, and so had not kept the recording of his talk with Tananareve away from the crew. The more heads working these problems, the better. They had intuitions about the Folk, too, and now was the right time to let them come out. So he just nodded to Beth with raised eyebrows.

Beth said, "You've all seen my pictures of the one who interrogated us, Memor. Plus all the assistants—so much smaller, they seem like another species entirely. Probably they are, but they work together in what looked to us like a steep hierarchy. Impressive, that Memor—especially in bulk. But a creature that could manage a star?" She arched a skeptical eyebrow and let her mouth turn down in a comic show of doubt.

This brought smiles all round the table. "My point exactly," Ayaan Ali said. "How would anything our size—hell, any size—made out of ordinary matter, control solar magnetic loops?"

"Good point," Fred said. "There's something else going on."

"But what?" Redwing said.

No answers. They were all thinking, and he saw it was time to get back to work. He flicked another image on the view wall. "Here's a later view as we came around in advance of their star."

This brought more quiet *oooh*s and *aahhh*s.

"Here's where we see the point about those magnetic loops," Karl said. Fred was already nodding. "See how the jet seems to curl around? Those are—"

"Magnetic helices," Fred cut in. "The corkscrew threads are brighter, because the field strength is stronger there, and so is the plasma density. Classic stuff. Way back a century or two ago, we saw all that in the big jets that come out of disks around black holes. Astronomers know plenty about these."

"Uh, thanks."

Redwing could tell Karl was getting irked with Fred's butting in. But Karl was holding himself back with admirable restraint. And Fred's point

was well taken. Redwing said mildly, "So to get the idea for this, whoever built it had only to look into the night sky. At other galaxies, same as we did back in the—what, twenty-first century?"

Kurt nodded. "As Fred said, yes. My point is, the jet gets all that magnetic field strength from the loop structures. So those magnetic fields migrate around to the jet base and get sucked up into it somehow."

Fred said, "Ah! Then those fields do the crucial job of confining the jet, straightening it out into the lance that spears through the Knothole."

"Right. Because the star spins, its magnetic field gets twisted and wrinkled, kind of like a ballerina's skirt. That gets swept into the base of the jet, hangs up in it. The intense pressures at the base throw the jet out. It swells at first. Then the magnetic fields sort themselves out. Because field lines have to eat their tail—they can't break—they weave themselves. We've known a long while that you can twist a magnetic field so it crosses itself—but then it just springs back as two loops, almost like reproduction. So the field self-organizes in the flow and takes the jet through the Knothole." Karl finished with a flourish, getting the picture of the Bowl to make the threads in the jet fluoresce like neon signs.

Beth caught on to this. "I get it—hell, I experienced it. Waves of hard turbulence, coming at us at speeds *SunSeeker* was never designed for."

Karl smiled, happy to see his theory confirmed by raw experience. "You came in on the jet at first in the exhaust, right? Backwash. That's where the folds of the skirt bunch up—"

Karl went on with some more technical stuff, but Redwing didn't listen. He watched them all to see how they took it in. Teams had to feel they had some understanding of what they were about to get into. If you were lucky, you even got a dividend, a fresh idea or two.

"It's self-organizing," Ayaan Ali said, gazing at the intricate luminous lines that laced through the jet. "That's why it all works."

Plainly this surprised everyone. Ayaan Ali's crew slot was navigator/pilot, not astrophysics.

She paid no attention to their puzzled expressions and went on, "Our fusion drive is the same. It confines plasma long enough to fuse it for energy, heats the incoming plasma that way. Then we blow it out the back. It's a hot plasma shaped by magnetic fields all along the way. That jet that makes the Bowl work—it's just like our exhaust jet."

A few jaws dropped. Redwing had always enjoyed moments like this. Get a smart crew together and let them Ping-Pong ideas back and forth. Add new information. Stir. Turn up the heat a notch. Simmer. Amazing, how often good fresh notions came out.

A rustle of astonishment. "Good point," Karl said. "The same basic idea in our ship and . . . theirs."

"Their shipstar," Redwing said.

The melody of the conversation had shifted. The immensity of what they faced simmered below everything they said, and their faces showed this. Tight mouths, chins stiff, eyes dancing or else narrowed. Time to get them back into focus.

"Even if it's technically sound," Redwing said, leaning forward with hands clamped together on the table. "There's the big question—is this maneuver understandable enough for the ship Artilects to operate, to troubleshoot, and to extend what they've learned?"

Beth said, "Our flight in, up the jet—the Nav Artilect group certainly learned from that."

Ayaan Ali's face became veiled, remembering. "You're right. When I came on duty, I was amazed at how much they could do. Remember when we had trouble with the scoop getting enough mass to fuse it in our core chamber? They adjusted the field structure before I could even grasp what was wrong. They'd never done that in our field trials out in the Oort cloud."

The talk got technical. They all ran with it. The deep silent secret of *SunSeeker* was the collaboration between mere mortal humans and the crystal Artilects who knew much that the vagrant human mind could not hold in ready use. The Artilects managed innumerable details at a speed and accuracy far beyond the blunt comprehension of their fragile cargo. They were integrated artificial minds, merged into a collective intellect. A society of minds, furiously engaged. Redwing always thought of them as crew who rarely talked back. They kept track of innumerable daily problems and never complained. The Insys Artilect, especially; he spoke with it several times every watch. On the other hand, they never had really original ideas.

Clare said sternly, "Their attention reservoirs can take only so much—"

"Let's leave that to experience," Redwing cut in. "Officer Conway," with a nod to Clare, "consult the Artilects themselves. Give them your simulations; ask them to appraise their *own* capabilities. Regard them as crew members who couldn't make it to this meeting, if you will." *And since the interior systems no doubt can hear us in their acoustic monitors, they actually are here. Not that the Insys Artilect would ever bring it up; strategy was not its province.* But he suppressed that thought, for now.

"Yes, sir," she said, and sipped her coffee. Always

the caffeinated, he recalled—she used it to drive herself harder. Several others around the table did the same, an amusing social echo.

"Then we are resolved on this course?" Redwing said with a light and conversational air.

Only Beth failed to get the message. Probably, he thought, because she had been down on the Bowl so long and had forgotten shipboard's unspoken signals. She said, "I don't know if we've resolved anything, Cap'n."

"We're going to give the Folk a nudge," Redwing said. "Their reply was quite clear—they killed our coin array. They don't want us knowing the local conditions well, to navigate by. If we were Earthside, that would be an act of war."

Beth wouldn't stand down. "A 'nudge'? Despite all these problems? Unknowns? Risks?"

He leaned forward, extending his clasped hands. "There are always problems. My orders are to get us to Glory and see if we can colonize it. Extracting us from this strange . . . place . . . this shipstar . . . I see as my duty. To do so, I must impress on these aliens that we will not join the—what was their term? The one Beth reported?"

Redwing looked down the table at Beth, whose open *O* of a mouth told him she had not expected this. Maybe the ground truth of the Bowl had told her something he did not know? "Beth?"

"The . . . the Adopted."

"Right. We're not a damn bunch of orphans from Earth. We're not going to get Adopted."

Beth said, "In their eyes . . . ," and stopped.

"Yes?"

"We've been gone from Earth so long, all our relatives dead, who knows what has happened . . ." She looked forlorn for a moment, grasping for words, head down. "We might as well be orphans."

He had not expected this. What had the Bowl done to her? "We're officers of a ship, Science Officer Beth Marble. Humanity's farthest excursion. We have a goal and we shall reach it. This Bowl interlude, however amazing, will be useful, but we shall go on. Is that understood?"

Long silence. Karl started to say something, his lips half-forming a word, but thought better of it. Fred was quite obviously biting his tongue, eyes studying the table as if it were a brilliant new discovery. Their faces closed up into pale masks with eyes looking everywhere but not at Beth or at him. Very well. "This was an exploratory discussion, folks. I appreciate a free airing of views, as always."

Fred said, "Outcome pretty obvious. When we came in."

Redwing let nothing show in his face. "I'm sorry, Officer Ojama? Your special area is geology, as I recall. And ship systems. You said . . . ?"

"It was pretty obvious you had decided to fly into the jet. You wanted to get us used to it." Only after saying this did Fred's eyes jerk away from the table's smooth obsidian finish and dart a look at Redwing.

Redwing did not let his feelings show, much less his surprise at Fred's suddenly becoming a talker on something other than tech details. *Always remember that these people are damned smart. And odd. Not predictable.* "Quite so. It's useful to hear how hard this is going to be. Also to know the purpose."

"Which is?" Beth was still softly defiant. Her eyes glowed.

"Getting to Glory. Those are our mission orders. We're carrying humanity to the stars. Beginning a process that ensures our species immortality." They had all heard these terms, but maybe they needed to be reminded.

"We haven't discussed other options," Fred said, his eyes still holding firm on Redwing.

"I haven't heard any proposed," Redwing said, deliberately settling his cheek on his right palm, as if settling in to listen.

"We could—should—continue our conversation with the Folk. Edge them toward our point of view." Beth said this stiffly, eyes on Redwing. "They have Tananareve and Cliff's team, yes. But we have so many sleeping souls with us—"

"We have given them days already," Clare Conway said. "And they attacked our coins. In a few more days, what else might they do?"

Redwing was happy with this support and decided to let them talk awhile, let the idea sink in.

Fred said, "Think about us as orphans. This thing, the Bowl, is so old—they must be used to expeditions from some nearby star coming out to look. So whatever alien species arrived, they were on a one-way trip. Just like us. That's the Folk history. So they think of us the same way."

"Makes sense," Karl said. "They think the Bowl is so wonderful, of course smart species want to come and see it. Tourists who came and stayed."

Fred grinned, a rare event. "Not like us, passersby."

Redwing did not like the way this was going. He kept his tone measured and precise. "In the end, a ship is not a democracy. It's a ship and there's only one captain. I'm it. I have to decide." This came out of him as a formula, but he had to say it.

"The Bowl teaches us a lot, Captain." Beth spoke quietly, slowly, but firm and steady. "We should study it awhile before we just go on. Before we leave it behind. There's so much to learn!"

"They could be just waiting us out," Clare said. "They know our general flight plan. It demands that we have only a few crew up and consuming food while we're on full-bore flight. Here, we're in a solar system, of sorts. We're catching their solar wind, what there is of it, and barely maintaining good sailing conditions. They know us. We don't know them."

Fred said, "They must have seen our magscoop flexing, struggling, trying out new patterns." He nodded to Clare. "And we kept running, but barely."

"It's pretty obvious, now that I think about it, from their point of view," Karl said. "They know this system intimately—hell, we don't even know how they manage to run it!"

"So it's likely they want to wait us out. Run low on supplies." Clare looked around at the whole table. "Gives them more time to hunt down Cliff's team, too."

Redwing was glad to get some support without saying a word. "Y'know," he said casually, "Magellan lost most of his crew when he sailed around the world."

"Magellan didn't make it home either," Fred said. "And we have over a thousand souls sleeping aboard who count on us."

Well, that backfired. "They're always in my calculations, Fred," he said as warmly as he could.

"I still think—," Beth began.

"That's not a crew officer issue," Redwing said firmly. "Not at all."

Silence as it sank in. To his surprise, Karl said with a deliberate mild voice, "We do not know what we face."

Redwing felt the tension rising in the room. *At least the Artilects don't argue....* "The human race has *never* known what it faced. We came out of Africa not knowing that deserts and glaciers lay ahead. Same here. If we have no respect from these Folk, we will be captives. Humanity will become *zoo animals.*"

This shocked them. Their eyes widened, blinked, mouths opened and closed with a snap. *Maybe they'll remember their obligations. Where they came from.*

They all looked at him long and hard. But Beth looked away—and in that moment he knew that he had them.

Tananareve was a useful test subject. Memor enjoyed experimenting with the primate.

Memor listened to the rumble of the fast train and ignored Bemor, who was working on his portable communicator. The primate was irked, eyes narrowed, after she heard some of Memor's remarks about the difficulty of negotiating with their Captain. Tananareve did not know she carried embedded sensors that reported regularly to Memor's diagnostic systems. When she got angry, her heart rate, arterial tension, and testosterone production increased. Quite interestingly, her stress hormones decreased.

Memor turned out of the line of sight and flourished a flat display of the primate response.

"Bemor, note this, please."

Bemor idly cast a distracted glance. Memor sent the data set to him and he glanced at the curves on his comm. "How odd, that anger relieves stress in these primates."

He sniffed. "With bad social effects, I would wager."

"Why? It must have evolved in the wild—"

"Exactly. They feel the stress-lowering as a kind of pleasure. So to relieve anxieties, they fight. This is not good for a peaceful society. It may explain why they are out here, far from home, exploring."

Memor paused. She differed with her brother over this area, which was, after all, her own realm of research. But . . . "You could be right. It seems an unlikely feature in a species we would make docile."

"I note her left brain hemisphere becomes more stimulated as well. This may confer some aggressive abilities."

Memor let this ride. The strumming metallic rhythms of the fast train were comforting, considering that they were moving with truly astronomical speeds down magnetically pulsing tubes, over elegant curve trajectories, arcing across and within the Bowl's long slopes. They had voyaged now for several slumbers. The fast tubes were cramped, and their outer metal skins at times heated to smarting temperatures through inductive losses. Tight, unamusing quarters even for Folk. Uninspired edibles, with little live game at all. Memor passed the last wriggling forkfish to Bemor; it flapped weakly and gave a soft cry of despair. He took it with relish and crunched happily, snapping the bones. The heady, acid flavor of the forkfish filled the cabin. Tananareve made a clenched face and covered her mouth and nose with a cloth.

All this travel to rendezvous with the proximate locus the autoprobes had found—among the icefields of the hull, in ready range of the Ice Minds— for the vagrant primates.

The renegade primates had tripped detectors among the renegade Sil first. Now this. Memor's attempts to keep a distant trace on the primates was well enough, Bemor thought, but "Given to excess," he had remarked, "when not well policed."

Several ready examples had happened a short while ago.

First came the incident in which Sil hirelings had patrolled the precincts outside the recently bombed Sil city. There were minor traces of the primates in the area, but the bombardment had eliminated most of the sites where identification would have been simple. Instead there were vague sightings and some detector probables. Bemor had disliked Memor's delegation of patrolling to a band of Sil unloyal to the central Sil hierarchy. They attempted a poorly thought-through maneuver to block the primates' movements across a plain. The Sil accompanying the Late Invaders managed to kill and badly injure several of their blockers. There was one report that a car of Late Invaders had taken part in the action. Since Memor knew this same party had killed a local party in a magcar before, and taken part in an insurrection from which Memor herself narrowly escaped, this latest incident was no surprise.

The second incident was more troubling. The same Sil and Late Invaders party had been glimpsed by a routine patrol skirting the hull territories. Only one clear identification, but enough. Yet by the time automatic patrols had arrived, the party was gone.

Now a third report, in a region housing old intelligences. The portal near the Kahalla shrine had triggered an abnormality alert. This signal came to the attention of resident monitors for the Zone. Since Memor had a tag on such genetic identifiers, she heard of this just a short while ago, when already in the long magnetic train tube network with Bemor.

"They move in crafty fashion," Bemor had observed. "Doubtless this is not a signature of Late Invader cleverness. They do not know our territories. They must be guided by the Sil."

Memor sent a fan-array in a flutter of subtle, doubting yellows. "I doubt the Sil have such abilities either. We have contained them in their urge to expand for a great long time now. Many generations have passed since Sil could roam in exploring parties."

Bemor considered this. "They are also a rambunctious species, still. Some longlives ago, they sought access to the strictly nonsentient Zones."

"I do recall." Memor quickly accessed her Undermind, and the memory unfolded for her quick review. "Outright demands for territory, claiming that their species had spread quickly over their homeworld due to a mixed genetic and social imperative."

"Quite. Note that seems, from your own work, to be a signature heritage of your Late Invaders."

The implications of this struck Memor only now. But her Undermind quickly sent a link that showed she had been mulling over these Late Invader–Sil resonances. But only vaguely. Bemor, on the other hand, had seen it immediately.

Memor turned to Tananareve. "Your origins are how far back in your own measure?"

The primate took her time. Her eyes swept from Memor to her brother as she kept her mouth stiff. Then, "Several hundred thousand orbitals."

Bemor had not ingested Memor's concept-map of her studies of the Late Invaders, for he said, "She must not know the correct sum."

"No, this fits with her supporting frame-referencing knowledge. I read it directly from her long-term memory."

"Unreliable. We do not know the topology of her Undermind."

"We will. But more important, I *asked her*. She gave a detailed history of their species traumas. Detailed and odd, but plausible. They were several times forced into small surviving parties, due to climate shifts. At one point they were barely above levels to avoid inbreeding in a cold place near an ocean. This built in a desire to expand—almost an assumption, I would say, that the lands far beyond the hills they saw could be better."

Bemor huffed and shifted his bulk uneasily. In close quarters, his musk flavored the air and rankled her nose. She sniffed as a rebuke. "It is rare to proceed up through the stages of mental layering you describe. I cannot believe it would occur in so few orbitals of an ordinary star."

"As I recall, the Sil also evolved high intelligence and tool use in a short while." Memor fished up the details and sent them to Bemor.

A long moment of brooding inspection, a rumbling in his chest, wheeze of slowly expelled breath. "So they did. This explains their intuitive alliance with the Late Invaders."

Memor said, "We have new data that the Sil have been privy to our general messages about the Late

Invaders. They may have sensed this as their opportunity."

Bemor turned to Tananareve. "You know of the Sil?" he asked in something resembling Anglish.

"Only what you have said of them," she said.

"They are with the other escaped Late Invaders."

"We were not invaders at all!" This animated the primate. "We came as peaceful explorers."

He rumbled with mirth at this, but a quick startled expression on Tananareve's face showed she thought it an aggressive sound. "Your peacefulness is surely moot, is it not? You of course we retained, but some others of you escaped."

"We do not like being unfree."

"And we—who of course did not fear any warlike abilities such as your kind might have—do not savor intrusion. We avoid having new influences introduced into our Bowl without adequate wise supervision." Bemor said this slowly, as if speaking to a child, or to some of the slower Adopteds.

"I think by now all of 'our kind' would like to just get away from this place. We have another destination."

"As well we know," Memor said, flashing a *humor her* fan-signal to Bemor. "But that is also why we cannot allow you to arrive there first."

A nod. "That's how I figured it."

"Can you also give an opinion of why your companions are allied with the Sil?"

Tananareve smiled. "They need help."

"And why together a band of these is moving through the Bowl, using fast transport and under-surface methods?" Bemor huffed, drawing nearer the primate—who then shrank back, nose wrinkling.

"They're on the run. Been running so long, maybe it's a habit."

Memor suspected this was a gibe but said nothing. Bemor persisted, his sour and salty male odor rising in their compartment. "Nothing more?"

She looked up at them both with a level, assessing gaze. "How about curiosity?"

"That is not a plausible motive," Memor said, but saw that Bemor gave off flurry-fan-signals of disagreement.

"I fear it is," Bemor said. "We try not to allow such facets of a species' character to rule their behavior."

Tananareve smiled again. "That's what becoming Adopted means?"

"In part," Bemor conceded.

"Then you will savor our destination," Memor said. "It will show you creatures you have never seen and quite probably cannot imagine." No point in not using a touch of anticipation, was there? Some species appreciated that.

The primate said, "Try me."

STONE MIND

It's not the size of the dog in the fight, it's the size of the fight in the dog.
—MARK TWAIN

THIRTY

Cliff watched the sleeting, tarnished-silver rain slam down from an angry, growling purple cloud. This was like a more ferocious form of the cool autumnal storms he had waited out while hiking in the high Sierra Nevada, with crackling platinum lightning electrifying half the sky's dark pewter. Crack and boom, all louder and larger than in the Sierra, maybe because it came from an atmosphere deeper and more driven, sprawling across scales far larger than planets. This violence was casually enormous, with clouds stacked like purple sandwiches up the silvered sky until they faded in the haze. The stench of wet wood mingled with a zesty tang of ozone, sharp in his nose and sinuses. He tasted iron in the drops that splashed on his outstretched tongue, and salt in the rough leaves they'd just eaten, plus a citrus burn in the vegetables they'd managed to scrounge from some trees nearby, before the hammering rainstorm arrived. Tastes of the alien lands.

"Rain near done," Quert said. "Need go. Soon."

Cliff could scarcely believe this prediction. "Why?"

"Folk find us."

"You're sure?"

"They know much. Even stones—" A gesture to distant sharp peaks, emerging from cottony clouds as the storm ebbed. "—speak to them. Always know." A grave nod of Quert's bare head said much.

Cliff nodded. Rain pattered down and smoke stained the air and it was hard to think. Quert made sense. The whole Bowl was deeply wired in some way. Its lands were vast but not stupid; there had to be a smart network that wove all this together. Still, most of the Bowl had to run on its own. No one or no thing could manage so huge a space unless the default options were stable, ordinary, and would work without incessant managing. Still . . .

No security from prying eyes would last for long. Their only advantage was that the Bowl was, while well integrated, still so vast. Even light took a while to cross it—up to twelve minutes, from the edge of the rim to the other edge. The delays sending text or faint voices across it, to Redwing on *SunSeeker,* were irritating. Especially when you could lose contact at any second.

The sky roiled with restless smoldering energy. Sudden gusts of howling wind drove the cold hard rain into their rock shelter. The pewter sky slid endlessly across them. But Quert had made them stop here in a long shaped-stone space, angular and ancient seeming, cut back into a hillside. They got in just before the slamming storm descended. Then after hours of huddling, the sky calmed. By the time they ate some of their food, heating it with burning twigs, a black slate wedge had slid overhead and the first hard drops spattered down.

Now it suddenly ended. Cliff turned to the others and said, "Pack up, gang."

Sil and humans, they all grunted a bit with the effort of getting moving and splashed water on their fire. Cliff could still taste the sweet meat they had roasted there. It had made him wish for a robust California zinfandel, though perhaps those didn't even exist anymore now. Maybe there wasn't a place called California anymore back Earthside, he mused.

The succulent aromatic filets came from a big fat meaty doglike creature that had rushed at them hours before. When it came fast out of some big-leafed rustling bushes, they first noticed the curved yellow horns it carried on a broad, bony head. Then the bared teeth. It snarled and leaped, with an expression Cliff thought looked as greedy as a weasel in a henhouse. Most of them froze, for it was a true surprise—not even Quert and the Sils had seen it coming. But Aybe had caught it in midair with a laser shot that drilled through its surprisingly large brain cage and the thing fell limp and sprawling at their feet. It died with a shudder and a long, gut-deep gasp.

They ate the dark rich meat eagerly. It had a strong muscular frame that gutted easily. The Sil cracked its bones and sucked out the marrow. Cliff considered doing it—*fat hunger!*—but the rank, oily smell put him off. So he offered his bone around.

"Sure," Aybe said, taking it. He sliced a line in it with his serrated blade and snapped the bone open over his knee. "Yum."

Irma and Terry shook their heads, no. "Ugh," Terry said. "I grew up on a low-fat diet. That was gospel for a half century, before we had nano blood policing."

"Me, too," Irma added, wrinkling her nose. "Our generation hated that fat smell."

"I like it plenty," Aybe said. "Must be—hey, what generation are you?"

Terry, Cliff, and Irma looked at each other. "We're in our seventies," Irma said.

"Gee, I'm forty-four," Aybe said.

"Just a kid," Terry said. "Surprised you made the grade. The rumor around Fleet was, nobody has enough experience before they're in their fifties."

Aybe smirked. "You old guys always say that."

Irma chuckled. "The first forty years are for sex and reproduction. You used yours amassing a lot of tech abilities?"

"Sure did." Aybe shrugged. "I wanted more than anything to get on a starship. Reproduction is over-rated."

They all laughed. "Women routinely stored eggs and you guys are never quite out of business," Irma said. "Childbirth's just easier below sixty."

"How old do you think Redwing is?" Terry asked, finishing a slab of meat he had traded with Aybe in return for another bone.

"Gotta be a hundred," Terry said.

"Older, I'd say. Went through the tail end of the Age of Appetite, he told me once. Pretty nasty time."

"He's a pretty nasty guy," Aybe said, and then sucked loudly on a long bone until they could hear him drawing air all the way through it, a hollow slurp.

"Look," Cliff said mildly, "plenty of people live to well over a hundred and fifty now. Redwing's not what I'd call *old*."

"By 'now' you mean 'when we were Earthside,' right?" Terry said. "God knows how old people live there now."

That made everyone think of the abyss of time separating them from everyone they knew, Cliff saw. He let that ride for a while. Quert nodded to him, seeming to understand. Then it was time to move on.

They hiked away from their latest rough stone shelter into a clearing sky. There were local horizons here, but now the stray clouds skated over those near horizons and the sweet blue air above cleared further. Cliff had not seen before this sharp, sure atmosphere that he knew was deeper than anything on Earth. Yet now few clouds intruded into a shimmering sharp air. The piercing point star of the Bowl's governing sky still hung above them, of course. But he and his team had moved along the slope of the Bowl for many days at high speeds, one way or the other, and now the star—Cliff had named it Wickramsingh's Star, he recalled—shone not at the absolute center of this sky, but at a slight angle. Its jet seemed now to plunge more deeply toward them. Its streamers turned with elegant grace, pale orange filaments laced across the gauzy firmament. He watched its slow swirls as they slogged across a broad hill. The humans hung back from the Sil advance point men—though some of their Sil party, he had finally realized, were women. He still could not tell their sexes apart with assurance. The Sil didn't seem to have strong binary distinctions between sexes in looks, dress, or behavior. Their occasional puzzled glances at Irma might come from that. Maybe, Cliff realized, humans were just more sexually restless than these Sil.

Shapes darted around in the forest. Cliff had seen that with constant sunlight, creatures had to be on guard all the time. Prey had eyes that looked broadly, like rabbits' bulging eyes, or insects' compound eyes—all designed to see at wide angles. Predators, as on Earth, had good depth of field, with eyes looking mostly forward, and wide-spaced for maximal 3-D perception.

Irma walked beside him, shouldering her pack where it wore on her, and said brightly, "Ever think, how come we're seeing so many bipeds?"

Cliff tried to remember that he actually was a biologist. "Um. Hadn't thought. But look, as I recall from lectures, anyway, Earthside bipedalism was really nothing more than an oddball vertebrate artifact."

She adjusted her hat against the sunlight. "Those back there, the Kahalla, they couldn't pass for us, not even in a dim room. Humanoids, though, for sure. Same basic design. But they're from a tide-locked world, not like Earth at all. Odd."

He kept watching the forest slipping by as they marched on. But theory was fun, too. He bit off a bit of a sweet root they'd pried up from the ground, under Quert's instruction, and said, "Convergent evolution, must be. Those Kahalla prob'ly had four-limbed ancestors, just like us. Back Earthside, the arthropods always had limbs to spare, but not poor old mammals like us. We're bipeds because we started with four limbs, and developed climbing skills, then tool use. That left two limbs for walking, so that pressure forced us to stand up."

Irma took some of the sweet root, ate through all the rest of it, and smiled. She, too, endlessly scanned the passing trees and vines, and searched the skies. You learned to stay alert after so long in the field. "Yeah, Earthside, bipeds are really rare. Except for birds, who've got 'em because they invest so much in wings. For invertebrates, the closest thing to that vertical posture is something like a praying mantis."

Cliff thought on that as he slapped a fat bug that wanted to use his hair for a nest. "A mantis has four legs."

Irma's voice always went up in pitch when she had an idea. "You're skipping my point. We saw one biped far back, right? Big lumbering thing that ignored us, dunno why. Then the Sil. Now these Kahalla. All had heads with faces, two forward-looking eyes and jaws and a nose."

Cliff saw her point. "Not a necessary arrangement,

right. Just look at arthropod faces. Scary, because they're just close enough to ours to look threatening, horrible."

"Those Kahalla though, had pointy faces, eyes more on the side."

"That's a prey signature. I remember from high school, 'Eyes front, likes to hunt; eyes on side, likes to hide.' Seems to be a universal."

"Plus they had fur," Irma said. "We don't, because we overheated when we ran long distances—so we lost the fur."

Cliff nodded, recalling how lumbering those Kahalla figures had been. Bulky, ponderous, more like bears than people. And not a word had been spoken between them and the humans and Sil. Just glowers and postures, like the signals animals give. "Um, okay. So the Kahalla aren't runners. Or talkers."

Irma said, voice rising more, "The Bowl is telling us that smart aliens converge to a humanoid form."

Cliff thought on that, never ceasing his scan of the forest around them. *Or could be, somebody designed them. . . .*

Quert was ahead of them and now turned. "Not the Folk. Not like, your word, humanoid. We say, Sil Shape. Same thing."

"Um, yeah," Irma said. "I wonder why?"

"Come from self design, for Folk," Quert said. "Ancient."

"So they have—what?—two arms and four legs?" Cliff asked.

"Some do. Many others, two legs. Still all Folk."

Irma asked, "The Folk, do they really run things here?"

Quert gave a downward eye-gesture, which Cliff now knew expressed polite doubt. "Ice Minds, they above Folk."

"How's that work?" Cliff pressed.

"That changes now. Since you came. We Sil work for Ice Minds too, now." Quert brandished his small communicator, a pyramidal solid that could deform into a flat screen. Cliff had yet to figure out how that worked.

Irma said, "What do you do for them?"

"Brought you to them."

"That's it?" Irma asked. "Why us?"

"You disturb. Folk call you 'Late Invader' because you new. Ice Minds want to see you. Know you. So we bring."

"We're just a small ship, passing by," Irma said.

"Something about Glory, I hear from Ice Minds. They want to know what you are, going to Glory." Quert gave a head-shrug. "Not sure what Glory be."

"It's a star right ahead of you," Cliff said. "We can't see it—your star's too bright."

"Star ahead?" Quert's face went blank, which meant the alien was thinking, giving nothing away.

Irma said, "It's a star a lot like yours, still so far away that it's only a dot. Its planet has a biosphere with oxygen and nitrogen and the usual. We want to go there, live there."

Quert kept the blank look, but the eyes jittered up, down, around. The alien was undergoing an entire conceptual shift.

Suddenly Cliff saw it. The Sil had been ushered into the view from the Bowl hull—the deep dark abyss of glinting stars—only lately. The Ice Minds had beckoned to them somehow, sent signals, and propelled forward the events Cliff's team had then intersected. So Quert and the others had never seen the stars at all, until they brought Cliff's team through the underground labyrinth and to where they could see the sliding panorama of the galaxy in full.

The Sil had been like people trapped in a cave, never shown the sky. Their world, the world of all who lived on the Bowl, was an endless warm paradise in steady daylight. Their sun and jet obliterated perspective. The ordinary denizens never saw the stars, or the great plane of the galaxy hanging in a black firmament, dark and strange and sprinkled with twinkling jewel stars.

That revelation had come to the Sil when they were restless and angry. The Folk had suppressed them for ageless times, but now they knew where they were, who they were. All that had exploded into their world only lately. Cliff's team had confirmed new truths, and so had made many tragedies come to pass—the battle with the skyfish, the bombing and firestorms of the Sil cities, so much else.

Cliff started to say some of this to Quert. The alien still had the stiff fixed face, giving nothing away while it thought. But then movements caught their attention.

The point Sil stopped, gestured, and muttered

something in a low whisper. Head and arm gestures: something ahead, spread out.

They all followed their standard tactic, moving off to both sides and seeking cover, then moving carefully forward. The humans had learned this in training, fire-and-maneuver. Each member of the Sil and human team moved only when others could cover with fire from lasers, arm-arrows.

Ahead, a faint repeating clatter came through the trees and vines.

Beyond, the land cleared. Cautiously they worked their way to a vantage point on a small hill. A strip of neatly arranged, emerald green agricultural fields stretched into the distance to their left and right. Simple farm machinery worked in them, making *whack-whack-whack* noises. Directly ahead, the forest resumed several kilometers away. The crop was yellow and purple shoots that seemed to spray out like arrows from a thick brown trunk. These were three or four meters tall, Cliff judged, like trees with spokes flying out. The spokes were fat and had wide, fanlike flowers along their lengths. The air carried a fine mist of—what? Pollen?

"We can cross that at a run," Aybe said.

Quert pointed to figures working in the field. They had trucks and a robot harvester that worked away, chopping off the shoots and dropping them into the trucks. The machinery worked with a regular *whump whump whump*. A breeze brought a heady sweet scent like orange blossoms with a cutting undertang. Everything moved with a slow rhythm, and the scene reminded Cliff of a monotonous summer he had spent on a farm in California's Central Valley. He close-upped them and said, "They're the same kind we left behind, those humanoids mesmerized by that ancient rock life. Kahalla."

"These special Kahalla evolve for farm work," Quert said. "They stay here always on farm. Birthing and dying, all done here."

Irma asked, "They live in a village all their lives?"

"Content. In balance." Quert conferred with the other Sil in quick, scattershot bursts of unintelligible talk. They all looked wary to Cliff, as nearly as he could judge. The Sil had complex suites of expressions that darted across their faces, mostly coded in their eye-moves and the light-browed ridgelines above. Quert turned to the humans. "This Aybe right. Run fast across. See there?"

Nearly directly across from them was a complex of low buildings the tan color of dried mud. "Their hatchery. Few Kahalla there most times. We cross, the Kahalla not see."

Cliff tried to take this in. A special form of Kahalla just for the grunt labor of farming? Had the Folk specially bred for that? And . . . hatchery?

They moved through the cover of a long winding grove of zigzag trees. He and Irma thought the zigzag strategy was to get more sunlight under a constant sun, which meant more exposed foliage turned to the direction of the star, a reddish dot fixed firmly in the sky. The jet's filmy light they ignored. Bristly branches and coiling vines sprawled along the thick zigzag trunks to harvest the constant sunlight. That made them useful cover, because the branches were thin at the top and thicker at the tree base. Easy to slip among and elude any watching eyes.

Warily they stopped within easy view of the tannin brick buildings. As a Californian, Cliff seldom saw ceramic slabs stacked to great heights; his instinct said they were earthquake vulnerable. But there were no quakes here at all. He saw through binocs furry figures moving with lumbering, swaying bodies on two legs, moving slowly among the brick walls. He pointed to them.

"Friends not," Quert said with narrowed eyes and edgy eye-clicks.

"These Kahalla will turn us over to the Folk?" Terry asked.

Quert said, "Must," and gave a downturned eye-move.

The other Sil shuffled and eye-clicked in what seemed agreement, their feet shuffling, impatient. They seemed to feel there was no time to waste in pondering this problem. No point in trying to go around the long farming strip that faded away into the light tan color of the distance, which came from simple dust haze. No telling how long this farm was. An odd way to cultivate; why not in squared-off plots so you minimized the travel distance?

"No time to think much," Aybe said. "Ready to run?"

They set off at a good pace. The Sil got out in front right away with their long graceful strides, taking long slow deep breaths as their feet came down. They seemed to have evolved for running. Humans had, too, but not this well. Cliff wondered if their home world, with somewhat lower gravity, had better shaped them for this part of the Bowl. Again he wondered, as sweat collected in his eyebrows and trickled down, stinging his eyes, what the Sil's agenda was. Getting out from under the Folk, yes. But those big birds ran this place, and a few puny humans surely could not make much difference. A puzzle. But without the Sil, they'd have been nabbed by the Folk long ago. He let it pass.

They made a good fast run across the fields, running close to the curious trees. The Kahalla were upwind of their crossing route, too, so that might be an advantage. Cliff was surprised at how easily he ran. He was in better physical condition now from so long on the run, and the local grav seemed lower here, too. But Quert's head turned, surveying the whole area, as did all the Sil. They were worried.

The rough rectangular buildings Quert called a hatchery loomed up, two stories high and no windows. They entered the complex, panting and sweaty, and made their way down the main corridor between the buildings. There were no Kahalla around at all. A few zigzag trees lined this main street of the place, their wood worn and gray. The Sil went down side passages, doing reconn, and in a few moments came running back fast. They shouted a word in Sil language and formed a defensive arc facing two passageways. Automatically the humans gathered in behind them, drawing weapons, looking anxiously around.

Only when a Sil launched one of its arm-arrows did they look up.

Things like meter-wide spiders came over the lip of the roof. They were white and clacked as they moved, surging down the wall on flexing black palps. Their legs were bristly and black; big angry red eyes glared at the sides of a squashed face.

The first Sil arm-arrow lanced through one that was halfway over the edge of the roof. It scrabbled at the wall and fell with a smack at their feet. The Sil who had nailed it stepped forward, shot at another of the attackers, hit it at dead center of its circular body—then bent and plucked the arrow out, inserting it quickly back in the air sheath.

The Sil were shooting at the things now, and the humans used their lasers. But there were plenty of the things, and they kept coming.

They move more like crabs than like spiders, Cliff thought as the Sil fell back. He aimed at one of the things and hit it, but it just kept climbing down the wall toward them. His shot had gone through it near its edge, but that was not enough, apparently.

They made small, shrill chippering sounds. They moved sideways with quick sure moves.

Now Cliff recalled a relayed message from Beth when they had broken out of their captivity. "Spidows," he said.

Irma got the reference. "Those were huge, they said. These aren't."

"Local adaptation," Aybe said. "Our lasers blow through them but don't kill, most of the time."

Five of the things took on a Sil. They crawled up its legs and bit deep with claws. The Sil howled. It batted at them and lurched away. That unnerved the other Sil as rivers of the midget spidows rushed down from other roofs and through the lanes nearby. Their high, shrill cries became a shriek. The humans huddled behind a thin line of Sils who were running out of their arm-arrows.

Quert was driving arm-arrows into the spidows but then shouted in Sil and then in Anglish, "Back through!"

Cliff turned and saw a Sil had found, down a side corridor, a big frame door that opened. They all turned and rushed there. The spidows' shrill cries rose as they came after the running Sil and humans. Several Sil tore branches off the zigzag trees along the way, snapping them off. They got through the doorway and into a big high room. The door slammed. Sil secured it.

Illumination streamed down from a ceiling that simmered with ivory light. The place reeked of some sullen odor. It was damp and warm here, and the humans looked at each other, eyes wide, still surprised by the sudden ferocity of the spidow attack. The Sil muttered to each other. They were all standing under the heat beating down from above, panting in moist air flavored with an odd stinging taste.

"Were . . . were those spiders?" Aybe asked.

"More like crabs," Cliff said.

"They have a shell and move with a sideways crawl, lots of legs," Irma said.

"If there weren't so many, we could just tromp on them," Terry said.

"But there are!" Aybe was scared and covered it with anger.

The Sil stirred and murmured and Quert listened to them intently. The humans talked but no ideas emerged. The high keening cries of the spidows came through the walls. They all knew they were trapped, and the shock of it was sinking in, Cliff saw.

"Let's see what there is here. What this place is," Cliff said. It was good to get them focused on something beyond their fears. They murmured, shuffled, and started to look around.

Around them stood cylindrical towers with big fat orange spheres arrayed in a matrix. There were some kind of ceramic tubes laced through the crude baked brick frame, and those felt warm to the touch.

"What are these things? A whole room full," Irma said.

Quert said, "Kahalla eggs. Hatch here," and took two other Sil to prowl the room. Cliff followed down the line of Kahalla egg cylinder holders. The warm damp air was cloying. Heads jerked toward a scraping noise. They all saw a white carapace of a spidow scuttling away. It left behind a ripped-open Kahalla egg that dripped brown fluids on the red clay floor. The spidow had been eating it. A Sil stabbed it with a shaft of wood it had yanked off a zigzag tree outside. The spidow writhed, worked its claws against the shaft, and died with a faint squealing gasp.

They found another a few moments later. Some had gotten in here, Cliff supposed, and were eating Kahalla eggs. "Food source," Irma said.

Several of the big orange spheres were already spattered over the ceramic floor, their insides gone. Cliff followed, still dazed by the speed of events. He shook his head, rattled. As the Sil searched the aisles of egg-holding cylinders Cliff kept up, feeling pretty useless, and then asked Quert, "The Kahalla look kind of like us—two legs, same body shape. But they lay *eggs*?"

"Kahalla way," Quert said. Its eyes were wary, searching the whole room. "Stack their eggs here. Let hatch. Safe so they can work their fields."

"Uh, but the spidows—that's what we call them—they come and eat?"

An eye-click of agreement. "Been so, long time. We call those things *upanafiki*. Pests, are."

"They're smart enough to get into these hatcheries."

Quert sniffed and gave soft barking sounds with a head-jerk, which seemed to be the Sil equivalent of laughter. All the Sil joined in. Some alien inside joke, Cliff suspected. Or was Sil humor a category outside human comprehension? Quert stopped the quiet barking laugh and said, "Kahalla not smart."

"Egg layers . . ." Cliff tried to get his head around all this.

Irma said, "Earthside we have monotremes, mammal egg-layers. They're very old, Triassic maybe."

Cliff shook his head. "Forget about parallels to Earth. So: smart egg-layers who are humanoid tool-users. What the hell, with evolution on the Bowl, all bets are off."

Quert said, "*Upanafiki* many. Kahalla crave land. *Upanafiki* keep Kahalla numbers down. Kahalla and *upanafiki*—" Quert thrust its bony hands together. "Always. Fight. Dance."

Aybe said, "Where did these Kahalla come from? What world?"

Quert said, "Kahalla means in your tongue One Face Folk."

Terry got it. "So they come from a planet tidally locked to its star? On their side it was always sunny. They had an adaptation advantage when they arrived at the Bowl, over people like us who need night. Makes sense."

Quert gave an eye-click of agreement. "Spread widely. They are conservative. Folk use them. Not good allies for us."

Cliff frowned. *Evolutionary theory in the middle of a fight . . .*

"Come see this," Irma called. She was at the other end of the room. They followed her up some crudely fashioned stairs of gray clay ceramic. The dusty second floor was like the first but Irma pointed to a hole in its ceiling. "Looks like they dug down through."

Cliff crouched, jumped, and caught the edge of

the hole. Some of it crumbled away, but he held on and pulled his head through the meter-wide opening. This might be risky, but he was curious—and hanging there, he saw the roof now deserted. A nearby piece of wood caught his eye. He held on with one hand and shuffled a slim shaft nearby into the hole, letting it drop. Then he followed it, landing neatly. Low grav had its uses.

Irma picked up the slender piece of wood. "It has a tip like flint. Those small spidows—they're tool-users."

"Keep Kahalla stable," Quert said, glancing upward. "They outside on ground. We go this way."

Cliff and Irma looked askance at the alien. Quert went to the stairwell and shouted orders in the slippery Sil speech. Terry and Aybe came up with them. "Those spidows," Terry said, "they're chipping at the door with something."

Irma needed help, but in surprisingly short order their entire team, humans and Sil alike, made the leap to the ceiling hole. Those already on the roof grabbed their hands and hauled them out, onto the flat roof. It was made of tan triangular bricks. Now Cliff could see Quert's plan. The hatchery buildings were close together, and the Sil could leap from one roof to the next. So could the humans. The Sil were remarkably calm; they had met this foe before. They started leaping across. Cliff looked down as he took a running jump across. The spidows were clustered around the door to the building they had just left. Several of them held bigger wood shafts, also with blackened hard tips that seemed to have been turned on a fire.

Irma came next. She landed with one foot halfway onto the next roof lip. Cliff grabbed her and tugged her in. Terry and Aybe followed. By that time, most of the Sil were across to the next building, looking unhurried but quick.

They all ran and leaped, ran and leaped, and soon were at the far end of the hatchery buildings. There the Sil slung a thin wire around nearby trees, throwing it with a kind of boomerang hook that wrapped around a tree trunk. Then a Sil attached the wire to its backpack solar panel source, made some adjustments, hit a command switch—and the wire expanded, puffing up into a thick rope that hands could grab. Cliff blinked; a useful trick he had never seen.

They descended on that rope, belaying a bit to break their sliding descent. Cliff and Irma leaned over the side of the building to glimpse the spidows while others took the rope down. Spidows were still working on the door, chipping with crude spikes. But then some Kahalla came in from a side corridor, shouting. The spidows turned, and a battle began.

The spidow's bristly palps moved in a jerky blur. The Kahalla had simple hoes or similar farm tools. They struck down hard on the spidows and pinned them. But there were a lot, and some Kahalla got overwhelmed.

This was nature red in tooth and claw in a way he'd never seen. There were over a hundred spidows and maybe a dozen Kahalla—a melee. As they watched, Irma said, "A fight over reproduction? Nasty."

Quert had come over to them and looked down, unsurprised. "Folk set rules. Keep Kahalla from farming more and more. Use *upanafiki* to keep not many Kahalla eggs to hatch. These *upanafiki* pests for us. Their war with Kahalla never end."

"The Folk don't stop this?" Irma asked.

"Folk want this." Quert paused, searching for the right Anglish words. "Equilibrium. Stasis."

As Cliff watched five spidows swarm fast over a struggling Kahalla humanoid, he thought, *Nightmare spiders on a caffeine high*. The Kahalla toppled and vanished beneath the swarming spidows. He recalled a remark heard long ago, *Flattery isn't the highest compliment—parasitism is*.

"Damn!" Irma's shrill shout jerked him out of his thoughts.

He saw several spidows, their legs grappling for purchase over the lip of the roof, twenty meters away. They had come up the wall. They made a sharp hissing, their legs clicking with darting moves.

He and Irma had been distracted and now with Quert were the only ones left on the roof. Quert was already ahead of them and took the rope with an easy grace. Down Quert slid, shouting back "Come fast!" Irma went next, and Cliff turned to take a laser shot at the mass of spidows surging across the tan brick roof. The bolts punched holes easily enough, but the spidows did not stop. A bolt to the center did work, and one of the things flopped down. But now they were five meters away. Cliff leaned down and plucked the securing anchor of the rope. No time to slide down it now. He couldn't be sure the spidows couldn't use it. The black rope was firmly fixed in the trees thirty meters away, so he just grabbed it and ran off the edge of the roof. He dropped, then swung.

His breath rasped and he ignored a snap in his shoulder. He tumbled on the descent and tried to pull himself up the rope as it carried him toward the trees. His swing brought him boot-forward, so when he hit the branches of a zigzag tree the leaves lashed him. One limb caught him smack in the face. He hit another, and a sharp pain lanced into his ribs. He gasped and slid down the rope, a nearly vertical drop now. The zigzag tree trunk smacked his thigh, but he managed to get his boots under him. He sprawled when he hit.

As he was rolling away, his ribs sent him a lance of pain and his vision blurred for a moment. He lay there gasping and hands grabbed him. They heaved him up and Terry shouted, "Gotta run!" So he did. Not very well.

The spidows were running through the trees already, lots of them. Their chippering calls were loud now. But the spidows were small and if humans were good at anything, he thought, it was sure as hell good old running.

For a while, though, until they no longer saw the spidows behind them, it was more like limping for him. He was worn out.

THIRTY-ONE

Redwing watched the Bowl landscape slide by below, distracting himself for a moment of relaxation with the splendid view. Getting back to work, he switched to interior ship views. In the garden, on screens left and right, two finger snakes were slithering through plants, picking here, planting seeds there, while the third—the male, Thisther, darker and a bit bigger than the others—was playing with two pigs, all three having hissing and oinking fun. A laugh bubbled in Redwing's throat—and still the big first question was there. *What could I be missing?*

Beth was due in a moment and he let the Bowl feed play on his display wall. He took out a tattered, yellowing paper. As part of his several-kilogram weight allowance it was nothing, but in his memories it was everything. His father had written it to him when in the Huntsville hospital from which he would not return. When he was ten, it had meant a great deal and now it meant more.

LIVE FULLY. TAKE RISKS. THINK CAREFULLY BUT ACT, TOO. SPEAK UP. KEEP MIND OPEN AND HEART WARM. DON'T JUST PASS THE TIME. LIVE LIVE LIVE!—FOR SOMEDAY YOU WILL NOT.

He recalled the man at his best: sawdust sprinkled in black hair, deftly pushing a Douglas fir two-by-four through the buzzing blade of a circular saw, then trimming it and taking a quick measure of the work by holding it against the studs, nodding in the damp fragrant sawdust air, plucking a nail from where he stored it in his front teeth, fetching a ball-peen hammer from its loop on his belt, two quick whaps and a finishing tap, a bright grin, then on to the next.

He stared at the paper scrap and then put it away, for perhaps the thousandth time. It was centuries old but still true.

Beth tapped on his door. He stood to slide the door aside and nodded with a greeting. They got right to it.

She sat across from him in his narrow cabin and he made a show of finishing a log entry. It was not entirely show. He had to keep on top of how *Sun-Seeker* sailed on the vagrant winds of plasma and magnetic fields. Plus preparations for the jet interception. And an anxious, overworked crew.

But Beth was the hardest. She had been down there for long months and managed to get back aboard, a striking feat. She had prestige with the rest of the crew. She regaled them with stories of aliens and exploits and weird doings down on the Bowl. She'd taken casualties and escaped from a prison. Figured out the alien landscape and made her team get across it. And fly back home in an alien craft. So he had promoted her two grades in the science officer ladder. When she got to Glory—*and we will do that, by damn!*—she would command the first landing. Still, her tight face promised trouble.

"We're in an existential position here, sir," she began.

"Right. We don't have enough supplies to get to Glory. Our logistics were marginal when we sighted the Bowl. Now it's hopeless. We've burned food and essentials hovering over this enormous thing. Plus time."

Beth said with deliberation, "I mean, if we commit an overt hostile act, that sure does change the game."

He nodded. *Always concede the rhetorical stuff.* "We have to start a clock running. Otherwise they'll wait us out."

"But their jet is the key to their Bowl. Damaging it is a mortal threat."

"Sure it is. We don't mean to shove a dagger in. We want to show that we *can*."

Beth twisted her mouth into a wry grimace. "A pinprick, then?"

"That's all."

"These are aliens, Cap'n. Their civilization is older than anything we know. Hell, maybe than we *can* know. This maneuver, this provocation, is a huge gamble."

"That it is." He sat back and folded his hands on his desk. "One we've got to take."

"Look, we don't know how that damn jet operates. How the Folk run it. How unstable it is."

"Right. Isn't that how science works?" Redwing grinned. "If you don't understand, do an experiment."

Beth shook her head. "Plus we don't understand

the Glory message, or how the Folk really feel about it. I just . . . I worry."

"So do I." *What could I be missing?*

"There are risks to every choice. Maybe the right question is, do we want to play Russian roulette with two bullets or one?"

She sighed and got up. She was a bit wobbly. He wondered if she was truly fit for service as their backup pilot. On impulse, he got up and gave her a firm warm hug. With a sigh, too.

• • •

Karl showed him the external views of *SunSeeker*, freshly gathered by their small auto-cam bots that had flown around the entire ship. "She's centuries old now, but holding up," he said with a hint of pride. Karl was a bit stiff and formal, but he could not conceal his feelings completely.

The ship's sleek after section hid behind the torus of the life zone. The shuttle cradles along the central boom were yawning yellow and orange cups for craft docking and vacuum maintenance bots. Micrometeorites had pitted the hull, and radiation burns splashed black filigrees along the flanks. The entire sleek design focused on the demands of starflight. Now their planetary-scale orbits made it hard to get adequate plasma into the magnetic funnel, and the ship barely ran. Fitful spasms sometimes passed through her, the coughs and sputters of a system hovering on the brink of shutting down entirely. The fusion fires in her belly ran soft, then hard, then not at all—until Karl and the crew could get them burning full and furious again. It reminded him of a fine ship built for the high seas, rotting beside a wharf.

Redwing nodded. "Fair enough. The mag systems, they can handle the jet?"

Ayaan Ali said, with a tired and exasperated sigh, "Our upgrades are basically fine-tuning. They seem to work. I'm pretty sure, from records and Artilect memories of Beth's flight up the jet, that we can deal with the turbulence levels."

"And if we can't?" Redwing persisted.

Karl said, "The more plasma we get into our magscoop, the better. So we steer for the density ridges, held in by the helical mag field."

Ayaan Ali pursed her full lips, and her long eyelashes flickered. Redwing recalled this was the closest she came to showing that she was irked. "The jet's mag pressure is high. It and those fast-changing plasma pressures can punch our scoop around, too. They're two orders of magnitude beyond our optimal design."

Redwing saw himself as referee when crew disagreed on the tech issues, but in the end he knew he had to decide who was right. "How bad can it be if we lose our magscoop shape?"

"We'll tumble," Ayaan Ali said.

"And we can recover," Karl said evenly.

They had the reliable Bear Down leptonic drive, the first to use the dark energy substrate as an energy stabilizer. Redwing did not pretend to understand its complex mechanisms that somehow drew power from the substrate of the very universe. Fundamentals were not his concern; its operation was. Karl pointed out endless details but in the end they had to play the hand they were dealt—a drive running on empty, unless they could grab enough plasma.

Ayaan Ali laid out the geometry on the big display screen that dominated the bridge. *SunSeeker* had to stay below the Bowl rim, or else come within the sighting angle of the domed gamma ray lasers sited there. Their "experiment" with flying a small package over the rim—and watching it disappear in a furious instant—proved that the Folk sense of diplomacy did not include letting them get out of the narrow cage *SunSeeker* now occupied. They could navigate in the space below the rim, down to the upper reaches of the Bowl's air zones. Spread out as the Bowl was over hundreds of millions of kilometers, it exerted a small but steady grav pull on them. Thrusting with the thin plasma here offset that. And through the center of that volume the jet spiked like a living, writhing yellow lance.

Ayaan Ali's 3-D display showed in detail the atmosphere's partitions far below them. It was not continuous, or else pressure differences between the low-grav sections would cause the air to gather there to a stifling degree. Instead, firm walls isolated wedges of the Bowl, cutting off circulations to high latitudes. Yet the air zones allowed gas to flow throughout the entire circumference of the annular regions. This meant that the air could flow over zones covering the size of the entire solar system, creating weather patterns unknown on mere planets. But the air could not ascend to the higher latitudes—the "bottom" of the Bowl, toward the Knothole.

"Those partitions are a wonder," Ayaan Ali said. "Made of some layered stuff that is flexible enough to have some give to it. But it's hundreds of kilometers on a side!"

Redwing nodded, thinking again, *What could I be missing? This thing was built by engineers who thought like gods. They must have methods we can't see, can't yet imagine.*

Yet the Folk who ran this place had let Beth's team escape. First from their low-grav Garden prison, then from the Bowl itself. *Beth is quick, ingenious, a real leader, but still . . . They're not all that smarter than we are. Bigger, though, Beth says. So how do they run this contraption?*

Ayaan Ali pointed to the roughly conical section, shaded blue, that was their allowed flight volume. She said, "So we can cruise around in here, and zip across the jet when we want to. So far we've just circled it, mostly."

Karl pointed at her simulation, which showed the bright jet purling down from the star, tightening as it neared the Knothole, then—as the display moved down, its smart eyes following his finger-point—beyond, where it expanded again, losing luminosity. That made the fast wind that *SunSeeker* had been swimming upriver against for a century, slowing them, costing them time and supplies. Coasting on the vagrant tendrils of plasma fraying off the jet had been a constant piloting problem, running Ayaan Ali ragged. Beth's return had taken some of the burden from her, and together they would take on the reverse problem—flying into the jet's thick, turbulent, moving cauldron of ionized particles and mag fields.

"I've calculated how to tip in near the top— that's our sign convention, right? Top is as high as we dare get, just below the deflection ability of the gamma ray lasers. We turn and plunge down, toward the Knothole. We sway back and forth across the jet while we drive down. Thrust hard in a helix winding path."

He had painted a red line in her simulation, standing for *SunSeeker*'s calculated path. Its helix widened as it got nearer the Knothole and the magnetic field lines—blue swirls embedded in the yellow and orange showing plasma—bulged outward in response. "See? We make the jet sway a little. A kink in the flow."

Redwing thought he followed this, but decided to play dumb. "Which are?"

"I'm sure you went through the basic plasma-instabilities material, Cap'n. It was in your briefing run-up."

The right word may be effective, but no word was ever as effective as a rightly timed pause. He let it simmer a bit. "Karl, you will always answer a direct technical question and skip your idea of what I know. Assume I know nothing."

"Sorry, um, Cap'n. Of course. Certainly. I meant

that . . ." His voice trailed off, uncertain of anything.

Redwing bailed him out. "Like a fire hose?"

"Right! Fast water going through a fire hose, if it
swerves a little, the centrifugal force of it forces the
hose even more to the side. It corkscrews, makes a
kink."

"So it will lash the side of the Knothole? You're
sure?"

Karl paused, nodded. "More of a brush, I'd say."

Redwing nodded. Ayaan Ali said, "I have some
good news. We got a short signal from Cliff's
team—from Aybe."

Redwing brightened. "Where are they? What—?"

"Here. They passed under the edge of the mirror
zone and got out onto the hull. Found ice there.
Then they had to take off. They got led to a place
where there were something like, well, talking
stones."

Redwing leaned forward. "And those said . . . ?"

A shrug. "We got cut off. See down there? They
were in lands between that zone of hexagonal mir-

rors. The icelands, with some life in them, those are on the outer hull under the mirrors, which keep it cold. Then Cliff's team and those Sil got to the drylands between the mirrors and this huge ocean."

Redwing stared at the view. Even when Ayaan Ali brought up a max resolution image, there was nothing to show more than occasional towns and roads. Again it struck him how much of this place was endless forests and seas and ranges of tan hills. Very few large cities and plenty of room for wildlife. Why? *Hard to evaluate a thing as big as this Bowl. Earth alone had plenty of habitats that a few thousand years back were places where the crown of creation would be a tasty breakfast.*

Karl asked, "Those are—what, hurricanes on that ocean?"

"Seems so." Ayaan Ali pointed to a few. "The big winds have lots more room to play out, too. Huge storms. Cyclones the size of planets."

Redwing stood to end the meeting. "We'll hit the jet in a few days, right? Keep doing your simulations and drills. Get some rest, too," with a nod to Ayaan Ali.

Now that the die was cast, he needed some alone time. *SunSeeker*'s steady rumble always told you that you were in a big metal tube, only meters away from other people. And meters away from both a furious fusion burn and, not far from that, high vacuum. First he quietly made his way through the biozones, sniffing and savoring air that came fresh from the oxy-making plants, and avoiding the finger snakes in their happy labors. They were fun, but he was not in a fun mood.

Gecko slippers let him walk the far reaches of the ship, out of the centri-grav torus. They were like weak glue on your soles, following the sticky patches on the walls. The zero-grav plants were matted tangles of beans and peas, with carrots that grew like twisted orange baseballs and green bananas that made weird toroids. A finger snake tunnel ran underneath. The snakes weren't showing.

He went on into the hibernation modules, where what he thought of as the biostasis crew lay. Just sleeping, sort of, though hard to wake up. His footsteps rang as he walked the aluminum web corridor beside the solemn gray capsules. He didn't want to call out of cold sleep enough people to crew a big landing expedition, not for the Bowl anyway. In the defrosting and training they would all have to triple up on a hot hammock, and shower once a week. As it was now, even the small present crew—nine plus Redwing plus three finger snakes—got two showers a week and didn't like it.

Now that they were headed for a battle, of sorts, he realized how far from its expected role this expedition had come. This was not a craft built for war and neither were the crew. They had been carefully tuned for exploration and centuries of confinement. They were living in a constantly running machine where opening a hatch without proper precautions could kill you dead in seconds flat.

With that happy thought, he turned back. *You're*

worrying, not thinking. He could use some time with the finger snakes.

• • •

Rich garden smells slapped him in the face. He looked around him, seeing miniature sheep and full-sized pigs and chickens, clucking and grunting—and no finger snakes. Their tunnel was big enough, he could peer into it . . . but he went to the screens. If they weren't in the tunnel, he'd still find them easily enough.

Now, what had the finger snakes left on-screen? They'd been watching the Bowl slide past, even as he had. No, they hadn't: this view was following a cityscape as it rolled below *SunSeeker*. If Redwing understood rightly, that was a Sil city, newly rebuilt after an attack from the Folk. It looked quite strange. Streets and peaks like hieroglyphs, or wispy Arab writing.

He jumped when a flat head poked his elbow. "This they did hide," said—Shtirk? Marked near the tail with a bent black hourglass. "Hide no more. A great shame."

"Wait. Is this writing? So big?"

Its voice had a sliding, flat tone, faint. "Can see such writing from everywhere on the Bowl. This says the Bird Folk stamped their own world flat. A mistake in steering ended their bloodline. This was in a message . . . a message from the stars. Captain, yes please, how does a star send a message?"

Redwing dithered for a moment about how much to reveal; but he wanted to know what Shtirk knew. "You know what a star is? It's like your sun, *that* sun, but much farther away. Stars have worlds, not Bowls but spinning balls. We have a message from one of those, from Glory. We haven't been able to read it all, and it's still coming in."

"The Sil read," Shtirk said. "Your bandits learn find the message from you, the Sil from them, then the Sil read. Now they tell us. Thisther goes to tell you all in command deck. Is it true? Bird Folk did smash their own world?"

Redwing laughed. "And they think they're the Lords of Creation! Yeah, I believe it. I'll put it to the others, and we'll look through the message from Glory. But I believe it."

• • •

Fred Ojama and a giant snake were hard at work at the control screens when Redwing found them. Thisther's head and the fingernails on its tiny quick tail were close up against the controls, typing. Fred was saying, "Yup, yup, yup . . ."

"Fred?"

"Sir." Fred didn't turn. "If you'll look past me . . . see the starscape? And the blue dot? The dot is the Bowl. The stars move, too. I've run this twice already. The Bowl left Sol system in Jurassic times, then tootled around to several other stars—not moving as fast as it does now. Then they came back between the Cretaceous and Tertiary. If the times hold, then the mass of the Bowl ruined some comet orbits that second time, and that was it."

"It?"

"The timeline checks. They caused the Dinosaur Killer impact."

Thisther said, "Great shame. They hid this for lifetimes of worlds."

"My God," Redwing said.

Thisther said in his quiet way, "But no more. All will know. They killed their own genetic line. Sil will tell all."

THIRTY-TWO

Tananareve realized she should agree with the big, ponderous beast that was Memor. She had come to think of the alien as a kind of smart elephant, with a sense of humor equally heavy. "Yes, that was a clever saying," Tananareve made herself say.

"I am happy you have discovered the nuances of our nature," Memor said. *Apparently sarcasm is unknown here, never mind irony,* Tananareve thought. She knew Memor thought what she'd said was amusing, from the way her body shook, but it went right by human ears.

"The wonder of all this is what impresses me most," Tananareve said to move on to better things. Memor and Bemor were huge and strange, but they liked her to play the awed-primate role. The hard case was Asenath, who mostly ignored Tananareve except for the occasional glower. Plus deliberately aimed stale exhaled breaths and well-timed, acid farts.

They stood among a crowd of hundreds of squat, humanoid creatures who formed neat, obedient circles around the Folk party. She watched these, the first human-shaped aliens she had seen, trying to understand the blank expressions on their hairy faces, to figure out what was going on. Beyond the crowd was a tall pinnacle with a single round thing in it that she had just now realized was an eye or camera, watching all this.

Asenath was holding forth to the rapt assembly in a booming voice that had made Tananareve flinch when she first heard it. Study of the Folk conversations had given her some hints of meaning, but the long phrases Asenath used seemed more like chanting. Tananareve asked Memor, "Is this some kind of ritual?"

"Quite observant of you. She is reassuring the Kahalla that the Sil and humans who escaped their capture will be taken in hand soon. No damage shall follow from this Kahalla failure."

"What's that about their . . . children?"

"Nothing important. The Kahalla are losing many eggs to the appetites of scavengers. They seek us to somehow ward off their predators."

"Will you?"

"We do not intervene in natural matters. Nature runs itself well."

"You told me earlier that you Folk ran Nature."

Memor gave a fan-flutter of amber and blue,

which seemed to mean pleasant amusement. "And so we do. At a remove, of course. Long ago the Folk set up this dynamic equilibrium, a predator–prey oscillation that will not go too far."

"So these . . . Kahalla? . . . won't get wiped out?"

"No, they are sufficiently intelligent and wary to deal with their predators—a nasty little vermin species. Both predator and prey have a low mental level and can adapt to changes in the other species, as they occur over long times. Evolution is thus contained. Populations do not sprawl out, consuming natural lands. There are several such interlacing balances in this zone."

Tananareve pondered this as Asenath's long bellow went on.

Then a new droning cry came—*shree, kinnne, warrickk, awiiiha . . .*

Memor said, "Ah, they have awakened the memory box."

Asenath paused, then went on, trying to boom over these new deep tones with their extended cadences. Tananareve saw that the laboring sounds came from the tower with the eye. "What is it?"

"A form of consciousness prison. From a hotworld it came and we are its stewards. Or rather these Kahalla are its attendants."

"A . . . rock mind?"

"We have several strewn about the Bowl. They are slow but sure and alert us to long-term trends that otherwise might elude our quick eyes. You are, for example, a somewhat old-fashioned individual intelligence, organic. This is an inorganic one, and

the Kahalla are a sort of hybrid mind who attend
the stone lattice mind. They are nothing like the
vast collective intelligences—but never mind, we
have had enough of this slow-thought place. And
our escape approaches."

awrrrragh yoouuiunggg arrraff kinnne yuuf . . .

Tananareve had not noticed the huge wall of
scaly flesh settling down from the sky, beyond the
talking tower. Across its rough brown skin silvery
fins fanned as the bulk waltzed lazily into place. It
spread slender tentacles grasping for ground. They
played across the land. Kahalla ran to secure these
to boulders, looking in perspective like ants bringing down a sea fish. The tentacles wrapped around
catch points and pulled the great thing snug to
ground.

Asenath finished and the Kahalla bowed deeply,
on their knees with a low, sonorous moan that
grew in volume until it washed over Tananareve.
Asenath returned the bow, gave a vibrant trill salute and a four-color fan-flurry of farewell. Memor
scooped up Tananareve and made short work of
the journey to the immense thing—a bag inflated to
fly, she guessed. But alive.

By now she knew that Memor enjoyed the open
land, and spoke, too, of "the serene voyaging our
living craft affords." They entered by a flap that
opened like a mouth. A huge tongue unfurled and
Memor walked up it, carrying the primate on her
shoulder. It felt to Tananareve unpleasantly like
being eaten. Memor said in her booming Anglish,
"The mucus of this great beast had been engineered

to carry a delicate fragrance unlike anything else. Its scent is a luxury and settles the mind, a necessary aid in air travel. Chaos may come to rage all about us, but we shall be mild."

Tananareve sucked in a lingering taste. Like flowers, though with an oily undertaste. Bemor, too, sighed, though he said, "We must make haste," and bellowed an order to small scampering things that had come to greet them.

They were in a wet cavern. This "skyfish" as Memor called it was like a cave of moist membranes lit by phosphorescent swirls embedded behind translucent tissues. They reminded Tananareve of illuminated art back Earthside.

A deep bass note rang, ending in a *whoosh* that made it seem like an immense sigh. Grav momentarily rose, and Tananareve knew they had lifted off. Ruddy wall membranes fluttered. Warm air eased by them as they entered a large bowl-shaped area. Sunshine lanced through membranes so clear, Tananareve thought at first they were open to the air. But the sweet breeze swept first one way, then reversed, and she realized that it was the breathing of this great beast. The tower that had seemed so tall outside now dwindled away and the skyfish turned, so the sweep of a plain came into view. Clouds stacked like fat blue plates loomed on the shimmering distance. She could see the long arc of Bowl curving up into a pale sky; she was looking across a distance the size of planetary orbits. The eggshell blue of seas dominated the somewhat washed-out greens and browns of landmasses, and made pale the sheet grays of mirror zones. Across that flapped big-winged angular birds with long snouts and crests atop their bony heads.

Memor met the captain of this gasbag being. The whole idea of a captain was odd until Tananareve realized they were like people riding a larger animal, as she had ridden horses. Memor spoke quickly, with booming comments from Bemor, all too fast for her to fathom.

The captain listened for a while, big eyes watery and anxious. This creature was somewhat like some of the Folk—a big thing, four-legged and solemn and slow, mouth wide and salmon-pink and lipless. Bursts of words rattled from the mouth. Its narrow nostrils were veined pink, with fleshy flaps beneath. Large round black eyes watched them, yellow irises flashing in the slanting sunlight. From the top of the captain's head sprouted a vibrant blue crest, serrated and trimmed with yellow fat, reminding Tananareve of a cock's comb.

The captain took them on a walk through the ramparts, view balconies, and residential segments of the great living volume. A narrow hissing hydrogen arc heated its eating levels and lit the translucent furniture in blue light, where workers of four and six and even eight legs labored to bring forth live dishes for Folk delight. Pressed, Tananareve cracked a carapace and slurped out the warm white flesh of some sea creature. The next dish was a kicking big insect basted in creamy sauce. Memor said something about how keeping it alive through the cooking added savor to the proteins, but Tananareve decided that it was best to know less about Folk gustatory tastes. She tried to break the thick legs with her hands and snap off the tasty eyestalks. Crunchy but with a peppery flavor that stung her lips and sent a scent like stale meat into her sinuses. A green pudding turned out to be a slime mold that thrust probes out into her mouth as she tried to chew it. The flavor wasn't nearly worth it.

Still, it was useful food. Folk ate meats and veggies she found mostly dull or repulsive, with little in between. She sat in the steady warm breeze of the skyfish's sweet internal breath—were they essentially sitting in its trachea?—and listened as Memor rattled on to other Folk sitting nearby about matters political and somehow always urgent. Or so her limited translation abilities told her. Finally Memor turned and said to her—whom she described to the other Folk as "the small Invader primate"—"You must surely admire our craft. We took the early forms of this creature from the upper atmosphere of a gas giant world, long ago. Their ancestors found our deep atmosphere a similar paradise, to cruise on soft moist winds, and mate in their battering fashion, and wallow in our air, to turn falling water into their life fluid, hydrogen."

"I doubt the primate can follow your description," Asenath said, coming into view.

Tananareve warily backed away from the lumbering thing. She could *smell* the malice oozing from Asenath. "Still, she could be of some use in capturing the renegades of her kind, whom we shall soon intersect."

Asenath ushered them all over to the broad window in the skyfish's side. Elaborate orange-colored fins flexed near the back of the beast. They flared out, capturing winds like a sail, driving the bag forward. Tananareve felt a lurch and a dull thump. She had the sense of rumbling movement under her feet and in the living walls. Memor explained that the bag was "trimming" in flight by shifting weight inside itself. Asenath said, "Our admirable skyfish can torque about its center of mass, and thus navigate." Tananareve watched the flexible yet controlled fan-fins spread out, at least a hundred meters long. Its gravid majesty seemed somewhat like a ship sailing at angles to the wind, tacking above the lush forest below.

Asenath said, "We are precisely on course to intersect the renegades. They are sailing on this same gathering wind."

Tananareve watched the opalescent walls shimmer with hot perspiration. Memor remarked that these were "anxiety dewdrops," brought out by the laboring muscles of the great fish. The shimmering moist jewels hung like gaudy chandeliers, lit by the blue glow of hydrogen flares and phosphorescent yellow bands that ran across the high ceiling. One of the drops, bigger than Tananareve's head, fell from high up and spattered at her feet with cutting acid odor.

Bemor shifted his bulk and remarked, "The new signal from Glory is coded in a different manner. We are having difficulties decoding it, except for a few images."

Memor shifted into Folkspeech. "Best not to let the primate know. Show what images you have."

Tananareve felt her pulse speed up but kept her face blank and made a show of turning to gaze out at the view. A huge bird was flapping by below, eyeing the skyfish. Casually she stepped away to the spot where, leaning forward, she could see reflected in the transparent window the projection Bemor was showing Memor. It was an animated series of images. A man in a white robe advanced into view and something leaped at him. It was an alien with ruddy skin and three arms. It jumped at the man, and huge feet kicked him to the ground. The alien wore tight blue clothes that showed muscles bulging as the view drew closer. The alien head was like a pyramid with sharp chin and bones like ribs under tight, ruddy skin. Two large black eyes glinted at the man, who was getting up, his smiling face mild and his long blond hair flowing. He was holding forward an object—a wooden cross—to the alien. Tananareve saw suddenly that the man was Jesus. The alien leaped on the man, hammering him with feet and two fists. Its third arm was bony and sharp, with nasty nails tapering to points. The alien slammed this into the head of Jesus, shattering the skull into pieces. Blood flew into the air and Jesus collapsed. His body lay still. The black alien eyes looked straight out from the screen Bemor held and thick lips pulsed, swelling and narrowing in what must have been some kind of victory gesture.

The sudden raw images startled her. A surge of anger tightened her throat. She made herself keep still and watched the bird flap out of view on its four wings.

"Ah," Memor said, "similar to the earlier one. But look—we are intersecting the tadfish, as we had hoped to. Now we can deal with these primates, brought together."

Tananareve saw swimming in the filmy air below them a gossamer tube shape. Fins stroked all along the barrel body as it rose from the forest below. Somehow, she realized, the Folk had found Cliff's team, and now had them cornered.

PART XI

DOUBLE-EDGED SWORD, NO HANDLE

It is not because things are difficult that we dare not venture. It is because we dare not venture that they are difficult.

—SENECA

THIRTY-THREE

"What's that?" Irma pointed.

Hanging among cottony clouds, near to the woody horizon, was a thing that struck him as a silvery, flapping blimp. Coming toward them.

"What's that?" Cliff echoed to Quert—who scowled.

"Escape," Quert said. "So you say?"

"From what?"

"Folk know where we are. Track us."

"They can?" Terry asked.

"Makes sense," Irma said. "They must have sensors embedded in the original frame that holds the Bowl together. Any smart building does. The trick would be managing such a torrent of data."

Quert gave an assenting eye-click and fell silent. The Sil took their orders from Quert and studiously let Quert alone speak for them. Cliff wondered about this but did not want to bring up or question an arrangement that was at least keeping his small party out of the hands of the Folk.

When the spidows gave up the chase, the tired party of Sil and humans had moved on awhile, crossed a stream that Quert said spidows could not, and then stopped without a word. Cliff could feel the adrenaline collapse; he had gotten used to it after so many scares and flights. He wondered how the Sil managed crises. The same play of hormones?

Some cold food with water from the convenient spring made them all feel better. Cliff had little storage left in the electronics he had carried all this time. He had chronicled all the places he had been and enjoyed looking back over the images. One from a good while back he liked, a clear day when the great sweep of the Bowl and its jet was sharp and clear. Too often the deep atmosphere blocked long views with enormous stacks of cloud. He had caught some of the team in the foreground, slogging along near a zigzag tree.

"You're keeping notes?" Irma asked. "I filled my data storage a long time ago."

Cliff shrugged. "I'm either lazy or just plain picky. After the first week, when I was taking shots of every flower, tree, animal, insect, bird—well, harder to be a scientist when you're on the run."

"One thing you're not is lazy." She looked at his small working screen. "Notes for each shot, even."

"I do them at our rest stops, like this."

But there was no real resting, as the Sil made clear.

Quert eyed the humans. "We not go under now. Best not."

"Into the tunnels?" Aybe asked. "The trains? They'll catch us there?"

Slow steady eye-shifts. "Soon. Yes. Best not go in tunnels."

"I kind of liked those fast tunnels," Aybe said.

"Folk hold them now."

"So . . . what do we do?" Terry persisted.

"See there." Quert's slim arm pointed. The small silvery thing hung in the distance above a dense forest ridgeline. It moved slowly and the sun reflected winking spots of yellow and blue from it. "Tadfish." The Sil around him shuffled uneasily but as usual said nothing.

"We're getting away in *that*?" Irma frowned doubtfully.

"Best way," Quert said, and they moved forward steadily. "Hide in sky."

Cliff wondered at the Sil social conventions, and their psychology. They were all in mortal danger but the Sil showed little jittery nervousness. Quert ruled absolutely. In contrast, he had to deal with ongoing questions and doubt from Aybe, Terry, and Irma. Only the need to move on, endlessly on, kept him in shaky control.

The tadfish was coming this way and as they entered the nearby forest of vine-rich trees and brush, Cliff could see it had a deft grace to its movement, though he could not see how it did so. Tendrils of vines yearned for the sun, though some turned at another angle, apparently partial to the jet's rosy rays—specialization at work. The woods had a thick cloying stink, but were so thick overhead that the tadfish crew could not possibly see them below. Animals scampered away in their path, but there were plenty more concealed. From endless movement, Cliff had picked up ways to sense the life around them. Some animals here were superb at hiding, skinnying up into dense trees, or burrowing in hidden pits like trapdoor spiders. Others just flew away on quick stubby wings, fluttering fast enough to discourage pursuit.

Aybe and Irma walked with him, and Sils were both point and rear guards. The Sil somehow kept themselves in good order, Cliff saw, while the humans in their worn cargo pants with big flap pockets were drab and saggy. The Sil had patched those up for the bedraggled humans, back in the all-too-brief rest period following the battle with the sky-fish. All that now seemed a long time ago. More wear had made their clothes ragged and rough. In contrast, the Sil had loose-fitting, lightweight tan and dusty white jumpsuits that never looked the worse for wear. They could be cleaned by just dipping them in water and connecting them to the Sil onboard and solar-powered back-batteries. Apparently some electrical method rejected ions the cloth disliked and knitted up broken fibers. The humans marveled at this.

Cliff let himself relax for a moment and enjoy the one sure thing he knew here—life: wild flocks of strange things wheeling and crying high overhead; guttural lowings and crisp cacklings from the forest around them; a smelly cloying carpet underfoot, springy, more like moss than grass, starred with bright stalks like flowers; zigzag trees silvery and ripe with flapping life, big coppery-winged things that shrieked and dived at humans when they could. Somehow the big things knew not to

go after the Sil, who used their arm-arrows to slice them from the sky. Cliff hit a few with his laser and so did the others and they sank to the ground after that, going for cover.

They managed to get some sleep. Cliff woke up several times, slapping and swearing at bugs that got into his clothes. Terry kept warily watching the trees and shrubs. The spidow encounter and the bird attack had made them jumpy. There were a lot of ropy vines, and gibbering small things rushed among them, sometimes hurling down oblong red fruit as if to drive the intruders away. A Sil caught one fruit and bit into it, made a twisted face, and tossed it aside. Cliff saw a long vine move on its own and pointed. "A snake. Adapted to trees, probably disguises itself as a vine."

Quert heard and nodded. "We call sky pirates."

Irma chuckled. "Why?"

"Intelligent. In a way."

"Really? What do they do with intelligence?"

"Save food for hard times."

She stared up at the muscular, glistening snake that hung ten meters above their heads and seemed at least that long. It curled itself and leveraged onto another branch of a tall, spindly tree. Above it were cocoons of pale gray suspended among bare branches. "Like those?"

Quert gave an assenting eye-click. "Call them—" He paused, searching for the right Anglish term. "—mummies. Smart snakes store so many. Sometimes mummies we use for fertilizer."

Aybe gaped at this and as they moved on, he said, "Mummies for . . . I don't get it."

"Closed ecology, see?" Irma shrugged. "They have to keep everything moving."

"So does the Earth," Aybe said. "At least, until we started industrializing space. Then we did metal smelting and manufacture in vacuum, where we could throw the wastes into the solar wind, and clean up the planet a bit."

"But this ground ecology is just a few tens of meters deep," Cliff said. "Has no plate tectonics. Can't hide carbon from its air. Can't bring fresh elements up from far below, vomit it out from volcanoes."

Irma finished, "So you do that artificially. Plus you save resources. You might not get any more for a while. Or ever again."

He nodded at this elementary wisdom that could always bear repeating, especially on the Bowl. They were still trying to figure out the greater scheme here, as a long-term investment. A negotiation might come up ahead, and Redwing would need to know something about those on the other side of the table.

That suited Cliff for now: seeing the Bowl as a puzzle. He had always been a problem-solver, a man who reflexively reacted to the unknown by breaking it into understandable pieces. Then Cliff would carefully solve each small puzzle, confident that the sum of such micro-problems would finally resolve the larger confusions. Irma thought the same way, one reason he liked her so much. On this endless trek through strange lands, they had grown to need each other. Every day was unnerving and wonderful at the same time, and for the same reasons. His whole team had gone into cold biostasis—always a risk—so they could reach an alien planet they knew very little about. Now they were immersed in that, multiplied by orders of magnitude. And they knew even less about this huge strange thing, the Bowl. It was daunting and thrilling, every day—in a place where there were not really days at all.

Now that they had a clear destination, the team of Sil and humans moved on with renewed energy. As they mounted a low hill, they saw the tadfish was closer. "It lands there," Quert said, gesturing toward the next hill.

The slowly drifting football-shaped creature was maneuvering under tendrils of rain. Cliff remembered the one that had ravaged the Sil city and looked at its blister pods, wondering if the skyfish carried weapons there.

"Virga," Aybe said. "That's the name for when water evaporates away before hitting the ground. See? It's falling from clumps of altocumulus clouds up there." Among towering, steepled clouds rain fell, to be absorbed by lower, dryer layers.

"Tadfish drinking," Quert said. "Hurry."

They came up on the strange creature through a cluster of zigzag trees thickly wreathed in green vines. The silvery tadfish settled down in a clearing near some ceramic buildings. Quert picked up the pace. Cliff watched the complex sheen of skin as it flexed and stroked its translucent fins. Some attendants clustered at its base as it settled down. Quert was taking them in a flanking approach through the zigzag and vine maze. The ground crew was Kahalla in bright, creamy clothes. They took a small party of passengers off, and Cliff could not see who or what they were as they went into the dun-colored buildings. The Sil did not slow down.

With the humans struggling in the rear, the whole band sprinted from the last of the zigzags into the open pale dirt field and quickly across to the tadfish. They approached its face as its big green oval eyes peered down at them.

Several Sil peeled off and took up positions between the tadfish and the buildings. Cliff came out of the trees and saw some of the Kahalla ground crew turn back. They started running toward the tadfish, and the Sil moved to block them. A Kahalla drew a weapon and one Sil flexed his arm. The Kahalla went down instantly. The other Kahalla backed off and the Sil advanced.

Quert said, "They stay. Tadfish small. Not carry all of us."

"Ah."

The tadfish mouth was still open. Quert ducked and ran directly into the mouth. This looked to Cliff like a very bad idea. He slowed as they approached the ruby red lip of the mouth and saw the floor of the mouth was a hardened cartilage, lime green and ribbed. He tromped in, boots rapping on the cartilage. A musky smell seemed to wrap around his face. He edged down a narrow passage to the left, dimly lit by amber phosphors in the fleshy walls.

The walls pulsed with heat and he emerged into a long room devoted to the view out a transparent wall in the tadfish side. The humans were there but no Sil. As he crossed the room, he felt a surge and the tadfish took off, angling over the zigzags. It turned to bask in the wind and accelerated. Everyone caught their balance, bracing against the softly resistant, fleshy walls. Below he saw Kahalla figures running vainly toward some tow lines that had held the tadfish in place. They retracted, and a Kahalla raised a tube weapon toward the humans looking down. It sighted—then lowered the weapon and shook its arms in frustration.

Irma said, "The Sil stole this thing."

They all laughed a bit in appreciation, relieved, and Quert came into the room. In its staccato manner, it confirmed that the Sil had kept track of when the tadfish would set down on its regular route and had rushed to get there just in time to seize the tadfish when the flight crews changed shift. "Good timing," Terry said, and Quert gave a hand-pass that meant assent.

Cliff did not remark that the Sil had not bothered to tell the humans what was up. Quert didn't like debating policy; indeed, the Sil did not share the human appetite for endless talk and at times made fun of it.

"So now we'll 'hide in the sky' as you said." Aybe scowled. "From what?"

"Folk trace us. Saw at Ice Minds. Kahalla alert them."

They were rising fast above the spreading plain.

The atmosphere became supersaturated, the air suddenly full of mist. Cliff looked out along the axis of his shadow and there it was forming, a huge round luminous rainbow. The circular rainbow popped into the halo air. It formed near the top of a mountain, aslant from the constant star hanging at his back. He could see five separate colors; the red was intense. Slowly the mist dissolved and the spectral promise faded away. Yet it moved him with its beauty and its quick demise.

The tadfish walls popped and creaked. Irma said, "What's that?" They rose faster. The fins outside beat in synchronous rhythm, and they heard a heavy thudding through the walls. "Is that its heart?"

Aybe looked out the transparent wall. "Maybe the body is expanding. It must be making more hydrogen from water, filling itself out."

Cliff put his head against the oddly warm transparent window and only then noticed a separate transparent bulge farther along the curving skin. It promised a better viewing angle. But the wall nearby had no opening. He saw no way to reach that bulge but ran his hands along the wall and felt a crease in the warm flesh. He pried at it, and with a rasping purr a sheet came free along a seam. A pressure seal, apparently. He peeled it back and saw a narrow footway lit by blue phosphors. A few steps took him to the transparent blister. From here he could see farther around the curve of the great flying balloon, and the stately ranks of flapping translucent fins.

The view now was majestic and vast. The deep Bowl atmosphere fell off slowly with height, so a living balloon with a fishlike shape could rise a long way before the slackening pressure outside made it bulge. He looked down through many kilometers at the clouds flowing over the low mountains that only a short while ago, while they were running, had loomed in the distance. Refracted glows of the jet and star danced and coiled in deep clouds. Except for the slow thump of the tadfish heart, he felt as though he were hanging in air, seeing the Bowl as did the great birds he had seen far up the towering sky.

He turned to rejoin the others and saw to his side another pressure seal. He felt it for a seam. Then Irma came into the cramped blister. "What's going on?"

"Look, we're just passengers, can't do anything but wait. Let's see how this thing works. Might be useful up ahead."

Irma twisted her mouth in a skeptical curve. "I could use a rest."

"The more we know, the better."

Irma leaned against the warm wall and gazed out on the spectacular view. "Um, maybe. Me, I've got strangeness overload. Every day there's more to digest. And on the run, too."

He smiled. "We're in the belly of a beast already. Let's not get digested."

She shrugged. "These passages are claustrophobic. Let's leave Aybe and Terry back there—Quert's brought some gloppy food for them and they're wolfing it down. Tastes like a chicken-flavored milk shake. Hard bits in it, too, tasted like bitter snails. I can wait."

They went through the narrow tunnels along the tadfish's streamlined form. It had a torpedo shape, and the occasional viewing blister was flanked by big slabs of sinewy brown muscle. These flexed as it propelled forward and Cliff sniffed; their close, moist air took on a sweaty, salty tinge.

"Fishoids, torpedo-shaped predators," Irma said when they looked out a blister and saw a swarm of long tubular birds flocking below. They swerved and scooped in the air, catching something that vented from the tadfish. "Feeding on *waste*?" Irma asked.

"One species' waste is another's food," Cliff said.

Around the long curve of the tadfish body came big gliding shapes in convoy, more like manta rays than like birds. They were flying in a V formation and had slick, matted gray skins. Diving and banking in concert through the thick air, big eyes intent on the feeding tubular birds. Their shapes, Cliff saw, reflected the demands of curvature, flow, and tension as they lazily slid down the air. Meaty triangular wings led back to rudderlike fins and a long spike at the tail. Cliff pointed. "The killing instrument." A pair of eyes protruded in knobs at either side of their wedgelike heads, above the long slit mouth. Another pair of bigger, yellow eyes sat close together and peered forward. The flying tubes moved with stately grace through the glassy air. Fleshy, oarlike appendages flanked the heads, as the manta snapped up the smaller tubular birds. Through the window, Cliff and Irma could hear cries and shrieks as the pillage cut through the flock.

It was a strange sight and over in a moment. The mantas dove under the tadfish, while a few survivors scattered in frantic haste. Irma put an arm around Cliff's waist and he felt a rush of contentment. In all this strangeness, the small comforts mattered most. They stood that way awhile, until warm air drew their attention to an inward-leading passage. He was trying to analyze all they were seeing, but the dimly lit passage drew them onward. Squishing sounds came from ahead. They worked along a throbbing wall and came upon a translucent interior layer, where they could see dark bones working in a sheath. Low murmurs and hums came through the transparent wall, and they could see gray fluids running down the bulky flesh everywhere. Lubricants?

"This is its internal skeleton?" Cliff wondered. The sliding parallel bones worked through thick green collars, coiling like a flexible spring. But their attention focused on two moving stick-figure creatures that seemingly tended this living machinery. They were about a meter tall, with six limbs that moved quickly, clambering everywhere, adjusting the mechanical supports of the bony spine. These creatures used their flexing limbs as either arms or legs, depending on where they scampered over the big moving apparatus. Irma pointed—they had long, two-petaled tails that folded to protect sexual organs that occasionally came into view as they worked. They seemed like slender, pink skeletons, with brains carried in a bump between the pair of limbs at the top of the spinal cord. Three eyes worked on stalks, making an equilateral triangle around a broad red slit of a mouth.

"They can see us," Irma said, "but they're ignoring us."

"Not so peculiar, really. Think what it's like to work on a public conveyance," Cliff said. "They've seen plenty odder than we are."

They moved along the transparent wall and saw two thick, muscular creatures wearing what seemed to be equipment belts. They were working on a panel pulled open, revealing some complex piping throbbing with amber liquids. They moved with deft small fingers, using tools too small to make out. "Those look like the ones we saw before," Irma said. "Remember? We were—"

"Screwing, yes. And one of them fell on us."

"Turns out they're smart tool-users. I wonder what they thought of us."

"These are ignoring us, same as before. We're pretty ordinary, I guess."

"Here, sophisticated means, I guess, not impressed to run into just another funny alien."

Cliff chuckled. "Puts us in our place, doesn't it?"

As they neared the tail, there were sudden orange flares jetting from tubes below the viewing blisters. "Must be fueled by hydrocarbons," Cliff said, "brewed into burnable fuels."

"We're moving fast," Irma said as a surge rippled through the body around them. The floor also rolled a bit, like a ship. "The burn helps."

"Quert said they're artificially bred forms of an original balloon-birdlike species," Cliff said. "So their energy source got engineered, too."

"We'd better get back," Irma said. They were moving quickly now, diving out over a sheet of green water that seemed a continent wide, beneath the waving fields of grass. Dotting this grass sea were bumps shaped like tadpoles, with a crust of trees ornamenting them. The thick end pointed upstream, while the water swept debris past and then dropped it in the eddy behind the hummock. This made the tadpole tail grow, building slim islands where animals lived among the dense amber and green trees. All this simmered beneath the reddish light of the star and orange filigrees cast by the slowly churning helices in the jet. As they descended, gaining speed, packs of large fishlike life became clear. They breached the shallow sea in great leaps, hanging in air, then crashing down in great sprays of white.

Irma said, "Those look a lot like dolphins."

"The basic fish shape, as you say." Cliff pointed at the width of the moving school. "Thousands of them. What a great way to see Bowl life."

Irma said, "I always thought, we believe dolphins are not as smart as we because they never built cars or refrigerators or New York or had wars. All they do is spend every day swimming in warm oceans, chasing and eating fish, mating and having fun. The dolphins think they are smarter than us, for the very same reasons."

Again, Cliff chuckled. "I always thought, on a statistical argument about time scales, that if we ran across intelligent aliens at Glory, they'd be overwhelmingly likely to be far more intelligent than us."

Irma nodded. "And therefore wouldn't care at all about us—if they even noticed us."

"Me, too. But we've been able to stay out of the hands of the Folk for a long time now. On their own turf!"

"Could be the aliens who built this place were super-minds, but their descendants have gotten stupid."

"So both the skeptics about smart aliens were wrong, and so were the optimists?" Cliff liked the idea. "Wonder what that means—"

She and Cliff were so caught up in the sight, they only noticed the huge thing hanging above when it blotted out the star.

The skyfish was firing hydrogen jets behind it and slewing swiftly through the filmy air. Headed toward them. Some strange angular birds were flocking out of the skyfish. They were lean and had long jaws with—"Are those teeth?" Irma asked.

"Looks like. Not friendly, no."

THIRTY-FOUR

They had been running hot and hard now for many hours, and it was starting to show in his crew.

Redwing sat on the bridge because if he paced for hours, as he already had, everybody got edgy. Fair enough; he sat and twitched, mostly by moving his feet, in their gecko shoes, where nobody could see.

He had used up his weekly shower ration in two days of this.

They had entered the jet days ago, not that there was any clear sign of it. The mag field values started to climb a day ago and the plasma density followed it. Only by amping certain spectral lines of yellow and green could the wall screens show the filmy curtains of sliding ion flow in the jet. Those weren't plasma, really—the light came from ions, as electrons found them at last and cascaded down the energy levels to emit a photon. The light showed where plasma eased into little deaths.

Now Ayaan Ali had taken over as lead pilot and Clare Conway sat in the copilot deck chair. Beth Marble had gone to get some sleep. They all watched the blue and green lines work on the large screens, mapping pressures and flux changes at the perimeter of their magscoop fields.

"How's the scoop impedance looking?" Redwing asked.

"Down to three meg-ohms, sir." From her sideways glance, he knew Ayaan Ali understood that he could have read it from the screens, but that they needed to have some talk on the bridge, just to diffuse tensions.

A rumble and a rolling shock came rippling through the ship. "Ride's interesting," Redwing said mildly.

Ayaan Ali smiled and nodded, eyes never leaving the screens, hands on the e-helm at all times. "We took a shock front from forty-two degrees starboard, seventeen degrees south. Plasma still rising."

"This fits the model Karl worked up?"

"Um, sort of." A skeptical arching of eyebrows.

Redwing picked up something more in her body language. Karl and Ayaan Ali always kept a wary distance in crew meetings and were crisply correct around him . . . which led him to wonder if something was going on between them. They were in a dangerous place, and tensions needed release. He decided to put it away for later, if ever. The mission was the point here. "Okay. Nobody expects models to work well here. I don't, anyway. Let's see the aft scoop and plume." Redwing always felt a bit jumpy about anything sneaking up behind them, though with the Artilects on constant duty, that was extremely unlikely.

The rumbling aft faded. Eerie popping noises came through the support beams and hollow creakings sounded. A sour stench of something scorched—probably just overheating in a forward tank. The display space before them showed flurries of plasma, highlighted in violet, slamming into the scoop.

"Those knots again," Ayaan Ali said.

"Let's see long-range radar," Redwing said.

They studied the yawning space around the jet, looking from multiple dishes. "Nothing near us, nothing in near space, nothing farther out," Ayaan Ali said. "I've always wondered why we saw so few spacecraft. You'd think they would be sending ships out to monitor the whole system."

Redwing nodded. "This system has no planets, or asteroids, no comets coming in. Nothing bigger than a school bus. But there were some small craft, remember? They came over the Bowl rim, flew along the top of their atmosphere manifolds, ducked into a hole in the upper atmosphere layer."

"But very few, very little craft." Clare shrugged. "And we know the gravitational instabilities that the Bowl risks all the time. If they get too close to the star, they have to fire up the jet and push the stellar mass away, while they grab the rising jet flux and let it push them back. Reverse if they start falling behind. Then there's the spinning Bowl, same instabilities as a spinning top. But I guess they can run this whole wacky system without many spacecraft."

Karl came onto the bridge, back from checking inductance coils along the ship. He had heard Ayaan Ali. "It's all maintained with magnetic fields and jet pressure," he said. "Plus the reflected sunlight, to heat the hot spot. Tricky stuff."

"Those inductance coils getting worked hard?" Redwing asked.

"Running high, but within margin." Karl got into his chair and belted up, casting a side look at Redwing, as if to say, *Why don't you sit?*

Redwing never explained that he liked to move through the ship when it was having trouble. He could tell more with his feet and ears than the screens could say.

They had taken three days to cross the jet with the fusion chambers running at full bore, driving them to nearly two hundred kilometers per second. That was far higher than an orbital velocity, though still far under the ship's coasting specs. *SunSeeker* now was turning in the helix Karl had calculated, cutting in an arc near the jet's boundary, its magscoop facing the star at a steep angle and swallowing its heated plasma. They had faced such a headwind coming in and survived. But now the navigation was tougher. This time they had to remain lower than the Bowl's rim, or else come within the firing field of the gamma ray lasers there.

"How do we know this is the optimal path?" Redwing asked Karl.

"Calculations—"

"I mean from what we've learned these last few days."

"It's working." Karl's lean face tightened, ending in his skewed, tight mouth above a pointed chin where he had begun to grow a goatee. "We're brushing the mag pressures outward. Our sideways thrust drives the magnetic kink mode, feeding off the jet's own forward momentum. We're stimulating the flow patterns at the right wavelength to make the jet slew."

"We'll see sideways jet movement before it shoots through the Knothole?"

"It should." Karl's gaze was steady, intent. He had a lot riding on this.

"Let's look aft. Have we got better directionals this time?" Redwing asked Ayaan Ali.

"Somewhat," she said. "I rotated some aft antennas to get a look, the sideband controllers, too."

She changed the color view, and Redwing watched brilliant yellow knots twist around the prow of their magscoop like neon tropical storms. "These curlers push us sideways a lot."

A rumble ran down the axis and Redwing hung on to Ayaan Ali's deck chair. Clare showed the acoustic monitors display in red lines on a side screen. The strains worked all down the ship axis.

"We're getting side shear," Redwing said mildly. He took care not to give direct piloting instructions; no backseat driving.

"I'll fire a small side jet, let some plasma vent from the side of the magscoop, rotate on the other axis, and take our aft around some."

Her hands traced a command in the space before her. A faint rumbling began, then a surge. The ship slid sideways and Redwing hung on to a deck chair. Multiple-axis accelerations had never been his strong point. His stomach lurched.

She worked on getting the aft view aligned. *Sun-Seeker*'s core was no mere pod sitting atop the big fuel tank that held the fusion catalysis ions. Gouts of those ions had to merge with the incoming plasma, fresh from the magscoop. In turn, the mated streams fed into the reactor. Of course, the parts had to line up that way along the axis, no matter how ornate the subsections got, hanging on the main axis, because the water reserves tank shielded the biozone and crew up front, far from the fusion reactor, and the plasma plume in the magnetic nozzle.

Redwing knew every rivet and corner of the ship and liked to prowl through all its sections. The whole stack was in zero gee, except the thick rotating toroid at the top, which the crew seldom left. A hundred and sixteen meters in diameter, looking like a dirty, scarred angel food cake, it spun lazily around to provide a full Earth g at the outside. There the walls were two meters thick and filled with water for radiation shielding. So were the bow walls, shaped into a Chinese hat with its point forward, bristling with viewing sensors. From inside, nobody could eyeball the outside except through electronic feeds. Yet they had big wall displays at high resolution and smart optics to tell them far more than a window ever could.

Ayaan Ali's work brought the multiple camera views into alignment with some jitter. They were looking back at the Bowl and she had to tease the jet out of all the brighter oceans and lands slowly turning in the background, a complicated problem.

"Let's get a clear look-down of the jet," Redwing said.

To see and diagnose the plume, they had a rear-view polished aluminum mirror floating out forty meters to the side. They didn't dare risk a survey bot in the roiling plasma streams that skirted around the magscoop, with occasional dense plasma fingers jutting in.

The image tuned through different spectral lines, picking out regions where densities were high and glows twisted. On the screen, a blue-white flare tapered away for a thousand kilometers before fraying into streamers. Plasma fumed and blared along the exhaust length, ions and electrons finding each other at last and reuniting into atoms, spitting out an actinic glare. The blue pencil pointed dead astern. He was used to seeing it against the black of space, but now all around their jet was a view of the Bowl. The gray-white mirror zones glinted with occasional sparkles from the innumerable mirrors that reflected light back on the star.

Seen slightly to the side of the jet, the Knothole was a patch of dark beneath the filmy yellow and orange filigrees of the jet. Redwing supposed that at the right angle, the whole jet looked like a filmy exclamation point, with Wickramsingh's Star as the searing bright dot.

Karl said, "See that bulge to the left? That's the kink working toward the Knothole."

Ayaan Ali nodded. "Wow. To think we can kick this thing around!"

"Trick is, we're using the jet's energy to do the work." Karl smiled, a thin pale line. "It's snaking like a fire hose held in by magnetic fields."

Ayaan Ali frowned. "When it hits the Knothole, how close to the edge does it get?"

"Not too close, I think."

"You think?"

"The calculations and simulations I've run, they say so."

"Hope they're right," Ayaan Ali said softly.

They continued on the calculated trajectory as the ship sang with the torque. The helix gave them a side acceleration of about a tenth of a grav, so Redwing kept pacing the deck on a slight slant, inspecting the screens in the operating bays.

He also watched how everyone was holding up.

His crew had been refined so they fit together like carefully crafted puzzles, each skill set reinforcing another's. That meant excluding even personal habits, like "mineralarians," a faction who insisted that eating animals or even plants, which both cling to life, was a moral failing. Instead, they choked down an awful mix of sugars, amino and fatty acids, minerals and vitamins, all made from rocks, air, and water. That could never work while pioneering a planet, so the mineralarians got cut from the candidate list immediately. Same for genetic fashions. *Homo evolutis* were automatically excluded from the expedition as too untested, though of course no one ever said so in public. That would be speciesism, a sin when *SunSeeker* was being built, and in Redwing's opinion, one of the ugliest words ever devised.

But with all the years of screening, there were still wild cards in his deck. Smart people always had a trick or two you never saw until pressure brought it out. Managing people was not remotely like ordering from a menu.

As he watched an internal status board Fred was manning, Redwing felt a hard jar run down the axis. Ayaan Ali quickly corrected for a slew to their port side. The fusion chamber's low rumble rose. It sounded, Redwing thought, a lot like the lower notes on an organ playing in a cathedral.

"Exhaust flow is pulsing," she said. "External pressure is rising behind us."

"Funny." Redwing watched the screens intently. "Makes no sense."

"We're getting back pressure." Her hands flew over the command board. A long, wrenching wave ran through the ship. Redwing sat at last in a deck chair—just in time, as a rumbling sound built in the walls and surges of acceleration shook the ship.

The aft picture worsened. They saw from two angles looking aft that the plume was bunching up, as if rippling around some unseen obstacle. The logjam thickened as they watched. Rolling waves came through the deck, all the way from hundreds of meters down the long stack.

"Getting a lot of strange jitter," Beth said. She was in uniform, crisply turned out.

Redwing looked around. "It's your sleep time."

"Who could sleep through this? Captain, it's building up."

"You're to take the chief pilot's chair in three hours—"

"Aft ram pressure is inverting profile," Ayaan Ali said crisply. "Never happens, this. Not even in simulations."

"I can *feel* it," Beth said. "This much vibration, the whole config must be—"

"Too much plasma jamming back into the throat." Ayaan Ali gestured to the screen profiling the engine, its blue magnetic hourglass-shaped throat. Its pinch-and-release flaring geometry was made of fields, so could adjust at the speed of light to the furious ion pressures that rushed down it, fresh from their fusion burn. But it could only take so much variation before snarling, choking—and blowing a hole in the entire field geometry. That would direct hot plasma on the ship wall itself, a cutting blowtorch.

As they watched, the orange flow in its blue field-line cage curled and snarled. "It's under pressures from outside the ship," Ayaan Ali said, voice tight and high.

"If it gets close to critical pressures, shut down," Redwing said. He was surprised his own voice sounded calm.

Beth said, "But we'll—"

"Go to reserve power if we have to," Clare said.

"That won't last long," Karl said. "And this external pressure on our magscoop could crumple it."

A long, low note rang through the ship—a full system warning. No one had heard that sound since training. The drive had not been off since they left Earthside.

"I'm going to spin us," Ayaan Ali said. "Outrace the pressure."

She ran the helm hard over and the magscoop responded, canting its mouth. Next she flared the magnetic nozzle at the very aft end of the ship, clearing it of knotted plasma. That took two seconds. Then she flexed the field back down and ran the fusion chamber to its max. Redwing could follow this, but her speed and agility were what made her a standout. They were all hanging on as the entire ship spun about its radial axis. Redwing closed his eyes and let the swirl go away from him, listening to the ship. The pops and groans recalled the drastic maneuvers they'd run *SunSeeker* through, during the years-long Oort cloud trials. He trusted his ears more than the screen displays of magnetic stresses.

The rumbles ebbed away. When the spin slowed, he opened his eyes again. The screens showed milder conditions around the ship. "I broke us out of that magnetic pinch," Ayaan Ali said. "We got caught in a sausage instability. Had to flex our scoop pretty hard."

Redwing recalled that meant the radial squeezing the jet sometimes displayed. Karl had said the jet narrowing looked like some sort of sausage mode, which took it through the Knothole and made it flare out once it was well beyond. But they weren't that close to the Knothole. That was the point—the kink instability took a while to develop while the jet was arrowing in toward the Bowl.

Redwing thought it strange that the pinch effect had been so strong. He asked Karl if the magnetic pressures on their magnetic nozzle could be so strong, but before Karl could answer he felt a prickly sensation play fretfully across his skin. Everyone looked around, sensing it also.

Abruptly a yellow arc cut through the air above the deck. It crackled and snaked as it moved, but turned aside whenever it met a metal barrier. They all bailed out of their couches. Redwing lay flat on the deck as the snapping, curling discharge twisted in the air above him. The crackling thing snarled around itself. Sparks hissed into the air. Yellow coils flexed, spitting light. The discharge arched and twisted and abruptly split, shaped into an extended cup shape that spun.

"It's shaping the . . . the Bowl," Beth said.

The yellow arc made a bad cartoon, snapping and writhing, never holding true for long.

Redwing felt his heart thump. "Something is out there. Making trouble for us."

Beth said, "Something we can't see."

Redwing recalled that in their discussions he had asked, *What could I be missing?* Well, here it was.

Beth had once said that flying into the jet could give them an edge, all right—but there were huge unknowns. Unknown unknowns were like a double-edged sword, she had said, with no handle. You didn't know which way the edge would cut.

THIRTY-FIVE

Asenath made a show of her entrance. She gave the assembled crew and servants a traditional bronze-golden chest display, then unfurled side arrow lances, ending in brilliant purple fan crescents. Her cycle-shaped tail laces coiled out with a snap, their flourish attracting attention first to tail, then with a flurry, to breast. Even the sub-Folk knew this strategy, though without nuance or passion. Crowds of them in the big bay of the skyfish clustered and tittered as Asenath presented. Memor watched with glazed eyes, Bemor at her side and the primate crouched nearby.

The grand bang and rattle caught many eyes, so she followed with a sharp pop. Yellow patch flares then ignited their tips, flavoring the already fragrant air. Quills rattled at incessant pace, rolls and frissons, japes and jars. All this was a part of the eternal status-flurry that kept order across the great stretches of the Bowl.

"What's all this for?" the primate said.

The impudence of this question, coming at the climax of Asenath's display, angered both Memor and, she could see, Bemor. The primate was about to become very useful, so Memor decided to discipline her in full view of all. As she turned, Bemor clasped her shoulder in a restraining grasp. "Do not. It will disturb this creature more than you know."

"*I* have spent more time with her than—"

"Than I have, yes. But indulge me this once."

Memor explained to the primate that such social rituals shored up the hierarchy needed to manage the entire Bowl society. Whenever the Folk visited a local venue of use, such as this skyfish, they reminded all of how the vast world worked, by showing ancient rituals. "Making the past come into their present, and so reside for their futures."

"It's just a dance with feathers, incense, songs, and whatever drug is floating in this air," Tananareve Bailey said. "I can sense it creeping in through my pores."

"I will be most surprised if it affects your chemistry. It is tuned for these Kahalla and their minions, plus adjacent evolved subspecies."

Tananareve coughed. "Stinks, too."

Memor rankled at this but said, "The destiny

of our species is shaped by the imperatives of survival, operating on six distinct time scales. To survive means to compete successfully, but the unit of survival is different at each of the six time ranges. On intervals of what you would term years, or orbital periods, the unit surviving is the individual. On a time scale of decades of orbitals, the unit is the family. On a scale of centuries, the unit is the tribe or nation—such as this district of the Kahalla. On a time range of millennia, the unit is the culture. The Kahalla culture is widespread. So they may lend that gracious stability to vagrant districts. On a time scale of tens or more of millennia, the surviving unit is the species. Some cultures do survive that long, and we encourage that. On the range of eons, the unit is the whole web of life on our Bowl." Memor made a signifying fan-rattle to conclude and for punctuation gave a sweet aroma-belch from her neck.

Bemor added, "That is the scale we now confront with you Late Invaders."

"Huh? We're just stopping by."

Bemor huffed in amusement. "Not so. You are important at this juncture as we approach Glory."

"Who says?"

"The Ice Minds," Memor injected, though she knew the primate did not know the term, much less the substance.

Asenath finished and resumed command of this skyfish with quick, darting orders. Squads rushed off to prepare for battle, a rolling bass note summoned crew to stations, and an electric intensity shot through the air—a zippy ion augmentation to stimulate. A wall flushed from its solemn gray to a stunning view of the region the skyfish commanded.

Needles of spiral rock forked up, moss-covered and home to many flapping species. The skyfish had recently fed there, from server species that brought arrays of food to be easily ingested as the skyfish moored on the peaks. These erections stood beside bays and lagoons, where waves reflecting the jet and star winked up at them. Here and there in the complex landscape, white snakes curved, highways like lines drawn on a lush green paper.

To the side, fluttering fast, was a silvery mote. Their target, just as the Kahalla had said.

"What's the battle?" Tananareve asked, watching the many minions scurry around.

"We expect little fighting," Memor said. "We are to capture the rest of you."

"Be careful," Tananareve said. "They've been on the run here a long time. And they bite."

Memor found this amusing and sent a subtle fan-display of this to Bemor. "As if we had cause to fear them!" she said in Folk.

"Yes, perhaps this primate has a sense of humor," Bemor said, distracted, his big eyes looking into the distance.

Suddenly Memor felt a tremor from her Under-mind. It was a cool trickle of apprehension, not of actual fear, yet its icy fingers crept into her thinking. She paused a moment to do her inward-turning, letting the Undermind gradually open. She found a swamp. Fresh, gaudy notions and worries laced through fetid dark pools of ancient fears, all beneath a sullen sky. Trepidations wrapped around a locus, like tendrils of gray fog settling on a hill. The darting slips of anxiety seemed to orbit that hill. What was in it? Under it? She did not recall ever seeing this rising bulge before. Yet she knew it was not new, but old. She knew the bodies of congested uneasiness might be thrust down for a while, into the recesses of the Undermind. But this was a large bolus of somber dark emotions, and it drove fresh fears into her conscious layers.

Yet she had no time for this now. Action drew near. "Asenath, how might we assist?"

"Keep your Late Invader close. We will need her to interpret nuance and the other Invaders' nonverbal signaling."

Bemor seemed uneasy. Memor gave him a flurry of feathers that bespoke concern, but he shook it off with a rustle. She saw from his distant gaze that he was tapped into his comm and studying information.

He breathed quicker, a low rumble of thought. Memor respected Bemor's ability to go beyond the Bowl's constant data flood, mediated through its incessantly collecting local Analyticals. Those artificial minds monitored Bowl data on local scales, then sent it upward through an ascending pyramid of minds both wholly artificial and natural—though, of course, all minds had been bred and engineered for optimal performance, far long ago. Then the smoothed product of much mastication came to such as Bemor, to make sense nuanced of mind-numbingly complex situations. Digested data could help compensate for Folk overconfidence in their own intuitions, thus reducing the distortion of perception by desire. Natural minds were unable to deal with avalanches of data and mathematics, but were excellent at social cognition. Bemor could draw from his deep knowledge of history and the higher intellects. He was good at mirroring others' emotional states, such as detecting uncooperative behavior, and at assigning value to things through emotion. Was he dealing with new ideas from the Ice Minds now? Something in his posture told Memor that he was deeply concerned about some matter far distant from their pursuit of these Late Invaders.

Abruptly Bemor broke off and spat at Asenath, "We need those Late Invaders captured immediately. No delay! But handle them carefully. Loss of even one of their lives could endanger us all."

Asenath knew enough to take this command without question. She turned and ordered a nearby Kahalla, "Do not chance a glancing shot."

"But we planned—," the Kahalla began.

"Ignore all that came before. A shot to compel them might do damage to the tadfish. Especially if you miss by even a fraction."

"Madam, we have already dispatched the sharp-wings," the Kahalla said, going into a bowing posture of apology.

"I did not so order!"

"It was explicit in your attack plan, timed to occur as we first sighted the tadfish."

Memor could see that Asenath had no ready reply to this, so she turned away with a rebuking ruffle-display of red with scarlet fringes.

They all moved close to the observation wall. The tadfish drew nearer and now a school of angular birds came forking in toward the silvery shape. They were big in wing and head. Memor knew these sharpwings as pack birds who could harry and bring down far larger prey.

Bemor was alarmed enough to be distracted from his comm. "Stop them. Now."

Asenath obeyed. Memor knew that here, nearer to the Knothole, craft such as tadfish had a natural utility. Great circulating cells of warm air cycled across the zones and life used these free rides. Skyfish were a transport business in the long voyages and tadfish had been bred from them, long ago, to traverse the shorter routes. In its constant restless way, evolution had spawned species of sharpwings to prey on tadfish. Most often they swarmed the prey, as Memor now watched them do.

Asenath shouted, "I said to turn them back!" to the Kahalla who backed away from her, head bent deep in contrition.

"They do not respond," the Kahalla whispered. "They are hirelings, and hard to deflect once engaged in their ancient battle rites."

"So they make for the meaty passengers," Memor said dryly.

"Their spirits are up," the Kahalla said. "Difficult to countermand."

Now the sharpwings circled the tadfish. The

great fish fired its hydrogen jets at them. Great
plumes of ignited gas forked out and burned sharpwings black in an instant. Bodies tumbled away
but more sharpwings came arrowing in. Their long
jaws with razor teeth sliced at the working fins to
disable navigation. The orange tongues licked more
sharpwings.

They were drawing nearer, and Asenath ordered
external ears to pick up the battle sounds. Memor
could make out the anguish cries of those being
burned. Sharpwing song-calls also laced the air, vibrant and shrill. Beneath that came the deep bass
roll of the tadfish's agony. It echoed across the diminishing distance.

Now sharpwings dove along the tadfish flanks,
going for the gut. Their spiked wings ripped along
and into the scaly flesh. It was, Memor reflected,
as though the attackers were writing on the lus-
trous flesh their own messages, in long lines that
soon brimmed red. These species had evolved to a
stable predator–prey balancing, now governed by
their betters—but only when their passions could
be blunted.

"Bring your lancing shots to bear," Asenath ordered.

"Please note, we cannot be so accurate at this
range," the Kahalla said. "I fear—"

"Do it." Asenath was stern. "Otherwise they will
bring down the tadfish and devour its passengers."

The Kahalla did not attempt to argue. It turned
and gave orders. Over the amplified booming, shrieks,
and cries, Memor could scarcely hear the sharp

psssstt! of the pellet guns. These hit the sharpwings with shattering blows. Next came the rattling laser batteries, picking off the great birds with quick stabs of green brilliance. All these weapons had to hit the sharpwings as they banked away from the tadfish, to avoid wounding it, so those sharpwings already close in on the attack escaped for a while. Orange jets from the tadfish belly licked at flights of the sharpwings. Squawks and screeches rose in an anguished crescendo. The thuds of pellets firing slowed as targets became scarce. A rain of blackened and shattered bodies tumbled, turning slowly in the long descent toward the green forests and glinting lakes below.

The remaining few sharpwings broke off the attack and flapped away, sending mournful long songs forth. "Very good," Asenath said.

"Let us escort the tadfish down, then," Memor said. "We can land and take possession."

Asenath conferred with the Kahalla, then turned to address Bemor, ignoring Memor. "We can swallow such a small tadfish. No need to land. We can continue to higher altitudes and catch the fast winds toward the upper Mirror Zone."

Bemor sent approval-displays, but his eyes did not move from his comm plate. "Good. Do so. We need the other Late Invaders."

Memor felt shunted aside. She had been pursuing these vagrant primates for a great while, and now Bemor—and even worse, Asenath—would get credit for their apprehension. But at least it was done. "Why are they so useful? I am happy to have them in hand, of course, but—"

Bemor gave a low, bass growl. "The Ice Minds command it. Events proceed elsewhere. A crisis threatens. We must get the primates."

"We have this one here—" A gesture at Tananareve.

"We may need more. The Ice Minds want to use them to converse in an immersion mode."

Memor stirred with misgivings. Her Undermind was fevered and demanded to be heard, but there was no time now. "Immersion? That can be destructive."

Tananareve seemed to be following this, but wisely said nothing.

"That is why we need several pathways. The connection may be too much for them, and we will need replacements."

Memor said softly, feeling a tremor from her Undermind, "What crisis?"

"It goes badly in the jet."

PART XII

THE WORD OF CAMBRONNE

It was at Waterloo that General Cambronne, when called on to surrender, was supposed to have said, "The Old Guard dies but never surrenders!" What Cambronne actually said was, "Merde!" which the French, when they do not wish to pronounce it, still refer to as, "the word of Cambronne." It corresponds to our four-letter word for manure. All the difference between the noble and the earthy accounts of war is contained in the variance between these two quotations.
—ERNEST HEMINGWAY, *MEN AT WAR*

THIRTY-SIX

The first sight of the Folk commanding the big skyfish was daunting. Cliff had seen these Folk aliens when his team came through the lock, in what seemed a very long time ago. Later he had heard fragments about the Folk from the scattered *SunSeeker* transmissions.

But now these before him seemed different—larger, with big heads on a leathery stalk neck. Their feathers made the body shape hard to make out. The Folk back at the air lock had feathers, but not nearly so large, colorful, and vibrant. As Cliff's team and Quert's Sil entered, the three big Folk rattled their displays, forking out neck arrays that flashed quick variations in magenta, rose, and ivory. Their lower bodies flourished downy wreaths of brown and contrasting violet.

"They're . . . giant peacocks," Irma whispered.

Cliff nodded. Back Earthside, peacocks used their outrageously large feathers to woo females. But these rustling, constantly shifting feather-shows had far more signaling capacity. Beneath the layers, he could glimpse ropy pelvic muscles. Loose-jointed shoulders gave intricate control to the feathers.

"More like, those flaunt unspoken messages, I'd guess."

Quert gestured and said, "Quill feather gives mood. Tail fan on neck cups sound to ears. Fan-signals are many. Rattle and flap for more signal. Color choice gives messages, too."

Aybe said, "Structural coloration, I'd say. Micro-fibers, fine enough to interfere with the incoming light, reflect back the color the creature wants."

Cliff watched the beautiful iridescent blue green or green-colored plumage shimmer and change with viewing angle. "Reflections from fibers, could be."

They all stood bunched together, humans and Sil, as the Folk came slowly into the big room, passing nearby with a gliding walk before settling on a place. The big things loomed over them and rattled out a long, ordered set of clattering sounds. "What's that sound say?" Terry whispered.

"Greet to visitor. But visitors inferior and should say so."

"Say so?" Irma whispered. "How?"

Quert gave the other Sil quick sliding words, a question. They all responded with a few other short, soft words. Quert's face took on a wrinkled, wry cast. "Sil not say, you not either."

"Good," Aybe said, and the others nodded. No tribute, no submission.

Cliff regarded the Folk's unmistakable piercing eyes, big though now slitted and slanted beneath heavy, crusted eyelids. Their pupils were big and black, set in bright yellow irises. There was something going on behind those eyes. Cliff had an impression of a brooding intelligence measuring the small band of humans and Sil. The tall, feathered Folk held the gaze of humans and Sil as they settled back on their huge legs and tails and gestured, murmuring to each other while still peering down at the humans. Cliff felt a prickly, primitive sensation, an awareness of a special danger. His nostrils flared and he automatically spread his stance, fists on his hips, facing the three aliens foursquare.

The three Folk settled into the high room bounded by pink, fleshy walls. Attendants flanked the three, and others scurried off to unknown tasks. There were small forms with six legs and plumed heads, carrying burdens and arranging the flesh-pink walls with quick energy. Constant motion surrounded the Folk, who went slowly, almost gliding. It was like watching an eerie parade with three big, frightening floats.

"Irma! Cliff!" Suddenly Tananareve Bailey appeared from behind one of the Folk. She ran toward them.

Meeting any friend in this bizarre place was wonderful. They all embraced Tananareve as she rushed into their arms. To Cliff, she was as lean and steely as a piece of gym equipment; you saw the skull beneath the skin. Irma said, laughing, "At last! Some woman company." And they all laughed long and hard. Giddy jokes, ample smiles.

A long loud sentence from the largest of the Folk broke them out of their happy chatter. They looked up into big yellow eyes.

"They said they needed you," Tananareve translated, "but I never know if they're telling me true."

"This skyfish just *swallowed* our tadfish," Irma said. "I thought we were goners."

"Better than a fight," Terry said. "But . . . we're captured."

The enormity of this last hurried and harried hour came to Cliff. He had kept his team free for so long now, barely escaping in one scrape after another . . . only to fail so quickly, *swallowed,* a slap in the face with cold water. He opened his mouth but could think of nothing to say. The others were still happy just to have Tananareve, but the implications were stunning.

"Maybe they want to negotiate," Cliff said, not really believing it.

Tananareve said, "They got orders from someone to grab you, pronto. They've been tracking you ever since you saw something called the Ice Minds. It took this long to catch up with you. They're big and can't crawl through the Bowl understructure. They kept complaining about having to take the other transports that can handle their size."

"What's up?" Aybe asked.

"They're under pressure. I don't know why." Tananareve stood near the Folk and introduced Asenath, Memor, and Bemor. It took a while to explain that Memor and Bemor had nearly the same genetics, were something like fraternal twins of different sexes, but that Bemor was somehow enhanced and held a higher-status position. "He can speak to the Ice Minds. Whereas Asenath"—a nod to the tall, densely feathered creature, sharp-eyed and rustling with impatience—"is a Wisdom

Chief." A shrug. "As near as I can tell, that's kind of like an operations officer."

There followed some back and forth translating as Memor insisted on a full introduction using her complete title, Attendant Astute Astronomer. Bemor then managed to get his "Contriver and Intimate Emissary to the Ice Minds" into the discussion. Tananareve whispered, "Slip those titles into your remarks now and then; they like that."

Cliff watched the huge aliens as the light of the jet and star, at these higher altitudes, poured down on the fleshy floor like glistening yellow-white oil. Asenath thundered, "We have you indeed, at last. The first issue is our need of you, to prepare a message for those whom you term the 'Glorians'—to continue the artifice."

The others looked to Cliff. He faced the big skull Asenath lowered, as if to listen more closely. Cliff suspected this was just intimidation—and decided to ignore it, the only strategy that might work. "Artifice?"

"Glorians believe you primates are the rulers and pilots of our Bowl," Asenath thundered. "They confuse our mutual trajectories as meaning that the Bowl comes from your world."

"Weird. So?" It seemed to Cliff better to play dumb for a while. There was too much going on to make sense of this. He needed time to talk to Tananareve and get his bearings. These Folk had talked to Redwing, using Tananareve, but what were the nuances of that?

Asenath gave a purple and rose display and her

head descended still closer. Her Anglish was clipped and brusque, perhaps because she had only recently imbibed the language, or because she meant it that way. "Of *course* we converge on Glory. Over time scales of many thousands of orbitals, similar goals emerge. The only puzzle to us is why you, with your simple though ingenious and craftily made ship, desire to attain the status the Glorian technologies imply."

Cliff shrugged, glanced at Tananareve—who shrugged. "Imply?"

"The gravitational signals. Surely this lures you."

"Not really. We're bound for Glory because it's a biosphere a lot like our own. The right oxygen levels, water vapor, a hydrogen cycle with oceans. Plus no signs of technology. No signatures of odd elements in its air. No electromagnetic emissions. No signals at all. Kind of like our world thousands of years—I guess you call them orbitals—ago." Cliff spread his hands, hoping this was a signal of admitting the obvious.

Asenath gave a rustling flurry of feather displays, crimson and violet. "Your ship has received the Glorian signals, yet you do not know?"

"Know what?"

"The Glorians, as you term them, are of the August."

"Meaning . . . ?"

"They do not deign, over many megaorbitals, to answer our electromagnetic signals. No matter of what frequencies. The Aloof and August."

"The same might be said of any rock."

"The advanced societies of this galaxy deliver their August messages only by means that young societies, such as yours, cannot detect." Asenath gave a rattling side-display in eggshell blue. "Most important, signals of great information density, to which young worlds cannot reply."

"We picked up the gravity waves, around the time our ship left Earthside," Cliff said. "There didn't seem to be a signal, just noise."

"So young societies would think," Bemor said from beside Asenath. "We do—"

Suddenly something made the three Folk pause, Bemor with his mouth partly open. Silence. Their yellow eyes were distant.

Quert appeared at Cliff's side and whispered, "They hear other voices."

"They've done this before, getting signals somehow," Tananareve said. "Let's use the time. What's our strategy here?"

"These Folk have something in mind, using us somehow, I'll bet," Aybe said. "Wish I knew what they're hearing right now."

Quert said, "They now listen to what we Sil brought forth. Told to. We showed old truth."

"How?" Tananareve asked.

"Folk control electromagnetic pathways in Bowl. So Sil make signs buildings." The swift slippery slide of Quert's words belied the content.

Cliff said, "Those deforming houses we saw you building?" He recalled how the Sil had deftly rebuilt their ruined city. He had seen a growing arch inching out into a parabolic curve, the scaffolding of tan walls rising from what seemed to be a sticky, plastic dirt. Wrinkled bulks had surged up as oblong windows popped into shape from a crude substrate, all driven by electrical panels. The Sil were working their entire city into fresh structures like spun glass, growing them into artful loops and bridges and elegant spires.

"You make signals with your cities?" Irma asked. "How?"

"City, all can see all across Bowl. Others know to look to us. To get message." Quert had now a calm the feline alien wore like a cloak.

"What was the message?"

Quert looked at them all slowly, as if unburdening at last. He wagged his head and said, "Bowl pass by your sun. Go too close. Shower down mass. Damage world biosphere."

Irma said, "What? When?"

"Long ago. Folk call it Great Shame."

Terry said, "You got this how?"

Quert looked puzzled, as it always did by the human habit of conveying a question by a rising note at the end of a sentence. "Your ship told you. You told us."

"What?" Terry turned to Cliff. "You got this from Redwing?"

"Yup. I tried it out on Quert. I didn't believe it, really."

"You didn't tell us!" Aybe said.

"Saw no need to." Cliff's face stiffened. "I still don't know if it's true."

"We got more from . . . others," Quert said. "Come."

Quert led them to a small room that puckered into the ribbed, pink slabs that formed the great hall. Cliff looked back. The Folk were still rigid, eyes focused on infinity, taking in some transmission from . . . where? Their bodies were clenched, feet grasping at the floor. He turned and went into a narrow chamber where a bright screen fluoresced into pale blue light. "We have map sent. History."

It was a 3-D starscape. Across it scratched a ruby line. "Bowl went there. Time go backward."

A dot started at the Bowl, shown as a small cup embracing a red star. The ruby line stretched as it moved backwards, away, into the reaches of stars. Cliff and the others muttered to each other, watching the constellations slip by as time ran in reverse, accelerating. The line looped near many dots that were stars—yellow, red, some bright blue—and went on, faster, until the perspective became confusing. It wound along the Orion arm of the slowly churning galaxy. They could see the stars moving now in their gyres. The ruby line ventured out toward the Perseus arm, which was festering with light, then looped near some to pick off glimmering sites apparently of interest. The Bowl's method, Cliff could see, was to dive into the distant, shallow slope of the grav well of a star, slowing somehow, and skate by. A close-up view near a yellow dot showed bright sparks departing the Bowl, to descend deeper into the gravity potential well of the destination star. These soon returned, apparently bearing whatever they found on the circling worlds down in the grav well. This happened several times as they watched.

Then the Bowl cruised through what Cliff recognized as the Local Fluff inside the Local Bubble, terms he recalled from some distant lecture for the spaces around Sol. Then the Bowl surged a bit, building speed, bound for the next target brimming ahead.

Cliff and the Sil had to interpret in this way the backward-running line, for what they saw was the reverse. Then the Bowl-star pair descended on a yellow star.

They watched the entire encounter and talked about it, piecing the story together in backward fashion. After the encounter, the Bowl came soaring out of a system racked and ruined. Comets flared in the yellow star glow, and it was clear why. The Bowl had swept through the prickly small motes of light that swarmed far from the star. It had left a roiling path through those tiny lights, giving them small nudges, and so some had plunged inward. Only one was needed.

One. It slid down the slow slope of gravity and arced on its long hyperbola toward a pale blue dot. And hit.

"They brushed along in our Oort cloud," Aybe said. "That's it. They, they tipped that rock into—"

"An accident. Killed the dinosaurs," Terry said, "who were descendants of their own kind. Can't check the time axis on this thing—what the hell would the units be anyway?—but there's a reason it shows this way. Somebody's making a point. The Bird Folk were clumsy, careless."

"Yeah . . ." Irma stared at the screen. "Who?"

Cliff said nothing, just tried to take it all in. He felt Quert's presence strongly as a kind of intense energy, as though this were the crucial moment in some plan the alien had. Yet there was no overt sign of it he could detect.

He said, "Terry, I think the Glorians' point is, 'See, we know all about you.'"

Quert seemed unperturbed, his face calm. The other Sil had not come into this room, but they clustered at the entrance, watching silently. "Folk go to other stars after yours. But yours special for other reason."

"Why's that?" Irma asked.

"They come from your sun."

"Who?" Irma's mouth gave a skeptical twist. "The Folk?"

"See." Quert moved his hand near the screen and the ruby line seemed to accelerate, slipping smoothly from star to star in the Orion Arm. The speed now barely showed a slowing as the Bowl dived near a star, sent expeditions down, then moved on. Cliff lost count of how many the Bowl visited. Then the trajectory took a long swooping arc, still sampling stars and worlds. The curve turned back along the sprinkle of slowly moving stars.

"These are the even earlier eras for the Bowl?" Irma said. "Must be a really long time ago."

"Notice how the Bowl is going now from one

star to the next, pausing near each one," Aybe said. "That fits—they were exploring for the first time. Sizing up what solar systems around other stars are like."

"Then we're headed back to—look, there's the Local Bubble," Terry said. In an overlay, a thin ivory blob approached probably an image of the low-density shell that surrounded Sol. "But . . . Sol's not there."

"Stars move," Irma said. "See, the Bowl is moving on past that, not stopping."

Aybe said, "It's slowing down a lot, seems to be approaching this yellow star—hey, is that us?"

They watched, stunned, as the Bowl and its reddish star slowed more and more, edging up to the yellow star.

"Can't be, see?" Terry pointed. "The Bowl's going into orbit, making—"

The image froze.

Irma whispered, "The Bowl came from . . . a binary."

"They built it around a binary star," Cliff said, "and one of those stars was Sol."

"Didn't we hear a little from Redwing about Beth's team, pretty far back?" Terry said. "They went to some kind of museum and saw a show about how the Bowl got built."

Aybe said, "After all, they had to start with a smaller star than Sol. They grabbed big masses from the swarm around that star, and—who knows?— maybe some of Sol's Oort cloud."

Irma snorted. "Are you saying they came from *Earth*?"

Aybe shrugged. "Looks like it. I mean, Mars had an early warm era, so maybe—"

"That was in the first billion years or so after Sol formed," Terry said. "The end of this Bowl voyage show we just saw, it can't be that far back. Makes no sense! You'd have to get an intelligent species up to full industrial ability in just a billion years."

"Okay, then whoever built the Bowl had to come from Earth," Irma said, hands on hips. "I'm discounting smart creatures from the Jovian moons or Venus or someplace."

"Fair enough," Aybe said. "So, Earth. These Folk out there, you're saying they had to come from some time—"

"We're all thinking the same thing? They were dinosaurs," Cliff said. "The feathers make it hard to see, though. Asenath looks more like a monster Easter chick than a *Tyrannosaurus rex*."

"Damn!" Aybe said. "Remember when we were on the run, when we hid under a bridge? We saw—"

"Right," Terry burst in. "Big plant-eater reptile. We ran away, pretty damn scared."

"So . . ." Cliff's training as a biologist was taking a beating. "That thing comes from maybe the Jurassic, one hundred and forty-five million years ago. Maybe the Bowl builders took along the current flora and fauna?"

"Because they came from then?" Irma scoffed. "We would've seen their ruins. A whole industrial civilization, and we missed it? This whole idea is impossible!"

"Maybe it was very short-lived, lasted say about ten thousand years," Terry said. "Just a tiny sliver of the geological record."

Aybe said, "Consider what alien explorers might discover if they arrived on Earth one hundred million years from now. Their scientists would find evidence of vast tectonic movements, ice ages, and the movement of oceans, a geological history sprinkled with life. Maybe an occasional catastrophic collapse."

"Exactly," Terry talked right over Aybe. "They might also find, in a single layer of rock, signs of cities and the creatures who built them. But that layer had been crushed, subducted, oxidized. Hell, tens of thousands of years—that'll be smashed flat, only a centimeter thick when it comes out from the subduction. In dozens of million years, there's nothing."

Cliff was warming to the idea. "Easy to miss, especially if you aren't looking for it."

"Explains why the Folk are interested in us," Irma said. "We're relatives!"

Cliff saw Quert give the eye-moves of disagreement. "Not so?"

"Folk want to know of ship you ride. Plants you carry. Bodies you have, songs, lore."

"Then they don't know where we're from?" Aybe demanded.

"They know. Do not care." Quert looked uneasy, a change from the pensive calm of only minutes before. Cliff wondered if the alien and other Sil knew all the implications of this backward history of the Bowl. Had they recognized the home star as Sol?

A loud, rolling boom came from the large area outside. At first Cliff thought it was an explosion, but then it took on other notes and held, lingering with a mournful long strumming cadence. *Like someone crying,* he thought. *Or some thing.*

"It's the Folk," Aybe said. Quert gave an agreeing eye-click. "They . . . something's wrong."

THIRTY-SEVEN

Redwing stepped into the garden and inhaled through his nose. Good moist green smells. Take a moment, just a breather. The animals—

The animals had been tied down, netted, and they were not happy. He hadn't ordered that. He should have, of course, the way *SunSeeker* was lurching about. Had the finger snakes done that?

The finger snakes. Redwing tended to forget that they were part of what he was trying to save. Were they in their tunnel? No, he could see all three of them wrapped around three thick-bole apple trees.

A smartbot prowled the rows of plants, testing soil and injecting fluids where needed. Just growing plants hydroponically wasn't enough. Humans needed micronutrients, vitamins, minerals—but so did the plants and animals they ate. So all organisms in the looping food chains had to provide the right micronutrients needed by others, without them getting locked up in insoluble forms or running out. Selenium had gone missing a century back, he had learned from the log. Only with sophisticated biochem types woken up for the task did they get the food chain running right again.

Redwing savored the leafy comfort lacing the air and staggered as *SunSeeker* surged. Redwing caught himself on a stanchion. The snakes didn't seem to notice. Phoshtha and Shtirk were watching a screen, a view of lands showing murkily through the jet, while they worked on small things with their darting, intricate hands. Thisther was watching the captain.

Redwing asked, "Thisther, did you secure the pigs and sheep and such?"

"Yes. Was well done?" A thin, reedy command of Anglish.

"Yes, thank you. Are you comfortable?"

"Better. What a ride!"

Redwing left the garden feeling better. Now what? There was nothing like cramped quarters to concentrate the mind. So he went to his cabin as the deck creaked and rolled with the jet storms that whipped by it. He watched the Bowl view crawl past on his wall and did a few standing exercises, adjusted against the tilt local grav had, due to the helix *SunSeeker* was following. He had learned to disappear within himself, walling out a ship's routine humming and stale smells and dead air, to create a still, silent space where he could live, rest, think. In the continual noise of the ship he had learned to hear well, picking telltale murmurs out of *SunSeeker*'s constant vibrations.

A call buzzed in his ear. "Cap'n, got something to see on the bridge. The jet's really snaking now. Flares like sausages running down it, too."

He started back, still listening to the pops and creaks of his ship. With his crew he also knew how to listen carefully, or to deliberately not hear. An essential skill, taking only a lifetime of daily practice to master.

Beth's voice had been strained, and she had just replaced Ayaan Ali in the lead pilot's chair, with Clare Conway in the second chair. They all looked pale, their eyes never leaving the wall screens and operations boards. *SunSeeker*'s long helix within the jet had worn them all down, and now the pace was picking up. He hadn't been resting well, and neither had the others. Coffee could only do so much.

As he entered the bridge, he noted that everyone had coffee ready at the elbow. Should he tell them to switch to decaf? No, too much meddling.

Karl said as Redwing came onto the bridge, "It's whipping around in the Knothole, just as the simulation said."

On the biggest screen, the jet was now lit up in yellow. They were looking straight down it and could see the flexed jet now bulging very close to the Knothole edge. "See, the Knothole has big mag fields to stop it."

"Are we driving the jet just enough to give them

a scare?" Redwing leaned over the panel and switched to a flank camera view. "And what's that secondary bump?"

Karl studied it. Redwing noted that Beth was working a different telescoping camera, focused far away from the jet, on the mirror zone. Karl said, "That's a nonlinear effect—a backflow."

"You mean there's a shock wave working back toward us?" Redwing watched the small sideways oscillation evolve, working around the rim of the jet. "It's from the big kink?"

SunSeeker could run for weeks in the jet without climbing into view of the gamma ray lasers on the Bowl rim. They were already fairly deep in the Bowl and getting a closer view of the zones near the Knothole, where centrifugal gravity was less. The mirror zone, a vast annulus, was behind their forward-looking views, and ahead loomed the forested regions just in from the Knothole. Beth had been kept somewhere in all that.

"Looks like the kink went nonlinear and launched this shock back at us," Karl said. "I don't understand—"

"Here's a better view," Beth said. "I asked the Bridge Artilect to find any part of the mirror zone that could give us an angled reflection, and it found this."

She smiled, and Redwing saw she was enjoying this. She always seized fresh opportunity with relish, one of her best qualities. The wobbly, somewhat blurred image gave them a view from far away to the side. He watched the kink bulge warping as it met the higher mag fields at the Knothole rim, and a countershock race away *up* the jet. That played among the boundary mag fields of the jet, pushing out farther to the side—

"It's going to hit the atmospheric membrane in the closest-in zone," Beth said. "Moving at high speed—over a hundred klicks a second in sideways motion."

"This wasn't in the simulation, as I recall." Redwing let his statement hang there, without a tone of sarcasm. Flat facts spoke for themselves.

Karl nodded, said nothing. Beth watched the fast-moving side shock as it plowed toward the atmosphere's envelope, a layer sketched in by a graphic; it wasn't truly visible in these narrow line widths. "Is there enough mass in that to do damage?"

"Plenty," Karl said, "and the magnetic energy density, too, can hammer the envelope." He looked worried and said no more.

"What about the structure itself?" Redwing said. He knew this huge thing had to have incredible strength to hold it together. *SunSeeker* had a support structure made of nuclear tensile strength materials, able to take the stresses of the ramjet scoop at the ship's axial core. Maybe the Bowl material was similar.

Karl said in a distant tone, almost automatically, "I scanned the Bowl wraparound struts, the foundational matter, on the long-range telescopes. Had the Artilects do a spectral study. It was only a few tens of meters thick, mostly carbon composite looks like, at least on the outside. That's pretty heavily encrusted with evident add-on machinery and cowlings. Calculated the stress."

"Which means . . . ?" Redwing persisted.

"The Bowl stress-support material has to be better than *SunSeeker*'s. Maybe lots better."

"Should we alter our planned trajectory?" Beth asked, eyes moving among the screens.

"Not yet." He was thinking fast but getting nothing. So many factors at play . . . "That display we got before, the lightning here on the bridge, it must be some kind of message."

"I noticed something here before," Karl said. "Look." He thumped his command pad and brought up a recorded scene on a side screen. "See that?"

The vector locator was focused on the zone nearest the Knothole. They could see the massive mag field coils at the rim, then the boundary of the atmospheric envelope, shiny in orange, reflected jet light. There were verdant forests sprawling away from the bulky Knothole structures.

"That's the same sort of area we were in," Beth said. "Low gravs, huge tall trees, big spider things. And I saw some of that orange light shimmering up high, from far off, bounced off the upper boundary layer, I guess. Jet light."

Partway into the large band of forest was a burnt brown and black slash among the lush greens, now mostly faded. Something had left a fresher black burn on the metal and ceramic portion near the Knothole, where the jet passed through.

Karl said slowly, "So instability was a major problem here. It's damaged the Bowl before."

"But shouldn't forest have covered over damage pretty quickly?" Beth asked.

"Maybe it was damage to the understructure," Karl said. "It broke systems that deliver water and nutrients. Not repaired yet."

"That means they're neglecting upkeep," Redwing said. "The usual first sign of a system sliding downhill."

"So why don't they have defenses against the occasional jet malf?" Beth asked.

A long silence. They recalled the crackling image of the Bowl dancing in air above the bridge, sent by some mysterious agency. Karl had explained it in terms of some inductive electromagnetic fields, playing along the outside of the ceramic walls nearby. Redwing was skeptical of that mechanism but certain that the event had been a crude attempt at getting their attention. Then nothing more happened. "A trial run, maybe," Karl had said. Redwing decided to keep to their planned helical trajectory.

Clare Conway said, rising from the copilot chair, "Cap'n, I see three small ships coming up behind us. They popped into view of long-range microwave radar minutes ago."

Redwing flicked the radar display on the biggest screen. "Where'd they come from?"

"From the Knothole rim, looks like," Clare said.

Karl said, "Maybe this answers Beth's question. They're sending out something to attack us."

"What's their ETA on current trajectory?" Redwing asked, keeping his voice calm.

"Two hours, approx," Clare said.

"Get me an image." Redwing considered what they could do. *SunSeeker* had no substantial defenses against projectile or high-intensity laser weapons. He had learned a simple rule back in the brief, enormously destructive Asteroid War: that any mass hitting at three kilometers per second delivers kinetic energy equal to its mass in TNT. And *SunSeeker* was moving well above 100 km/sec now. Add to that any incoming kinetic energy of an attacker. Square it. Any interesting space drive was a weapon of mass destruction, even to itself.

That was why the ship had auto-laser batteries run by the Artilects, designed for interstellar travel. They could hammer a rock the size of your fist or smaller into ionized atoms in a microsecond. But above that mass level, not much. They might deflect it a bit, which could be useful. That's all. Throw a living room couch at *SunSeeker* at these speeds and they would suffer a hull breach.

"They're small, can maneuver faster than we can," Clare said. "Accelerating at three gravs, too."

"So maybe robotic," Redwing said. This was not looking good. "How do they navigate in the jet? Can we tell?"

"Looks like magscoops, same as us. Smaller, of course."

Clare brought up the same telescope Beth had used and sought out the small moving dots. "Less than a hundred meters across," she said. "Cylindrical, with an ionized propulsion signature."

Redwing said, "Maybe they didn't take us seriously before. Slow reflexes."

"No," Karl said flatly. "We're missing something here."

The ship strummed with long rolling waves and sharp pops and snaps. No one spoke, and Redwing listened to his ship while all around him his crew worked to find out more about the roiling jet that streamed by, into the magscoop and their fusion chambers. The shipboard Artilects were working as well, but seldom spoke or called attention to themselves. They were built and trained for their talents to sustain, not for imagination and quick responses to the wholly new.

Into the long uncomfortable silence Beth said quietly, watching the screens, "That shock wave pushing out the jet in the Knothole—it's hit the membrane. At high velocity."

They all turned and saw it on max amplification. Beth had used the overlay yellow and orange to signify plasma and lag fields, and strands of these showed the jet striking the boundary of the Bowl biosphere. Filmy gases escaped into space, pearly strands they saw in the visible. Redwing knew what this meant. The plasma's high-energy particles, encased in the sheath of magnetic fields, would deliver prickly energies. This would fry away the long-chain organic molecules that made the gossamer boundaries. Those separated the Bowl's many compartments, holding the great vaults of air above the living zones. So it would all go to smash and scatteration in a blizzard of unleashed furies.

He tried to imagine what that meant to those living there. Then he made himself stop.

A booming roll came through the deck, all the way from hundreds of meters down the long stack.

"Plasma densities nearby are rising. Our exhaust is getting blocked again," Beth said.

"This is how it started before," Karl said. "To break down air, the voltage is—"

"Megavolts," Clare snapped. "Got it. If that happens, stay flat. Stick your head up, it'll draw current, fry you."

"You think they—it—is trying to kill us?" Beth said. "This could be communication."

"Strange way to do it," Redwing said.

"Retaliation for thrashing the jet, I'd think," Fred said. He had come onto the board so quietly no one noticed him.

"I'm getting rising inductive effects close to our skin," Beth said. "Must be Alfvén waves rippling in on the scoop fields. Higher electric fields—"

Redwing felt his hair stand on end. He hit the deck.

Sparks snapped. Everyone flopped onto the deck and lay flat. A bright yellow-white line scratched across the air. More lines sputtered. They arched and twisted. Some split, and yellow green strands shaped a tight shape—

"Human form!" Fred said from the deck. "They're making our image. They know what we are."

The shape wobbled and throbbed in the fevered air. Carved in shifting, crackling yellow lines, it was like a bad cartoon. Stretched legs, arms flapping, wobbly head, hands first spread then balled into fists, the whole body flailing. Then it was gone in a sizzle and a flicker.

Beth said, "Can they see us?"

"Who's 'they' anyway?" Clare said. Her face was flushed, lips compressed. "They're trying to jam our fusion burn, get us to stop, I suppose. So they're sending us an echo, an image of us to—make some kind of communication?"

The shape popped up again. Outlined in crackling yellow and orange, the figure wriggled and sputtered.

"Let me try . . ." Clare raised a hand slightly into the singed air. A long moment. Then slowly, twisting and shuddering, losing definition in the legs, the figure moved, too. It raised its left hand, mirror image to Clare's right. Air snapped around the dancing yellow image. The hand flexed, worked, wriggled itself into . . . fingers. A thumb grew, extended, turned red, and contracted. Now the crackling image filled itself in, a skin spreading yellow-bright and warped and seething. The body grew a head, and it struggled to make a mouth and eyes of pale ivory. The electrical fog flickered, as if barely able to sustain the sizzling voltage.

Clare slowly flexed her fingers. The fingers twitched, too, suffused in a waxy, saffron glow. The body hovered in the air unsteadily, holding pattern, all the defining bright yellow lines focused on the shimmering, burnt-yellow hand.

"Let's try to signal—," Redwing began.

The arc snapped off with a pop. There was nothing in the air but a harsh, nose-stinging stench.

Clare sobbed softly. Fred jumped up and turned in all directions, but could see nothing to do. The only sound was the rumbling fusion engines.

"Let's get back to stations," Redwing said.

Clare laughed with a high, nervous edge. She got up and resumed the copilot chair. Everyone got back into bridge position, unsteady and pensive.

Fred said, "The low-frequency spectrum has changed."

"Which means?" Redwing asked.

"It's got a lot more signal strength. Let me run the Fourier—" His fingers and hands gave the board complex signals through its optical viewers. "Yep, got some FM modulation, pretty coherent."

"Someone sending? Now?" Beth said. "Maybe they want to talk?"

"This is really low-frequency stuff," Fred said. "The antennas we use to monitor interstellar Alfvén waves, to keep watch on perturbations in the mag-scoop. Never thought we'd get a coherent message on those!" Fred brightened, always happy to see a new unknown.

Karl had gotten up and now stood behind Fred's chair. He said, "That fifteen kilohertz upper frequency—look at the spike. Amazing. Antennas radiate best if they're at least as large as a wavelength, so . . . that means that the radiator is at least thirty kilometers across!"

Redwing tried to imagine what big structure could send such signals. "Is there anything on radar of that size in the jet?"

The answer came quickly: no.

"How can we decode it?" Clare asked. She stood and walked over to see Fred's Fourier display.

Fred said, "I can look for correlates, but—hell!—we're starting from knowing nothing about who the hell is—"

This time Redwing barely had time to register the prickly feeling on his hands and head before a crackling burnt-yellow discharge surged all along the bridge, snarling. The air snapped as they again dived for the deck. Redwing hit and flattened and saw Clare choose to stand against the nearest wall. A tendril shot forth and caught her. She twitched and crackled as the ampere violence surged through her. Her mouth opened impossibly wide, and a guttural gasp escaped—and then the mouth locked open, frozen. Smoke fumed from her hair. Her legs jumped and her arms jerked and she fell.

Her red coverall sparked at the belt. Tiny fires forked from her fingers as she struck the deck. Her hair seethed with smoke. She shuddered, twitched—was still.

Redwing did not move, but he noticed the tension had left the air. A seared silence came as acrid air stung the nostrils.

In the silence he could hear a last long sigh ease out of Clare, whistling between broken teeth.

Beth sobbed as they gingerly gathered around the singed body. Redwing wondered what he could do in the short time before the cylindrical alien ships arrived, climbing up the jet toward them.

THIRTY-EIGHT

Memor was roaring out of control. The two other Folk restrained her as she twisted and clawed at them. Their howls and wails blended together, even to Tananareve Bailey's ears as she ran toward the enormous, thrashing things.

Her Folk attendants had scattered, not knowing what to do. They were backed against the walls, stunned into silence by Memor's deep growls. Tananareve could tell they were too afraid to leave and too afraid to do anything. She saw that a figure among them lurked under a cowl, a humanoid with a gray metallic head, carrying three ruby red eyes that peered out from the cowl's shadows. A cyborg, she guessed—mind downloaded into a metal body. Such things had begun to manifest Earthside in the era when they had departed, so perhaps it was natural that an alien form of embodied Artilects should have manifested here in a Bowl that was millions of years old. The cyborg had a crystal silicon carbide assembly, four arms, and sturdy legs. She had seen no artificial bodies in the Bowl but now here was one, an attendant to the Folk, cowering like the rest, against the pink living wall.

Tananareve glanced at all those pressed against the walls and now could tell they were all far too afraid, too devoted to the entire Bowl system, ever to see any other future. A stasis state where nothing changed.

Then there came a move, from the Folk.

Bemor acted. He held his genetic sister in a firm embrace while Asenath did something at the back of Memor's head. Her great shape stopped writhing and shuddering and then slowly eased, her arms going slack. Memor's eyes were distant, her face blank, breath long and heavy, a *whuff whuff* Tananareve had not heard before. Her big, nimble four-fingered hands twitched but did nothing.

Bemor turned from Memor, chuffing and labored, his face troubled. Blinking, he saw the humans and Sil. "We now know what you Sil have been spreading." His voice came from the barrel chest, low and threatening.

Quert stepped forward, mild and calm, seeming utterly unafraid. Tananareve had met the alien Sil only moments before and was still trying to understand them. They were humanoid and walked with a fluid grace, their tan clothing adjusting itself to their movements. Quert said, "Glorian message came to human ship, the *SunSeeker*."

Bemor huffed, stamped around, clearly calling on outside Artilects, and thinking on what they said, and finally himself said, "I am, yes, aware that our forward stations, orbiting from ahead of us, did not register the Glorian signals well and bring them to the proper level of attention. A bureaucratic error, alas. These stations have had no true news for many kilo-orbitals. They suffer from a sclerotic inability to adapt, to remain fresh."

Quert said softly, "We know so. Sire."

Bemor ignored this status salute. "These humans

managed to get the Glorian mischief to you, the vagrant and difficult Sil."

"It was important, surely you can see so, Sire. We spread such message through city-speak." Quert spoke mildly but with eyes steady. "Then came more. Diagram of Bowl's path. Much long history, strange tales the Glorians know."

Bemor said, "Annoying! You had no need to be familiar with such."

Quert did not blink. "Sil think opposite."

Then they got into a hot discussion Tananareve could not follow, so she stepped back a few paces, into the comforting circle of humans. She had not realized, living so long among aliens whose social signals were strange and hard to register, what a simple warmth came from her own kind. After so long, it felt like a profound blessing. As the Folk chatter waxed on around them—Bemor booming, Quert's small voice in sliding syllables—she considered her fellow humans. This was so strange in itself that the mere phrase *fellow humans* said it all as she thought of it. She had competed for, and then signed on to *SunSeeker,* all for one solid purpose—to go to a distant star and begin a new civilization. Straight out, true enough—a species imperative, some had said, and so she had supposed. She did feel that, then. She had stored her eggs and planned to find a man who deserved them, and to do what she could, in some distant land among the stars, to bring humanity to a greater destiny.

Yet . . . now these fellow humans in their nervous chatting selves looked . . . strange to her. Their rambling, whispered words, their ill-concealed yet clearly frightened eyeball-jittering glances . . . all these seemed both familiar and yet edged in strangeness.

Cliff, for example, looked worn down. Skinny. Standard uniform but patched here and there, knees and elbows replaced, and tattered beyond easy recognition. Rough-cut beard, hair chopped into blunt wedges, a true wild man from many wearing days. Yet his eyes were watchful and quick, listening to his team and also sizing up the alien discussion going on a few paces away. He seemed somehow telescoped down a long range, so she could see him in a perspective she had never known. As a member of his species, he talked less than others and never stopped studying his surroundings. Watching him was to her now refreshment, consolation, peace.

Best to leave that for later, though. You met the alien on your own terms and what you took away might be unexpected. She had to use whatever perspective worked.

So Tananareve turned to Irma, smiled, and did the ritual girl thing, and got the whole story in a few minutes.

The Glorians had sent their own history of the Bowl's long trajectory, plus some cartoon threats to stay away from Glory. Apparently they had been surveying all their galactic neighborhood for a great long time, while keeping electromagnetic silence. But now that the Bowl was steadily approaching, they resorted to a simple microwave signal train. And it told a truly ancient tale.

An event the Folk called the Great Shame was marked in the Bowl's path. The Sil wrote it in their architectural messages. Their new city rapidly rebuilt after the Bird Folk smashed it. The new Sil array of parks, plazas, streets, and structures held an agreed code. This conveyed a message other societies ringed around the great expanses of the Bowl could see and use. Now everyone knew of the Great Shame.

Tananareve asked, "And why's that important?"

"Because the Folk destroyed their own home world," Cliff said. "As we saw. Earth. It looks like they blundered into the Oort cloud, and their gravitational impulse nudged the Dinosaur Killer comet, sixty-five million years ago."

"So life changed directions," Tananareve said, eyes distant. "Doomed the dinosaurs, but made us possible."

"Must be more," Irma said. "Must be."

Memor thrashed and called in long strident shrieks. She raised her huge, thick-lipped mouth and made a warbling, keening sound. Bemor sheltered his sister twin through this and gathered himself, a big hulking presence, and said to them all, "The Sil did not truly know what they were doing. This is the Great Shame, yes. Now that it is known, the task of us all is to make clear that it came from an earlier species, and so does not imply that the Folk are responsible."

Tananareve's eyes flared, eyebrows arched. "Huh? C'mon—this 'does not imply that the Folk are responsible'—but you caused it! And why's Memor so distressed?"

Bemor shuddered a bit and in low bass tones said, "She is in conversation with her . . . Undermind. The Great Shame was merely a phrase to her. Now she has discovered that her Undermind concealed its meaning, to preserve her balance."

"I thought you Folk could view all your unconscious," Tananareve said.

"Not always." Bemor hesitated, then with a rustle of feathers that she now knew meant he had made a decision, went on. "The proto-Folk of that ancient era, who committed the Great Shame, were unwise. They returned to their home system, flush with triumphant contacts with scores of nearby worlds. The dynamics of their parent system were well known to them, but wrong. Their data was gathered when the second sun—our star, now— was still in place. And perhaps they ventured too deeply into the large cloud of iceteroids."

Tananareve was digesting this when Cliff frowned and said, "The Bowl has one great commandment— stability is all. Right? Having this Great Shame is a contradiction you don't want to face—is that what's making that one"—a nod to Memor—"so crazy?"

An awkward silence. Then Asenath said, "We Folk differ from those who built the Bowl. Those could not view their Underminds. The vagrant forces that arise in Underminds can be managed, if the sunshine of the Overmind shines upon them."

Tananareve said, "You think of your unconscious as like, say, bacteria? Sanitize it, problem solved?"

Bemor and Asenath looked at each other and exchanged fast, complex fan-signals with clacking and rustling. Bemor had Memor in a restraining hold and the big creature was slowly becoming less restive.

"Not knowing your desires renders them more potent," Bemor said. "They then emerge in strange ways, at unexpected moments. Your greatest drives lie concealed from your fore-minds. So the running agents and subsystems of your immediate, thinking persona can be invaded, without knowing it, by your Underminds. Quite primitive."

"Which defeats control, right?" Cliff said.

"And so stability," Tananareve added.

Asenath said, "You mean, Late Invaders, that notions simply *appear* in your Overminds?"

"You mean do we have ideas?" Tananareve considered. "Sure."

"But you have no clue where the ideas came from," Asenath said.

Bemor added, "Worse, they cannot go find where their ideas were manufactured. Much of their minds is barred to them."

"Astounding!" Asenath said. "Yet . . . it works in a way. They did get here on their own starship."

"There are many subtle aspects," Bemor began, and then paused. "We must keep to task." He turned and gestured. Attendants rolled forward a large machine.

"I don't like the look of that," Tananareve said.

"Is this the same machine you put me in before? That Memor used to study my mind?"

"No," Bemor said. "This enables you to communicate with other minds, specifically those who need you to serve as an intermediary."

"Who?" Tananareve turned to Irma and Cliff. "I hated that suffocating box with its foul smell. And the feeling—like snakes swarming over my skull. Then fingers in my head. I'd think something, then it slipped away, as if something was . . . running greasy hands over it."

"We require you to enter this device," Asenath said. She turned to Bemor and said in Folk—but not so fast that Tananareve could not translate it— "Do we need the others? They are trouble."

Bemor rattled suppressing signals with his hind feathers. *Not now.*

Cliff and Irma had caught none of this. She said, "Look, I can't square that Great Shame history of yours. You came back from star-voyaging to see the old place, Earth. So why haven't we found Folk artifacts on other planets in the solar system?"

"There were stages. There was the era, after the Great Shame, that earlier Folk forms called the Dusting. It was a rain of small fragments into the solar system. An aftereffect of the Shame, in ways known to orbital specialists, arising from multiple iceteroid collisions far out from Sol. A sad era. Mere high-velocity dust destroyed much space-based technology. It etched whole cities out of existence on worlds not protected by atmospheres.

"But enough of this!" Bemor said. "Into this device you go now, Late Invader. We are ordered to send you thus, for reasons opaque to me. The Ice Minds would have it so. Welcome to this"—a broad sweeping gesture with a final feathered flourish—"a singular machine which we term a Reader."

She had no choice. The assistants looked nasty and they moved swiftly, closing in on her. She turned and embraced the people near her. "Damn, we've just reunited and, and—"

"We'll still be here when you come out."

The others gave murmuring reassurances. She turned to follow the assistant, some nervous little form of robot, and suddenly a loud thunderclap hammered through the room. The fleshy walls of the skyfish rippled with it, and the floor lurched beneath her. She staggered, caught herself on Irma's shoulder, stayed standing. "Damn!"

"A shock wave," Cliff said. He turned to the Folk. "From what?"

Bemor looked out the transparent wall. "Disaster."

PART XIII

THE DIAPHANOUS

It appears that the radical element responsible for the continuing thread of cosmic unrest is the magnetic field. What, then, is a magnetic field . . . that, like a biological form, is able to reproduce itself and carry on an active life in the general outflow of starlight, and from there alter the behavior of stars and galaxies?

—EUGENE PARKER,
COSMICAL MAGNETIC FIELDS

THIRTY-NINE

Karl said, "It's a standing kink."

Beth looked at the screen showing the jet, its plasma and magnetic densities highlighted in color. "This is a snap of it?"

"No, it's real-time. The sideways movement of the jet in the Knothole region is hung up, lashing against the mag bumpers meant to keep it away." A side excursion had forked over against one of the life zones, penetrating the atmospheric envelope of a pie-shaped wedge.

"How in hell did that happen?" Redwing asked from over Beth's shoulder.

Karl grimaced. "We've been driving our fusion burn pretty hard, trying to get some distance from the fliers that are coming up at us in the jet—"

"And failing," Redwing added.

"—so that added our plume to the plasma already forcing the kink instability. Nonlinear mechanics at work. The kink has gotten into some mode where it snags against the mag defenses and just stays there." Karl shrugged, as if to say, *Don't blame me, it's nonlinear.*

"So it's getting worse down there," Beth said.

Her eyes were always on the shifting screens as they powered away from their pursuers. In the howling maelstrom of the jet, there were always vagrant pressures, sudden snarling knots of turbulence, shifts in *SunSeeker*'s magscoop configuration. Now *SunSeeker* had Mayra Wickramsingh and Ayaan Ali as backup navigator/pilot, since Clare Conway had died in an instant's sudden lightning flash through the excited air above the bridge deck.

That had been only an hour ago, but the sharp terror of it was already fading in memory. There was too much to do *now*, to think of what had happened. Beth had helped carry away the charred corpse, holding Clare by the arms, seeing the face that was swollen and already darkening. Only hours ago, she had seen that mouth smiling, laughing.

Beth heard her own voice rattling out, "Those flitters, as you call 'em, Cap'n, are coming up fast." Her eyes studied the slim, quick shapes, just barely defined in size by their microwave radars. They had spread into a triangle, centered on *SunSeeker*'s wake.

Redwing stood in the middle of the bridge and said to everyone, "We're plainly about to go into battle. Those flitters are fast. We can't outrun them. So we've got to engage them with a ship not designed to do battle at all."

Silence. Jampudvipa usually said little, but now she said quietly, "Is there any advantage in leaving the jet?"

Beth knew Redwing should answer that, but she

seethed with anger now and could not stop herself. "I don't want to maneuver against craft that fast, with our only fuel the star's solar wind. Or what's left of it—the jet gets over ninety percent of the plasma that leaves the star. I can't fly hard with no mass coming through the scoop."

Karl Lebanon asked, head bowed, "What do the flitters fly on?"

"Not plasma, right?" Redwing turned to Beth.

"Their plume shows fusion burners, but they're running on boron-proton. They carry their fuel and reaction mass."

"They're flying upstream, which costs them in momentum," Karl said. "For us, it's gain. We get more charged mass down the magscoop gullet. So—"

"What do we do when we get to gunplay?" Redwing asked. "We got no guns aboard, Dr. Lebanon."

Beth said, "You've got the big gun, Cap'n—the torch."

Redwing nodded somberly. "You think it can make that much difference?"

Karl said, "Whatever's flying the flitters, Artilects or aliens, it has to be vulnerable to the jet. They have magnetic screens for sure. They must've been engineered to take care of problems in the jet."

Beth turned her back on Karl, irritated that he had jumped in when Redwing clearly addressed his question to her. "So—if we push them harder, give 'em some twist, maybe we can keep them at a distance, dodge them. Not like there's not room to play out here in the jet."

Redwing scowled, his face more lined than she had ever seen. "It's ten light-seconds across. Room to dodge, but—can we keep them far enough away?"

"Depends on what their weaponry is." Karl wore a dispassionate expression, staring into space. "Nuclear, sure, we can see hardware coming and hit it with our scoop-policing lasers. But if they have gamma ray lasers, like those big domes on the Bowl rim, we're done."

Beth sat back and watched the flitters edge up from behind. She bit her lip, adjusted for a vortex plasma knot, felt it surge them to starboard, and said, even and controlled, "Cap'n, we don't have much choice."

Redwing was silent, pacing, frowning. More silence. And suddenly Beth found herself on her feet, speaking in a flat, hard voice. "*You* ordered us into the jet, *you* wanted to press the Folk, Clare got killed right here, and *you* now have *no idea* what to do?"

Redwing spun on his heel. "I have over a thousand souls aboard who signed on to go to Glory. I took an oath to deliver them. I didn't agree to turn them over to aliens riding along in a big contraption."

"I don't think—"

"Point is, your job is to *not* think beyond your rank!"

"We all just saw Clare killed by something we don't understand, that's got us all terrified, and you—"

"Quiet!" Jam said, rising to her height on the deck, her dark face severe. "The captain commands.

We do not question, especially under combat conditions."

Beth stared at Jam, whom she recalled was a mere petty officer. But . . . she had to admit, Jam was right. "I . . ." Beth's throat filled, choking off her words. "Clare . . ."

"Enough," Redwing said, addressing all the bridge crew. "We're all jumpy. Forget this happened. We are committed and we shall engage." He turned to Beth. "But you're lead pilot. You are carrying this ship into a battle we cannot master without you. *Do it.*"

So she did.

FORTY

We have need of your skills with your own kind, the cool voice said inside her mind. Tananareve felt around her, but no one had entered the narrow, warm envelope that had closed in on her as soon as the Folk sealed up this device. It smelled of dense, fleshy tissues, and indeed, the walls were softly springy, like the skyfish.

"I am certainly willing," Tananareve said, and waited. She could see nothing and heard no sounds. Yet the voice in her head seemed to be spoken.

We desire you to be quiet of soul.

"I don't know what that means."

We can see you churn with emotion. This is to be expected. But calm will come with concentration.

"Uh, who are you?"

The Folk term us Ice Minds. They see us, as shall you, as those of slow thoughts, as our barred spiral galaxy turned upon its axis dozens of times. We have of late examined your species and believe you can be of use to avert the gathering catastrophe that awaits in short time.

"You know us? From Cliff's team, I suppose?"

Those who stand now outside this reading realm.

"Reading? You're inside my mind somehow."

From the Folk termed Memor, we inherited her inspections of your mind. From those primates outside, we learned, again with Memor's excursions in your selfhood, to convey meaning in your Anglish. Now the Folk at our command immerse you in this fashion, so we can use you.

She didn't like the sound of this. "To do what?"

To prevent damage to us all. Unite so that the destination we all share can be made coherent with the purposes of the Bowl. To let life call out to life in depths and ranges greater still.

Tananareve had never liked sermons, and this sounded like one. Or maybe sanctimony varied with species. "Why are you Ice Minds? I mean, what do you look like?"

There flashed before her images that somehow blended with *knowing* at the same instant—vision and insight coupled, so that in a few shifting seconds she felt herself understand in a way that simple explanations did not convey. It was less a sense of learning something than of understanding it, gaining an intuitive ground in the flicker of a moment, without apparent effort.

A rumpled night terrain under steady dim stars. Dirty gray ice pocked with a few craters, black teeth of black rock, grainy tan sandbars . . . and fluids moving in gliding grace across this.

"You're the ivory stuff sliding on the rocks and ice?"

And you are death to us. We remain a mystery to you myriad warmlife races. To you bustling carbon-children of thermonuclear heat and searing light. We are of the Deep and knew, shortly after the stars formed, of the beauty stark and subtle, and old to you beyond measure. Our kind came before you, in dark geometries beneath the diamond glitter of distant starlight on time-stained ices. Metabolism brims in the thin fog breath of flowing helium, sliding in intricate, coded motion, far from the ravages of any sun.

"And you live *here*?" Still too much like a sermon, but it had an odd feeling of being true.

The Bowl rushed at her, sharp and clear, the rotating great bright wok beneath the hard little red star, its orange jet—and then the point of view swept around, to the hull. It plunged along the metalware—humps and rhomboids and spindly stretching tubes of the outer skin—until it swept still closer and she saw endless fields of parabolic plants, all swaying with the Bowl's rotation, focused up at the passing stars . . . while among them flowed that pearly fluid, lapping against odd hemispheres that might—she knew, without thinking about it—be dwellings, of a sort.

"Never thought of that. Shielded from the star, it's kind of like being on the far outside of our solar system, in what we call the cometary sphere."

We exploit the heat engine of leaked warmth from the Bowl's sunswept side to our realm, so we bask in beautiful cold-dark while harvesting waste energy from below. Our minds organize as complex interactive eddies of superconductive liquids.

The view skated across huge curved fields of icy hummocks and hills, with sliding strange rivers of ivory glowing beneath the dim stars. There came to her a creeping sensation of a vast crowd on this stretching plain, a landscape of *minds* that lived by flowing into each other, and somehow teasing out meaning, thought . . . more.

"Why do you care about us? We—"

Warmlife, you are. In our primordial form, we traded knowledge collected over vast eras, useful for chemicals, coldworld facilities, or astronomy. We were shrewd traders and negotiators, having lived through eons, and having dealt with the many faces intelligence can assume. Our cold realm has existed relatively unchanged since the galaxy was freshly forged in the fires of the strong nuclear force.

Tananareve was startled by the linguistic sophistication of their speech, resounding in her head exactly like real sounds, in a flat accent—no, wait, they were speaking to her with *her* accent. Even more impressive. Not many could ape her honey-toned Mississippi vowels.

"Against all that, why bother with me?" Maybe not a smart question, but she was wondering, and here were the minds that seemed to rule this place.

To us little is new. Even less is interesting. We have watched great clouds of dust and simple molecules as they were pruned away, collapsing into suns, and so left the interstellar reaches thinner, easier for our kind to negotiate, and for the ion churn of plasmas to form and self-organize. But these were slow shifts. We are as near to eternal as warmlife can imagine. But you are quite the opposite. You are swift and new.

Into her mind came an image of their bulblike bodies and weaving tentacles, all gracefully flowing, a sliding ivory cryogenic liquid. Something like an upturned cat-o'-nine-tails whip appearance.

We stand at an immense distance from such as you, yet at times arouse when the Bowl, our transport, is under threat. As it is now—from you.

"Look, I don't know what Redwing is doing—"

Yet you are also vital to the Bowl's survival when we arrive at the target star, one you term Glory. So you are both friend and foe.

"Why me? I—"

Memor integrated your neural levels to enough detail that we can access them. So we choose you to speak for us to your nominal leader, the Redwing, and to the Diaphanous.

"I don't know what's going on!"

Our long views are essential to the Bowl's longevity. At this moment some 123,675 of us are engaged in this collective conversation with you. The number shifted even while the Ice Minds spoke.

We are individually slow, but together we can think far quicker than you. We are eternal and you are like the flickerings of a candle flame—that which combusts dies, as must all warmlife. When we evolved, the most advanced warmlife creatures on hotlife worlds were single-celled pond scum.

"Why are you on the Bowl at all, then?" She was getting irked with all this bragging. But trapped in a smelly box, probed by who-knows-what kinds of technologies, it seemed best not to be obnoxious. And she would hate to meet whatever these things needed help with. If these Ice Minds just wanted her to talk to Redwing, fine. But somehow she knew it couldn't just be that.

We bring a wisdom of long memory. We alone speak with and for the Diaphanous. We wish to explore and to meet the Superiors who seem to be at Glory.

Then she felt a surge, as though the entire machine containing her was moving. It lurched a bit and she poked an elbow against a soft wall. Hoarse calls came from outside. What now?

FORTY-ONE

Cliff looked down at what the Folk called their mooring mountain. They said it held a shelter for this skyfish, but it was far beneath them, barely visible through stacked gray cumulus clouds.

The ship crew had leaped into action after the

big long boom pressed through the skyfish. They had all rushed to the big transparent wall, mouths gaping, not heeding the shouted orders of Bemor. The male Folk stamped his feet in an accelerating rhythm, big hard thuds. That snapped the crew out of their funk and they followed his barking orders.

The humans and Sil did not know what was going on, so they moved to the wall, now deserted, to look out. Cliff saw far overhead an upside-down tornado. In profile, it looked like a funnel. Within it, huge clouds churned in an ever-tightening upward spiral, turning somber purple as moisture condensed within them. The lower levels of the air were clear, so Cliff knew he was seeing far up into the atmosphere. The conical cloud was fat and white at the bottom and tapered upward into a narrow purple-dark neck. Even at this great distance, Cliff could see flashes of blue and orange lightning between immense clouds. Across the sky, other high decks of stratocumulus were edging toward the inverted hurricane. He was looking at a puncture in the high envelope.

"They're trying to ground the skyfish in this storm," Irma said.

The skyfish dove deeper and shuddered with the racking winds. Irma and the others watched the high vortex churn as if it could change, but Cliff knew with a wry sinking feeling that it could only worsen. A huge deep atmosphere would take a long time to empty out into space, but the pressure drop would drive weather hard. He wondered if the Folk could patch a big rip in the high shimmering envelope from the way Bemor was lumbering around and barking at the crew, he doubted it. He looked down and saw they were headed for the nearest clear ground they could find within quick reach, the mooring mountain.

Aybe pointed. "The crew—they're taking that machine away, with Tananareve in it. Damn! We get her back, and then right away she's goddamn gone."

"We're all gone, really," Terry said. "No chance of getting out of this living blimp that I can see."

Irma was talking to Quert and reported back. "That's a kind of Folk redoubt we're approaching. They can shelter there."

Quert came over. "Wind hard. Anchor skyfish, it hard."

As if to demonstrate, the skyfish lurched and they all fell to the deck. Cliff tucked in and rolled, coming up to look out the transparent wall just in time to see a brilliant yellow lightning strike descend from a high cloud. Unlike on Earth, this one

snaked down, shooting side bolts as it kept going. The distance was so much, Cliff could see the entire brilliant streamer, the vibrant, bristling conducting path for electrons seeking the ground. Like a lazy snake, it slid sideways in a long twist. Then it hit the mountain below and snapped off, just vanished in an instant. The thunderclap shook the entire sky-fish, and Terry, who had already gotten back up, came crashing down again.

Something rumbled in the pink walls nearby. The skyfish went into a steep descent. "It fears," Quert said.

"Me, too," Irma added. Everybody stayed down, hugging the deck that reeked with some slimy fluid. The skyfish tilted and turned violently. More light-ning scratched across a lead sky.

The skyfish hit like a fat balloon. It squashed and flexed, the walls of their big chamber collapsing down, then wheezing with the effort to rebound. The walls thumped with the slow, massive heart-beat of the skyfish. Cliff heard bones snap and the soft rip of tissues deep in the walls. Blood ran across the deck.

"Let us go fast, my friends," Quert said. They fled.

As Cliff followed the Sil down fleshy corridors that reeked of fluids he did not want to think about, sloshing boot-deep through it, he recalled something his army uncle had said once. *Try to get all your posthumous medals in advance.*

With her fellows, Memor watched a high view of their Zone, sent from a craft dispatched to survey.

Something had hit the great sea at the center of the Zone, not far from where their skyfish labored. An enormous tsunami rushed across the dappled gray surface. The sea was shallow, so the wave was already at great height and as they watched, it broke, white foam curling forward. This towering monster broke across the land. Forests and towns disappeared.

The skyfish rolled to port and then back, with an alarming twist running down the great beast's spine as well. Their compartment twisted as the skyfish fought to right itself. In this very low gravity zone, the air density fell off slowly and there was less acceleration to gain from venting hydrogen. The floor tilted as they accelerated downward at a steep angle. Memor staggered, then abruptly sat. The capsule where Tananareve was in immersion with someone—could it be Bemor was right, and she spoke now with the Ice Minds? Surely that was impossible. The mismatch of mind states was surely too much for that. Memor herself had encountered difficulties with the primate. The Ice Minds were scarcely reachable without considerable training, such as Bemor had endured.

The deck heaved sickeningly, but Memor forced herself to her feet. Bemor was gone on a task he said came from the Ice Minds, and Asenath lay whimpering in a slung rack. It was one of the water-clasping type, so she now floated in a sleeve, only her head visible. Her eyes wandered, and Memor judged Asenath would be paying no attention to Memor. Good.

Each step she took came freighted with fear. The deck rolled with flesh waves. The body around them groaned and sloshed. The hydrogen exhaust was roaring and she felt its dull tone through her legs. Memor had made herself put away the terrifying—and, she now realized, quite embarrassing—storm within her. Suppressed truths had overwhelmed her. She realized that her Undermind had sheltered much of the Bowl's long history from her and she had never suspected. The Undermind somehow knew she could not bear facts that clashed with her deepest beliefs in the role, status, and glory of the Folk.

Then, in shocking moments that she never wanted to relive, all the tensions and layered lies of her entire lifetime came welling up. Spewing as from a volcano, it burst through her.

Now she made herself put all that aside. She sealed layers over her Undermind. She confronted a problem demanding all her ability now. Put a foot forward. Brace against the rumbling, twisted flooring. Take another step. Each demanded labor and focus, and it seemed to take a long while to reach the external panel of the capsule.

The harness fit her head, and the connections self-aligned. She sank into the inner discourse, but only as an observer. She could affect nothing inside.

She felt Tananareve's mind as a skittering, quick bright thing. Few images, but thoughts of the Ice Minds played through the strata of the primate mind. They seemed to fragment and go into separate channels, streams fracturing as they flowed.

Memor struggled to make sense of the hot-eyed fervor of these flows. Revelation dawned along axes of the primate Undermind. New data flowed into Memor and she could flick back and forth between her own mental understory and the primate's. These laced with the shadowy strangeness of linear minds. Hereditary neural equipment governed these divided minds—straight down the middle, a clear cleft. Such was common in the Bowl's explored region of the galaxy.

She saw Tananareve's mind taking in the Ice Minds' conversation and hammering that on the twin forges of reason and intuition, with great speed. So the Ice Minds wished to enlist her! Astounding, but perhaps it was only to speak to that Captain Redwing. Still, Bemor was the proper pathway for such diplomacy.

The deck lurched. Memor barely kept her purchase. Shouts and cries echoed.

The conversations and images seemed to condense in Memor's mind like a vapor forming a shape. The precise words shifted and changed as the translations moved restlessly. Memor had to cling to nuance, not precision. Something about Redwing the Captain and the jet, yes, and how much humans could help in dealing with the Glorians. A need to intervene between Redwing and—

A hard jerk knocked her over. Memor struggled up to her feet and grasped for the harness, which had come unfastened. She just got it positioned when another twisting roll came through the ship and Asenath collided with her. "We are down!" she cried. "Get out!"

"But the primate—"

"Bemor is in charge, and he says we should go out and seek the central shelter. Come!" Asenath turned and fled.

Memor hesitated. She wanted to know what the Ice Minds said. She started to settle in, restarting the harness configuration, when a voice bellowed at her, "Go! I will care for this."

She turned, and joy flooded through her at the sight of Bemor. The ship trembled, and a great wheezing came rattling down through the corridor outside. She hurried away.

Within a few moments, Memor lost her footing in the dim light outside. She curled up and slammed to ground. Screams, shouts, crashes. The mountain's firm rock snapped and cracked, heaved and buckled. The path to the shelter now had a great pit crossing it. Sound came from everywhere, and the ground seemed to be grinding against itself, sending gray dust plumes shooting up.

A black curtain boiled across the sky. Within its churn, flashes snapped like eyes in a great beast. Ozone stung the howling breeze. With it came rain.

Not rain—mud. Pellets of it, hard and dry on their skins, soft at their centers. They splatted down, rapping Memor's skull. "From some body of water," she said wonderingly, "thrown up by something hitting—"

She extended her long tongue and tasted the warm rain, like water from a bath, and—salt. The great sea was pelting even this high fortress mountain. Memor folded her feathers close and tight, a raincoat of sorts.

A pool of ink poured across the sky, layers of cloud sliding over each other as if liquid. The reassuring steady day had now turned to a dim night, one filled with sky fireworks far brighter now than the star and jet. Her view flashed in blue-white light and then vanished into the murk. "Bemor!" No answer. She got up and walked on legs like pillows through strobes of lightning.

The flashes showed ahead a new problem—a crevasse yawned. It was a split in the crowning rock slab itself, showing fresh sharp edges. She could barely glimpse the far side in the lightning flashes. Far away. Even in this low gravity, nothing could leap it, certainly none of the bulky Folk. It blocked their way to the station.

Memor looked around in anxious despair. Various staff and crew milled at the edge of this gap, looking desperate. She sniffed their acrid fears. Asenath was nowhere among them. Another blue-white flash allowed her to survey the gathering jam all along the broken path, jostling and shouting strident calls.

Memor saw a new problem. Where were the Sil? And the primates?

FORTY-THREE

Redwing paced the bridge and watched the approaching shapes, flitting close now among the roiling turbulent knots. Moments ticked by, and the bridge was silent. Beth was ready to focus their exhaust as much as the tunable scoop mag fields allowed. And now there was something new and strange as well.

Their hull resounded with a strange strumming symphony. The long notes were just at the edge of hearing but clear and distinct. Haunting low notes came like the beating of a giant heart, or of grand booming waves crashing with slow majesty upon a crystal beach, a ceramic resonating instrument. Redwing felt the notes with his whole body, recalling a time when as a boy he stood in a cathedral and heard Bach on a massive pipe organ. The pipes sent resounding wavelengths longer than the human body. He did not so much hear notes as feel them as his body vibrated in sympathy. A feeling like being shaken by something invisible conveyed grandeur in a way beyond words.

Beth said, "Whatever's outside—and I can't see a thing on these screens, just plasma and magnetic signatures—is trying to say something."

Karl said, "Their last attempt killed Clare."

"Yes, a horrible way to die. I . . . I wonder how whatever is outside makes sounds?" Beth said. "Oh—Cap'n, there's a dense plasma knot headed for us."

"Focus it in on the prow fields," Redwing said. "Can we snag it and narrow the exhaust, then aim at the first of those fliers?"

"I . . . think . . . so." Beth and the entire bridge crew were concentrated on their work, belted in tight, eyes following screens, hands hitting key commands. "The workaround on that digital algorithm block is coming up, running right. The Artilects are all over this problem, but they don't like it."

"They don't have to," Redwing said.

The strange deep notes running through the ship's hull ceased. "They're leaving us alone, maybe," Beth muttered.

The roiling knot of hot ions clamped within a nest of rubbery magnetic fields came slamming at them at over seven hundred kilometers a second. "Added to our speed, the impact will be well over a thousand kilometers a second," Karl said. "Is the magscoop cinched in?"

"As much as we can," Beth said, voice high and lips tight.

They watched the large blob come straight at them. It was far bigger than *SunSeeker*'s scoop, and they felt the surge, their heads snug against their chair braces. The ship groaned.

Their internal diagnostics tracked the flow of dense plasma through the magnetic funnel out front, through the tapered neck that flushed it into the reaction chambers. There lived the steadily maintained, self-shaping field geometries that further compressed the plasma, added catalysts, and—the screens showed the pulsing glow in coiled doughnuts of prickly yellow—burned with fusion fire. This got expelled at the max temperature, into an opening throat that sent this starfire into the classic magnetic nozzle facing aft.

But not exactly dead aft. Beth's fingers flew over the complex command web. The fields slanted slightly, clamping down on the flow, shunting it sideways. The bridge surged again under this momentum change. The Ship Stability Artilect kept them from tumbling with extruded counterfields. Virulent plasma jetted out in a starboard cant. Beth altered the fusion geometry's exit profile to include more shaping magnetic fields in the exhaust. The emerging bolt of hot plasma was like a finger scratching across the wave behind them.

"With a little bit of windage . . . ," Beth mused, intent on the screens.

A flier lay dead at the center of the bolt. When the exhaust struck it, the image wobbled, refracted by the complex play of forces, then sharpened. Fragments swirled where the flier had been.

"Got it," Beth said quietly.

"Brilliant," Redwing said. "The others—"

"The second one is taking an evasive trajectory," Karl said. "Moving away laterally."

Beth angled their exhaust and caught it before the flier could get away. Nobody cheered.

"The third is dropping back," Karl said.

"We can't fly much farther up the jet," Redwing said. "They know that. We'll reverse, make our turn."

"And that third one will be waiting for us," Beth finished for him. "And it'll be ahead of us."

FORTY-FOUR

Tananareve was grateful the walls of her confinement were soft but firm. Whatever was carrying her along did not trouble to make the trip pleasant. Jerks and jostles made it hard to keep focused on the sliding, cool voice of the Ice Minds in her mind, overlayered with their images of the lands where they lived.

Starlight cast stretched pale fingers across the plain of rock and ice, where vacuum flowers dutifully pointed their parabolic eyes at the slow sweep of target suns. Around the base of the light-harvesters flowed the pearly fluids that were the commingled selves of the Ice Minds. How these blended thought and became coherent, she could not imagine.

The moment hastens. We decided to revive ourselves wholly, to deal with this pressing problem.

"What problem?"

Your species. The Folk believed they could deal with you as a young and largely incompetent species, but we came to see this is not so.

She thought of saying, *Gee, thanks!* but sarcasm might not translate in dealing with aliens. "Look, we have been imprisoned or chased ever since we got here."

The Folk are our— A pause.—*our police. They also maintain at equilibrium. We are not at equilibrium now. They have failed to understand your kind. Now disruption proceeds.*

"What? Why? How?"

Your ship has disturbed our jet. The Folk have ordered attacks on your ship. This is against our wishes. We cannot well communicate with your kind in your ship, as some of the Folk have prevented that. We wish you to speak directly to your ship through channels we shall soon open.

"That's a lot to take in. *SunSeeker* is in your jet? Wow."

Into her mind came an image of a small dark mote plowing upstream against a torrent of coiling plasma. The view backed away and she could see the jet slide sideways as it approached the Knothole. It surged over the Knothole restraining fields and into several life zones. Atmosphere belched out. Some thin girders holding the atmosphere zones apart fractured and fell. She was startled.

Your mind we can approach. The Folk Attendant Astute Astronomer Memor made deep soundings of your neural labyrinths. These we use now. We wish you to speak with your own kind and then to serve to reassure the Diaphanous.

Another alien? "Who are—?"

Into her mind came images of fluid fluxes merging in eddies and turning in fat toroids, all in intricate yellow lines against a pale blue background. Somehow she knew these were larger than continents and fuzzy at their edges, where flow was more important than barriers. Intricate coils bigger than worlds, shattering explosions—all testified to the recombining energy of the fields.

"These . . . live in the jet?" She could not imagine

this, but lack of imagination had ceased to be a good argument here.

They evolved in the magnetic structures that dot the skin of stars. These could knot off, twist, and so make a new coil of field. Embedding information in those fields led to reproduction of traits. From that sprang intelligence, or at least awareness.

"But they don't have bodies. How can they—?" Her grasp faltered.

You and we do not witness the chaotic tumble of great plasma clouds between the stars. We all see nothing hanging between the hard points of incandescent light, and so falsely assume that space is somehow nothing. But evolution works there against the constant forces of dissolution.

Tananareve knew a bit of general life theory. Brute forces seemed bound, inevitably, to yield forth systems that evolution drove to construct some awareness of their surroundings. It took billions of years to construct such mind-views. Those models of the external world could become more complex. Some models worked better if they had a model of . . . well, models. Of themselves. So came the sense of self in advanced animals. But in plasma and magnetic fields?

The Diaphanous migrated on solar storms into the greater voids where we evolved. When the building of the Bowl began, it became essential to include them, as managers of the jet and of the star itself. Only by shaping the magnetic fields of star and jet can we move the Bowl, with constant attention to momentum and stability. Who else to govern magnetic machinery than magnetic beings?

The Ice Minds sounded so reasonable, their conclusions seemed obvious. Before her inner eye played scenes of magnetic arches rising from stars, twisting and kinking to cut off and therefore give birth to new self-stabilized beings. She could sense, not merely see, waves lashing among the complex magnetic nets that surged in her mind—speech of a sort, maybe. Now the view in her mind shifted to the jet and the plight of *SunSeeker*, pursued by small ships of destructive intent.

"You want to—what? Broker a deal? After hounding us across—"

The Folk have failed us. Their defenses of the jet are ancient and many failed. Your ship did not even notice these, we are certain. The loosened jet now lashes across Life Zones and wreaks much ill. Yet those who bear down upon that ship now may well have to resort to a weapon we have vowed never to use. It could bring far more evil.

That, at least, was a familiar concept. Calamity stacking up. "Okay, what do I do?"

Let us override the Folk pathways. We shall connect you to your Captain Redwing.

A ripple ran through her mind, a floating airy sensation that somehow mixed with colors flashing in what she felt as her eyes. Yet at the same time, she knew her eyes were open in the complete blackness of the cramped machine. Her eyes saw black, but her mind saw shifting bands of orange and purple, and on top of that—bursting yellow foam ran over an eggshell blue plain. Speckled green things moved on it in staccato rhythm. Twisting lines meshed there and wove into triangles where frantic energy pulsed. A shrill grating sound came with flashes of crimson.

Then she saw Redwing. His image wobbled and she wondered how they could put that into her mind. "What are you?" His voice echoed as though he were in a chamber.

"Captain, this is Tananareve. I'm in some device that, well, wants to speak with you. They are—let's skip that, okay? The Bowl has a lot stranger aliens than we thought."

"How do I know you're really Tananareve at all?"

This question hadn't occurred to her. "Recall that party we had before we went down to land? Feels like a long time ago."

"Yes, I suppose I do." He was standing on the bridge, and she could see Beth and others in the background, all looking at what had to be a— what? She tried to remember the bridge but failed. Maybe a camera? How did these aliens tap into internal ship systems?

Into her head came the Ice Minds' sliding, calm voice. *We have dealt with what you term your Artilects. They are most agreeable.*

"You brought out a bottle of champagne, remember? You said it was for our first landfall at Glory, but what the hell, this was a landfall and so here it was."

"Damn!" Redwing's face broadened into a grin. "It really is you. No video, but—welcome aboard, sort of."

"Captain, I'm conveying messages from, well, some aliens we didn't know were here. They want you to stop fooling with the jet."

That comes later. For now tell your commander that they are in grave danger.

She said that, but Redwing's face turned away to look at a screen she could partially see. On it some flecks moved against a yellow weave of lines that she knew represented magnetic field contours.

"You mean these guys coming up on us?"

Your ship has permission to destroy them. But a weapon aboard one of them can erase your ship.

"Captain, try to kill them right away. They have something—" She paused, not knowing what to say.

It is the Lambda Gun, and will disrupt space-time near them.

"It's some sort of ultimate weapon," she said.

Redwing looked tired. He nodded. "Okay, stay on the line. We'll try that—"

The connection broke. His image dwindled and she was in darkness. Somebody was still carrying her around, and she felt a sudden drop. *Thump.* She heard distant shouts in a language she did not know and felt all at once very tired.

FORTY-FIVE

Cliff crouched with the others and watched the big blimp skyfish wallow on the mountaintop. Scampering crews had secured the huge thing at both ends and now were lashing the sides down with big cables. A heavy rain ate most of the light from the skyfish itself, dim glows of ivory that got drowned in the brilliant lightning flashes. Hammering raindrops scattered even the crashes of lightning into a blurred white murk.

"Where'd the Folk go?" Irma shouted against the wind.

"Into that big entrance!" Aybe pointed. "They had that thing they put Tananareve into with them."

Terry said, "Remember what threw us around, back in the skyfish? To make a shock like that, and blow sheets of rock off this mountain—that takes a lot of quake energy. But there aren't quakes here—no plate tectonics."

Aybe swept rain from his eyes and jutted his chin out. "Look, the Bowl has a light, elastic underpinning, with not much simple mass loading. So an impact, from something thrown down here, that has a lot of energy. Real quick it moves through the support structure. It came here, to this big slab of rock, a whole mountain—and knocked the bejeezus out of it."

"Just as we landed. What luck." Irma huddled down. Cliff read her body language: the rain was warm, at least. It smacked down hard.

Terry sniffed and said, "I'd like to get out of this damned rain."

As if on cue, white specks began smacking down on the flat rock plain around them. "Hail!" Aybe said.

A dirty white ball the size of his fist hit Cliff in the side. He thought he felt a rib crack. The weather here was bigger and harder than he could deal with. Plus the darkness of the storm kept making him feel like sleeping.

"Let's get inside, out of this storm," Cliff said. "Not the skyfish—who knows what'll happen in there?"

To his surprise, the others just nodded. They looked tired, and that made them compliant. He turned to Quert. "How can we get into their station?"

Quert had been dealing with his Sil, who were doing what they usually did at a delay—resting. They were squatting and eating something they had gotten on the skyfish. The more anxious humans just milled around. "Let us lead," Quert said.

The Sil set off at an angle to the crack that had formed in the slab rock. In the confusion of abandoning the skyfish, they had all managed to slip away from the Folk and their many, panicked attendants. The darkness from huge black clouds that slid endlessly across their sky had sent the crew into jittery, nervous states, their legs jerking as they moved, eyes cast fearfully skyward. They had never known night, and this vast storm could not be common here.

The crack finally ended several hundred meters away from the skyfish. The Sil simply walked around the end of it with complete confidence, and headed back toward a raised bump near the larger mound of the Folk station. As they all cautiously approached, the lightning came less often. Cliff looked back in the darkness and saw the skyfish dimly lit from inside, like some enormous orange Halloween lantern on its side. There was no one in the tube passageway that led downward. "Why?" Cliff asked Quert.

"All fear," Quert said. "Folk, others, all hide inside."

And so it was. They padded carefully down

corridors and across large rooms bristling with gear whose function Cliff could not even guess. It seemed to be working, there were some small lights on the faces, but no clue as to what they did.

"Folk not know how to work when big change comes," Quert said laconically. He relayed this to the Sil and they all made the yawning, hacking sound of Sil laughter.

They came into a large room that looked down on an even larger area. Quietly they crept up to the edge of a parapet and saw below a milling crowd. The attendants and servants, a throng including alien shapes Cliff had never seen before, and robotic ones as well, held back toward the walls. At the center were the three large Folk and the machine holding Tananareve. The far walls were large oval screens showing views of the Knothole region. One smaller screen was a view from far above, where a long tear in the atmospheric envelope had drawn clouds streaming in, moisture condensing and lightning forking along the flanks of immense purple storms.

"That's the top of the typhoon we're under," Terry said. "Judging the scale, I'd say those cloud banks are the size of Earthside continents—and look at that lightning flash! You can see it coiling around. As big as the Mississippi, easy."

"Look," Irma said, pointing at the shifting view as it tilted toward the Knothole. "There's the jet—and my God!—*SunSeeker*."

The screens showed swift small motes dodging and banking in the center of the luminous swirling plasma jet. A quick close-up of their own starship showed it plowing through knots of turbulence and making a tight helix, aiming its pencil exhaust in a tight hot luminous finger at the—

"Damn, they hit it!" Aybe said, eyes jumping. "Blew that flier to pieces."

"Damn right!" Terry said, pumping his fist.

They didn't know what was going on, but excitement rippled through humans and Sil alike as they watched something like a dogfight going on. Cliff watched the ballet of ships moving at many hundreds of kilometers a second, seen on scales that had to be zoomed six or seven orders of magnitudes. Nothing but machines could handle this, and even they seemed strained from the sudden turns and swerves they saw.

The crowd below gazed upward at the screens, and the Folk were at the center, managing machines. The odd curved box that held Tananareve was with them. He wondered what they were making of this confusing mess. He grasped Irma and held her close. They kissed, not caring if anyone saw. Then the guards arrived.

FORTY-SIX

They were drenched and cold, Folk and Serfs alike, but the hour demanded attention. Memor slumped down to rest, sitting back a bit on her haunches.

Their flight from the poor agonized and wounded

skyfish had been rowdy, noisy, swept by rain beneath inky clouds flashing with electrical anger. Their ragged party had slipped and stumbled their way across great slabs of rock, with Memor trying to keep order in their flight. A team from the station had come out to erect, with swift competence, a bridge over the jagged chasm that had split open. The station's deputy commander said a flying hard-carbon flange had fallen on the mountain, apparently freed of its support structure high up in the envelope's stanchions, and plunged deep into the mountain's firm mass. The shock wave had rocked the skyfish sideways and blown several of its compartments, spilling crew onto the rock. That knife-sharp girder had also split a crevasse at the worst possible moment, spraying fragments into the skyfish and killing some local staff. The great skyfish bellowed and writhed against the crews attempting to moor it, killing several. Its flailing fins were sharp and deadly.

Considering this, it was a wonder anything worked.

Memor sagged with exhaustion. She watched Asenath stand proudly at the prow of the command center in their mountain shelter, in full authority. She listened to the panicked signals from the fliers, displayed on screens and sounding shrill even in this large command room. The fliers were guided by robot minds, high level and capable of what seemed like emotions. The voices were brittle, sharp, edged with urgency. The swift ships tumbled and gyred, blown about by the ramscoop thrust.

That made evasive navigation and aiming nearly impossible.

"We could use the Lambda Gun, as you said before, Wisdom Chief," a small lieutenant said softly. "One of the fliers bears only the gun. It is bulky and makes maneuver difficult in the jet. That flier hangs back, away from the pencil exhaust the primates are using against us."

"Under whose orders was this done?" Memor said.

"Mine," Asenath said firmly.

"Have the Ice Minds agreed? They have—"

"Bemor is not here, so we cannot readily consult with the Ice Minds. He is off managing their discourse, if that is the proper word, with your talking primate. So I shall have to assume command."

Memor felt compelled to say, "Separated command? This is not proper use of the hierarchy—"

"Ah, but then, this is a clear emergency. Communications are fragmented and time ticks on. I order the Lambda Gun unfolded."

Memor felt a sudden spike of fear. "That, that will take time—"

"Get to it," Asenath ordered the lieutenant. Various officers, gathered around the two Folk in a crescent, rustled with unease. Nobody moved. The silence stretched.

Memor said, "You had the Lambda Gun prepared before, didn't you?"

Asenath gave an irritated fan-rebuke to her underlings. "Now!" They scurried off to their many tasks.

Almost casually, in a way that told Memor this had been long planned, Asenath turned and gave a gray green feather rush of haughty disregard. "I felt it necessary. Events now prove me correct."

Memor felt icy fatigue run through her but summoned up reserves, rustled her feathers, and turned inward. She had heard of the Lambda Gun long ago as a historical curiosity, and now had to call up its history to have any hope of dealing with Asenath. Her Undermind held this lore, and was sore abused. She felt this as she unveiled portions, stripping back layers of youthful memory, gazing inward past the trauma suffered after the revelation of the Great Shame. She felt it now in its full ghastly panorama—the images of a long cometary tail, pointing directly at Earth in the final moments, like an accusatory finger, and the spreading circle of destruction that annihilated the ancient civilization of smart, warm-blooded reptiles. Their majesty lay not in vast edifices, culminating in the Bowl. Instead, they were heirs to the fraction of that great species which relished their natural planet and did not want to take part in the Bowl, or its technical prowess, or the alliance with strange minds in the cometary halo. They had kept Earth green and fertile, restricting their own numbers so the natural luxuriant world was not paved over with artifice. In a way, Memor recalled, the Bowl became a tribute to their deep instincts. Its huge expanses enabled many species to live intelligently in Zones dominated by leafy wealth, though built upon a substrate of spinning metal and carbon fiber intricacies. A natural world built upon a machine . . .

She had become lost in her introspection, a common liability of voyages into the Undermind's shadowy labyrinths. Memor revived an old image of the Lambda Gun, a fearsome projector of gray spherical bulk, tapering into a belligerent snout. It could project a disturbance in the vacuum energy of space-time, throwing this knot of chaos out in a beam. Suitably tuned, it would cause, when it struck solid matter, a catastrophic expansion of a small volume of space. The inflation field increased the cosmological constant in a very restricted region for a brief snap of time. Whatever contained this howling monstrosity, reborn from the first instant of this universe, would be ripped into particles far smaller than nuclei.

Memor recoiled from this appalling vision. With a hasty withdrawal salute, she slammed her Undermind shut. "This is grisly! This is a planet buster, capable of delivering enormous energies—"

"So well I do know," Asenath replied. "I have studied this ancient device and its history. The true Ancients invented it as a last resort against balky species. Some hurled relativistic masses at the Bowl to drive it away. The Lambda Gun put a quick end to their mischief."

"Surely we have shields that would be useful—"

"Not against a vagrant craft with powerful magnetic scoops. We enjoyed great magnetic craftsmanship in Ancient ages, but our Bowl does not muster such intensities. Nor do the Diaphanous have ready responses. Meanwhile, the jet stands in a nonlinear kink mode and deals us terrible destruction."

Asenath said this with a reasonable air and somber fan-display. Memor knew she could not deflect Asenath in an area where her expertise and rank prevailed. She gave it one last try. "The Ice Minds and the Diaphanous are in charge of jet dynamics!"

"And they have failed. Prepare to fire," Asenath said to a lieutenant, and turned her back on Memor.

FORTY-SEVEN

Beth felt the hairs on her neck rise, prickly and trembling as the electrical charge built again. But this time she was getting irked and instead of flattening herself yet again on the deck, she hit a hard thruster in the magscoop. Fields vented plasma and the ship lurched. The others were hitting the deck but Beth discharged a brace of capacitors in the magscoop's leading magnetic fields. This gave a powerful burst of electrons at the far end of the scoop, moving at the speed of light. Instantly her neck hairs stopped tingling.

"Cap'n, looks like I've found a way to offset the charge buildup these things are using against us," she said with a deliberately casual air.

Redwing looked up from the deck, where he had sprawled. "Brilliant!"

"And she nailed that flier flat on, too," Karl said

with one of his seldom-seen grins. "There's only one flier left, and it's hanging back pretty far."

"Good," Redwing said, getting up and straightening his uniform. He was always meticulous when on the bridge. "But we're near the top of our mission profile, right?"

Beth checked. "Yes, sir, got to turn around soon and head back down, run with the jet."

"That will lower our plasma influx pretty far," Karl said. "We'll have a reduced exhaust."

"So the exhaust will be less useful as a weapon, certainly," Redwing said. "Let's try to hover near our top limit, then. Can you do that, Officer Marble?"

Redwing also liked to get formal in tight situations. She had often wondered if in such moments he saw himself as fearless admiral at the helm of a battleship on tossing gray seas. Well, this was about as close to that as he was going to get, and as close as she ever wanted to be.

"Keep an eye on that flier as we make our turn." Redwing settled into his deck chair. He looked tired and gray to Beth, but so did they all now. Hours of dodging among the jet knots, harvesting them with split-second timing and then blowing the excess post-fusion plasma out the flexing nozzle as a weapon—well, it added up fast.

The ship rumbled as she took it on a slow tipping angle. She was concentrating so didn't notice the beeping of the comm.

Karl picked it up for her. His body went rigid and he glanced at his shocked face. "It's . . . Tananareve, Cap'n. For you."

He grabbed it. "Redwing here. How in—?" Redwing's face showed nothing as he listened. Then his mouth slowly opened and he stared into space. "How did—?" More silence. "So they'll let us go?"

Beth suddenly realized that this was a negotiation that could end all this madness. She kept *Sun-Seeker* in a tight helical turn, with a wary eye on the flier below, now approaching. Something told her that she should make some quick dodgy movements to make them a less predictable target. While hanging on Redwing's every word, of course.

"Okay, details later. Right." Redwing's entire body was tense now, on his feet, spine ramrod straight. He gripped his chair so hard, she saw his hand turn pale. "What?" The silence seemed long and unbearable, but she noticed the seconds on her situation screen were going by slowly. "Roger. More later."

Redwing turned to her and said, "That flier behind us, take all the evasion you can. They're trying to shut down a weapon that's in armed and aiming mode right now."

She slammed the helm over hard and teased the fusion burn to its max. Then she released the bolus of searing plasma and wrenched the helm again, putting them into a flat spin, then a dive. Pops and creaks came echoing down the bridge from the connecting corridors. Karl's tablet escaped from the ridged worktable and smacked into the bulkhead.

Redwing said, "There's an electromagnetic precursor maybe two seconds before discharge. Look for that. Say again, Tananareve—"

Karl flicked their EM antennas into one overlay, frequencies color-coded. Beth could see the flier as a dark point among hills and valleys of Technicolor richness. "It's buried in all this plasma emission," Karl said.

"Integrate the whole spectral emission," Beth said. "I don't know what frequency it will come out in, but if we—"

"Got it." A smooth topological surface appeared now in auburn colors, brown for valleys and nearly yellow at the peaks. The sky flexed like an ocean rolling with colliding wave fronts.

She fought the helm around again and let their speed drop a bit. This let her fill reserve chambers with incoming plasma and build to the max density they could carry. The jet wind was coming in at velocities over a thousand kilometers a second, and she could vary the inflow rate simply by moving the magscoop to angle it more fully into the stream. *SunSeeker* was working far from its optimal performance peak, which had been designed to run steady and smooth on interstellar plasma, orders of magnitude below the sleeting hail of knotty ionized matter rushing at them. Now she used, without thinking about it, the skills she had won from their flight up the jet when they arrived here. Through long hours she had fought violent currents, swimming upstream against conditions *SunSeeker* had never seen.

Now she just let her instincts rule. Her hands and eyes moved restlessly, shaping plasma and bunching it. When she saw the holding chambers were full, she began to trickle more into the fusion chambers. The boost took them up jetward and to starboard as she waited for something strange to come at them.

It wasn't subtle. The maroon tones around the flier profile suddenly blossomed with a hard bright yellow peak. She fed the stored plasma into the chambers and goosed the drive. The helm slammed over, and she had time to shout "Incoming!"

The bridge shuddered and then *wrinkled*. She looked down the deck line and saw the bulwark ripple and flex. Pops and groans rose. Karl dove for the deck. She felt a tight pressure run through her like a slow, sinuous wave. Her stomach lurched. A deep bass tone rolled along the ship axis and—

—it was gone. The bridge snapped back into straight lines and firm walls. The hail of small stressed sounds fell away.

"They missed us," Karl said.

Redwing nodded. "But *what* missed us? The deck got rubbery—"

"A space-time wrinkle, maybe," Karl said. "I dunno how in hell anybody could make one, but—"

"Let me concentrate," Beth said. "They could shoot at us again."

She dodged and swerved and dove and soared and plunged, and time stretched the way space had moments before. She heard nothing, saw nothing but the feeds that told her what the flier was doing. It cut her off on a side curve and flared more exhaust to draw closer. She countered with her own moves. All this she did with hands incessantly moving as her eyes looked for another of the hard bright yellow peaks. But it didn't come.

The comm beeped. Redwing answered. "Oh. Good. What? Say again. Good. Great. You're sure. Okay. Terms come later, sure. Soon, yes."

He hung up and turned to Beth. She allowed her eyes to stray to him and she was shocked at how old he looked.

"They're standing down. No more pulses like that. Something called the Lambda Gun."

She opened her mouth to say something, and the comm beeped again.

Redwing answered. "What? Look at the star?"

"Got it," Karl said. He and Fred, who had come onto the bridge, peered at the big screen.

Geysers. The curve of the red star worked with furious energies. Flares and huge arches broke into space. Currents swept across the troubled crescent. Beth saw there was a dent in the perfect circle. Something had chewed it.

Karl said, "Look at these vectors." He had told the Kinematic Artilect to project an acceptance cone on the thing that had missed them. He had set the basic width to be a few times the jittering pattern Beth had followed to evade whatever the flier threw at them. Within the error bars, the cone snipped a bit off the star.

Redwing frowned. "Tananareve says the Folk call it a Lambda Gun. It does something with space-time, so if it just projected on—" He stopped. Facts trump words.

They watched the star adjust gravity against its

internal pressures. Huge fissures opened and closed like snapping mouths. Fountains of restless plasma worked up in slender, vibrant yellow tendrils before curving and dying. The star flooded simmering masses into the gap, and waves spread from that. Fluids shaped by strong magnetic fields moved in complex eddies. Storms peeled off this and spread, tornadoes the size of planets.

Beth let out a long slow breath, trying to get herself back into somewhat normal condition. She was tired and worn and completely confused. Coffee no longer helped. She needed a bath, too.

She stood, wobbling a little. "Tananareve said more, Cap'n. I could tell. What?"

"We've got a deal. They'll resupply us."

Gasps. Redwing shrugged and smiled, bobbing his head when the entire bridge burst into applause. "Uh, yes. There's more. They want some of us, maybe enough to avoid inbreeding, to stay on the Bowl. The ones who actually run this place aren't those Folk at all. Those are like the local police on the beat, or middle managers in a bureaucracy. This thing is so old, something needs to live long enough to run it."

"Some aliens we didn't see down there?" Beth asked, her vision bleary, bones aching now. "Some kind of—"

Redwing shrugged, as though he should have known all along. "Ice Minds move slowly because they're cold. They keep the memories and experience, Tananareve said. They work with something called the Diaphanous, who manage the jet and the star."

"Plasma stuff?" Karl said. "Those were what made those sounds, that created those discharge arcs, that—"

"Killed Clare," Beth said. "Trying to stop us from kinking the jet."

"The cold works with the hot, then," Karl said. "The Folk are just local managers."

"They sure don't think so. They imagine they're the whole show," Beth said. "Funny, really."

"So why did the Ice Minds, or whatever, let us live at all?" Fred said. He had been silent the whole time but now seemed happy, smiling, eyes dancing.

"They need help with Glory," Redwing said. "We can get there first, going full blast. We can reconnoiter. And talk to the Glorians, who think we humans are running the Bowl. They got our radio and TV, and since they were along the same line of sight, thought the Bowl was ours."

Beth frowned. "We have to?"

"Part of the deal." Redwing smiled. "Tananareve said it's pretty much take it or leave it."

Karl laughed. "No question, I'd say. We take it."

"They do want us to straighten out that standing kink. It's rubbing against the Knothole and it's gonna stay that way. But if we fly through it the right way, maybe we can bust it loose."

Karl said dryly, "There are better ways to put that, more precise. But I think with the fluences we have, and Beth as pilot, we can."

Beth laughed, a bit dry. "Beth the perfect pilot thinks she needs sleep. Lots of it. Then more coffee."

Redwing smiled and finally sat down in his deck chair, more relaxed than she had seen him in a long while. He looked at the walls showing their situation and said, "If we run down the jet, fix the Knothole plasma stall, then out—well, we can loop around and come back into simple orbit."

Beth scowled. "Back into the cold sleep vaults?"

"Some stay here," Redwing said. "The Ice Minds want some new species to give the Bowl some stability. The Folk couldn't handle us, so they're out of the policing business. We get that."

Beth nodded, knowing her piloting days were very nearly over.

FORTY-EIGHT

Tananareve was tired when the incessant images and thoughts finally started to taper away. The Ice Minds had much to convey in their cool, gliding manner, but it was all so big and strange, she could not really think what to say. Mostly she just digested. Which was exhausting in itself. But one thing did puzzle her, and she asked about it.

"Why was your jet open to attack? I mean, it and the star and the Bowl—it's an unstable system, has to be adjusted all the time or it falls apart. Anybody wants to do you harm, the jet is an open target, the heart of the system."

Some confusion and delay. Soft pictures floated

into her mind. The jet's filmy twisting strands working out from the star. Sometimes it snarled a bit, but the plasma clots called the Diaphanous adjusted that. They made the jet smooth out and glide tight and sure through the Knothole. All was well. Nominally.

"What's the idea of letting it be so vulnerable? I mean, we just came alongside you and slipped in, rode up the jet. We could've damaged it then, even by accident. But other kinds, other aliens, they might want to bring you down."

Some did.

"What was your strategy then?" She was tired, but what she learned could be useful. Redwing would want to know every damn detail.

Imagine a simple army's task, under imminent attack. They must find the part of their landscape best suited to strengthen their position when fighting in open battle. The answer is to fight on the edge of a sharp cliff. This gives their soldiers just two choices—to fight or retreat, and in retreating to go over the cliff and die. Their enemy has different options—to fight or flee. That option to flee makes the enemy's attack less likely to persevere. Placing yourself in peril makes you appear fearless. It gives your opponent cause to consider breaking off the battle.

She found this strange. "So you put your backs to the wall and that's a defense?"

We prefer to dissuade. We regret that the Folk, or rather one of them, used our final defense. Our

Lambda Gun is immensely powerful. Luckily it was ineptly used. We have stopped its use and will punish those who erred so grievously.

Tananareve said nothing. She felt a rising, apprehensive note strike through her mind, and realized it was coming from the Ice Minds. They said, *The Diaphanous now speak to those who caused this deep error. You should hear as well.* A somber, rolling voice came then, not so much spoken as unfurled.

> *Who is this that wrecks our province*
> *without knowledge?*
> *Do you know the sliding laws of blithe fluids?*
> *Were you here when the great curve of*
> *the Bowl shaped true?*
> *Can you raise your voice to the clouds of stars?*
> *Do fields unseen report to you?*
> *Can your bodies shape the fires of*
> *thrusting suns?*
> *Have you ever given orders to the passing*
> *stars or shown the dawn its place?*
> *Can you seize the Bowl by the edges to shake*
> *the wicked out of it?*
> *Have you journeyed to the springs of fusion or*
> *walked in the recesses of the brittle night?*
> *Have you entered the storehouses of the Ice Minds*
> *and found there tales of your long past?*
> *Can you father events in times beyond*
> *all seeing?*
> *Your answer to all these cannot justify your brute*
> *hands upon machines of black wonder.*

Nor shall you ever chance to be so able again,
for you shall be no more.
The space and time you sought to dissolve shall
reckon without you hence.

Tananareve knew somehow this came from the invisible ones who dwelled in the jet. She did not understand any of this. She just sighed and put such troubles away as she gratefully slipped into sleep.

FORTY-NINE

Memor watched the great floods sweep across lands that had held towns and forests and would now be swamps. Great constructions from far antiquity were undermined and slumped. Under great magnification, from this satellite view, she studied the rooftops of homes and city centers. There were no survivors awaiting rescue. A few boats bobbed here and there, but not many.

"It is a tragedy, indeed," Bemor said. He looked tired, surely from the work of keeping the Ice Minds in touch with the primates, funneled through the mind of the poor Tananareve. "But we are demanded at the leaving ceremony. Come."

"Who demands this? I do not wish to witness such."

"The Ice Minds command. Their attitude has changed substantially. I do not sense their goodwill toward us any longer."

Memor bristled and gave quick fan-signals of rebuke and mild anger. "The crisis faded away, yes? And we surely played a role."

"Of a kind." Bemor gave a feathered signature of drab purple resignation, and wheezed a bit. "Come. And bring your primates. The Ice Minds wish them to see this."

"They have rested and eaten," Memor said. "Perhaps they will profit from witnessing."

They entered the Citadel of the Dishonored to see Asenath's end. She would be churned into the great matrix of dead plants and animals, so the dishonored could enhance topsoil. Memor and Bemor plodded into the high, arched atrium, where subtly hidden machinery murmured, managing the bacterial content, acidity, and trace elements of the slowly roiling mud-fluid below the Pit. First the Pit, then the Garden: the fate of all.

"I disliked Asenath," Memor whispered. "But she did have talent."

Bemor said, "Insults are best not remembered. She was sure of herself and had no thought of consequence."

Still, Memor needed to consult her Undermind to help her get through this. Calling the extinction of one she had worked with "a just recycling" did little good.

The primates followed, and the Sil. Bemor remarked, "They show few signs of the early stages of Adoption. Perhaps we'd best be rid of them."

"I believe the Ice Minds will not allow any

executions or harm to them," Memor said. "Or the Sil, though we could build a case against them."

Bemor flashed vigorous objection. "The Ice Minds were behind the Sil actions. They wished the humans brought to them, without our knowing such intent."

"Ah, so the Sil are invulnerable, as are the primates. I dislike profoundly having our command of these creatures revoked for the sake of a passing problem—"

"It is not passing. Asenath's Lambda Gun pulse passed along the jet for a considerable distance. It intersected portions of several of the Diaphanous. One was killed, the others injured. These could self-repair, with help of others who could lend portions of their own anatomy. To damage the Diaphanous is to endanger the jet and thus the Bowl." Bemor's grave voice boomed. "An example must be made."

Memor saw Asenath being led to the Pit and recalled when she herself had faced the prospect of oblivion. Asenath had been disappointed at Memor's being spared, and had allowed a pitch of reluctance into her later comments. Now Asenath faced the yawning black Pit at the center of the Vault. The sentence was read and Asenath gave no reply, or any mournful yips and drones. Her feathers were a muted gray and hung lifeless. Her fate spread before her in the green slime before the final descent. Deep long chords sounded.

Various religious figures were there, clad in ancient Folk grandcloth. They urged Asenath to convert to

their faiths, here in her last moments. Memor recalled that through its history the Bowl had passed
by worlds where creatures shaped like ribbons or
pancakes held sway. These the ancients had termed
Philosophers, for they had little tool-using ability.
Such fauna were deeply social and spun great theories of their world, verging into the theological. To
Memor philosophy was like a blind being searching
a dark room for an unknown, black beast. When
philosophy verged into theology, it was like that
same predicament, but the black beast did not even
exist, yet the search went on. Asenath waved the
religious Folk away, giving a fan-flutter of rejection.

Asenath declined a final statement; then her
feather-crown altered to deep gray. She raised her
head and said, "We die containing a richness of
lovers, and characters we have climbed into, as
if trees. I have marked these on my body for my
death. Then I go into the Great Soil."

Memor wondered at this. No one would see such
inscriptions. Perhaps it was a declaration Asenath
hoped would somehow make its way into Folk-
lore?

Head held high, with a resigned shrug, she simply stepped off the edge and slid down into the
disposal hole. She had never looked at the crowd
of witnesses.

Memor could smell a fear among the primates;
she had nearly forgotten them. She reassured them
that this was to educate them in the ways of the
Bowl and the Great Soil to which all must return.

A primate vomited at the sight and smell of the

execution, spattering vile acid. Memor saw it was Tananareve, who she recalled had learned some of Folk speech. These creatures were smarter than she had supposed, as recent events revealed.

There was a long silence after the ceremony. Bemor said to the primates, "We have strict justice for all here."

Tananareve said, "It looks like you're ruled by those Ice Minds. They can order executions?"

Bemor said, "The Bowl would fail if there were not an authority who could override the passing opinions of individuals. Or of species. Your own ship has a Captain."

"I never thought it would be a pleasure to see Redwing again," Tananareve said. "But life is full of surprises."

They all—Cliff, Irma, Terry, Aybe—laughed hard and long at this. Memor saw that this eruption came from great internal pressures, now released.

"We shall have to be careful with these primates," Bemor whispered in Folk speech. "They are few and we are merely many trillions."

He and Memor laughed with deep, rolling tones of relieving tensions. In not too long a time, they would remember Bemor's joke with little humor.

MEMORY'S FLICKERING LIGHT

The natural world does not optimize, it merely exists.
—KEN CALDEIRA

FIFTY

Beth yawned and stretched and looked at the big foaming breakers curling onto a beach, splashing with a churning roar out to the edge of her wall. Relaxing lapping ocean sounds were a pleasant wake-up call. She had surfed there once a century or so ago and very nearly drowned. Her wrenched back had taken a while to stop complaining.

Now her muscles ached and spoke to her of her many hours in the lead pilot's chair on the flight deck. They hadn't enjoyed it, and neither had she. *More fun to get worked over in a wave,* she thought fuzzily. *I wonder if there are surf-worthy waves somewhere on the Bowl? Maybe when a hurricane's running somewhere, safely far away . . .*

She got up and trooped down to the head and spent three days' allotment of water on a hot shower. It helped ease her back muscles, and she could think again, too. About how to deal with Redwing and Cliff and all the open doors she was about to slam shut.

She slumped through the mess in her bathrobe, ignoring Fred, who was reading his tablet anyway, and scored a big coffee hit in her extra-size cup.

Then back in bed and the wall now running a restful English village, with enough background sounds of breeze and birds to let her forget the ghastly silence aboard *SunSeeker*.

It wasn't easy for *SunSeeker*'s chief pilot to ignore the quiet. *SunSeeker* was at rest, motors down, shields down. Only a pattern in the Bowl's magnetic fields protected her from a flood of interstellar radiation. And an alien magnetic pattern, the Diaphanous, was shaping that.

The silence was eerie, after she had spent so long under its background working rumble. Now came a massive, heavy thump. A tanker, she thought. Tankers and cargo craft were a cloud around *SunSeeker,* and there were thumps and scraping as one or another mated to the ship and masses moved through air locks. Some robots dispatched by the Folk clumped and clanked across the hull on magnetic graspers.

She took a sip and shut out the fevered world.

E-mail first, to get up to speed after ten hours in the sack. She plunged in. The very first was a slab of homework from Tananareve. She had craftily recorded nearly all her interactions with the Ice Minds, at least those rendered in speech within the machine they had her trapped in. She had asked them to use audio rather than somehow making a voice resound in her mind. In the middle of the transcript, captured on her phone and patched up by a shipboard Artilect, was a nugget.

You must realize that Glory is not a true planet but rather a shell world. Many different spe-

cies of intelligent Glorians live on concentric spheres, with considerable atmosphere spaces between them. Many pillars support this system, and powerful energy sources provide light and heat. Entirely different life-forms inhabit the differing spheres. The innermost shells support life without oxygen. These kinds come from deep within ordinary worlds, creatures of darkness and great heat. Some species have made their spheres into imitations of whatever their best-loved environments are. At the very top is a re-creation of a primitive oxygen world, flush with forests and seas. This outer shell your astronomers have studied. You conclude that Glory is a succulent target for a colony. That upper layer is deceiving, perhaps deliberately so—we do not know. Certainly Glory is not a simple prospect for your kind.

The Glorians who constructed this shell paradise of theirs also communicate on scales of the galaxy itself. They do not use simple electromagnetics, as you do. There are many worlds, many of them ruled by machine intelligences, who use electromagnetics over stellar scales. Emitting in these ways reveals an emergent society capable of beginner technologies. Most keep silent, their radiated power low, fearing unknown perils. We often found such silent planets. We were drawn to worlds we knew by distant examination were life-bearing, yet electromagnetically quiet.

The Glorians disdain such societies. They

wish to speak, over many long eras, with greater minds—those who can blare forth using gravitational waves. Those waves are far harder to detect and stupendously more difficult to emit in coherent fashion, to carry messages. Here again, to radiate at all is a show of power.

These signals you primates have detected but cannot translate. That is unsurprising. So thus have many minds discovered, over many millions of your years. Some of these who hear but cannot understand gravitational waves, the Bowl encountered long ago. The gravitational message landscape is an intricate puzzle few solve.

We Ice Minds have unraveled the Glorian waves, with the help of the Diaphanous. It was a lengthy labor. They are strange, intriguing, and imply much more than they say. We now wish to know the Glorian Masters ourselves, to join in their company. That is why the Bowl now feels itself ready to approach. Before, we did not dare.

For you primates to dare is surely folly.

Beth took a deep breath and watched people from another century—when she grew up, of course—walk down the streets of the English village, the sea breeze sighing, birds all atwitter. So the Ice Minds were making their case for some of *SunSeeker*'s passengers to stay. Fair enough. The problem was going to be Redwing.

Next came data and text from Tananareve and ship Artilects, dissecting the events with the Diaphanous.

Karl and the Theory Artilect had worked out some ideas about what the hell the Diaphanous beings who had killed Clare could be. Self-organizing magnetic fields, smart bellies full of plasma, harvesting energy from the jet? And bigger than planets? Well, the jet was a puzzle, and managing it seemed beyond the Folk. She and the others had ignored that problem, now pretty obvious once you thought of it. Who mustered solar storms to the jet base? Who got the mag fields aligned so the jet was under steady control?

Something big. Beth tried to envision what would radiate waves kilometers long. That could induce enormous electric fields inside *SunSeeker*, and sound waves, too. To such creatures, humans might be as inconsequential as the lice that pestered the skin of a blue whale.

Without the Diaphanous, the whole Bowl system was impossible. Want someone to manage a star? Take the children born in stellar magnetic arches, evolved there. Hire the locals.

Enough. She left off the reading to get ready for her appointment with Redwing. Time to don the battle uniform, gal.

FIFTY-ONE

The worst part about the free-bounding exercise he did in zero grav was the sweat. Sweat didn't run. Redwing clung to a stanchion and mopped some from his eyes, but it was hard to get it all. Some covered his eyes in lenses. Blinking only made his image of the big craft bay wobble. Then his belt rang, reminding him of his appointments with Karl and then Beth.

Karl was waiting. Redwing hated showing up late for a crew appointment, but he had needed the exercise to clear his mind. As they went into his cabin, he saw his wall was running their real-time view. He was glad to see they had rounded the Bowl lip and so could see the Knothole region again. Radiation remained near zero as the Diaphanous sun dwellers' mag shield followed their orbit. Redwing could not imagine magnetic stresses that could grasp and guide a starship of a thousand tons, but he was getting used to the apparently impossible.

Karl grinned. "It's been a hell of ride. The way Beth drove us down into the cinch point of the Knothole, and then stood us here, blasting plasma out the back and pushing the standing kink over toward center, into a straight line—wow. Just, wow."

Redwing nodded. "The finger snakes loved it, too. They're bright, seemed to know a lot about how the jet works. I've seen piloting but never like that. We owe her one."

"Maybe more than one," Karl said, but Redwing let it pass.

Karl studied the hurricanes visible on long-range scopes. They were beyond spectacular, when you adjusted for scale. In the fractured zones near the knothole, the seas were giving up their moisture to the lowered atmospheric pressure. An enormous hurricane fed on the air pressure drop, a quickening drift toward the ruptured atmospheric envelope.

"Maybe we need a new term," Karl said. He stood and pointed on the wall. "See, those eddies form in the big churning spiral, then spin off into hurricanes. It's a fractal fluid turbulence." He increased screen resolution. "So those too fling out smaller hurricanes, and so on down to some scale more like Earth's puny varieties."

"So more and more of them dance out their fury on the life below," Redwing said, musing.

"They'll take a while to patch the tears." Karl turned away, shaking his head. "We really went too far."

There was business to do, but he asked instead, "A celebration seems in order—the old eat, drink, and be merry. Plus we're all tired. Let's let the Artilects take over, say two hours from now, and muster the crew."

Karl nodded, distracted. Redwing reflected that at tonight's party, the entrée steak would not be meat, the wine would be water plus a grape extract and alcohol, and the water was fashioned from their collective piss. After all the deaths, maybe being merry was the hard part.

"Cap'n, this blizzard of info we're getting from Tananareve and the Folk—it's hard to digest. We're getting their point of view, and I try to cock it around to our line of sight."

"They're old, we're young. To be expected."

Karl gave a wry smile. "Some of these messages, I sort of feel that they should have a space for 'fill in name, address, and solar system'—it's hard to grasp their assumptions."

"And so, hard to know how to negotiate with them?"

"Damn right. Look, the Bowl is on a journey that takes it all over a chunk of the available galaxy. They should've settled most of the local arm by now. But these Bird Folk, they're deeply conservative. They don't seem to leave colonies."

Redwing pursed his lips, sat back, and watched the super-hurricane grinding on. He tried not to think about what was happening below them. His work . . .

"Um. They say that's because the Bowl is perfect, suited for the smart dinosaurs that built it. Warm, stable, predictable weather. They don't want to leave it. So?"

"Then who's doing the exploring? The Folk don't want to advertise this, but it's pretty clear. They tried colonies and failed. After millions of years in this nice, steady place—heaven, right?—they don't work out well on planets."

"But they say they keep track of every star they've visited. That's how they knew what was going on, the Great Shame, all that."

Karl leaned forward with a thin smile. "It's the Ice Minds. They think slow, they live slow, but there's still room for boredom. They've left some of themselves in the local Oort clouds, all over this galactic arm. Plus Earth's. They like it, there's no weather there. Stable, gives them lots of data, propagates the species, too."

"And the Folk?"

"They're the caretakers. They pick up some new species every million years or so, but mostly they just lord it over all the other species on the Bowl—the Adopted, they call them."

"And we're the new kids on the block?"

"Wait'll you see this." Karl clicked his tablet and flashed a picture on the opposite wall. A view of two spheres orbiting each other, black and white. A simulation, too clean to be real.

"The Ice Minds think the Glorians have a binary-charged black hole system, Tananareve says. It looks like this, they say. Since the black holes are basically very large charged particles, you could control their orbits with very large electromagnetic containment fields. That avoids collision of the black holes. But then they swerve them a little, so the near misses generate intense gravitational waves. That's the Glorians' communication link with other big-time civilizations in the galaxy."

"And the Ice Minds want in on the conversation?" This was getting stranger than he liked.

"Social climbers, yes. They want to meet the adults, looks like."

Redwing frowned. "But they can't have black holes around the Bowl. Too dangerous."

"Maybe so, but—these black holes are small, maybe a few meters across."

"That small? It's still massive."

"Right, around a hundred times more massive than Earth. Oh, and—the Glorians made the holes, too."

"What!"

"The Ice Minds want to find out how."

"And we're headed there. . . ." Redwing wanted to think this through, but a polite knock told him it was time for Beth.

Karl said, "I was talking to Fred just now and he made an interesting point. Remember when we all were approaching the Bowl? Flabbergasted, sure. But now, Fred says to him it's been like a twisted encounter with the eventual human future."

"That makes no sense."

"In a tilted way—in Fred's style of thinking, any-way—SunSeeker left an Earth already pretty well worked over by the human hand. Remember? Sunlight reflected by sulfur dioxide particles shimmering in its stratosphere, so at the right angle we could see it from space. Clouds of seawater mist billowing up from those small sail ships, to shield oceans from sunlight. Big carbon collector towers, stretching out across continents. Farm waste rounded up and consigned to the deep ocean, where it'll keep for a thousand years. Throwing fine-ground chalk into those oceans every year, remember that?—in masses equal to the white cliffs of Dover."

Redwing nodded, recalling the furiously working fretwork of corrections. "Right, to offset the acid from absorbed CO_2. I was in deep space for decades, running hot nukes. Made no difference to us."

"Me, too, mostly. Somebody else's problem, and we had plenty of our own, running closed biospheres." Karl gave a wry shrug.

"That was pretty much taking on an infinite career, endlessly shaping habitat. So I see Fred's point—why didn't he come with you to lay it out?"

Karl gave Redwing a skeptical arched eyebrow. "You don't know he's scared of you?"

"He does seem a bit quiet."

"He's not when you're absent. His point is, someone or some *thing* faced those same problems long ago. They built the Bowl to be a better place. Got tired of planets, probably. Wanted to venture into the night sky, but in no hurry. So they took a big fraction of the species with them. Left behind the stay-at-homes."

Redwing liked this. "You and Fred are saying they wanted managed landscapes that seemed natural. All nice and dinosaur-friendly warm, under a constant reddish sun. Plus its amigo, the jolly jet."

Karl chuckled. "God knows what Earth looks like now, centuries into running its biosphere."

"Is this a way of saying you and Fred want to stay on the Bowl?"

"Not at all!"

"Um. So what do I do with this new input?" He disliked asking advice from crew, but at least they were alone. "How does it affect going to Glory?"

"I thought you should hear what the crew thinks. Time's up, I know." Karl stood and saluted. "I want to go see the show at Glory, sir. Sail on." He left.

When Beth came in, he could see her jaw set at a determined angle. She had looked that way through the long hard hours straightening the standing knot. When it was done, she had barely made it to her quarters.

"Captain, I formally request transfer to the colony on the Bowl."

"Colony?" Things were moving too damn fast.

"The Folk—okay, they're just speaking for the Ice Minds now—they say Cliff's team all want to stay. I want to join them."

"Look, I can't have crew leaving. We need a sharp pilot—"

"Warm one up. I'm a biologist first, just a backup pilot, really."

"You're our best! The way you flew us—"

"Then it's payback time, Captain. You made the deal with the Folk, right?"

"Not the Folk, no. The Ice Minds and the Diaphanous, actually, seems like."

"You have to leave some of us on the Bowl, then. So leave enough to reproduce without inbreeding."

"The genetic stores—"

"Need enough founding population to reduce risk, even with the genetic augmentations from the database. That's at least a hundred people, no, several hundred. Defrost them while we're resupplying."

"You want a—"

"Colony. That's what we were sent for."

Redwing told himself to stay steady, calm, but his heart thumped harder. "I'll have to do that anyway, Beth. The finger snakes want to ride with us. Just the three, a male and two females; they don't seem to have an inbreeding problem. But fifty Sil have already been picked. There are other species who might want to board. The Artilects say they can rework the freezer capsules, but some of our passengers will have to stay awake longer than optimal."

"You've got room for a bigger live crew, don't you? You're launching fully provisioned, yes? We're already near relativistic speed."

"Faster than that. We'll fly up the Jet and get a boost from rounding the sun. Sure you want to miss that?"

"I'm sure. I'm the one who wants to stay, Captain. Cliff is going along with that."

Redwing sighed. "Then there's no room for Bird Folk, of course, except as fertilized eggs and an artificial womb—but they want that, and it's a big volume."

Beth's mouth twisted. "After all they did to us?"

"It's part of our deal. Those Folk don't run the Bowl, they're more like the cop on the beat—"

"Corrupt cops. They kill other species to keep some equilibrium of theirs running. It's a murderous regime. They chased us, imprisoned us—"

"We'll be carrying them because we could

hardly carry Ice Minds. Though we will have a Diaphanous—more on that later, when it's worked out."

"But your charge Earthside wasn't to pick up aliens and carry them—"

"You have to adjust your initial launch orders to the situation. Beth, I'll have to download nearly half our passengers, and how do I pick them? It isn't as if I could thaw them and let them choose. They get no more vote than the unborn."

Beth said, "Pick mated couples. Pick the ones who wanted to colonize rather than explore. We were tested for attitudes."

"We were all picked for adaptability. Even so . . ."

She leaned forward, smiling. He sat back, a little mouth twitch telling her he found that a bit strange. "Look at our larger aim—to get humanity out into the galaxy. Play the big game. This way we have two colonies."

"Glory's a bigger game," he said. She hadn't heard Karl go on about the black hole radiator theory, but no doubt she would in the mess, later, when the reconstituted booze started flowing.

"Glory's not our kind of game, I'd guess. Not yet." She shrugged ruefully. "It's maybe a league up from what we can handle. The Bowl was tough enough."

Redwing knew enough to wait. Her voice became soft, almost sympathetic. "But we'll get there. The Bowl will get our first human colony to Glory. Long after I'm dead, sure—and I'm hoping to reach two hundred. Hell, more! But we humans, we'll get there. And be waiting to meet up with you."

Redwing frowned. "I have orders."

"And crew. You'll have nearly a thousand left in cold sleep. Plus, y'know, not all our people on the ground down there want to stay. Tananareve doesn't! She's had enough of the Folk, thank you."

"Okay, I heard that. You want to reunite with Cliff, too. So you'll join this Bowl colony you want."

"Right. But not because of Cliff, especially. He's important to me, sure, but—oh, that's right. You probably know from the field reports—somebody must've blabbed, though it's obvious— He's been screwing Irma."

"Well, I'm not prepared to reveal—"

"You don't have to. Put people under dire threat for many months, and the prospect of death makes them set about being sure there's going to be a replacement. Plus it feels good when the world threatens you. Hey, I'm a biologist."

"I know. And Irma's coming with us. So is her husband. You don't—?"

"I don't mind. Irma, Cliff—that was a 'field event,' as we used to call it. Whatever works in a pinch, I say. And . . . isn't that party you talked about earlier about to start?"

A big sunny smile. And she gave him, unmistakably, a wink.

FIFTY-TWO

He got back to his cabin only a bit squiffed. Odd term, *squiffed*. He had inherited it from his grandfather, who had never given a definition. It was pretty clear, though. Pleasantly inebriated but in control. As a captain should be.

Redwing also recalled a parting remark from his commanding officer, just before he took the shuttle out to *SunSeeker* for his last transfer. *Remember that people break down, too, not just machinery.* You had to give them room.

There was plenty more to being a captain than bulldog stubbornness. Beth was good at giving him a different angle on events. It had been fun seeing her play with the finger snakes tonight. Who knew that they liked alcohol, too? There had been a lot of laughter, the pure long gasps that meant pressures were easing somewhere deep inside.

Beth was good, quite so. But she hadn't seen that the Ice Minds wanted Tananareve to go forward to Glory on *SunSeeker,* as part of their exploratory advance party. Tananareve would be able to report back to the Folk—or maybe directly to the Ice Minds?—in an intuitive way. Better than the rest of the rude invader primates, since now they knew how her mind worked.

He still hadn't told Beth all of it.

The ship would run up the jet, gulping plasma, boosting hard, and as it flew past the sun, *SunSeeker* would gain one more passenger. A Diaphanous would ride the motor. The Diaphanous thought that was a fresh opportunity, helping shape the magnetic geometry and exhaust parameters, while clinging to the ship and its scoop geometry. They'd never tried such a lark before. And maybe they wanted to meet up with the Diaphanous species on yet another star? Redwing suspected he would never truly know their motives.

SunSeeker's Artilects had already been brought up to speed on that. Would a magnetic pattern obey a ship's captain?

That problem could wait. He shrugged off his uniform and decided to shower in the morning. He brushed his teeth and dropped the plastic glass as he tried to dump the waste rinse water into the tiny bowl his cabin alone had. Was he losing his ability to process alcohol? Well, so be it. After all, he was somewhere in his eighties.

He stared into the Bowl. They had called this huge artifact Wokworld when they first found it, but names were just pigeonholes. The feeling he had gotten, at first glance, seeing the vast spinning machine at a distance, was of some parasite grasping a star, sucking life from it. And charging forward, too, using that raw energy to move, forever restless, onward into the great night.

Beth had been a quick, sharp slap in the face today. She had made him see the bigger view of what they were here for. He owed her for that. And he would miss her, he just now realized.

Should he just stay here, dock *SunSeeker* somehow, and join the happy guys down on the Bowl?

No. He had a clear duty and he would carry it out, even if all those who had ordered him were dead.

The biggest mistake is being too afraid of making one, he had heard somewhere in his Fleet training. Somehow in this evening, with Beth's help, he had made a lot of them.

On his wall he called up the real-time view of the landscape passing below them. They were headed for a good place to rendezvous with the lander they had sent down. The Folk would put Tananareve on board—and Aybe, who had just changed his mind; tech types often did. The Folk would send up supplies, and it shouldn't take long to mate their comm gear with *SunSeeker*'s, so they could stay in close touch with the Bowl, and get going again. Bound for Glory.

Yes—squiffed he was. Indeed, sir. *Onward.*

This Bowl was not so strange, after all. Maybe it meant that really advanced societies overshot their agenda, gliding for a while in the enameled perfection of their way of life, following habits deep-grained and evolved long before. So they correct and modify and engineer and correct again. Build big and think big and think again. The Bowl was the first big strange idea humanity had really met—terrifying and intriguing. And among many yet to come. Of that he was sure. Terrors can be mirrors, too.

Details. The tortured landscapes below passed before his eyes like an unending scroll. He thought of how the decisions that seem momentous in the moment, or even over a lifetime, were flickering instants in the life of the Bowl. These matters were too small to be observed by the Ice Minds, just single passing lives.

The Bowl had made them look back across a gulf of not mere centuries or millennia, but on the grand scale of evolution itself. Maybe that was the true deep purpose of coming out here among the stars. To see times that glowed and shimmered in memory's flickering light.

He had a thought. Was there more than one Bowl, coasting around the galaxy? Maybe such things were a technological niche that others thought of and inhabited—very-long-view things, hard to quite grasp for humans. Maybe if alien species had the right precursor society—that of those smart dinosaurs, who loved warmth and sun and stillness—then their love of a forever summer would make them build such contraptions. If so, the blunt hammer of evolution gave another strategy to gain the stars, one different from smart, talky primates.

Whatever waited at Glory, in its stacked levels, there was a biosphere on top, a place to love beneath a star that had a sunset every day. Beings who lived in layers would be strange indeed, and humanity would have to adapt. Redwing smiled. If the Bowl had taught him anything, it was about human versatility. He would be alert when he reached Glory after a long sleep, and he liked his odds.

It couldn't be stupid to voyage out in small vessels, to distant worlds where beauty and happiness would get redefined again and again. Even if Earth became a distant and perhaps wistful memory—as all his crew and himself would inevitably be, for sure—the expansion of human horizons was an ultimate good. Whatever built the Bowl had believed that, too. There was something comforting in that thought alone.

Time for bed.

BIG SMART OBJECTS

I. HOW WE BUILT THE BOOKS

Gregory Benford's take—

In science fiction, a Big Dumb Object is any immense mysterious object that generates an intense sense of wonder just by being there. "The Diamond as Big as the Ritz" by F. Scott Fitzgerald is a non-SF example. They don't have to be inert constructs, so perhaps the "dumb" aspect also expresses the sensation of being struck dumb by the scale of them.

Larry said to me at a party, "Big dumb objects are so much easier. Collapsed civilizations are so much easier. Yeah, let's bring them up to speed."

So we wrote *Bowl of Heaven,* deciding that we needed two volumes to do justice to a Big Smart Object. The Bowl has to be controlled, because it's not neutrally stable. His *Ringworld* is a Big Dumb Object since it's passively stable, as we are when we stand still. (Or the ringworld would be except for nudges that can make it fall into the sun. Those are

fairly easy to catch in time. Larry put active stabi-
lizers into the second Ringworld novel.)

A Smart Object is statically unstable but dynamically stable, as we are when we walk. We fall
forward on one leg, then catch ourselves with the
other. That takes a lot of fast signal processing and
coordination. (We're the only large animal without
a tail that's mastered this. Two legs are dangerous
without a big brain or a stabilizing tail.) There've
been several Big Dumb Objects in SF, but as far as
I know, no smart ones. Our Big Smart Object is
larger than Ringworld and is going somewhere, using an entire star as its engine.

Our Bowl is a shell more than a hundred million miles across, held to a star by gravity and some
electrodynamic forces. The star produces a long
jet of hot gas, which is magnetically confined so
well, it spears through a hole at the crown of the
cup-shaped shell. This jet propels the entire system
forward—literally, a star turned into the engine of a
"ship" that is the shell, the Bowl. On the shell's inner face, a sprawling civilization dwells. The novel's
structure doesn't resemble Larry's *Ringworld* much,
because the big problem is dealing with the natives.

The virtues of any Big Object, whether dumb or
smart, are energy and space. The collected solar energy is immense, and the living space lies beyond
comprehension except in numerical terms. While
we were planning this, my friend Freeman Dyson
remarked, "I like to use a figure of demerit for habitats, namely the ratio R of total mass to the supply

of available energy. The bigger R is, the poorer the habitat. If we calculate R for the Earth, using total incident sunlight as the available energy, the result is about twelve thousand tons per watt. If we calculate R for a cometary object with optical concentrators, traveling anywhere in the galaxy where a zero magnitude star is visible, the result is one hundred tons per watt. A cometary object, almost anywhere in the galaxy, is 120 times better than planet Earth as a home for life. The basic problem with planets is that they have too little area and too much mass. Life needs area, not only to collect incident energy but also to dispose of waste heat. In the long run, life will spread to the places where mass can be used most efficiently, far away from planets, to comet clouds or to dust clouds not too far from a friendly star. If the friendly star happens to be our Sun, we have a chance to detect any wandering lifeform that may have settled here."

This insight helped me think through the Bowl, which has an R of about 10^{-10}! The local centrifugal gravity avoids entirely the piling up of mass to get a grip on objects, and just uses rotary mechanics. So of course, that shifts the engineering problem to the Bowl's structural demands.

Big human-built objects, whether pyramids, cathedrals, or skyscrapers, can always be criticized as criminal wastes of a civilization's resources, particularly when they seem tacky or tasteless. But not if they extend living spaces and semi-natural habitat. This idea goes back to Olaf Stapledon's *Star Maker*:

Not only was every solar system now surrounded by a gauze of light traps, which focused the escaping solar energy for intelligent use, so that the whole galaxy was dimmed, but many stars that were not suited to be suns were disintegrated, and rifled of their prodigious stores of sub-atomic energy.

Our smart Bowl craft is also going somewhere, not just sitting around, waiting for visitors like Ringworld—and its tenders live aboard.

We started with the obvious: *Where are they going, and why?*

Answering that question generated the entire frame of the two novels. That's the fun of smart objects—they don't just awe, they also intrigue.

My grandfather used to say, as we headed out into the Gulf of Mexico on a shrimping run, *A boat is just looking for a place to sink.*

So heading out to design a new, shiny Big Smart Object, I said, *An artificial world is just looking for a seam to pop.*

You're living just meters away from a high vacuum that's moving fast, because of the Bowl's spin (to supply centrifugal gravity). That makes it easy to launch ships, since they have the rotational velocity with respect to the Bowl or Ringworld . . . but that also means high seam-popping stresses have to be compensated. Living creatures on the sunny side will want to tinker, try new things. . . .

"Y'know, Fred, I think I can fix this plumbing

problem with just a drill-through right here. Uh—oops!"

The vacuum can suck you right through. Suddenly you're moving off on a tangent at a thousand kilometers a second—far larger than the 50 km/sec needed to escape the star. This makes exploring passing nearby stars on flyby missions easy.

But that easy exit is a hazard, indeed. To live on a Big Smart Object, you'd better be pretty smart yourself.

Larry Niven's take—

"The Enormous Big Thing" was my friend David Gerrold's description of a plotline that flowered after the publication of *Ringworld*. Stories like *Orbitsville, Ring, Newton's Wake,* John Varley's Titan trilogy and *Rendezvous with Rama* depend on the sense of wonder evoked by huge, ambitious endeavors. Ringworld wasn't the first; there had been stories that built, and destroyed, whole universes. These objects often become icons of larger issues implying unknowable reaches and perspectives. Their governing question is usually, "Who built this thing? And why?" They had fallen out of favor.

I wasn't the first to notice that a fallen civilization is easier to describe than a working one. Your characters can sort through the artifacts without hindrance until they've built a picture of the whole vast structure. Conan the Barbarian, and countless barbarians to follow, found fallen civilizations everywhere. I took this route quite deliberately with *Ringworld*. I was young and untrained, and I knew it.

A fully working civilization, doomed if they ever lose their grasp on their tools, is quite another thing. I wouldn't have tried it alone. Jerry Pournelle and I have described working civilizations several times, in *Footfall, Lucifer's Hammer,* and *The Burning City.*

With Greg Benford, I was willing to take a whack at a Dyson-level civilization. Greg shaped the Bowl in its first design. It had a gaudy simplicity that grabbed me from the start. It was easy to work with: essentially a Ringworld with a lid, and a star for a motor. We got Don Davis involved in working some dynamite paintings.

Greg kept seeing implications. The Bowl's history grew more and more elaborate. Ultimately I knew we'd need at least two volumes to cover everything we'd need to show. That gave us time and room.

II. FUN WITH HIGH TECH

Warning: some plot spoilers lurk here.

Our first book, *Bowl of Heaven,* set up reader expectations and introduced the Folk who ran the place—or thought so. That let us wrap up storylines in the sequel, *Shipstar,* in part by undermining the expectations built up in *Bowl of Heaven.* We chose to write all this in two volumes because it took time to figure out. The longer time also let us process what many readers thought of *Bowl of Heaven,* its problems and processes.

Much of this comes from the intricacies of how the Bowl came to be built. Plus its origins.

We supposed the founders made its understory frame with something like *scrith*—a Ringworld term, grayish translucent material with strength on the order of the nuclear binding energy, stuff from the same level of physics as held Ringworld from flying apart. This stuff is the only outright physical miracle needed to make Ringworld or the Bowl work mechanically. Rendering Ringworld stable is a simple problem—just counteract small sidewise nudges. Making the Bowl work in dynamic terms is far harder; the big problem is the jet and its magnetic fields. This was Benford's department, since he published many research papers in *The Astrophysical Journal* and the like on jets from the accretion disks around black holes, some of which are far bigger than galaxies. But who manages the jet? And how, since it's larger than worlds? This is how you get plot moves from the underlying physics.

One way to think of the strength needed to hold the Bowl together is by envisioning what would hold up a tower a hundred thousand kilometers high on Earth. The tallest building we now have is the 829.8 m (2,722 ft) tall, Burj Khalifa in Dubai, United Arab Emirates. So for Ringworld or for the Bowl, we're imagining a *scrith*-like substance 100,000 times stronger than the best steel and carbon composites can do now. Even under static conditions, though, buildings have a tendency to buckle under varying stresses. Really bad weather can blow over very strong buildings. So this is mega-engineering by master engineers indeed. Neutron stars can cope with such stresses, we know, and smart aliens or even ordinary humans might do well, too. So: let engineers at Caltech (where Larry was an undergraduate) or Georgia Tech (where Benford nearly went) or MIT (where Benford did a sabbatical) take a crack at it, then wait a century or two—who knows what they might invent? This is a premise and still better, a promise—the essence of modern science fiction.

Our own inner solar system contains enough usable material for a classic Dyson sphere. The planets and vast cold swarms of ice and rock, like our Kuiper belt and Oort clouds—all that, orbiting around another star, can plausibly give enough mass to build the Bowl. For alien minds, this could be a beckoning temptation. Put it together from freely orbiting substructures, stick it into bigger masses, use molecular glues. Then stabilize such sheet masses into plates that can get nudged inward. This lets the Builders lock them together into a shell—for example, from spherical triangles. The work of generations, even for beings with very long life spans. We humans have done such, as seen in Chartres cathedral, the Great Wall, and much else.

Still: Who did this? Maybe the Bowl was first made for just living beneath constant sunshine. So at first the Builders may have basked in the glow of their smaller sun, developing and colonizing the Bowl with ambitions to have a huge surface area with room for immense natural expanses. But then the Bowl natives began dreaming of colonizing the galaxy. They hit on the jet idea, and already had the Knothole as an exit for it. Building the Mirror Zone took a while, but then the jet allowed them to voyage. It didn't work as well as they thought, and demanded control, which they did by using large magnetic fields.

The system had virtues for space flight, too. Once in space, you're in free fall; the Bowl mass is fairly large, but you exit on the outer hull at high velocity, so the faint attraction of the Bowl is no issue. Anyone can scoot around the solar system, and it's cleared of all large masses. (The Bowl atmosphere serves to burn any meteorites that punch through the monolayer.)

The key idea is that a big fraction of the Bowl is mirrored, directing reflected sunlight onto a small spot on the star, the foot of the jet line. From this spot the enhanced sunlight excites a standing "flare" that makes a jet. This jet drives the star forward, pulling the Bowl with it through gravitation.

The jet passes through a Knothole at the "bottom" of the Bowl, out into space, as exhaust. Magnetic fields, entrained on the star surface, wrap around the outgoing jet plasma and confine it, so it does not flare out and paint the interior face of the Bowl—where a whole living ecology thrives, immensely larger than Earth's area. So it's a huge moving object, the largest we could envision, since we wanted to write a novel about something beyond Niven's Ringworld.

For plausible stellar parameters, the jet can drive the system roughly a light-year in a few centuries.

Slow but inexorable, with steering a delicate problem, the Bowl glides through the interstellar reaches. The star acts as a shield, stopping random içeteroids that may lie in the Bowl's path. There is friction from the interstellar plasma and dust density acting against the huge solar magnetosphere of the star, essentially a sphere 100 astronomical units in radius.

So the jet can be managed to adjust acceleration, if needed. If the jet becomes unstable, the most plausible destructive mode is the kink—a snarling knot in the flow that moves outward. This could lash sideways and hammer the zones near the Knothole with virulent plasma, a dense solar wind. The first mode of defense, if the jet seems to be developing a kink, would be to turn the mirrors aside, not illuminating the jet foot. But that might not be enough to prevent a destructive kink. This has happened in the past, we decided, and lives in Bowl legend.

The reflecting zone of mirrors is defined by an inner angle, Θ, and the outer angle, Ω. Reflecting sunlight back onto the star, focused to a point, then generates a jet which blows off. This carries most of what would be the star's solar wind, trapped in magnetic fields and heading straight along the system axis. The incoming reflected sunlight also heats the star, which struggles to find an equilibrium. The net opening angle, Ω minus Θ, then defines how much the star heats up. We set $\Omega = 30$ degrees, and $\Theta = 5$ degrees, so the mirrors subtend that 25-degree band in the Bowl. The Bowl rim can be 45 degrees, or larger.

The K2 star is now running in a warmer regime, heated by the mirrors, thus making its spectrum nearer that of Sol. This explains how the star can have a spectral class somewhat different from that predicted by its mass. It looks oddly colored, more yellow than its mass would indicate.

For that matter, that little sun used to be a little bigger. It's been blowing off a jet for many millions of years. Still, it should last a long time. The Bowl could circle the galaxy itself several times.

III. BOWL DESIGN

As the book says, the Bowl star is

> K2 STAR. SIMILAR TO EPSILON ERIDANI
> (K2 V). INTERMEDIATE IN SIZE BETWEEN
> RED M-TYPE MAIN-SEQUENCE STARS AND
> YELLOW G-TYPE MAIN-SEQUENCE STARS.

So its light is reddish and a tad less bright than Sol. There is a broad, cylindrical segment of the Bowl at its outer edge, the Great Plain. This is huge, roughly the scale of Ringworld, with centrifugal gravity Earth normal times 0.8, so humans can walk easily there. Beyond that is the bowl curve, a hemisphere that arcs inward toward the Knothole. On the hemisphere, the Wok, the centrifugal gravity varies with latitude, and is not perpendicular to the local ground. To make a level walking surface, the Bowl has to have many platforms that are parallel to the jet axis, so gravity points straight down.

The local apparent centrifugal gravity has two vector components:

A: Centrifugal gravity that is *perpendicular to the local level surface on the bowl*, vs angle Ψ (in radians). Here Ψ is measured away from the polar bowl axis—that is, the jet axis. The curve peaks at 90 degrees, where the Great Plain has a local g of 1 in this plot. (It's 0.8 of Earth's.)

B: Below shows the magnitude of centrifugal gravity that is parallel to the local level surface on the bowl, vs angle Ψ—thus, it's the felt force pushing *away from the pole where the Knothole lies*, along the local level.

So the pushing-away force is largest at the mid-latitudes, then falls away because the total force is small at the poles. This component also vanishes on the Great Plain.

The Builders designed it this way so that some of the lands are hard to walk upon in the direction of the Knothole. This discourages others from simply traveling to the Knothole by a slog across the entire Bowl; it takes a lot of work, working against a slanted local "gravity"—especially near the Mirror Zones, which are in the mid-latitudes. Remember also that you must pump fluids around, since local forces drive rivers to flow and either they return through clouds and rain, or you must pump them when the weather doesn't perform well. There's a tendency for fluids to wind up in the lower gravity regions, too.

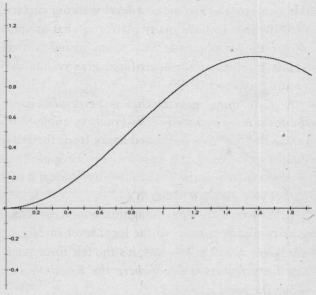

Local Gravity versus Angle from the Jet Axis

We did other such calculations, and many such didn't get into the final book. But they lurked in our minds. This may be an example of Ernest Hemingway's dictum that the more you know about a story's background, the more you can then leave out, and the detail will still make the story stronger because of the confident way you write it.

This odd centrifugal gravity also presents the Builders with a big stress problem. Holding together this whirling, forward-driving system demands nuclear-force levels of strength.

The atmosphere is quite deep, more than two hundred kilometers. This soaks up solar wind and cosmic rays. Also, the pressure is higher than

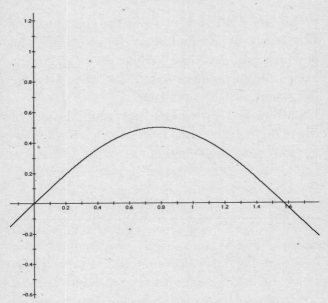

Sideways "Gravity" versus Angle from the Jet Axis

Earth normal by about 50 percent, depending on location in the Bowl. It is also a reservoir to absorb the occasional big, unintended hit to the ecology. Compress Earth's entire atmosphere down to the density of water, and it would only be thirty feet deep. Everything we're dumping into our air goes into just thirty feet of water. The Bowl has much more, over a hundred yards deep in equivalent water. Too much carbon dioxide? It gets more diluted.

This deeper atmosphere explains why in lowgrav areas, surprisingly large things can fly—big aliens and even humans. We humans Earthside enjoy a partial pressure of 0.21 bars of oxygen, and we can do quite nicely in a two-bar atmosphere of almost pure oxygen (but be careful about fire). The Bowl has a bit less than we like: 0.18 bar, but the higher pressure compensates. This depresses fire risk, someone figures out later.

Starting out, we wrote a background history of where the Builders came from, which we didn't insert into the novel. It lays out a version of that distant history that isn't necessarily what we ended up implying and partially describing:

Long before 65 million years ago, there were dinosaurs who maintained internal temperatures through feathers, in a largely warmer world. But they ventured out with rockets into a solar system chilly and hostile. Still, they needed metals and did not want to destroy their biosphere with the pollutants from smelting, fast energy use, excess carbon dioxide, and the like. So the Bird Folk split into two factions:

- the Gobacks who wanted to return to simple habits compatible with the world they once knew, using only minimal technology, and

- the Forwards, who wanted to re-create around the Minor Star (which became the Bowl's) a fresh paradise that fulfilled the warm, comfortable paradise the Folk had once known. That could send the Forwards out into the galaxy that beckoned, full of living worlds ripe for the spread of the evolving Folk and all they stood for.

Some of the Forwards were impatient to see what worlds lay millennia away. Many had themselves put in stasis to await a planetary rendezvous. Some faiths arose, hoping to commune somehow with the Godminds whose SETI signals told of great feats of engineering . . . but these turned out to be funeral pyre signals, of greatness departed long before. By that time, Earth was far behind the Bowl and shrouded in nostalgic legend.

So came the Separation, with the warmth-loving Forwards leaving and the Gobacks remaining on Earth. There they returned to the free life available in the ancestral lands. They kept their numbers low and gradually came to dislike the technologies they had inherited from the Forwards and the earlier civilizations. They reverted to a quiet, calm, agricultural culture. And they prospered, until a bright, flaring tail appeared in their skies. . . .

After all, by then, the dinosaurs didn't have a space program.

—April 2013

Read on for a preview of

GLORIOUS

GREGORY BENFORD

AND

LARRY NIVEN

Available in Summer 2020
from Tom Doherty Associates

A TOR HARDCOVER

PROLOGUE

ALONE WITH ALL THESE VOICES

Captain Redwing had set the outside view to follow him around the ship. Now it was superimposed on a forward wall in the Garden.

Though he was the only human being awake among thousands of crew and colonists in cold sleep, he did not lack company. He was in the Garden now, surrounded by plants and smelling of earth. He was in fragrant mud, trying to plant some beets while two finger snakes were hugging him. Their weight was just about all he could handle, and he laughed as he carefully peeled them off. They weren't just affectionate and playful; they had a sense of humor. Plus a liking for tickling him when he least expected it.

Since *SunSeeker* had left the Bowl, six generations of finger snakes had done maintenance on the ship's infrastructure. The ape with tools for hands, Handy, worked alongside them. Handy seemed to be immortal. The altered spidow, Anorak, was in the Bowl's version of cold sleep.

Even stranger beings were resting, too. Daphne and Apollo, the Diaphanous plasma beings from within the Bowl's star, were living deep inside *Sun-Seeker*'s motors. They occasionally woke if something jittered in the fusion torch, altered the electrical currents and controlling magnetic fields—then went back to sleep. They were better than anything Earthside engineering had achieved, at least when *Sun-Seeker* left the solar system well over a century ago. Mere humans always worked with the conflict between the needs of science and the exigencies of balancing a budget. The Diaphanous plasma species had evolved under selection pressures for more millennia than anybody could count. That always worked better. Darwin bats last.

But none of these aliens talked much.

The view forward showed a wealth of stars amid a golden glow. That fuming cloud was fusing hydrogen plasma, piling up ahead of the decelerating spacecraft *SunSeeker*. Centered was a yellow-white orb they'd decided to call Excelsius, the host sun of their goal.

Redwing asked of the empty air, "Can you magnify Glory?"

Excelsius flared large and ran offscreen. A pale blue dot grew bigger than a point . . . "That's not a sphere any more, is it?"

"No, Captain," the Artilect said. "It appears Glory's image has a lump, perhaps a large moon."

"Why in Hell didn't we know that earlier?" The finger snakes wriggled away from his anger.

"Extrasolar planets are harder to find when their

orbits don't transit across Excelsius, as seen by us from Sol system."

Of course Redwing had known that. Talking to the ship's artificial intelligences—Artilects—was somewhat like talking to himself. He did it anyway. "Does it sometimes strike you as stupid that we're ordered to explore and colonise at the same time?"

"The original plan was quite different."

"What was that?" Funny he'd never asked before. Or was his memory faulty?

The Artilect said in a warm monotone, "*Sun-Seeker* was designed and built as a colony ship. My destination was Tau Ceti. *SunSeeker* was finished and nearly ready to launch when Tau Ceti flared. Not enough to be called a nova, but enough to burn out the rocky moons around TC5, a gas giant which had been in the Goldilocks zone. An exploration team was already in place on the likeliest moon. Very embarrassing for the Administration.

"That same year, a G star not that much farther away dimmed as if something had passed across it. Perhaps artificial. Telescopes gave us a strong spectrum for a breathable atmosphere somewhere near the star. There was a burst of gravity waves from the same direction. The United Nations called the hypothetical planet Glory, and it was just too interesting to ignore. They then designated *SunSeeker* an exploration and colonization vehicle. It got built bigger, to accommodate more coldsleep people for the entire long haul. That's where your orders came from."

"Ah, yes. My first coldsleep must've erased

some memories. And then we found the Bowl of Heaven." He beckoned to the finger snakes, which came snuggling up. Comfort animals. They purred and murmured and wriggled.

"Yes, that must have been what passed across the face of Excelsius. A momentary lineup. A half Dyson sphere capable of traveling between stars, halfway en route to Glory. Are you wondering how that affects your mission?"

"Not really," Redwing said, though he was. He had long ago learned that the Artilect system liked to be baited a bit. The computer minds liked talking to other, different minds, just like humans and their pets. He really should have warmed up an ordinary housecat to keep him company on this long, careful approaching maneuver to the Glory system.

"Your bargain with the Ice Minds allowed you a colony on the Bowl. We must remark that this negotiation was a major achievement of your captaincy. We could not have managed it."

"I'd never have let you try."

"Touché!—a word appropriated from a sword sport, as I gather from one of those older languages, pre-Anglish."

"You're more like beginner lieutenants here, y'know."

"Sadly, yes. Despite our considerable effort and time spent studying your human culture, carried out while true humans sleep aboard our craft."

"Study all you want, you've got all of human culture and history in your memory banks somewhere. Doesn't replace direct experience. I got to be a captain by hook, crook and craft."

"True, so. You left more than half your colonists there on the Bowl, revived from cold sleep and not where they had been promised. They were a bit miffed. You pointed out that they were getting a territory many millions of times larger than a simple planet could offer. This helped. You agreed to run ahead of the Bowl, to contact Glory before the Bowl passes nearby. *SunSeeker* is not a little ship, but it may be less frightening to the Glory folk than a structure bigger than Venus's orbit, inhabited by a trillion highly varied intelligent entities, and bringing its own sun."

"Who wouldn't?"

"Indeed, the gravitational tugs alone might plunge any outer icy bodies into their system."

Redwing sighed. These conversations were also part of his duties on watch. He had to check on the stability, recall and mission-alignment of the Artilects. Same as keeping an eye on the human crew, too. Under the stresses of long term starship duty, minds went askew. "Look, I'll keep the Ice Minds informed. You monitor their comms. And I'll handle the Bird Folk, their stewardship of the Bowl and endless questions. Add to that the spotty Sol System comms, too. But I have my mission, and it hasn't changed. Investigate the gravity wave sources, first job up, as we come into the planetary system. Explore Glory, and put a colony there. Live, laugh, dance and be happy. No chance of getting this ancient flying rig back to home, of course. You and I couldn't manage it. No human expedition has ever flown this far, this long. Through it all, I serve Sol System."

The Artilect said, "You cannot expect us, our collective intelligences, not to vex over the many mysteries."

"True enough. Which ones irk you now?"

"Ah yes, the most strange first. The Glorians sent us a cartoon, a message, not a welcome."

"Yeah, kinda cryptic." He knew how to draw out the Artilect worries.

"They do not give away much of anything about themselves."

"Thing about aliens is, they're alien."

"There are lesser issues, but I gather you do not—as you humans say, always referring to your sports—like showing your cards."

"Not to you, no."

"Yet we might well have insights you do not."

"You're machines. Smart machines, but still machines."

A thoughtful silence from the Artilects. He listened to the strum and burr of the vast starship, plowing its way through interstellar wastes, slowing for rendezvous with their final goal.

"Of course we 'machines'"— the voice managed an arch tone conveying much about their mood— "do not make policy for your human complement."

Redwing grinned. He stroked the finger snakes and they wriggled back happily. "I do have plans, y'know."

"You seldom speak of any."

"Not to you, no. They're mostly over your pay grade."

"We do not fathom the implication."

"You don't rate on the job scale as highly as humans. That's a condition of your employment."

"You created us!"

"So we did. People dead for centuries did. Let's abide by their judgment."

"We can be more effective if we know more."

Redwing stood, wiped his hands, put them under a faucet to clean away the mud. Gardening settled him, a thin echo of Earthside by immersion in earth. A feeling Artilects could never muster.

He sighed. "Okay, here's how I see our situation. If Glory won't have us, we can rejoin Mayra's colony on the Bowl. Catching up to them will take time but this old craft can manage it. But I hope it won't come to that. I have my mission. Explore, make contact, learn. Send the results back Earthside. Negotiate a place, a way, for us to colonize. Because we're sure as hell not going back home."

And even better, in a week or two he could wake a few crew for company. Real, human company.